The Last Kids on Earth are creating
THEIR OWN COMIC BOOK!

JACK, **QUINT**, **JUNE**, and **DIRK** are about to face a challenge unlike any they've faced before . . . At their local comic book store, the kids make a startling discovery: they've read every last issue of their favorite comic, Z-Man, and no new issues are coming . . . ever! (Thanks a lot, apocalypse.) Nooo!

Our heroes have but one choice: continue Z-Man's legacy by writing and illustrating **THEIR OWN COMIC BOOK!** Step one? Knock off their beloved Z-Man and cast themselves as super-rad, super-goofy superhero protectors of the mysterious city of Apocalyptia. What could possibly go wrong? Just about everything!

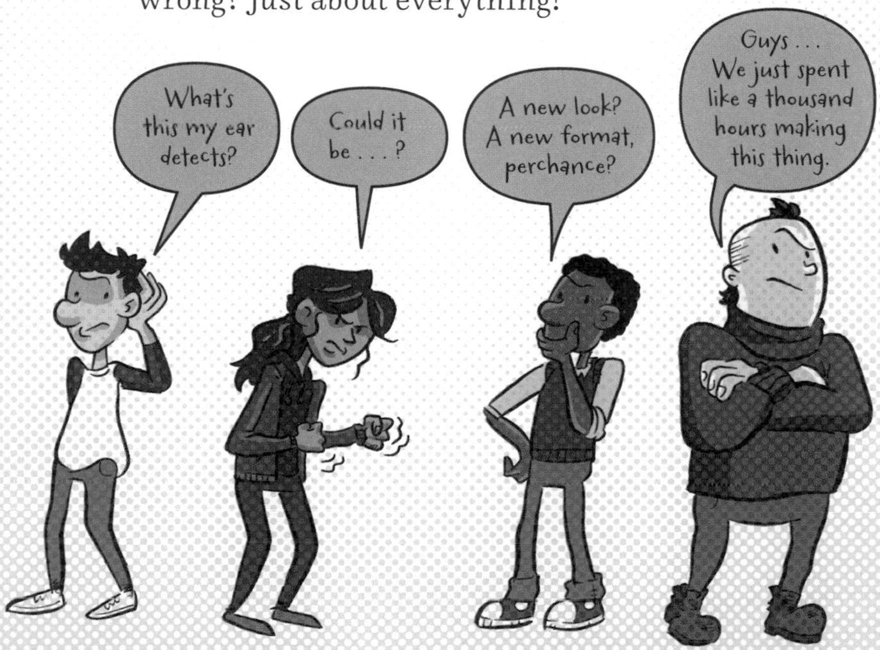
What's this my ear detects?
Could it be . . . ?
A new look? A new format, perchance?
Guys . . . We just spent like a thousand hours making this thing.

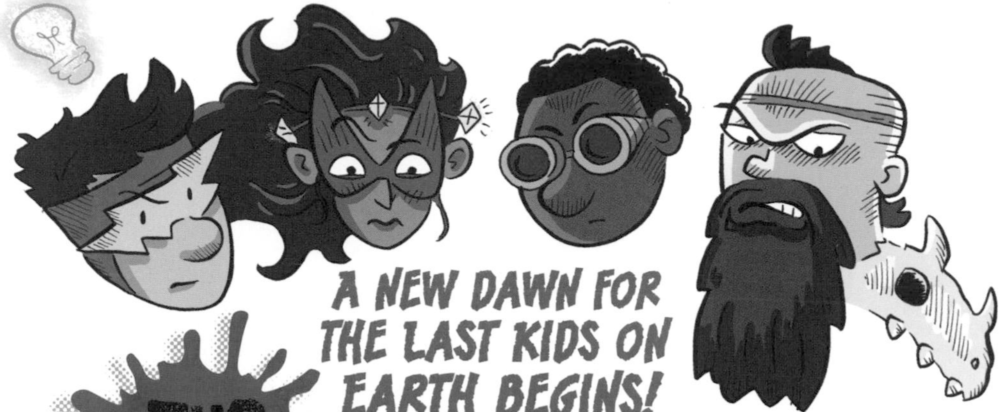

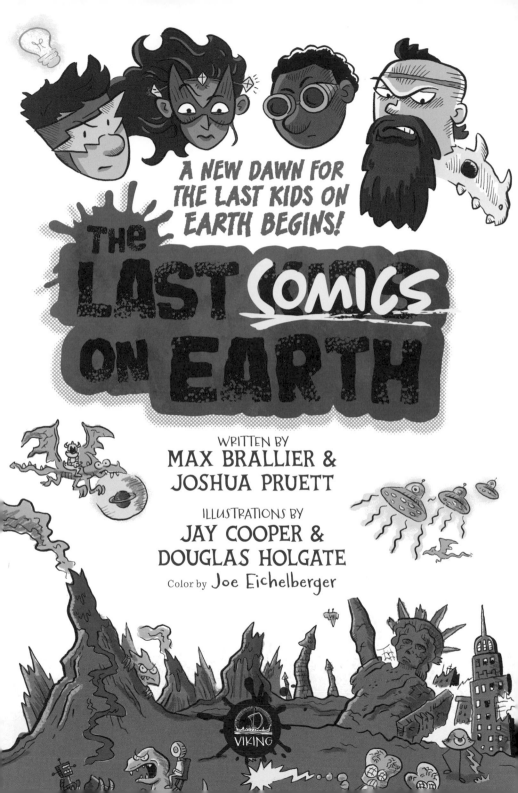

A NEW DAWN FOR THE LAST KIDS ON EARTH BEGINS!

THE LAST COMICS ON EARTH

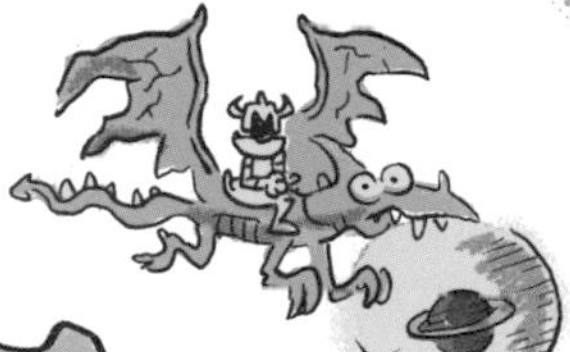

WRITTEN BY
MAX BRALLIER & JOSHUA PRUETT

ILLUSTRATIONS BY
JAY COOPER & DOUGLAS HOLGATE

Color by Joe Eichelberger

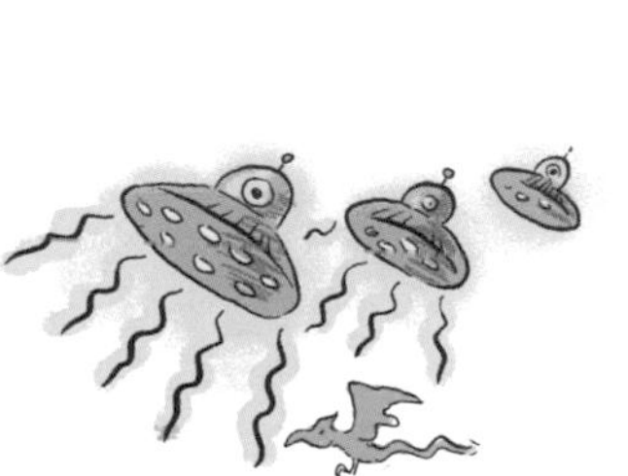

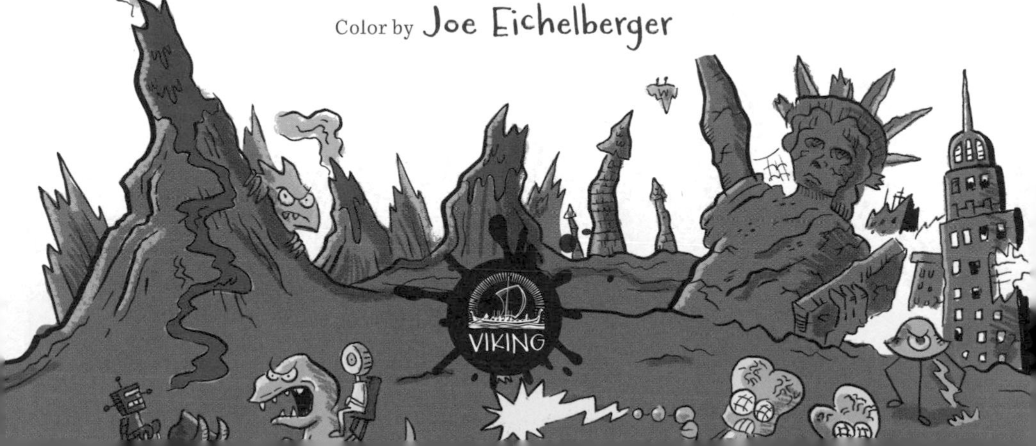
VIKING

VIKING
An imprint of Penguin Random House LLC, New York

First published in the United States of America by Viking,
an imprint of Penguin Random House LLC, 2023

Stock photo on page 24 courtesy of Unsplash.
Stock photos on pages 87 and 126 courtesy of Deposit Photos.

Visit us online at penguinrandomhouse.com.

Library of Congress Cataloging-in-Publication Data is available.

Manufactured in China

ISBN 9780593526774

10   9   8   7   6   5   4   3   2   1

TOPL

Book design by Jim Hoover and Chris Dickey   Color by Joe Eichelberger

For all the daydreamers
—M. B.

For Shari,
who bought me my first comic book
from a 7-Eleven spinner rack.
Love you, Mom.
—J. P.

For the Delgonquins.
I'm thankful for the people I have found.
—J. C.

CHAPTER ONE
THE COMIC WITHIN THE COMIC BOOK

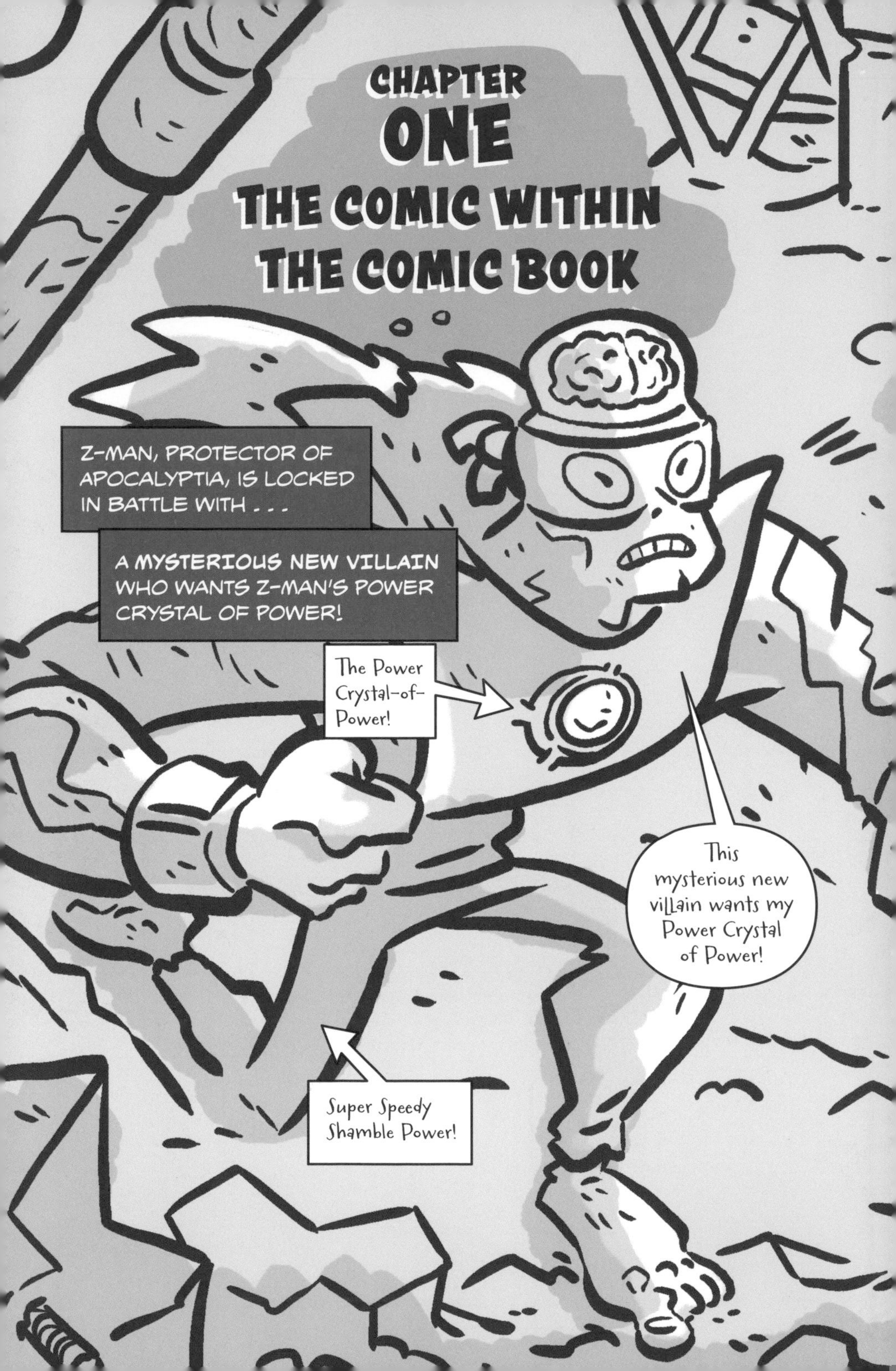
Z-MAN, PROTECTOR OF APOCALYPTIA, IS LOCKED IN BATTLE WITH . . .
A MYSTERIOUS NEW VILLAIN WHO WANTS Z-MAN'S POWER CRYSTAL OF POWER!
The Power Crystal-of-Power!
This mysterious new villain wants my Power Crystal of Power!
Super Speedy Shamble Power!

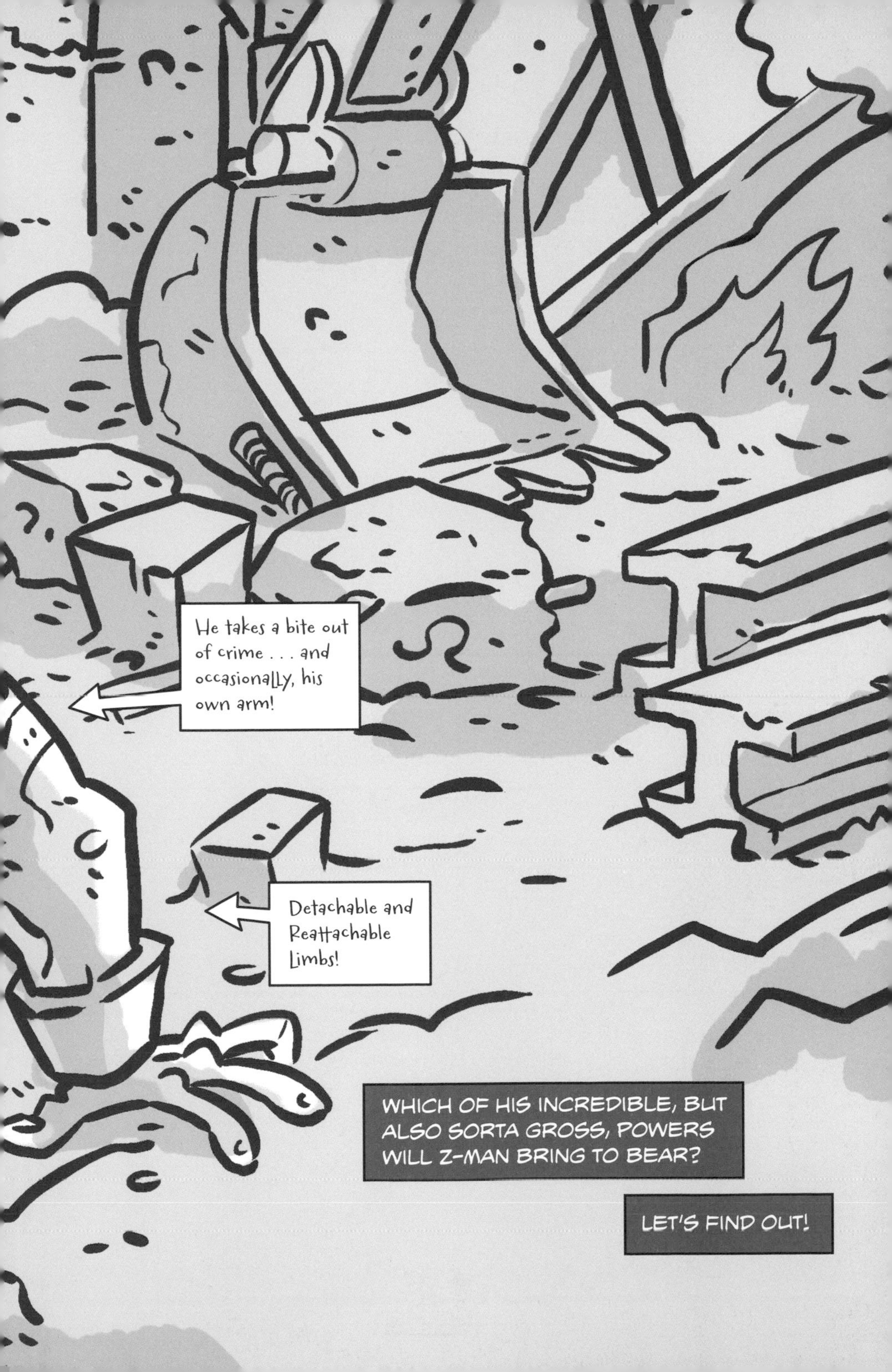

He takes a bite out of crime . . . and occasionaLLy, his own arm!
Detachable and Reattachable Limbs!
WHICH OF HIS INCREDIBLE, BUT ALSO SORTA GROSS, POWERS WILL Z-MAN BRING TO BEAR?
LET'S FIND OUT!

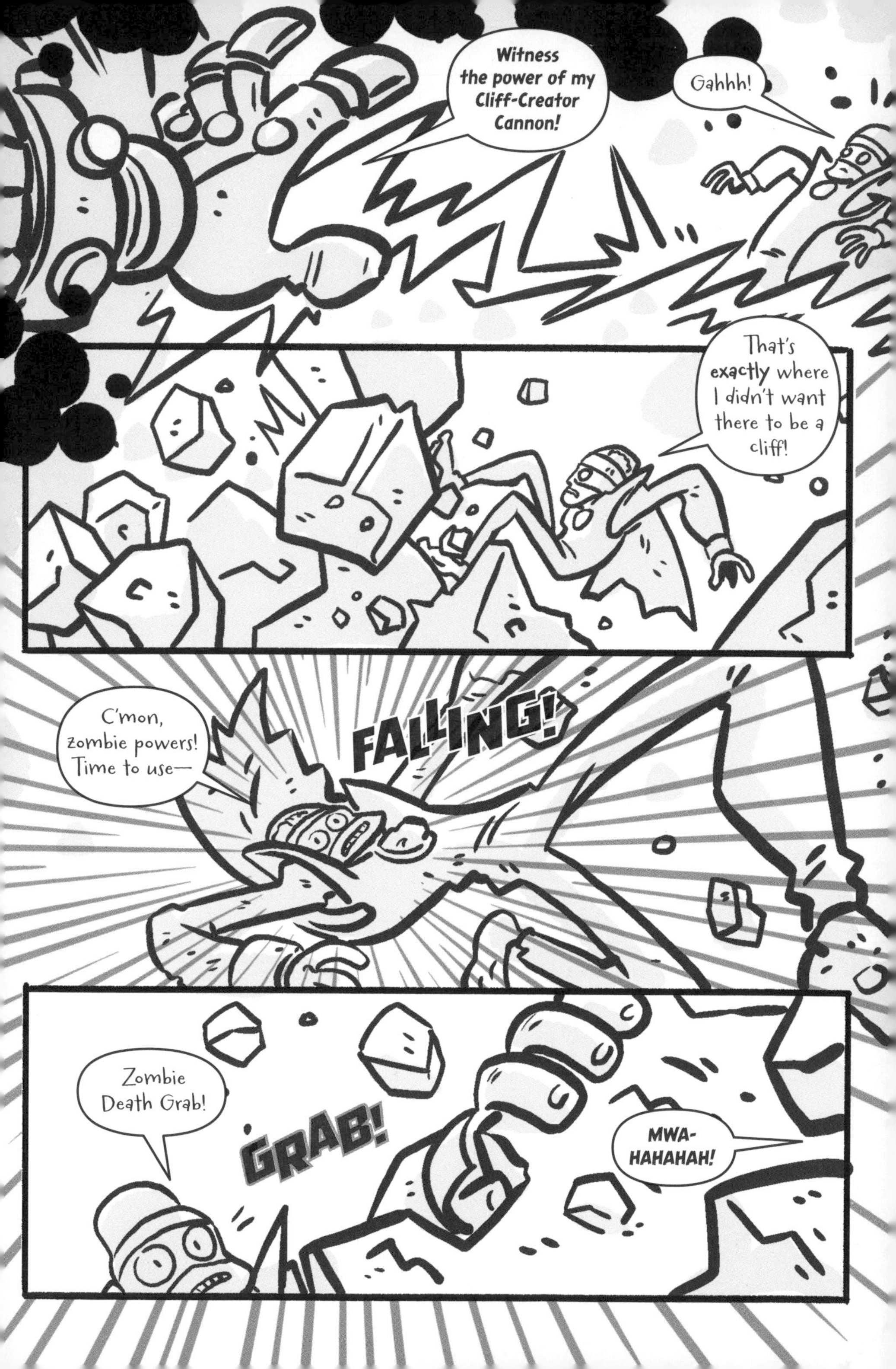
Witness the power of my Cliff-Creator Cannon!
Gahhh!
That's exactly where I didn't want there to be a cliff!
C'mon, zombie powers! Time to use—
FALLING!
Zombie Death Grab!
GRAB!
MWA-HAHAHAH!

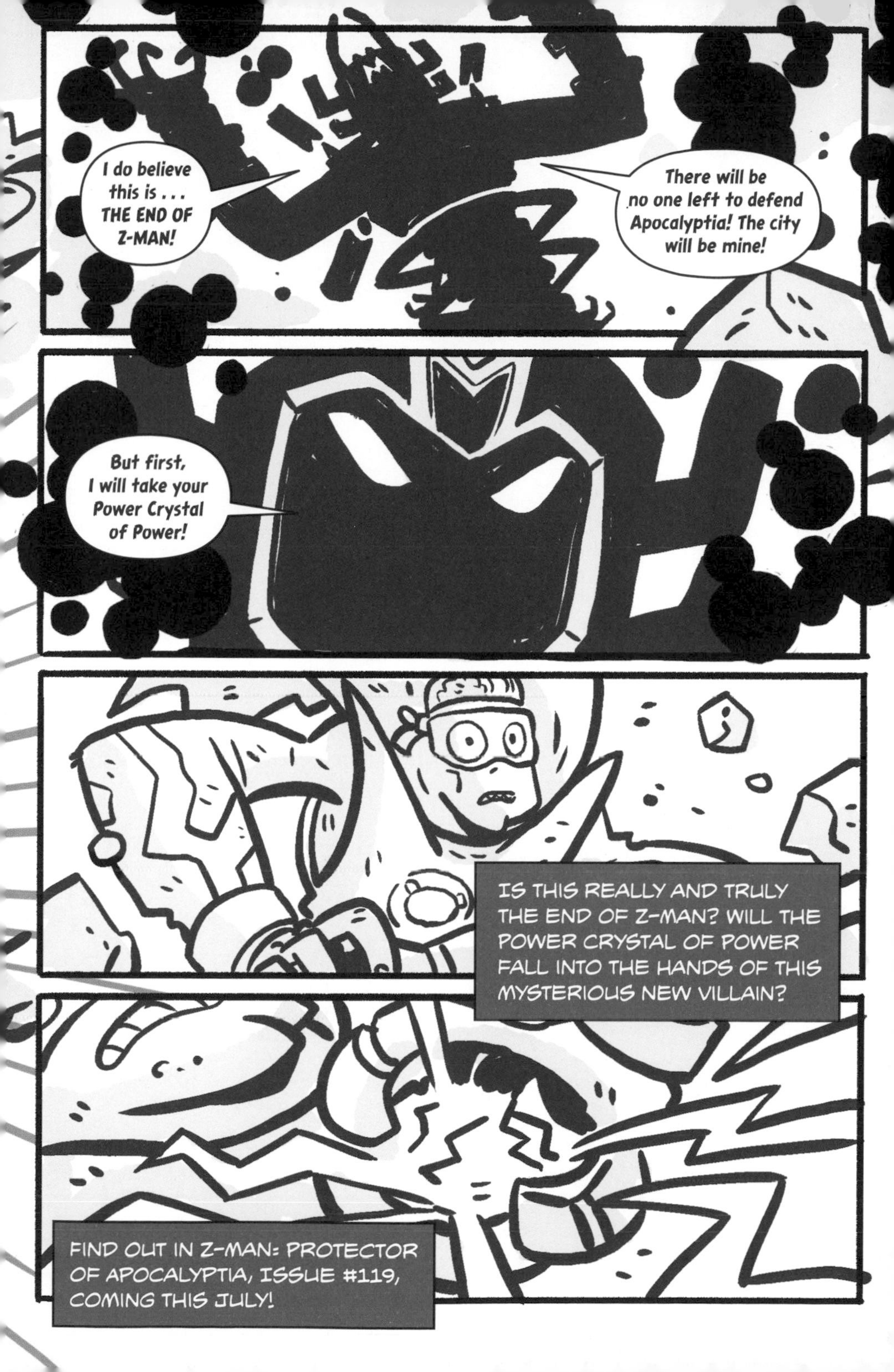
I do believe this is . . . THE END OF Z-MAN!
There will be no one left to defend Apocalyptia! The city will be mine!
But first, I will take your Power Crystal of Power!
IS THIS REALLY AND TRULY THE END OF Z-MAN? WILL THE POWER CRYSTAL OF POWER FALL INTO THE HANDS OF THIS MYSTERIOUS NEW VILLAIN?
FIND OUT IN Z-MAN: PROTECTOR OF APOCALYPTIA, ISSUE #119, COMING THIS JULY!

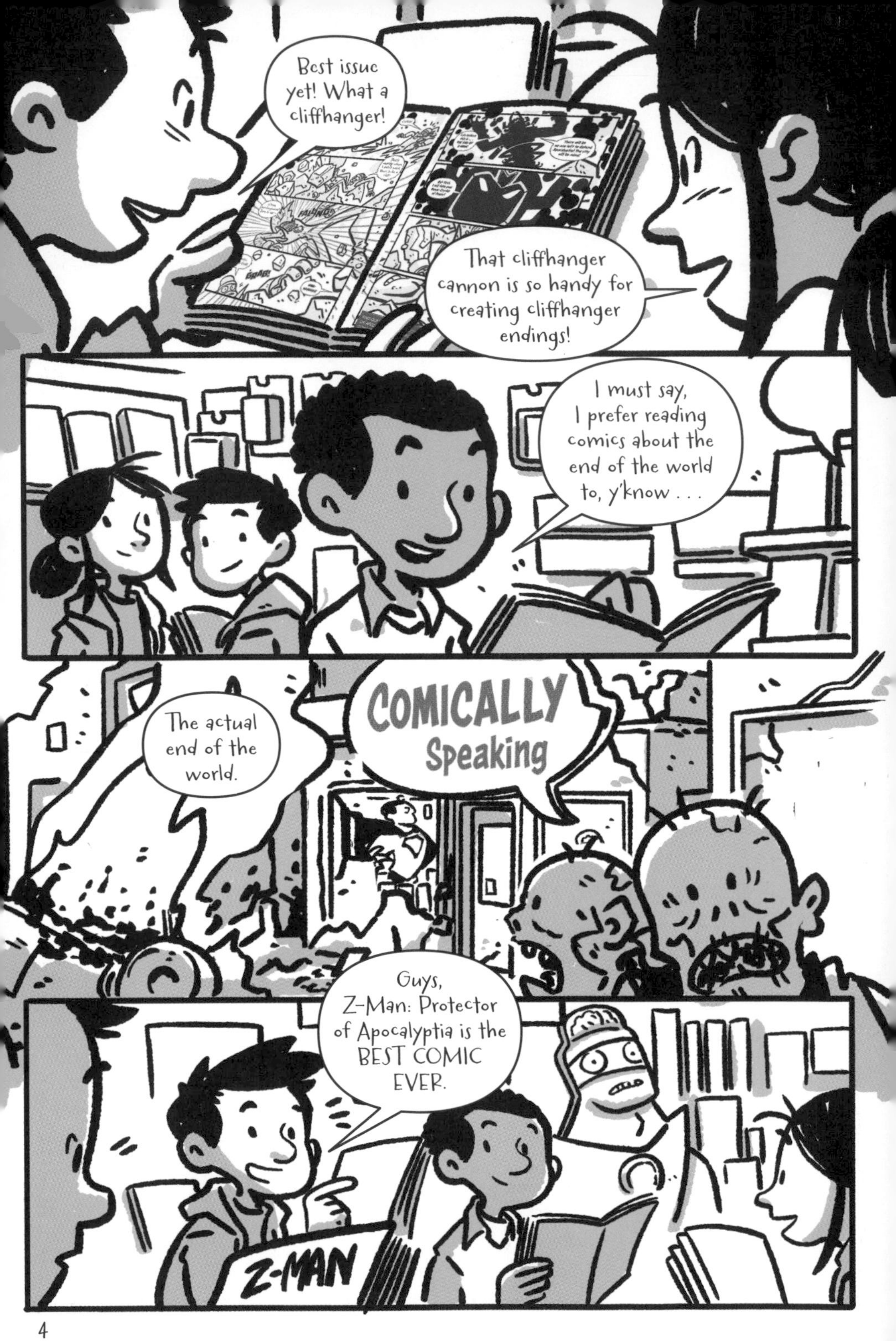
Best issue yet! What a cliffhanger!
That cliffhanger cannon is so handy for creating cliffhanger endings!
I must say, I prefer reading comics about the end of the world to, y'know . . .
The actual end of the world.
COMICALLY Speaking
Guys, Z-Man: Protector of Apocalyptia is the BEST COMIC EVER.
Z-MAN

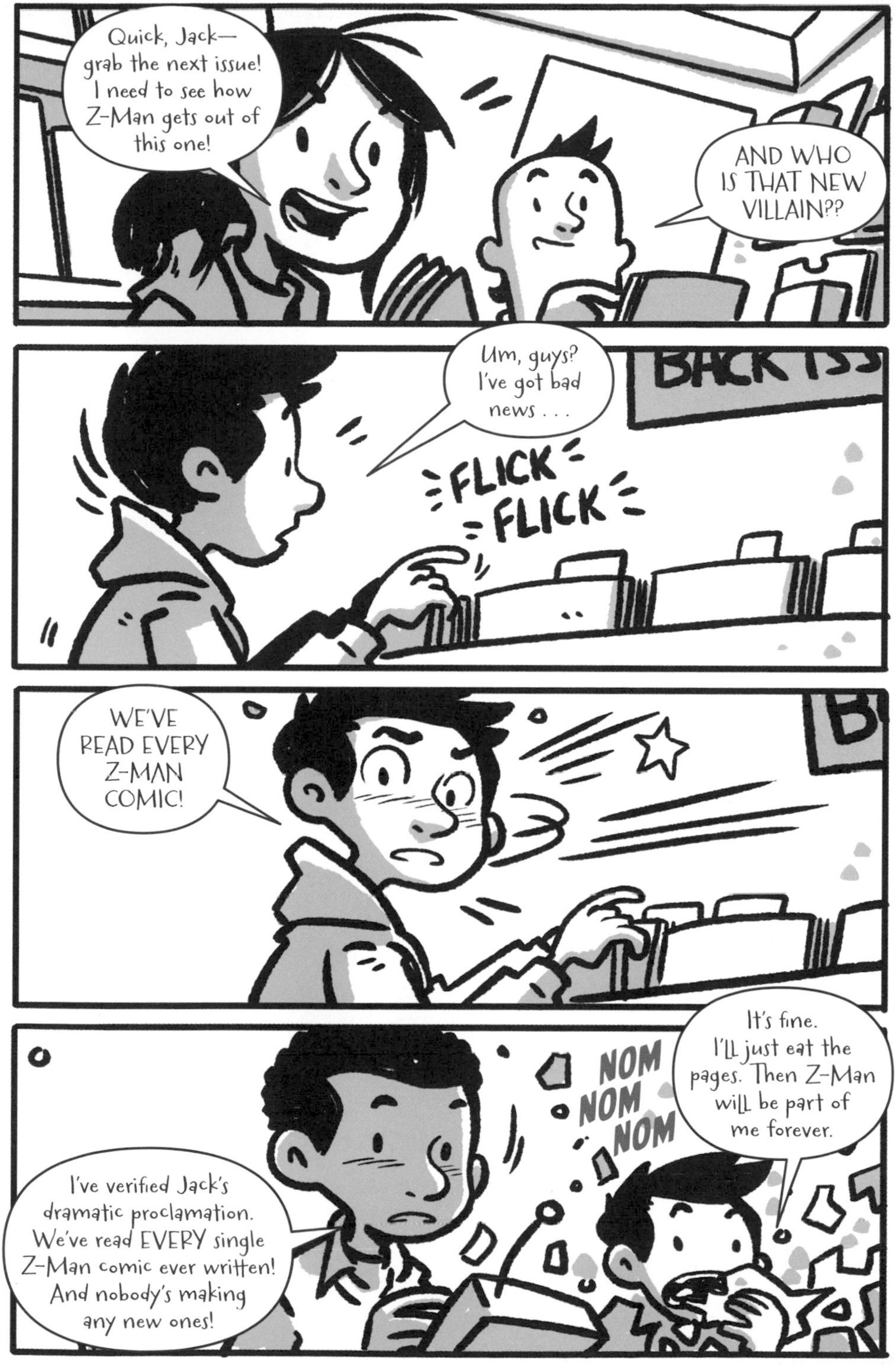
Quick, Jack—grab the next issue! I need to see how Z-Man gets out of this one!
AND WHO IS THAT NEW VILLAIN??
Um, guys? I've got bad news . . .
BACK ISS
FLICK
FLICK
WE'VE READ EVERY Z-MAN COMIC!
It's fine. I'LL just eat the pages. Then Z-Man will be part of me forever.
NOM
NOM
NOM
I've verified Jack's dramatic proclamation. We've read EVERY single Z-Man comic ever written! And nobody's making any new ones!

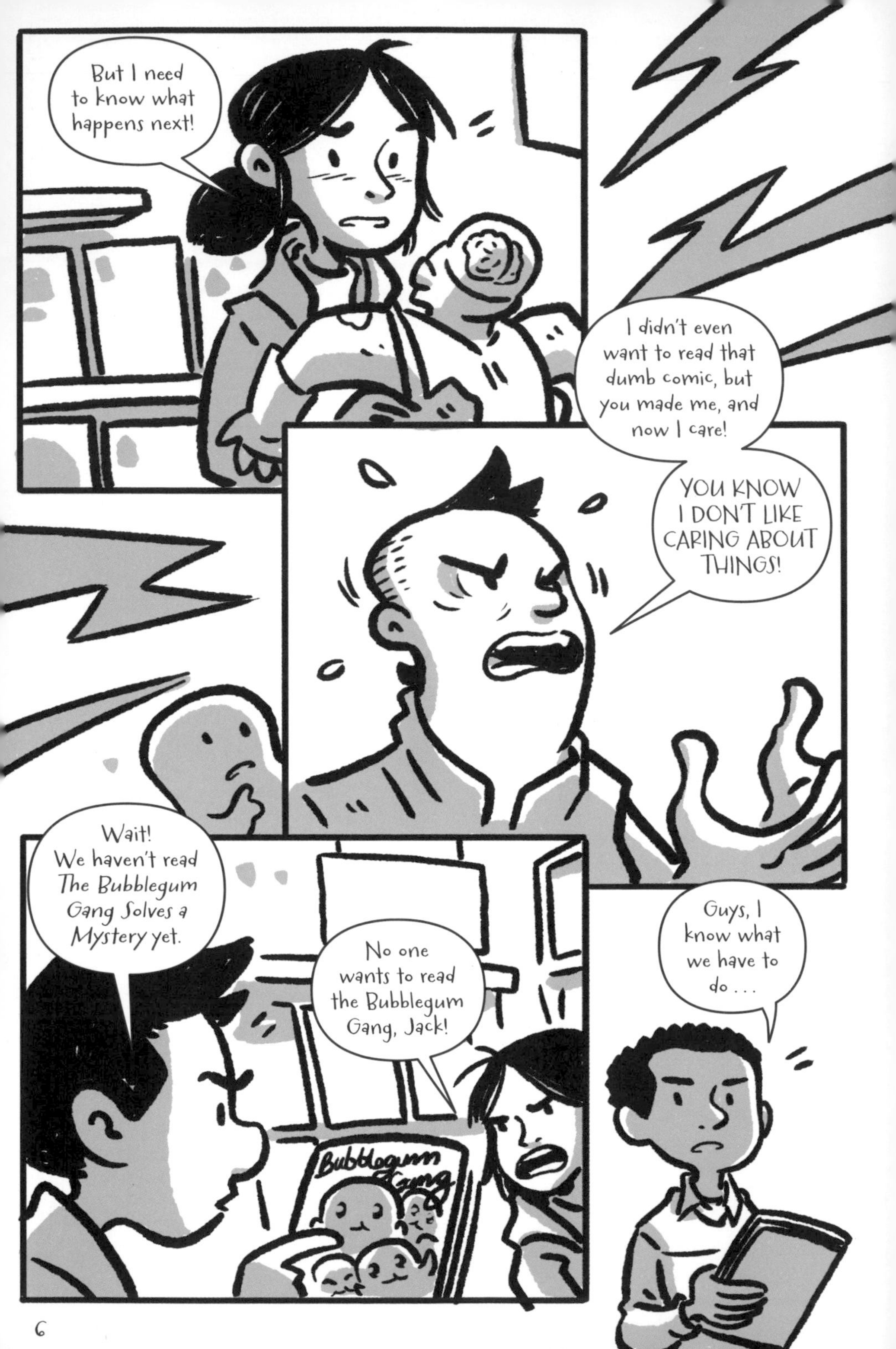
But I need to know what happens next!
I didn't even want to read that dumb comic, but you made me, and now I care!
YOU KNOW I DON'T LIKE CARING ABOUT THINGS!
Wait! We haven't read The Bubblegum Gang Solves a Mystery yet.
No one wants to read the Bubblegum Gang, Jack!
Bubblegum Gang
Guys, I know what we have to do . . .

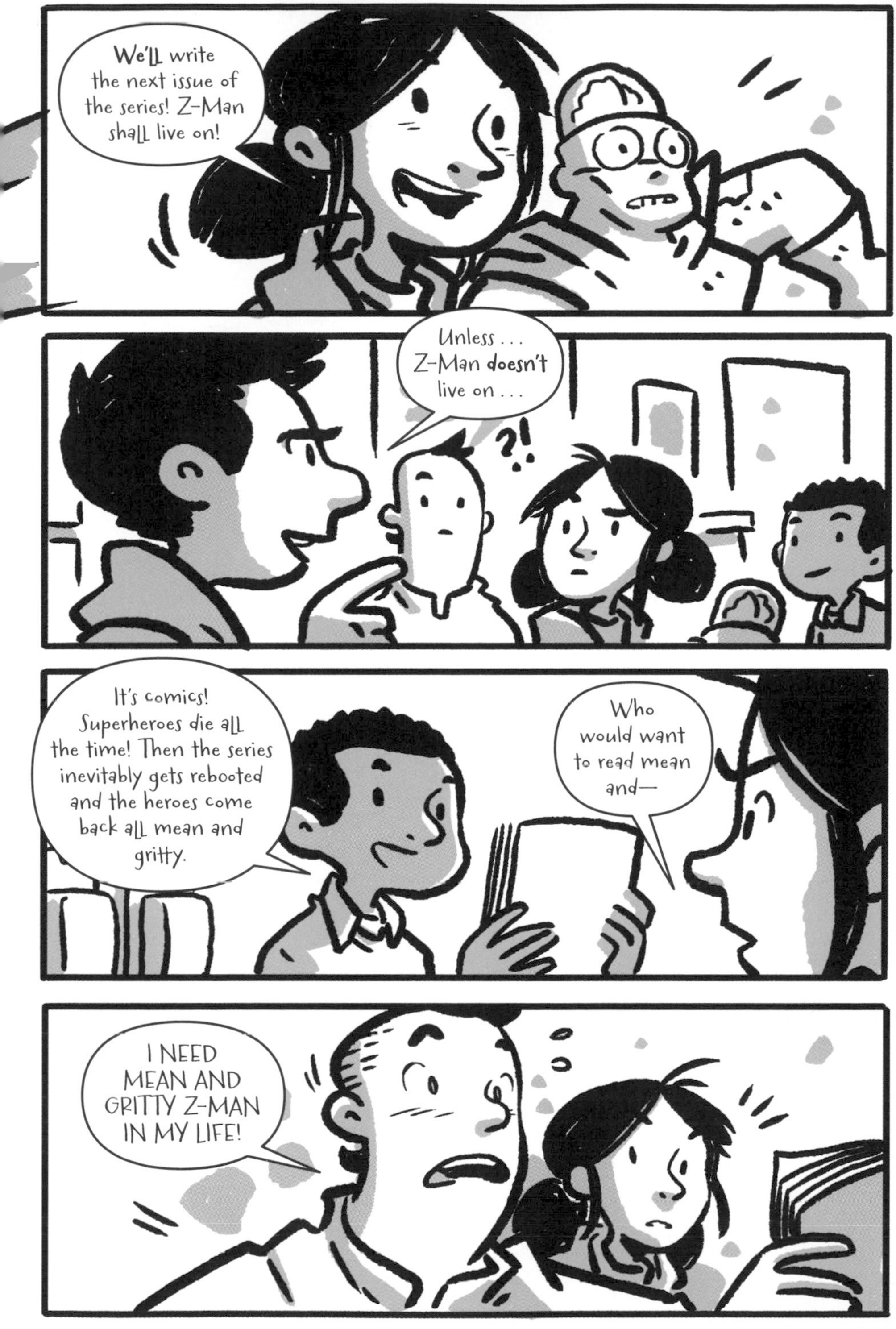
We'll write the next issue of the series! Z-Man shall live on!
Unless . . . Z-Man doesn't live on . . .
?!
It's comics! Superheroes die all the time! Then the series inevitably gets rebooted and the heroes come back all mean and gritty.
Who would want to read mean and—
I NEED MEAN AND GRITTY Z-MAN IN MY LIFE!

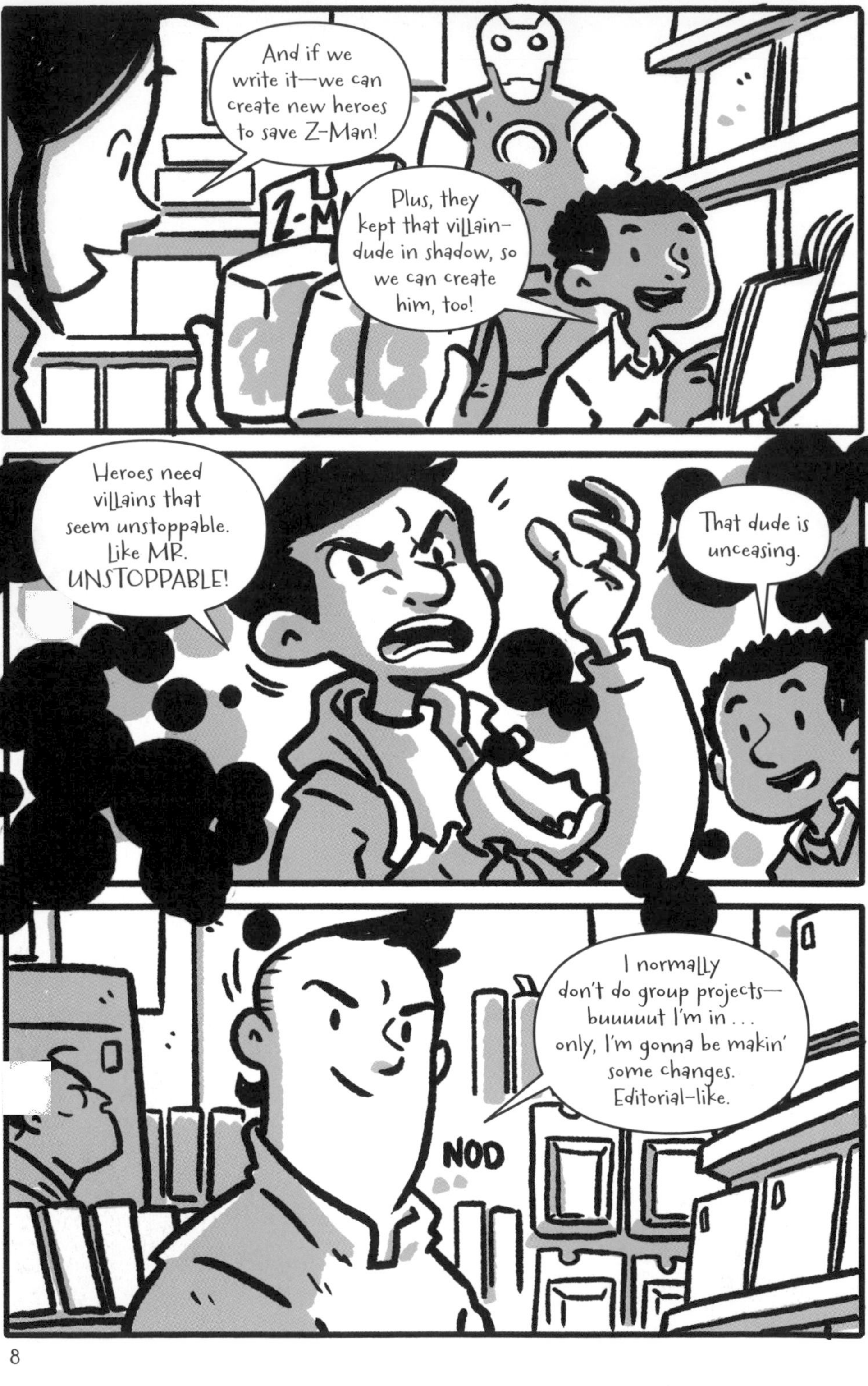
And if we write it—we can create new heroes to save Z-Man!
Plus, they kept that villain-dude in shadow, so we can create him, too!
Heroes need villains that seem unstoppable. Like MR. UNSTOPPABLE!
That dude is unceasing.
I normally don't do group projects—buuuuut I'm in . . . only, I'm gonna be makin' some changes. Editorial-like.
NOD

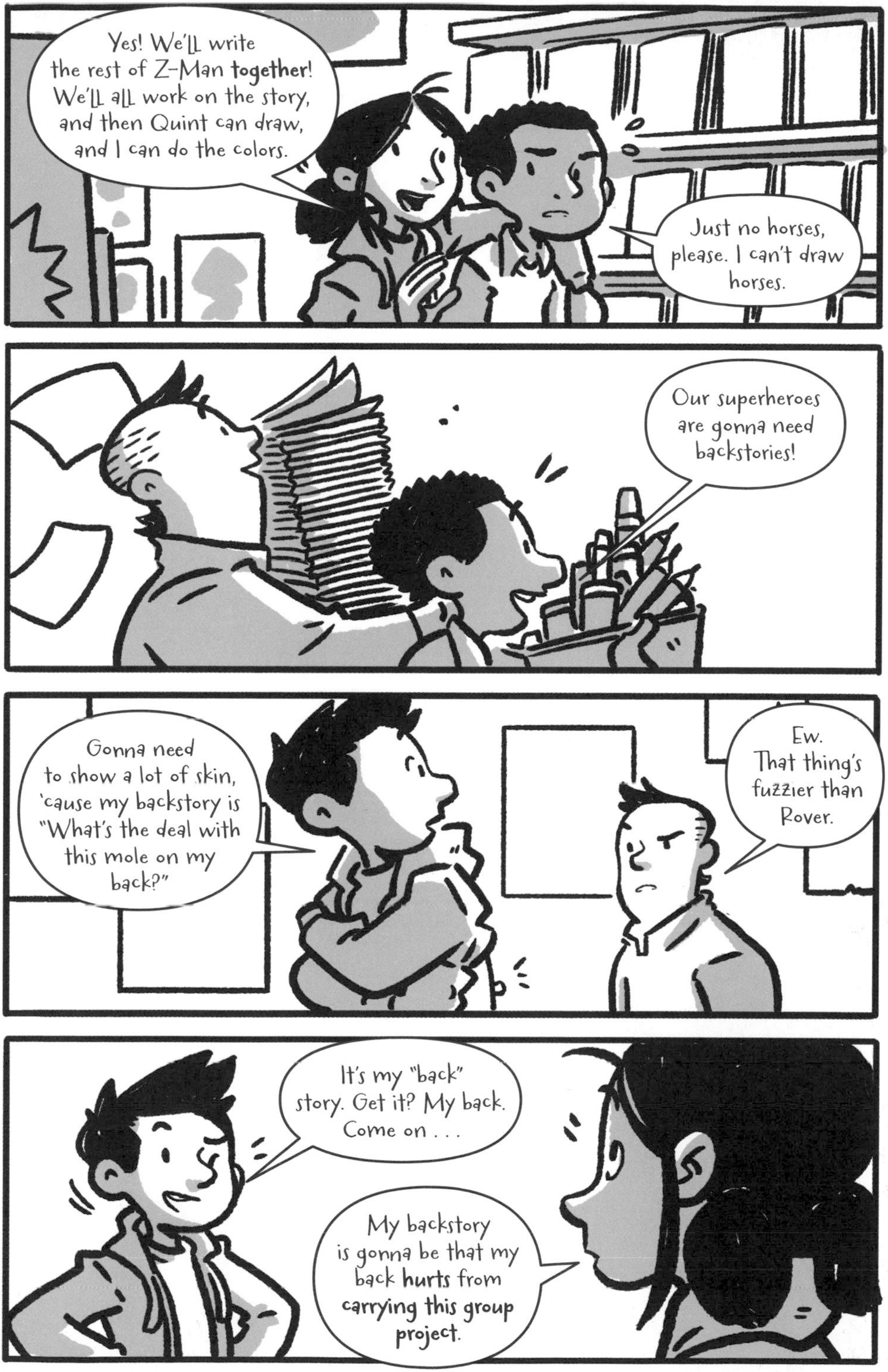

Yes! We'll write the rest of Z-Man **together**! We'll all work on the story, and then Quint can draw, and I can do the colors.
Just no horses, please. I can't draw horses.
Our superheroes are gonna need backstories!
Gonna need to show a lot of skin, 'cause my backstory is "What's the deal with this mole on my back?"
Ew. That thing's fuzzier than Rover.
It's my "back" story. Get it? My back. Come on . . .
My backstory is gonna be that my back **hurts** from **carrying this group project**.

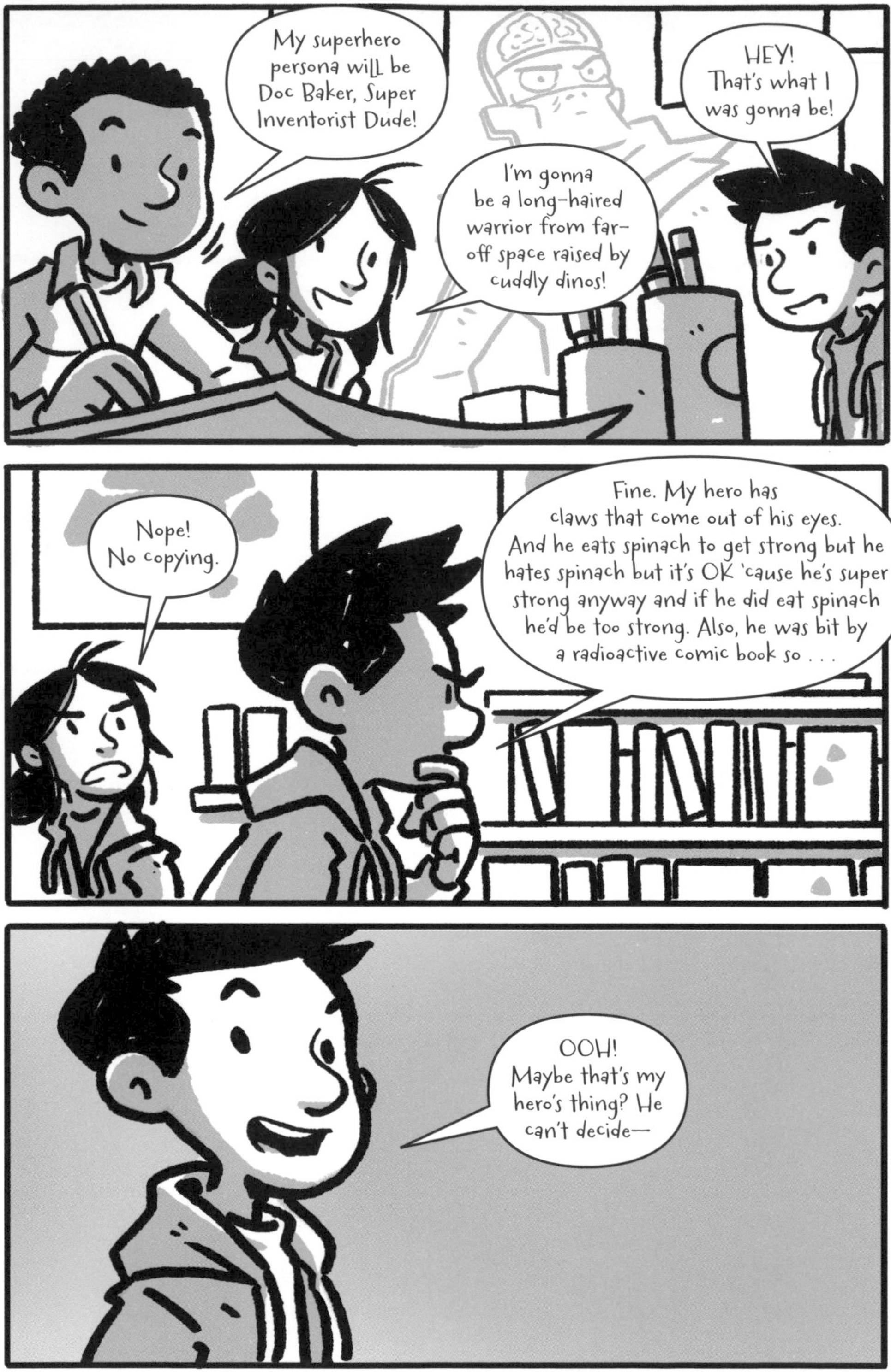
My superhero persona will be Doc Baker, Super Inventorist Dude!
I'm gonna be a long-haired warrior from far-off space raised by cuddly dinos!
HEY! That's what I was gonna be!
Nope! No copying.
Fine. My hero has claws that come out of his eyes. And he eats spinach to get strong but he hates spinach but it's OK 'cause he's super strong anyway and if he did eat spinach he'd be too strong. Also, he was bit by a radioactive comic book so . . .
OOH! Maybe that's my hero's thing? He can't decide—

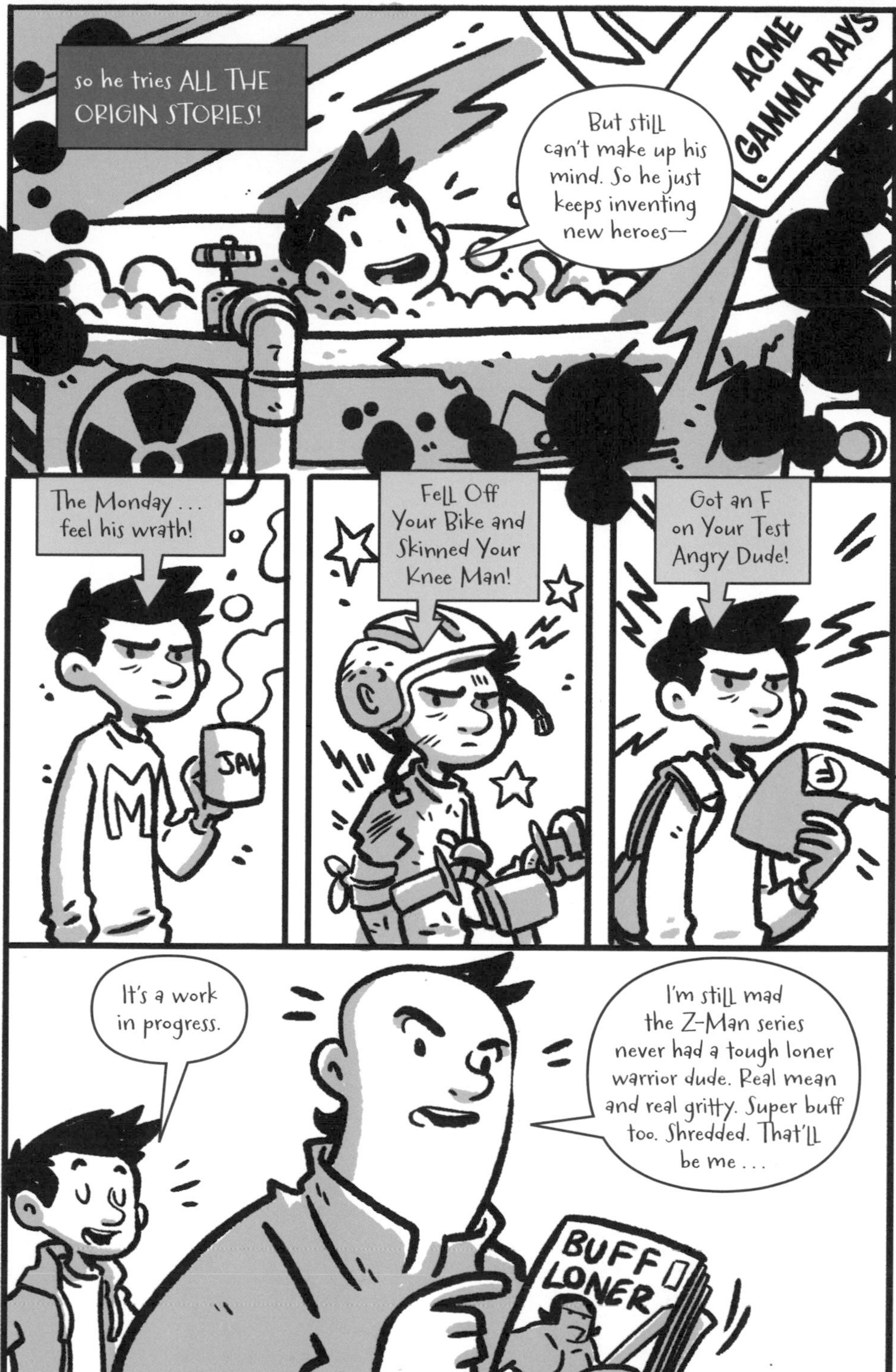
so he tries ALL THE ORIGIN STORIES!
But still can't make up his mind. So he just keeps inventing new heroes—
ACME GAMMA RAYS
The Monday . . . feel his wrath!
JAV
Fell Off Your Bike and Skinned Your Knee Man!
Got an F on Your Test Angry Dude!
It's a work in progress.
I'm still mad the Z-Man series never had a tough loner warrior dude. Real mean and real gritty. Super buff too. Shredded. That'll be me . . .
BUFF LONER

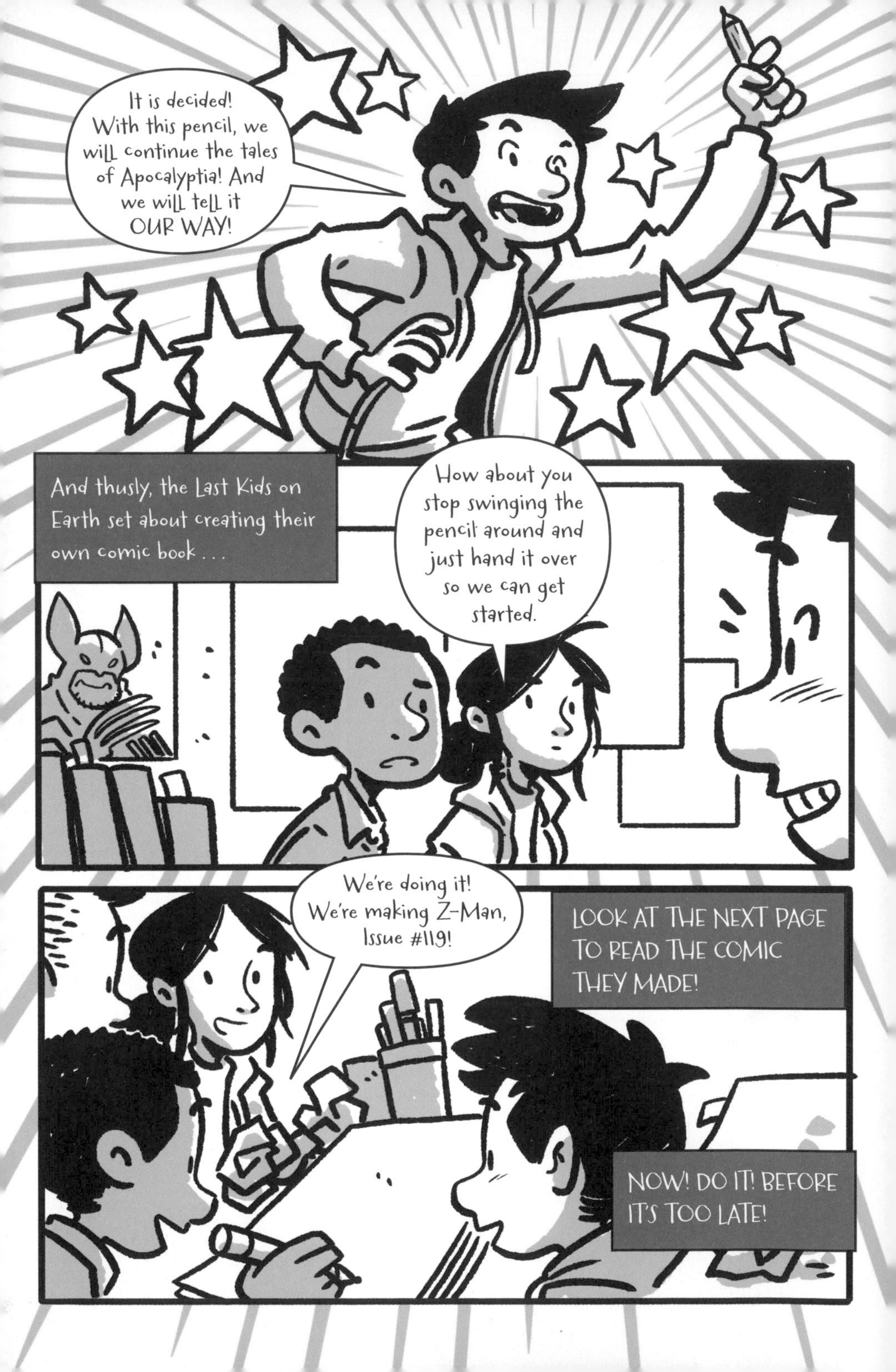
It is decided! With this pencil, we will continue the tales of Apocalyptia! And we will tell it OUR WAY!
And thusly, the Last Kids on Earth set about creating their own comic book . . .
How about you stop swinging the pencil around and just hand it over so we can get started.
We're doing it! We're making Z-Man, Issue #119!
LOOK AT THE NEXT PAGE TO READ THE COMIC THEY MADE!
NOW! DO IT! BEFORE IT'S TOO LATE!

CHAPTER TWO

JACK, JUNE, QUINT & DIRK IN . . .

THE LEGACY OF Z-MAN!

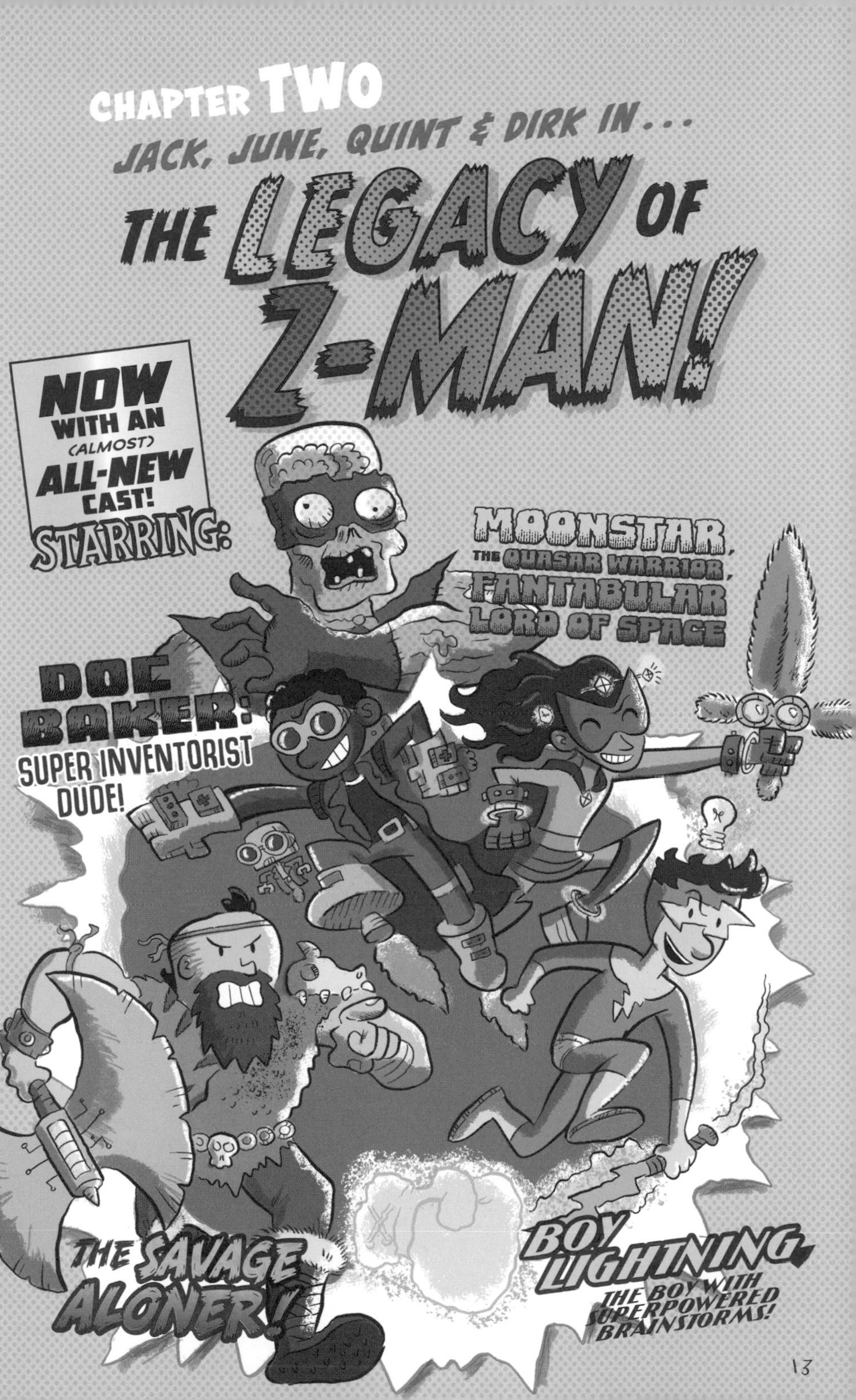
NOW WITH AN (ALMOST) ALL-NEW CAST!
STARRING:
MOONSTAR, THE QUASAR WARRIOR, FANTABULAR LORD OF SPACE
DOC BAKER: SUPER INVENTORIST DUDE!
THE SAVAGE ALONER!
BOY LIGHTNING, THE BOY WITH SUPERPOWERED BRAINSTORMS!

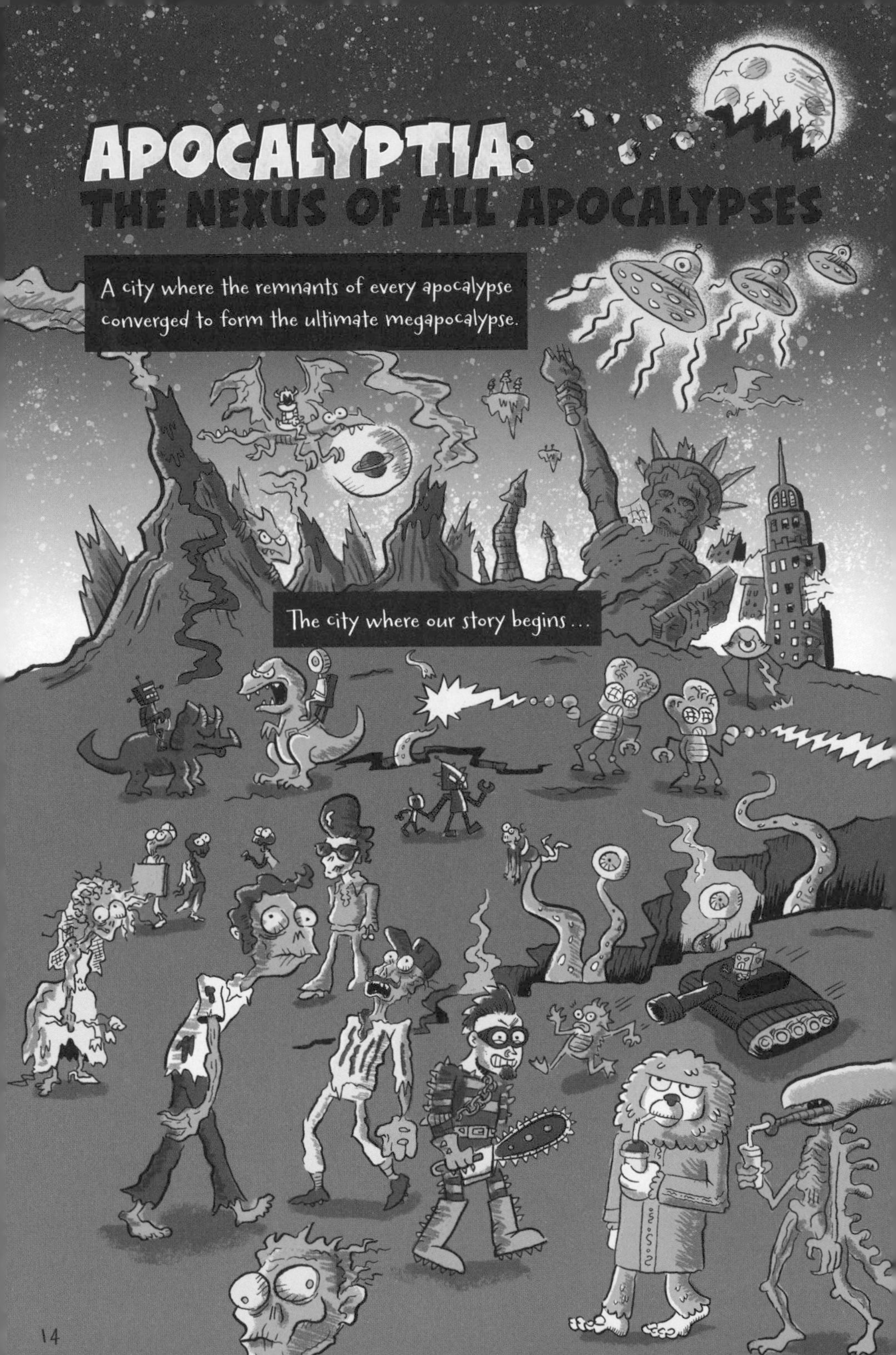
APOCALYPTIA:
THE NEXUS OF ALL APOCALYPSES
A city where the remnants of every apocalypse converged to form the ultimate megapocalypse.
The city where our story begins . . .

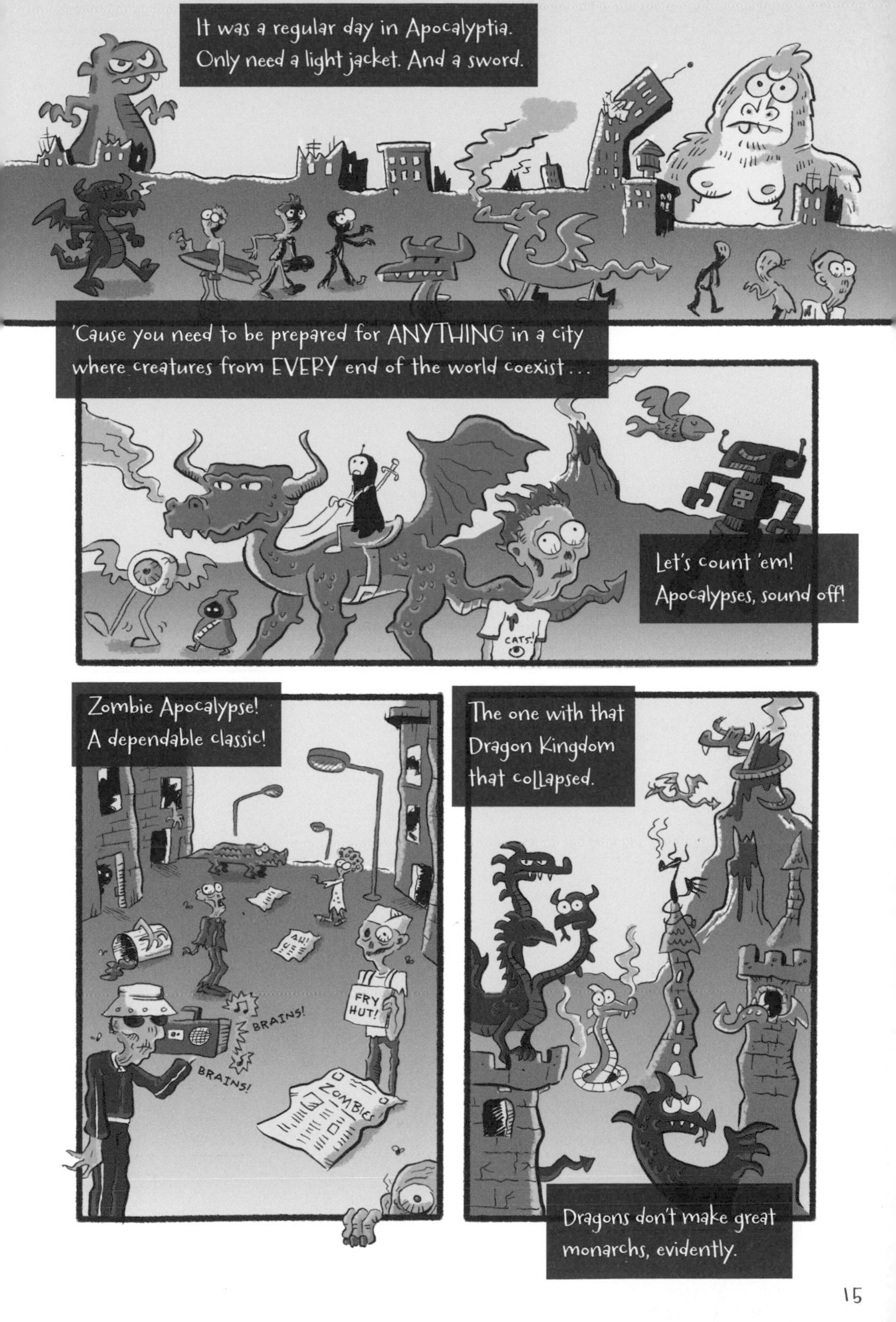
It was a regular day in Apocalyptia. Only need a light jacket. And a sword.
'Cause you need to be prepared for ANYTHING in a city where creatures from EVERY end of the world coexist . . .
CATS!
Let's count 'em! Apocalypses, sound off!
Zombie Apocalypse! A dependable classic!
AH!
FRY HUT!
BRAINS!
BRAINS!
ZOMBIES
The one with that Dragon Kingdom that collapsed.
Dragons don't make great monarchs, evidently.

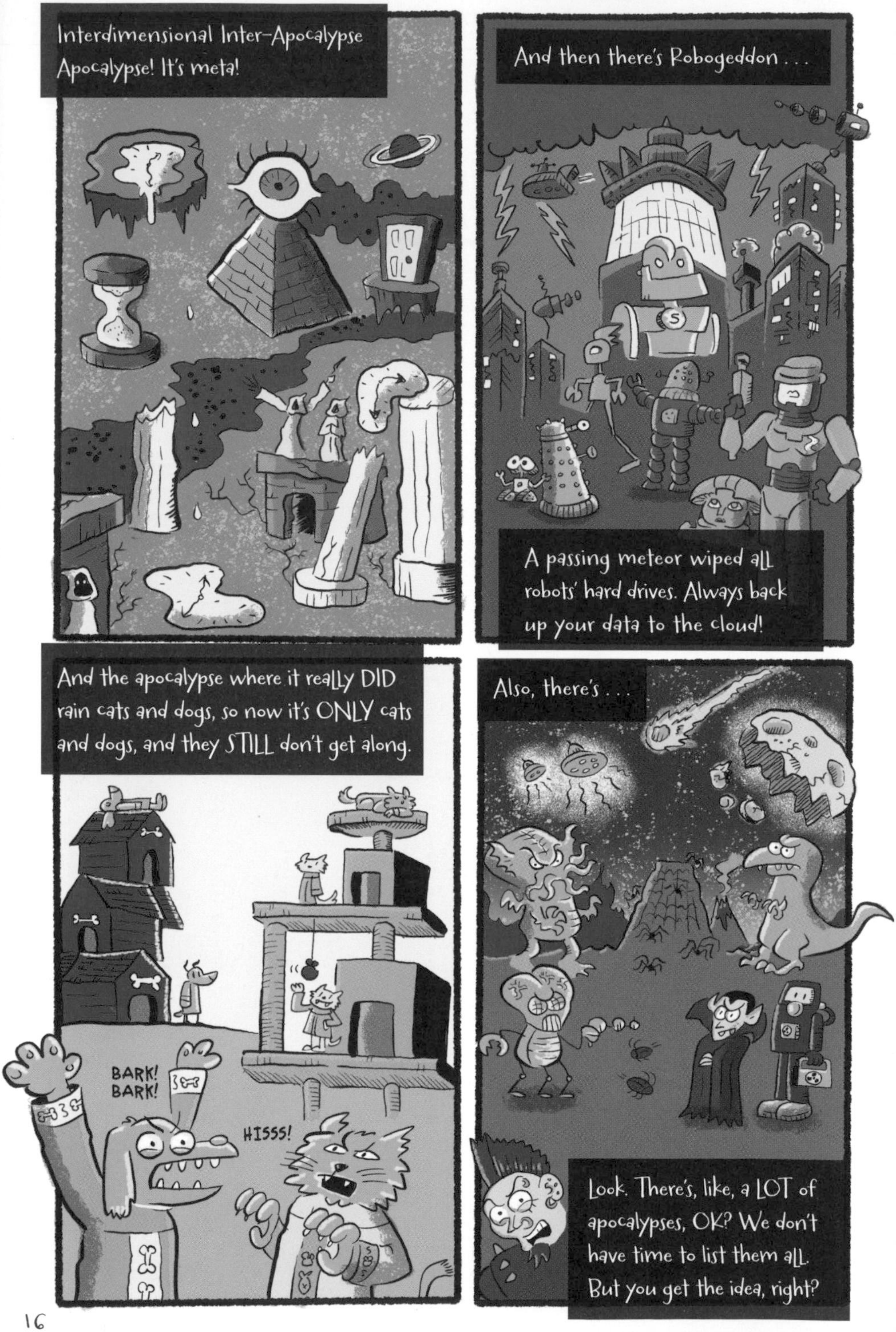
Interdimensional Inter-Apocalypse Apocalypse! It's meta!
And then there's Robogeddon . . .
A passing meteor wiped all robots' hard drives. Always back up your data to the cloud!
And the apocalypse where it really DID rain cats and dogs, so now it's ONLY cats and dogs, and they STILL don't get along.
BARK! BARK!
HISSS!
Also, there's . . .
Look. There's, like, a LOT of apocalypses, OK? We don't have time to list them all. But you get the idea, right?

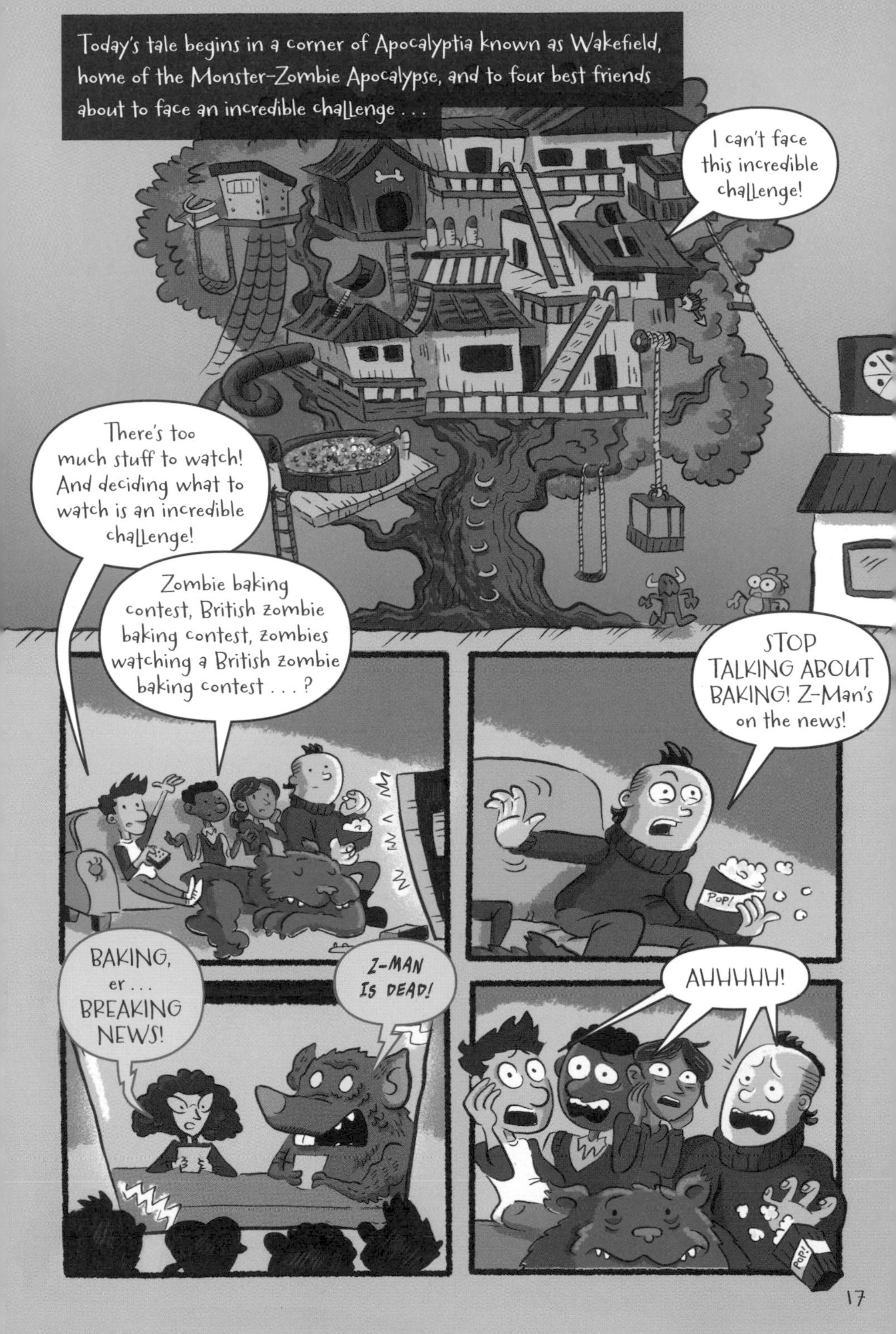
Today's tale begins in a corner of Apocalyptia known as Wakefield, home of the Monster-Zombie Apocalypse, and to four best friends about to face an incredible challenge . . .
I can't face this incredible challenge!
There's too much stuff to watch! And deciding what to watch is an incredible challenge!
Zombie baking contest, British zombie baking contest, zombies watching a British zombie baking contest . . . ?
STOP TALKING ABOUT BAKING! Z-Man's on the news!
POP!
BAKING, er . . . BREAKING NEWS!
Z-MAN IS DEAD!
AHHHHH!
POP!

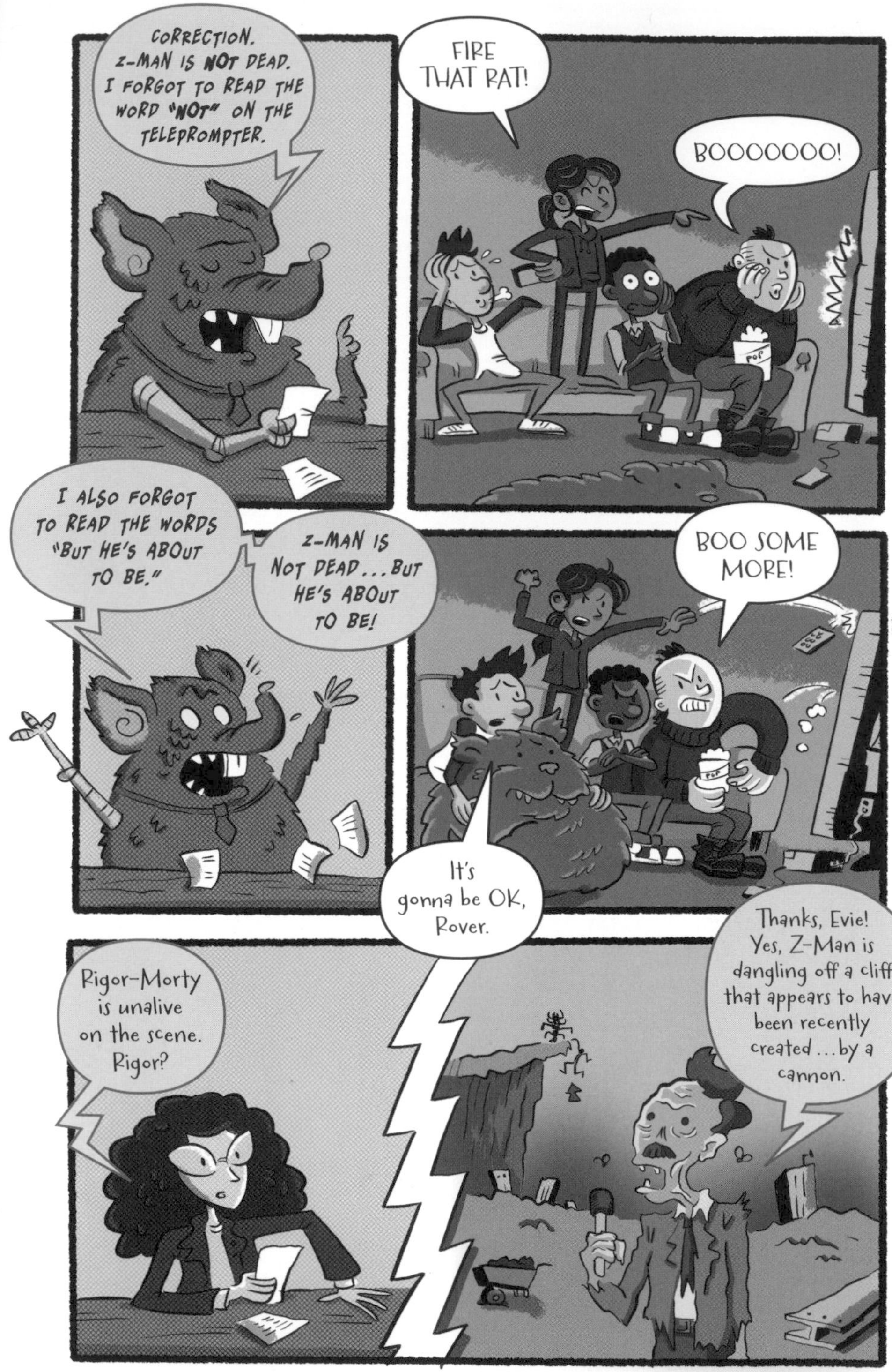
CORRECTION. Z-MAN IS **NOT** DEAD. I FORGOT TO READ THE WORD "**NOT**" ON THE TELEPROMPTER.
FIRE THAT RAT!
BOOOOOOO!
I ALSO FORGOT TO READ THE WORDS "BUT HE'S ABOUT TO BE."
Z-MAN IS NOT DEAD . . . BUT HE'S ABOUT TO BE!
BOO SOME MORE!
POP
It's gonna be OK, Rover.
Rigor-Morty is unalive on the scene. Rigor?
Thanks, Evie! Yes, Z-Man is dangling off a cliff that appears to have been recently created . . . by a cannon.

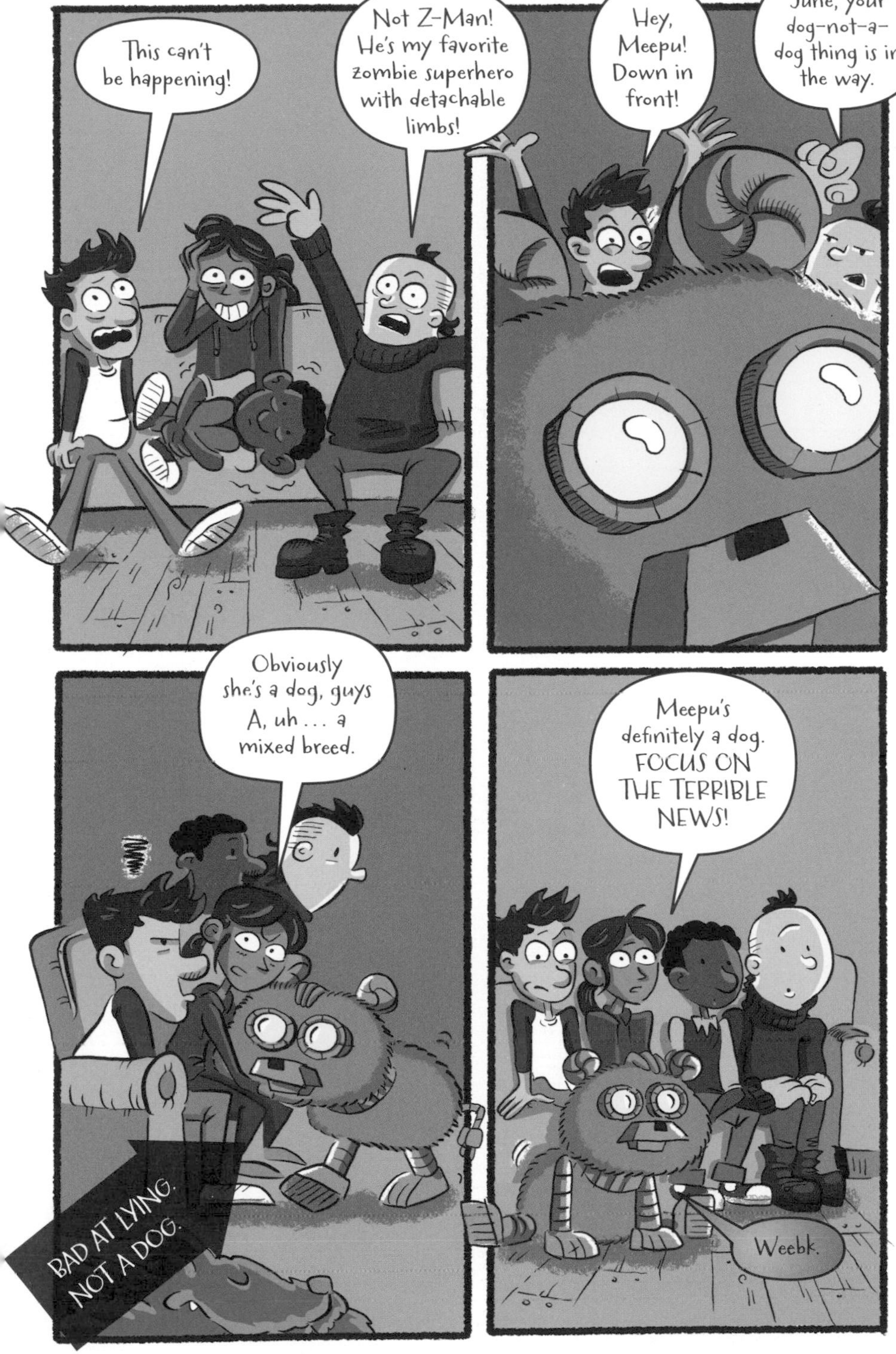
This can't be happening!
Not Z-Man! He's my favorite zombie superhero with detachable limbs!
Hey, Meepu! Down in front!
June, your dog-not-a-dog thing is in the way.
Obviously she's a dog, guys A, uh . . . a mixed breed.
BAD AT LYING. NOT A DOG.
Meepu's definitely a dog. FOCUS ON THE TERRIBLE NEWS!
Weebk.

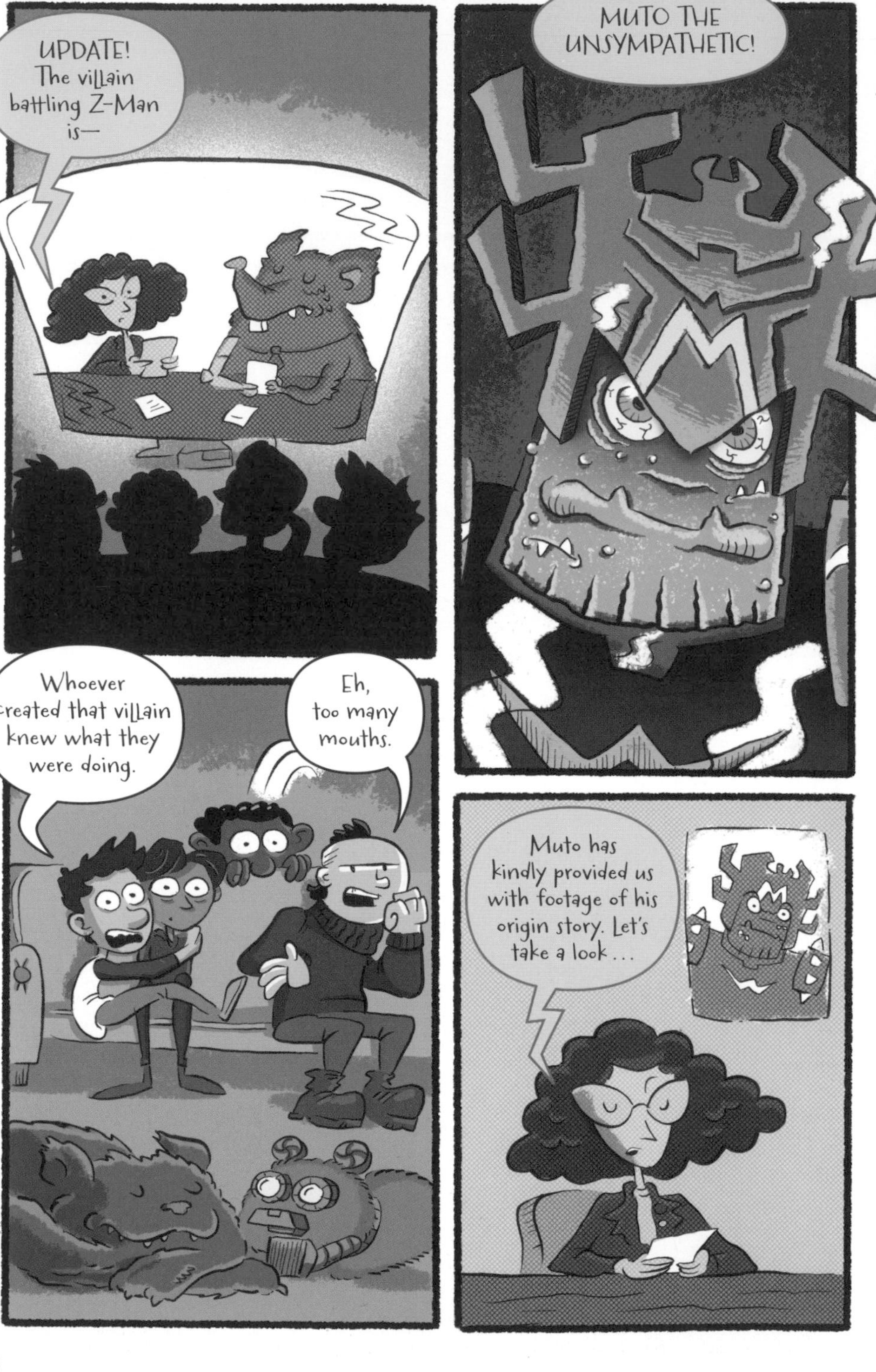
UPDATE! The villain battling Z-Man is—
MUTO THE UNSYMPATHETIC!
Whoever created that villain knew what they were doing.
Eh, too many mouths.
Muto has kindly provided us with footage of his origin story. Let's take a look . . .

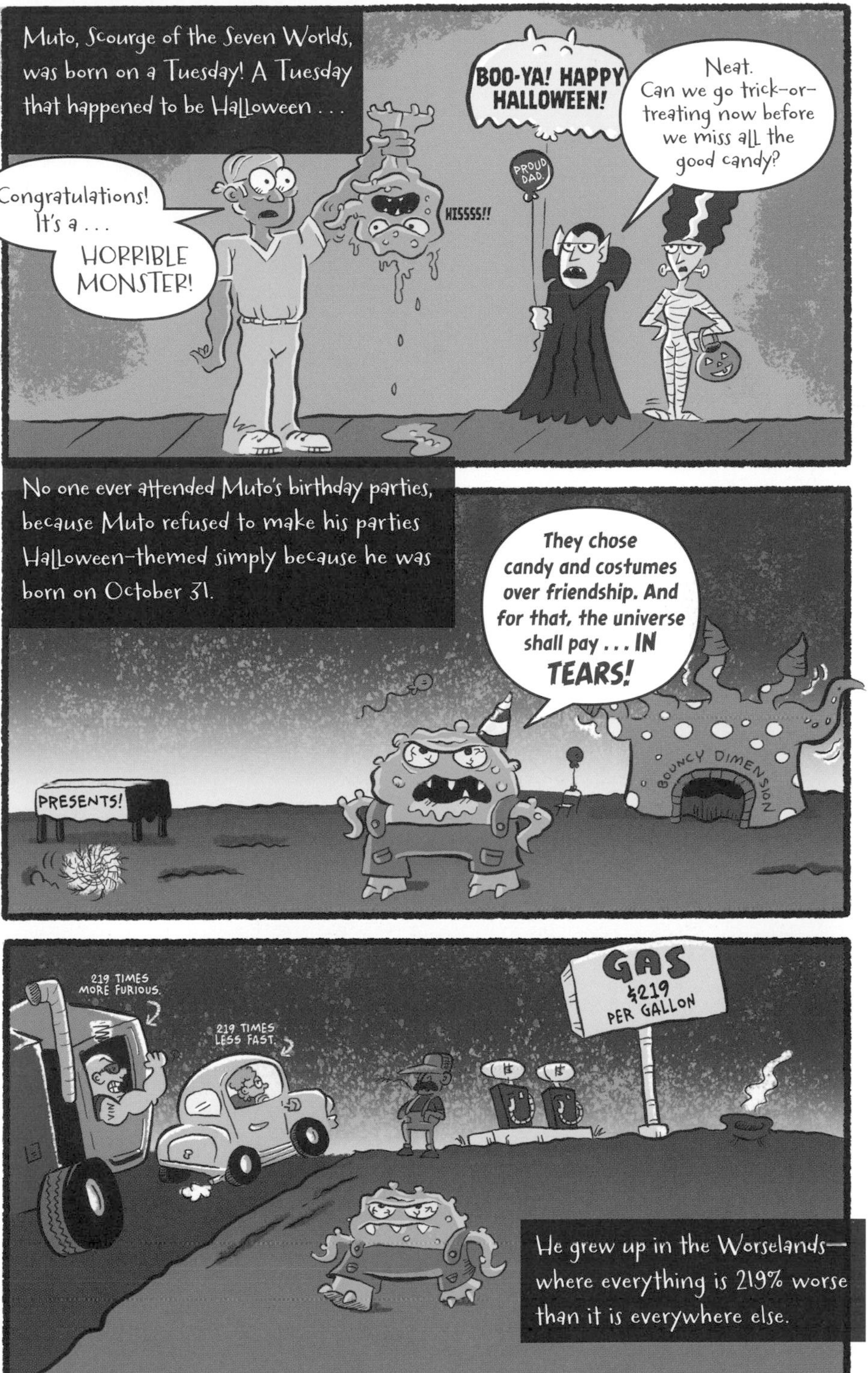
Muto, Scourge of the Seven Worlds, was born on a Tuesday! A Tuesday that happened to be Halloween . . .
Congratulations! It's a . . . HORRIBLE MONSTER!
HISSSS!!
BOO-YA! HAPPY HALLOWEEN!
PROUD DAD.
Neat. Can we go trick-or-treating now before we miss all the good candy?
No one ever attended Muto's birthday parties, because Muto refused to make his parties Halloween-themed simply because he was born on October 31.
They chose candy and costumes over friendship. And for that, the universe shall pay . . . IN TEARS!
PRESENTS!
BOUNCY DIMENSION
219 TIMES MORE FURIOUS.
VIN
219 TIMES LESS FAST.
GAS
$219
PER GALLON
He grew up in the Worselands—where everything is 219% worse than it is everywhere else.

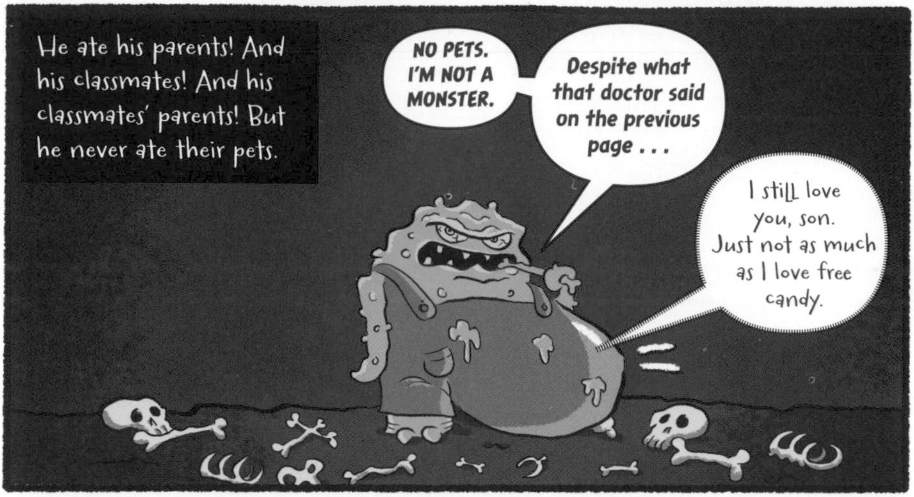
He ate his parents! And his classmates! And his classmates' parents! But he never ate their pets.
NO PETS. I'M NOT A MONSTER.
Despite what that doctor said on the previous page . . .
I still love you, son. Just not as much as I love free candy.

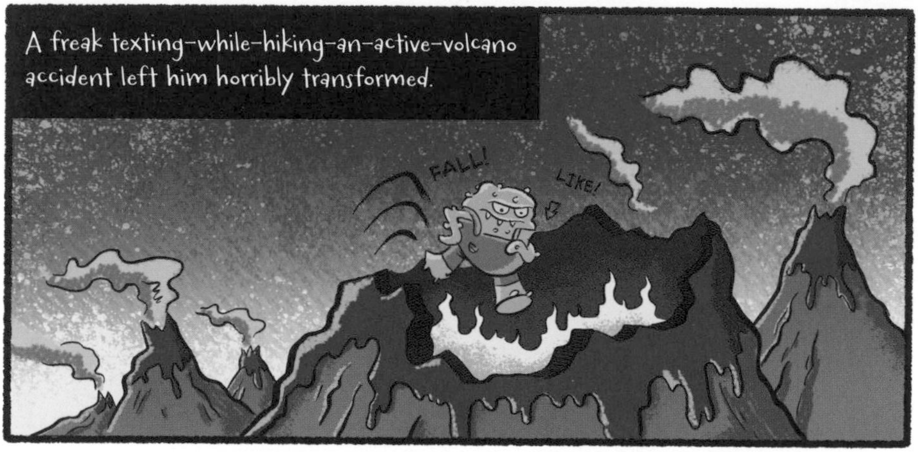
A freak texting-while-hiking-an-active-volcano accident left him horribly transformed.
FALL!
LIKE!

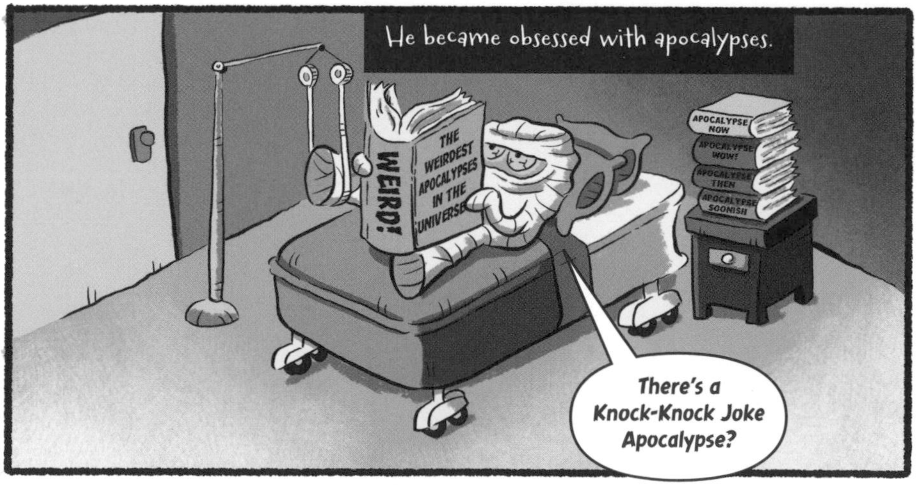
He became obsessed with apocalypses.
WEIRD!
THE WEIRDEST APOCALYPSES IN THE UNIVERSE
APOCALYPSE NOW
APOCALYPSE WOW!
APOCALYPSE THEN
APOCALYPSE SOONISH
There's a Knock-Knock Joke Apocalypse?

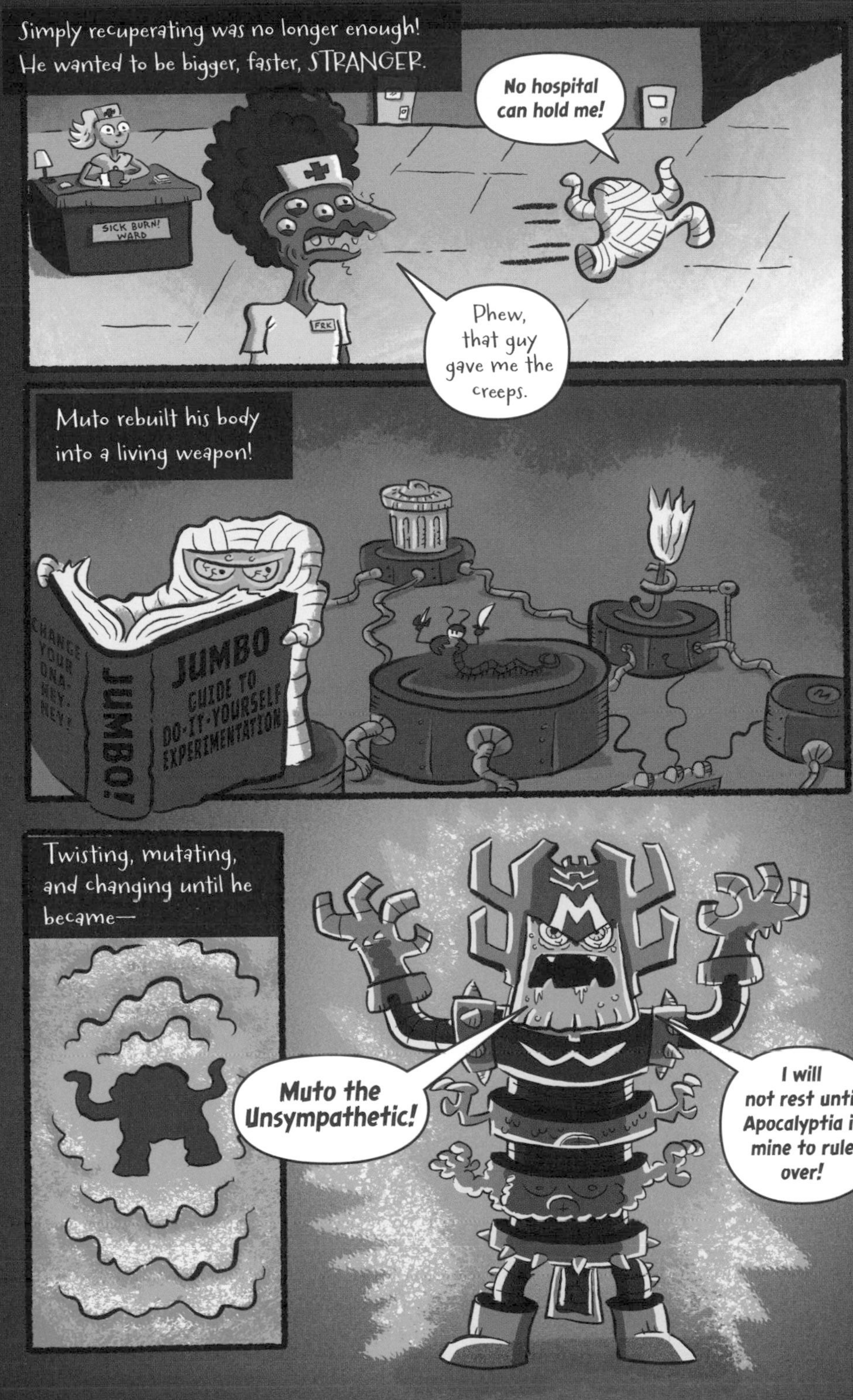
Simply recuperating was no longer enough! He wanted to be bigger, faster, STRANGER.
SICK BURN! WARD
No hospital can hold me!
FRK
Phew, that guy gave me the creeps.
Muto rebuilt his body into a living weapon!
CHANGE YOUR DNA-HEY-HEY!
JUMBO
JUMBO GUIDE TO DO-IT-YOURSELF EXPERIMENTATION
JUMBO!
Twisting, mutating, and changing until he became—
Muto the Unsympathetic!
I will not rest until Apocalyptia is mine to rule over!

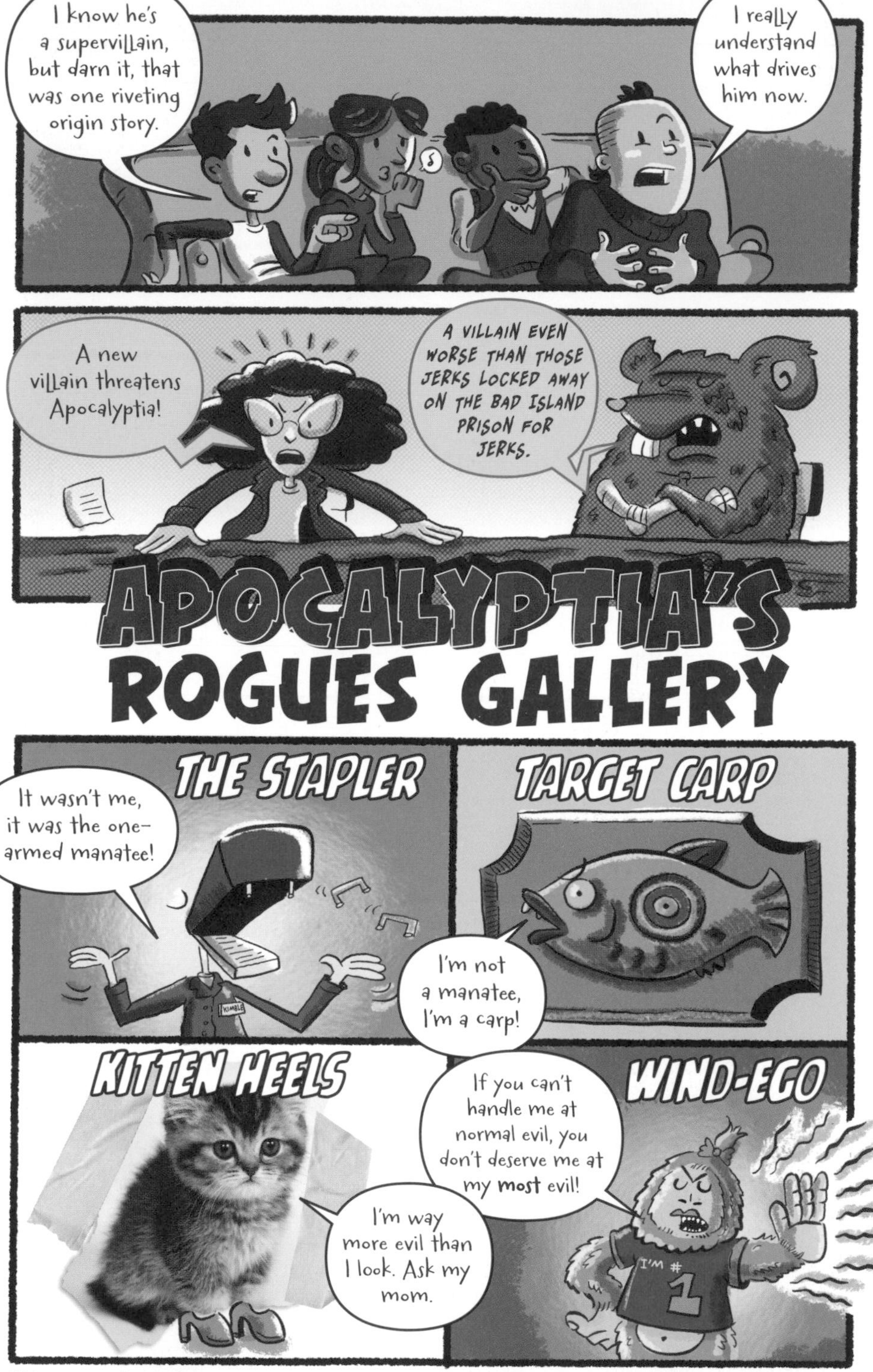
I know he's a supervillain, but darn it, that was one riveting origin story.
I really understand what drives him now.
A new villain threatens Apocalyptia!
A VILLAIN EVEN WORSE THAN THOSE JERKS LOCKED AWAY ON THE BAD ISLAND PRISON FOR JERKS.
APOCALYPTIA'S ROGUES GALLERY
THE STAPLER
It wasn't me, it was the one-armed manatee!
KIMBLE
TARGET CARP
I'm not a manatee, I'm a carp!
KITTEN HEELS
I'm way more evil than I look. Ask my mom.
WIND-EGO
If you can't handle me at normal evil, you don't deserve me at my **most** evil!
I'M # 1

*EDITOR NOTE: QUINT, ASK BEFORE YOU CUT PICTURES OUT OF MY KITTEN MAGAZINES! —DIRK

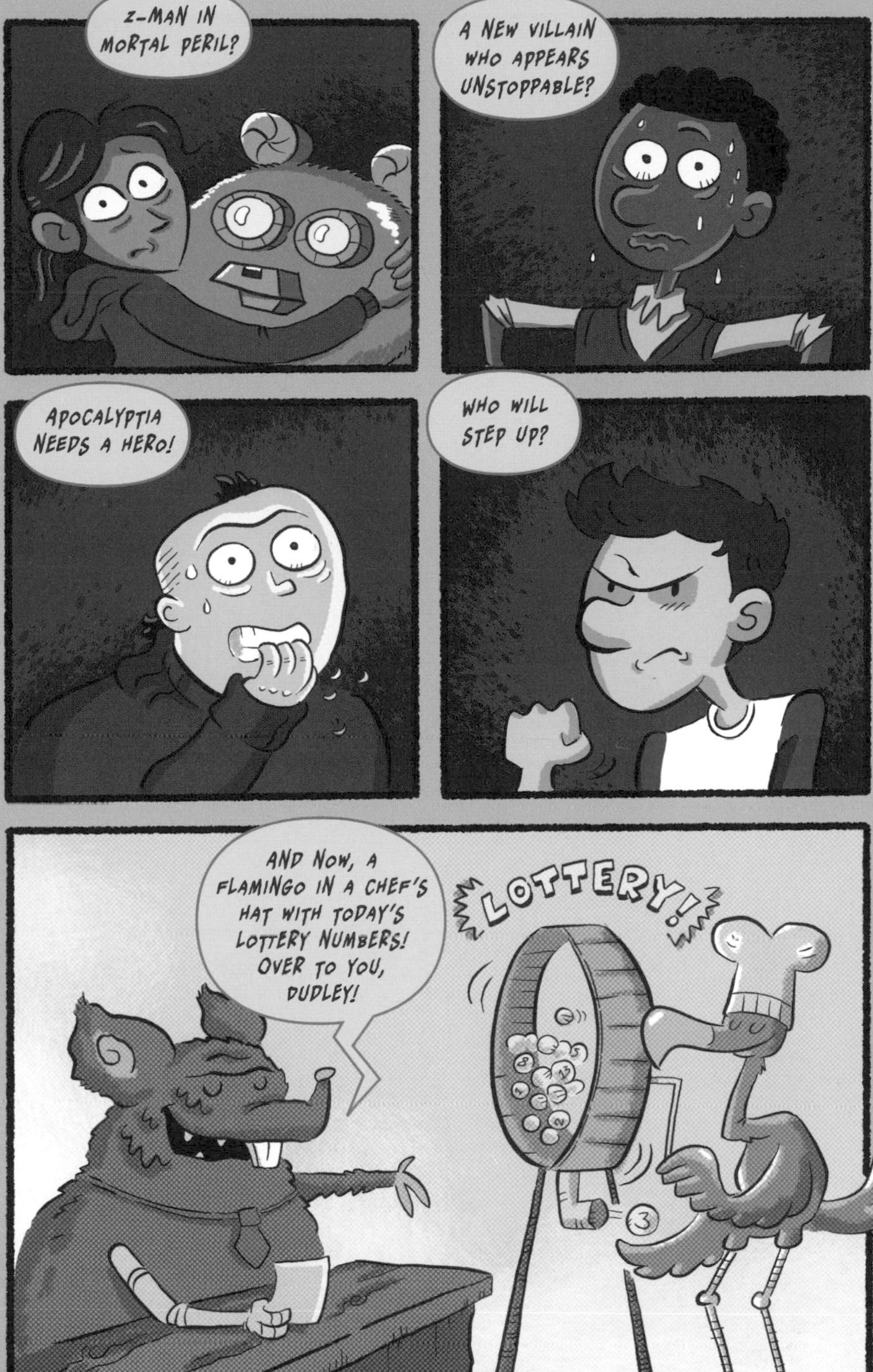
Z-MAN IN MORTAL PERIL?
A NEW VILLAIN WHO APPEARS UNSTOPPABLE?
APOCALYPTIA NEEDS A HERO!
WHO WILL STEP UP?
AND NOW, A FLAMINGO IN A CHEF'S HAT WITH TODAY'S LOTTERY NUMBERS! OVER TO YOU, DUDLEY!
LOTTERY!

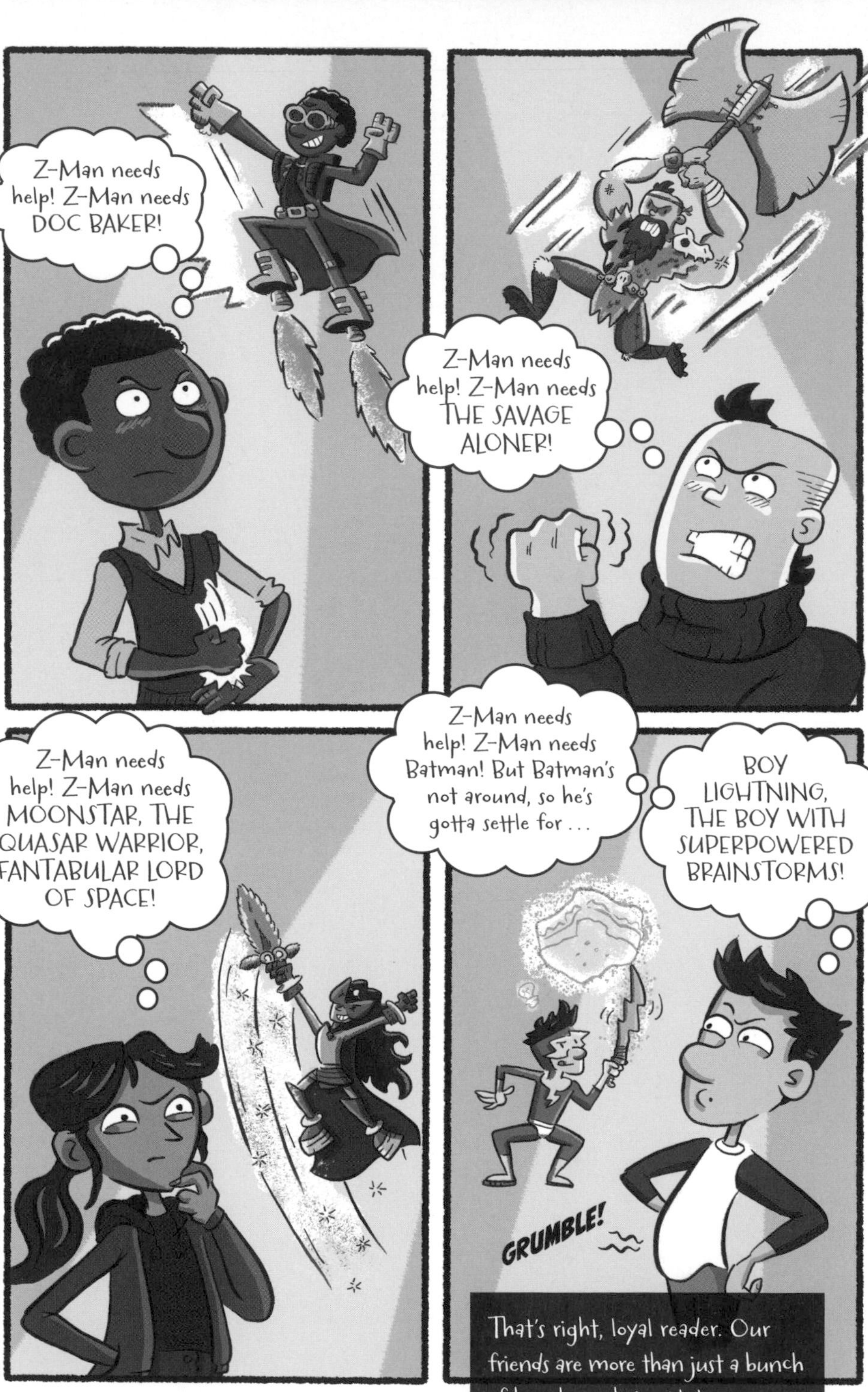
Z-Man needs help! Z-Man needs DOC BAKER!
Z-Man needs help! Z-Man needs THE SAVAGE ALONER!
Z-Man needs help! Z-Man needs MOONSTAR, THE QUASAR WARRIOR, FANTABULAR LORD OF SPACE!
Z-Man needs help! Z-Man needs Batman! But Batman's not around, so he's gotta settle for . . .
BOY LIGHTNING, THE BOY WITH SUPERPOWERED BRAINSTORMS!
GRUMBLE!
That's right, loyal reader. Our friends are more than just a bunch of beanbag-chair potatoes . . .

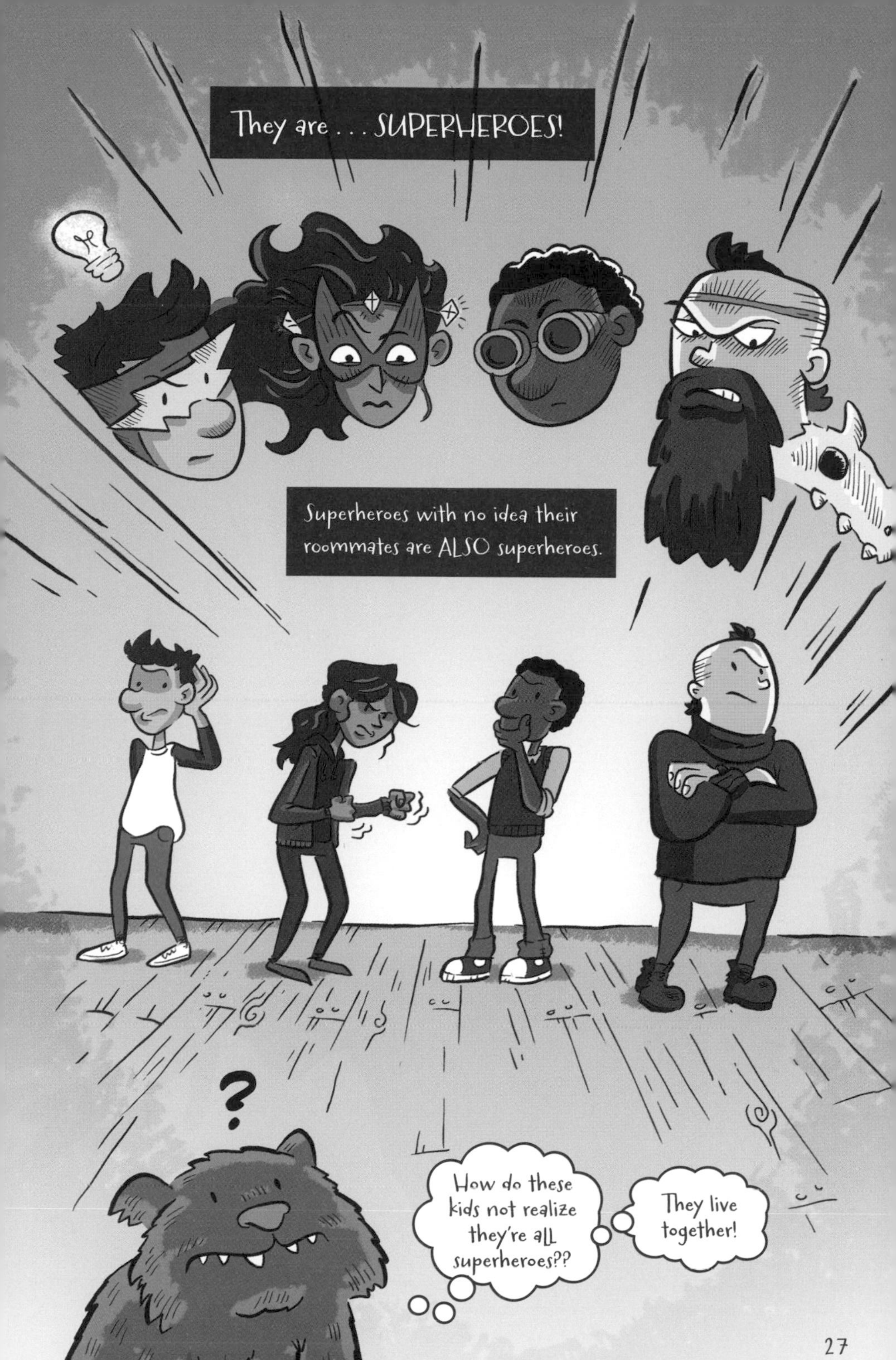

They are . . . SUPERHEROES!
Superheroes with no idea their roommates are ALSO superheroes.
?
How do these kids not realize they're aLL superheroes??
They live together!

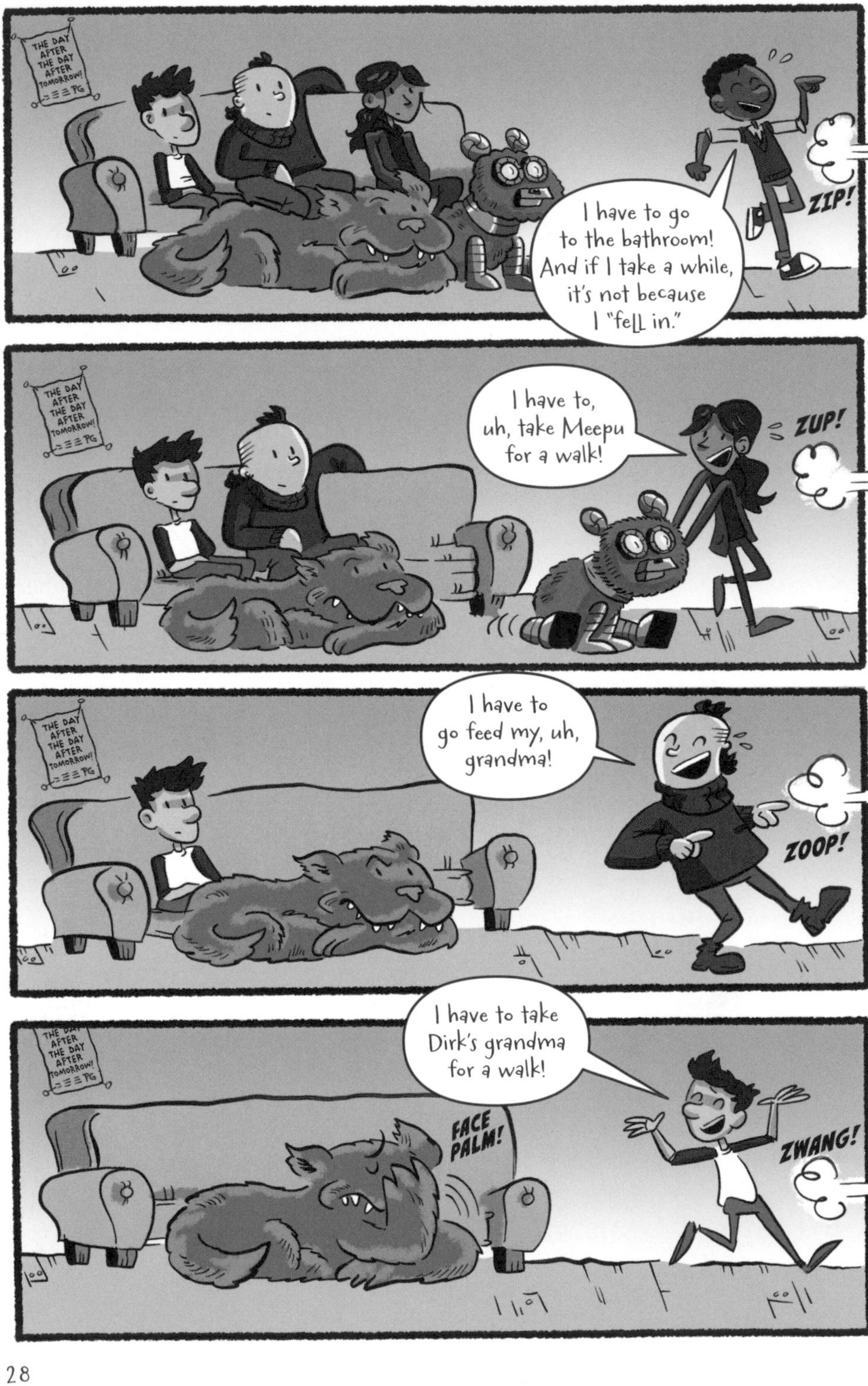
THE DAY AFTER THE DAY AFTER TOMORROW!
PG
I have to go to the bathroom! And if I take a while, it's not because I "fell in."
ZIP!
I have to, uh, take Meepu for a walk!
ZUP!
I have to go feed my, uh, grandma!
ZOOP!
I have to take Dirk's grandma for a walk!
FACE PALM!
ZWANG!

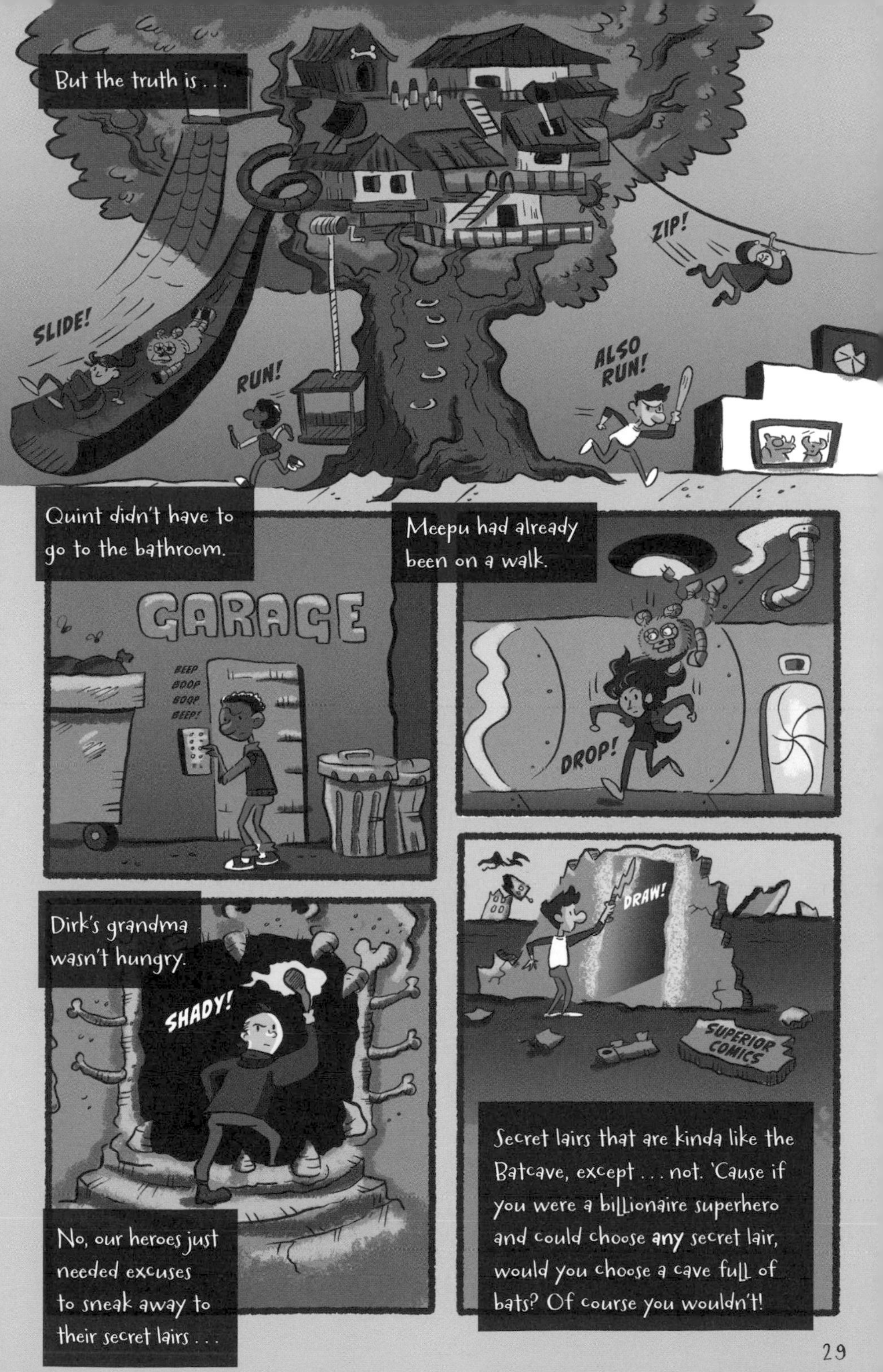
But the truth is . . .
SLIDE!
RUN!
ZIP!
ALSO RUN!
Quint didn't have to go to the bathroom.
GARAGE
BEEP BOOP BOOP BEEP!
Meepu had already been on a walk.
DROP!
Dirk's grandma wasn't hungry.
SHADY!
DRAW!
SUPERIOR COMICS
No, our heroes just needed excuses to sneak away to their secret lairs . . .
Secret lairs that are kinda like the Batcave, except . . . not. 'Cause if you were a billionaire superhero and could choose **any** secret lair, would you choose a cave full of bats? Of course you wouldn't!

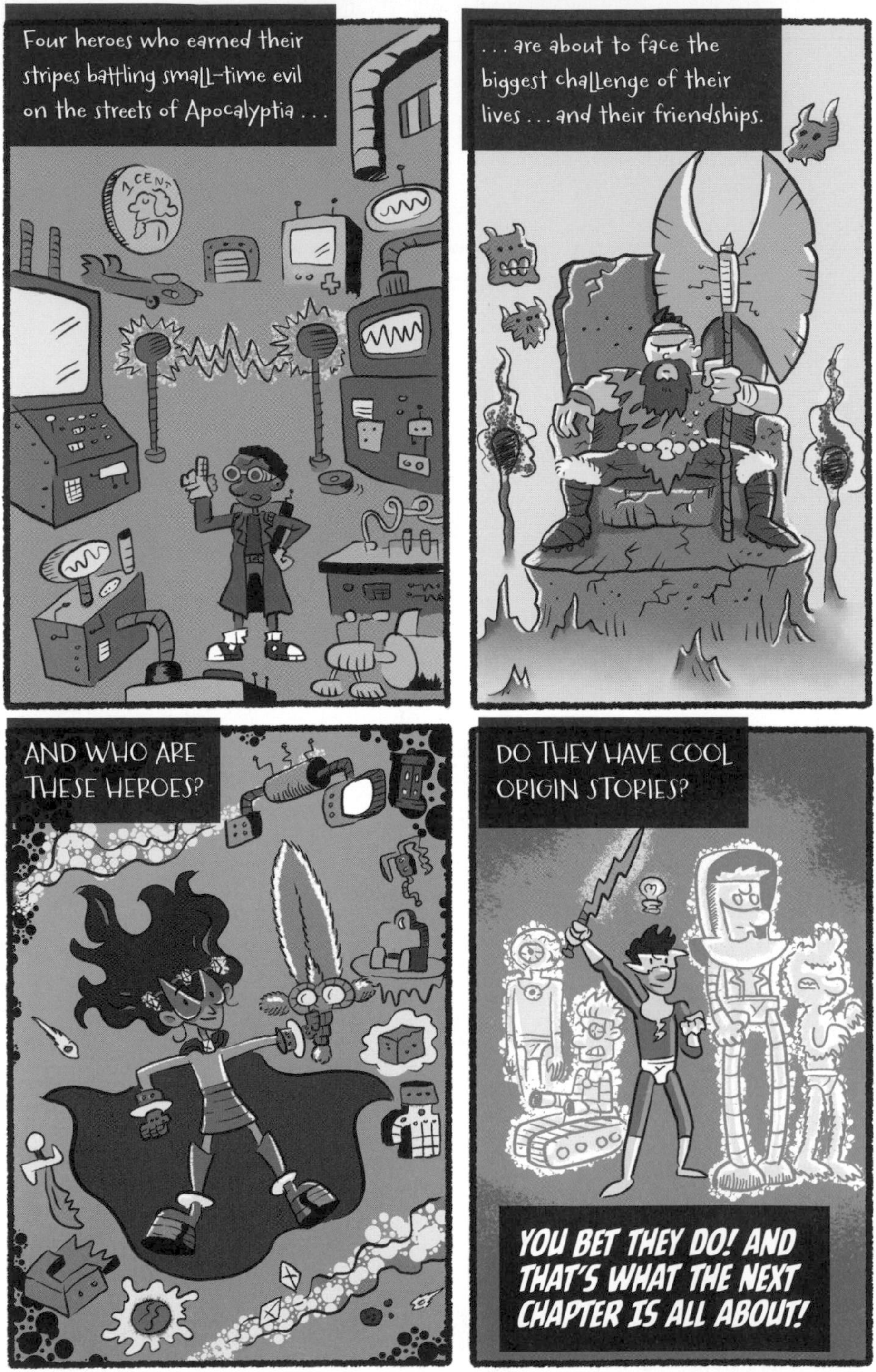
Four heroes who earned their stripes battling small-time evil on the streets of Apocalyptia . . .
1 CENT
. . . are about to face the biggest challenge of their lives . . . and their friendships.
AND WHO ARE THESE HEROES?
DO THEY HAVE COOL ORIGIN STORIES?
YOU BET THEY DO! AND THAT'S WHAT THE NEXT CHAPTER IS ALL ABOUT!

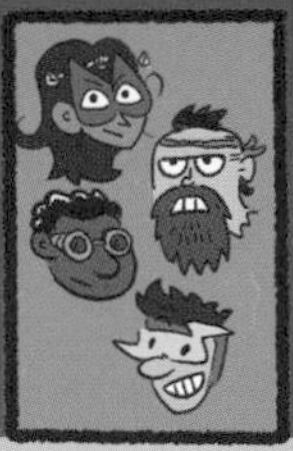

CHAPTER THREE

FOR THE FIRST TIME, ANYWHERE, THE AMAZING ORIGIN STORIES OF . . .

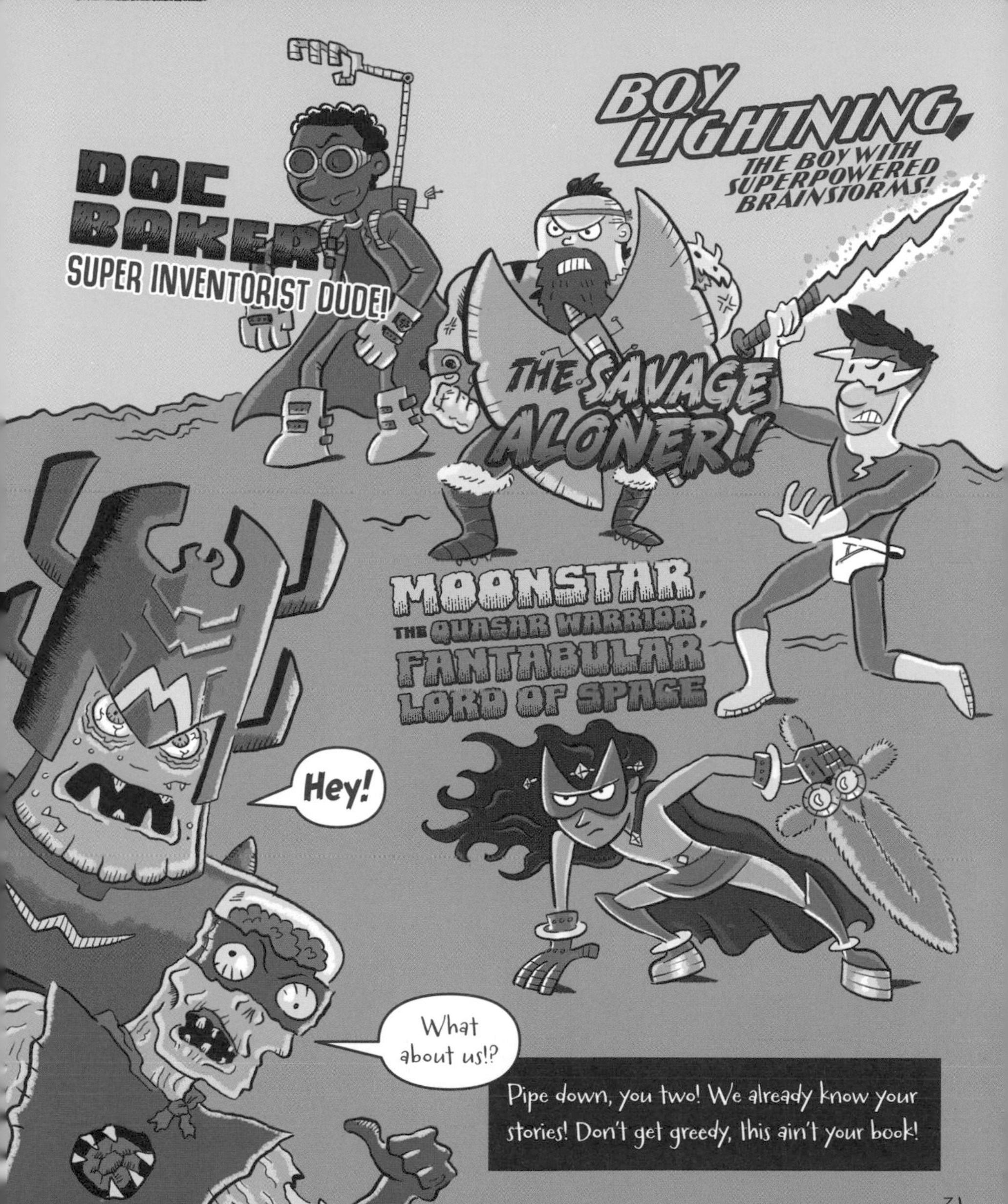

DOC BAKER, SUPER INVENTORIST DUDE!
BOY LIGHTNING, THE BOY WITH SUPERPOWERED BRAINSTORMS!
THE SAVAGE ALONER!
MOONSTAR, THE QUASAR WARRIOR, FANTABULAR LORD OF SPACE
Hey!
What about us!?
Pipe down, you two! We already know your stories! Don't get greedy, this ain't your book!

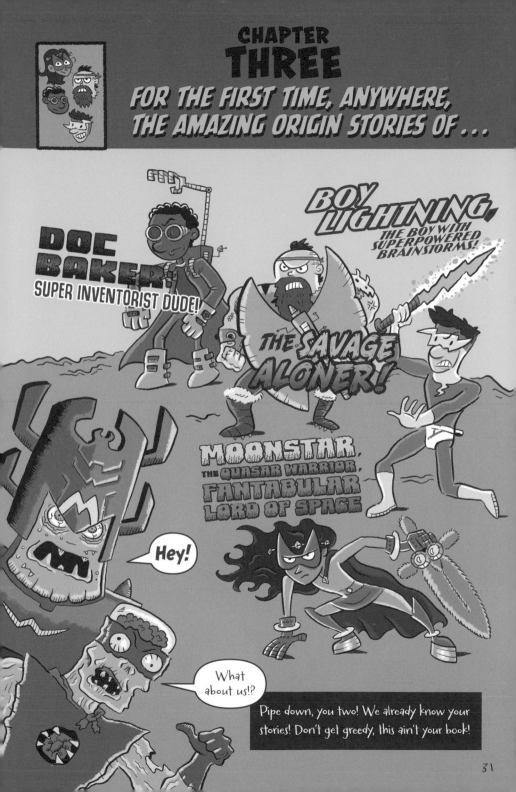

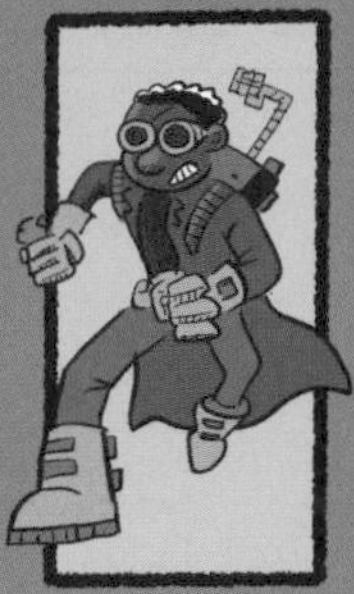

THE ORIGIN OF . . .

DOC BAKER: SUPER INVENTORIST DUDE!

Half man, half machine, **ALL HERO.**

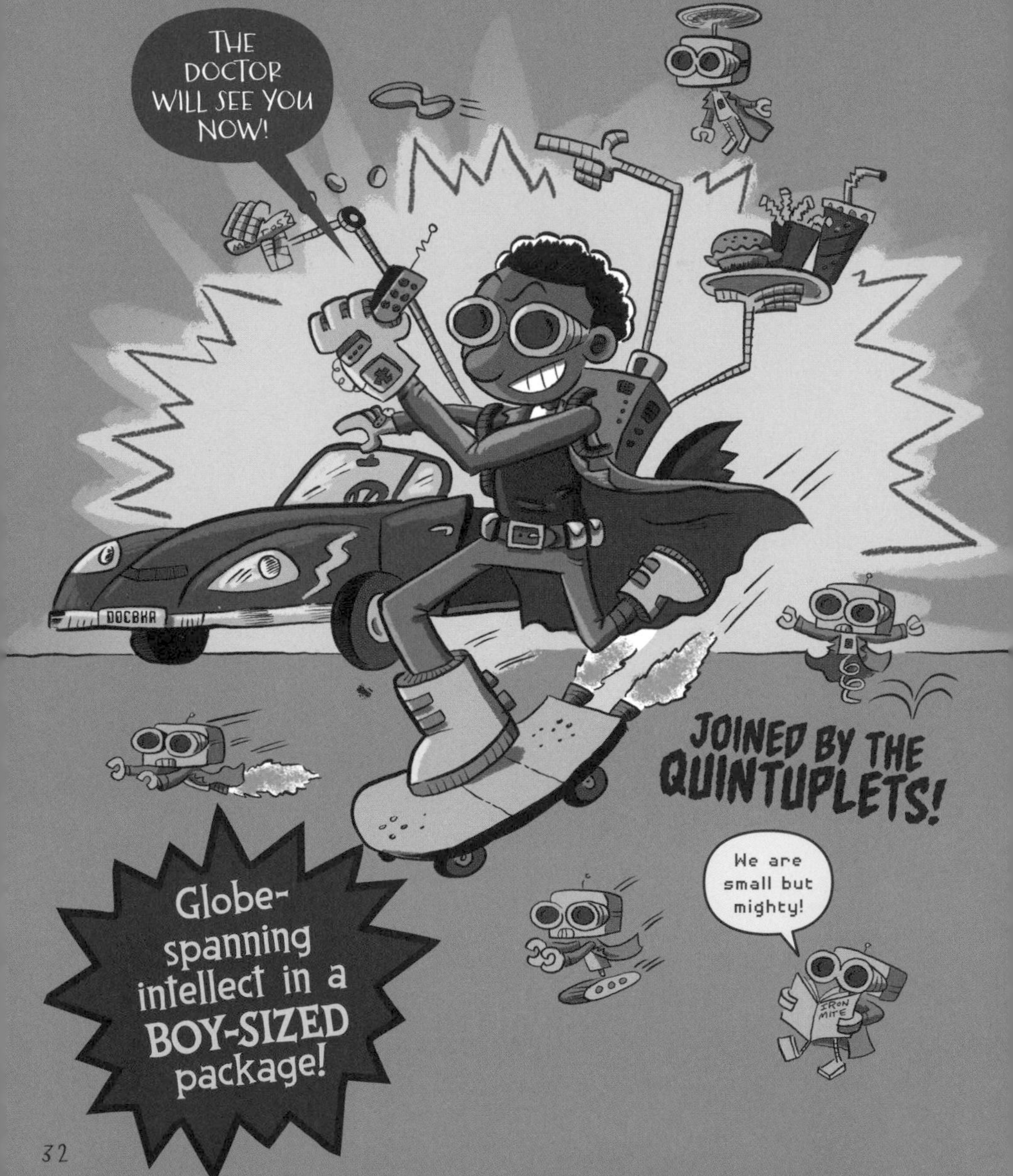
THE DOCTOR WILL SEE YOU NOW!
DOCBKR
JOINED BY THE QUINTUPLETS!
We are small but mighty!
IRON MITE
Globe-spanning intellect in a BOY-SIZED package!

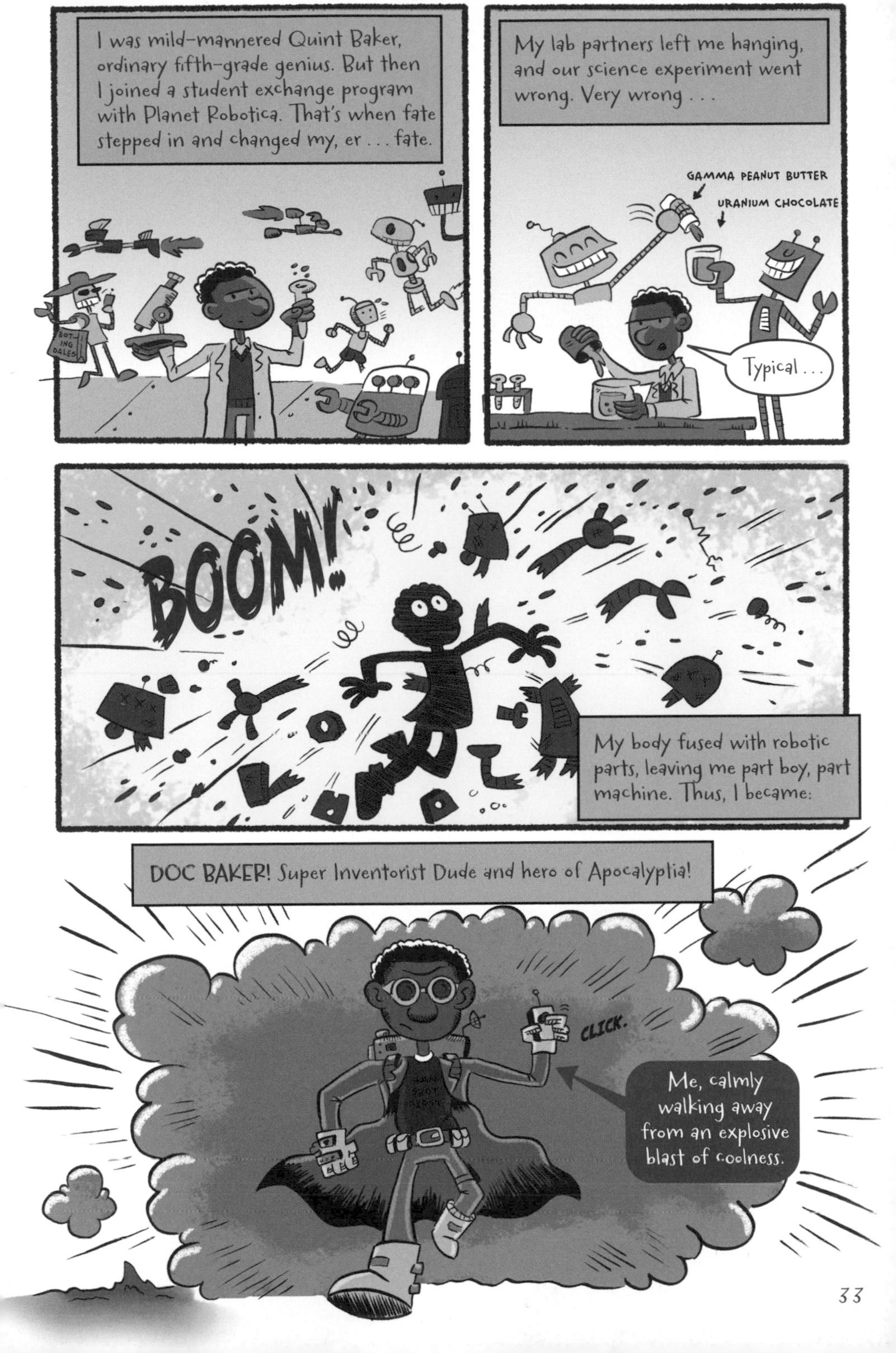
I was mild-mannered Quint Baker, ordinary fifth-grade genius. But then I joined a student exchange program with Planet Robotica. That's when fate stepped in and changed my, er . . . fate.
BOT-ING DALES
My lab partners left me hanging, and our science experiment went wrong. Very wrong . . .
GAMMA PEANUT BUTTER
URANIUM CHOCOLATE
Typical . . .
BOOM!
My body fused with robotic parts, leaving me part boy, part machine. Thus, I became:
DOC BAKER! Super Inventorist Dude and hero of Apocalyplia!
CLICK.
Me, calmly walking away from an explosive blast of coolness.

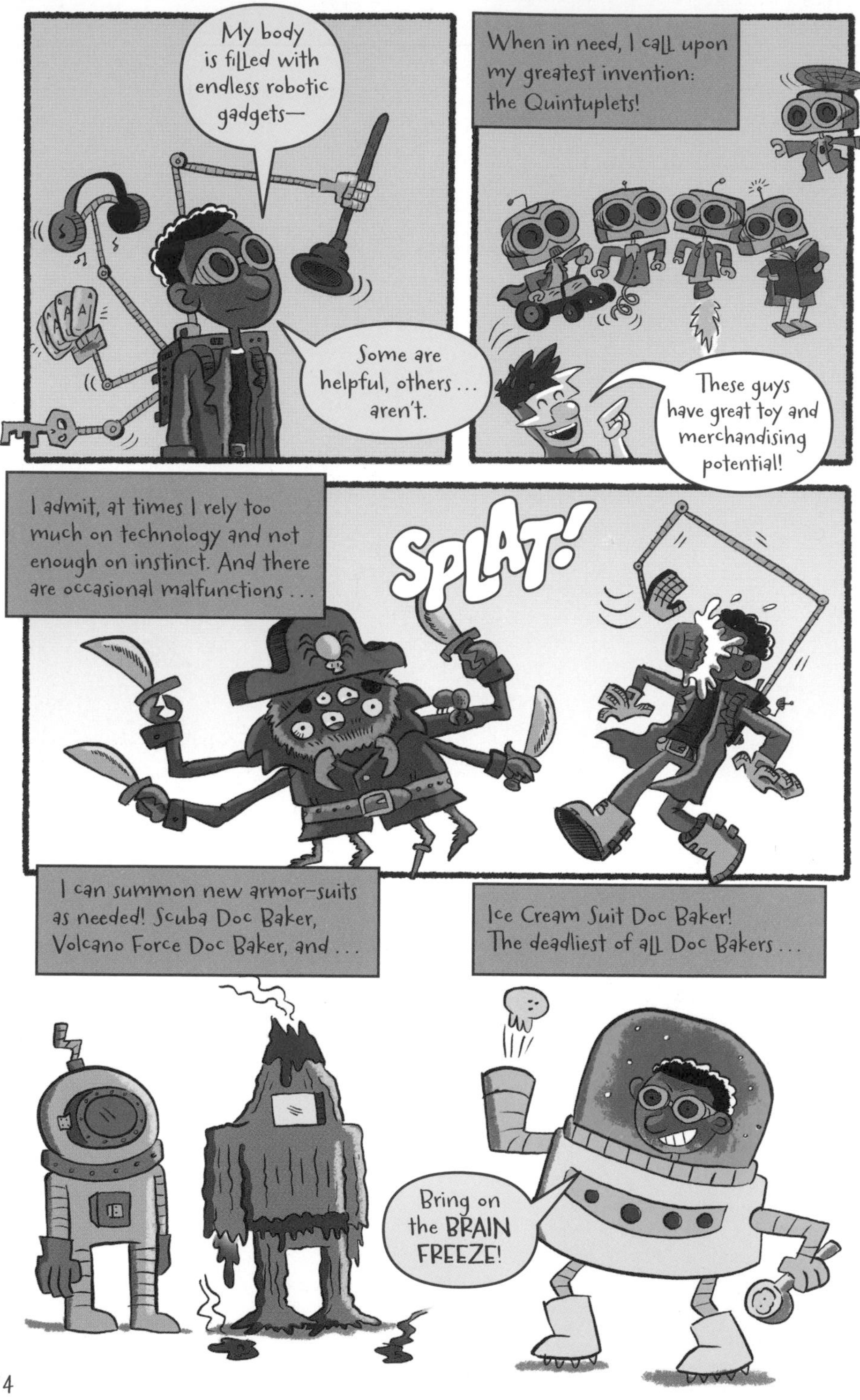
My body is filled with endless robotic gadgets—
Some are helpful, others . . . aren't.
When in need, I call upon my greatest invention: the Quintuplets!
These guys have great toy and merchandising potential!
I admit, at times I rely too much on technology and not enough on instinct. And there are occasional malfunctions . . .
SPLAT!
I can summon new armor-suits as needed! Scuba Doc Baker, Volcano Force Doc Baker, and . . .
Ice Cream Suit Doc Baker! The deadliest of all Doc Bakers . . .
Bring on the BRAIN FREEZE!

DOC BAKER'S SECRET LAIR: THE IMPOSSIBLE LAB!

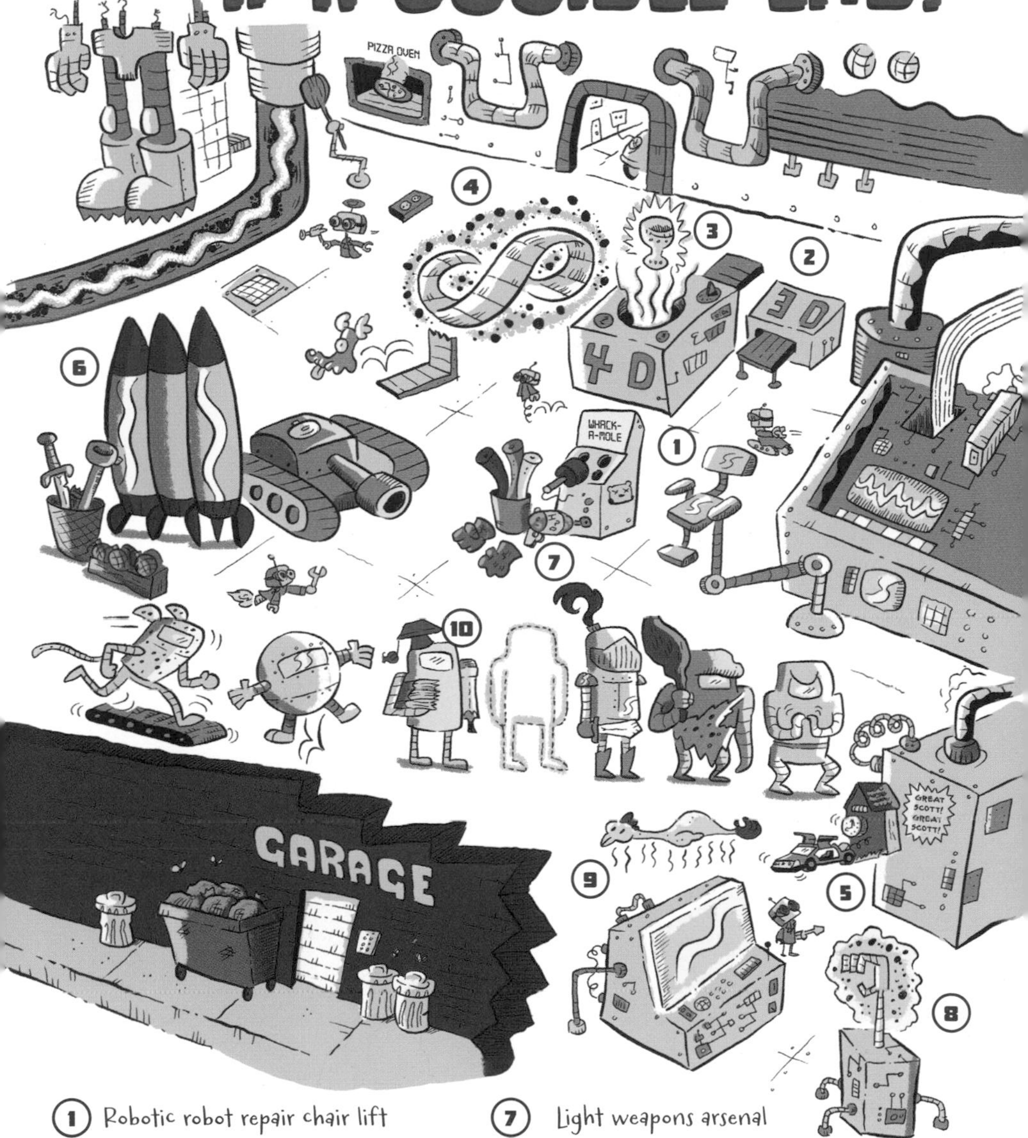
PIZZA OVEN
4
3
2
3D
4D
6
WHACK-A-MOLE
1
7
10
GREAT SCOTT! GREAT SCOTT!
GARAGE
9
5
8

1. Robotic robot repair chair lift
2. 3D printer
3. 4D printer
4. 8D printer
5. Miniature time travel vehicle storage
6. Heavy weapons arsenal
7. Light weapons arsenal
8. Proto-neutrino back scratcher
9. Rubber Hover Chicken
10. Cheetah Speed Doc Baker, Rubber Bouncy Ball Doc Baker, Book Report Doc Baker, Invisible Doc Baker, Medieval Doc Baker, Primeval Doc Baker, Almost Evil Doc Baker

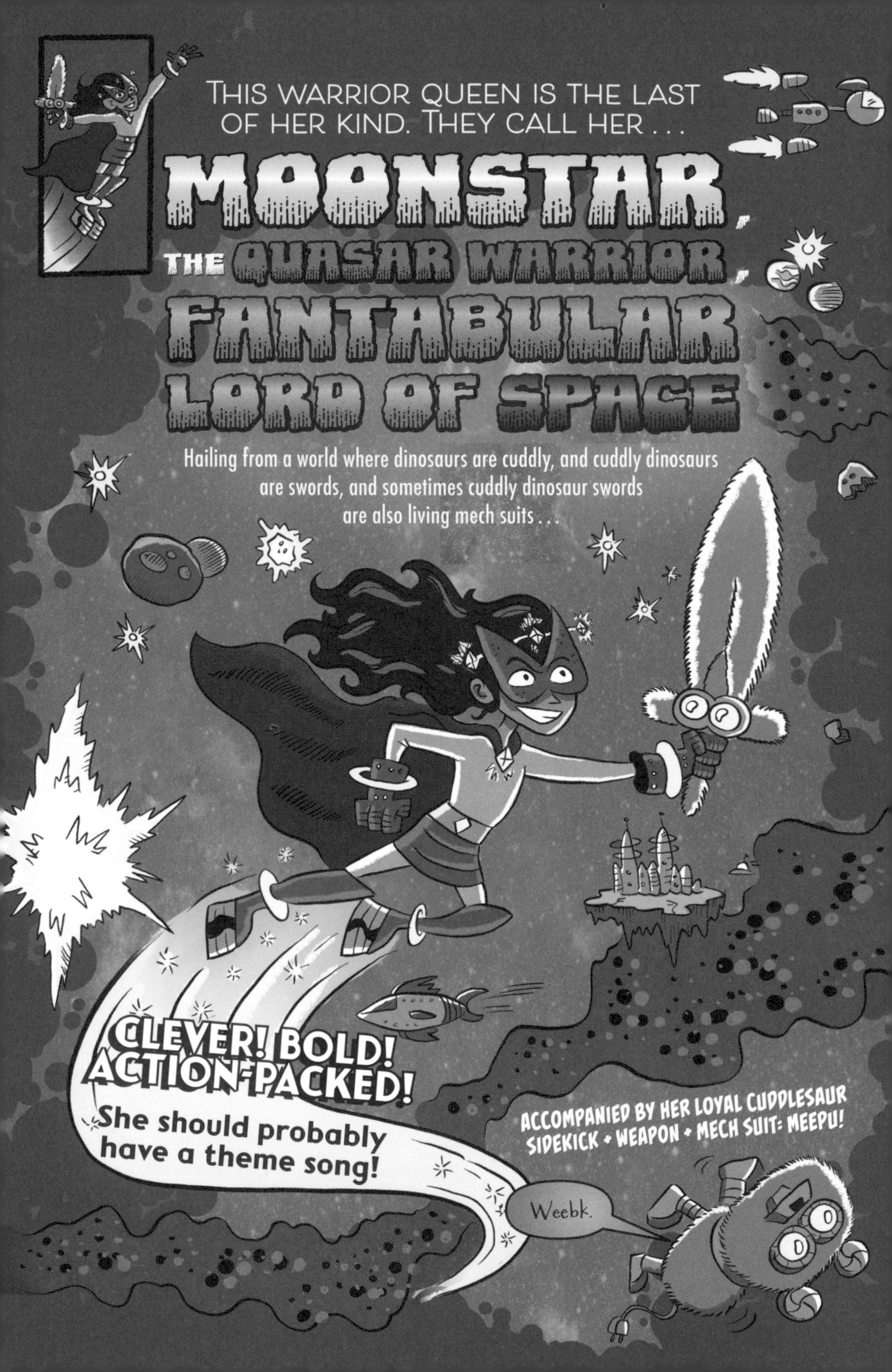
THIS WARRIOR QUEEN IS THE LAST OF HER KIND. THEY CALL HER . . .
MOONSTAR, THE QUASAR WARRIOR, FANTABULAR LORD OF SPACE
Hailing from a world where dinosaurs are cuddly, and cuddly dinosaurs are swords, and sometimes cuddly dinosaur swords are also living mech suits . . .
CLEVER! BOLD! ACTION-PACKED!
She should probably have a theme song!
ACCOMPANIED BY HER LOYAL CUDDLESAUR SIDEKICK + WEAPON + MECH SUIT: MEEPU!
Weebk.

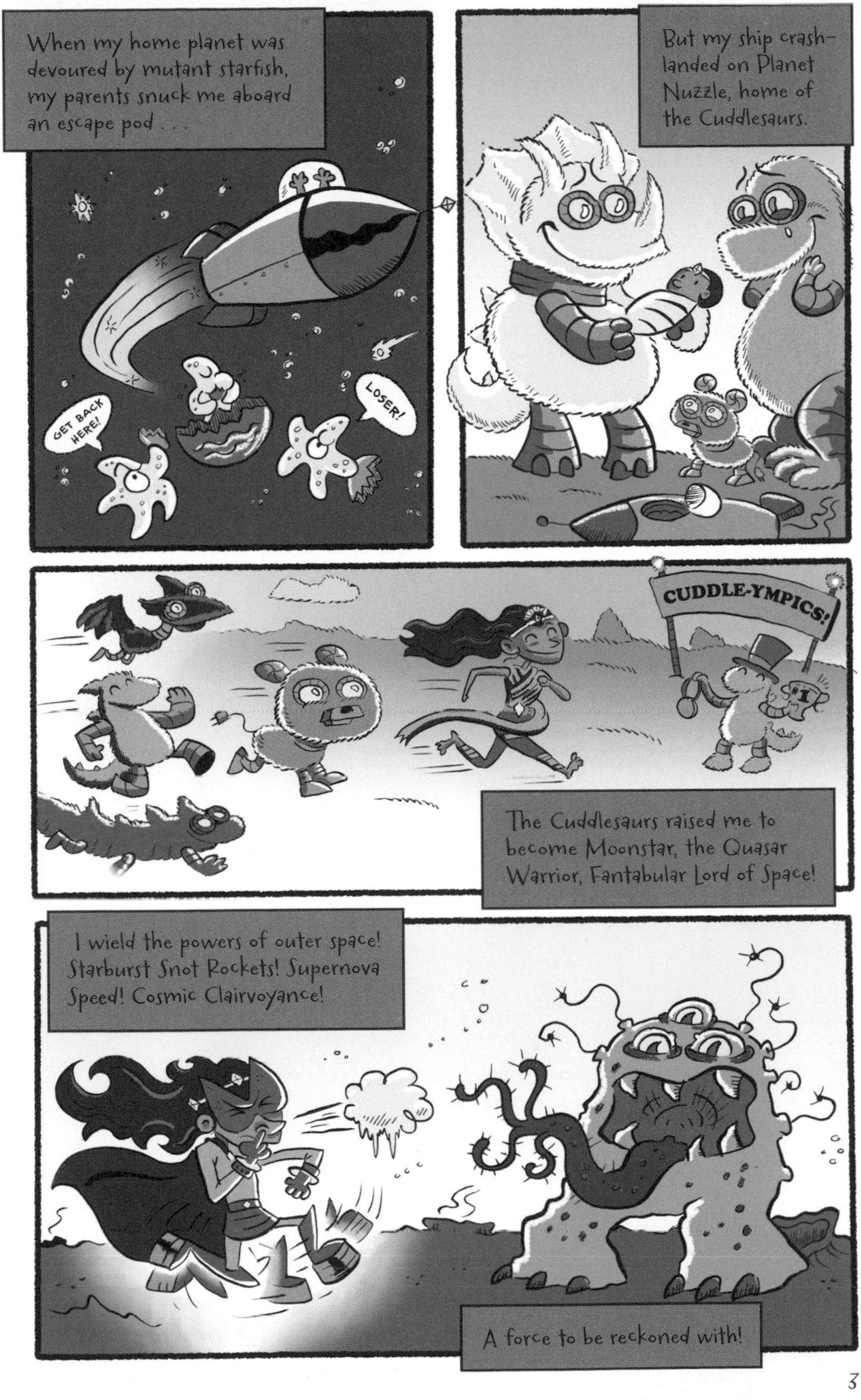
When my home planet was devoured by mutant starfish, my parents snuck me aboard an escape pod . . .
GET BACK HERE!
LOSER!
But my ship crash-landed on Planet Nuzzle, home of the Cuddlesaurs.
CUDDLE-YMPICS!
#1
The Cuddlesaurs raised me to become Moonstar, the Quasar Warrior, Fantabular Lord of Space!
I wield the powers of outer space! Starburst Snot Rockets! Supernova Speed! Cosmic Clairvoyance!
A force to be reckoned with!

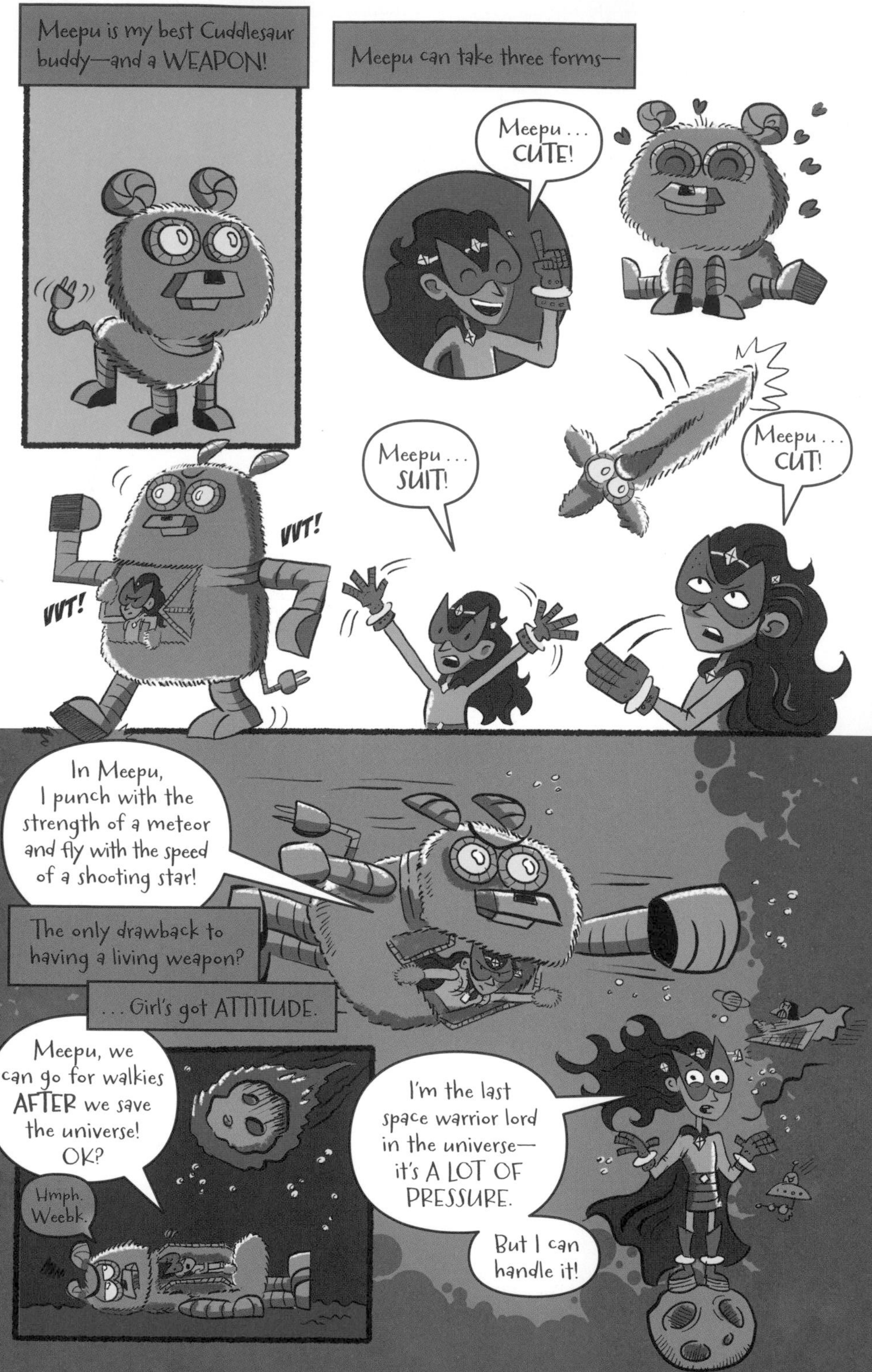
Meepu is my best Cuddlesaur buddy—and a WEAPON!
Meepu can take three forms—
Meepu . . . CUTE!
Meepu . . . CUT!
Meepu . . . SUIT!
VVT!
VVT!
In Meepu, I punch with the strength of a meteor and fly with the speed of a shooting star!
The only drawback to having a living weapon?
. . . Girl's got ATTITUDE.
Meepu, we can go for walkies AFTER we save the universe! OK?
Hmph. Weebk.
I'm the last space warrior lord in the universe—it's A LOT OF PRESSURE.
But I can handle it!

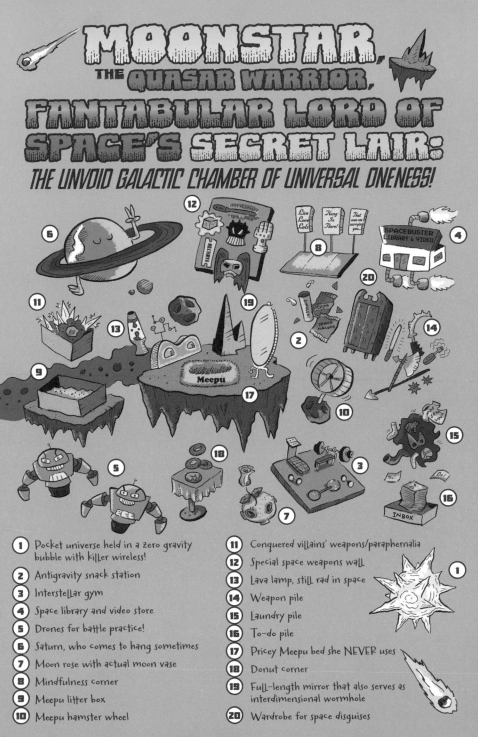

MOONSTAR, THE QUASAR WARRIOR, FANTABULAR LORD OF SPACE'S SECRET LAIR:

THE UNVOID GALACTIC CHAMBER OF UNIVERSAL ONENESS!

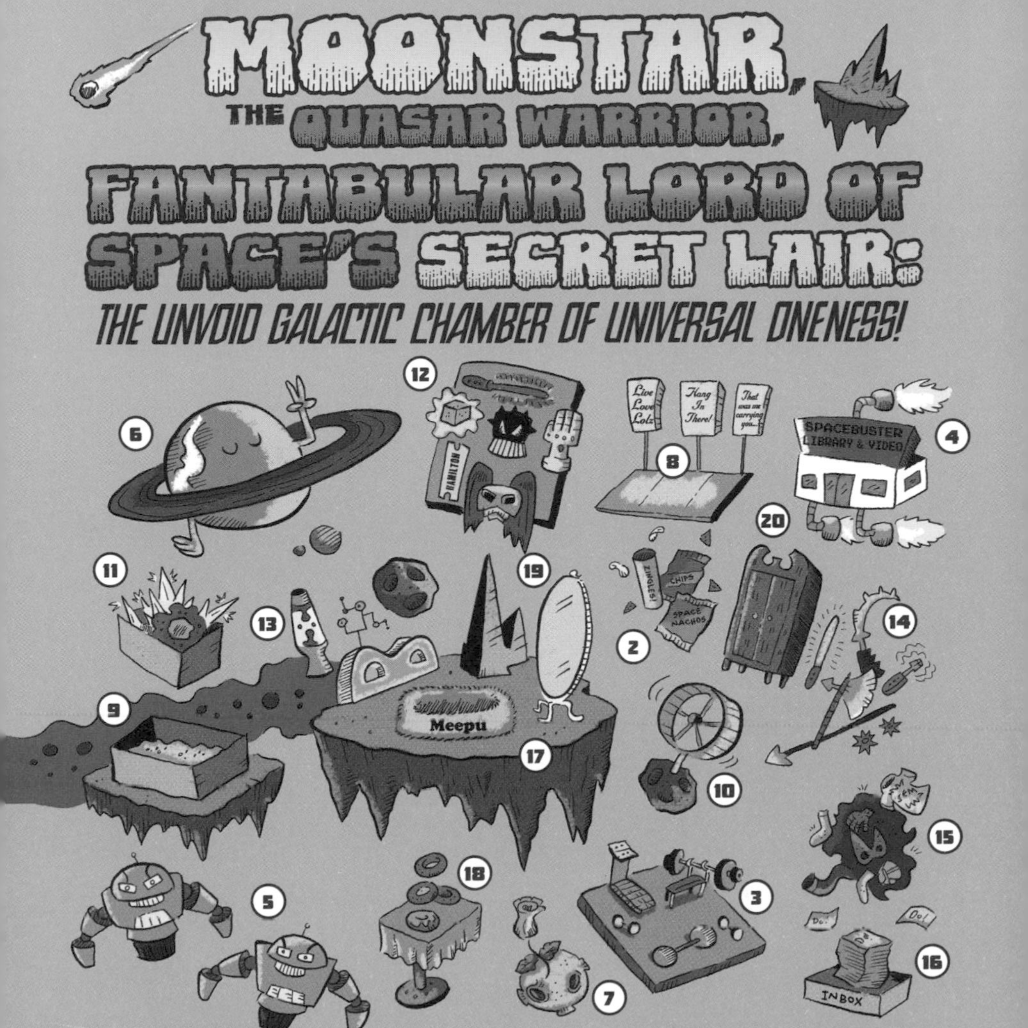

Live Love Lolz
Hang In There!
SPACEBUSTER LIBRARY & VIDEO
HAMILTON
ZINGLES!
CHIPS
SPACE NACHOS
Meepu
INBOX
Do!
Do!

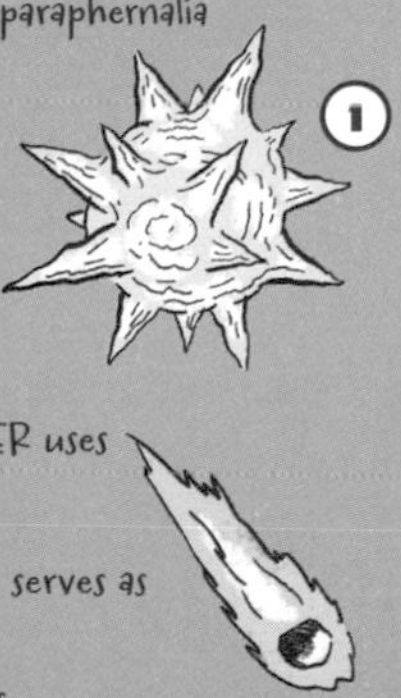

1

1. Pocket universe held in a zero gravity bubble with killer wireless!
2. Antigravity snack station
3. Interstellar gym
4. Space library and video store
5. Drones for battle practice!
6. Saturn, who comes to hang sometimes
7. Moon rose with actual moon vase
8. Mindfulness corner
9. Meepu litter box
10. Meepu hamster wheel
11. Conquered villains' weapons/paraphernalia
12. Special space weapons wall
13. Lava lamp, still rad in space
14. Weapon pile
15. Laundry pile
16. To-do pile
17. Pricey Meepu bed she NEVER uses
18. Donut corner
19. Full-length mirror that also serves as interdimensional wormhole
20. Wardrobe for space disguises

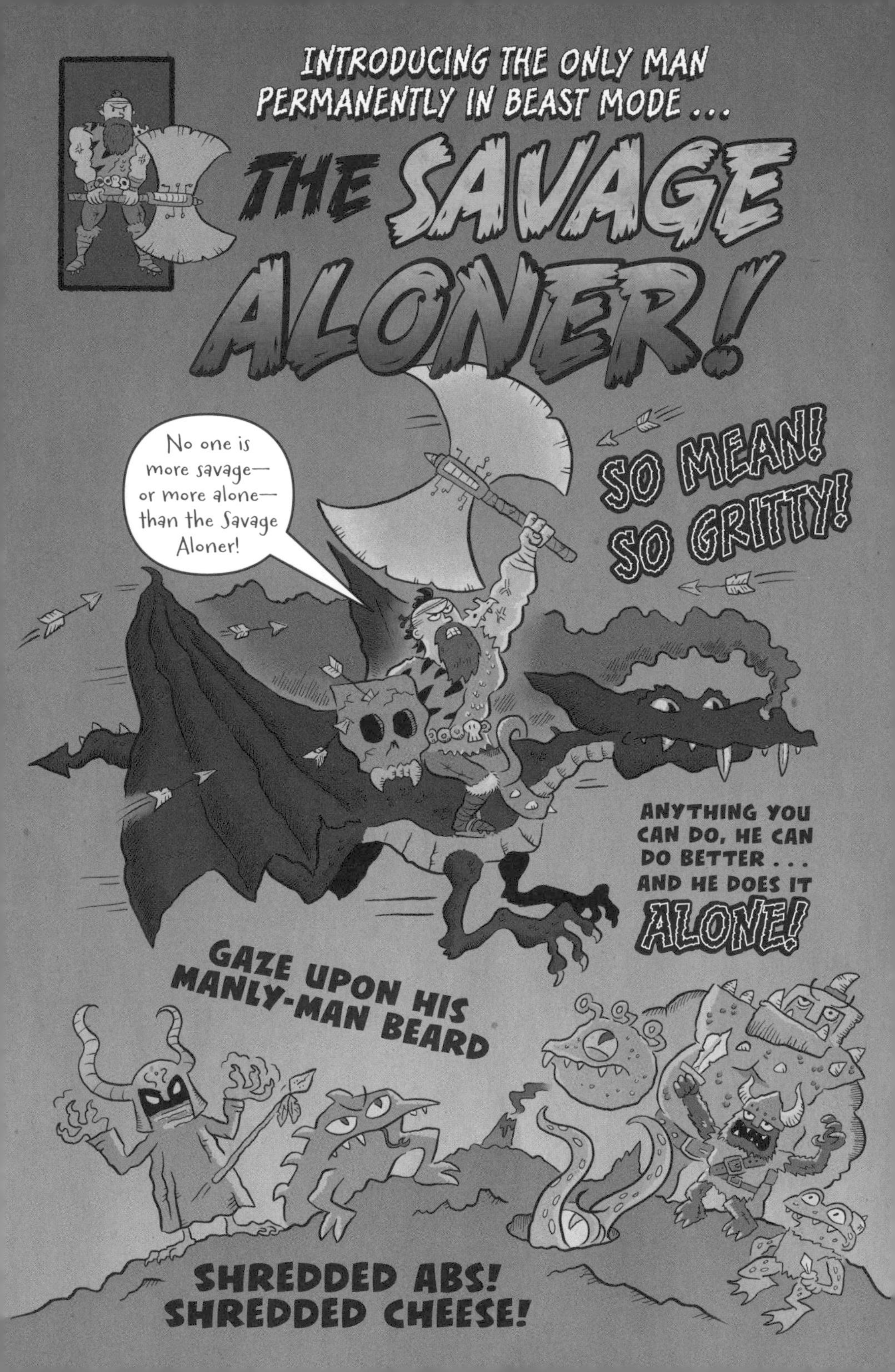
INTRODUCING THE ONLY MAN PERMANENTLY IN BEAST MODE ...
THE SAVAGE ALONER!
No one is more savage—or more alone—than the Savage Aloner!
SO MEAN! SO GRITTY!
ANYTHING YOU CAN DO, HE CAN DO BETTER . . . AND HE DOES IT ALONE!
GAZE UPON HIS MANLY-MAN BEARD
SHREDDED ABS! SHREDDED CHEESE!

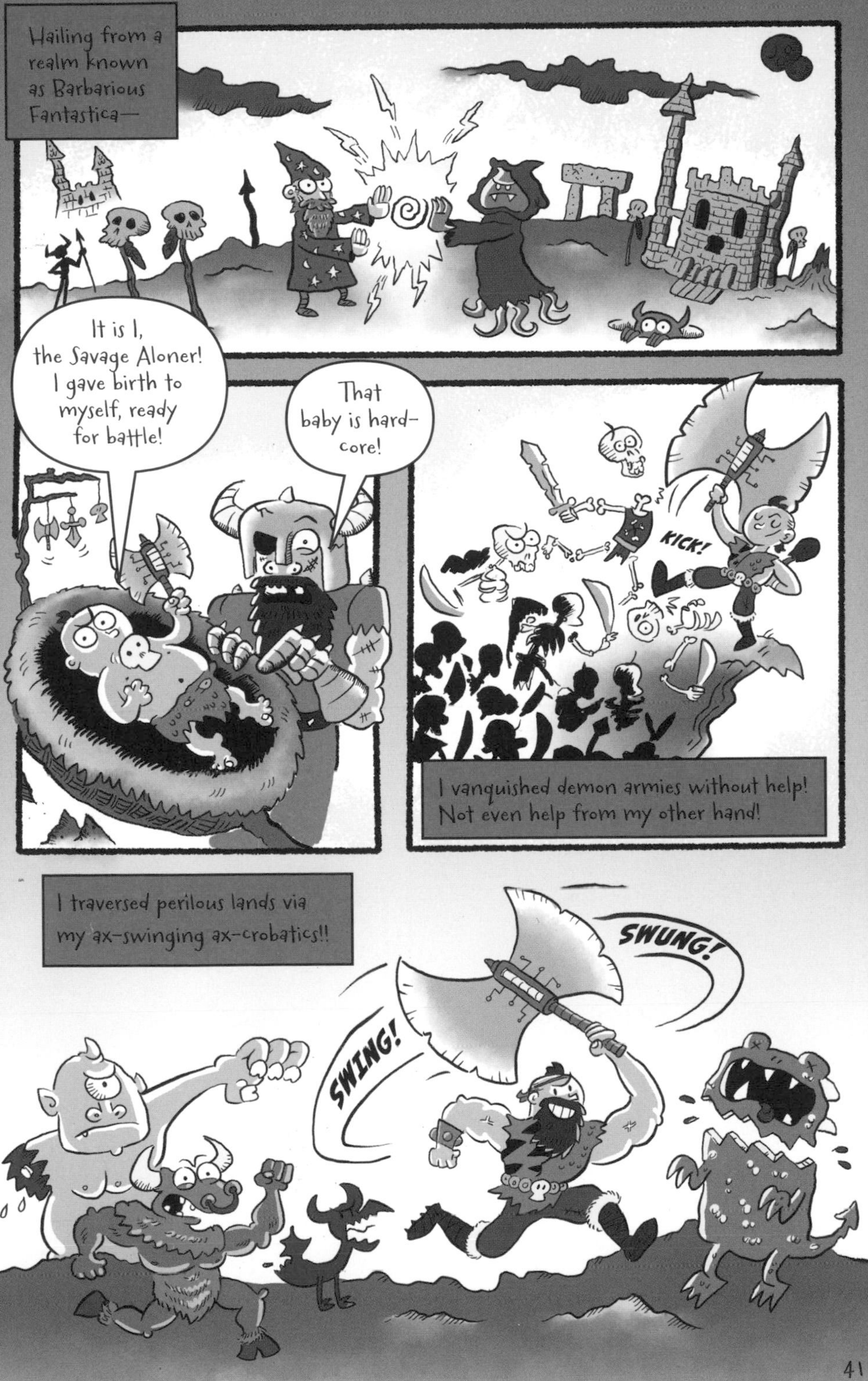

Hailing from a realm known as Barbarious Fantastica—
It is I, the Savage Aloner! I gave birth to myself, ready for battle!
That baby is hard-core!
KICK!
I vanquished demon armies without help! Not even help from my other hand!
I traversed perilous lands via my ax-swinging ax-crobatics!!
SWUNG!
SWING!

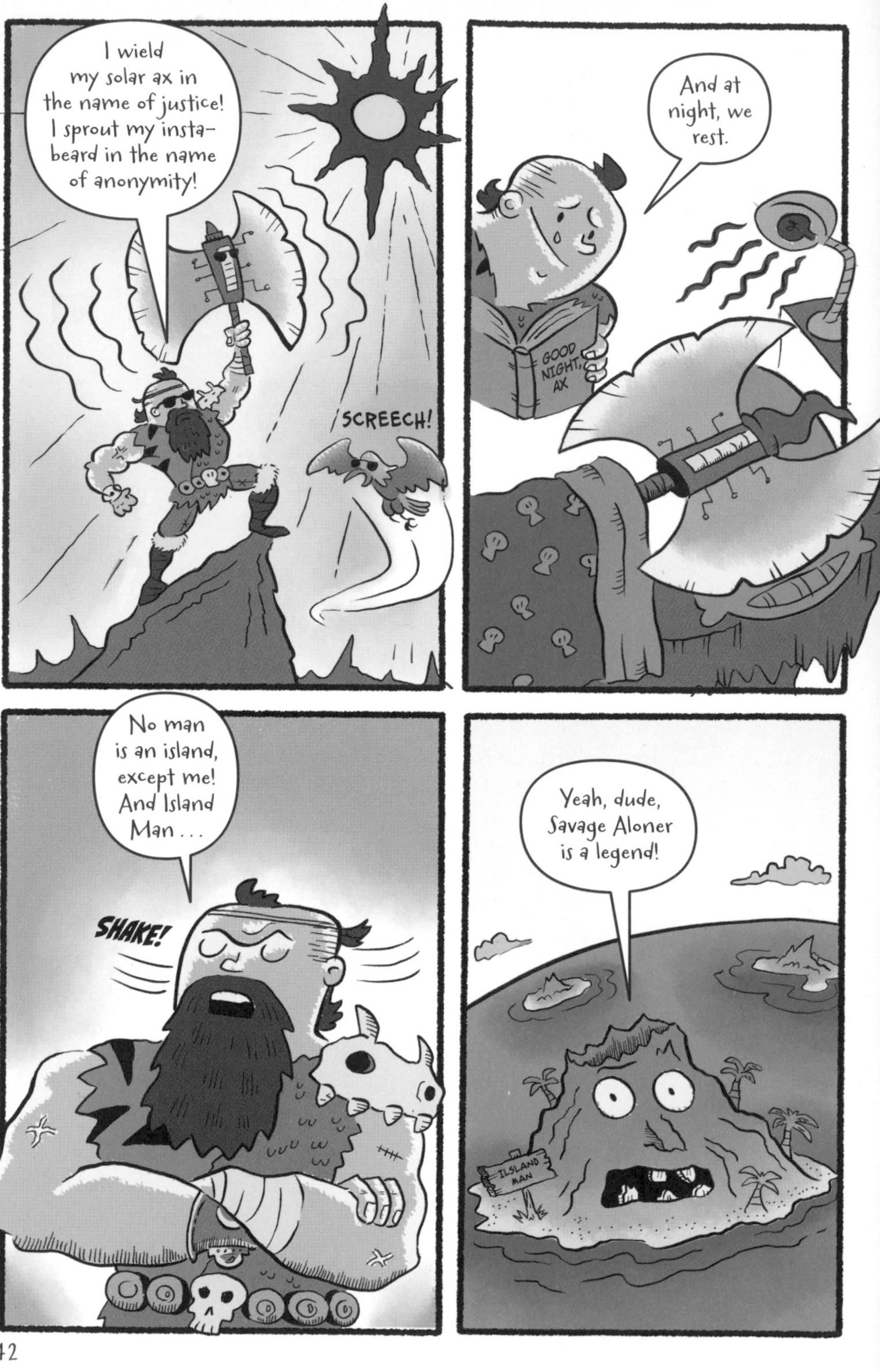

I wield my solar ax in the name of justice! I sprout my insta-beard in the name of anonymity!
SCREECH!
And at night, we rest.
GOOD NIGHT, AX
No man is an island, except me! And Island Man . . .
SHAKE!
Yeah, dude, Savage Aloner is a legend!
ILSLAND MAN

THE SAVAGE ALONER'S SECRET LAIR: THE ROOM WITH A THRONE IN IT!

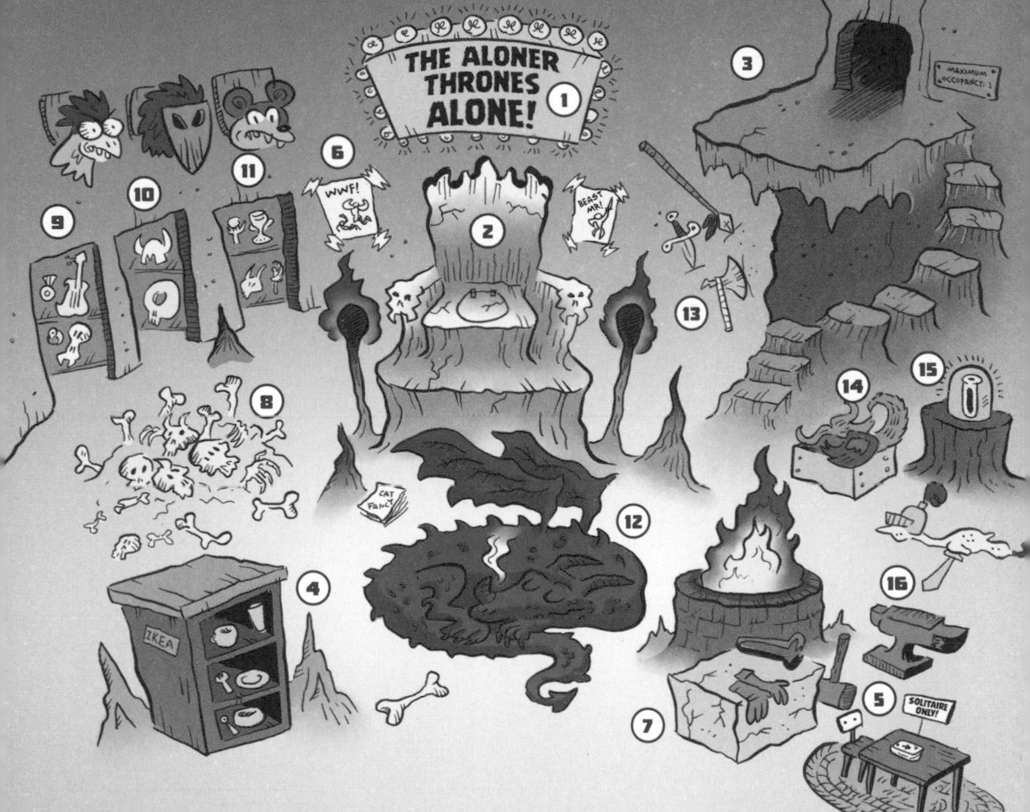
THE ALONER THRONES ALONE!
MAXIMUM OCCUPANCY: 1
WWF!
BEAST MR!
CAT FANCY
IKEA
SOLITAIRE ONLY!

1. The Aloner thrones ALONE.
2. The throne doubles as a toilet. Don't tell anyone.
3. Area for standing alone
4. Dish cabinet (only one of everything)
5. Card table (SOLITAIRE ONLY)
6. Inspirational wrestling posters
7. Blacksmith shop for making more weapons
8. Pile of skeletons generously donated by enemies
9. Trophy room
10. Other trophy room
11. Third trophy room
12. Dragon-skin rug (dragon just sleeping)
13. Wall meant for stabbing
14. Used beard storage
15. Beard growth serum
16. Medieval rubber chicken

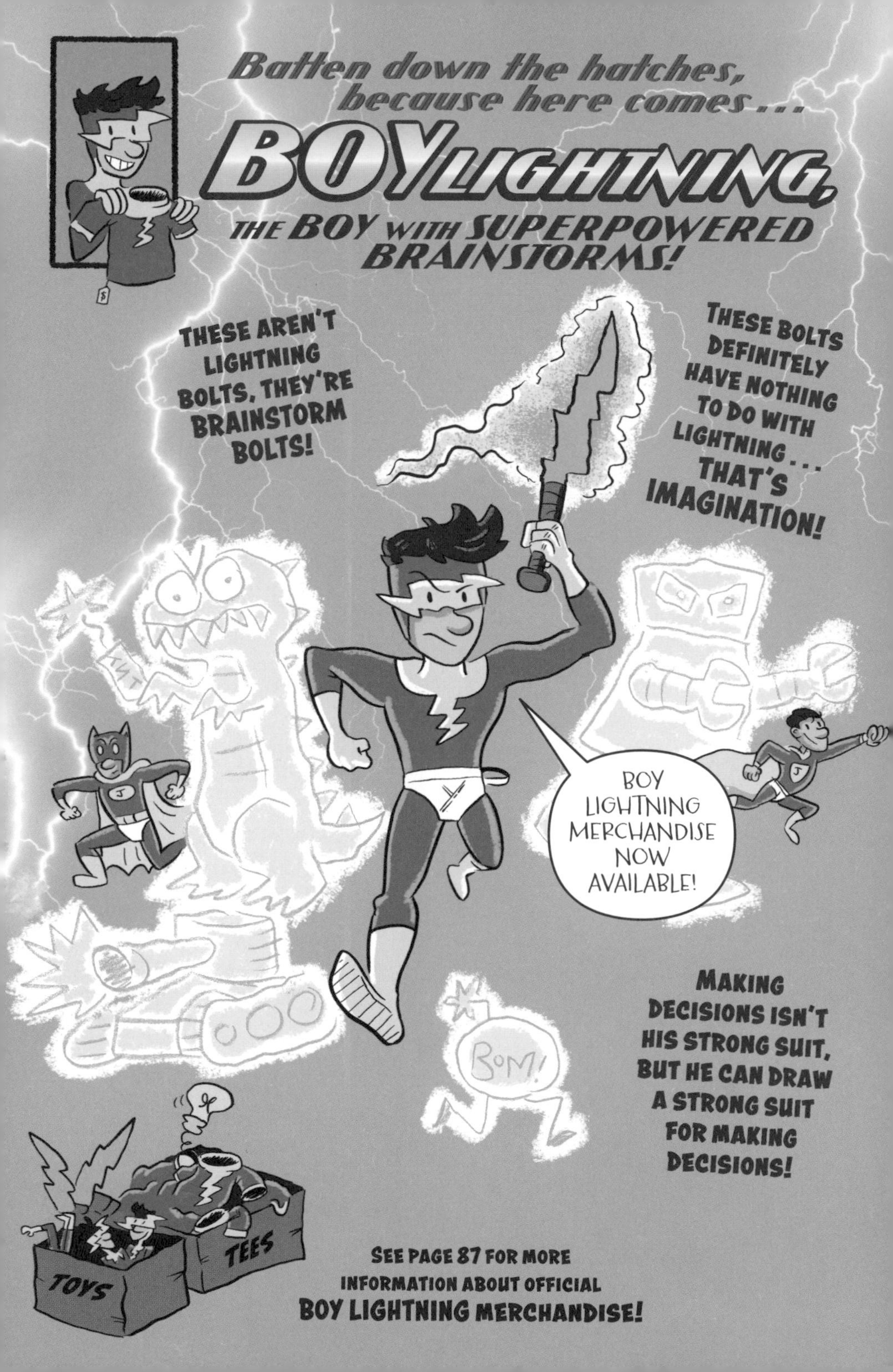

Batten down the hatches, because here comes . . .
BOY LIGHTNING,
THE BOY WITH SUPERPOWERED BRAINSTORMS!
THESE AREN'T LIGHTNING BOLTS, THEY'RE BRAINSTORM BOLTS!
THESE BOLTS DEFINITELY HAVE NOTHING TO DO WITH LIGHTNING . . . THAT'S IMAGINATION!
BOY LIGHTNING MERCHANDISE NOW AVAILABLE!
BOM!
MAKING DECISIONS ISN'T HIS STRONG SUIT, BUT HE CAN DRAW A STRONG SUIT FOR MAKING DECISIONS!
TEES
TOYS
SEE PAGE 87 FOR MORE INFORMATION ABOUT OFFICIAL BOY LIGHTNING MERCHANDISE!

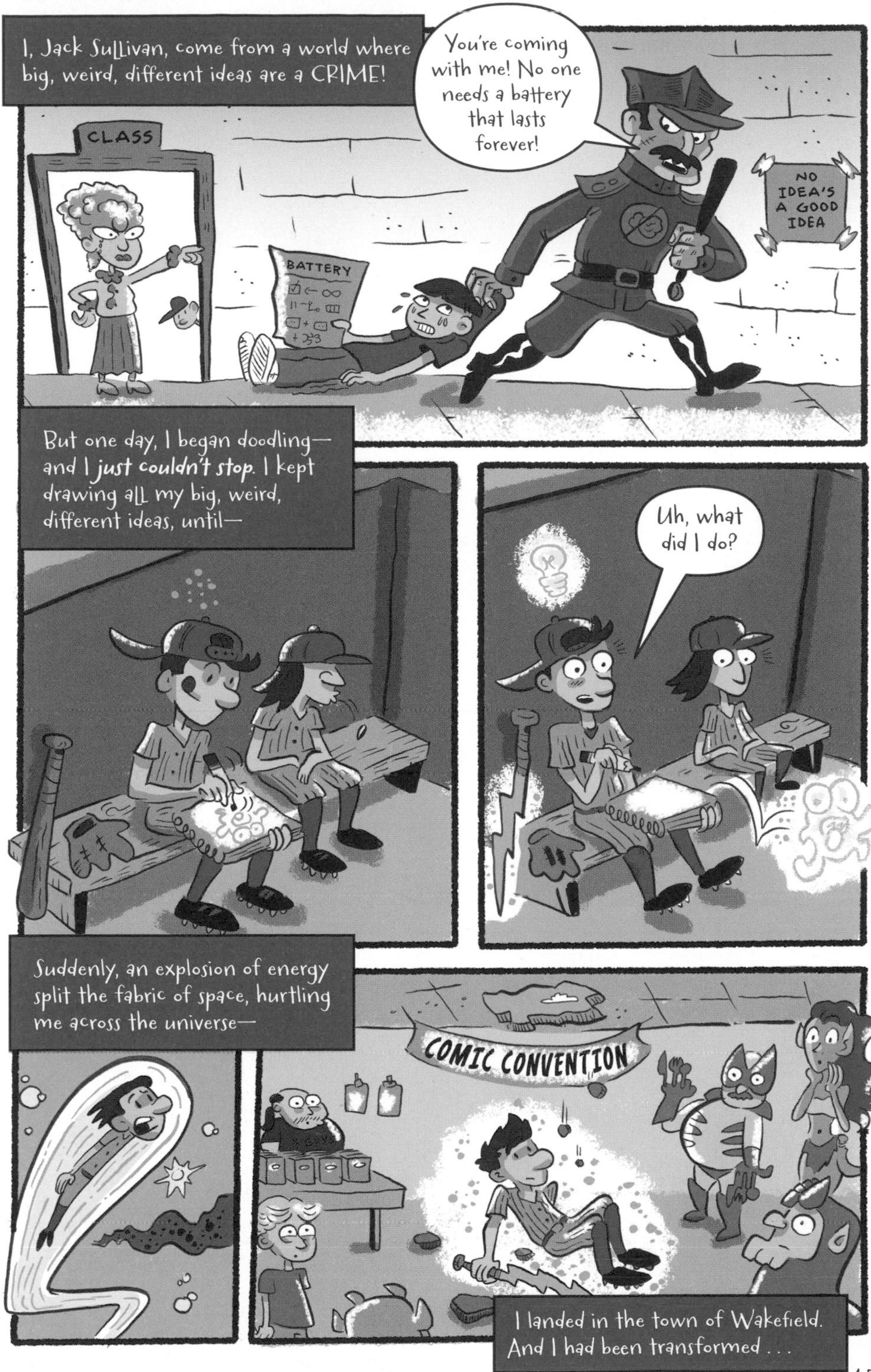

I, Jack Sullivan, come from a world where big, weird, different ideas are a CRIME!
CLASS
You're coming with me! No one needs a battery that lasts forever!
BATTERY
NO IDEA'S A GOOD IDEA
But one day, I began doodling— and I **just couldn't stop**. I kept drawing all my big, weird, different ideas, until—
Uh, what did I do?
Suddenly, an explosion of energy split the fabric of space, hurtling me across the universe—
COMIC CONVENTION
I landed in the town of Wakefield. And I had been transformed . . .

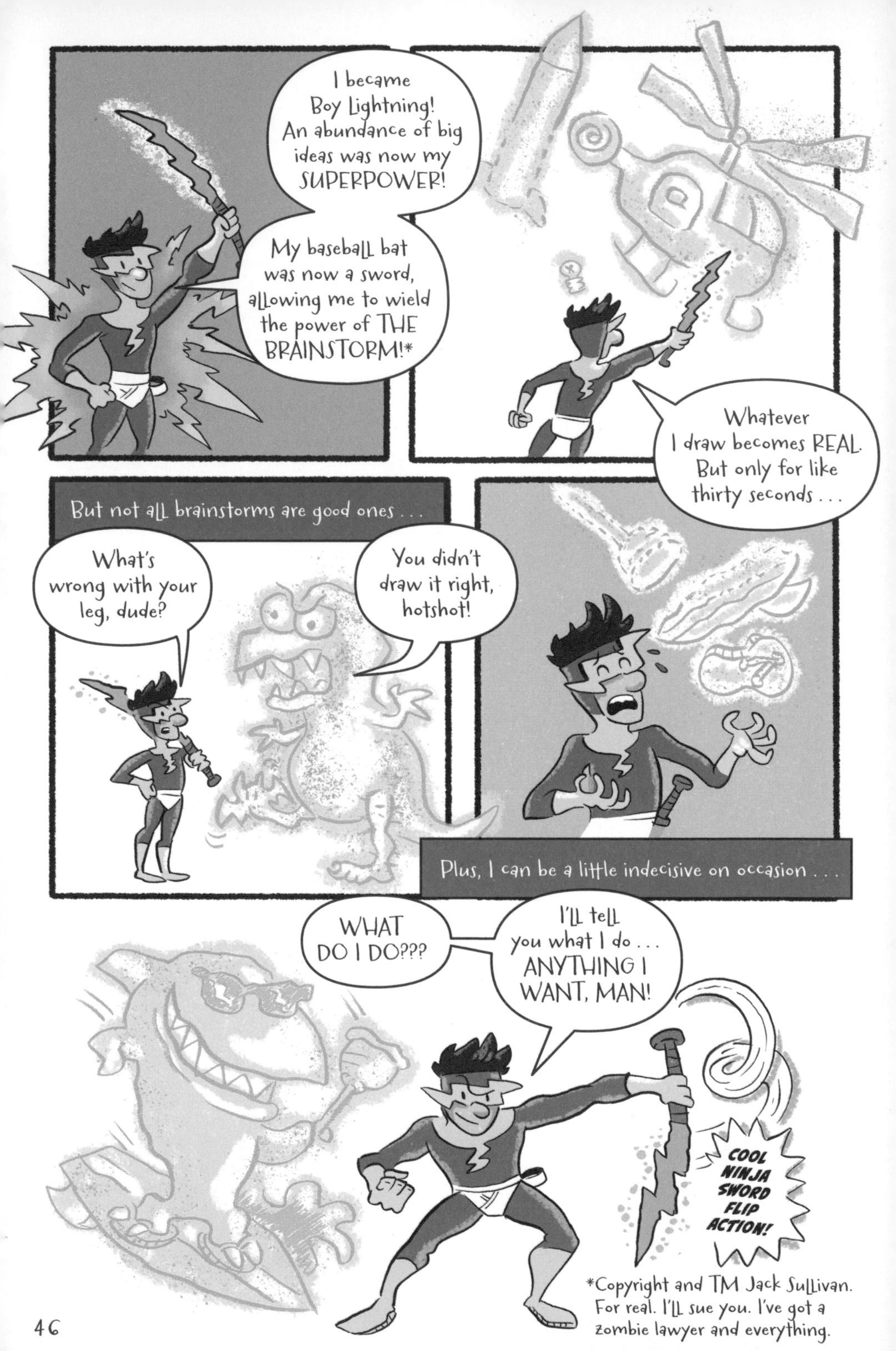
I became Boy Lightning! An abundance of big ideas was now my SUPERPOWER!
My baseball bat was now a sword, allowing me to wield the power of THE BRAINSTORM!*
Whatever I draw becomes REAL. But only for like thirty seconds . . .
But not all brainstorms are good ones . . .
What's wrong with your leg, dude?
You didn't draw it right, hotshot!
Plus, I can be a little indecisive on occasion . . .
WHAT DO I DO???
I'll tell you what I do . . . ANYTHING I WANT, MAN!
COOL NINJA SWORD FLIP ACTION!
*Copyright and TM Jack Sullivan. For real. I'll sue you. I've got a zombie lawyer and everything.

BOY LIGHTNING'S SECRET LAIR: THE LIGHTNING LAIR

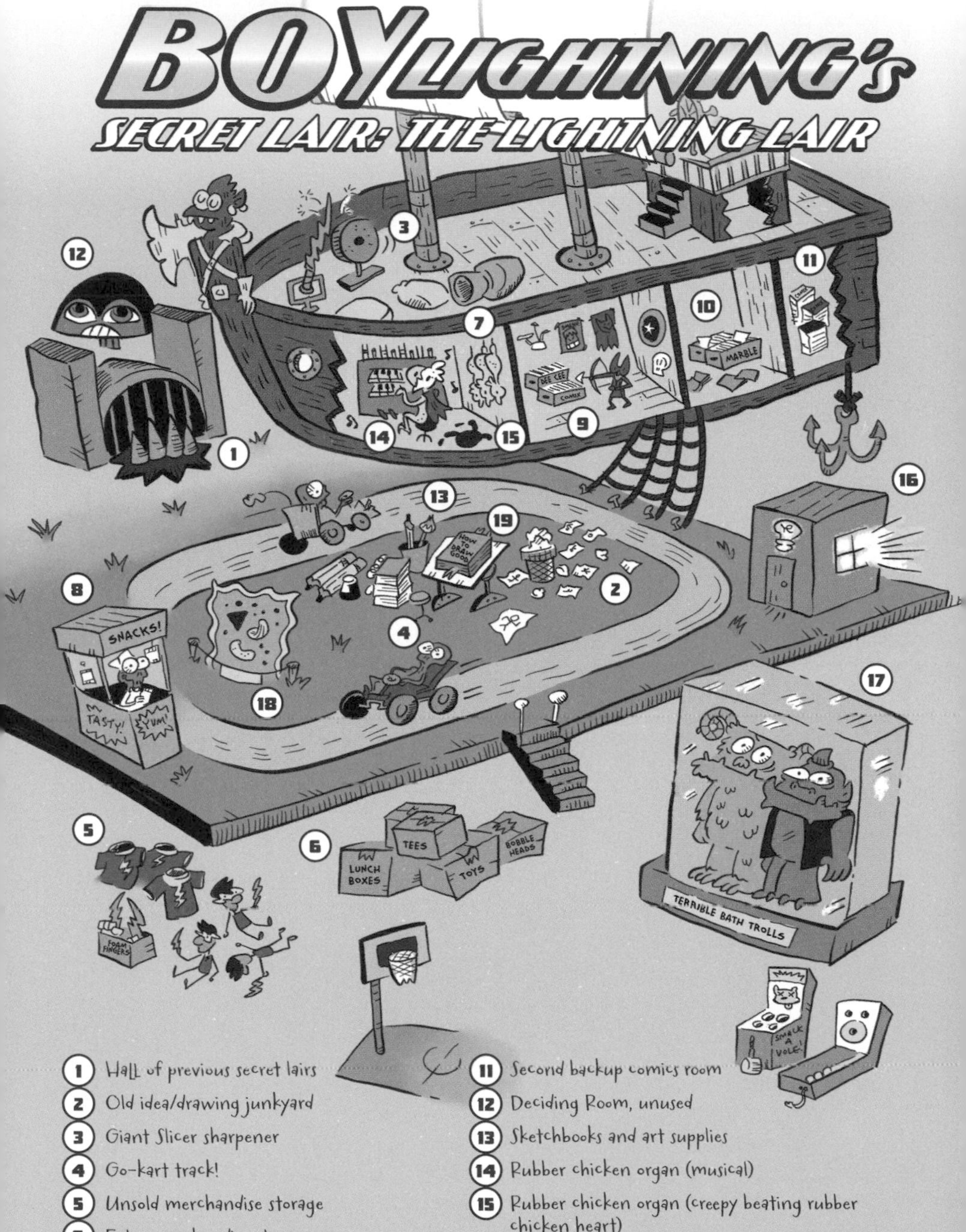
SNACKS!
TASTY!
YUM!
HOW TO DRAW GOOD
DEE CEE COMIX
MARBLE
TEES
LUNCH BOXES
TOYS
BOBBLE HEADS
FOAM FINGERS
TERRIBLE BATH TROLLS
SMACK A VOLE!

1. Hall of previous secret lairs
2. Old idea/drawing junkyard
3. Giant Slicer sharpener
4. Go-kart track!
5. Unsold merchandise storage
6. Extra merchandise storage
7. Rubber chicken closet
8. Snack emporium
9. Collectibles and comics room
10. Backup comics room
11. Second backup comics room
12. Deciding Room, unused
13. Sketchbooks and art supplies
14. Rubber chicken organ (musical)
15. Rubber chicken organ (creepy beating rubber chicken heart)
16. Light bulb closet
17. Giant monster display case
18. Gateway to snack dimension, use with caution
19. *How to Draw Good* book

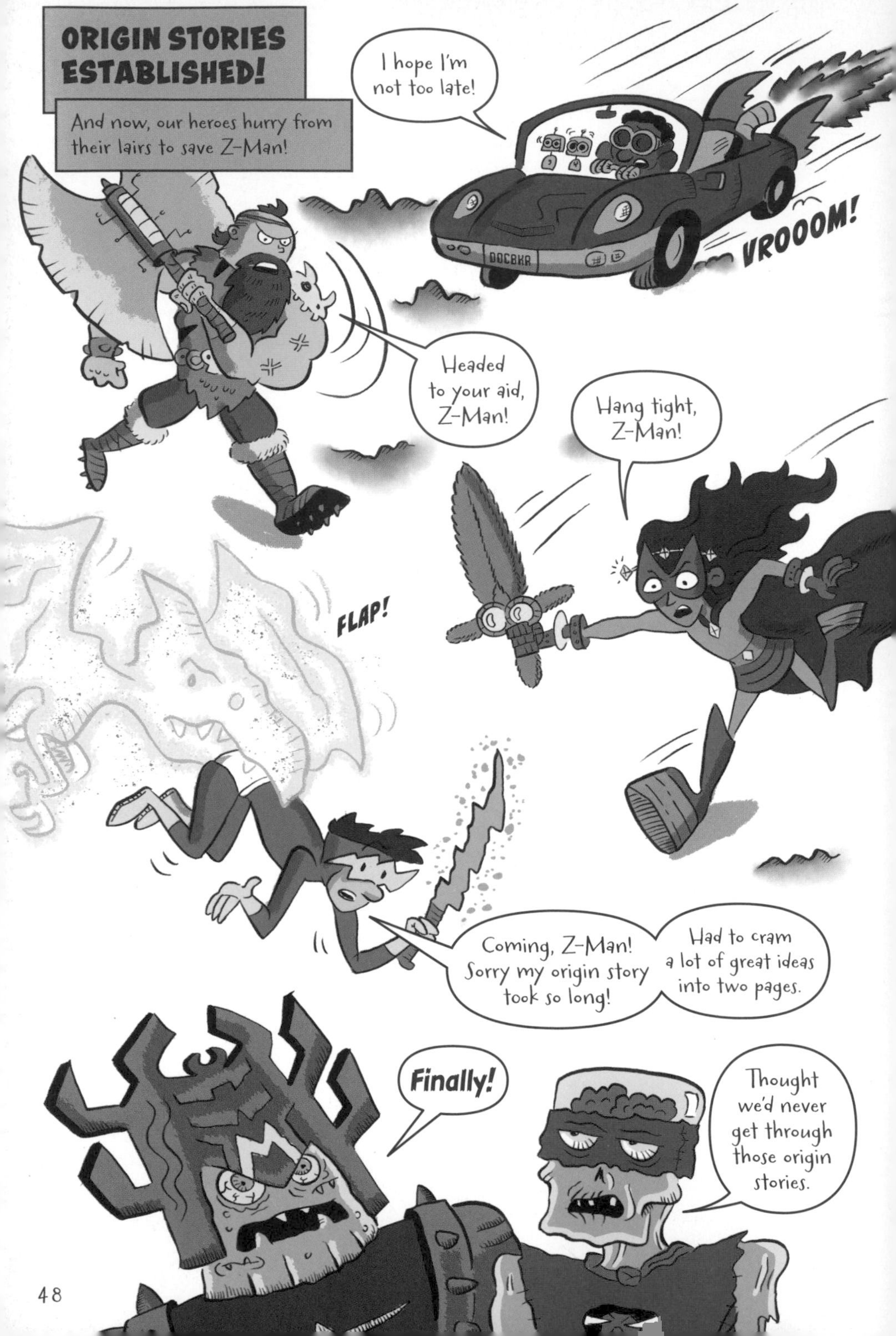
ORIGIN STORIES ESTABLISHED!
And now, our heroes hurry from their lairs to save Z-Man!
I hope I'm not too late!
DOCBKR
VROOOM!
Headed to your aid, Z-Man!
Hang tight, Z-Man!
FLAP!
Coming, Z-Man! Sorry my origin story took so long!
Had to cram a lot of great ideas into two pages.
Finally!
Thought we'd never get through those origin stories.

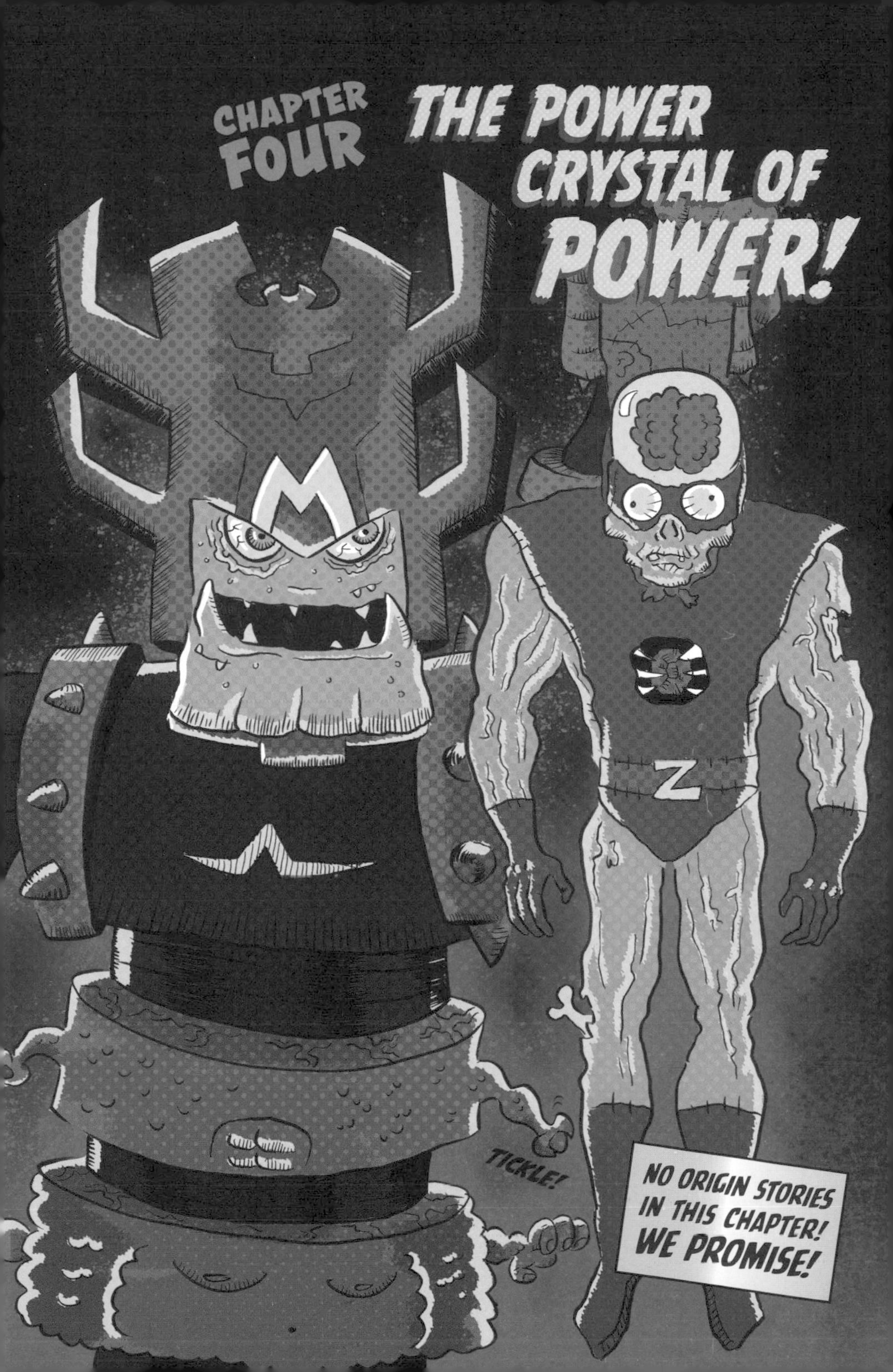
CHAPTER FOUR
THE POWER CRYSTAL OF POWER!
TICKLE!
NO ORIGIN STORIES IN THIS CHAPTER! WE PROMISE!

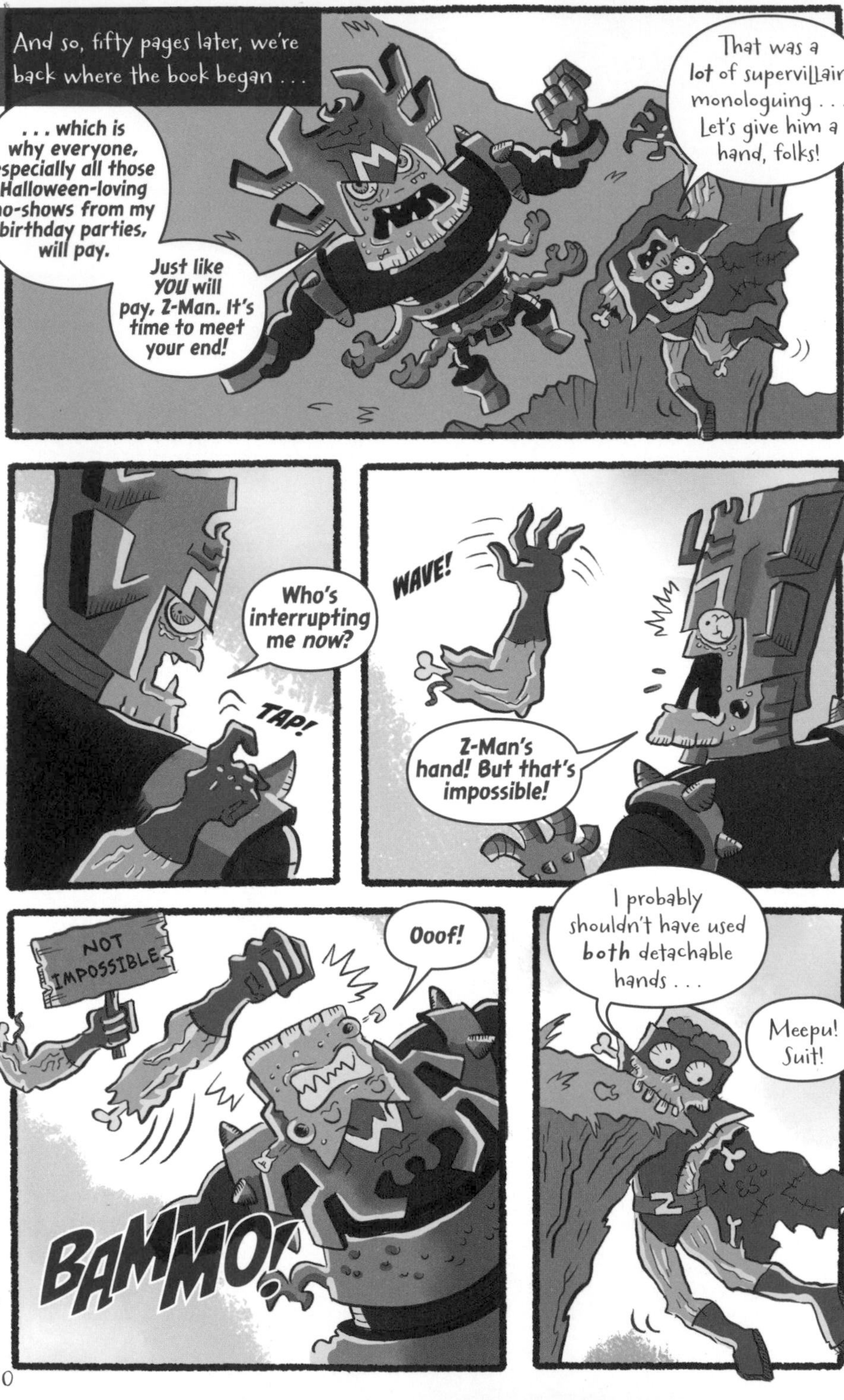

And so, fifty pages later, we're back where the book began . . .
. . . which is why everyone, especially all those Halloween-loving no-shows from my birthday parties, will pay.
Just like YOU will pay, Z-Man. It's time to meet your end!
That was a lot of supervillain monologuing . . . Let's give him a hand, folks!
Who's interrupting me now?
TAP!
WAVE!
Z-Man's hand! But that's impossible!
NOT IMPOSSIBLE
Ooof!
BAMMO!
I probably shouldn't have used both detachable hands . . .
Meepu! Suit!

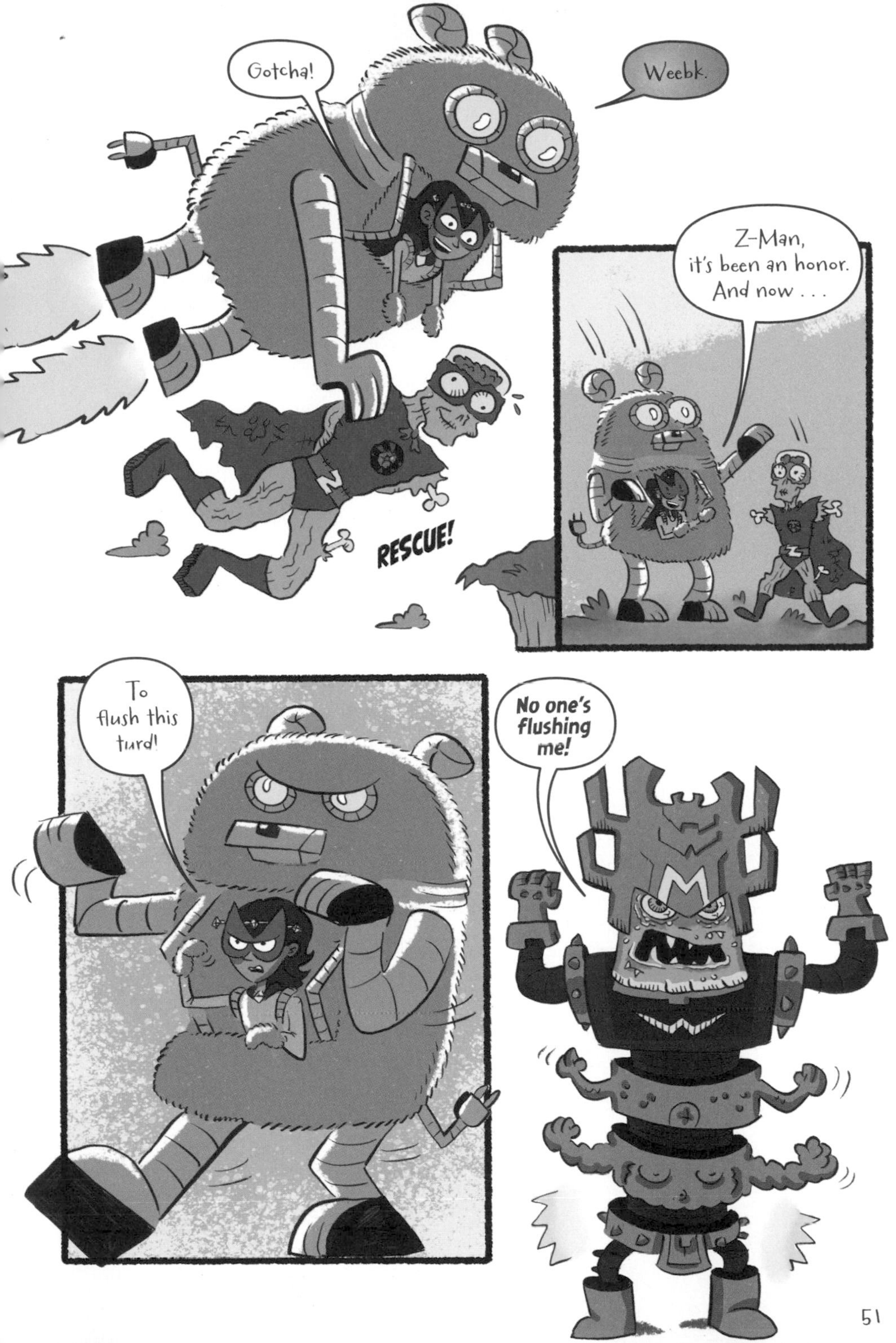
Gotcha!
Weebk.
RESCUE!
Z-Man, it's been an honor. And now . . .
To flush this turd!
No one's flushing me!

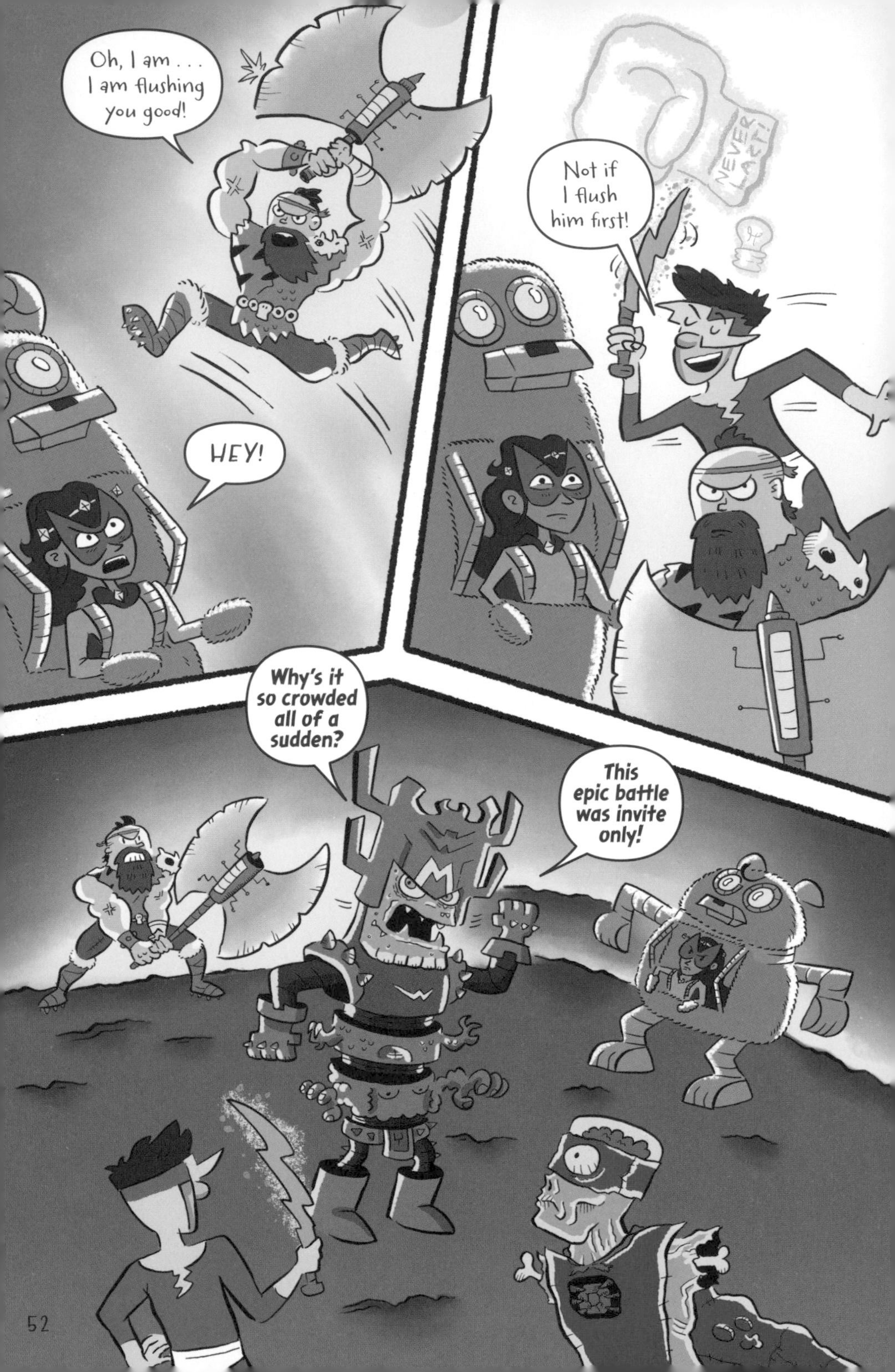
Oh, I am . . .
I am flushing
you good!
Not if
I flush
him first!
NEVER LAST!
HEY!
Why's it
so crowded
all of a
sudden?
This
epic battle
was invite
only!

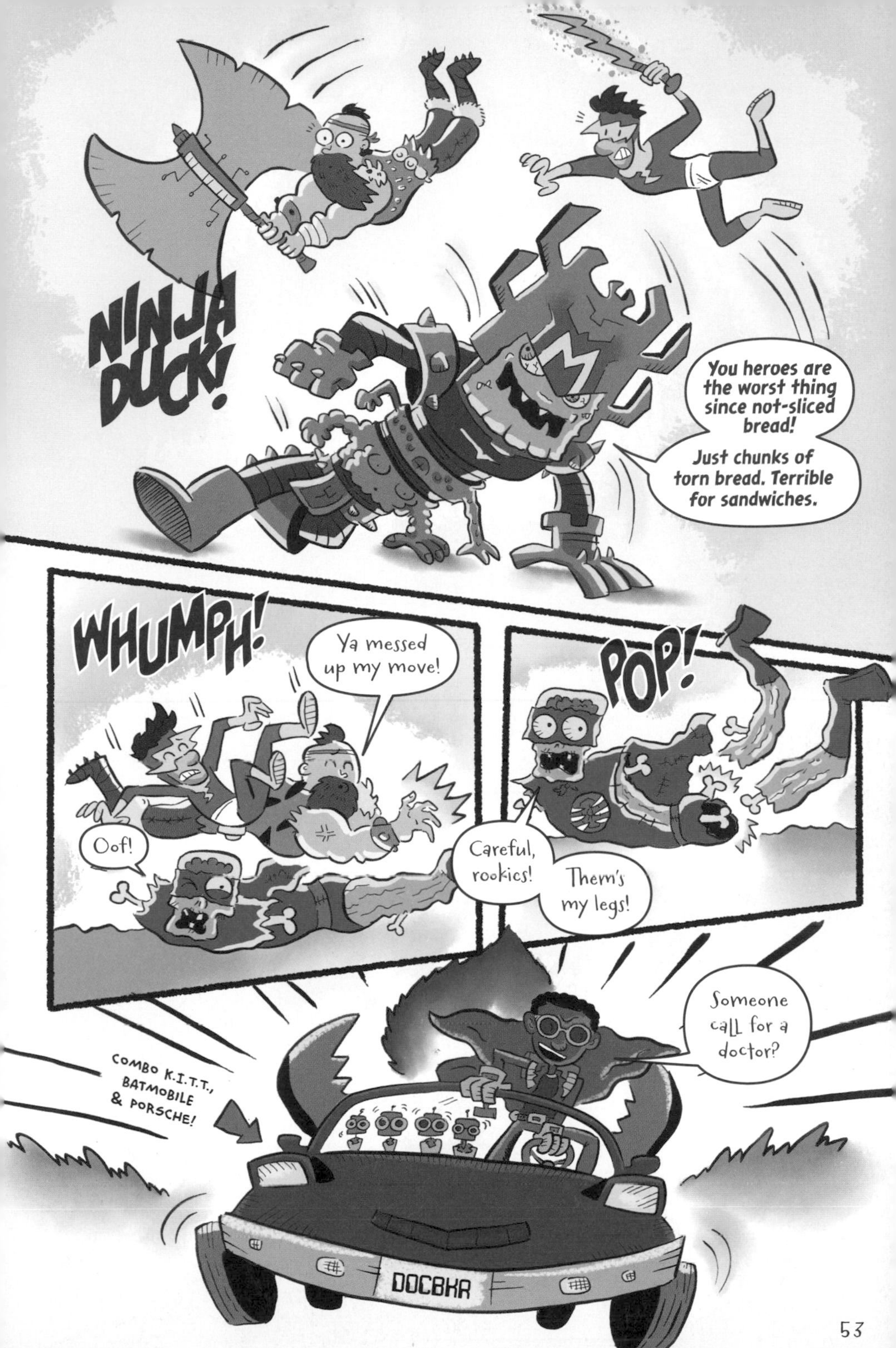
NINJA DUCK!
You heroes are the worst thing since not-sliced bread!
Just chunks of torn bread. Terrible for sandwiches.
WHUMPH!
Ya messed up my move!
Oof!
POP!
Careful, rookies!
Them's my legs!
COMBO K.I.T.T., BATMOBILE & PORSCHE!
Someone call for a doctor?
DOCBKR

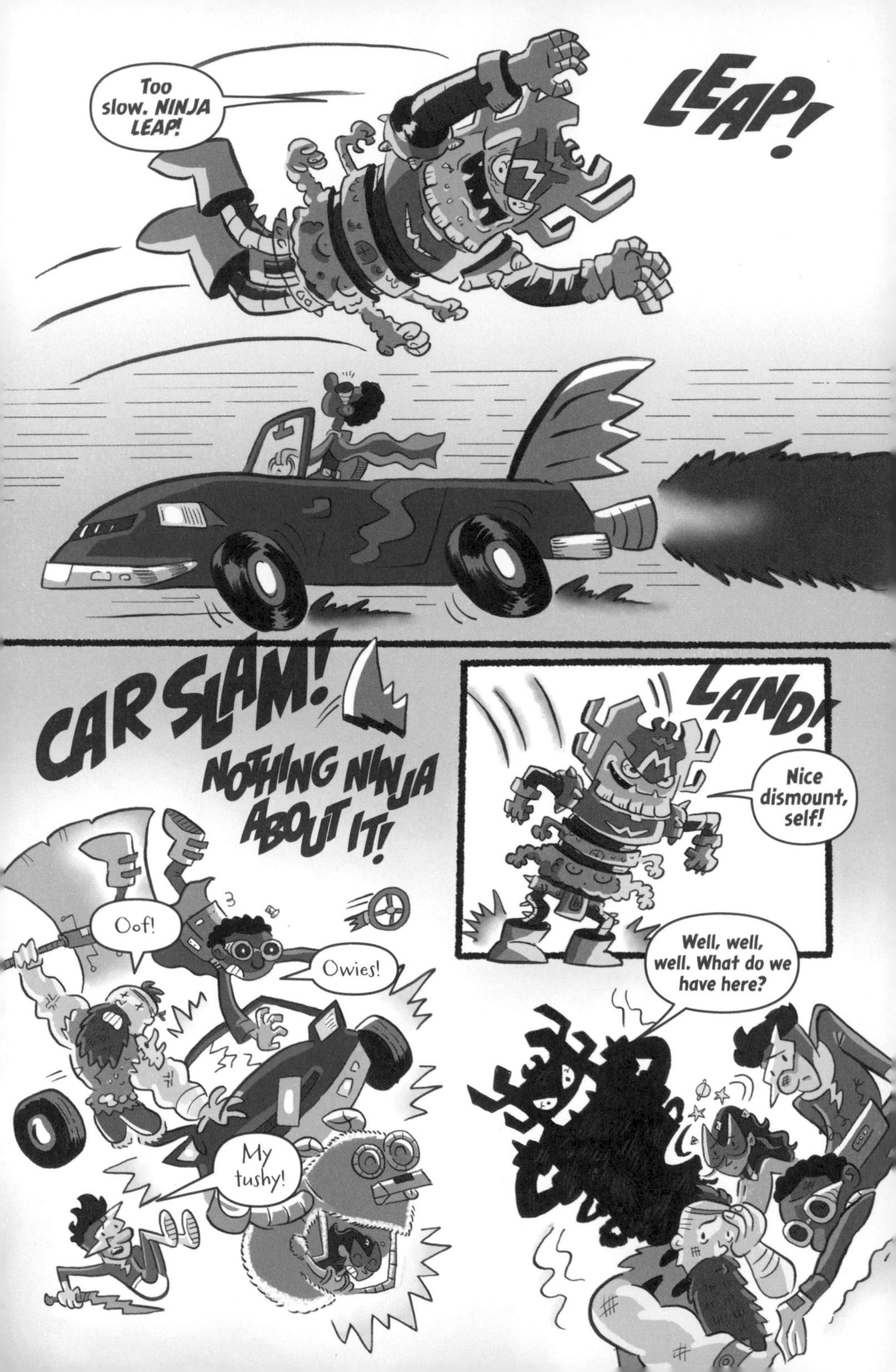
Too slow. NINJA LEAP!
LEAP!
CAR SLAM!
NOTHING NINJA ABOUT IT!
Oof!
Owies!
My tushy!
LAND!
Nice dismount, self!
Well, well, well. What do we have here?

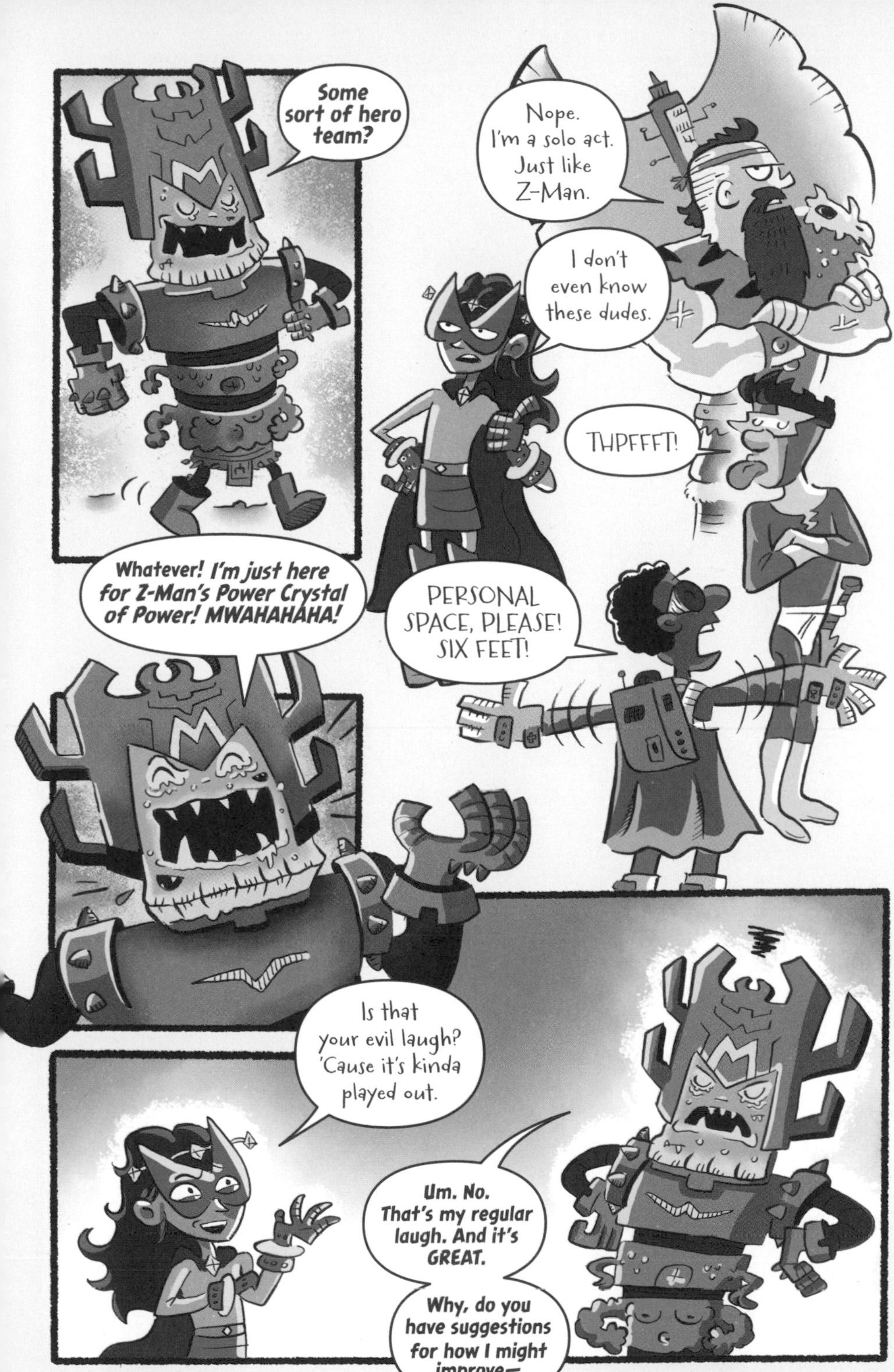
Some sort of hero team?
Nope. I'm a solo act. Just like Z-Man.
I don't even know these dudes.
THPFFFT!
Whatever! I'm just here for Z-Man's Power Crystal of Power! MWAHAHAHA!
PERSONAL SPACE, PLEASE! SIX FEET!
Is that your evil laugh? 'Cause it's kinda played out.
Um. No. That's my regular laugh. And it's GREAT.
Why, do you have suggestions for how I might improve—

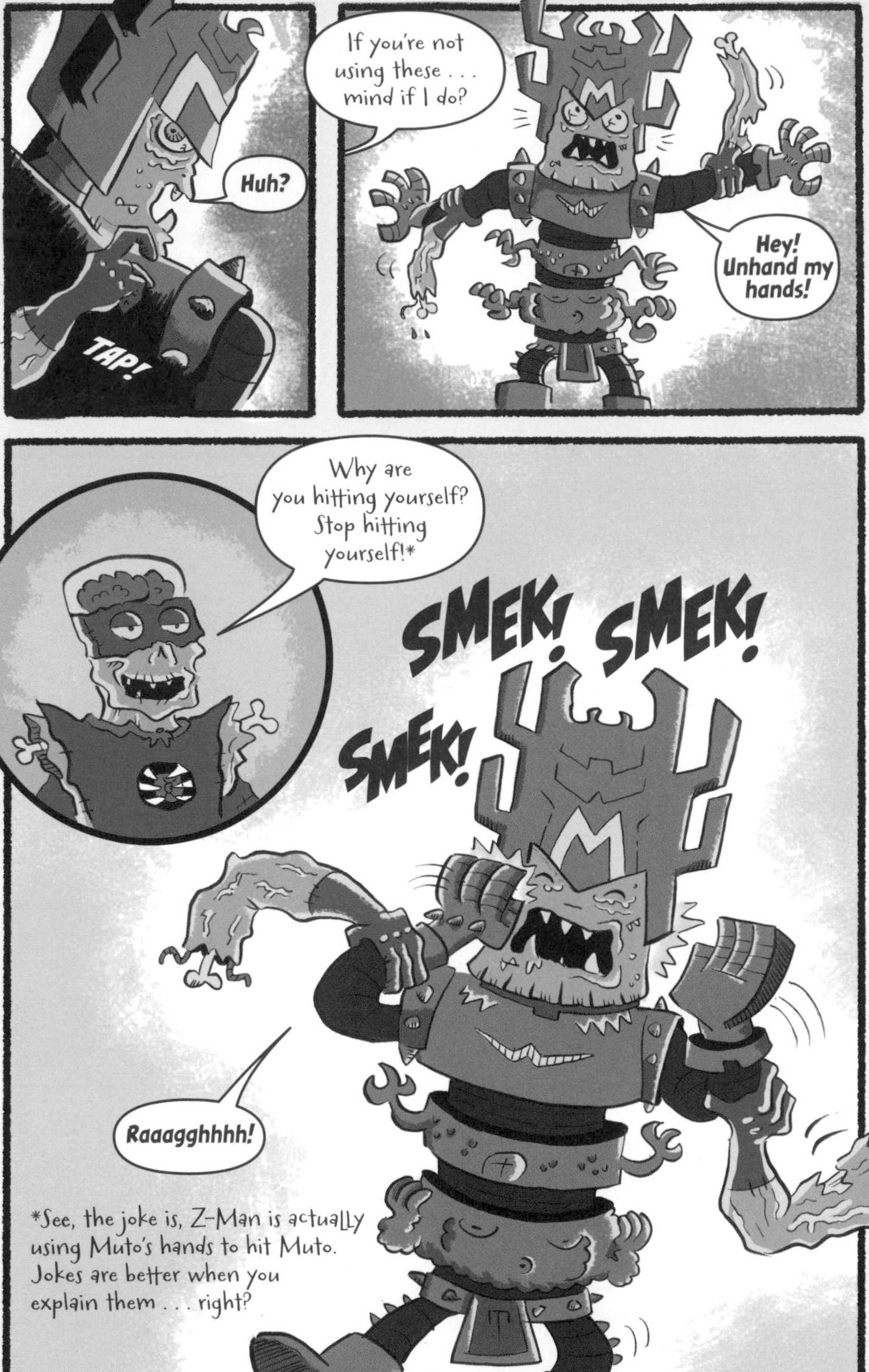
Huh?
TAP!
If you're not using these . . . mind if I do?
Hey! Unhand my hands!
Why are you hitting yourself? Stop hitting yourself!*
SMEK! SMEK! SMEK!
Raaagghhhh!
*See, the joke is, Z-Man is actually using Muto's hands to hit Muto. Jokes are better when you explain them . . . right?

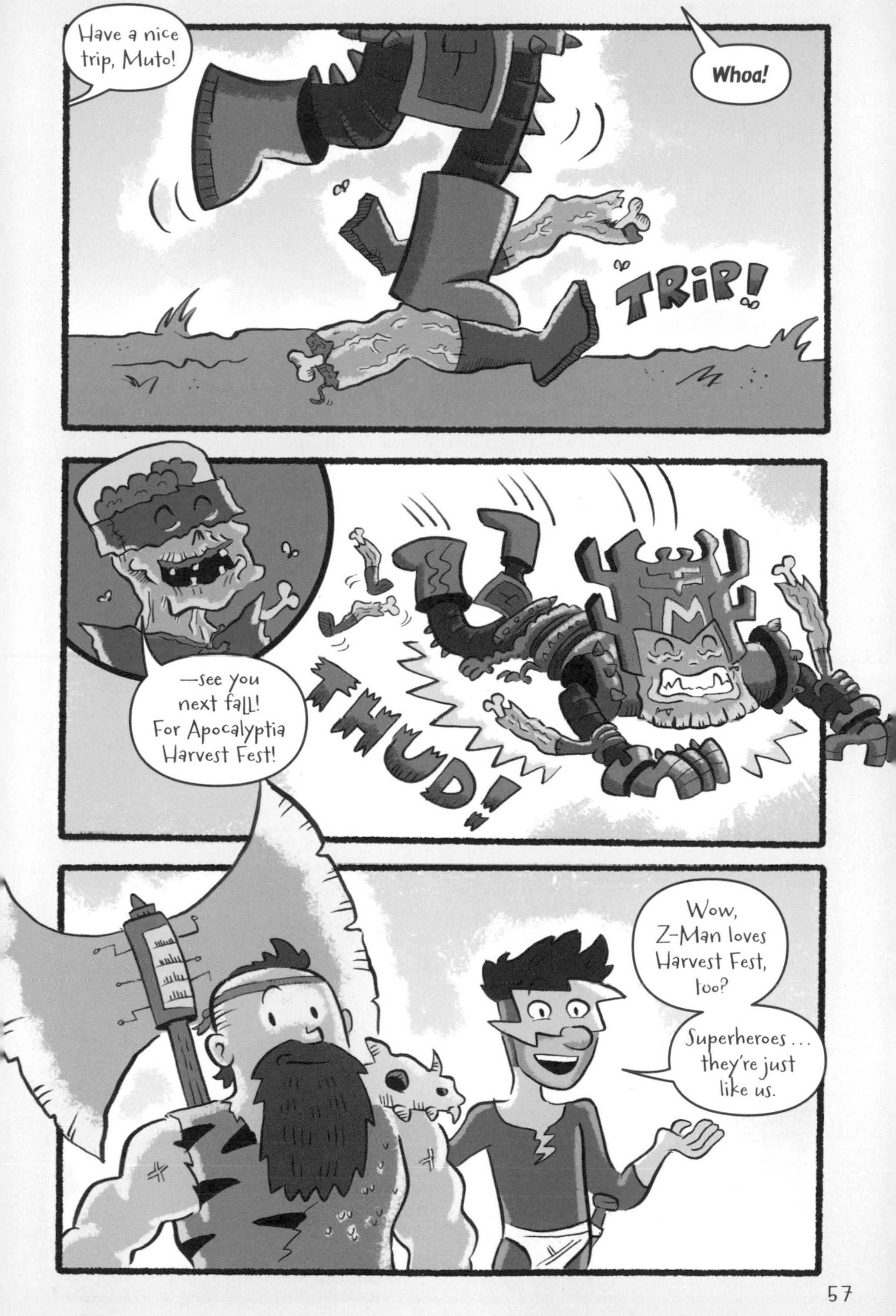
Have a nice trip, Muto!
Whoa!
TRIP!
—see you next fall! For Apocalyptia Harvest Fest!
THUD!
Wow, Z-Man loves Harvest Fest, too?
Superheroes . . . they're just like us.

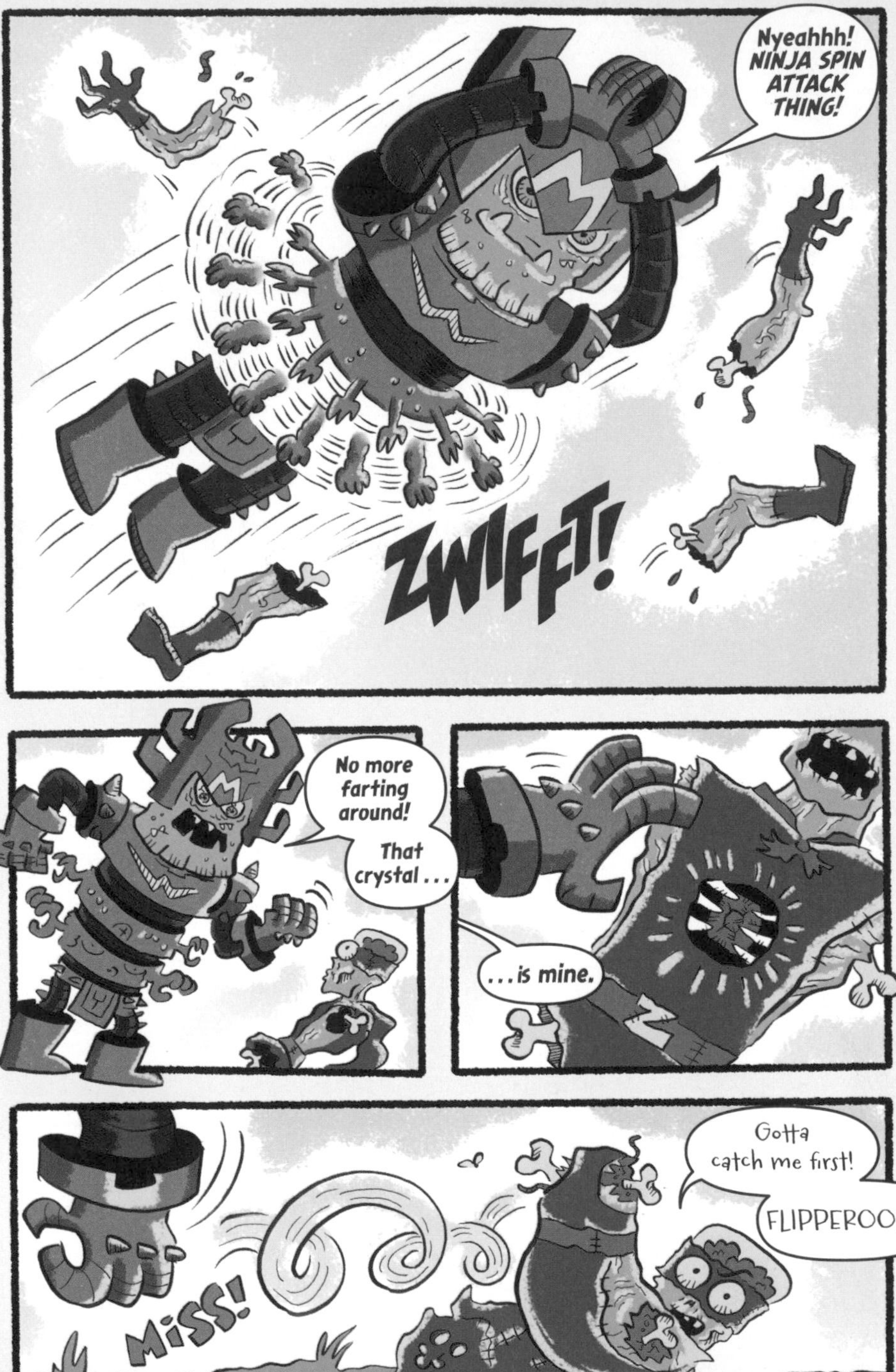

Nyeahhh! NINJA SPIN ATTACK THING!
ZWIFFT!
No more farting around!
That crystal . . .
. . . is mine.
Gotta catch me first!
FLIPPEROONI!
MISS!

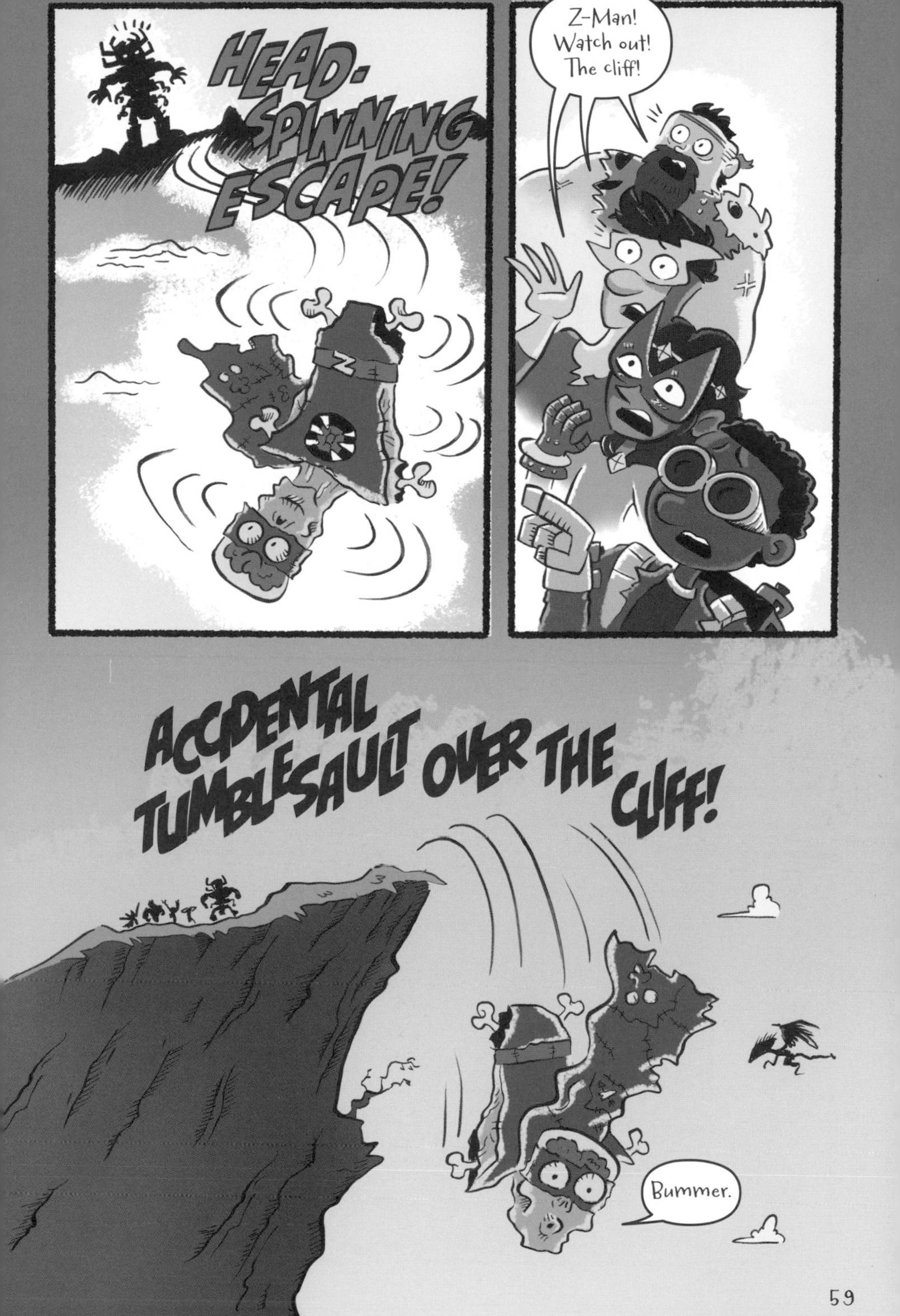
HEAD-SPINNING ESCAPE!
Z-Man! Watch out! The cliff!
ACCIDENTAL TUMBLESAULT OVER THE CLIFF!
Bummer.

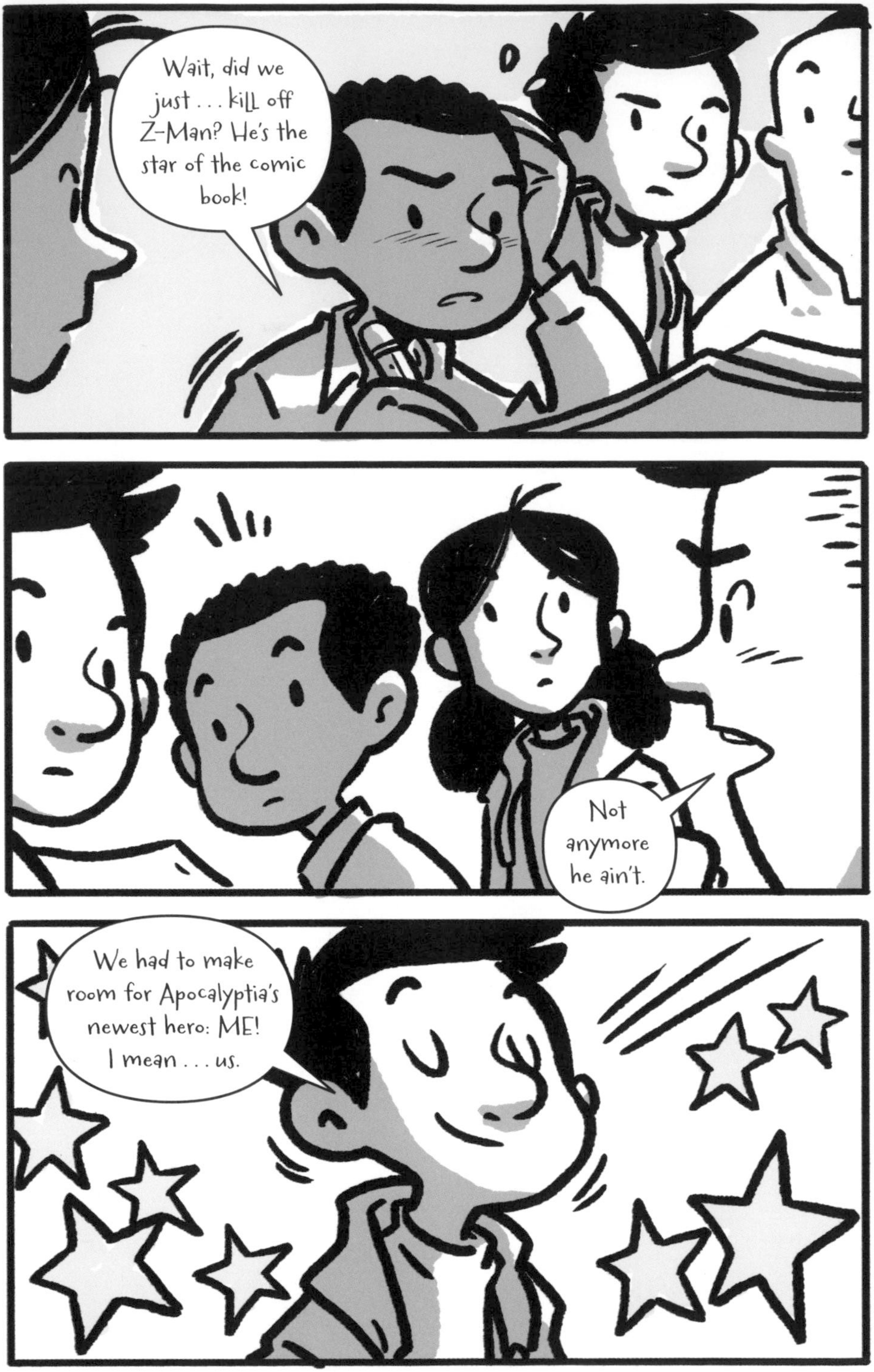
Wait, did we just . . . kiLL off Z-Man? He's the star of the comic book!
Not anymore he ain't.
We had to make room for Apocalyptia's newest hero: ME! I mean . . . us.

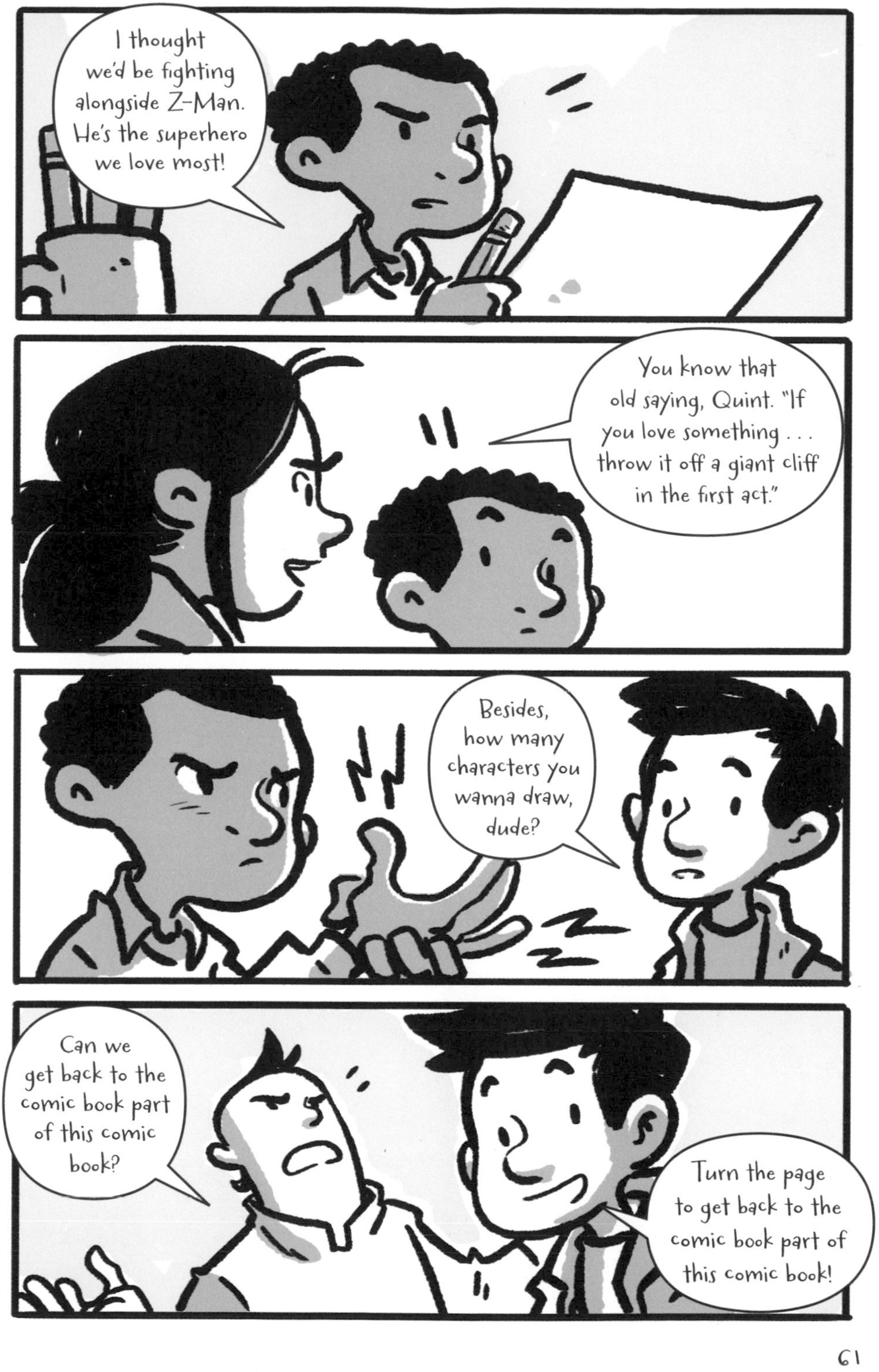
I thought we'd be fighting alongside Z-Man. He's the superhero we love most!
You know that old saying, Quint. "If you love something . . . throw it off a giant cliff in the first act."
Besides, how many characters you wanna draw, dude?
Can we get back to the comic book part of this comic book?
Turn the page to get back to the comic book part of this comic book!

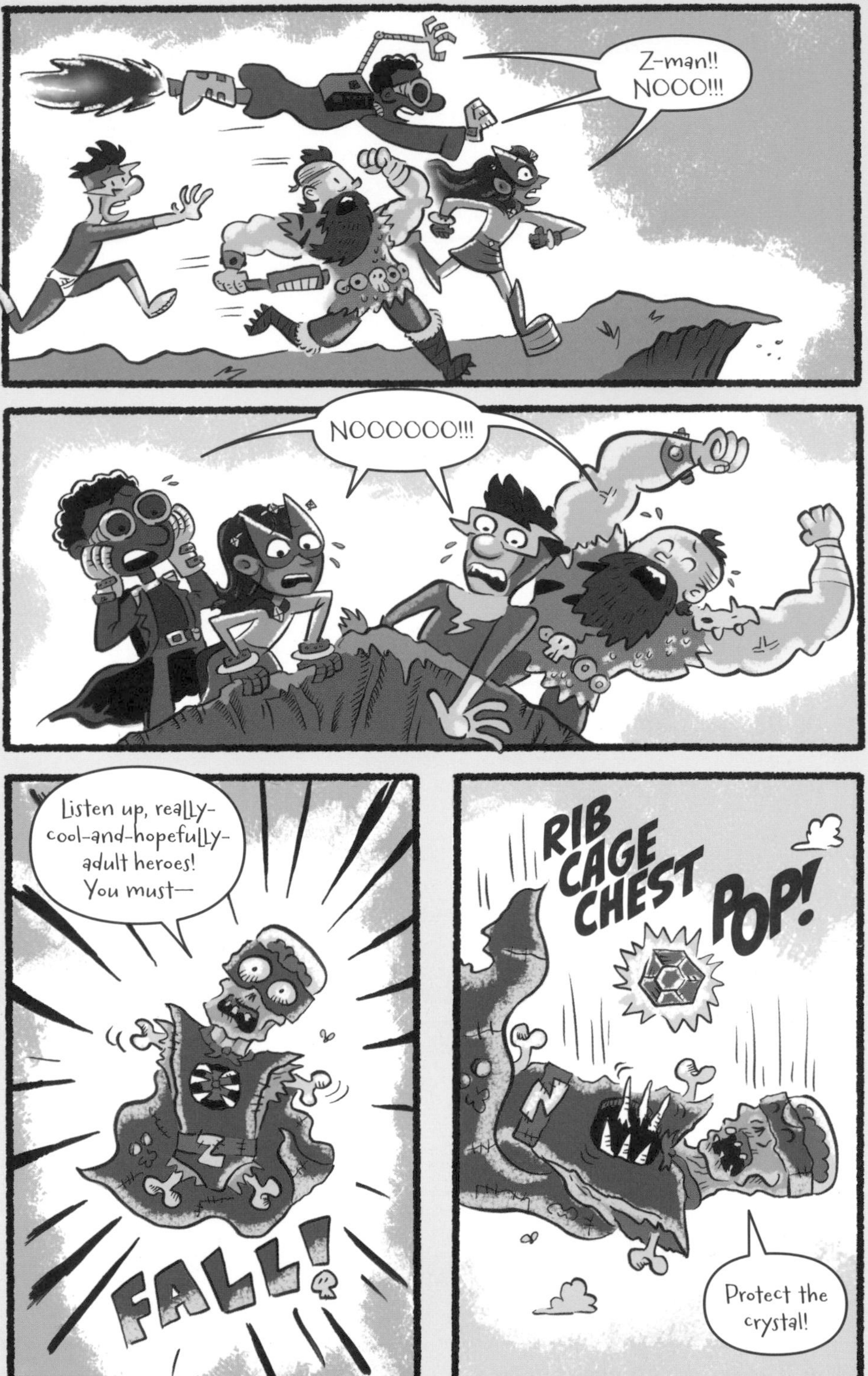
Z-man!! NOOO!!!
NOOOOOO!!!
Listen up, really-cool-and-hopefully-adult heroes! You must—
FALL!
RIB CAGE CHEST POP!
Protect the crystal!

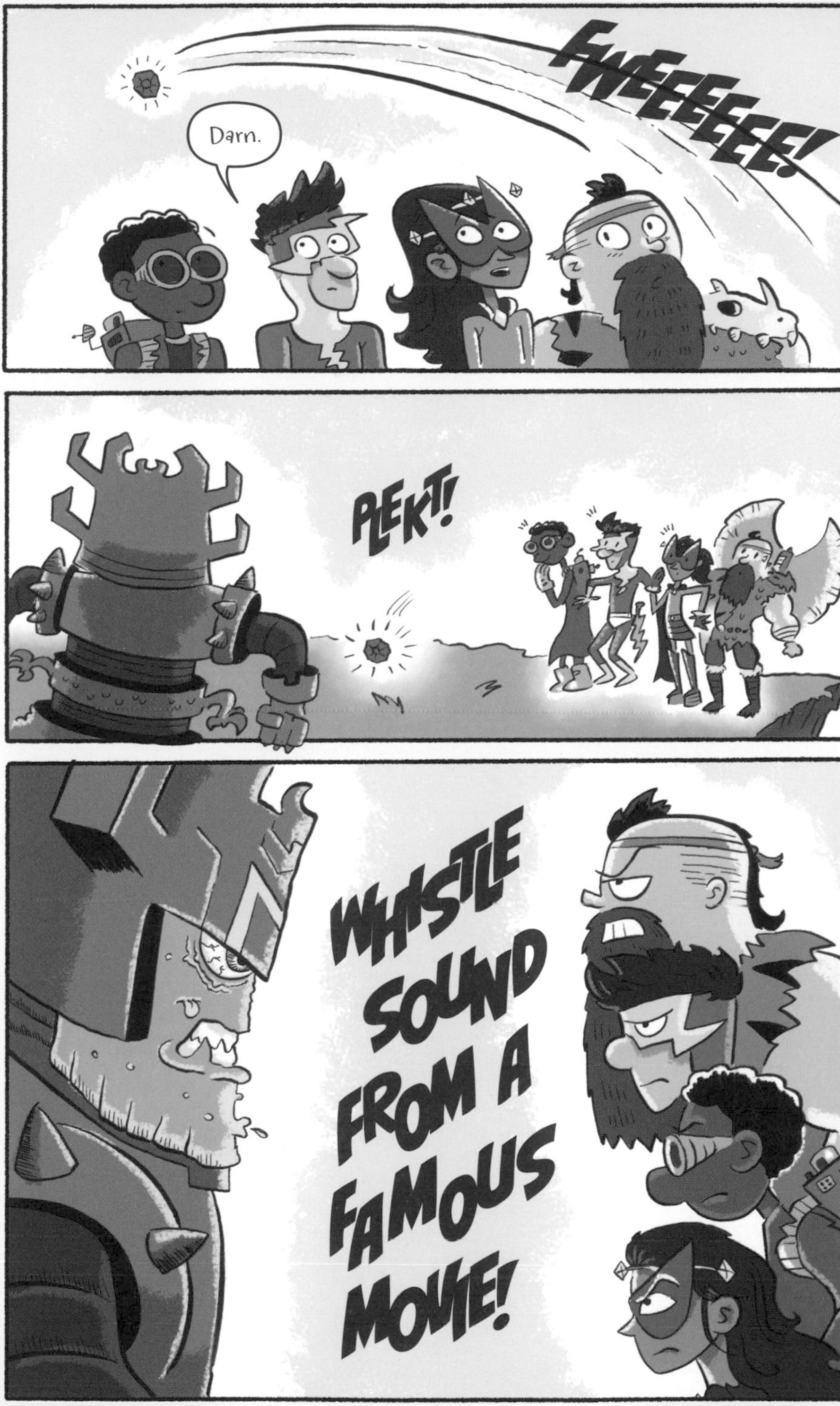
FWEEEEEEE!
Darn.
PLEKT!
WHISTLE SOUND FROM A FAMOUS MOVIE!

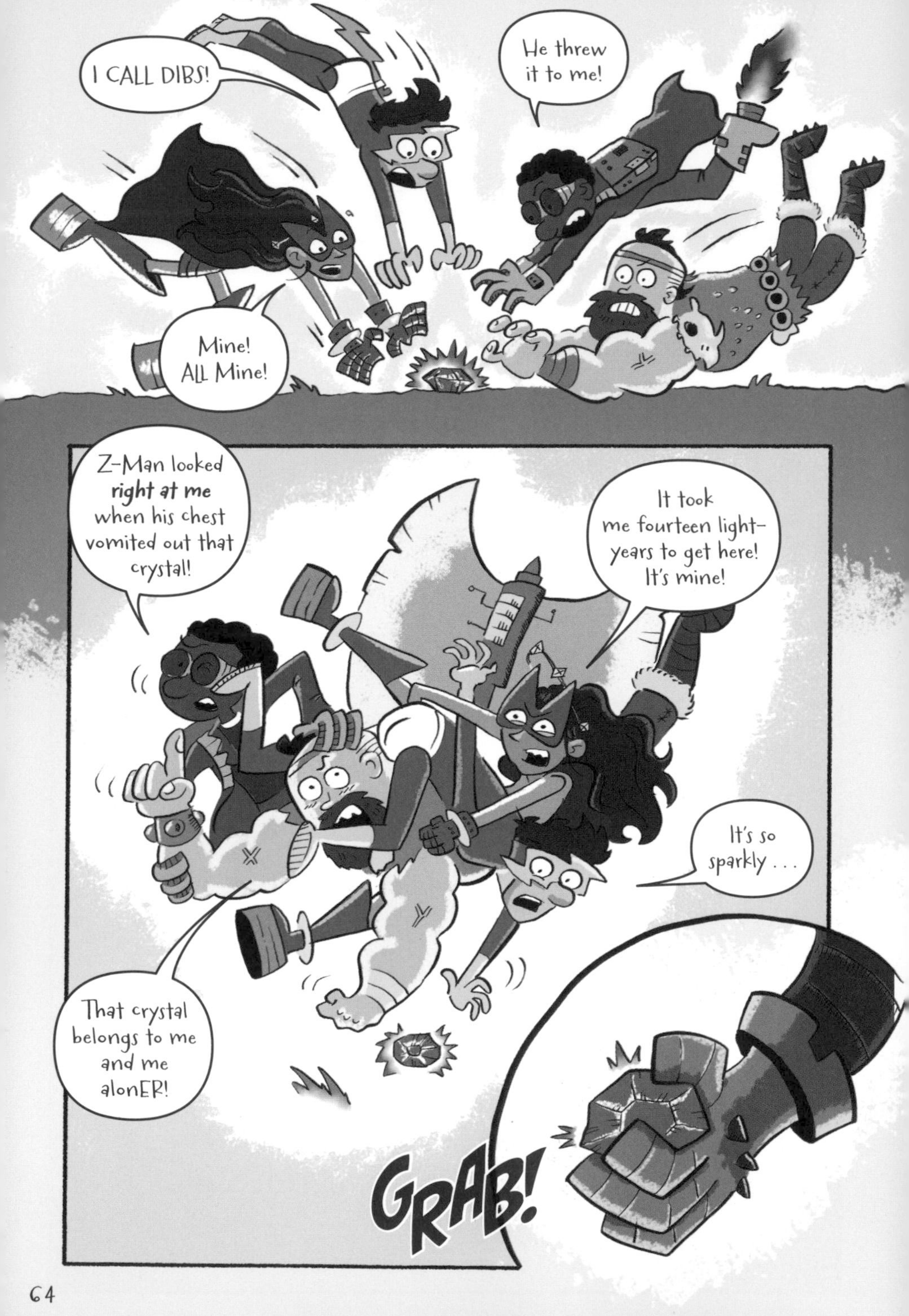
I CALL DIBS!
He threw it to me!
Mine! ALL Mine!
Z-Man looked **right at me** when his chest vomited out that crystal!
It took me fourteen light-years to get here! It's mine!
It's so sparkly . . .
That crystal belongs to me and me alonER!
GRAB!

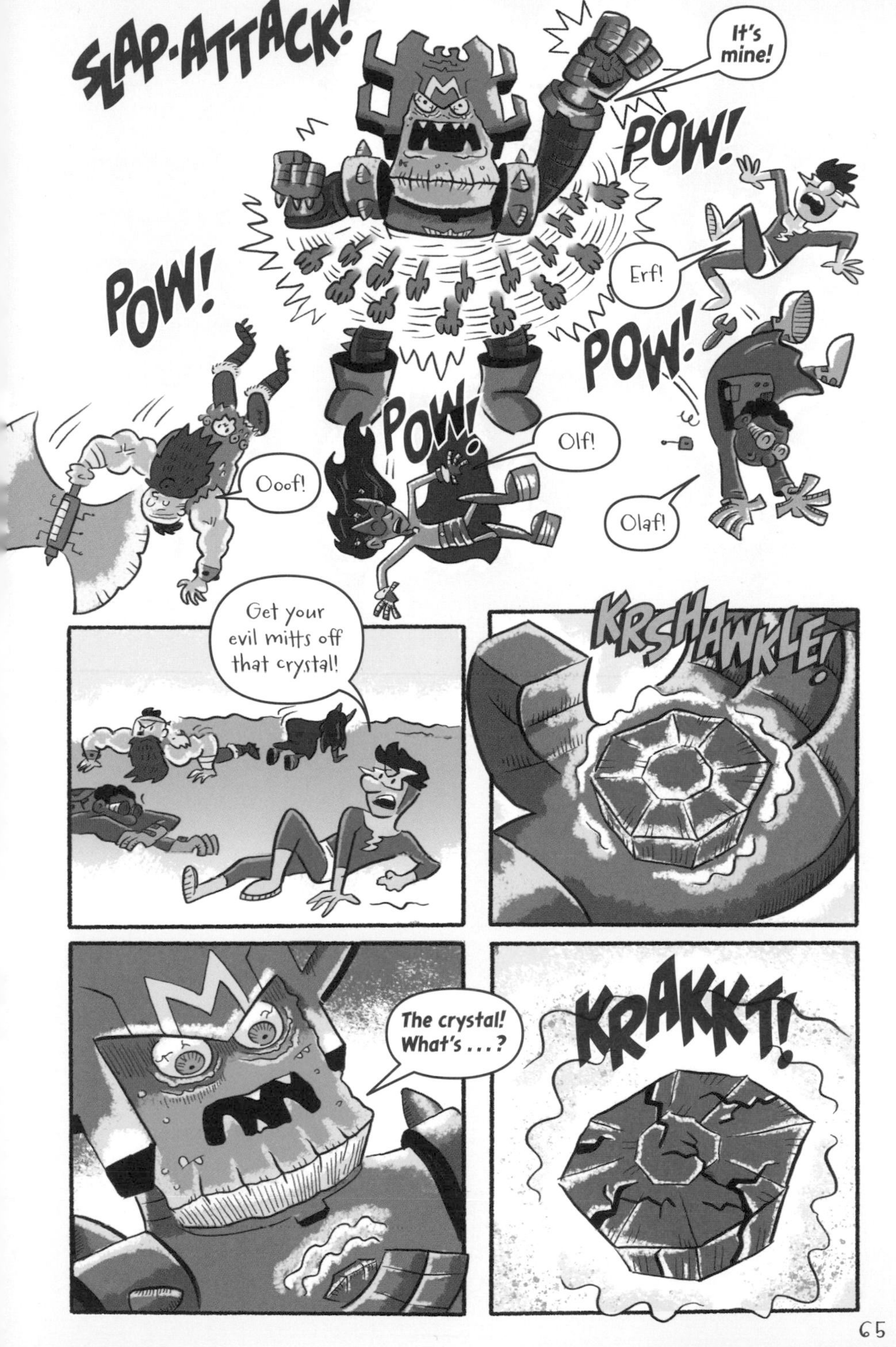
SLAP-ATTACK!
It's mine!
POW!
POW!
Erf!
POW!
POW!
Olf!
Ooof!
Olaf!
Get your evil mitts off that crystal!
KRSHAWKLE!
The crystal! What's . . . ?
KRAKKT!

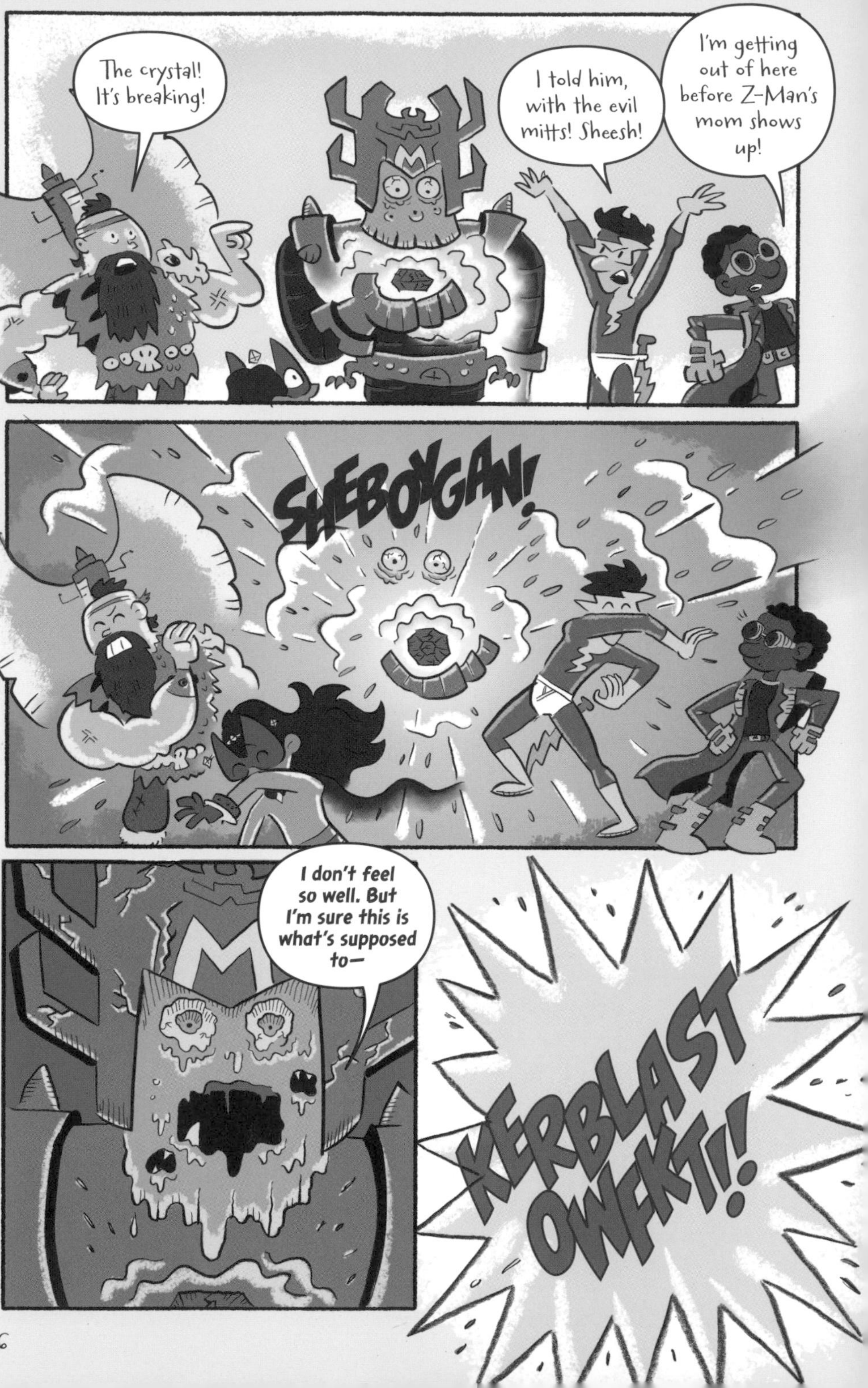
The crystal! It's breaking!
I told him, with the evil mitts! Sheesh!
I'm getting out of here before Z-Man's mom shows up!
SHEBOYGAN!
I don't feel so well. But I'm sure this is what's supposed to—
KERBLAST OWFKT!!

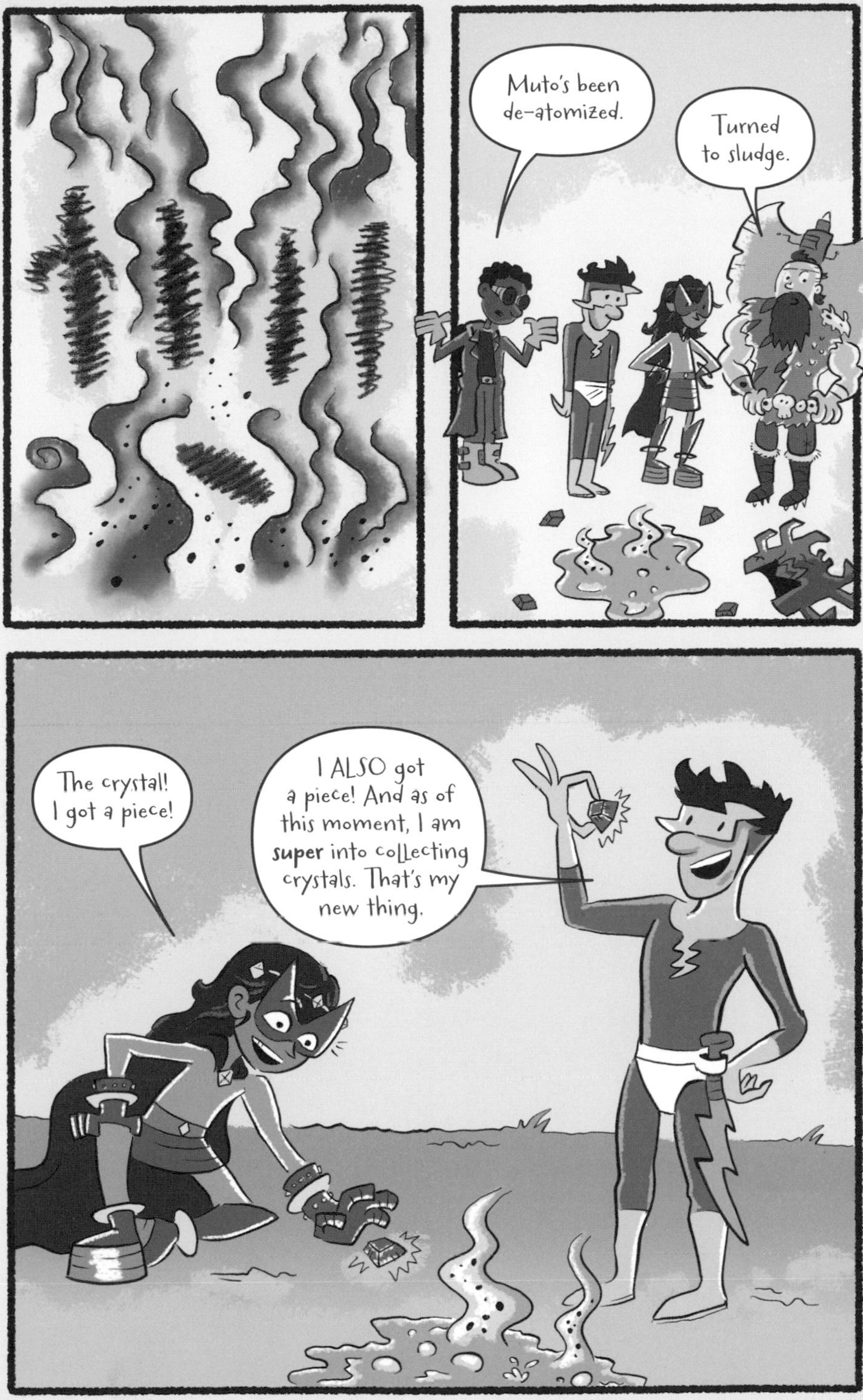
Muto's been de-atomized.
Turned to sludge.
The crystal! I got a piece!
I ALSO got a piece! And as of this moment, I am **super** into collecting crystals. That's my new thing.

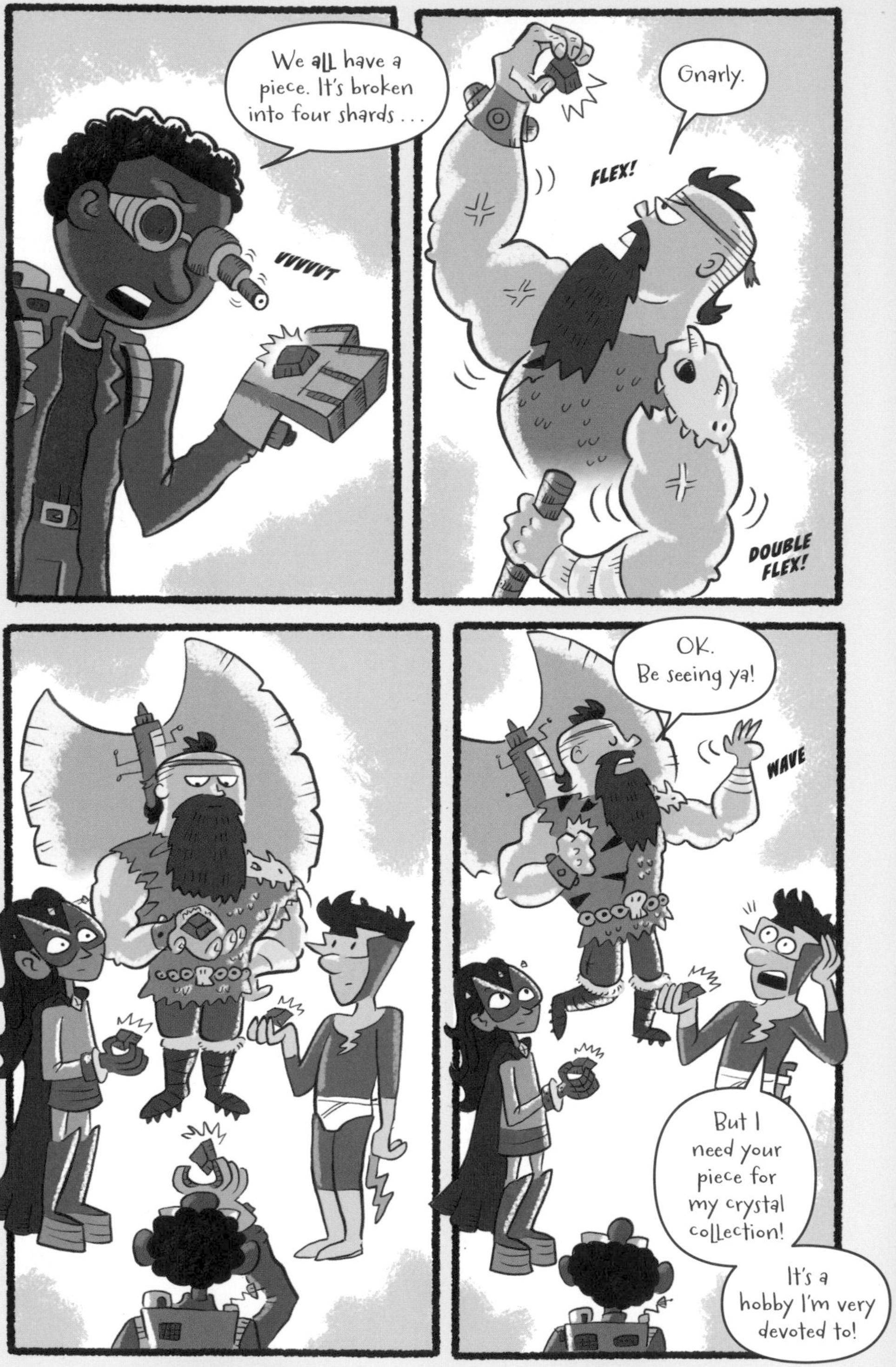

We ALL have a piece. It's broken into four shards . . .
VVVVVT
Gnarly.
FLEX!
DOUBLE FLEX!
OK. Be seeing ya!
WAVE
But I need your piece for my crystal collection!
It's a hobby I'm very devoted to!

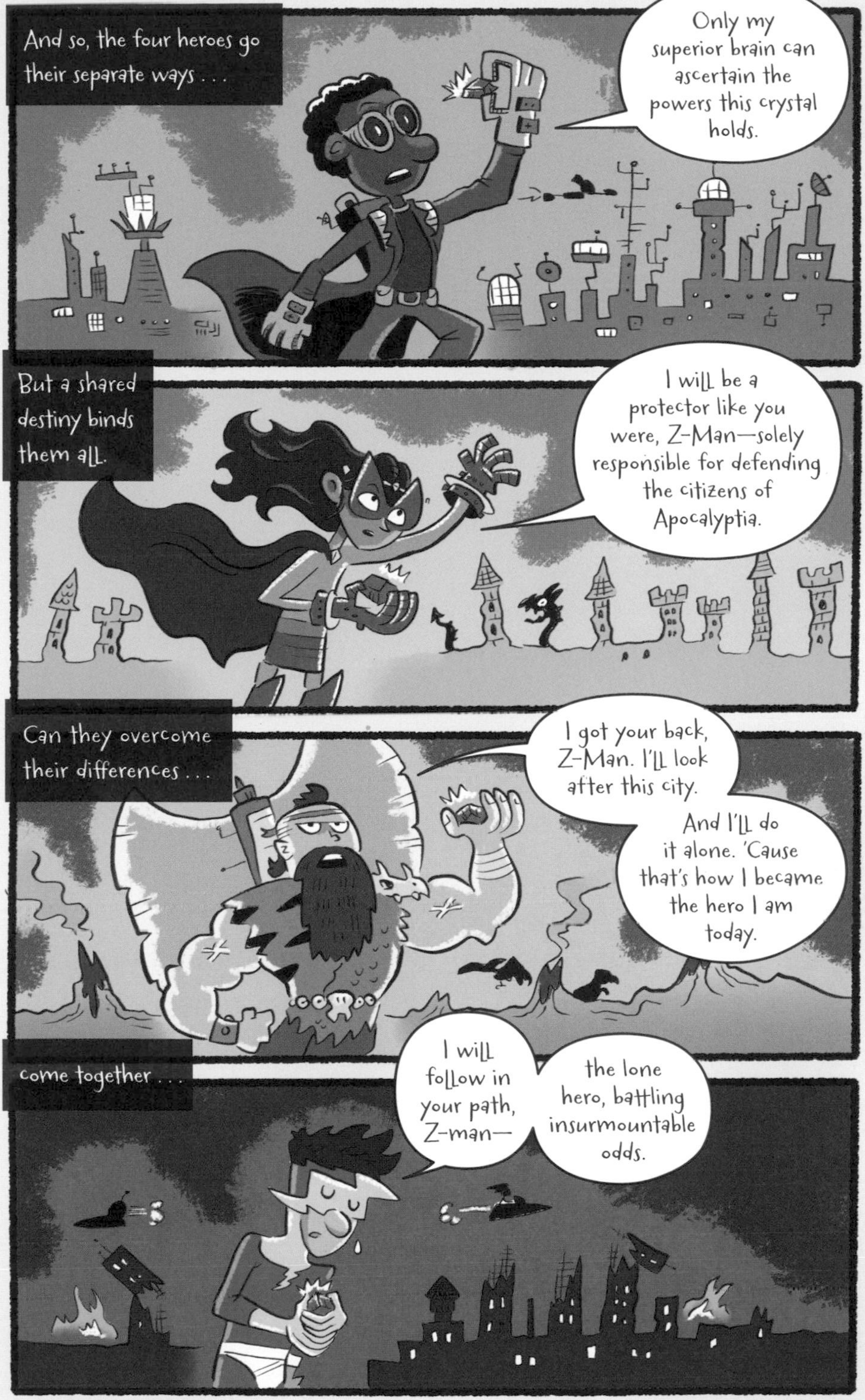

And so, the four heroes go their separate ways . . .
Only my superior brain can ascertain the powers this crystal holds.
But a shared destiny binds them all.
I will be a protector like you were, Z-Man—solely responsible for defending the citizens of Apocalyptia.
Can they overcome their differences . . .
I got your back, Z-Man. I'll look after this city.
And I'll do it alone. 'Cause that's how I became the hero I am today.
come together . . .
I will follow in your path, Z-man—
the lone hero, battling insurmountable odds.

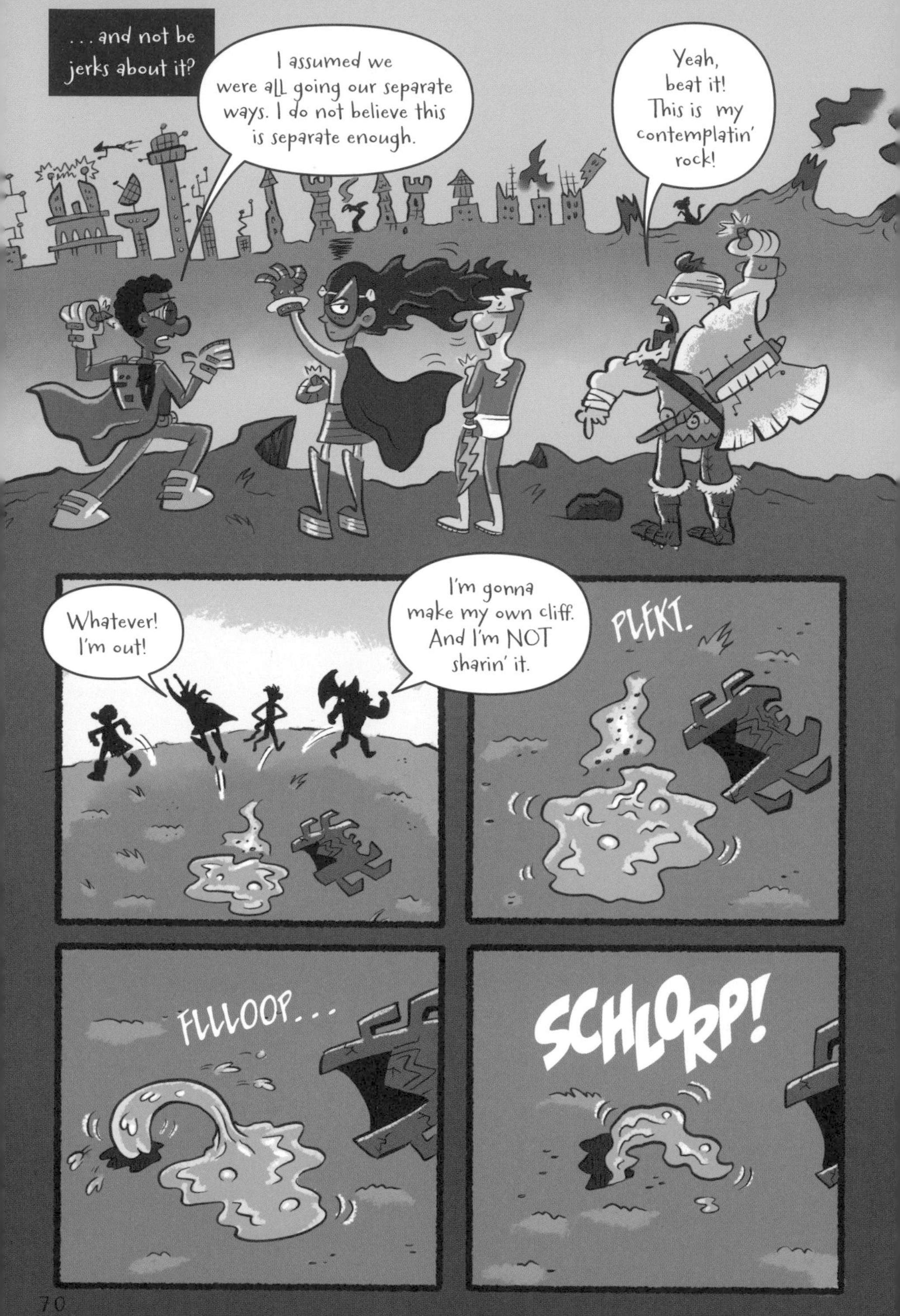
. . . and not be jerks about it?
I assumed we were aLL going our separate ways. I do not believe this is separate enough.
Yeah, beat it! This is my contemplatin' rock!
Whatever! I'm out!
I'm gonna make my own cliff. And I'm NOT sharin' it.
PLEKT.
FLLLOOP. . .
SCHLORP!

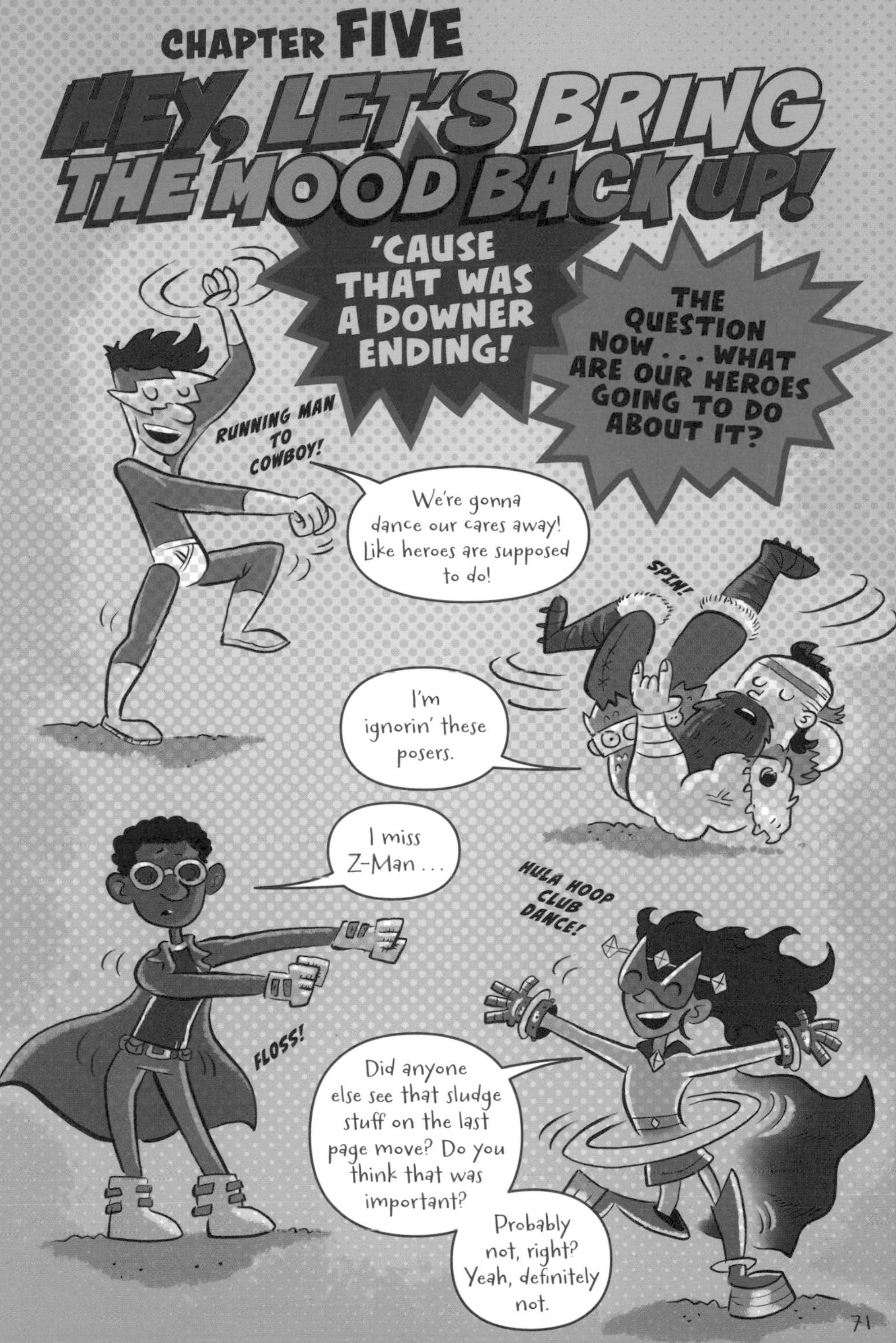

CHAPTER FIVE
HEY, LET'S BRING THE MOOD BACK UP!
'CAUSE THAT WAS A DOWNER ENDING!
THE QUESTION NOW . . . WHAT ARE OUR HEROES GOING TO DO ABOUT IT?
RUNNING MAN TO COWBOY!
We're gonna dance our cares away! Like heroes are supposed to do!
SPIN!
I'm ignorin' these posers.
I miss Z-Man . . .
HULA HOOP CLUB DANCE!
FLOSS!
Did anyone else see that sludge stuff on the last page move? Do you think that was important?
Probably not, right? Yeah, definitely not.

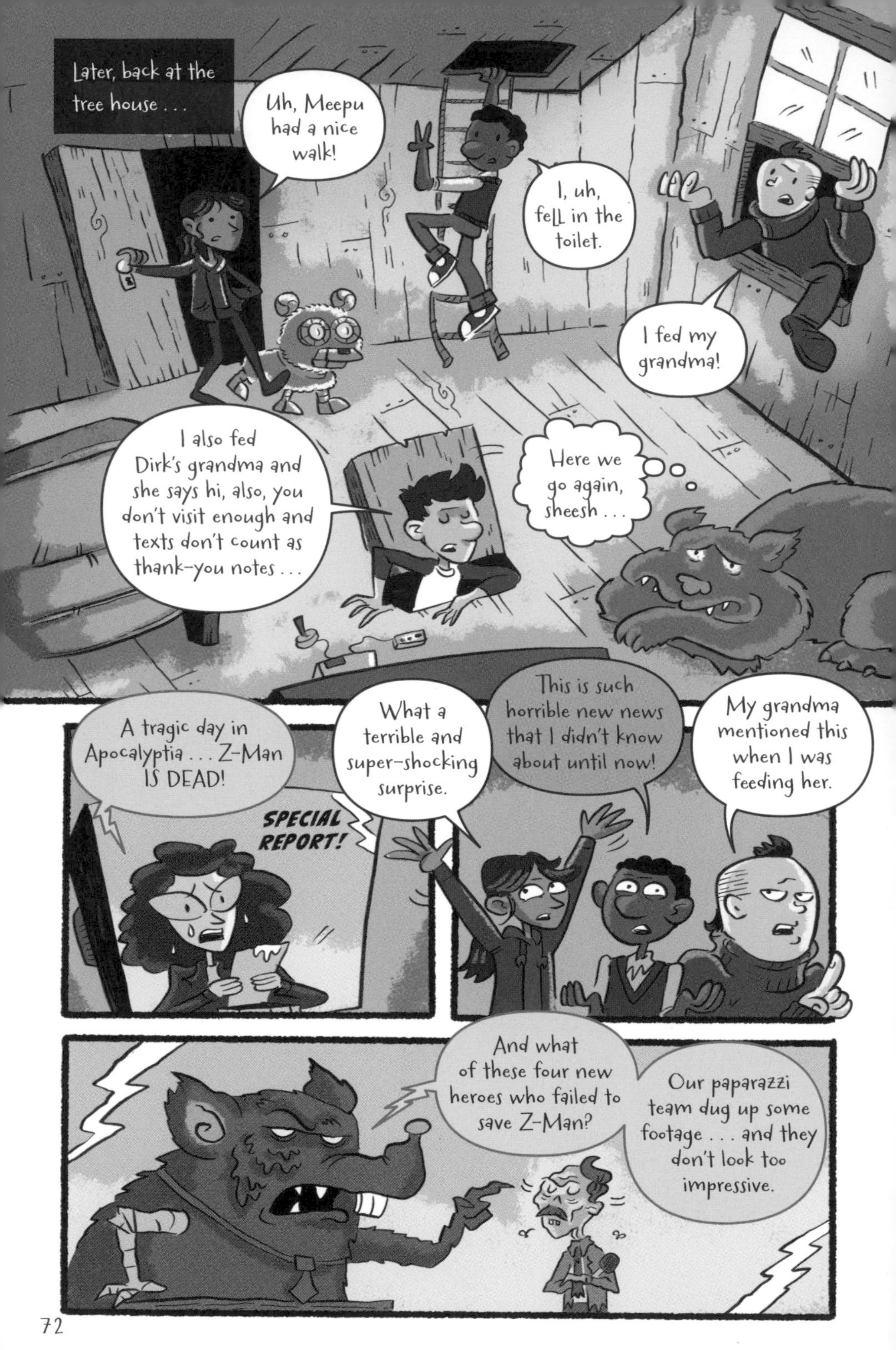
Later, back at the tree house . . .
Uh, Meepu had a nice walk!
I, uh, fell in the toilet.
I fed my grandma!
I also fed Dirk's grandma and she says hi, also, you don't visit enough and texts don't count as thank-you notes . . .
Here we go again, sheesh . . .
A tragic day in Apocalyptia . . . Z-Man IS DEAD!
SPECIAL REPORT!
What a terrible and super-shocking surprise.
This is such horrible new news that I didn't know about until now!
My grandma mentioned this when I was feeding her.
And what of these four new heroes who failed to save Z-Man?
Our paparazzi team dug up some footage . . . and they don't look too impressive.

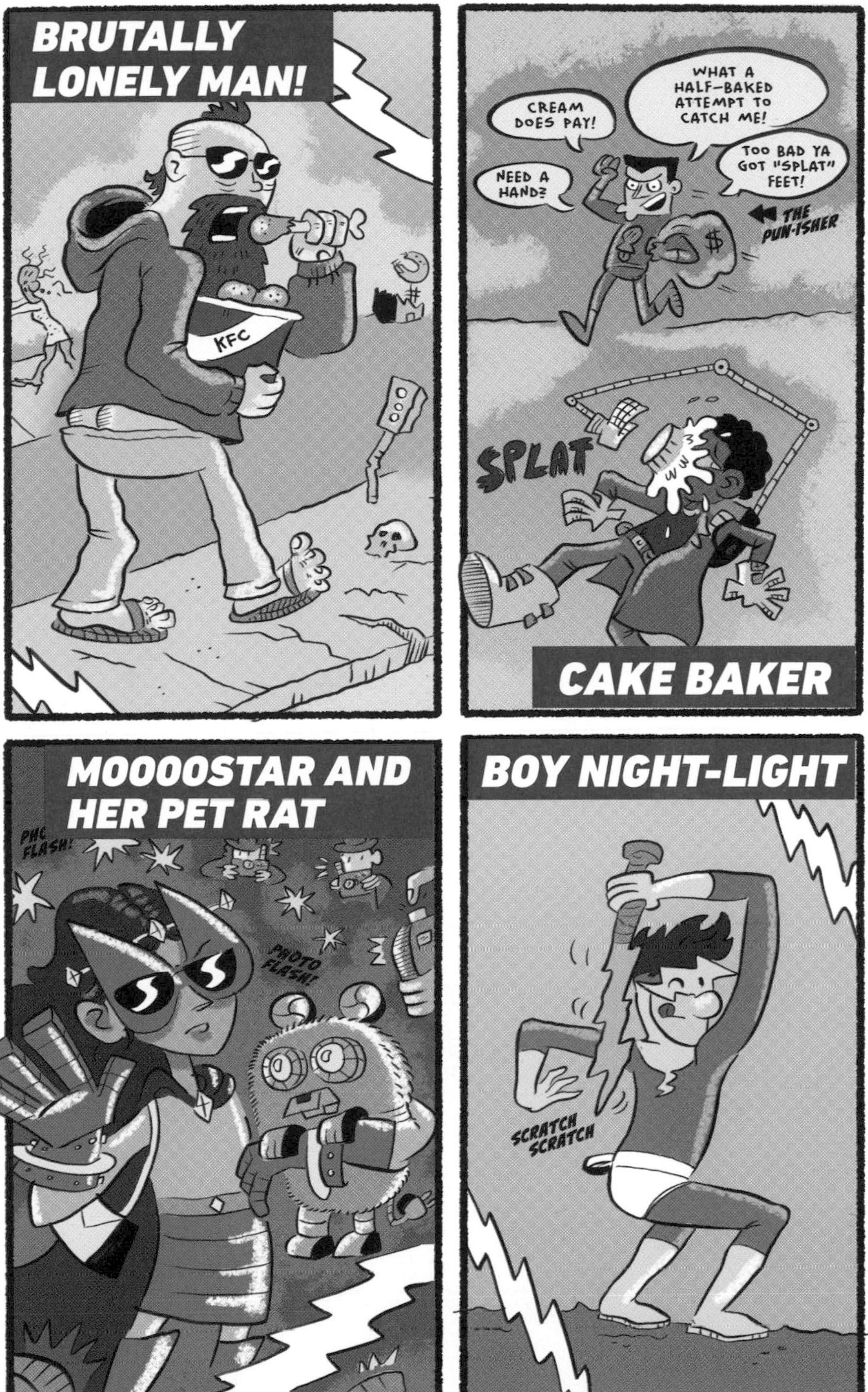
BRUTALLY LONELY MAN!
KFC
CREAM DOES PAY!
WHAT A HALF-BAKED ATTEMPT TO CATCH ME!
NEED A HAND?
TOO BAD YA GOT "SPLAT" FEET!
THE PUN-ISHER
SPLAT
CAKE BAKER
MOOOOSTAR AND HER PET RAT
PHOTO FLASH!
BOY NIGHT-LIGHT
SCRATCH SCRATCH

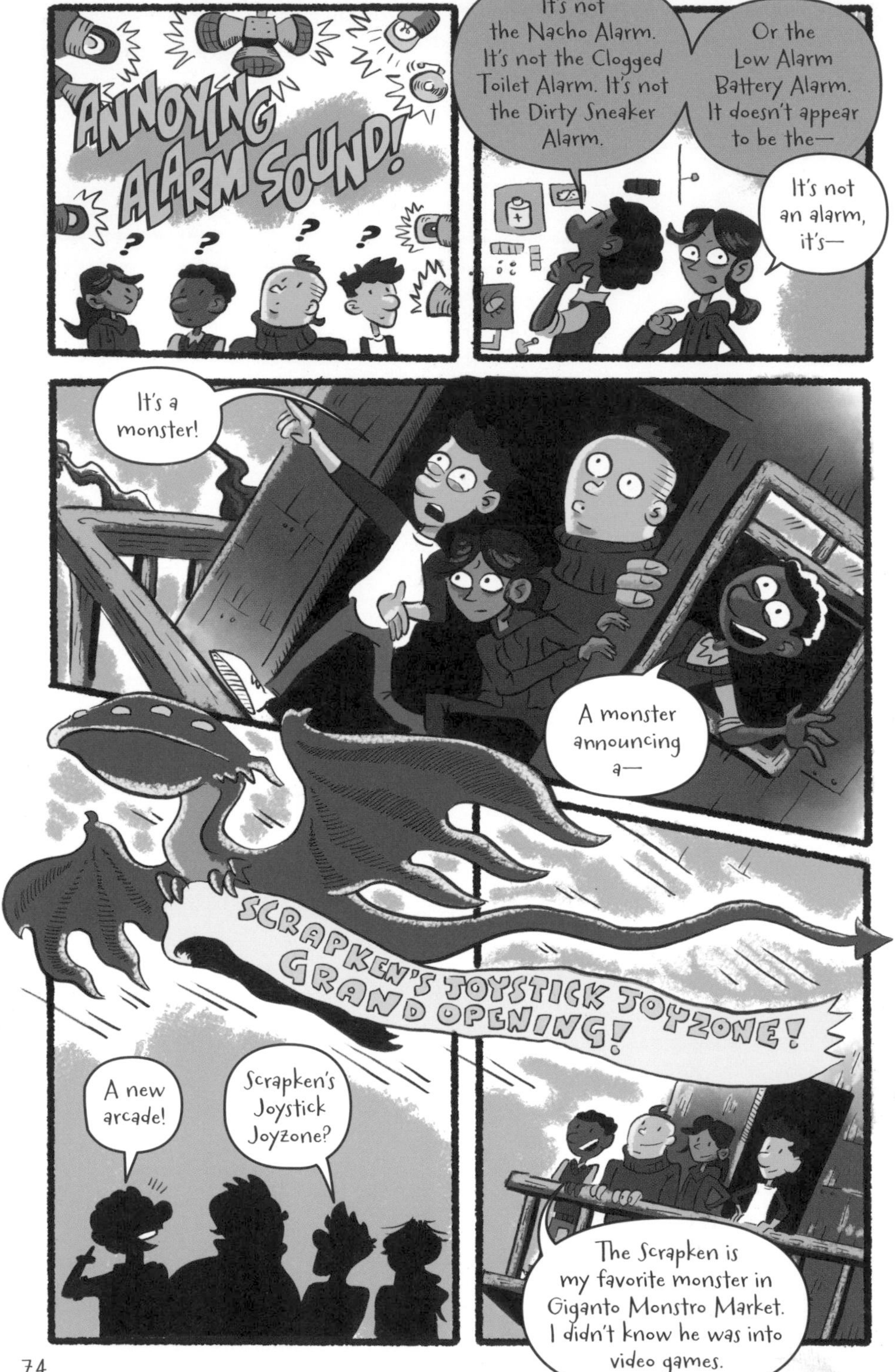
ANNOYING ALARM SOUND!
It's not the Nacho Alarm. It's not the Clogged Toilet Alarm. It's not the Dirty Sneaker Alarm.
Or the Low Alarm Battery Alarm. It doesn't appear to be the—
It's not an alarm, it's—
It's a monster!
A monster announcing a—
SCRAPKEN'S JOYSTICK JOYZONE! GRAND OPENING!
A new arcade!
Scrapken's Joystick Joyzone?
The Scrapken is my favorite monster in Giganto Monstro Market. I didn't know he was into video games.

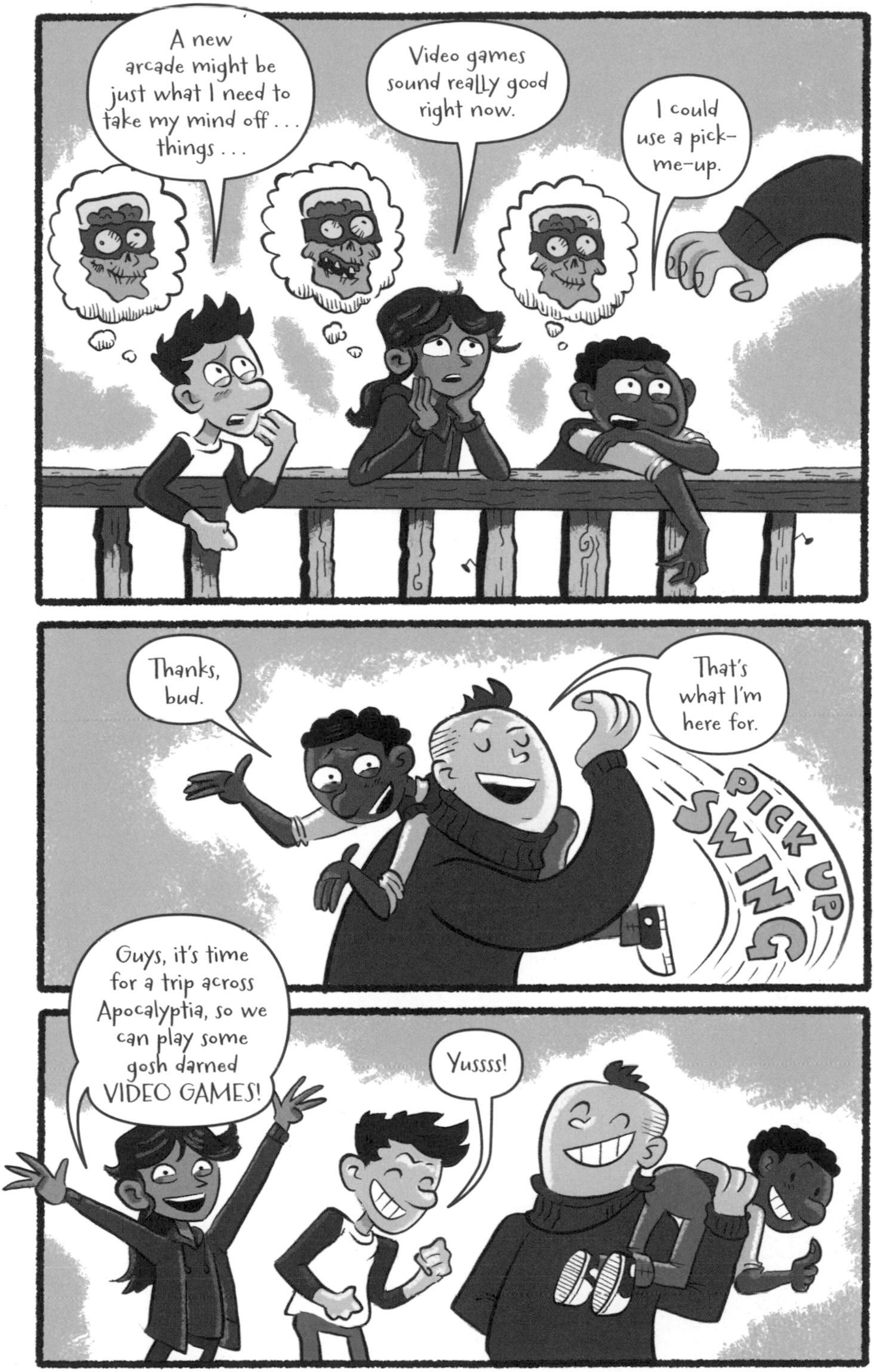
A new arcade might be just what I need to take my mind off . . . things . . .
Video games sound reaLLy good right now.
I could use a pick-me-up.
Thanks, bud.
That's what I'm here for.
PICK UP SWING
Guys, it's time for a trip across Apocalyptia, so we can play some gosh darned VIDEO GAMES!
Yussss!

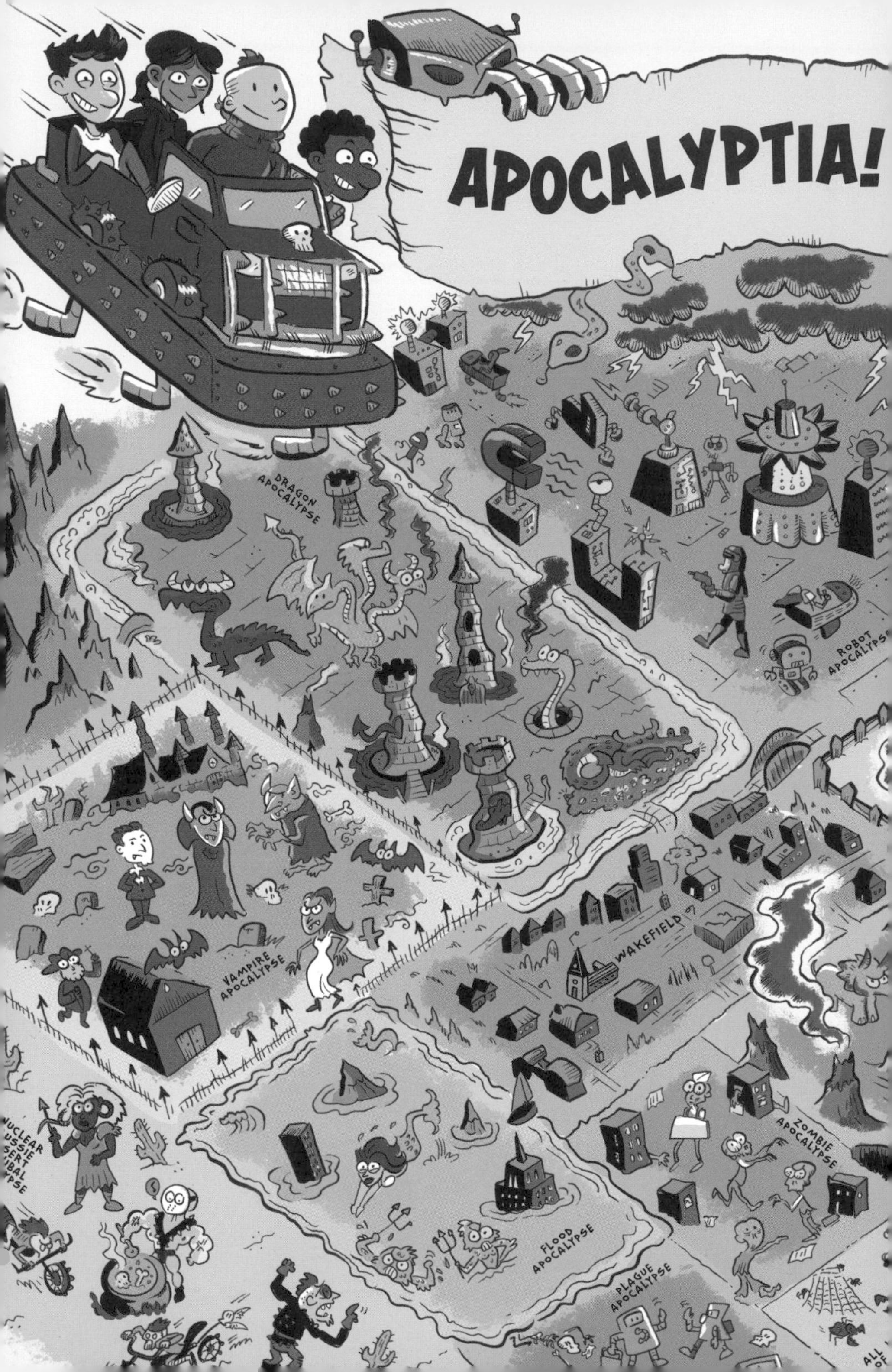

APOCALYPTIA!
DRAGON APOCALYPSE
ROBOT APOCALYPSE
VAMPIRE APOCALYPSE
WAKEFIELD
ZOMBIE APOCALYPSE
FLOOD APOCALYPSE
PLAGUE APOCALYPSE
NUCLEAR
USSIE
SERT
IBAL
YPSE
ALL OF

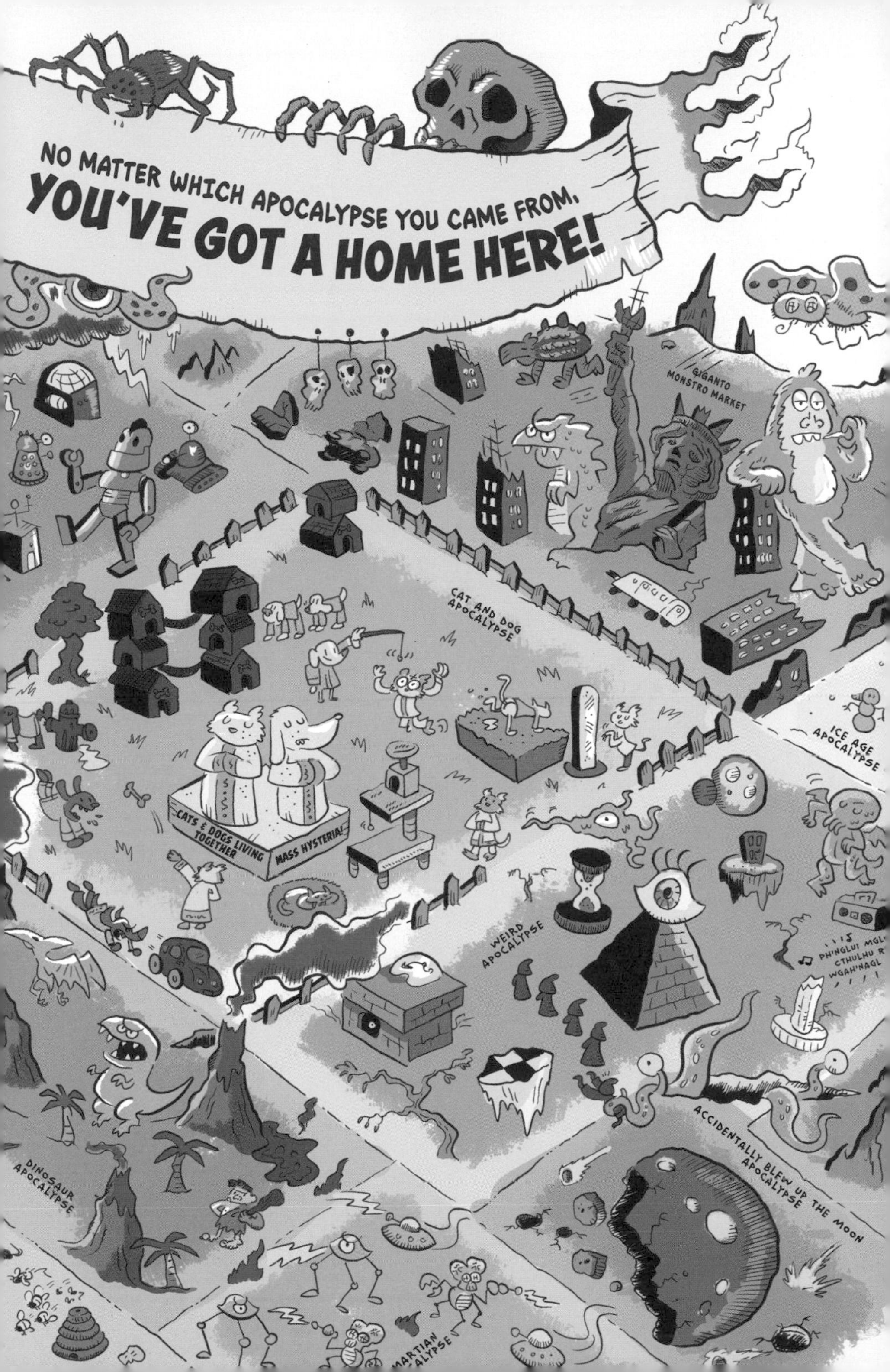
NO MATTER WHICH APOCALYPSE YOU CAME FROM,
YOU'VE GOT A HOME HERE!
GIGANTO MONSTRO MARKET
CAT AND DOG APOCALYPSE
ICE AGE APOCALYPSE
CATS & DOGS LIVING TOGETHER
MASS HYSTERIA!
WEIRD APOCALYPSE
PH'NGLUI MGL
CTHULHU R
WGAH'NAGL
ACCIDENTALLY BLEW UP THE MOON APOCALYPSE
DINOSAUR APOCALYPSE
MARTIAN
ALYPSE

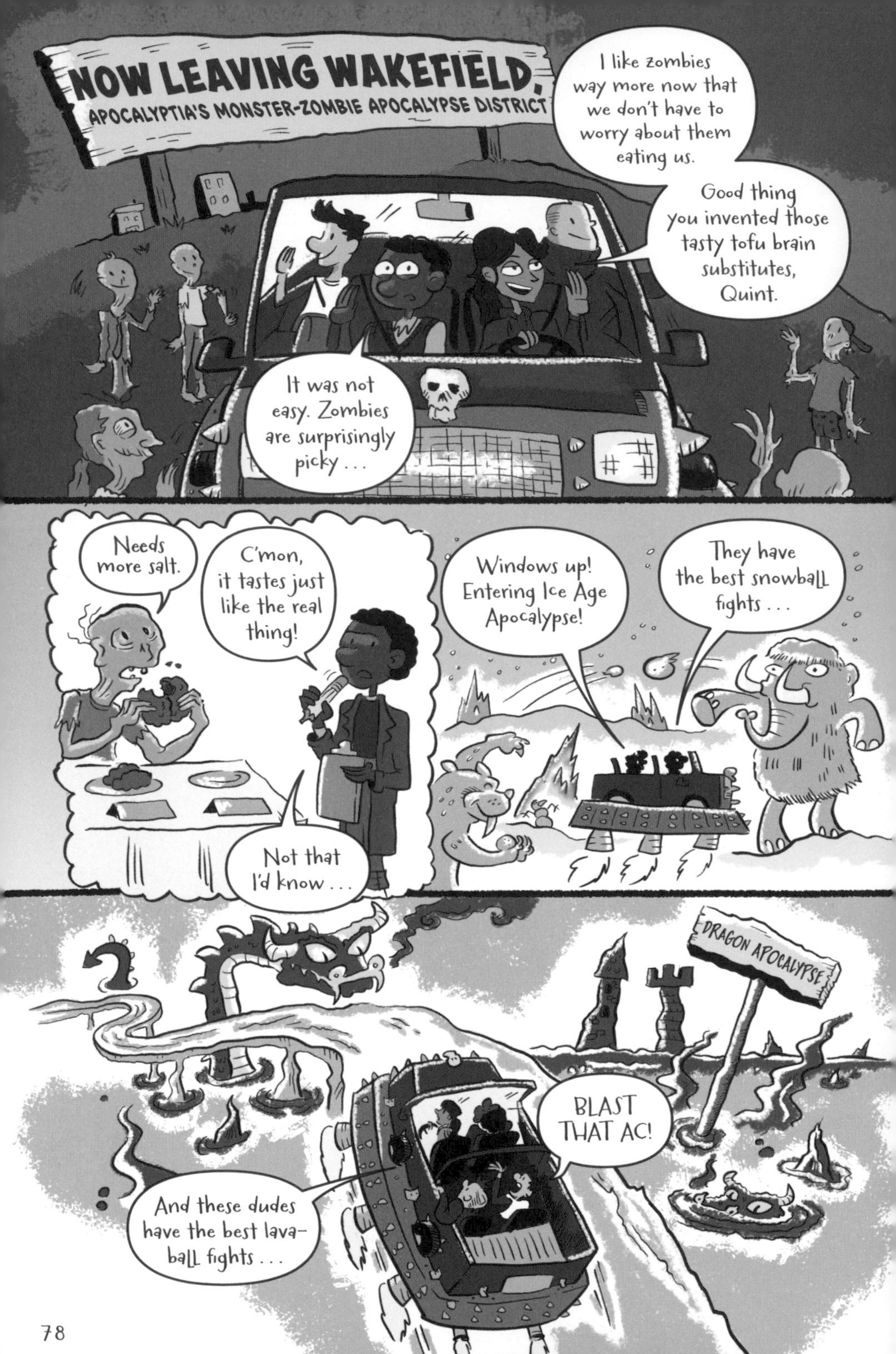
NOW LEAVING WAKEFIELD,
APOCALYPTIA'S MONSTER-ZOMBIE APOCALYPSE DISTRICT
I like zombies way more now that we don't have to worry about them eating us.
Good thing you invented those tasty tofu brain substitutes, Quint.
It was not easy. Zombies are surprisingly picky . . .
Needs more salt.
C'mon, it tastes just like the real thing!
Not that I'd know . . .
Windows up! Entering Ice Age Apocalypse!
They have the best snowball fights . . .
DRAGON APOCALYPSE
BLAST THAT AC!
And these dudes have the best lava-ball fights . . .

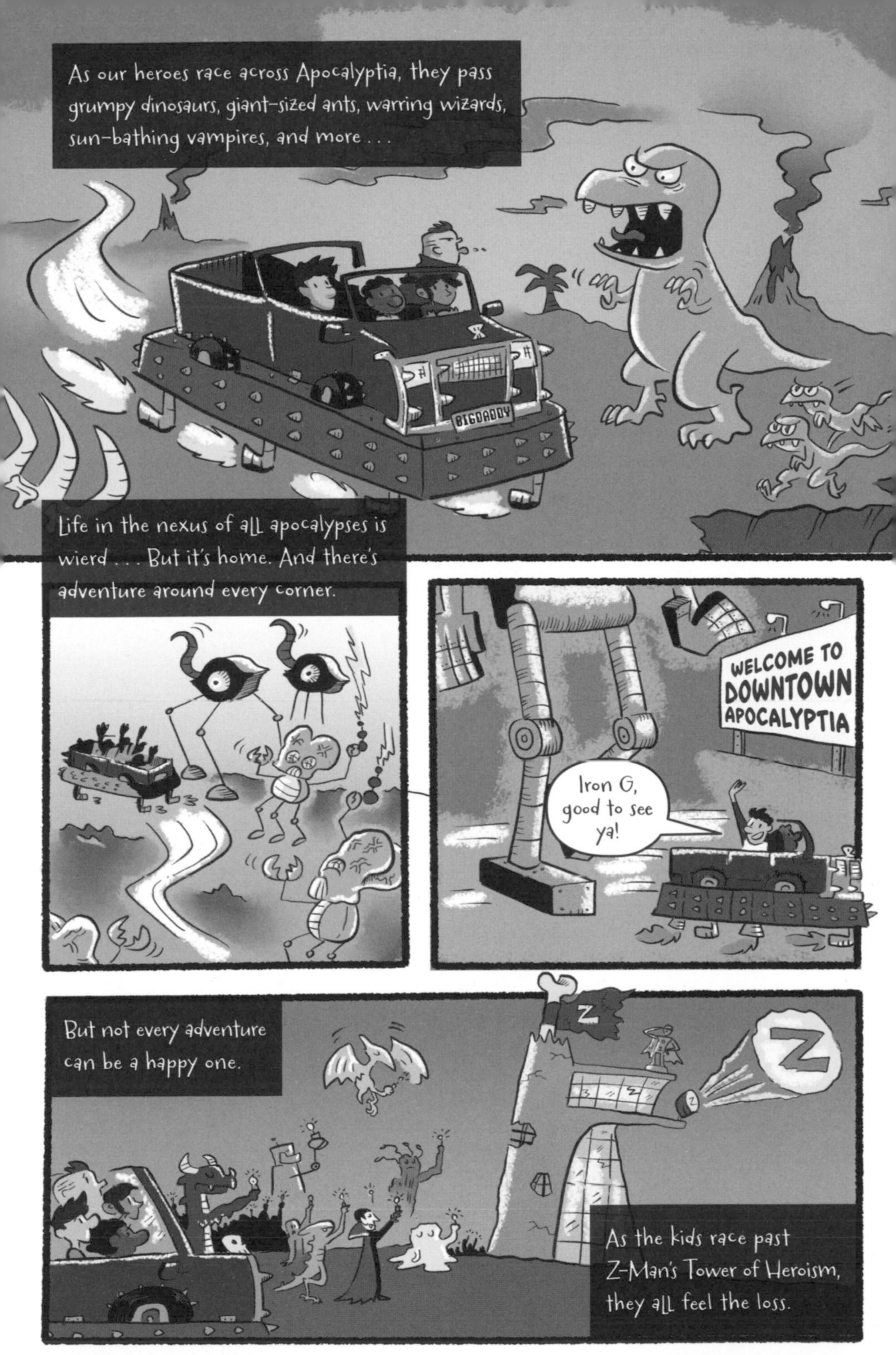
As our heroes race across Apocalyptia, they pass grumpy dinosaurs, giant-sized ants, warring wizards, sun-bathing vampires, and more . . .
BIGDADDY
Life in the nexus of all apocalypses is wierd . . . But it's home. And there's adventure around every corner.
WELCOME TO DOWNTOWN APOCALYPTIA
Iron G, good to see ya!
But not every adventure can be a happy one.
As the kids race past Z-Man's Tower of Heroism, they all feel the loss.

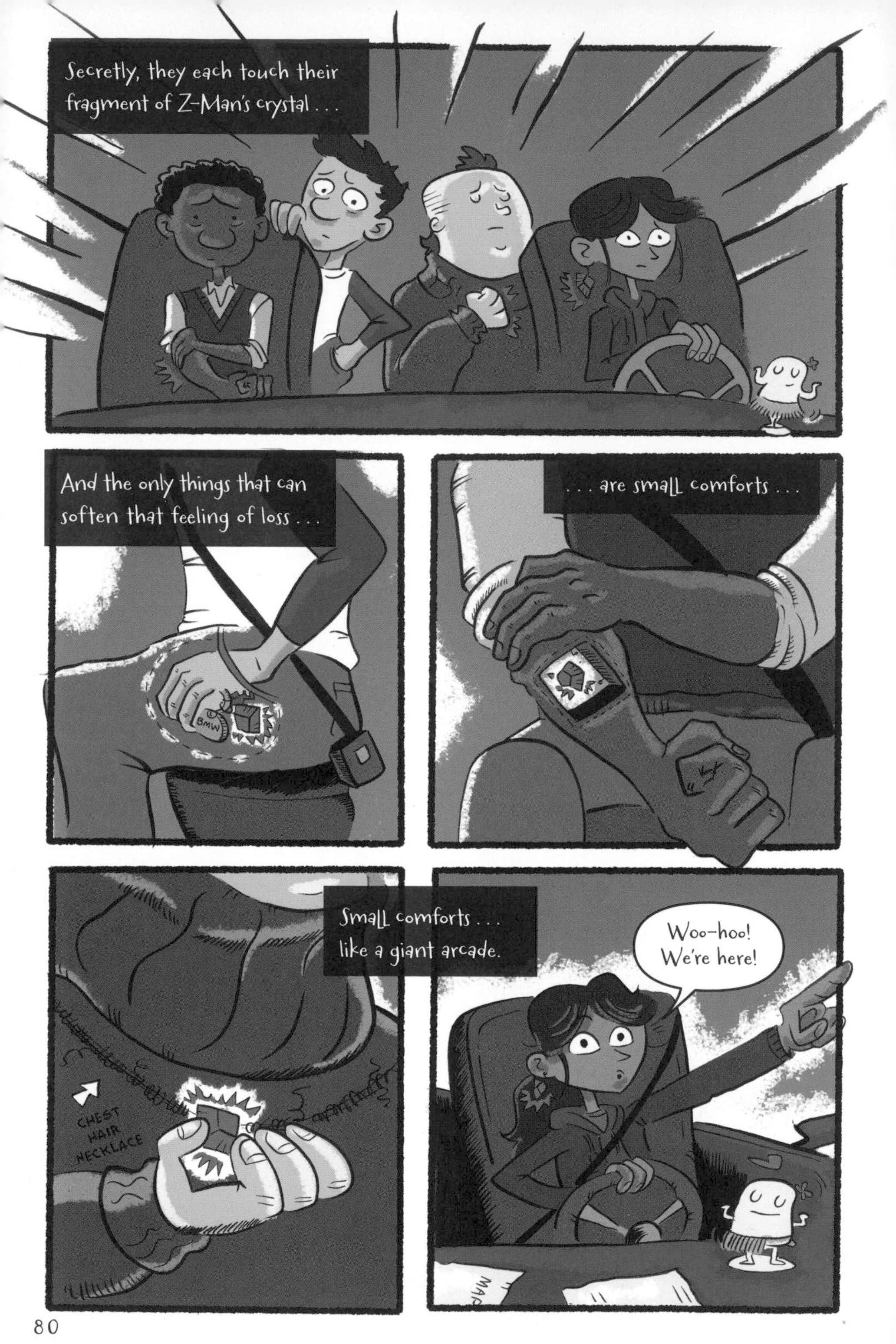
Secretly, they each touch their fragment of Z-Man's crystal . . .
And the only things that can soften that feeling of loss . . .
BMW
. . . are small comforts . . .
Small comforts . . . like a giant arcade.
CHEST HAIR NECKLACE
Woo-hoo! We're here!

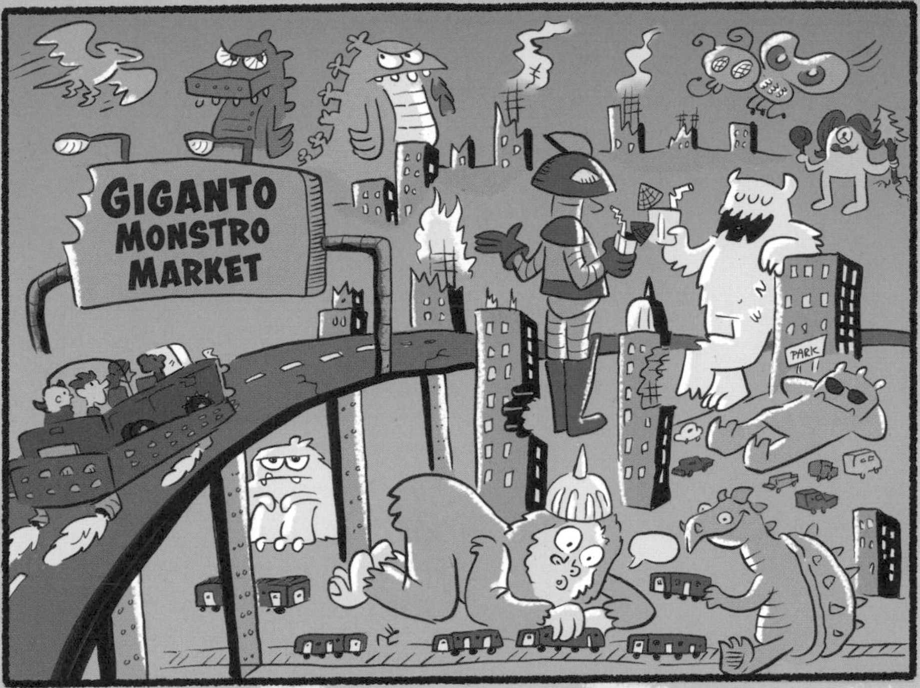
GIGANTO MONSTRO MARKET
PARK

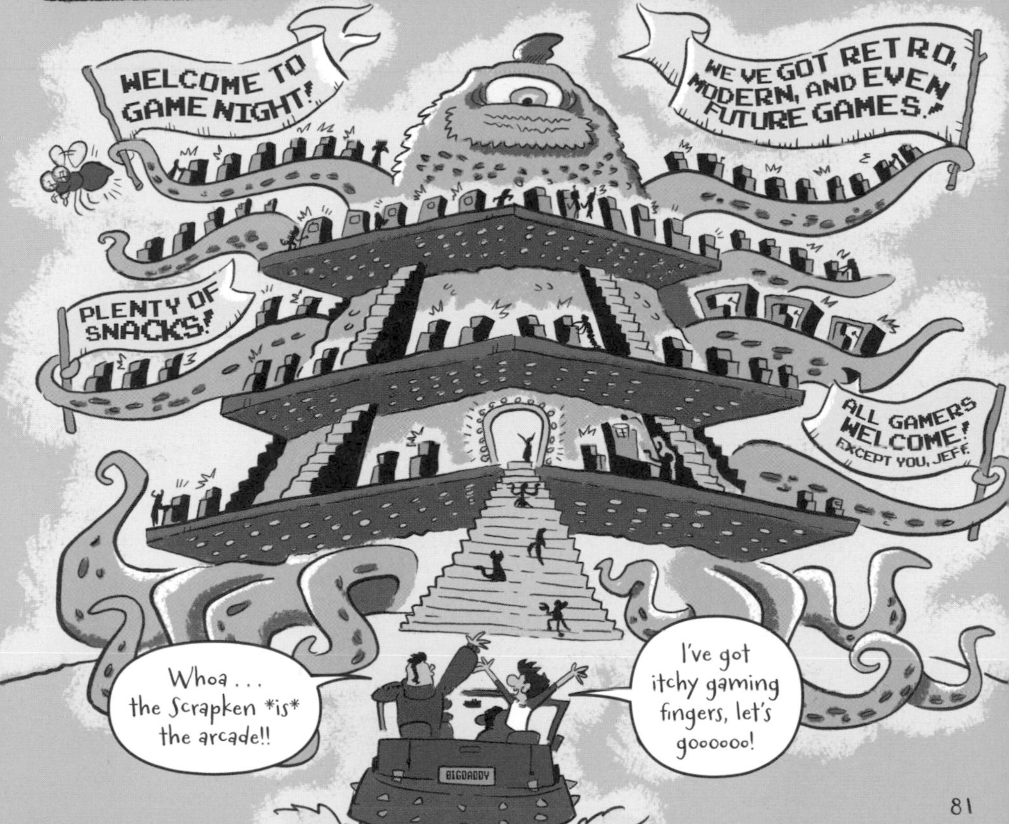
WELCOME TO GAME NIGHT!
WE'VE GOT RETRO, MODERN, AND EVEN FUTURE GAMES!
PLENTY OF SNACKS!
ALL GAMERS WELCOME! EXCEPT YOU, JEFF.
Whoa . . . the Scrapken *is* the arcade!!
I've got itchy gaming fingers, let's goooooo!
BIGDADDY

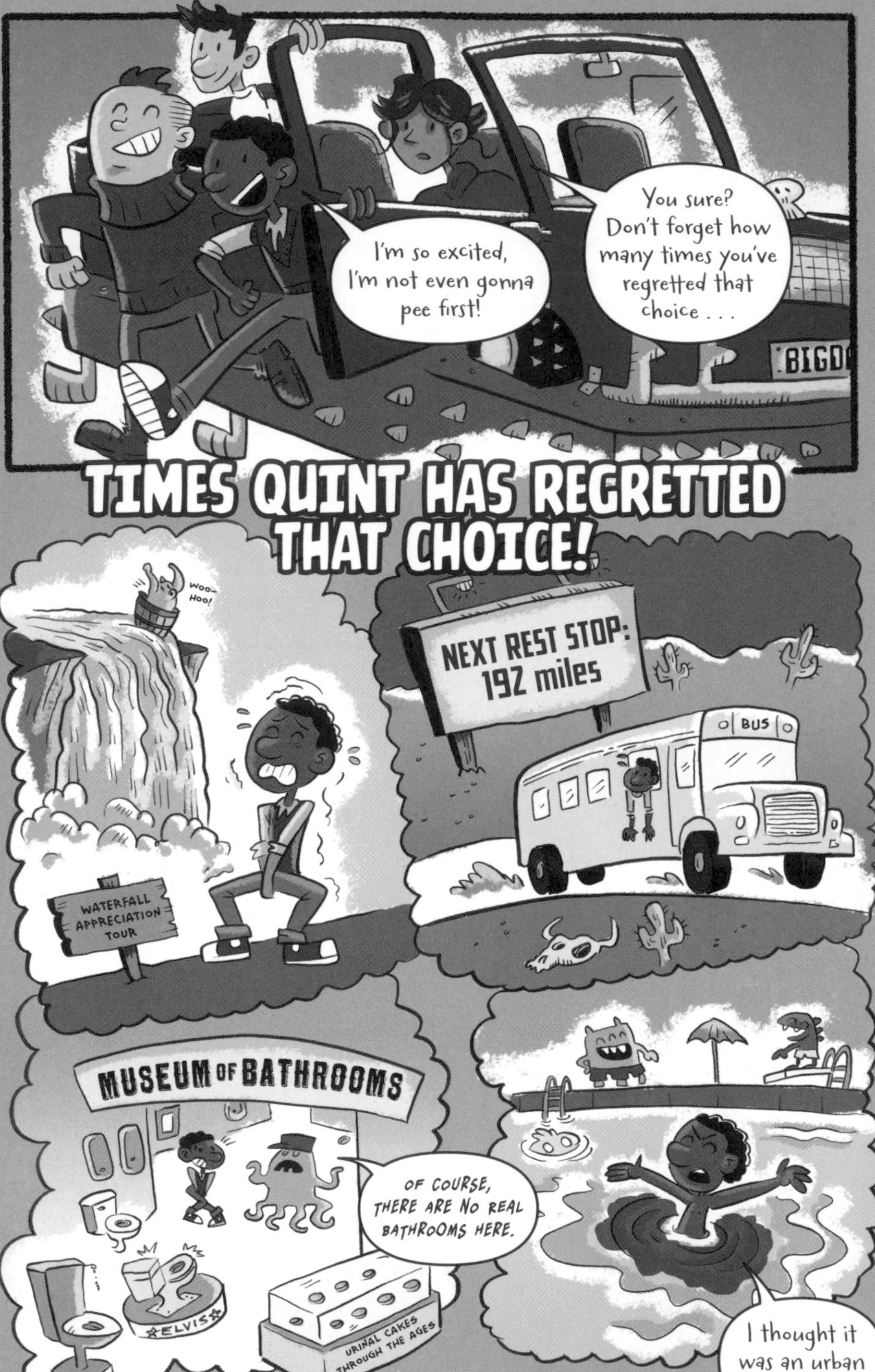
I'm so excited, I'm not even gonna pee first!
You sure? Don't forget how many times you've regretted that choice . . .
BIGD
TIMES QUINT HAS REGRETTED THAT CHOICE!
WOO-HOO!
WATERFALL APPRECIATION TOUR
NEXT REST STOP: 192 miles
BUS
MUSEUM OF BATHROOMS
OF COURSE, THERE ARE NO REAL BATHROOMS HERE.
ELVIS
URINAL CAKES THROUGH THE AGES
I thought it was an urban legend!

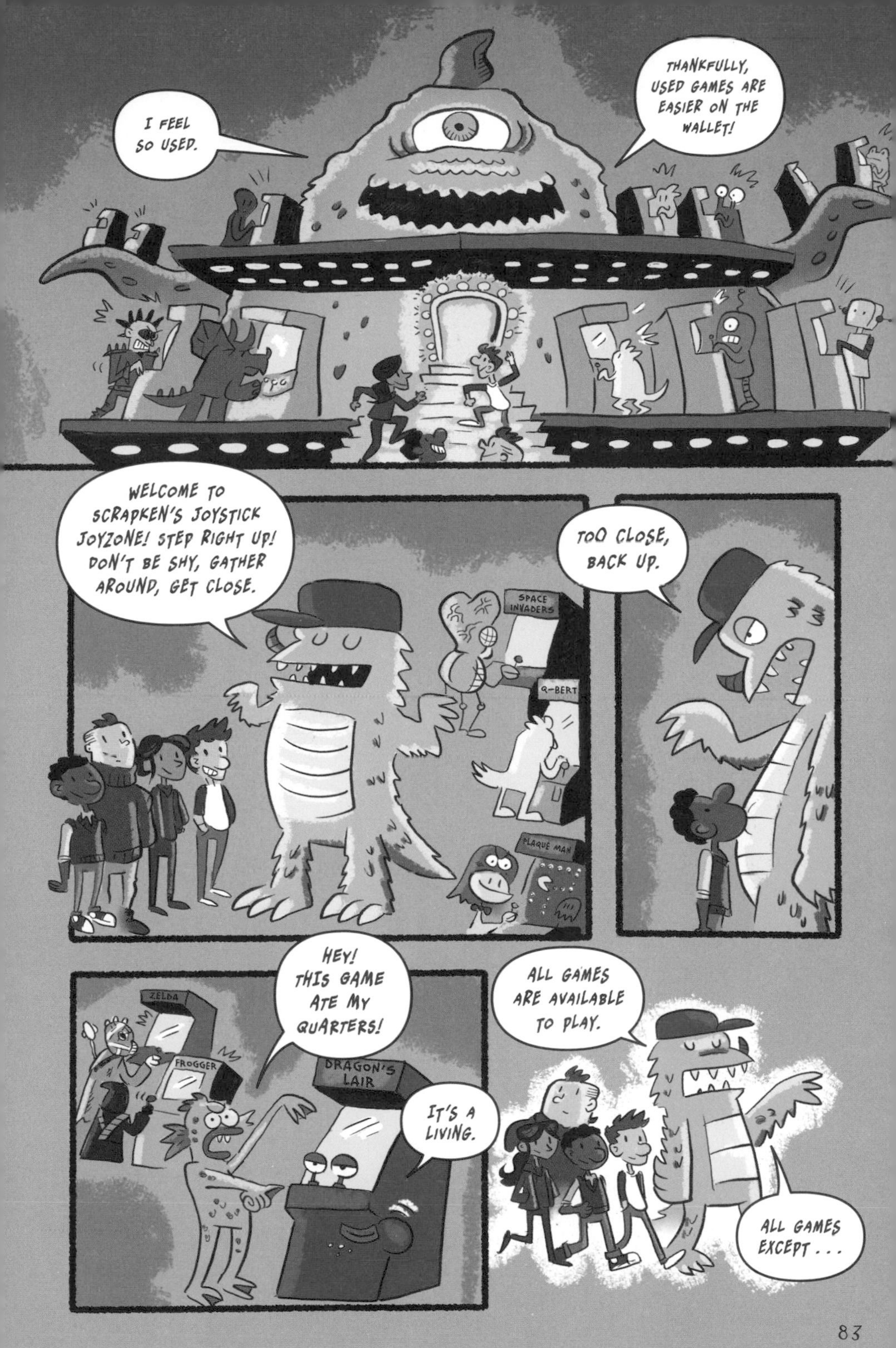
I FEEL SO USED.
THANKFULLY, USED GAMES ARE EASIER ON THE WALLET!
WELCOME TO SCRAPKEN'S JOYSTICK JOYZONE! STEP RIGHT UP! DON'T BE SHY, GATHER AROUND, GET CLOSE.
SPACE INVADERS
Q-BERT
PLAQUE MAN
TOO CLOSE, BACK UP.
ZELDA
FROGGER
HEY! THIS GAME ATE MY QUARTERS!
DRAGON'S LAIR
IT'S A LIVING.
ALL GAMES ARE AVAILABLE TO PLAY.
ALL GAMES EXCEPT . . .

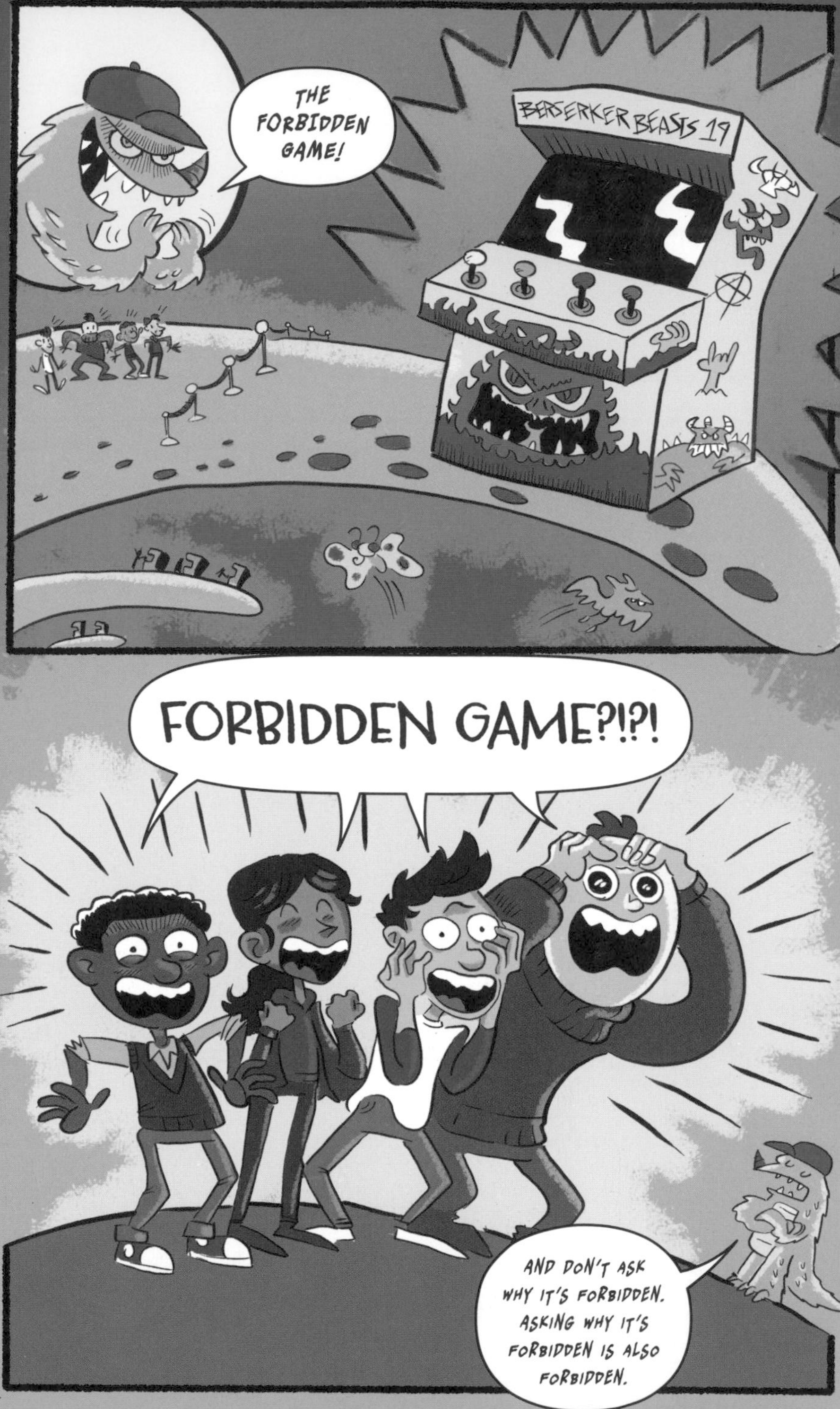
THE FORBIDDEN GAME!
BERSERKER BEASTS 19
FORBIDDEN GAME?!?!
AND DON'T ASK WHY IT'S FORBIDDEN. ASKING WHY IT'S FORBIDDEN IS ALSO FORBIDDEN.

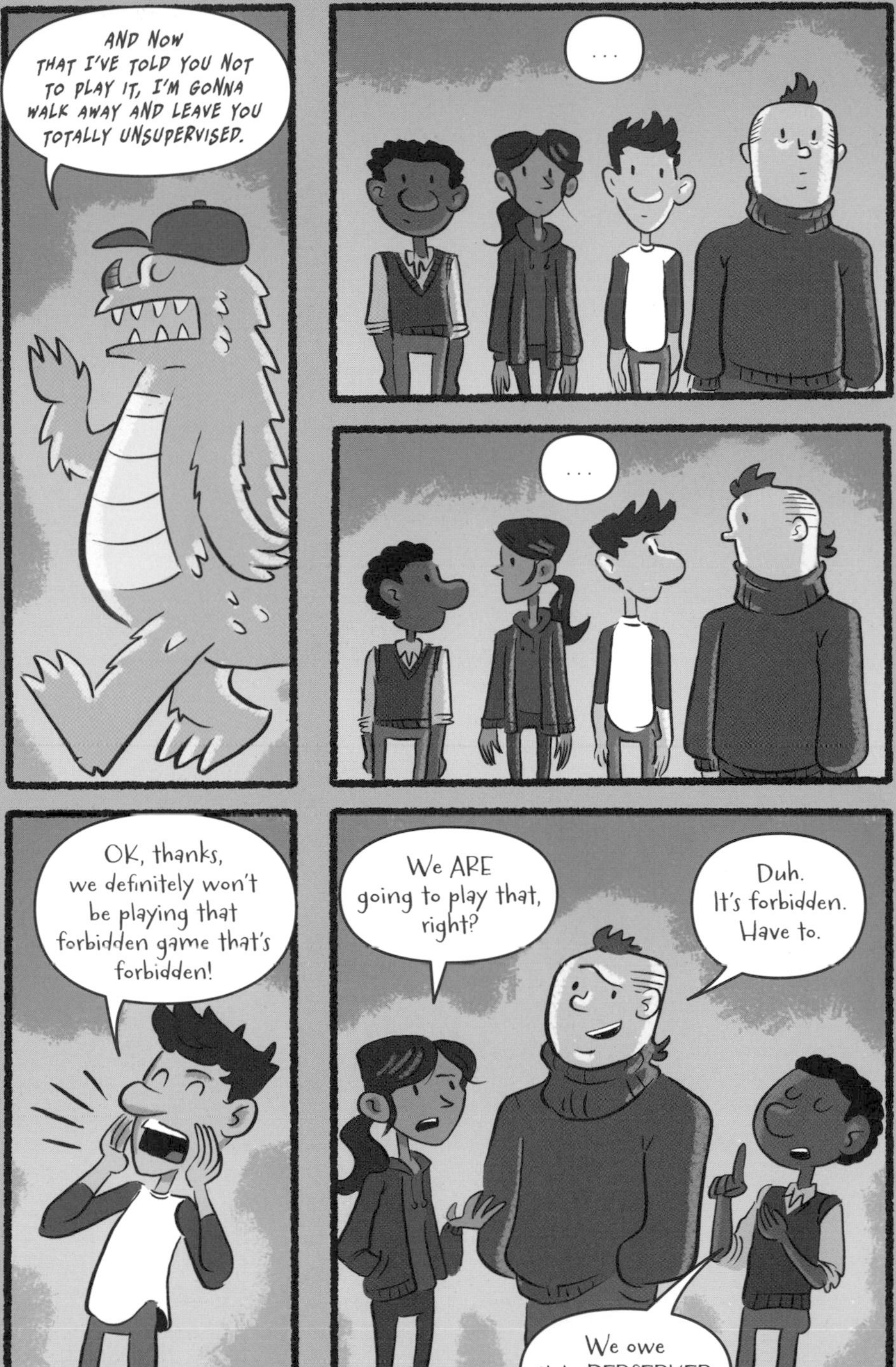
AND NOW THAT I'VE TOLD YOU NOT TO PLAY IT, I'M GONNA WALK AWAY AND LEAVE YOU TOTALLY UNSUPERVISED.
...
...
OK, thanks, we definitely won't be playing that forbidden game that's forbidden!
We ARE going to play that, right?
Duh. It's forbidden. Have to.
We owe it to BERSERKER BEASTS 1–18.

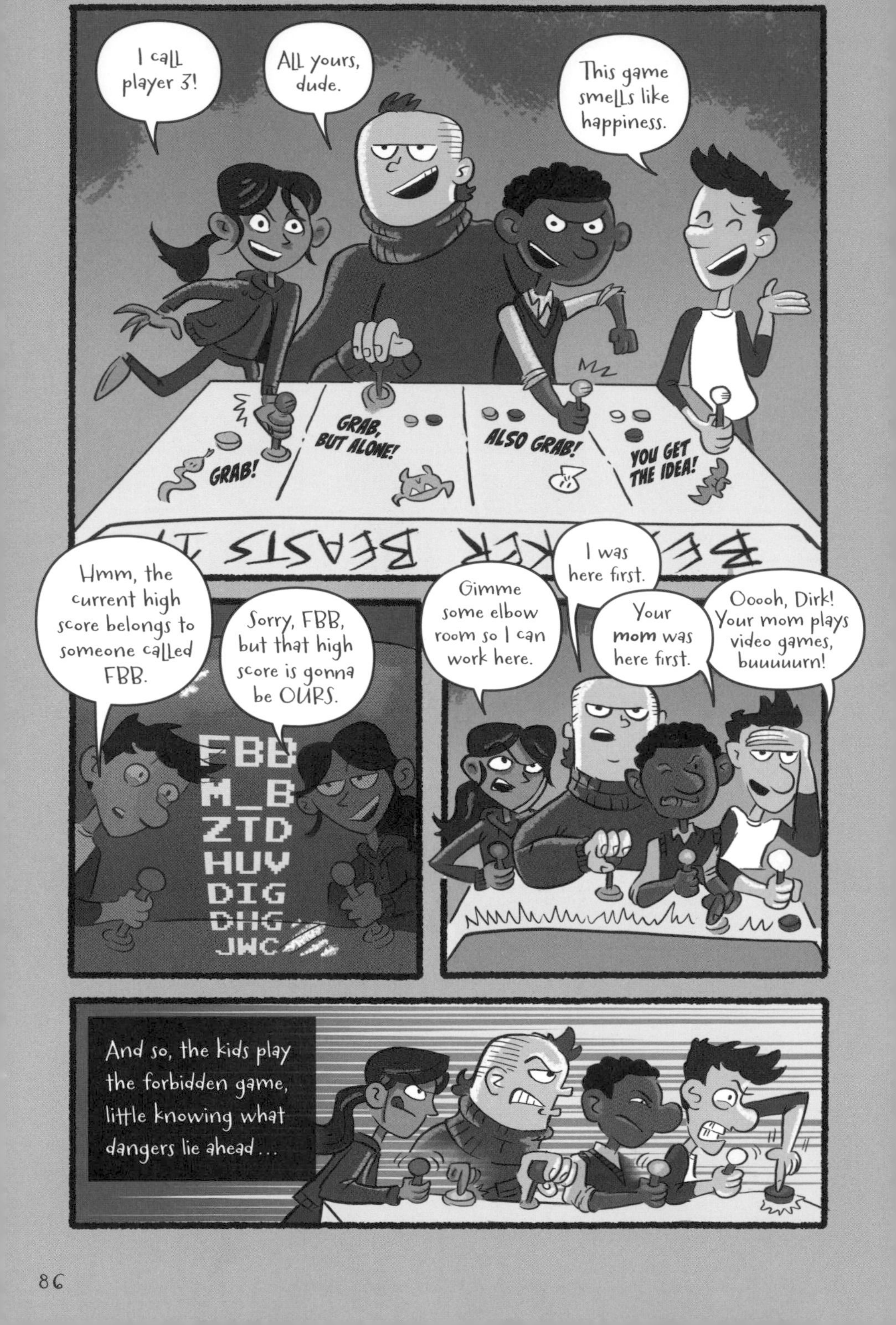
I call player 3!
All yours, dude.
This game smells like happiness.
GRAB!
GRAB, BUT ALONE!
ALSO GRAB!
YOU GET THE IDEA!
Hmm, the current high score belongs to someone called FBB.
Sorry, FBB, but that high score is gonna be OURS.
FBB
M_B
ZTD
HUV
DIG
DHG
JWC
Gimme some elbow room so I can work here.
I was here first.
Your mom was here first.
Ooooh, Dirk! Your mom plays video games, buuuuurn!
And so, the kids play the forbidden game, little knowing what dangers lie ahead...

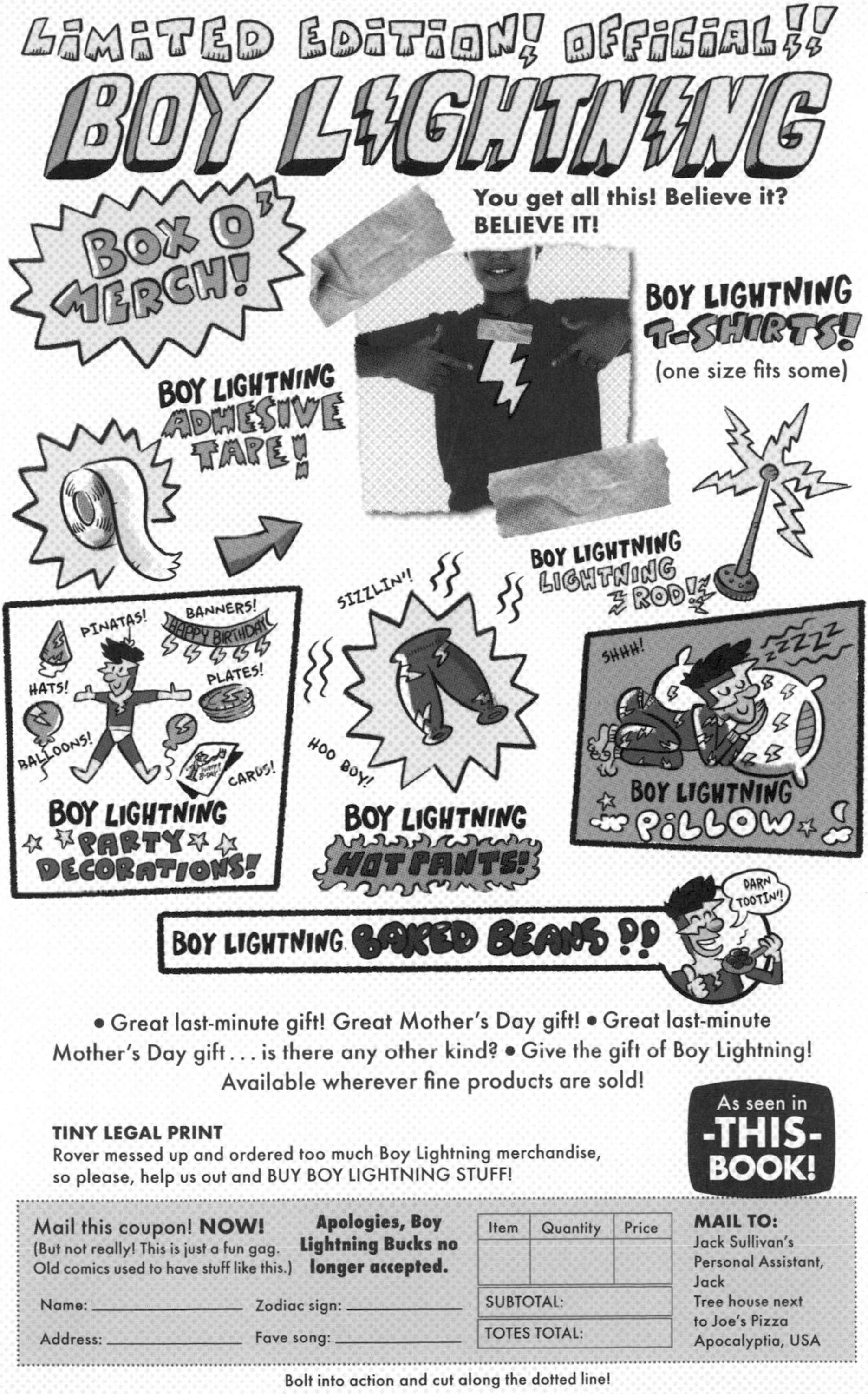
LIMITED EDITION! OFFICIAL!!
BOY LIGHTNING
BOX O' MERCH!
You get all this! Believe it? BELIEVE IT!
BOY LIGHTNING T-SHIRTS!
(one size fits some)
BOY LIGHTNING ADHESIVE TAPE!
BOY LIGHTNING LIGHTNING ROD!
PINATAS!
BANNERS!
HAPPY BIRTHDAY
HATS!
PLATES!
BALLOONS!
CARDS!
BOY LIGHTNING PARTY DECORATIONS!
SIZZLIN'!
HOO BOY!
BOY LIGHTNING HOT PANTS!
SHHH!
ZZZZ
BOY LIGHTNING PILLOW
DARN TOOTIN'!
BOY LIGHTNING BAKED BEANS ?!

• Great last-minute gift! Great Mother's Day gift! • Great last-minute Mother's Day gift . . . is there any other kind? • Give the gift of Boy Lightning! Available wherever fine products are sold!

As seen in -THIS- BOOK!

TINY LEGAL PRINT
Rover messed up and ordered too much Boy Lightning merchandise, so please, help us out and BUY BOY LIGHTNING STUFF!

Mail this coupon! **NOW!**
(But not really! This is just a fun gag. Old comics used to have stuff like this.)

Apologies, Boy Lightning Bucks no longer accepted.

Name: ____________ Zodiac sign: ____________

Address: ____________ Fave song: ____________

Item	Quantity	Price
SUBTOTAL:		
TOTES TOTAL:		

MAIL TO:
Jack Sullivan's
Personal Assistant,
Jack
Tree house next
to Joe's Pizza
Apocalyptia, USA

Bolt into action and cut along the dotted line!

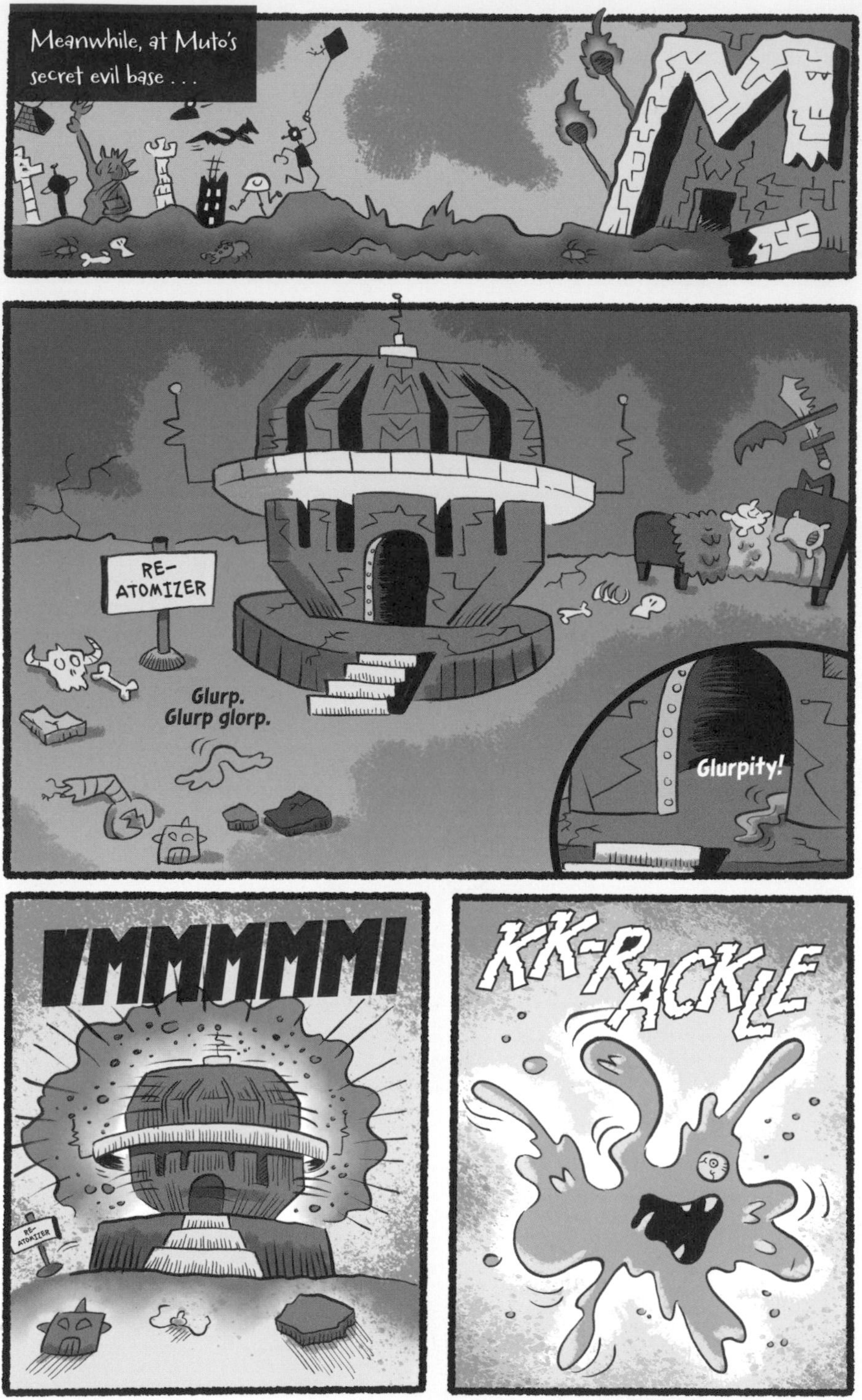
Meanwhile, at Muto's secret evil base . . .
RE-ATOMIZER
Glurp. Glurp glorp.
Glurpity!
VMMMMMM!
RE-ATOMIZER
KK-RACKLE

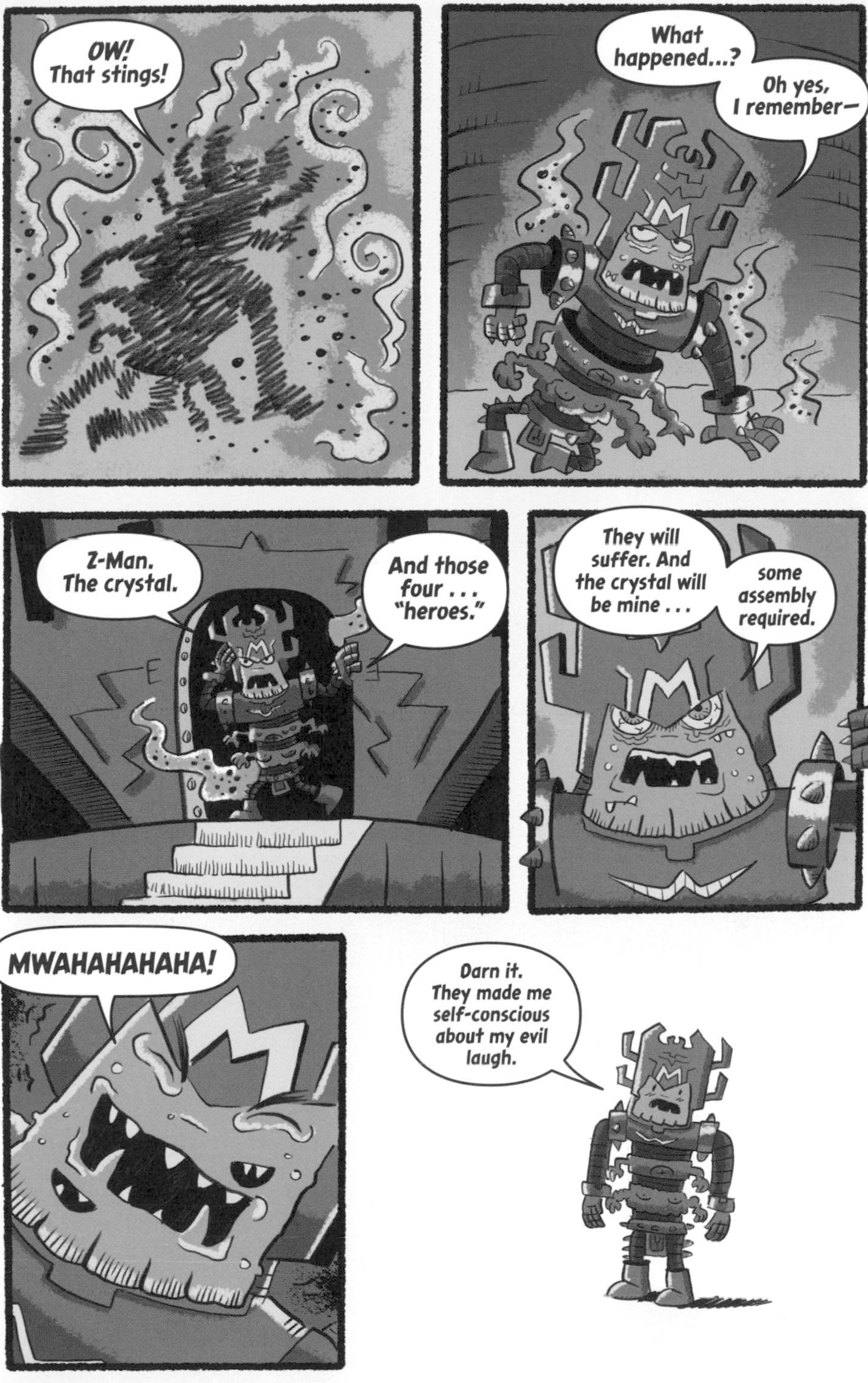
OW! That stings!
What happened...?
Oh yes, I remember—
Z-Man. The crystal.
And those four . . . "heroes."
They will suffer. And the crystal will be mine . . .
some assembly required.
MWAHAHAHAHA!
Darn it. They made me self-conscious about my evil laugh.

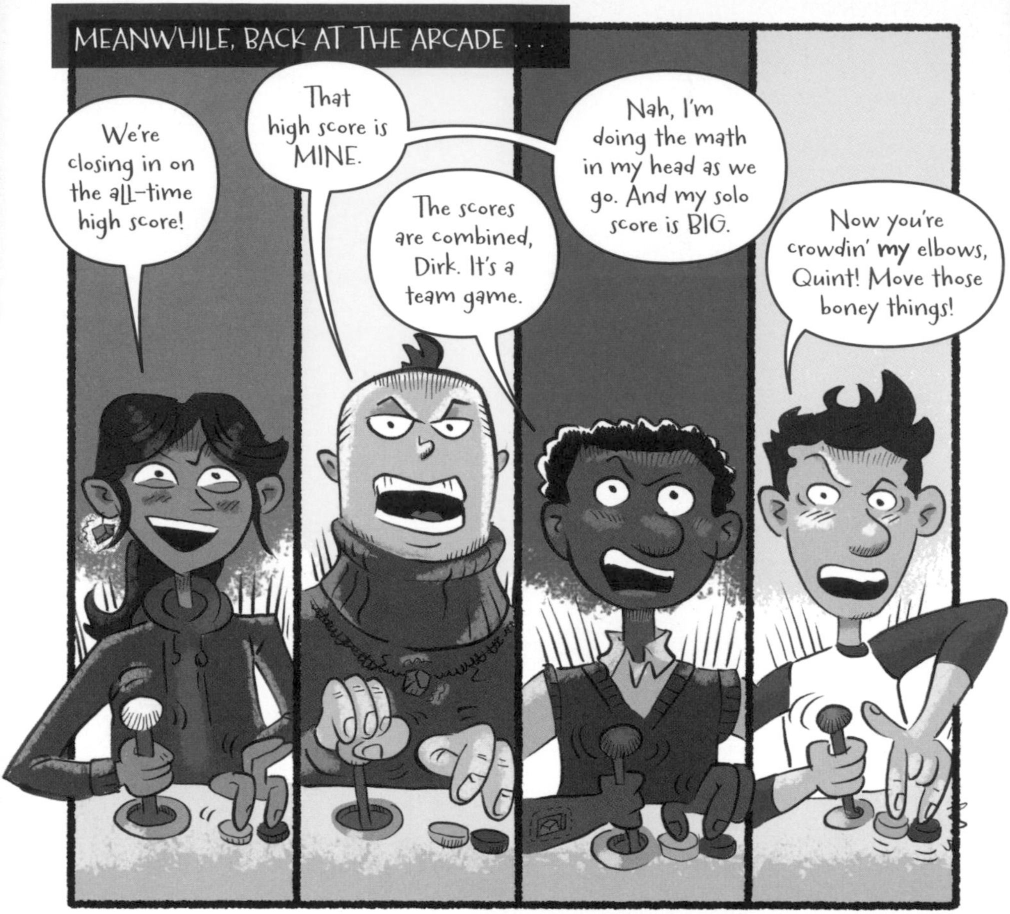
MEANWHILE, BACK AT THE ARCADE . . .
We're closing in on the all-time high score!
That high score is MINE.
The scores are combined, Dirk. It's a team game.
Nah, I'm doing the math in my head as we go. And my solo score is BIG.
Now you're crowdin' my elbows, Quint! Move those boney things!

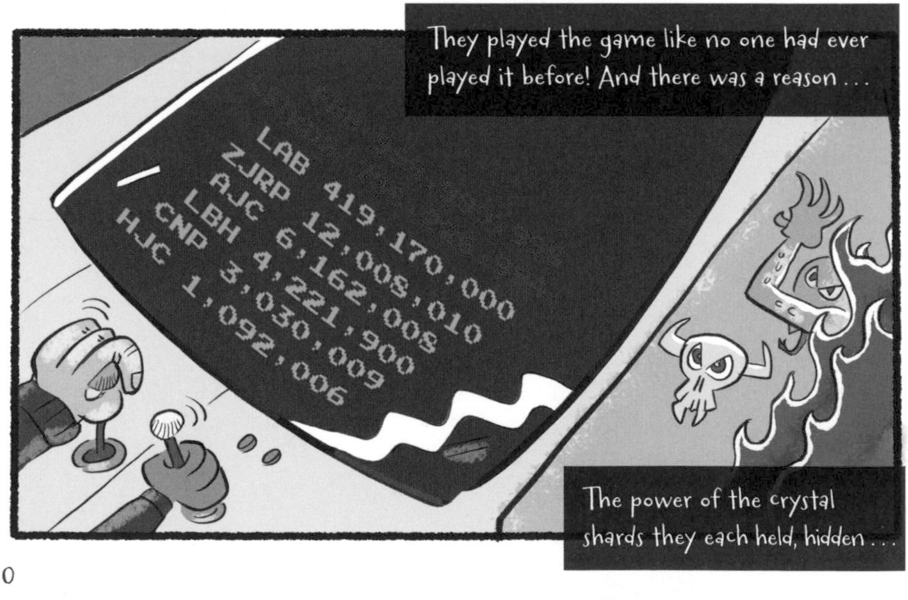
They played the game like no one had ever played it before! And there was a reason . . .
LAB 419,170,000
ZJRP 12,008,010
AJC 6,162,008
LBH 4,221,900
CNP 3,030,009
HJC 1,092,006
The power of the crystal shards they each held, hidden . . .

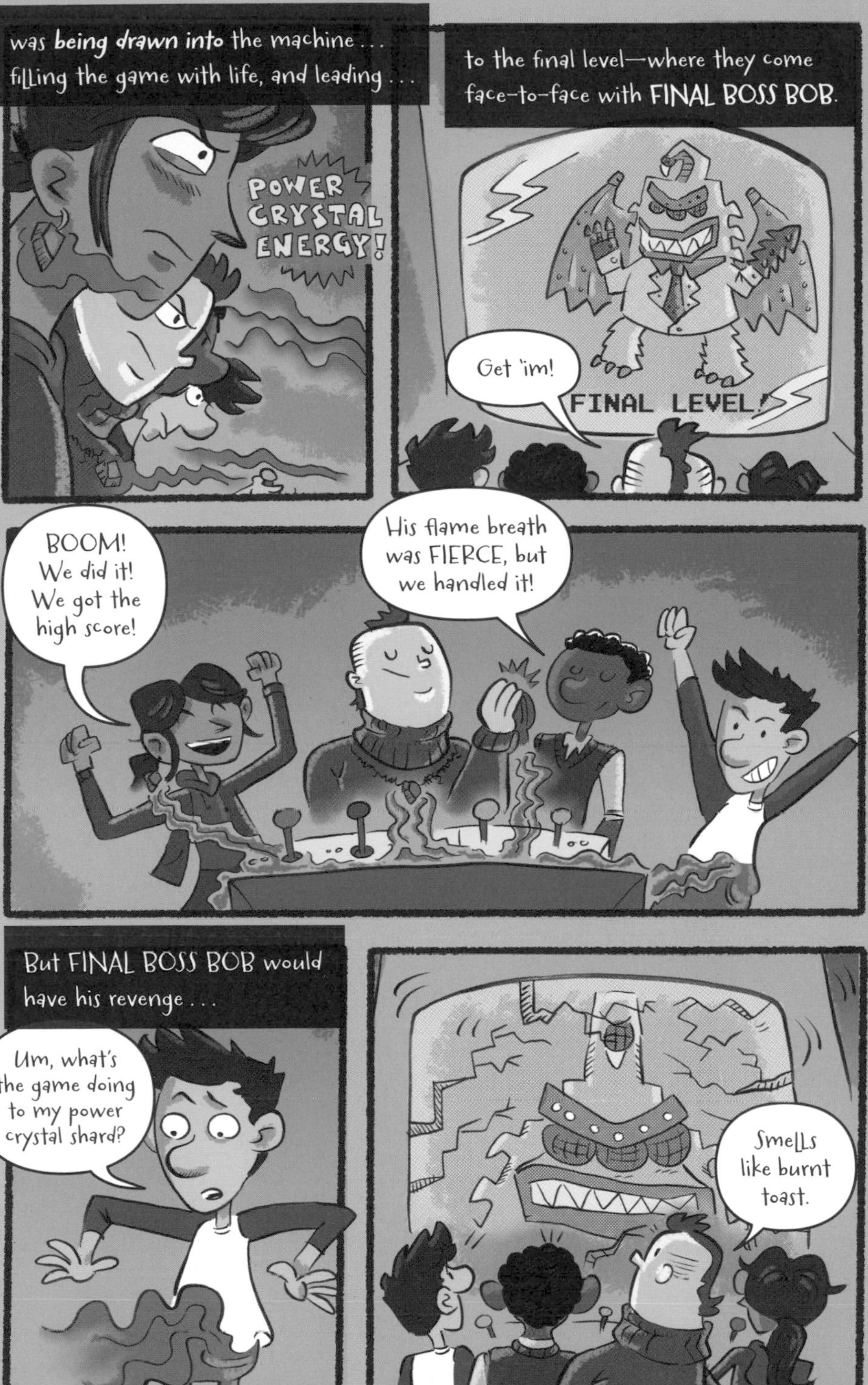
was being drawn into the machine . . . filling the game with life, and leading . . .
POWER CRYSTAL ENERGY!
to the final level—where they come face-to-face with FINAL BOSS BOB.
Get 'im!
FINAL LEVEL!
BOOM! We did it! We got the high score!
His flame breath was FIERCE, but we handled it!
But FINAL BOSS BOB would have his revenge . . .
Um, what's the game doing to my power crystal shard?
Smells like burnt toast.

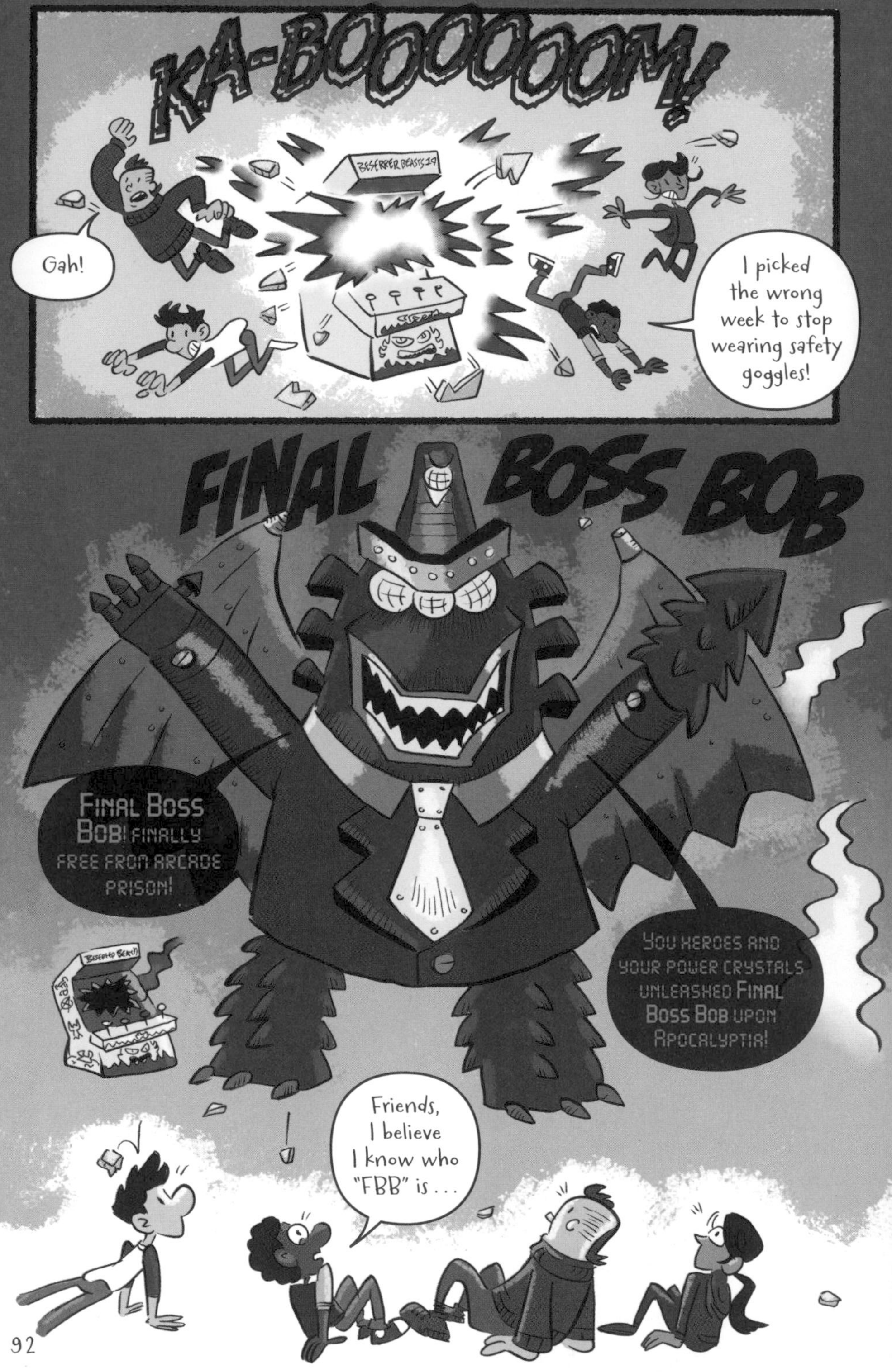
KA-BOOOOOOM!
BESERKER BEASTS 17
Gah!
I picked the wrong week to stop wearing safety goggles!
FINAL BOSS BOB
FINAL BOSS BOB! FINALLY FREE FROM ARCADE PRISON!
YOU HEROES AND YOUR POWER CRYSTALS UNLEASHED FINAL BOSS BOB UPON APOCALYPTIA!
Friends, I believe I know who "FBB" is . . .

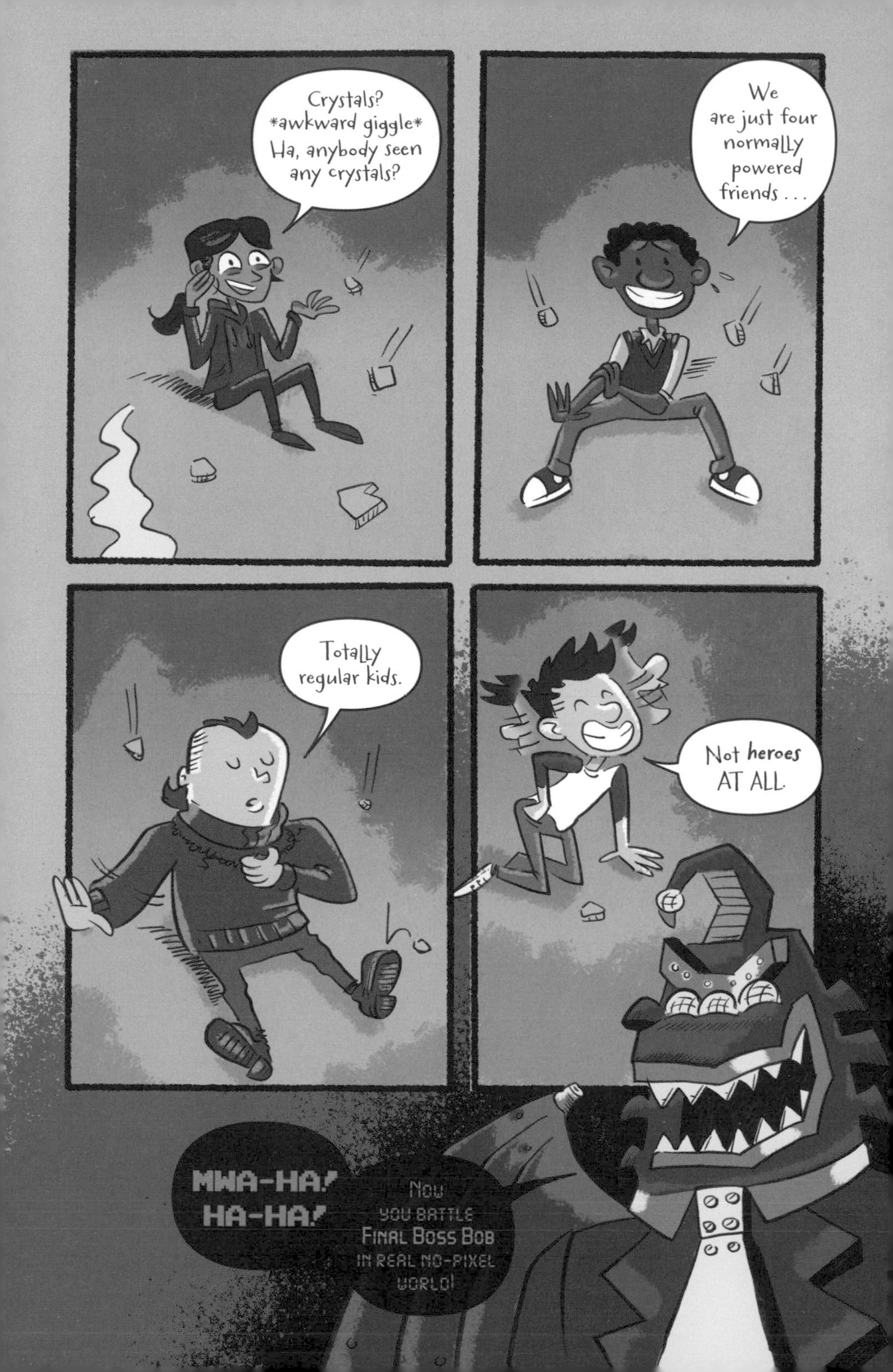
Crystals? *awkward giggle* Ha, anybody seen any crystals?
We are just four normally powered friends . . .
Totally regular kids.
Not heroes AT ALL.
MWA-HA! HA-HA!
NOW YOU BATTLE FINAL BOSS BOB IN REAL NO-PIXEL WORLD!

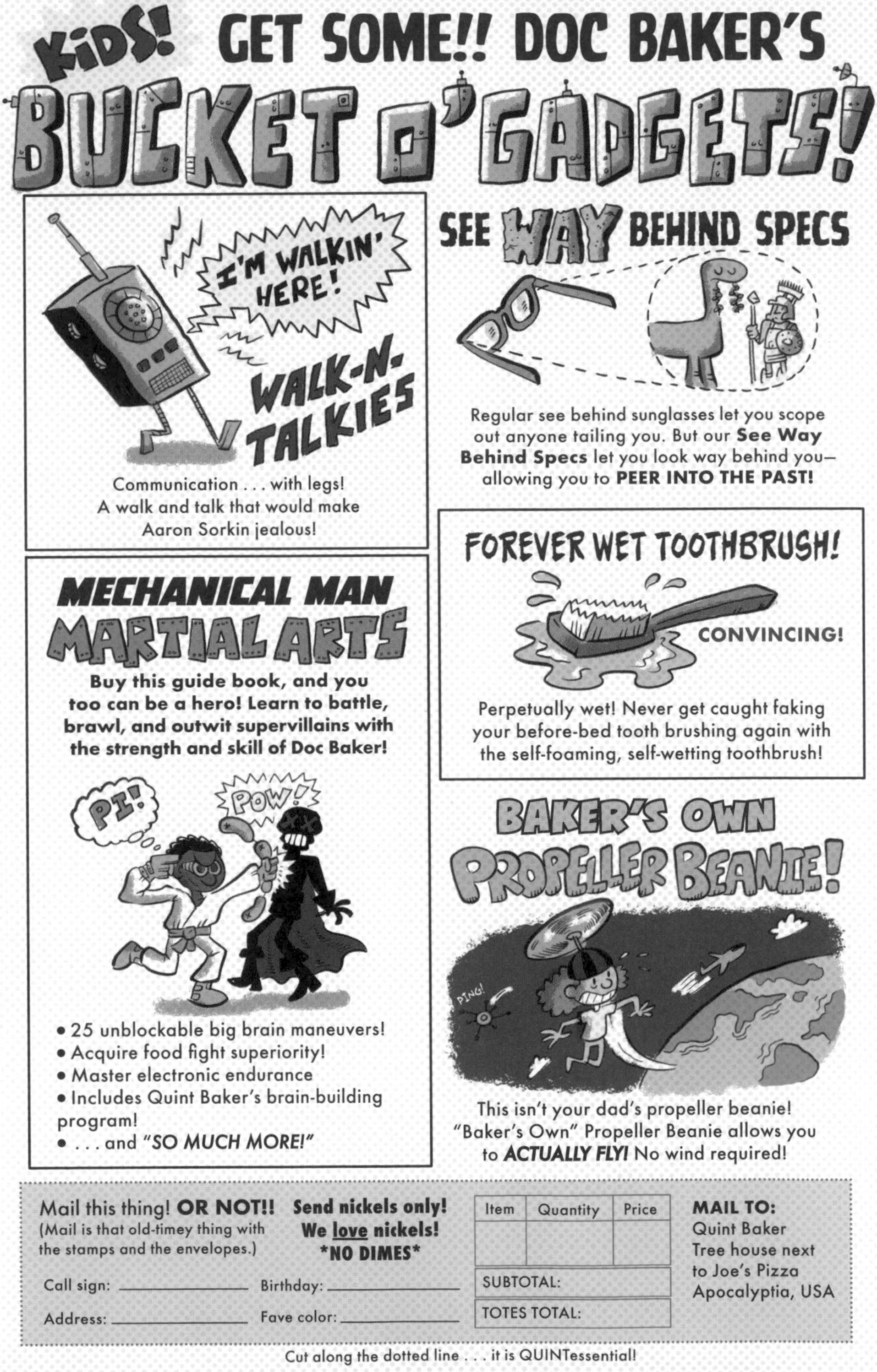
KIDS! GET SOME!! DOC BAKER'S
BUCKET O' GADGETS!
I'M WALKIN' HERE!
WALK-N-TALKIES
Communication . . . with legs!
A walk and talk that would make Aaron Sorkin jealous!
SEE WAY BEHIND SPECS
Regular see behind sunglasses let you scope out anyone tailing you. But our See Way Behind Specs let you look way behind you—allowing you to PEER INTO THE PAST!
FOREVER WET TOOTHBRUSH!
CONVINCING!
Perpetually wet! Never get caught faking your before-bed tooth brushing again with the self-foaming, self-wetting toothbrush!
MECHANICAL MAN MARTIAL ARTS
Buy this guide book, and you too can be a hero! Learn to battle, brawl, and outwit supervillains with the strength and skill of Doc Baker!
PI!
POW!
• 25 unblockable big brain maneuvers!
• Acquire food fight superiority!
• Master electronic endurance
• Includes Quint Baker's brain-building program!
• . . . and "SO MUCH MORE!"
BAKER'S OWN PROPELLER BEANIE!
PING!
This isn't your dad's propeller beanie! "Baker's Own" Propeller Beanie allows you to ACTUALLY FLY! No wind required!
Mail this thing! OR NOT!!
(Mail is that old-timey thing with the stamps and the envelopes.)
Send nickels only! We love nickels! *NO DIMES*
Call sign: ____________ Birthday: ____________
Address: ____________ Fave color: ____________
Item | Quantity | Price
SUBTOTAL:
TOTES TOTAL:
MAIL TO:
Quint Baker
Tree house next to Joe's Pizza
Apocalyptia, USA
Cut along the dotted line . . . it is QUINTessential!

CHAPTER SIX
BOSS FIGHTIN' FUN!

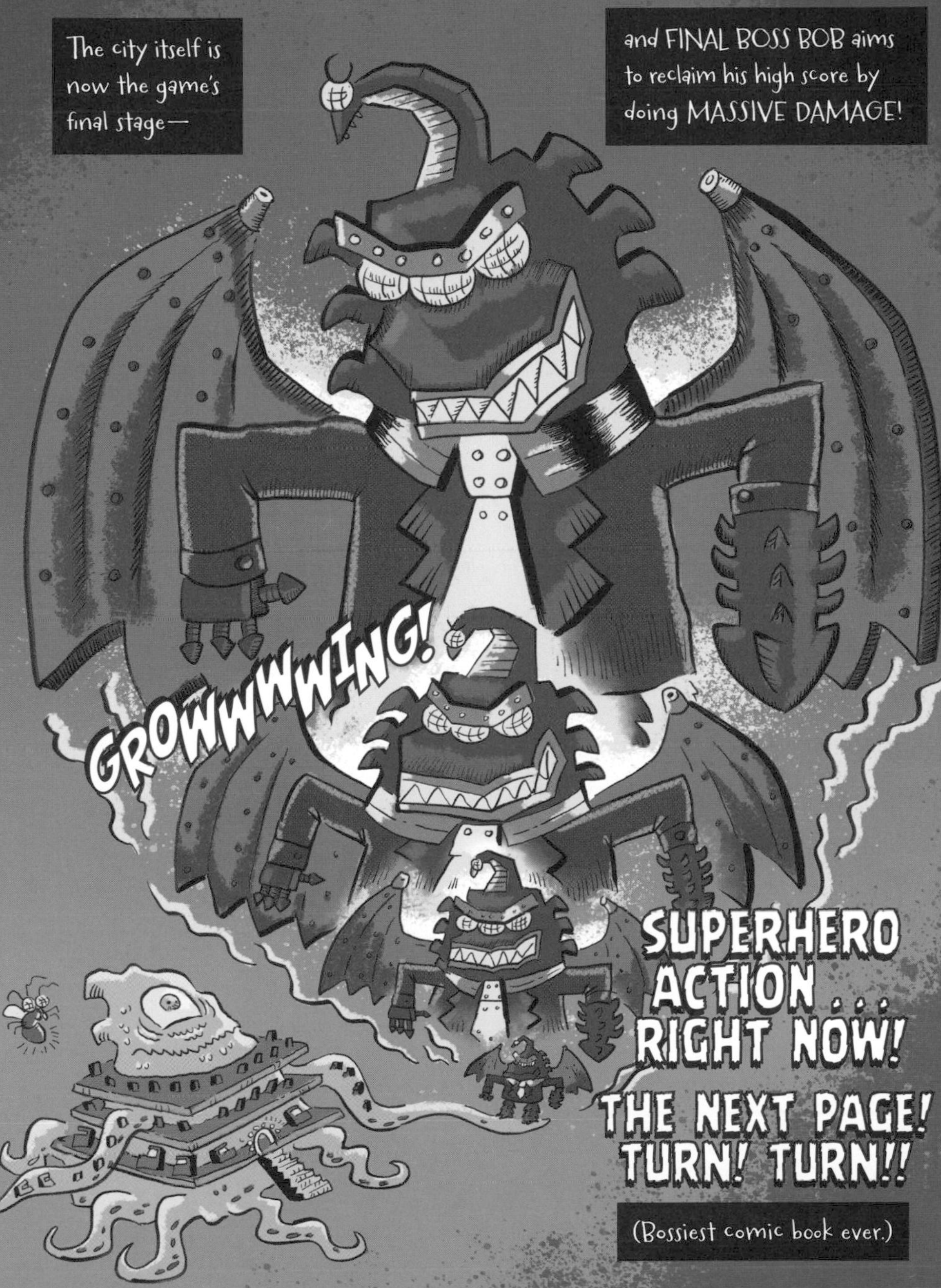
The city itself is now the game's final stage—
and FINAL BOSS BOB aims to reclaim his high score by doing MASSIVE DAMAGE!
GROWWWWING!
SUPERHERO ACTION . . . RIGHT NOW!
THE NEXT PAGE! TURN! TURN!!
(Bossiest comic book ever.)

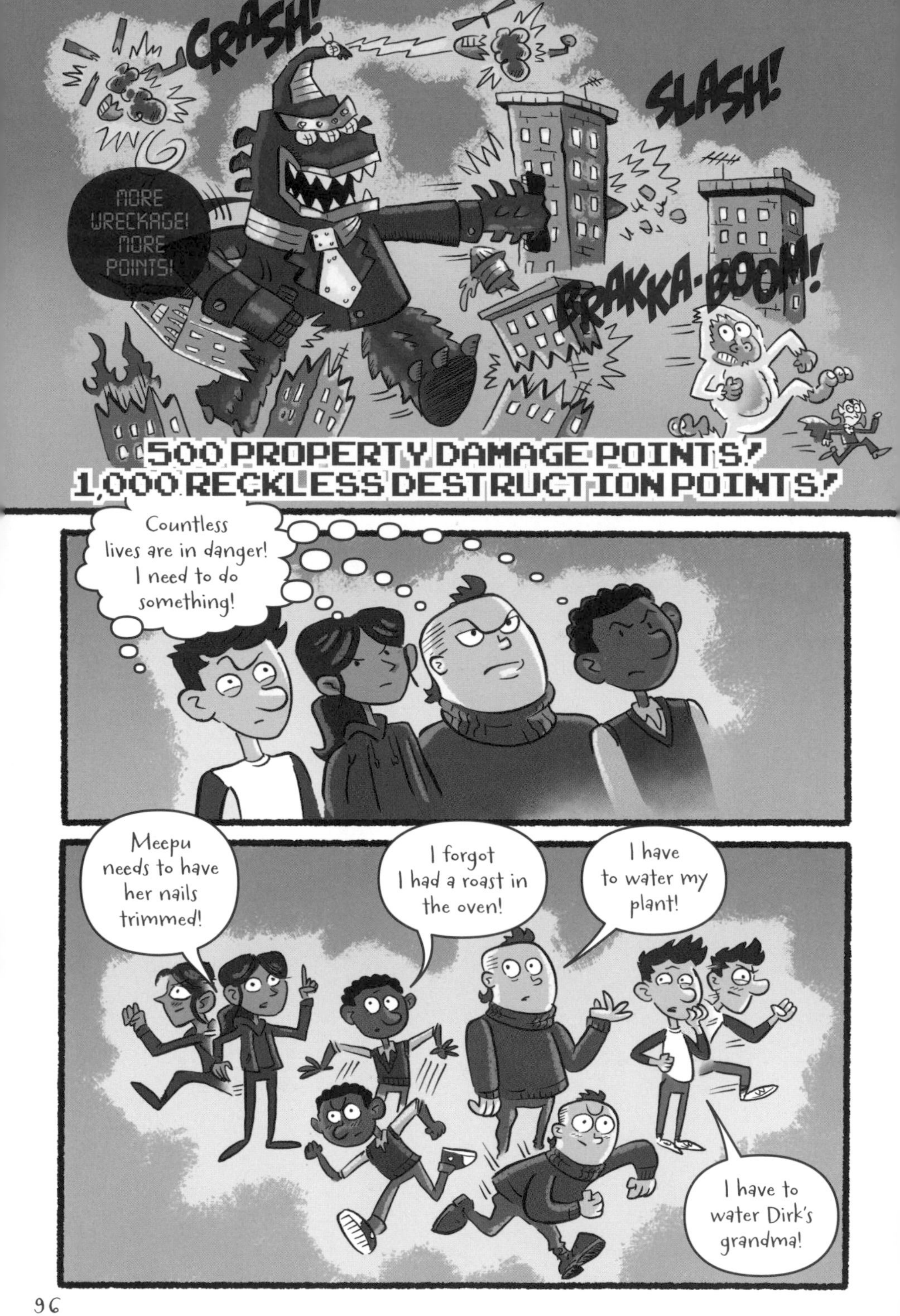
CRASH!
SLASH!
MORE WRECKAGE! MORE POINTS!
BRAKKA-BOOM!
500 PROPERTY DAMAGE POINTS!
1,000 RECKLESS DESTRUCTION POINTS!
Countless lives are in danger! I need to do something!
Meepu needs to have her nails trimmed!
I forgot I had a roast in the oven!
I have to water my plant!
I have to water Dirk's grandma!

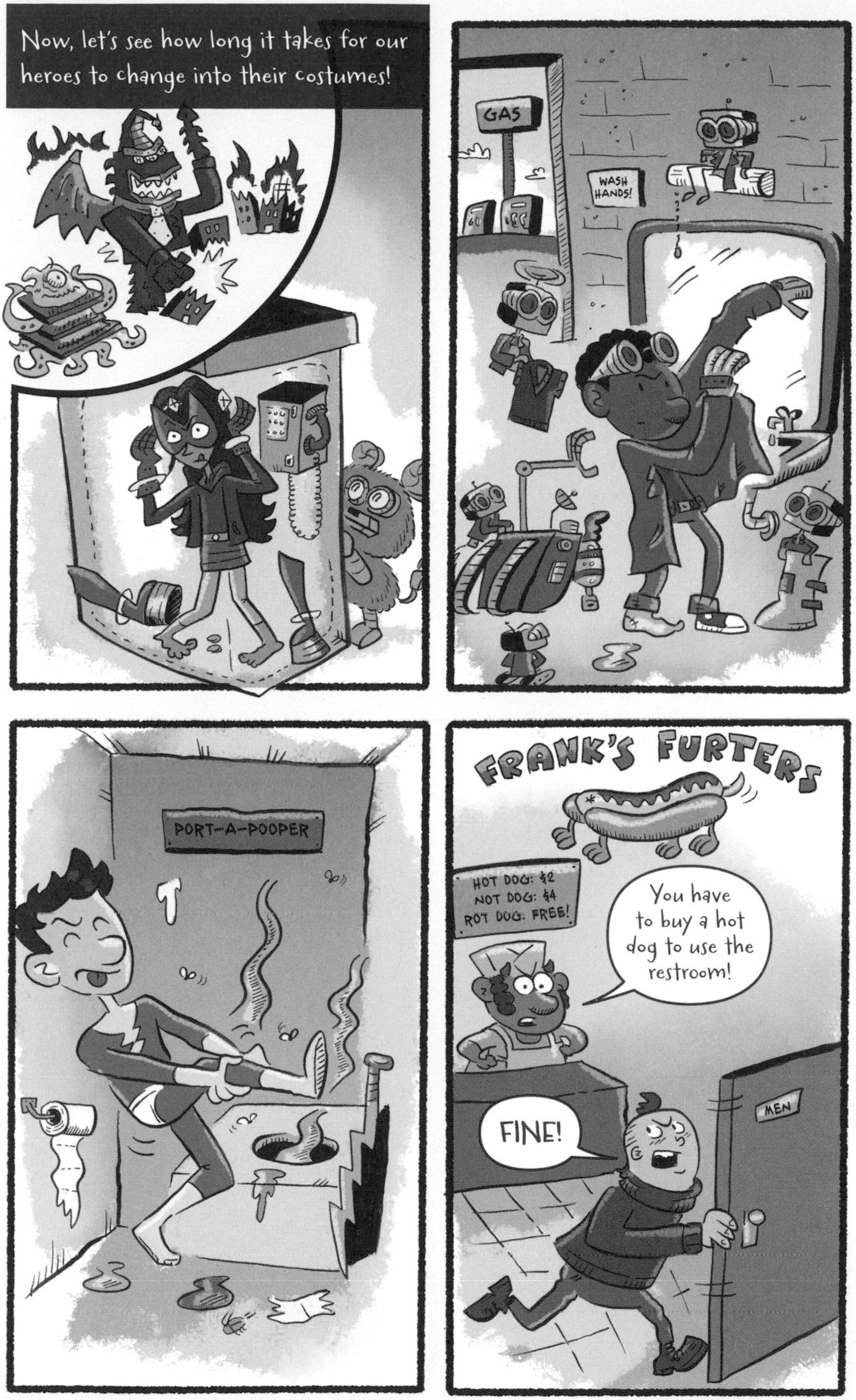
Now, let's see how long it takes for our heroes to change into their costumes!
GAS
WASH HANDS!
PORT-A-POOPER
FRANK'S FURTERS
HOT DOG: $2
NOT DOG: $4
ROT DOG: FREE!
You have to buy a hot dog to use the restroom!
MEN
FINE!

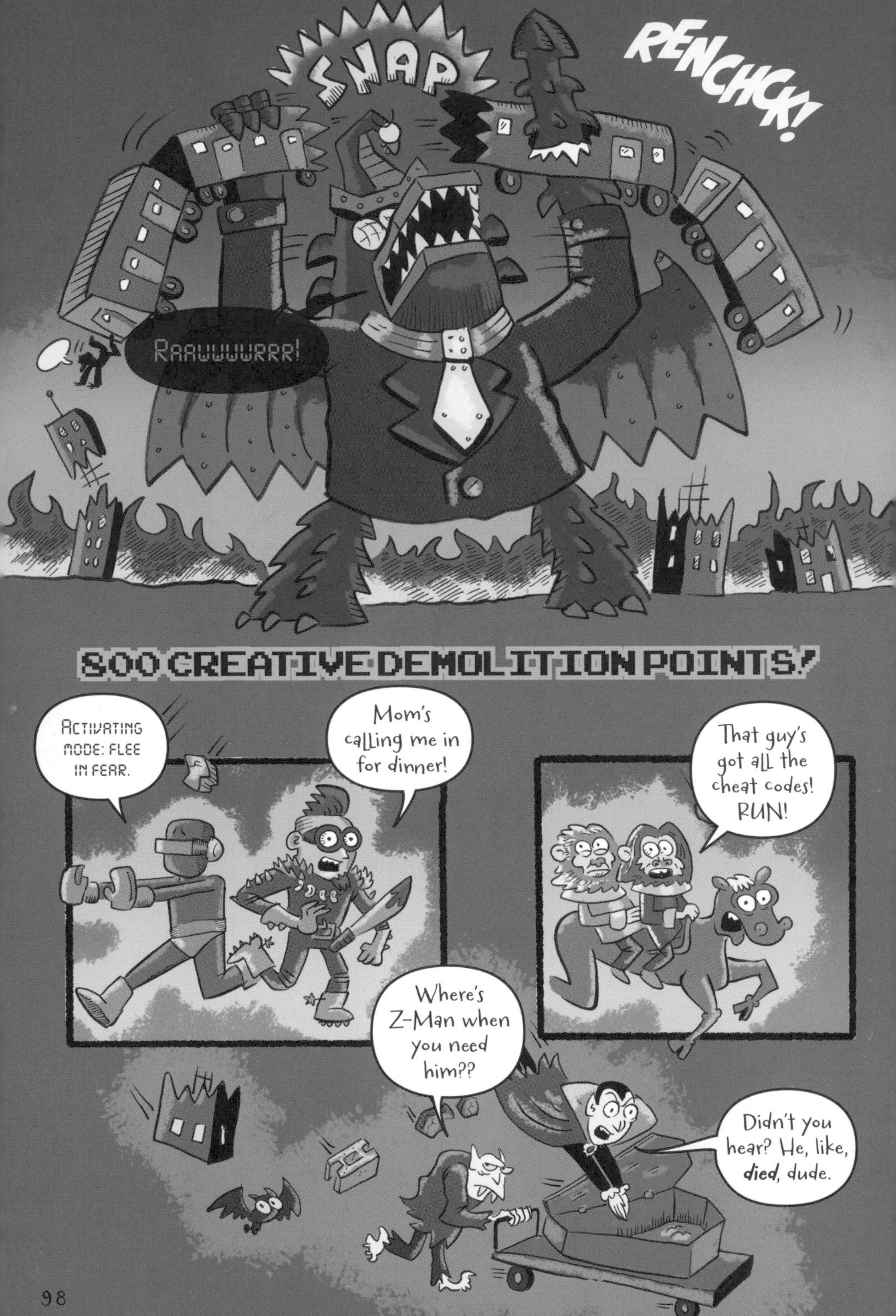
SNAP
RENCHCK!
RAAUWWURRR!
800 CREATIVE DEMOLITION POINTS!
ACTIVATING MODE: FLEE IN FEAR.
Mom's calling me in for dinner!
That guy's got all the cheat codes! RUN!
Where's Z-Man when you need him??
Didn't you hear? He, like, died, dude.

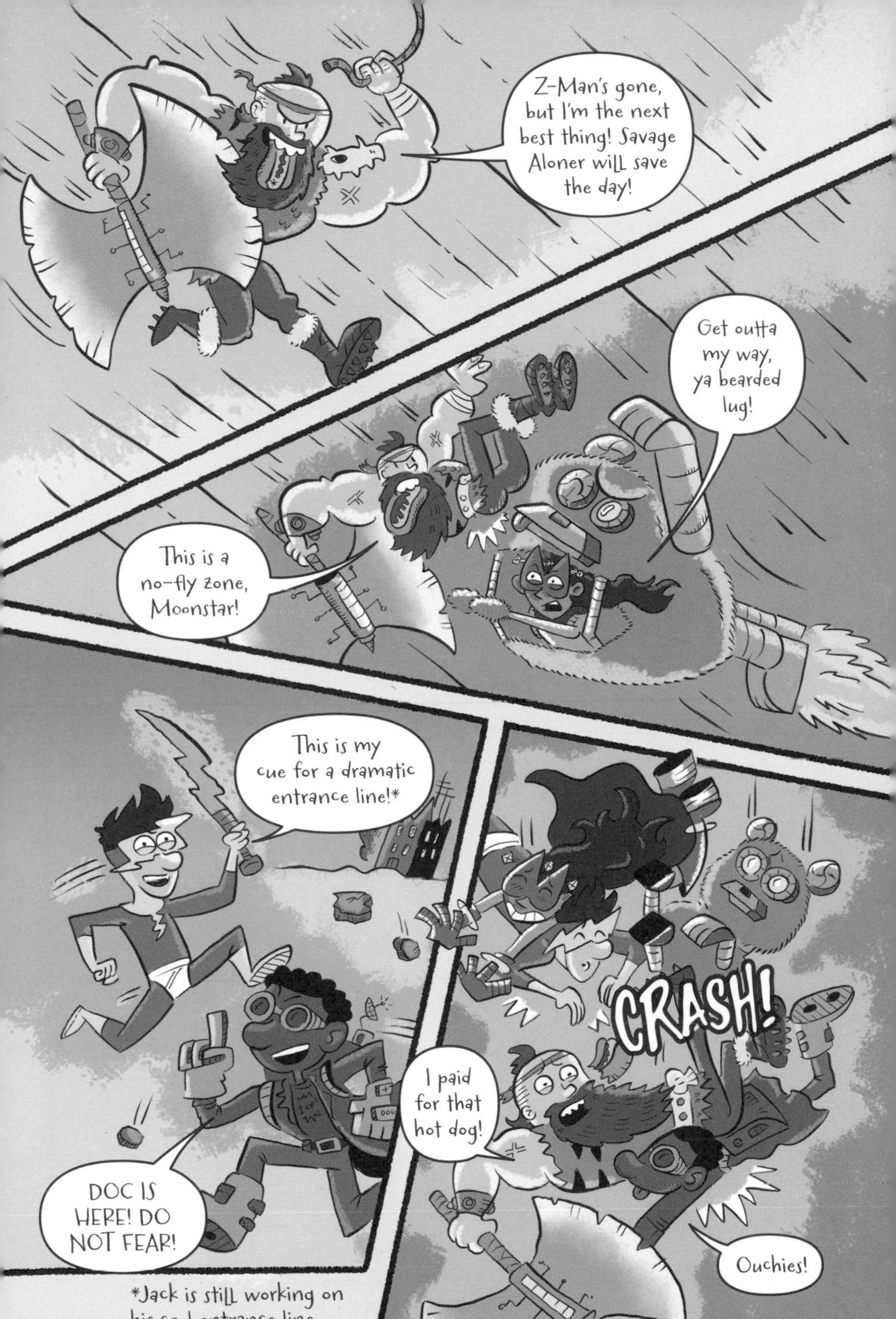
Z-Man's gone, but I'm the next best thing! Savage Aloner will save the day!
Get outta my way, ya bearded lug!
This is a no-fly zone, Moonstar!
This is my cue for a dramatic entrance line!*
DOC IS HERE! DO NOT FEAR!
CRASH!
I paid for that hot dog!
Ouchies!

*Jack is still working on his cool entrance line.

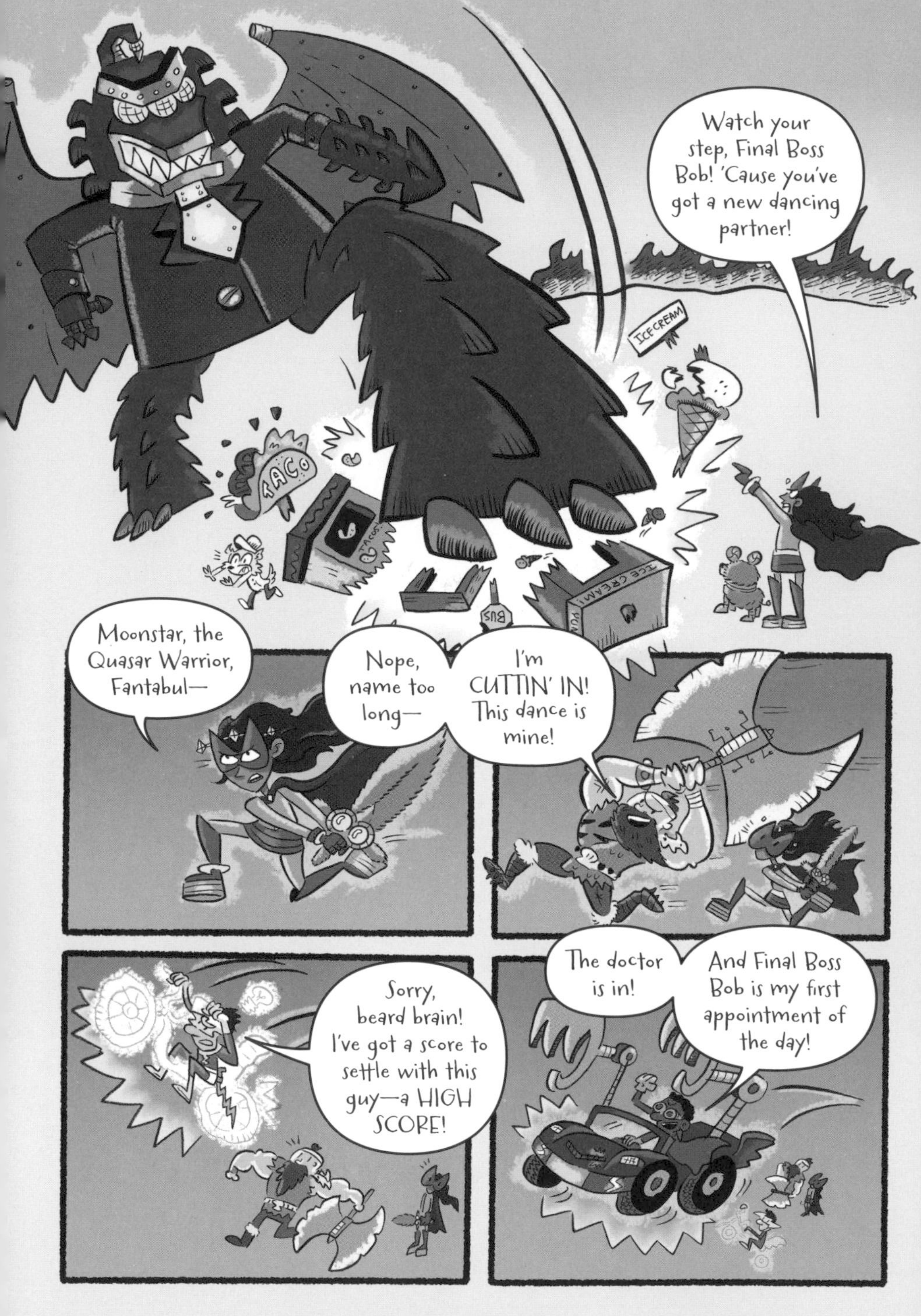
Watch your step, Final Boss Bob! 'Cause you've got a new dancing partner!
ICE CREAM
TACO
TACOS
BUS
ICE CREAM!
Moonstar, the Quasar Warrior, Fantabul—
Nope, name too long—
I'm CUTTIN' IN! This dance is mine!
Sorry, beard brain! I've got a score to settle with this guy—a HIGH SCORE!
The doctor is in!
And Final Boss Bob is my first appointment of the day!

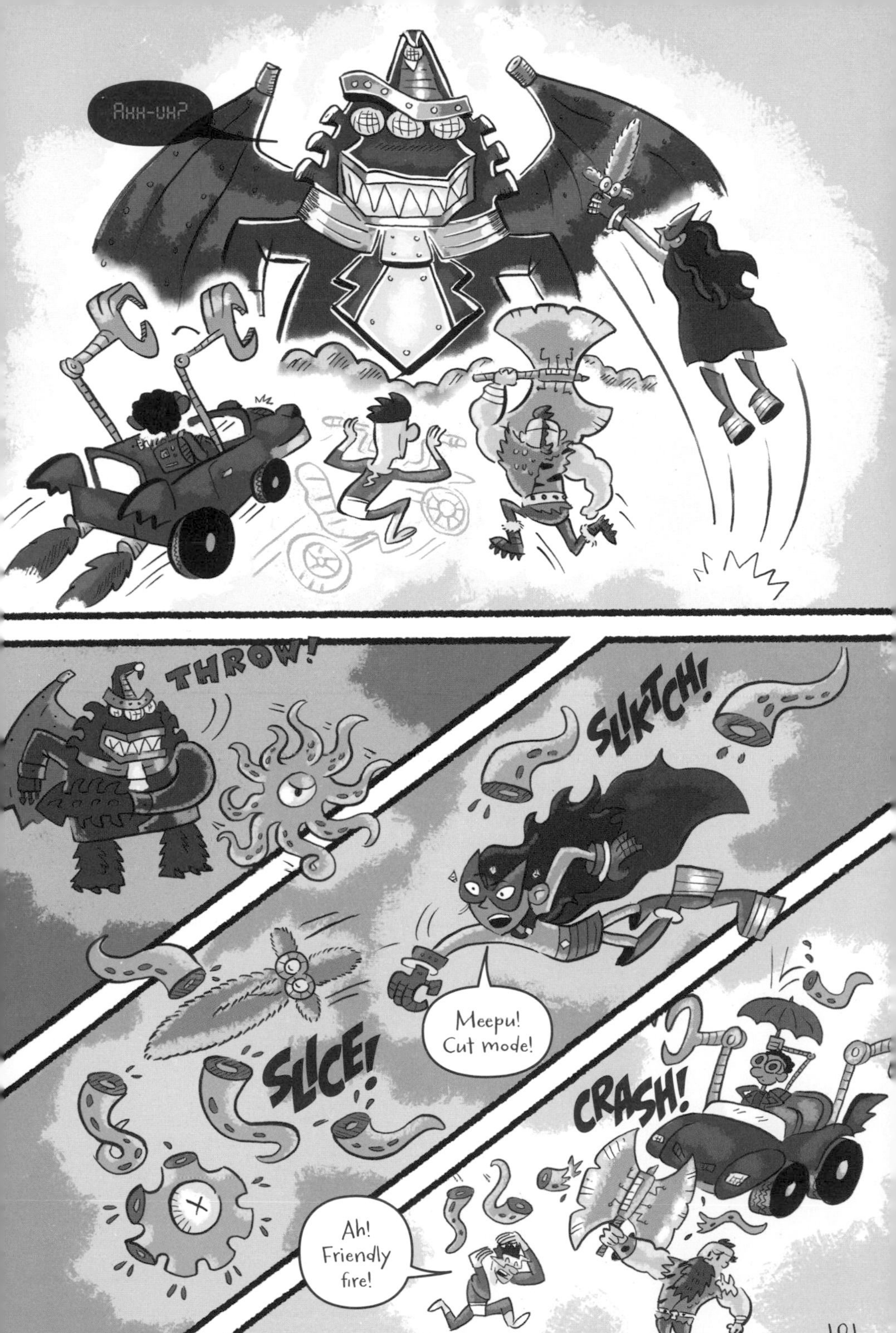
Ahh-uh?
THROW!
SLIKTCH!
Meepu! Cut mode!
SLICE!
CRASH!
Ah! Friendly fire!

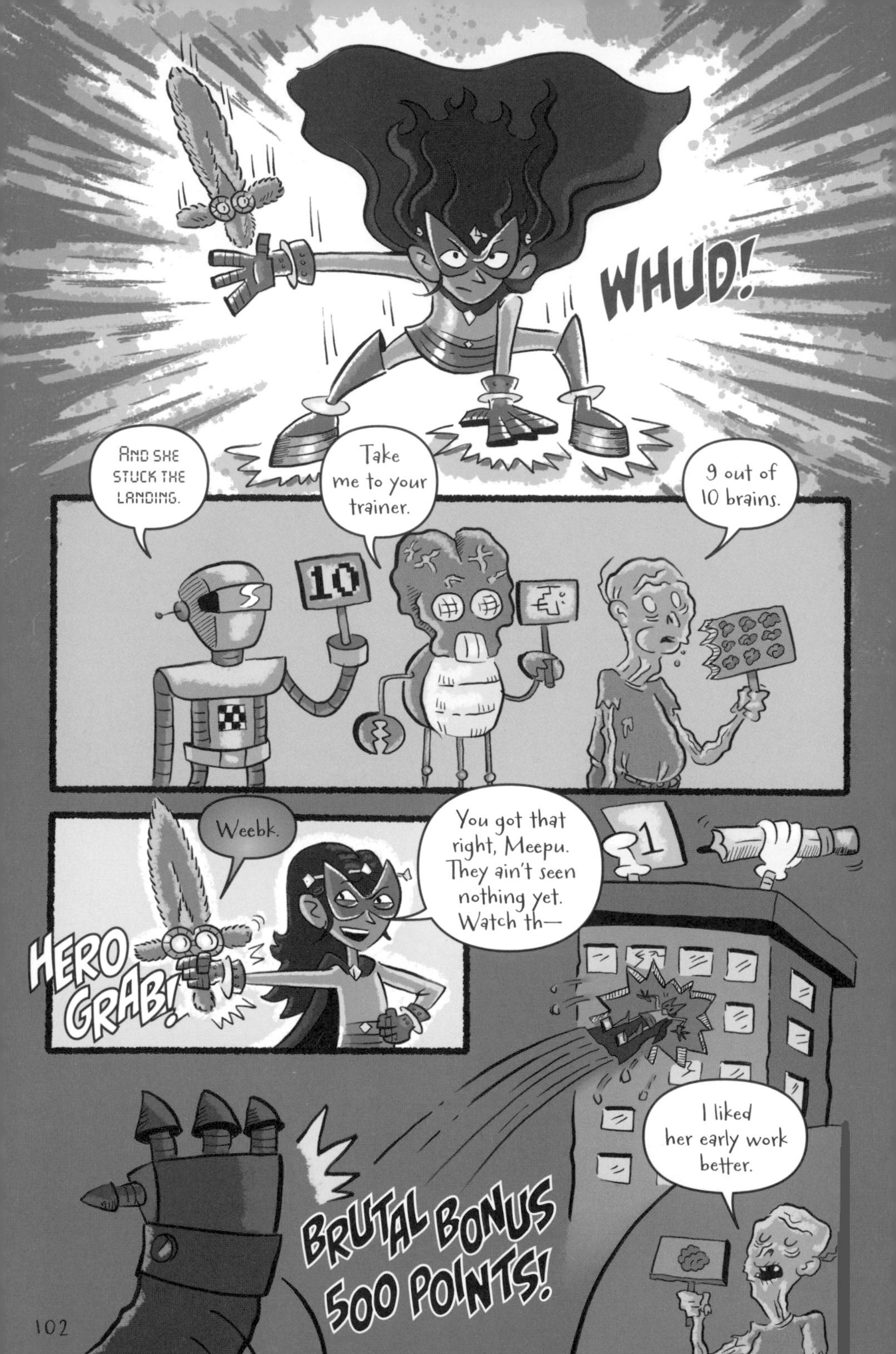
WHUD!
AND SHE STUCK THE LANDING.
Take me to your trainer.
9 out of 10 brains.
10
Weebk.
You got that right, Meepu. They ain't seen nothing yet. Watch th—
HERO GRAB!
1
BRUTAL BONUS 500 POINTS!
I liked her early work better.

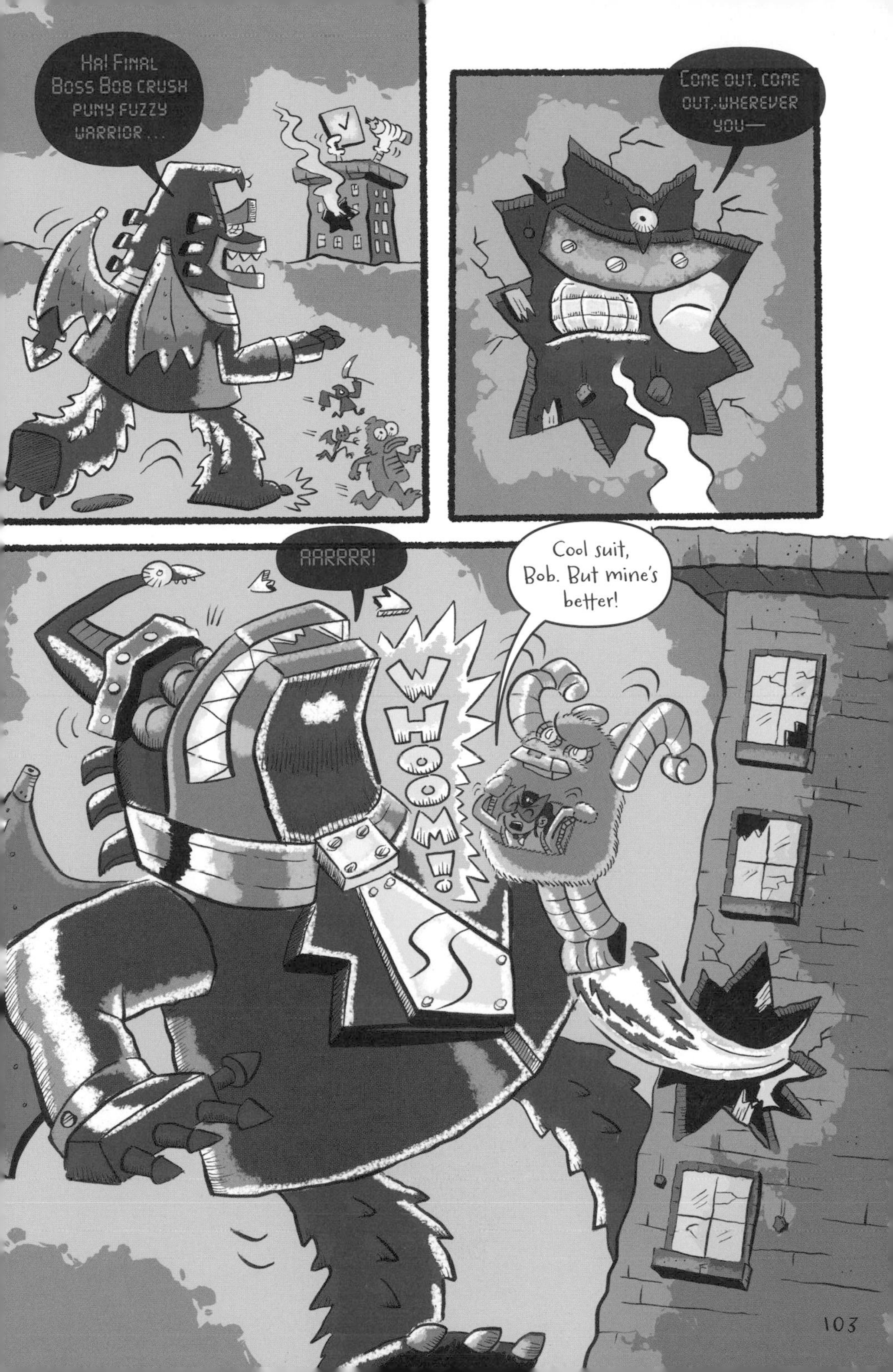
HA! FINAL BOSS BOB CRUSH PUNY FUZZY WARRIOR . . .
COME OUT, COME OUT, WHEREVER YOU—
AARRRR!
Cool suit, Bob. But mine's better!
WHOOM!

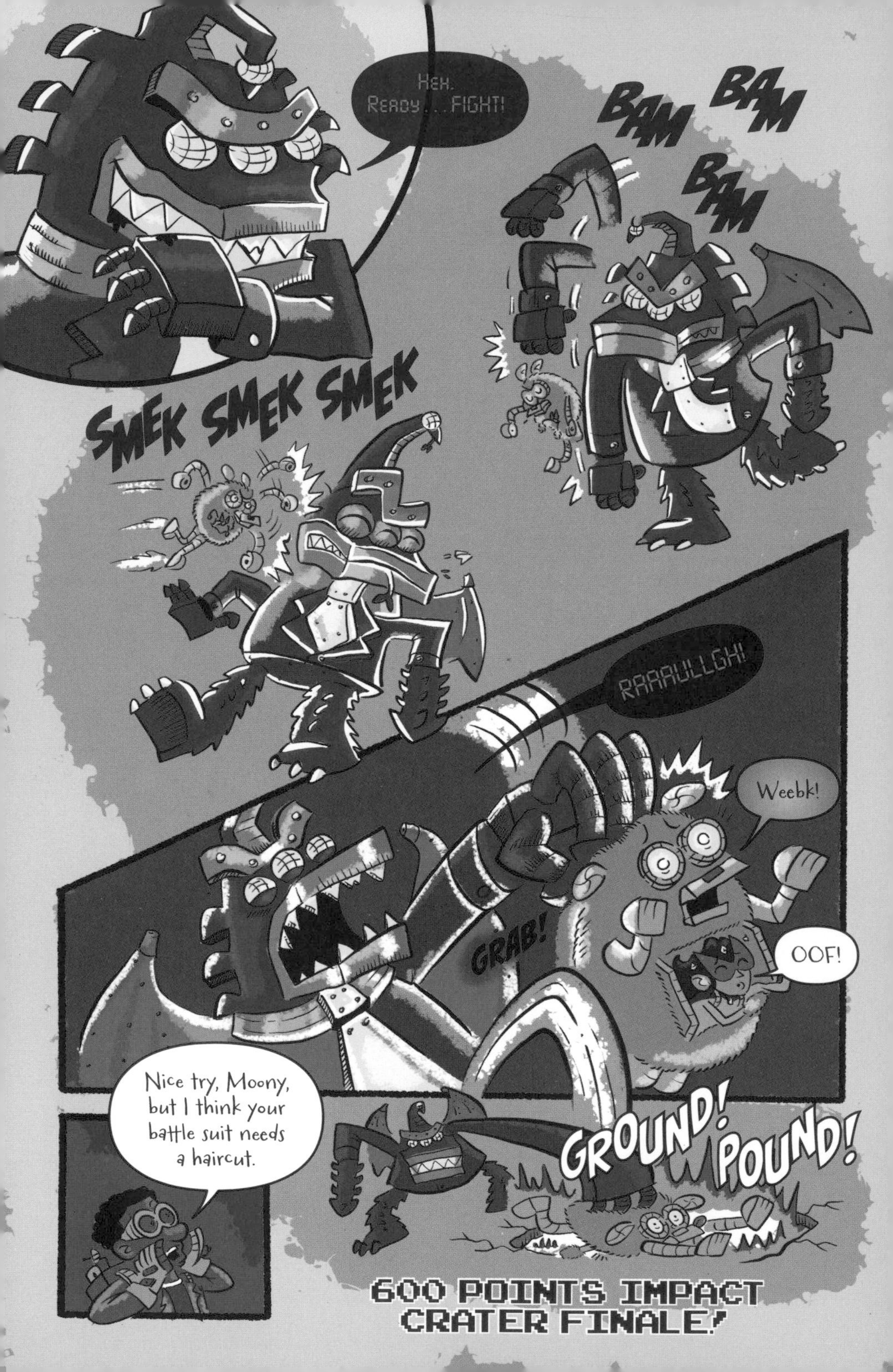
Heh.
Ready...FIGHT!
BAM BAM BAM
SMEK SMEK SMEK
RAAAULLGH!
Weebk!
GRAB!
OOF!
Nice try, Moony, but I think your battle suit needs a haircut.
GROUND! POUND!
600 POINTS IMPACT CRATER FINALE!

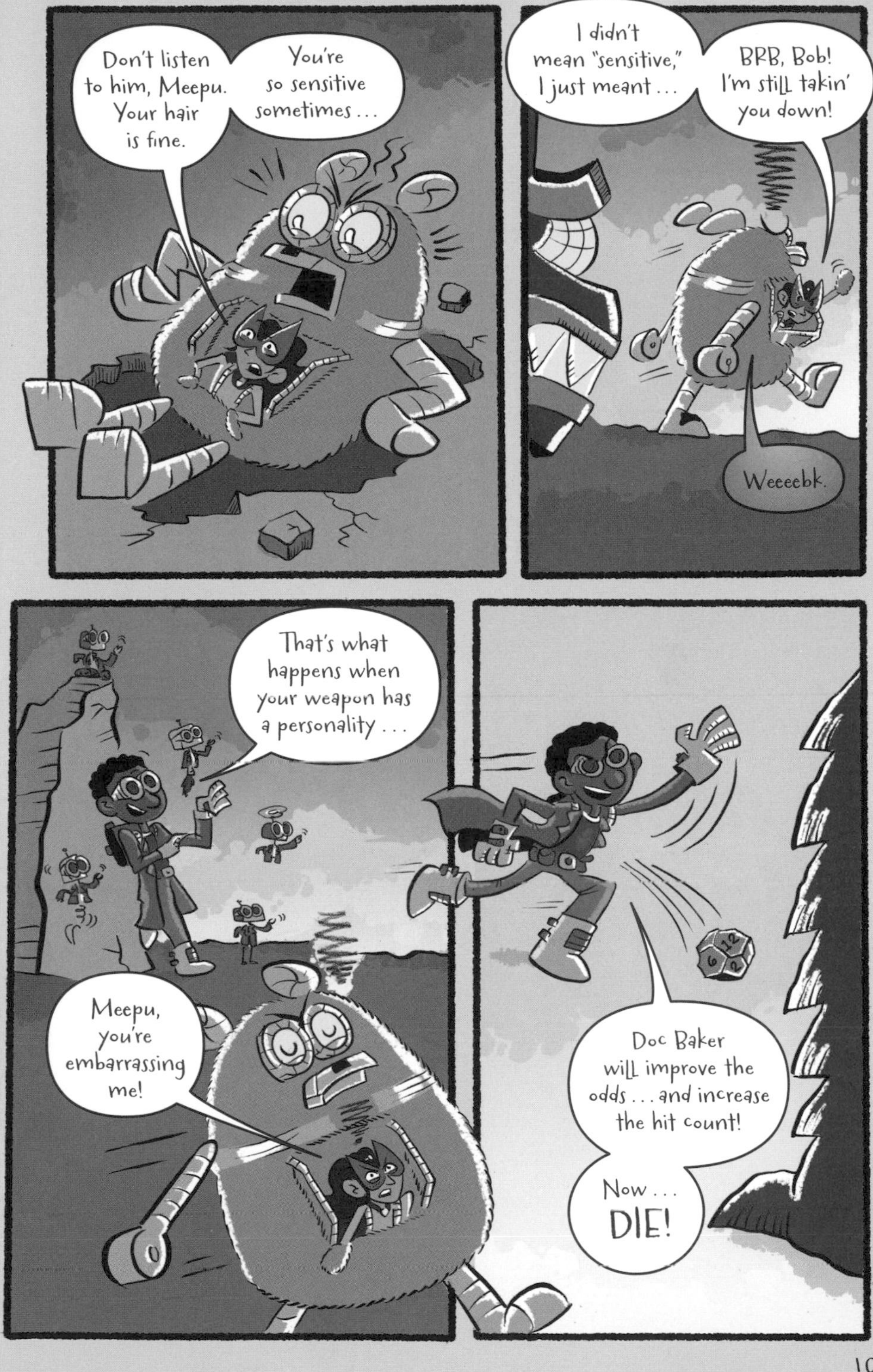

Don't listen to him, Meepu. Your hair is fine.
You're so sensitive sometimes . . .
I didn't mean "sensitive," I just meant . . .
BRB, Bob! I'm still takin' you down!
Weeeebk.
That's what happens when your weapon has a personality . . .
Meepu, you're embarrassing me!
Doc Baker will improve the odds . . . and increase the hit count!
Now . . . DIE!

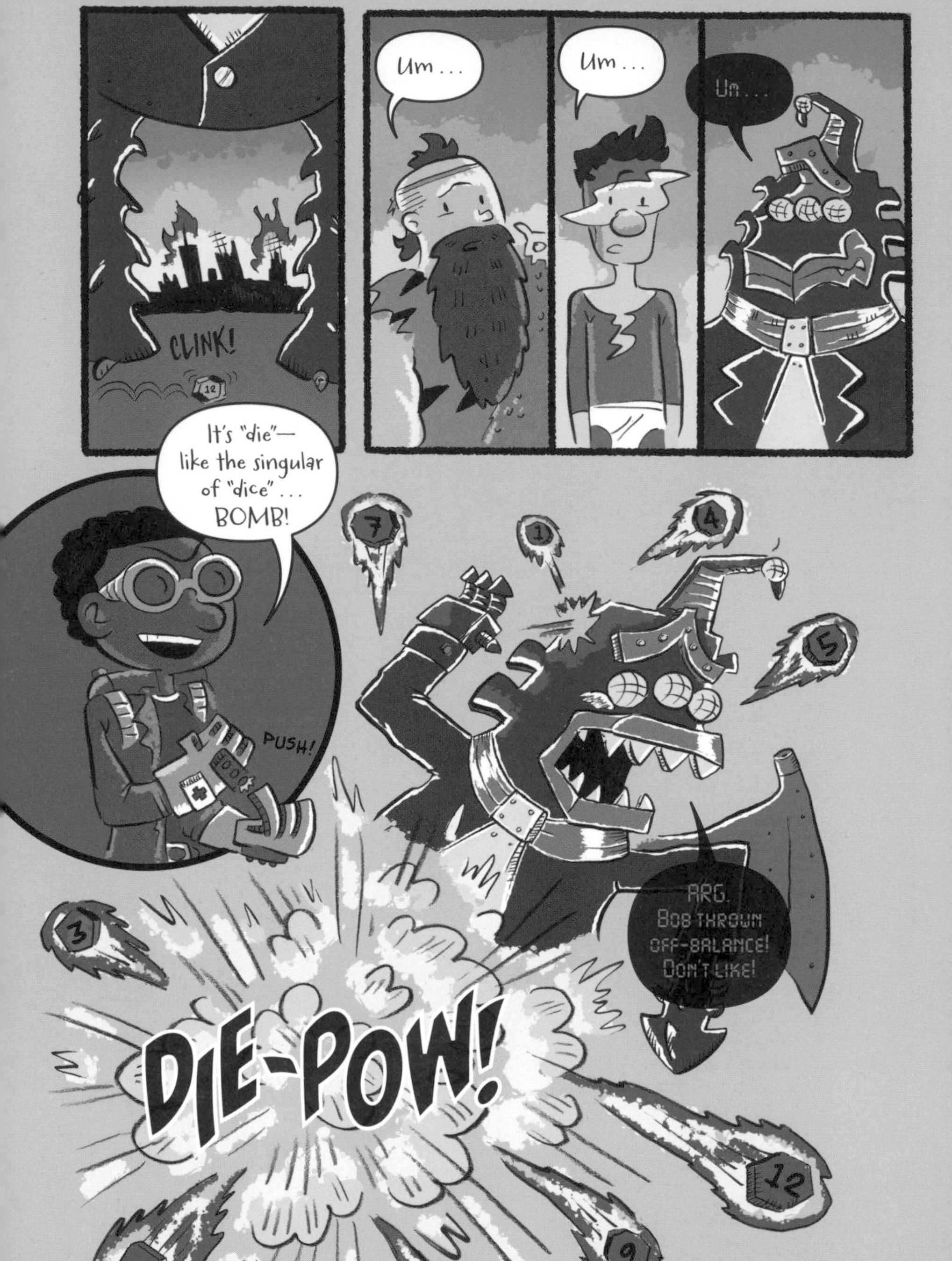
CLINK!
Um...
Um...
Um...
It's "die"— like the singular of "dice"... BOMB!
PUSH!
ARG. BOB THROWN OFF-BALANCE! DON'T LIKE!
DIE-POW!

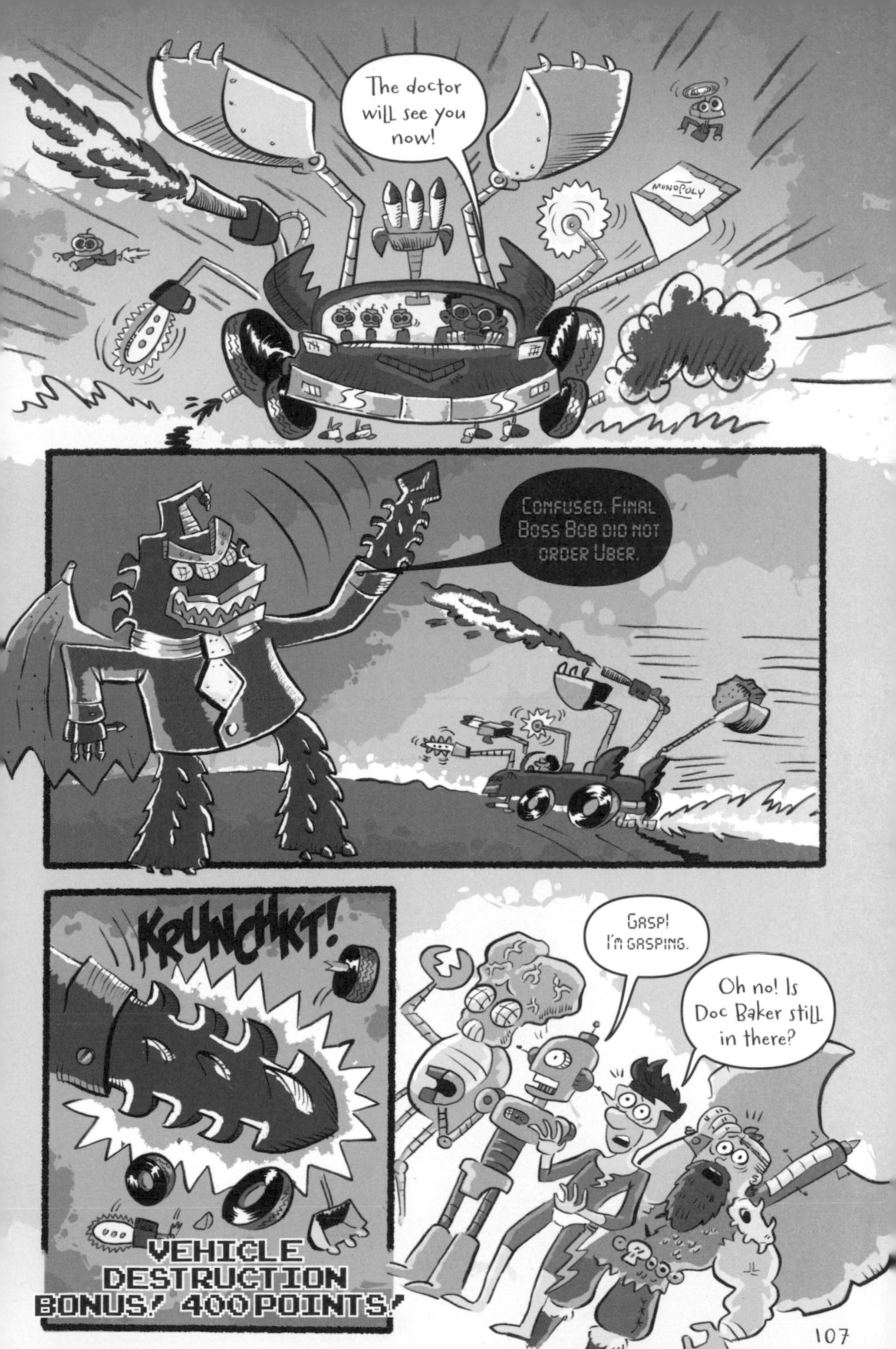

The doctor will see you now!
MONOPOLY
CONFUSED. FINAL BOSS BOB DID NOT ORDER UBER.
KRUNCHKT!
VEHICLE DESTRUCTION BONUS! 400 POINTS!
GASP! I'M GASPING.
Oh no! Is Doc Baker still in there?

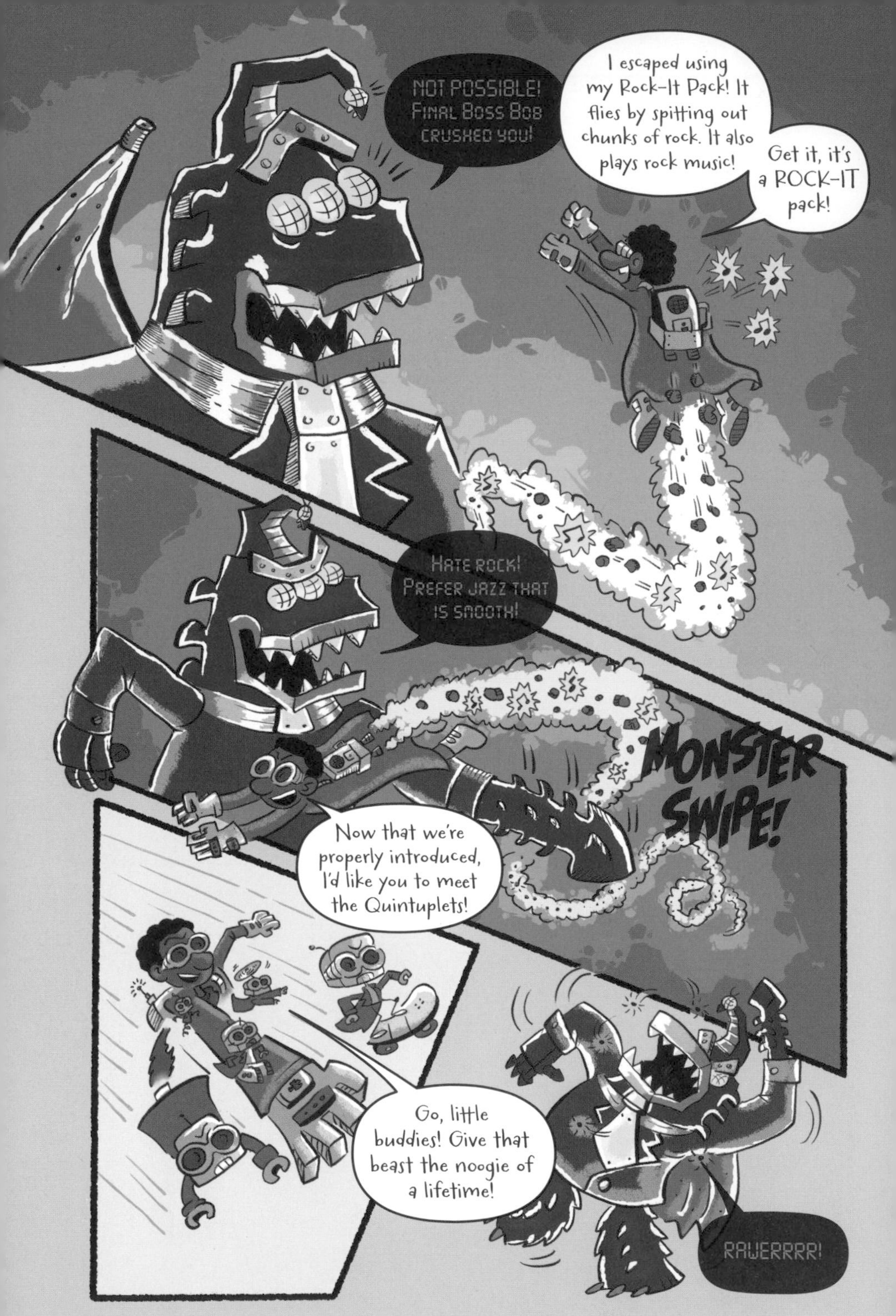
NOT POSSIBLE! FINAL BOSS BOB CRUSHED YOU!
I escaped using my Rock-It Pack! It flies by spitting out chunks of rock. It also plays rock music!
Get it, it's a ROCK-IT pack!
HATE ROCK! PREFER JAZZ THAT IS SMOOTH!
MONSTER SWIPE!
Now that we're properly introduced, I'd like you to meet the Quintuplets!
Go, little buddies! Give that beast the noogie of a lifetime!
RAWERRRR!

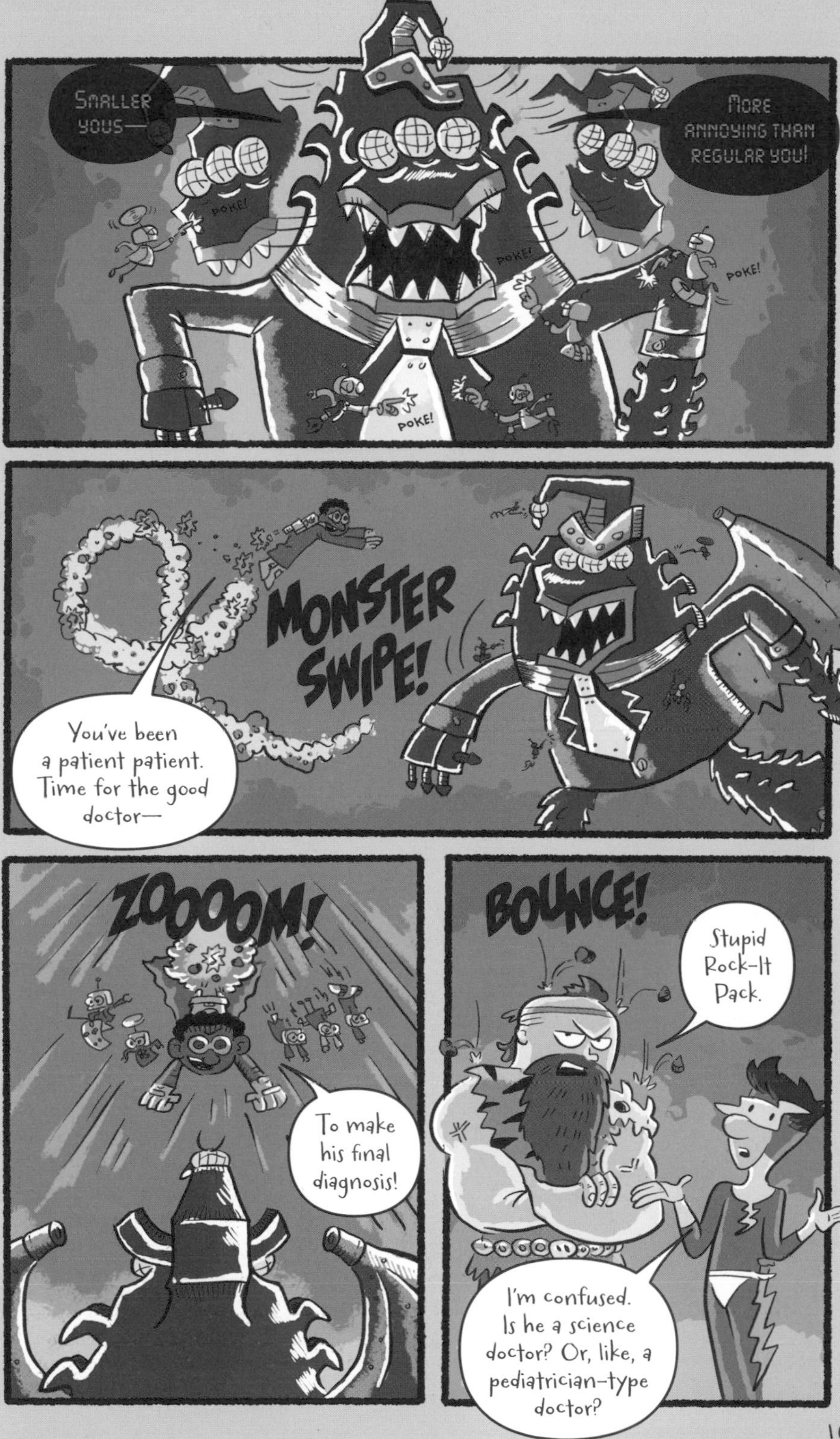
SMALLER YOUS—
MORE ANNOYING THAN REGULAR YOU!
POKE!
POKE!
POKE!
POKE!
MONSTER SWIPE!
You've been a patient patient. Time for the good doctor—
ZOOOOM!
To make his final diagnosis!
BOUNCE!
Stupid Rock-It Pack.
I'm confused. Is he a science doctor? Or, like, a pediatrician-type doctor?

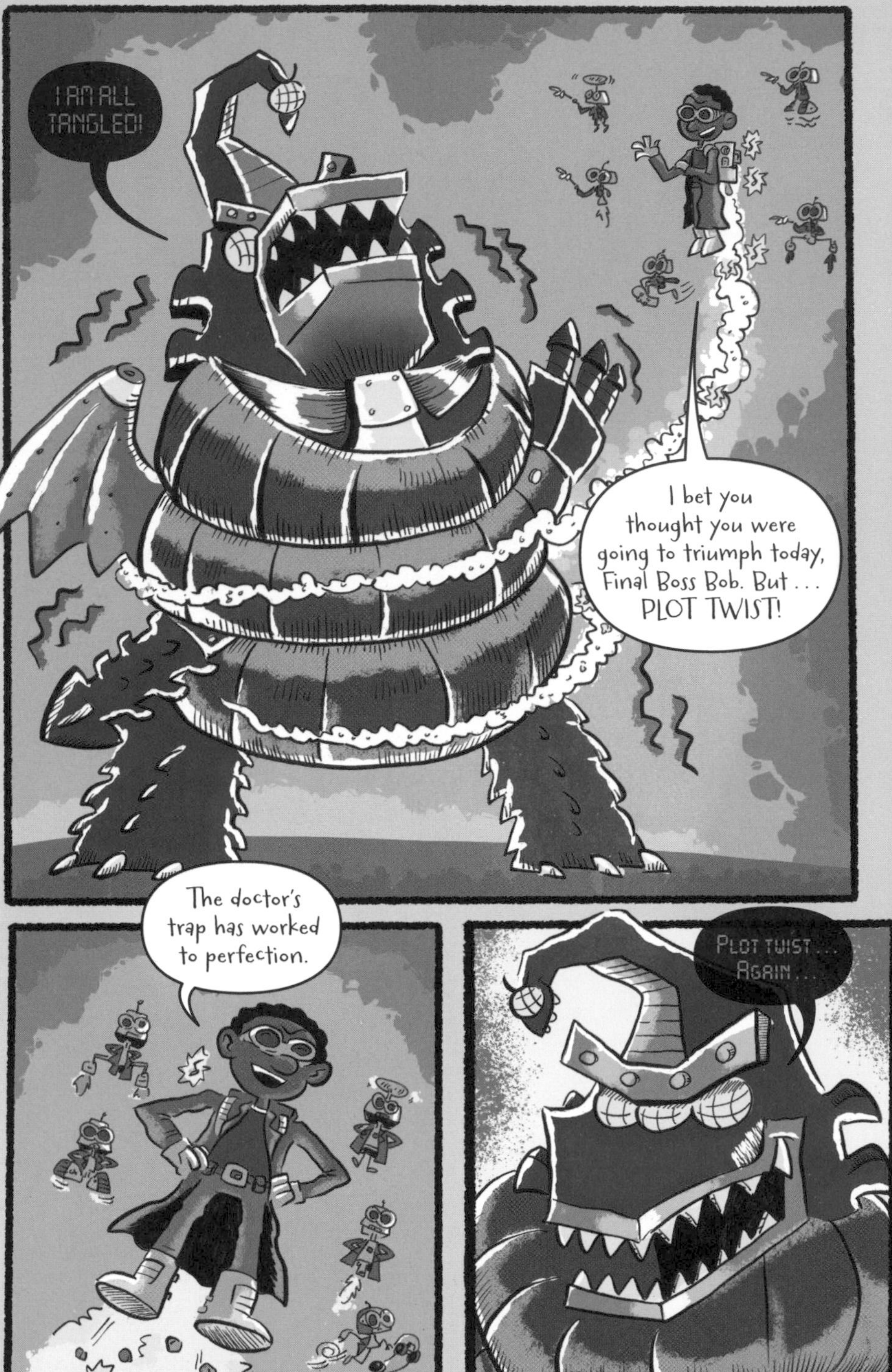
I AM ALL TANGLED!
I bet you thought you were going to triumph today, Final Boss Bob. But . . . PLOT TWIST!
The doctor's trap has worked to perfection.
PLOT TWIST . . . AGAIN . . .

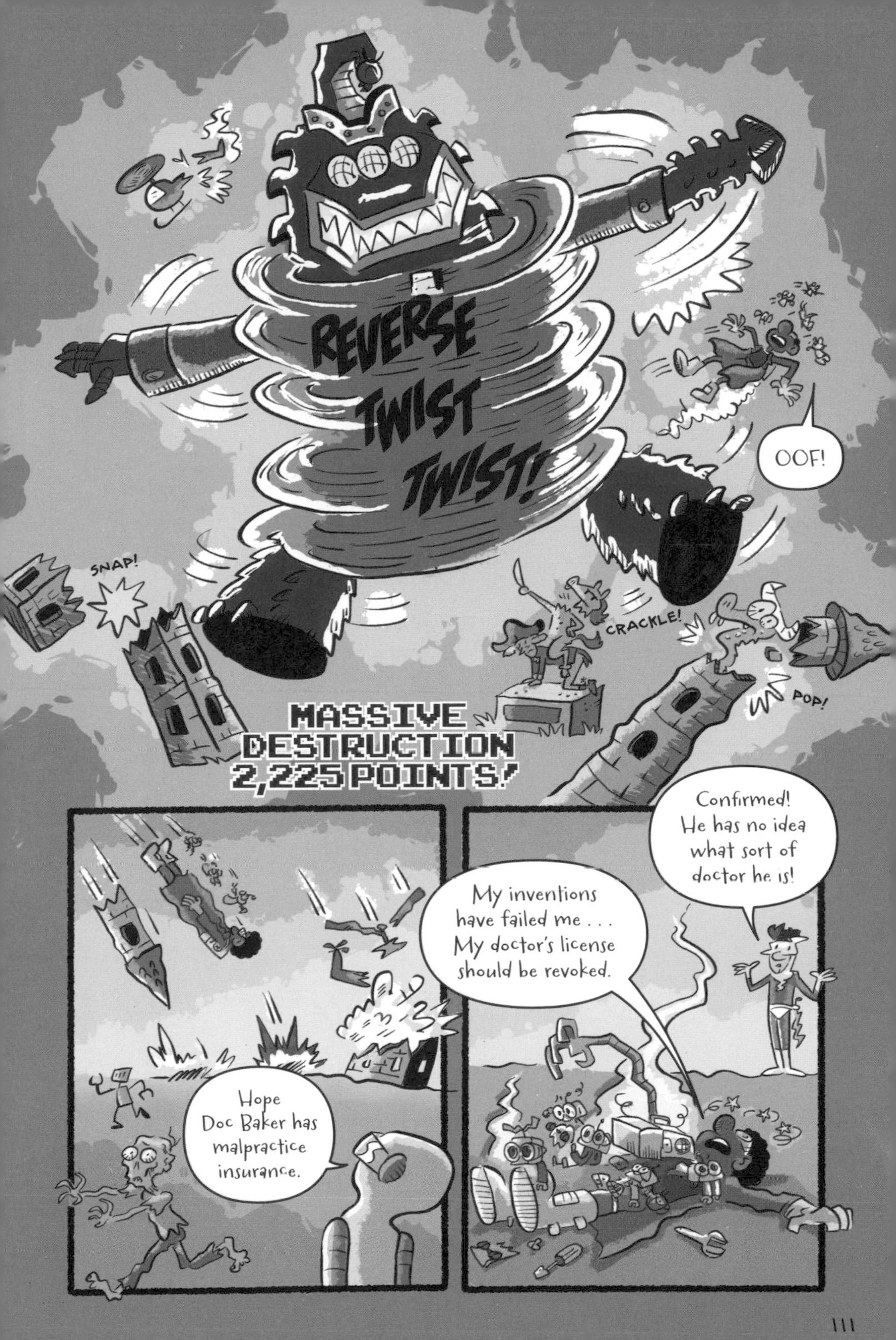
REVERSE TWIST TWIST!
OOF!
SNAP!
CRACKLE!
POP!
MASSIVE DESTRUCTION 2,225 POINTS!
Hope Doc Baker has malpractice insurance.
My inventions have failed me . . . My doctor's license should be revoked.
Confirmed! He has no idea what sort of doctor he is!

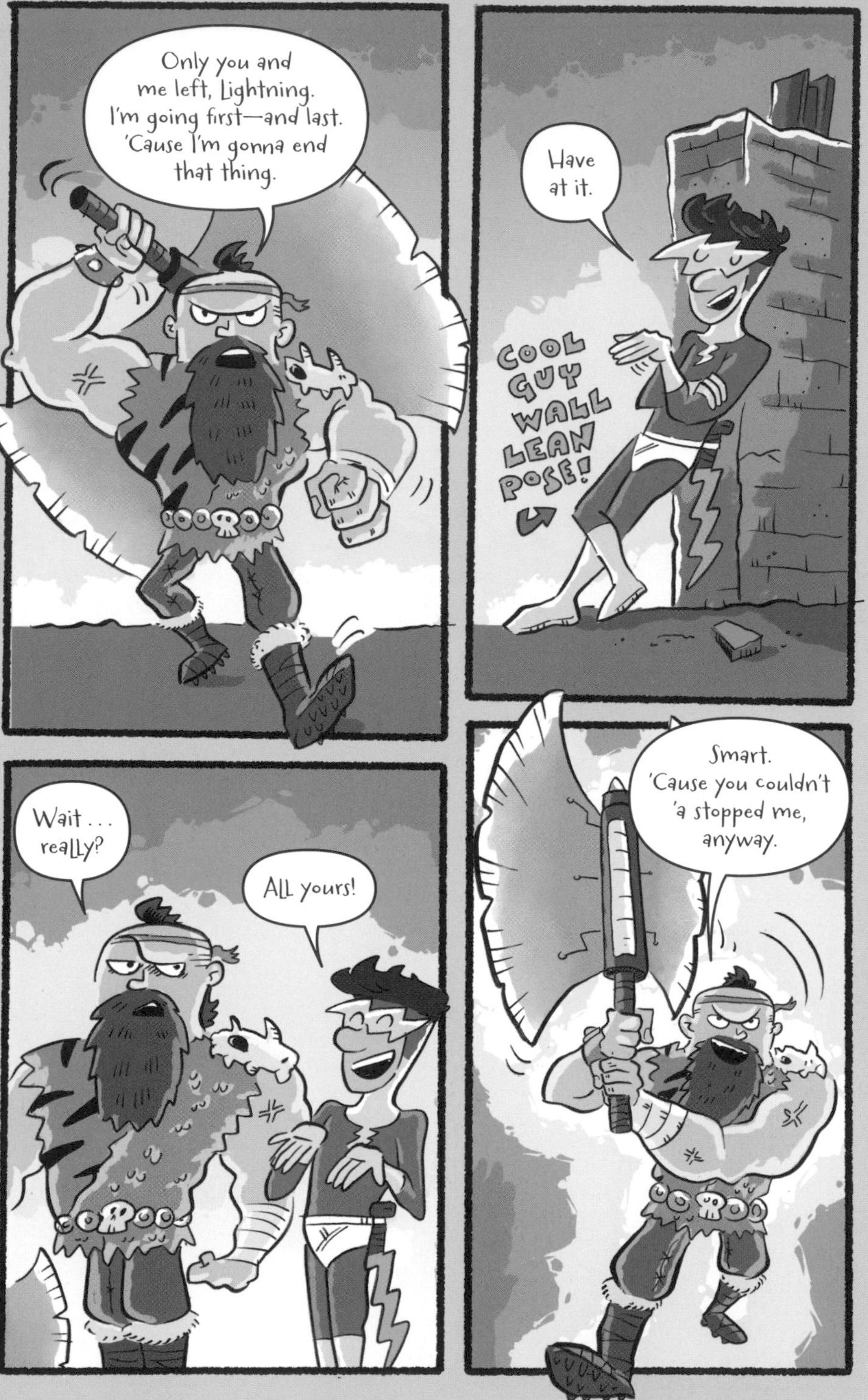
Only you and me left, Lightning. I'm going first—and last. 'Cause I'm gonna end that thing.
Have at it.
COOL GUY WALL LEAN POSE!
Wait . . . really?
ALL yours!
Smart. 'Cause you couldn't 'a stopped me, anyway.

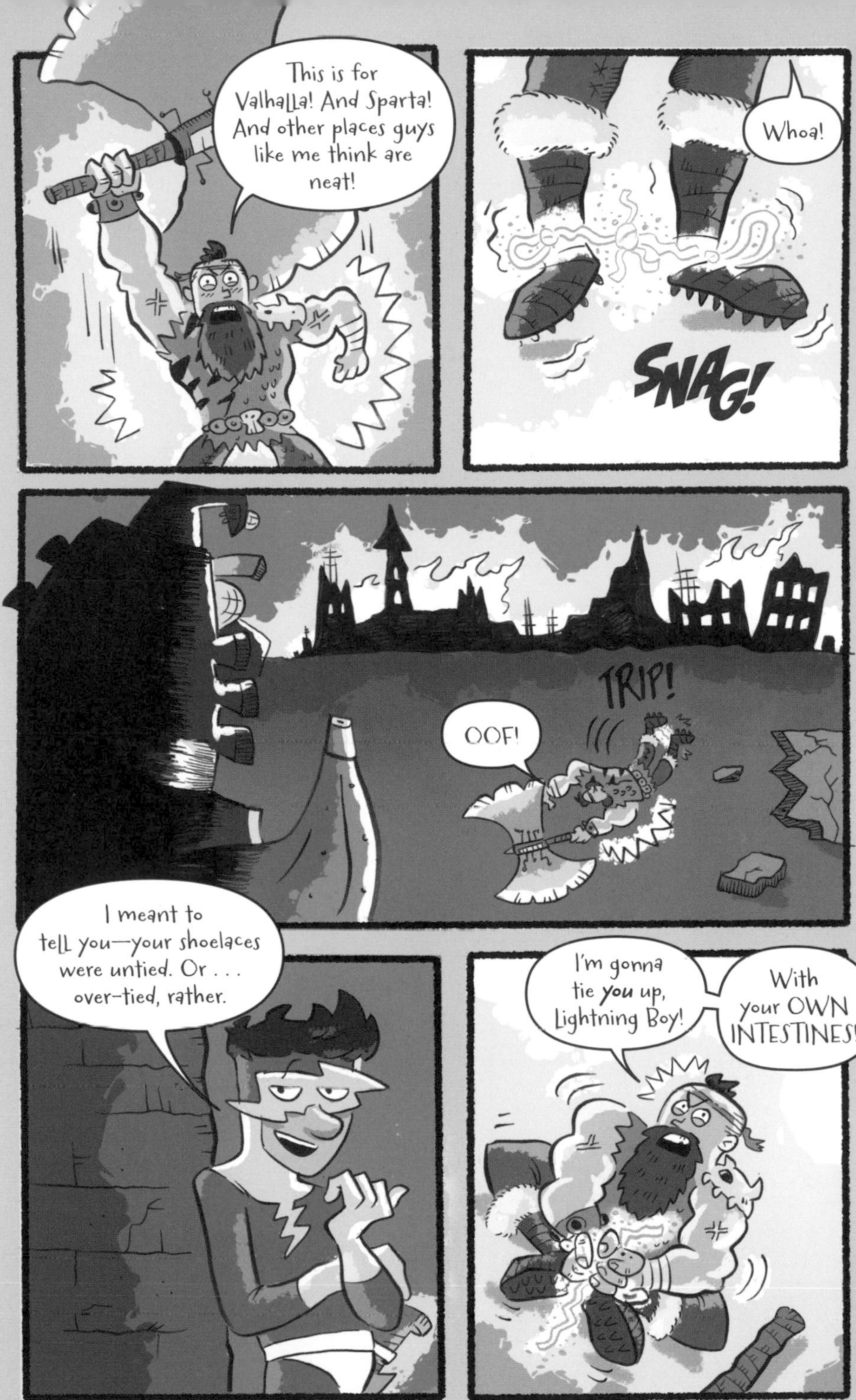
This is for Valhalla! And Sparta! And other places guys like me think are neat!
Whoa!
SNAG!
TRIP!
OOF!
I meant to tell you—your shoelaces were untied. Or . . . over-tied, rather.
I'm gonna tie **you** up, Lightning Boy!
With your OWN INTESTINES!

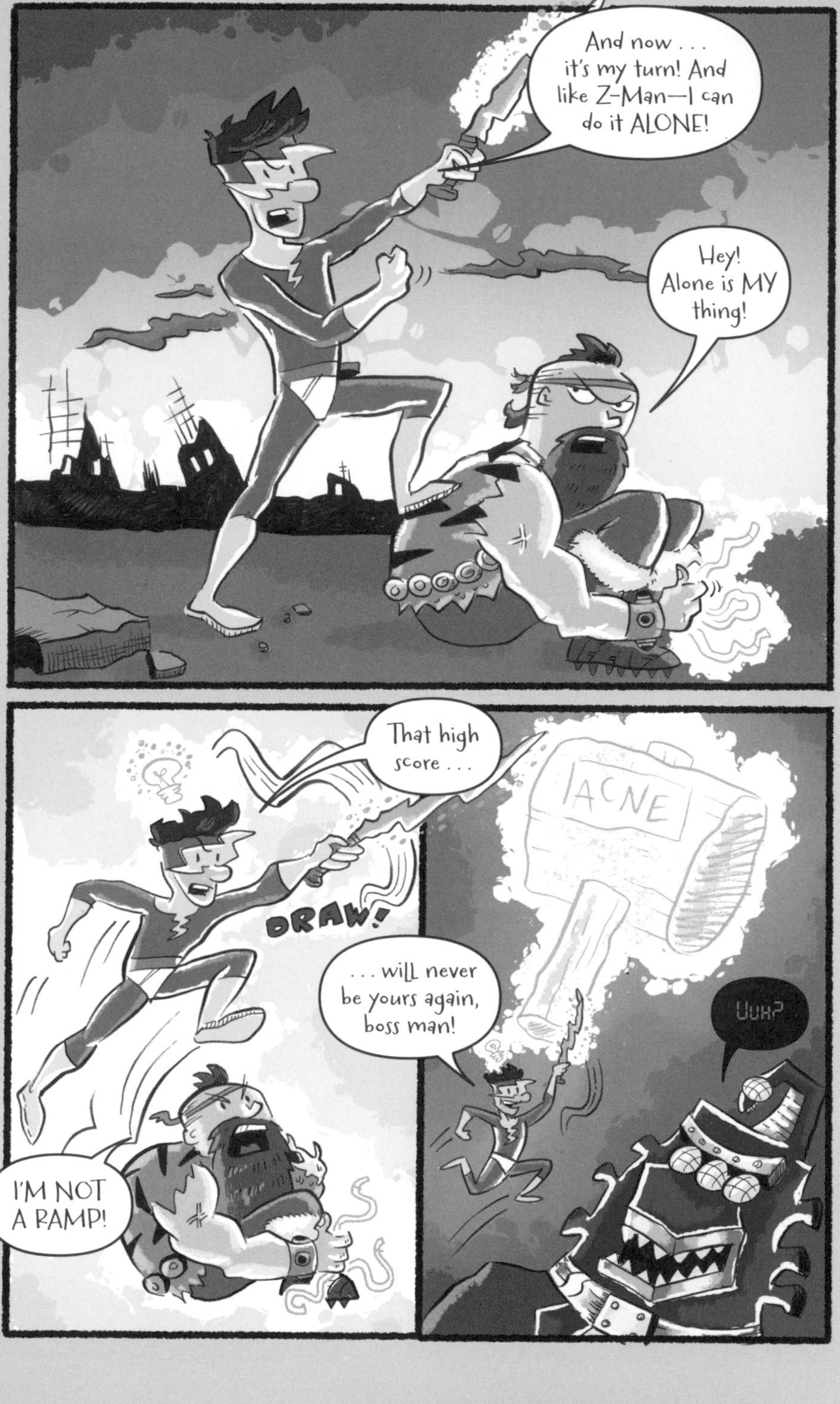
And now . . . it's my turn! And like Z-Man—I can do it ALONE!
Hey! Alone is MY thing!
That high score . . .
DRAW!
ACNE
I'M NOT A RAMP!
. . . will never be yours again, boss man!
UUH?

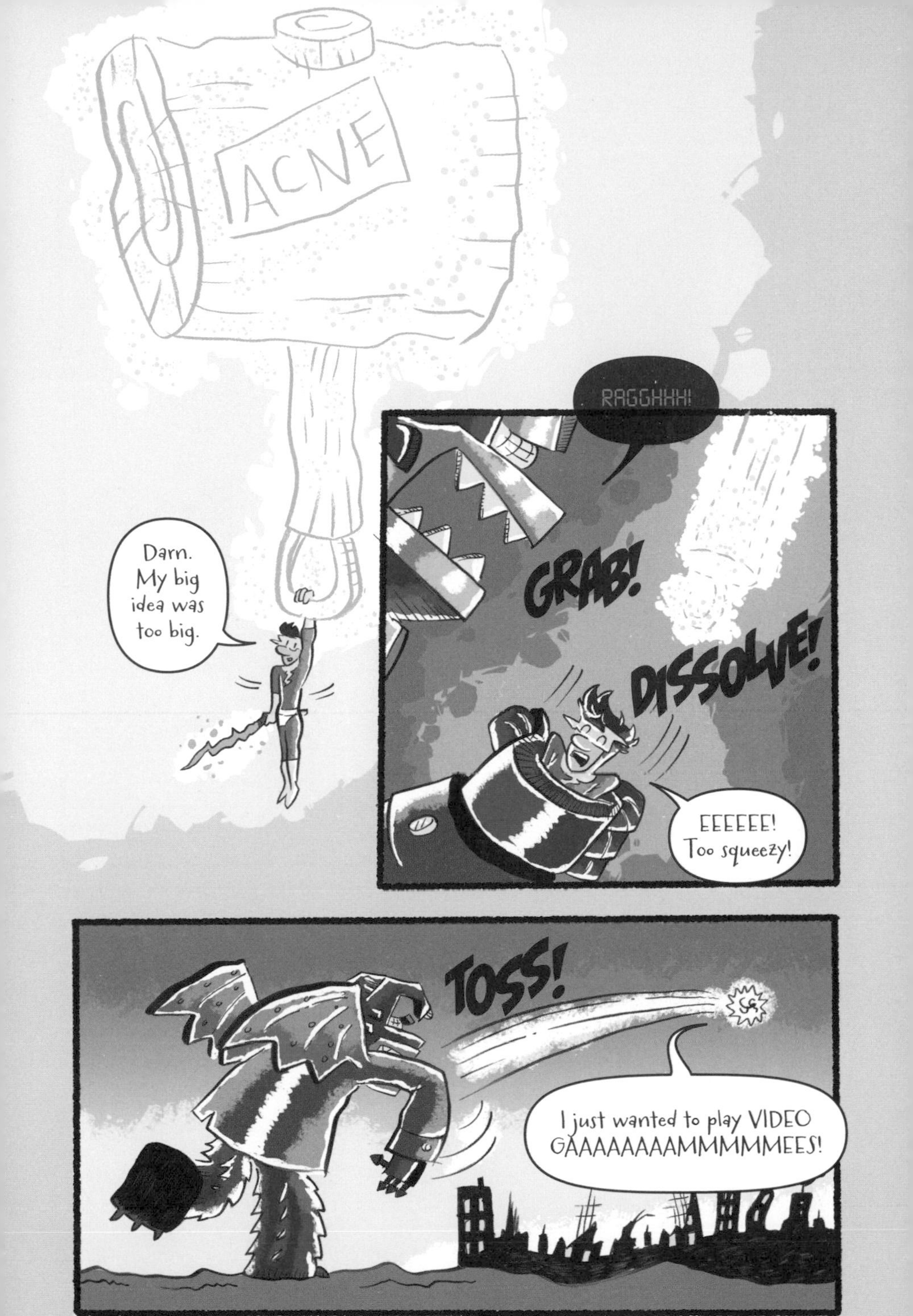
ACNE
Darn. My big idea was too big.
RAGGHHH!
GRAB!
DISSOLVE!
EEEEEE! Too squeezy!
TOSS!
I just wanted to play VIDEO GAAAAAAAAMMMMMEES!

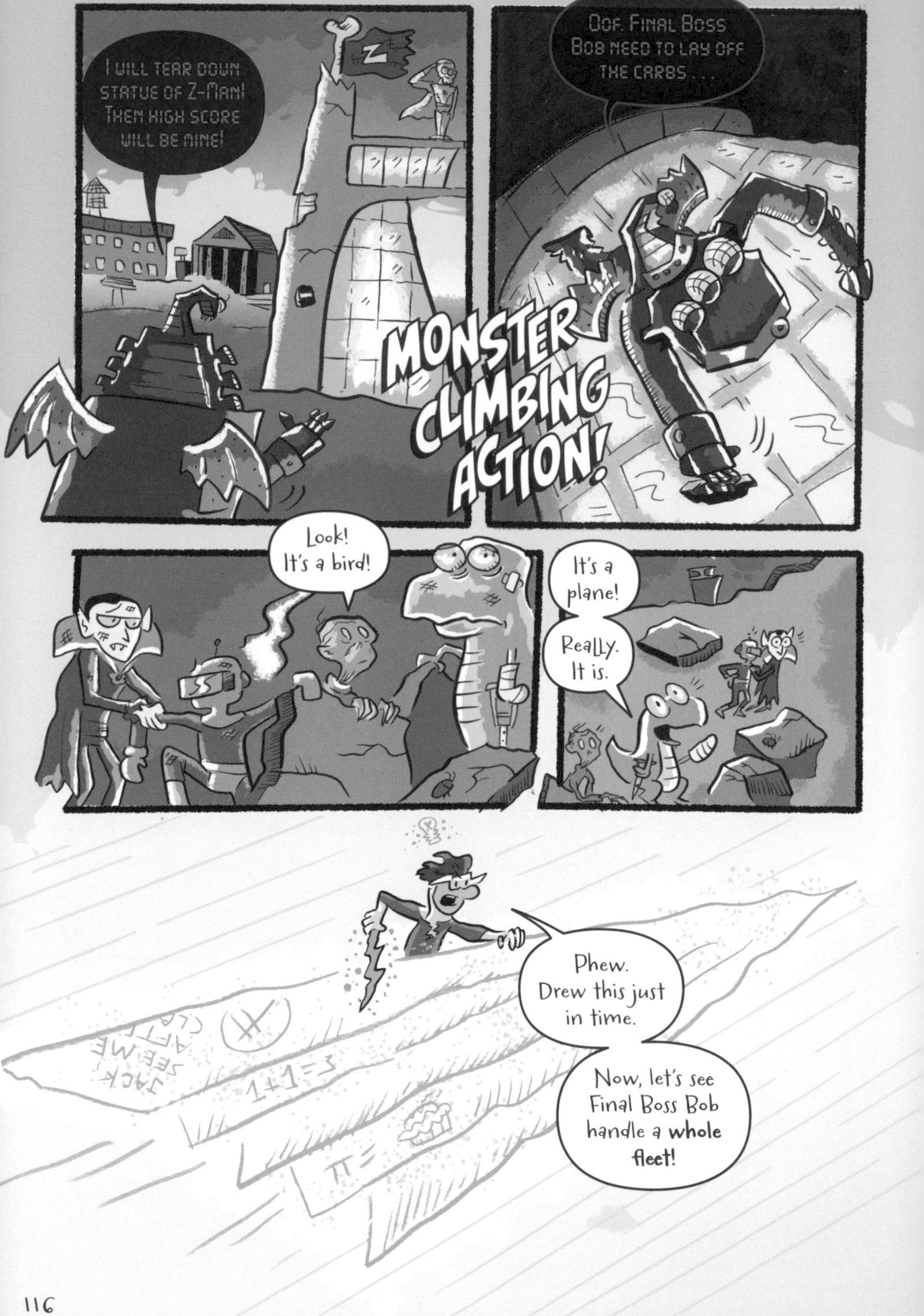
I WILL TEAR DOWN STATUE OF Z-MAN! THEN HIGH SCORE WILL BE MINE!
OOF. FINAL BOSS BOB NEED TO LAY OFF THE CARBS . . .
MONSTER CLIMBING ACTION!
Look! It's a bird!
It's a plane!
Really. It is.
JACK SEE ME AFTE CLA
1+1=3
π=
Phew. Drew this just in time.
Now, let's see Final Boss Bob handle a **whole fleet**!

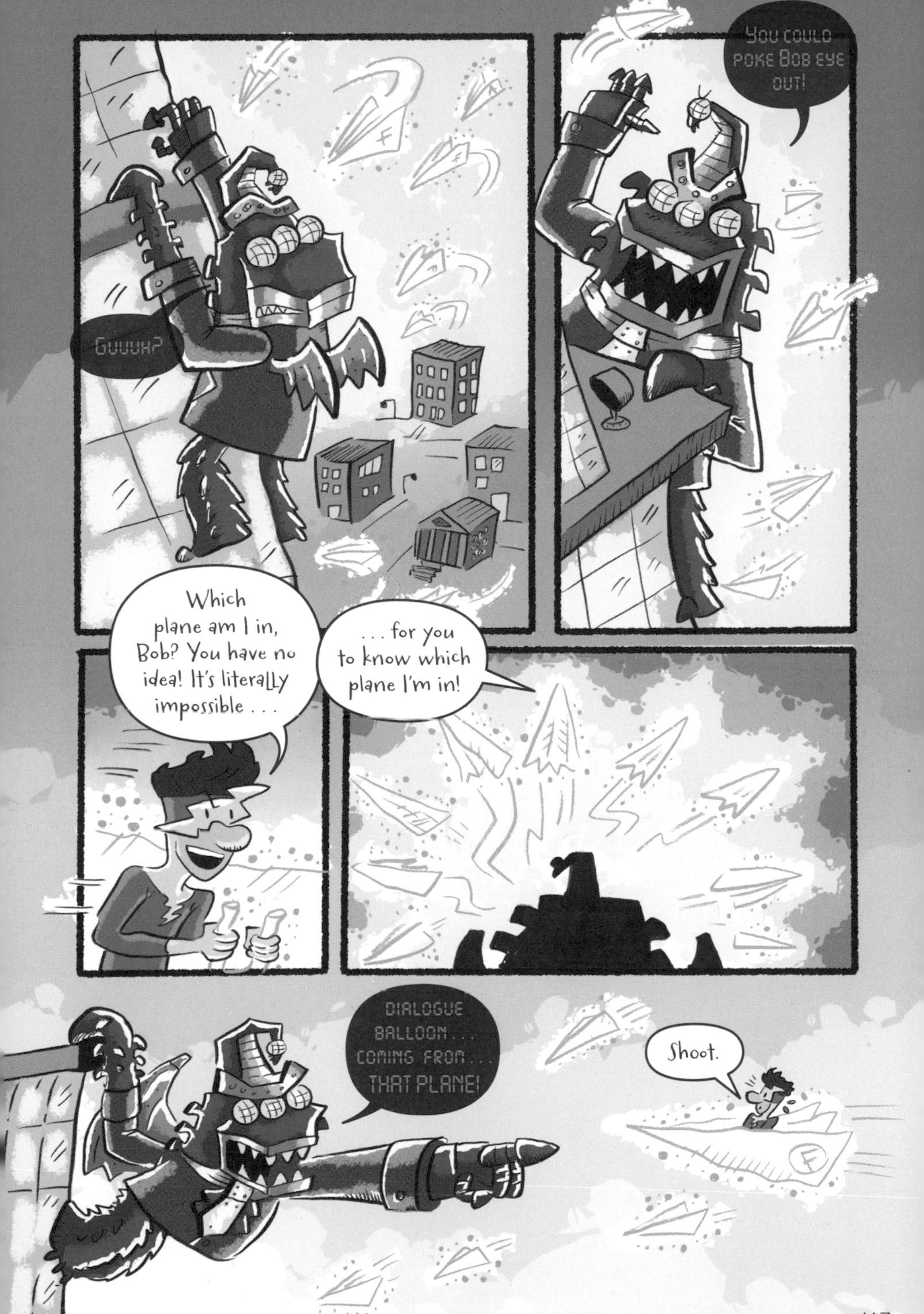
GUUUK?
YOU COULD POKE BOB EYE OUT!
Which plane am I in, Bob? You have no idea! It's literaLLy impossible . . .
. . . for you to know which plane I'm in!
DIALOGUE BALLOON . . . COMING FROM . . . THAT PLANE!
Shoot.

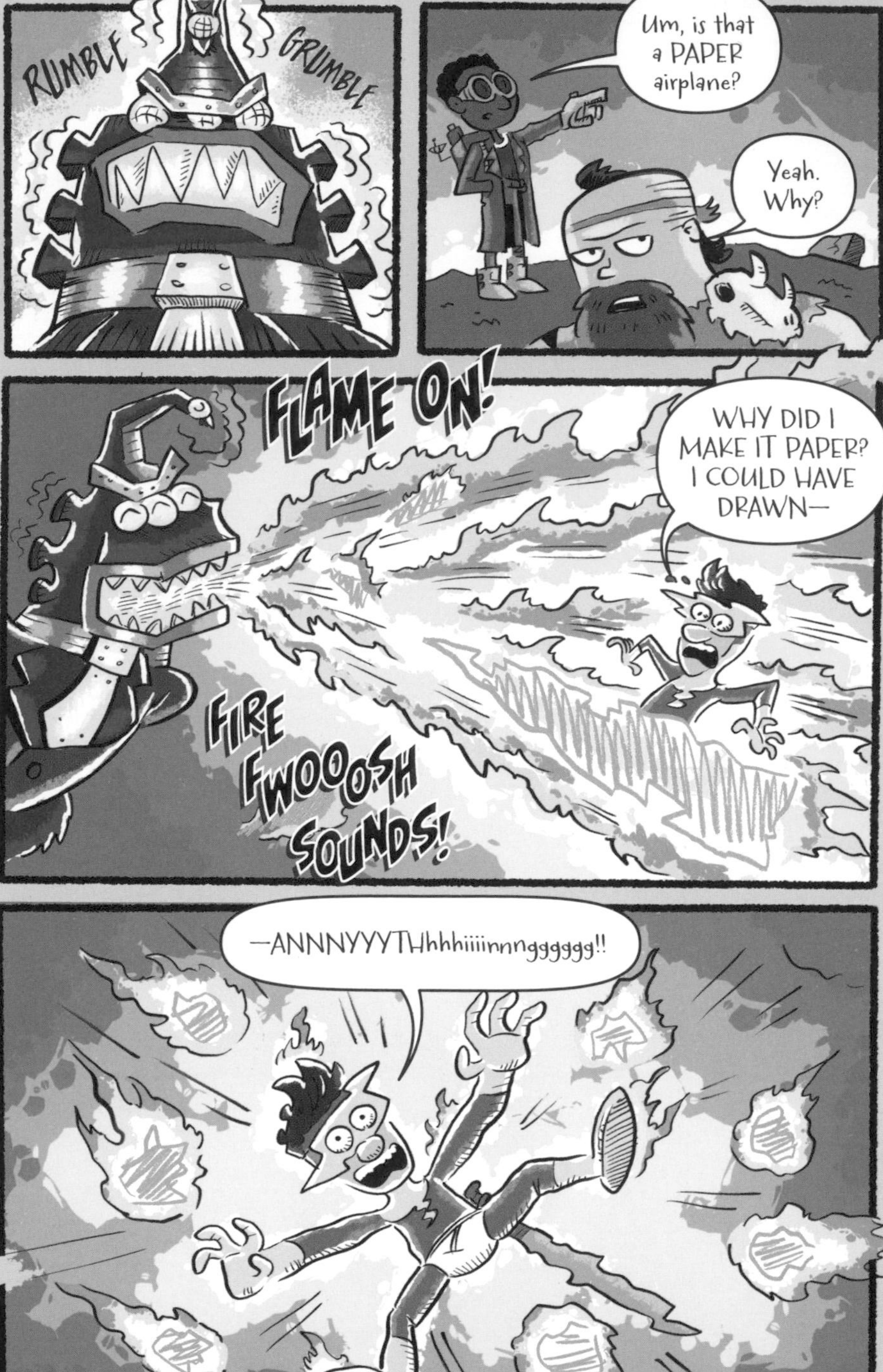
RUMBLE
GRUMBLE
Um, is that a PAPER airplane?
Yeah. Why?
FLAME ON!
WHY DID I MAKE IT PAPER? I COULD HAVE DRAWN—
FIRE FWOOOSH SOUNDS!
—ANNNYYYTHhhhiiiinnngggggg!!

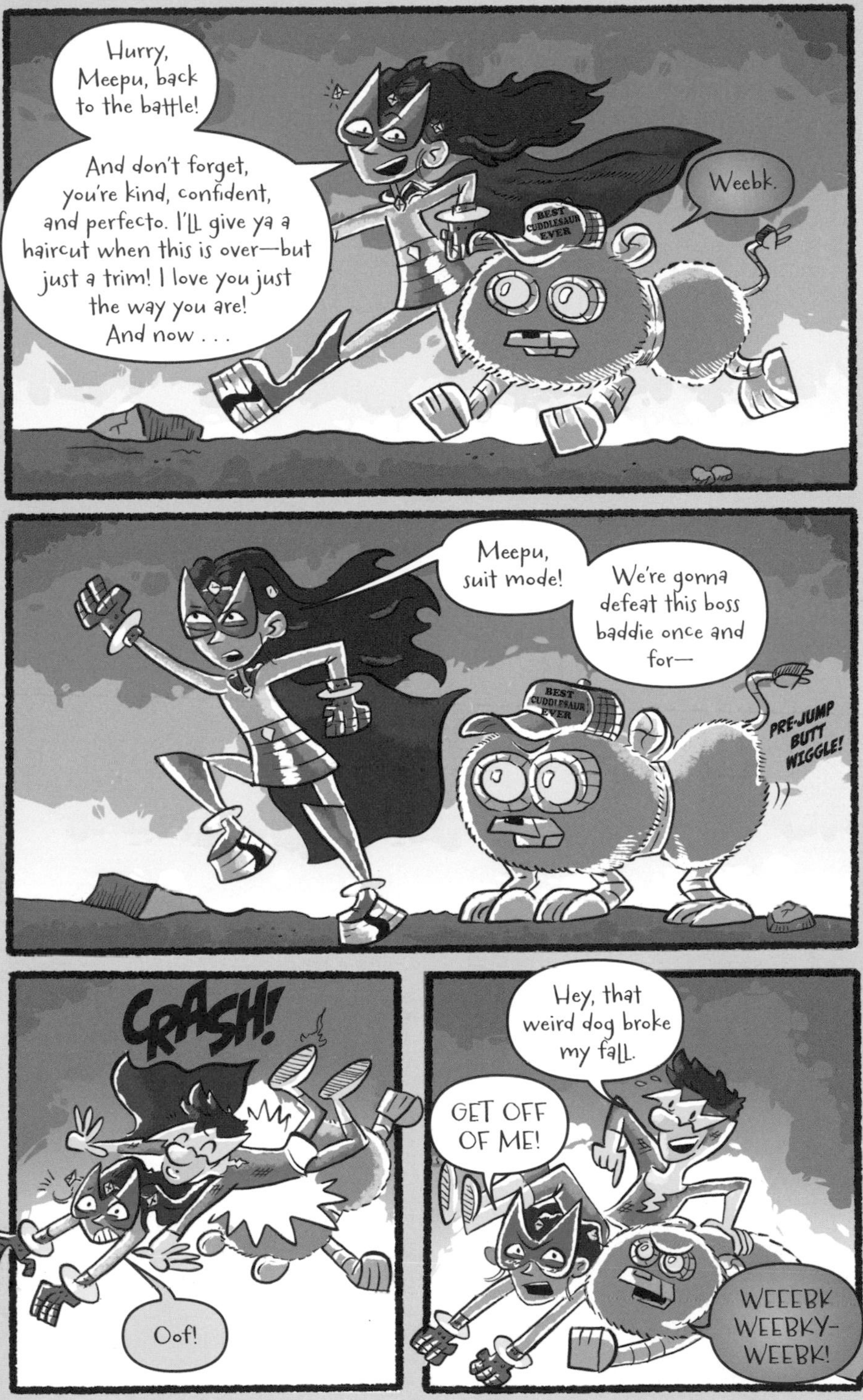
Hurry, Meepu, back to the battle!
And don't forget, you're kind, confident, and perfecto. I'll give ya a haircut when this is over—but just a trim! I love you just the way you are! And now . . .
BEST CUDDLESAUR EVER
Weebk.
Meepu, suit mode!
We're gonna defeat this boss baddie once and for—
BEST CUDDLESAUR EVER
PRE-JUMP BUTT WIGGLE!
CRASH!
Oof!
Hey, that weird dog broke my fall.
GET OFF OF ME!
WEEEBK WEEBKY-WEEBK!

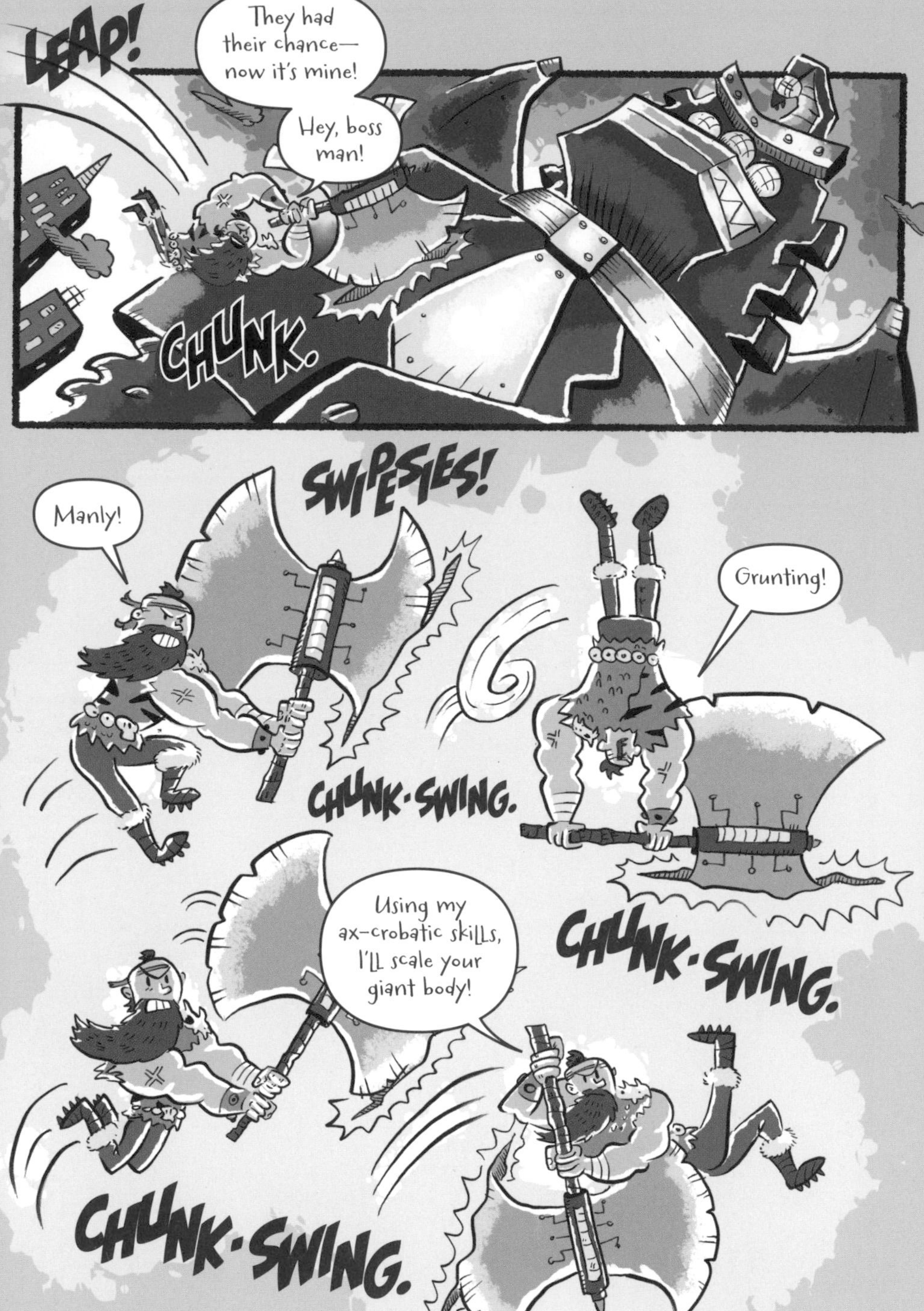

LEAP!
They had their chance—now it's mine!
Hey, boss man!
CHUNK.
SWIPESIES!
Manly!
Grunting!
CHUNK-SWING.
CHUNK-SWING.
Using my ax-crobatic skiLLs, I'LL scale your giant body!
CHUNK-SWING.

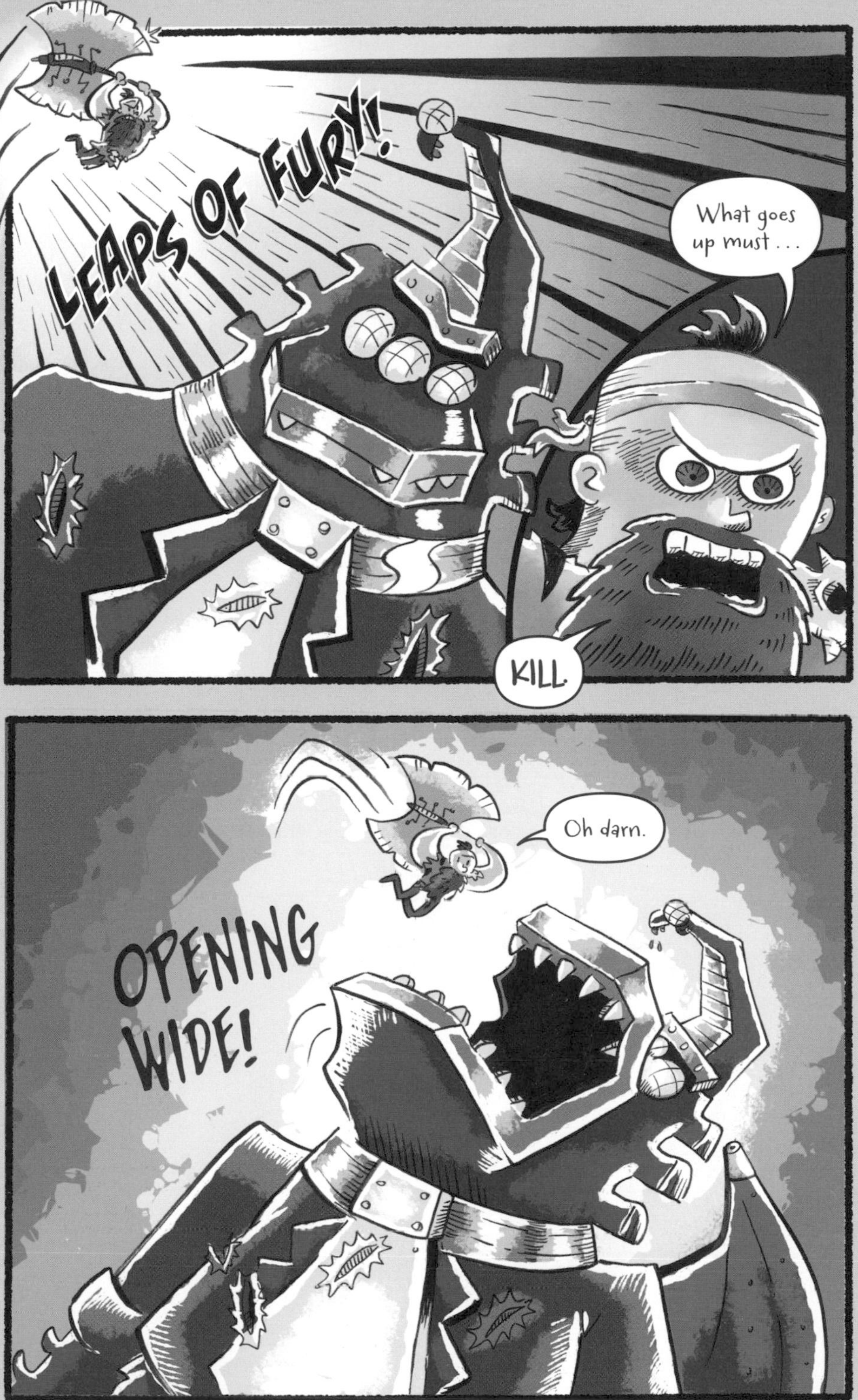

LEAPS OF FURY!
What goes up must . . .
KILL.
Oh darn.
OPENING WIDE!

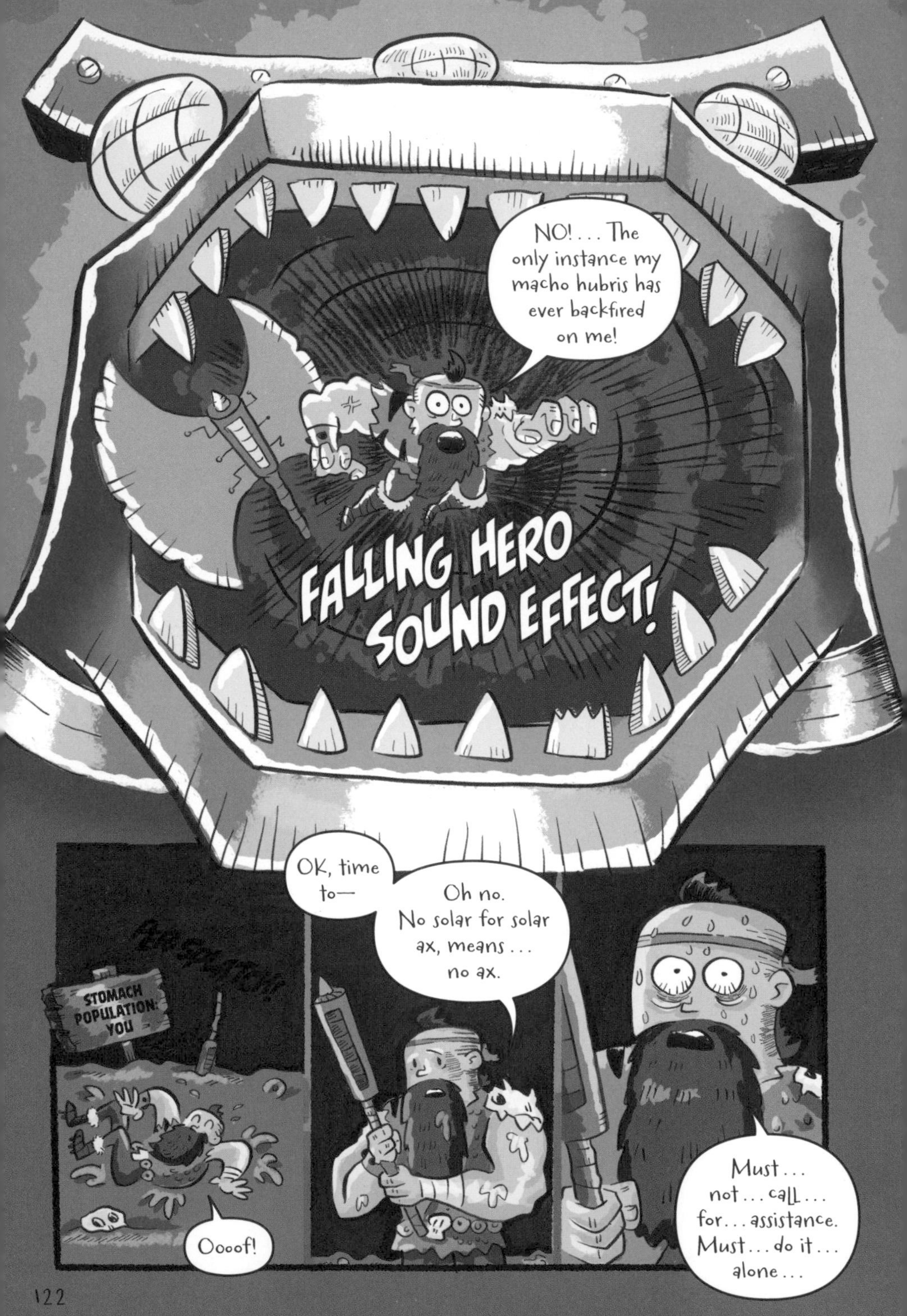
NO! . . . The only instance my macho hubris has ever backfired on me!
FALLING HERO SOUND EFFECT!
STOMACH POPULATION: YOU
Oooof!
OK, time to—
Oh no. No solar for solar ax, means . . . no ax.
Must . . . not . . . call . . . for . . . assistance. Must . . . do it . . . alone . . .

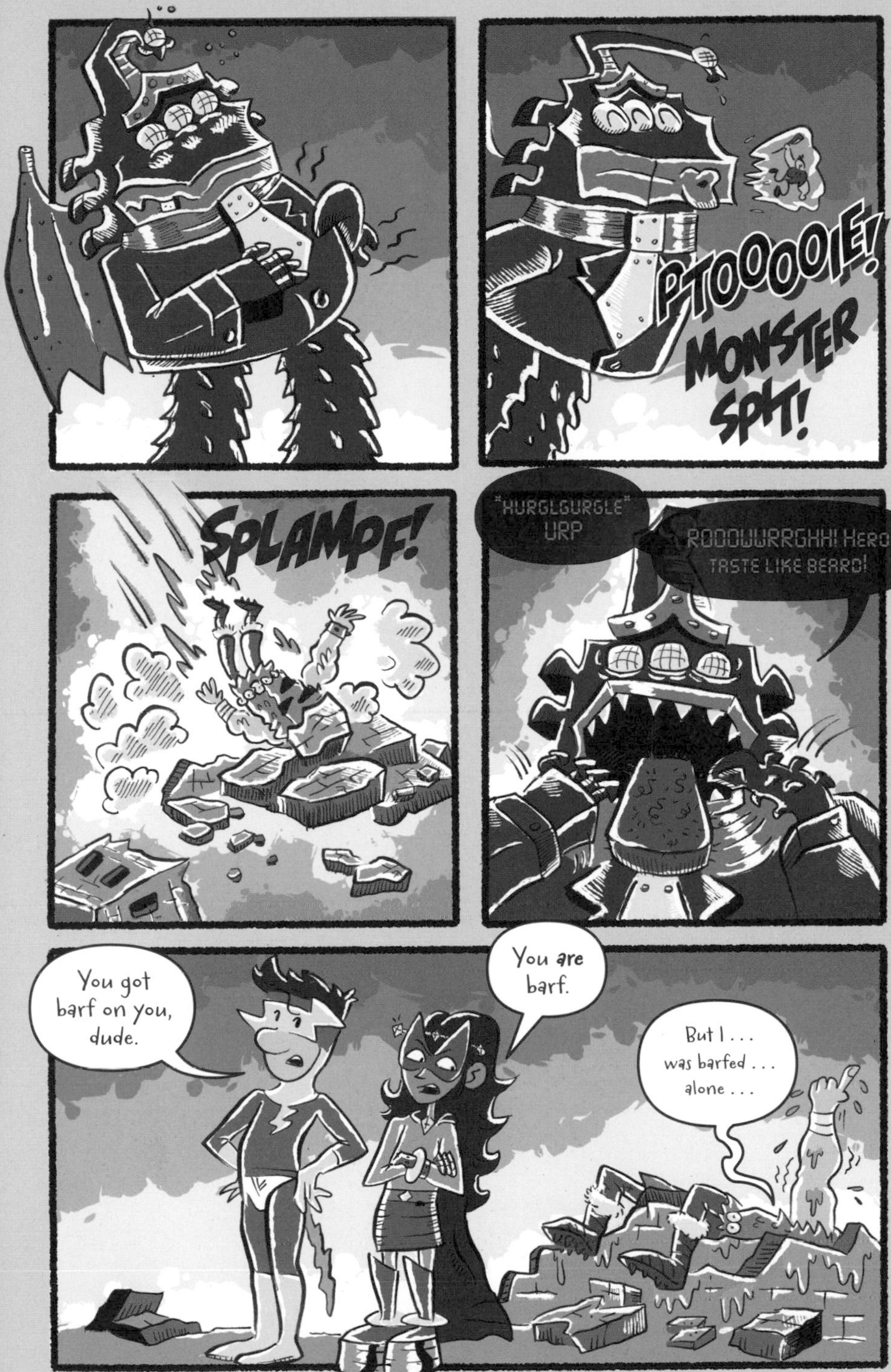
PTOOOOOIE!
MONSTER SPIT!
SPLAMPF!
"HURGLGURGLE" URP
ROOOWURRGHH! HERO TASTE LIKE BEARD!
You got barf on you, dude.
You are barf.
But I . . . was barfed . . . alone . . .

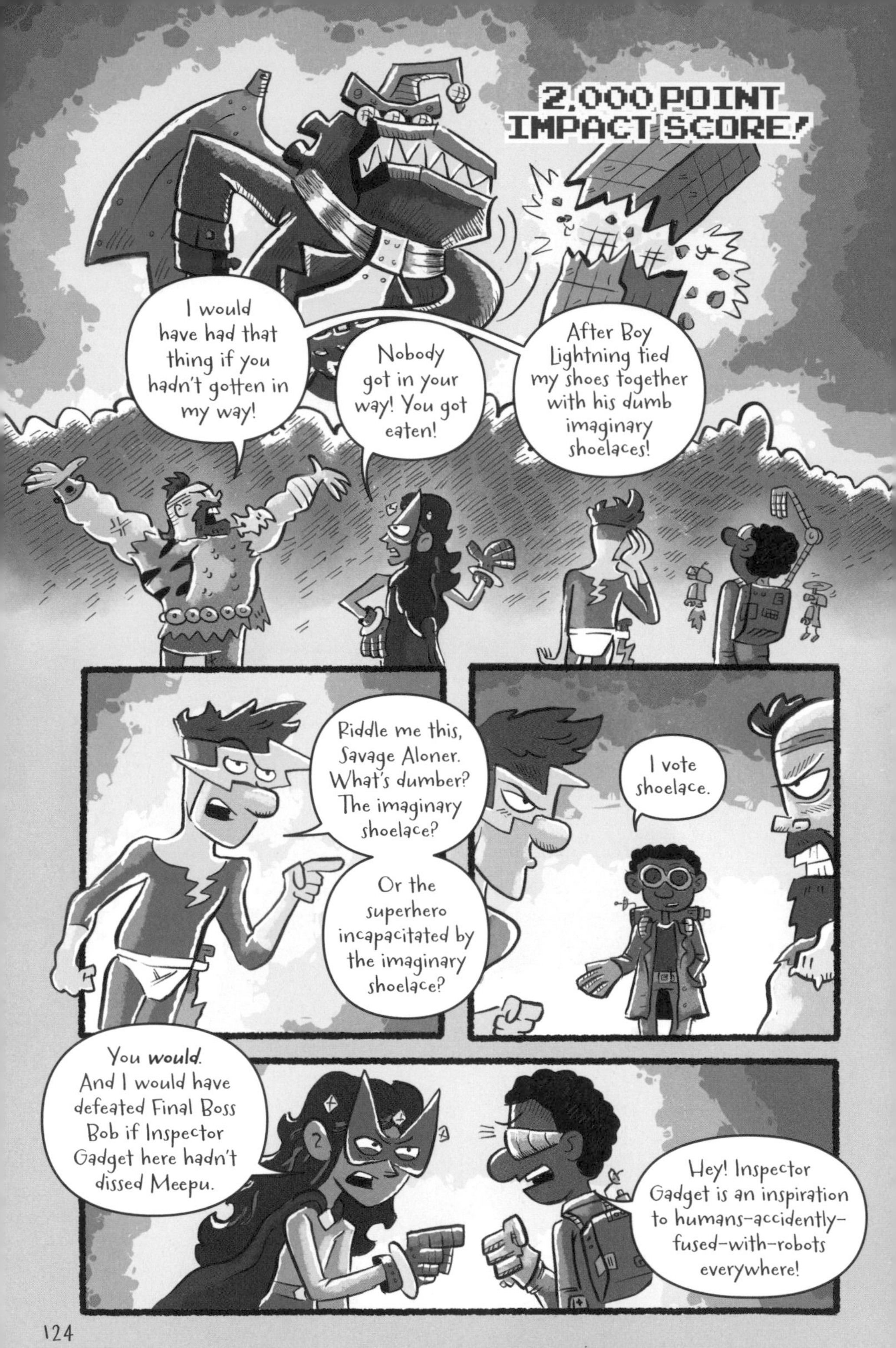
2,000 POINT IMPACT SCORE!
I would have had that thing if you hadn't gotten in my way!
Nobody got in your way! You got eaten!
After Boy Lightning tied my shoes together with his dumb imaginary shoelaces!
Riddle me this, Savage Aloner. What's dumber? The imaginary shoelace?
Or the superhero incapacitated by the imaginary shoelace?
I vote shoelace.
You **would**. And I would have defeated Final Boss Bob if Inspector Gadget here hadn't dissed Meepu.
Hey! Inspector Gadget is an inspiration to humans-accidently-fused-with-robots everywhere!

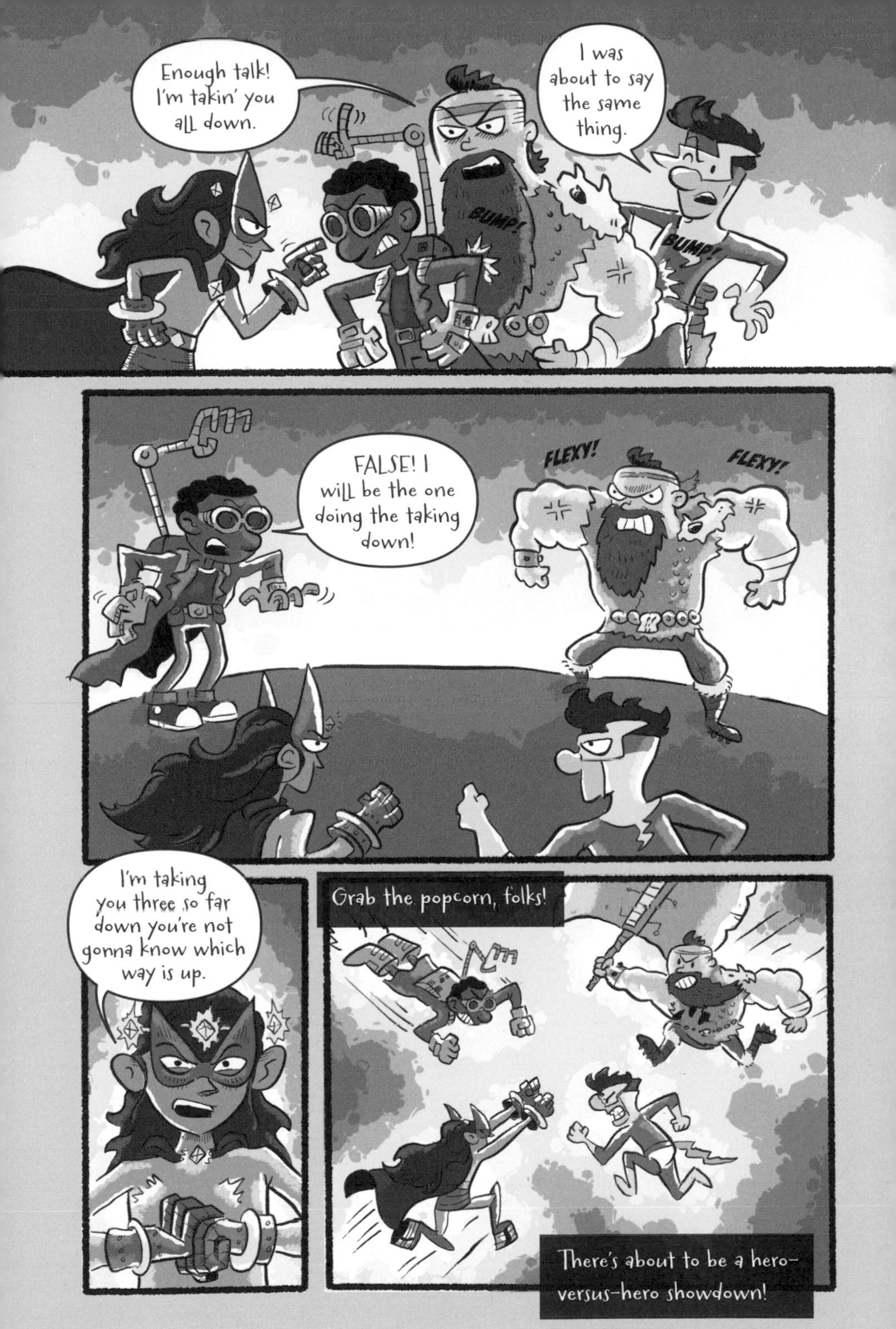
Enough talk! I'm takin' you all down.
I was about to say the same thing.
BUMP!
BUMP!
FALSE! I will be the one doing the taking down!
FLEXY!
FLEXY!
I'm taking you three so far down you're not gonna know which way is up.
Grab the popcorn, folks!
There's about to be a hero-versus-hero showdown!

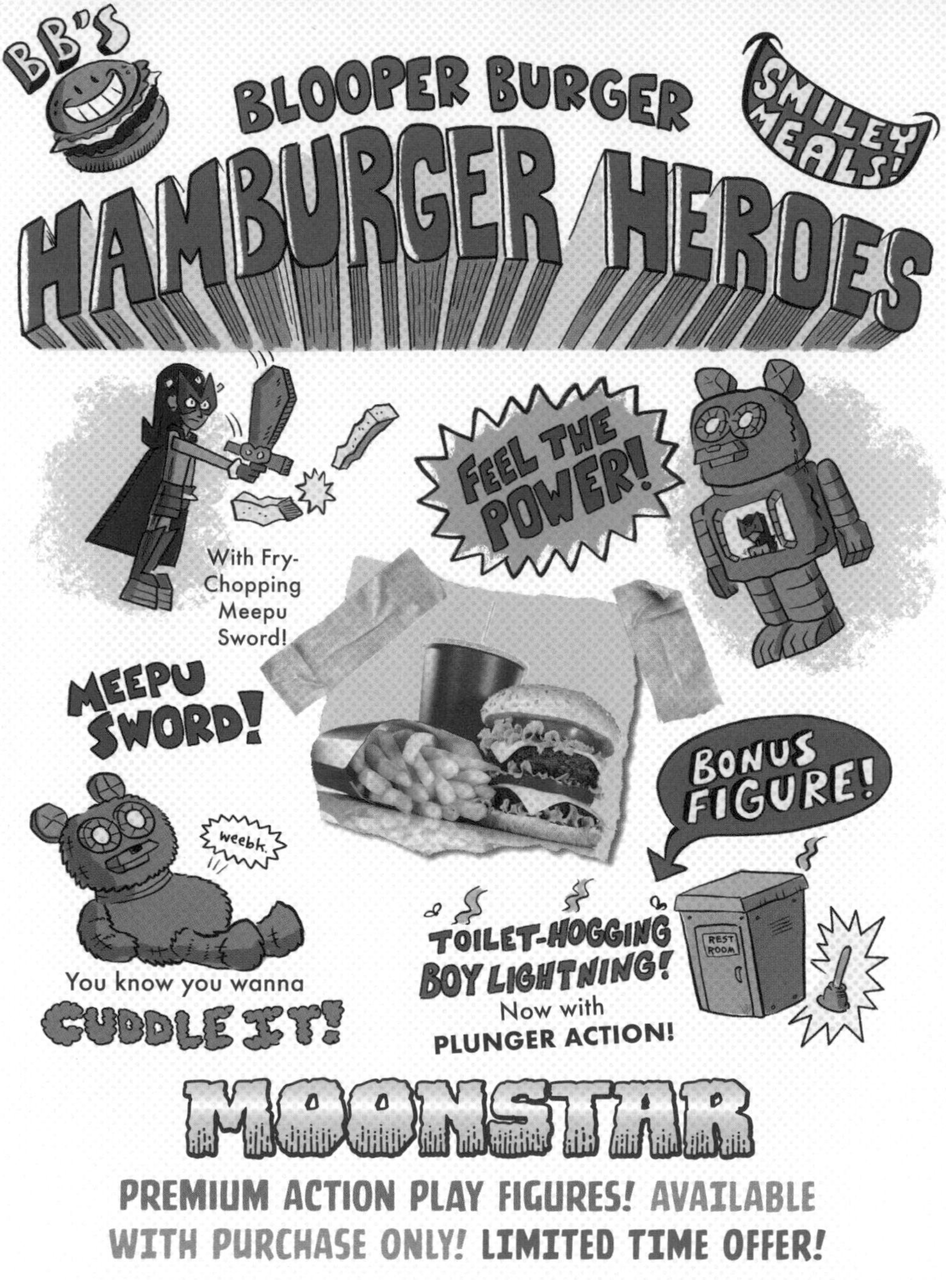
BB'S
BLOOPER BURGER
SMILEY MEALS!
HAMBURGER HEROES
FEEL THE POWER!
With Fry-Chopping Meepu Sword!
MEEPU SWORD!
weebk.
BONUS FIGURE!
REST ROOM
You know you wanna
CUDDLE IT!
TOILET-HOGGING BOY LIGHTNING!
Now with
PLUNGER ACTION!
MOONSTAR
PREMIUM ACTION PLAY FIGURES! AVAILABLE WITH PURCHASE ONLY! LIMITED TIME OFFER!

LEGAL STUFF
A Smiley Meal consists of a Blooper Burger or Blooper Bites of ChickenMeatProduct, Crispee Fries or Banana Chips, and Liquid Sugar Beverage!** Cost is 49 cents above the price of the meal. Limited time only. While supplies last. **Pure Wretch juice and Meathook milk excluded from offer.

Caution: May contain small parts. Not intended for children under 3 . . . but trust us, they're gonna want to play with these bad boys! Ask about special toys for kids under 3. We don't have any, but feel free to ask. WHY ARE YOU STILL READING THIS—GET BACK TO THE COMIC!

CHAPTER SEVEN
FOES AND FRIENDS, FIGHT!

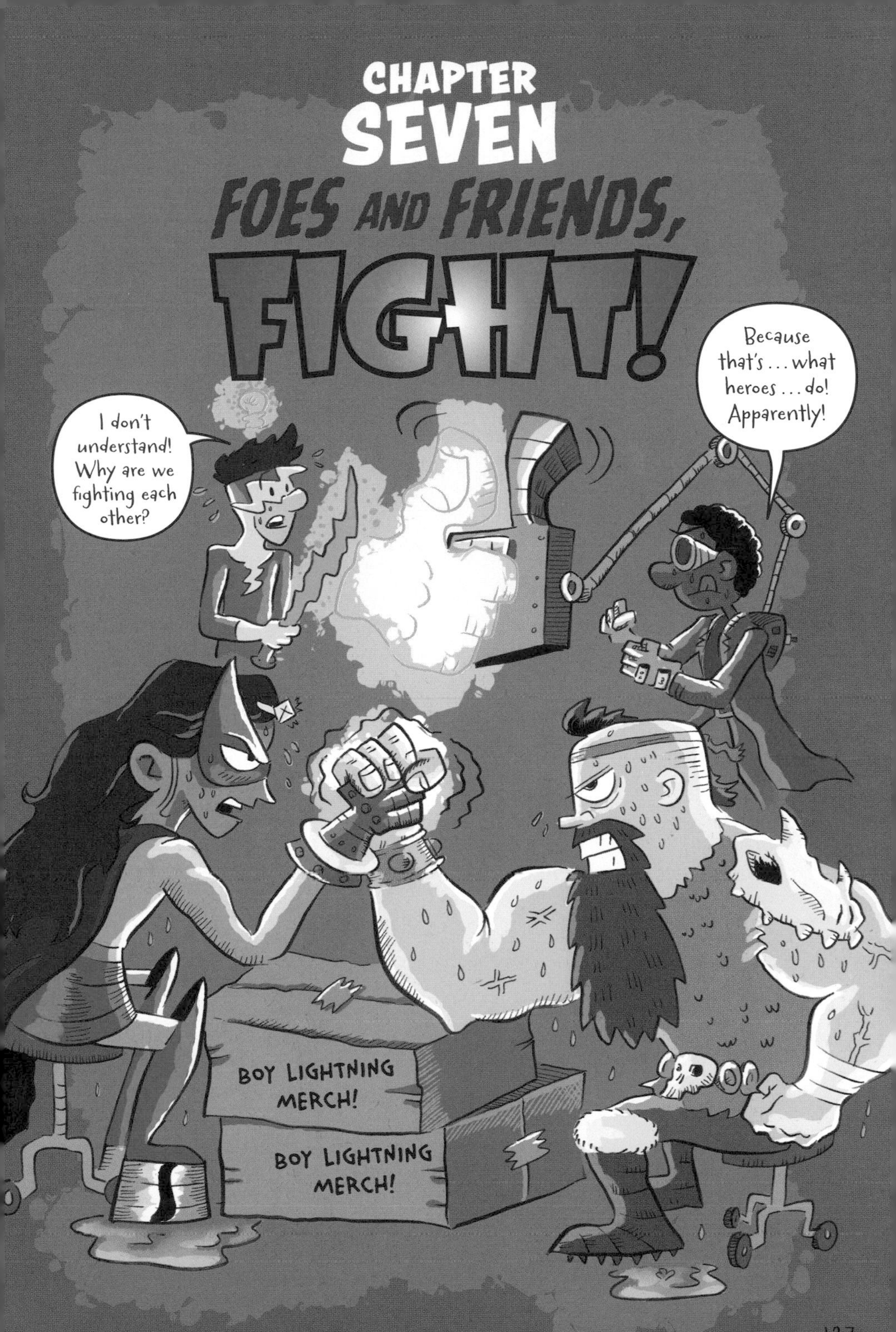
I don't understand! Why are we fighting each other?
Because that's . . . what heroes . . . do! Apparently!
BOY LIGHTNING MERCH!
BOY LIGHTNING MERCH!

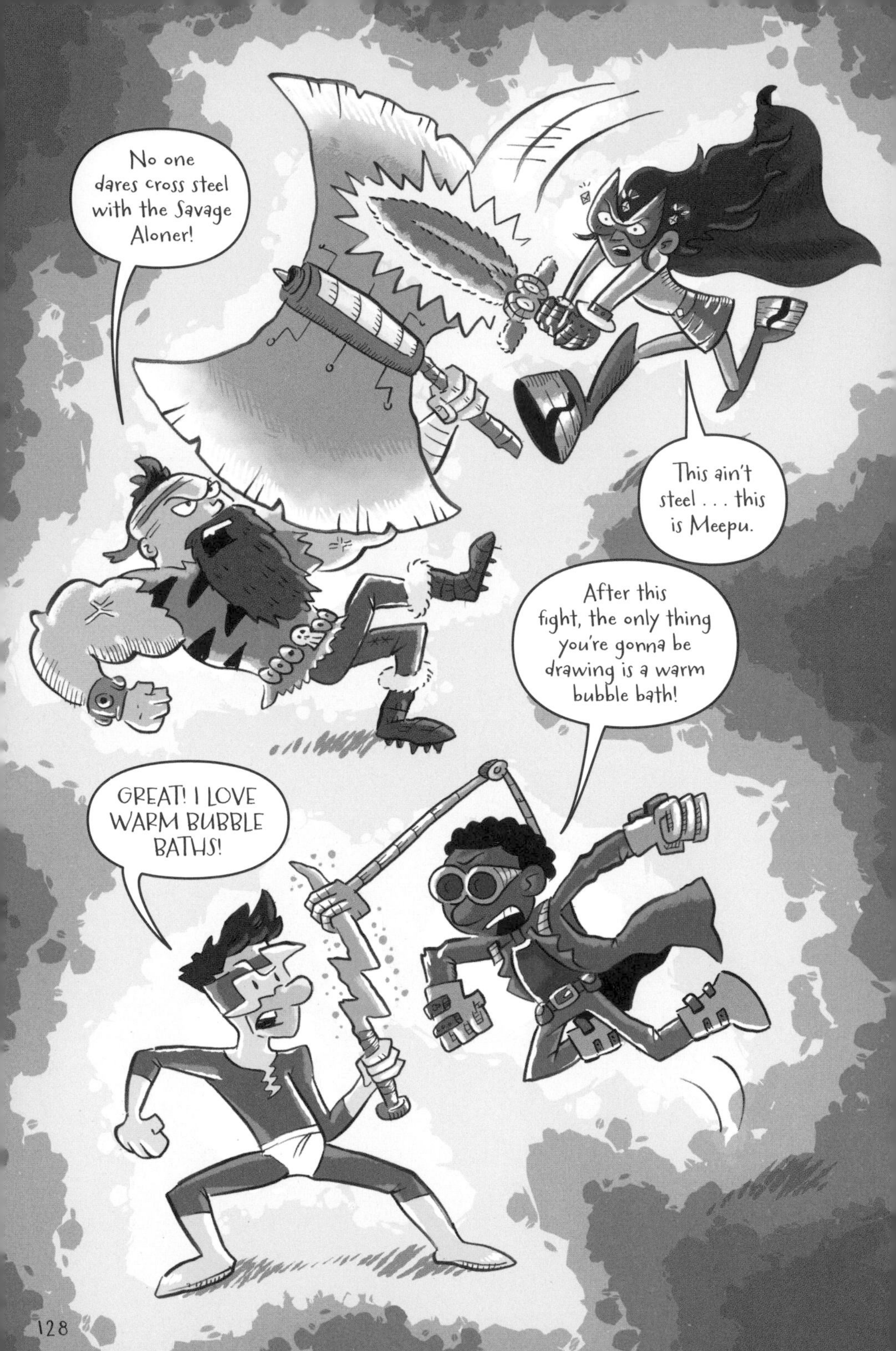
No one dares cross steel with the Savage Aloner!
This ain't steel . . . this is Meepu.
After this fight, the only thing you're gonna be drawing is a warm bubble bath!
GREAT! I LOVE WARM BUBBLE BATHS!

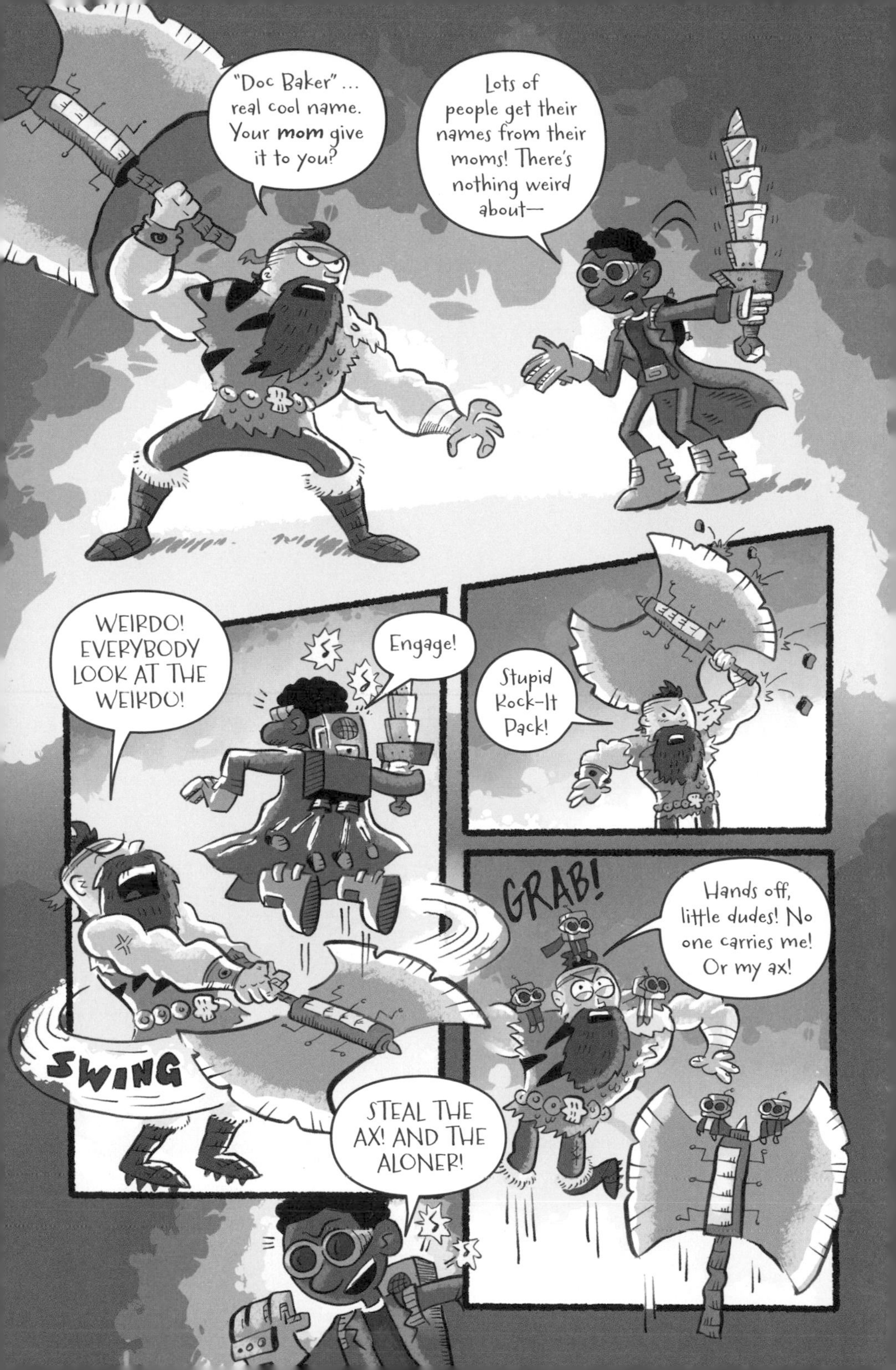
"Doc Baker" ... real cool name. Your **mom** give it to you?
Lots of people get their names from their moms! There's nothing weird about—
WEIRDO! EVERYBODY LOOK AT THE WEIRDO!
Engage!
Stupid Rock-It Pack!
SWING
GRAB!
Hands off, little dudes! No one carries me! Or my ax!
STEAL THE AX! AND THE ALONER!

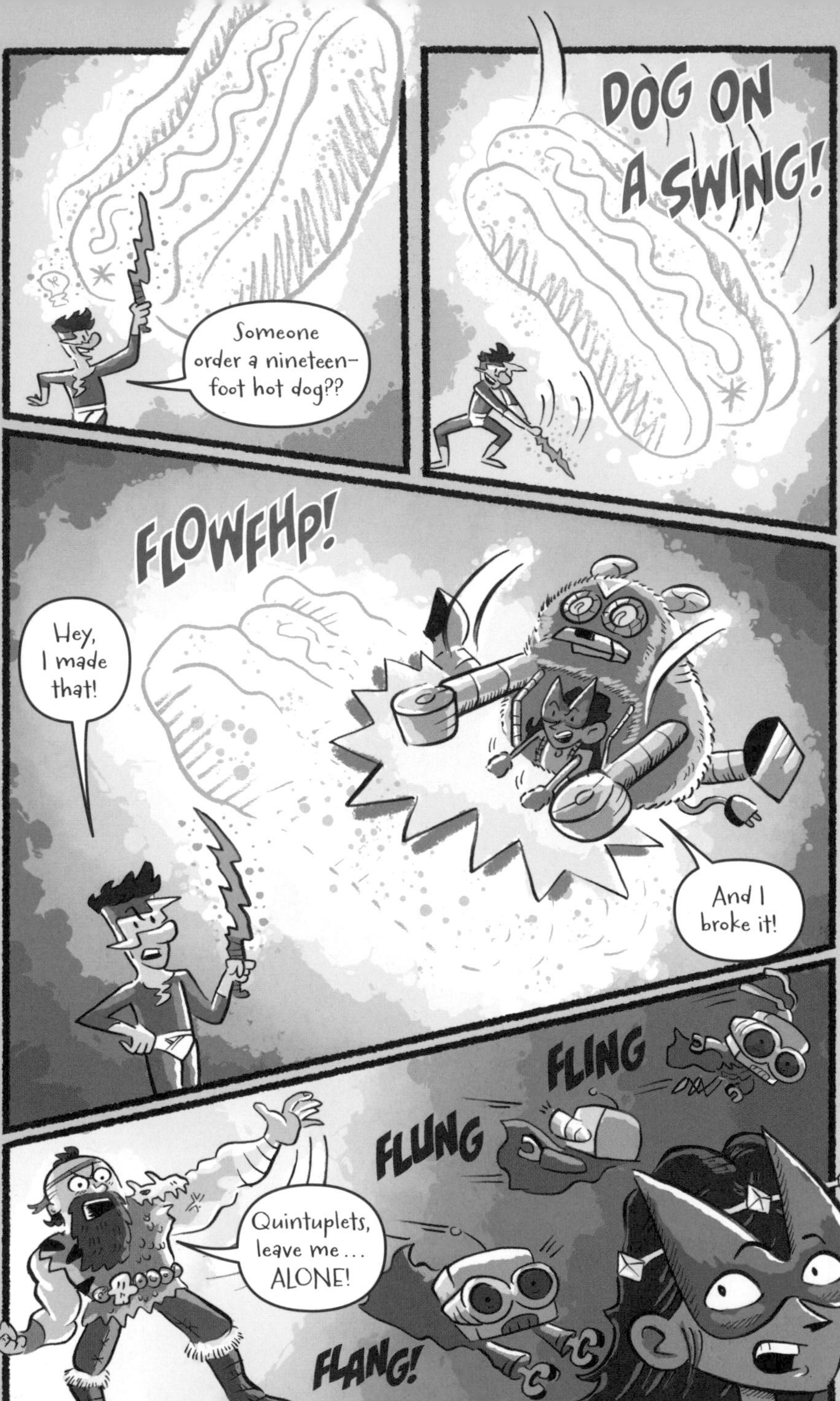
Someone order a nineteen-foot hot dog??
DOG ON A SWING!
FLOWFHP!
Hey, I made that!
And I broke it!
FLING
FLUNG
Quintuplets, leave me... ALONE!
FLANG!

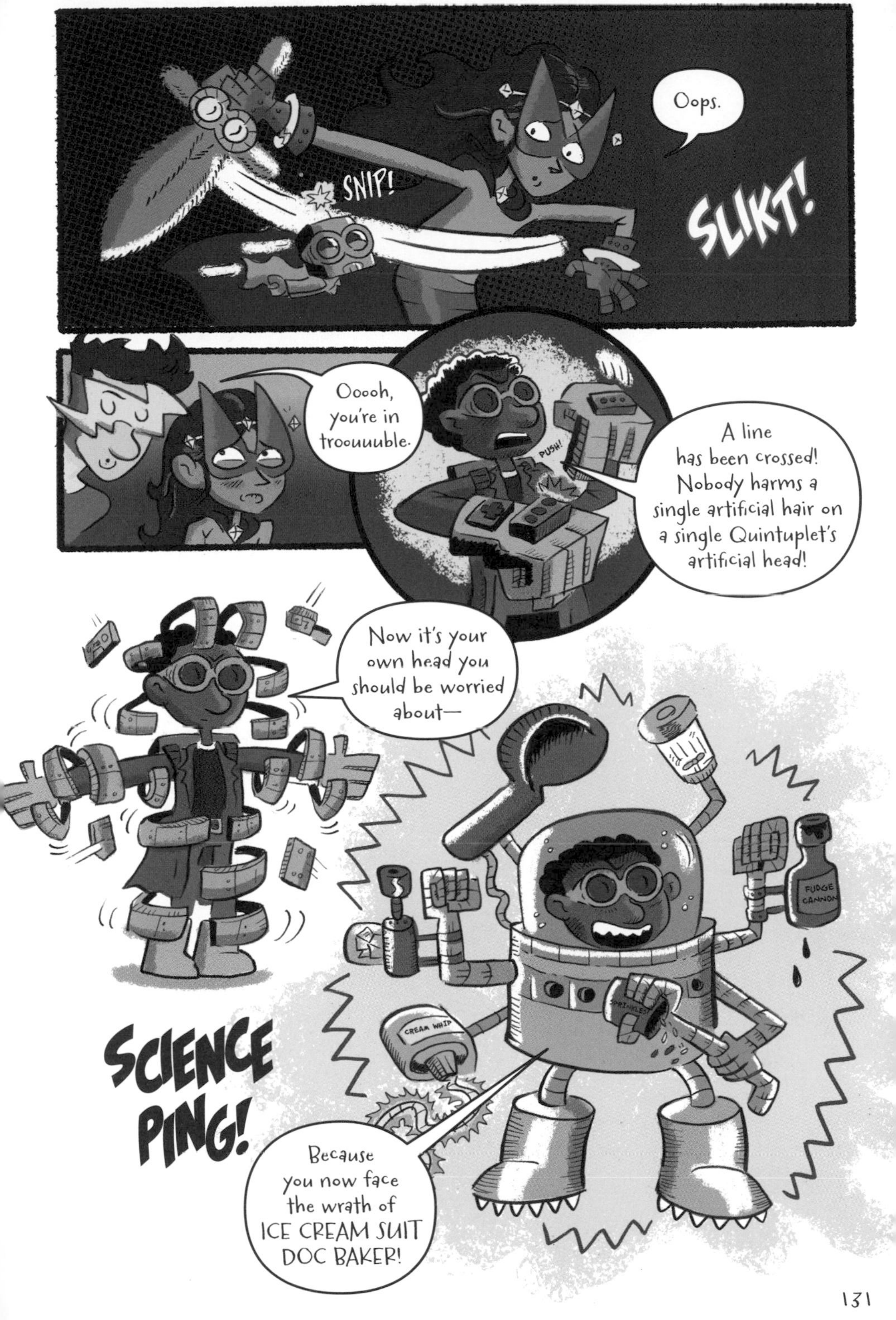

SNIP!
Oops.
SLIKT!
Ooooh, you're in troouuuble.
PUSH!
A line has been crossed! Nobody harms a single artificial hair on a single Quintuplet's artificial head!
Now it's your own head you should be worried about—
FUDGE CANNON
CREAM WHIP
SCIENCE PING!
Because you now face the wrath of ICE CREAM SUIT DOC BAKER!

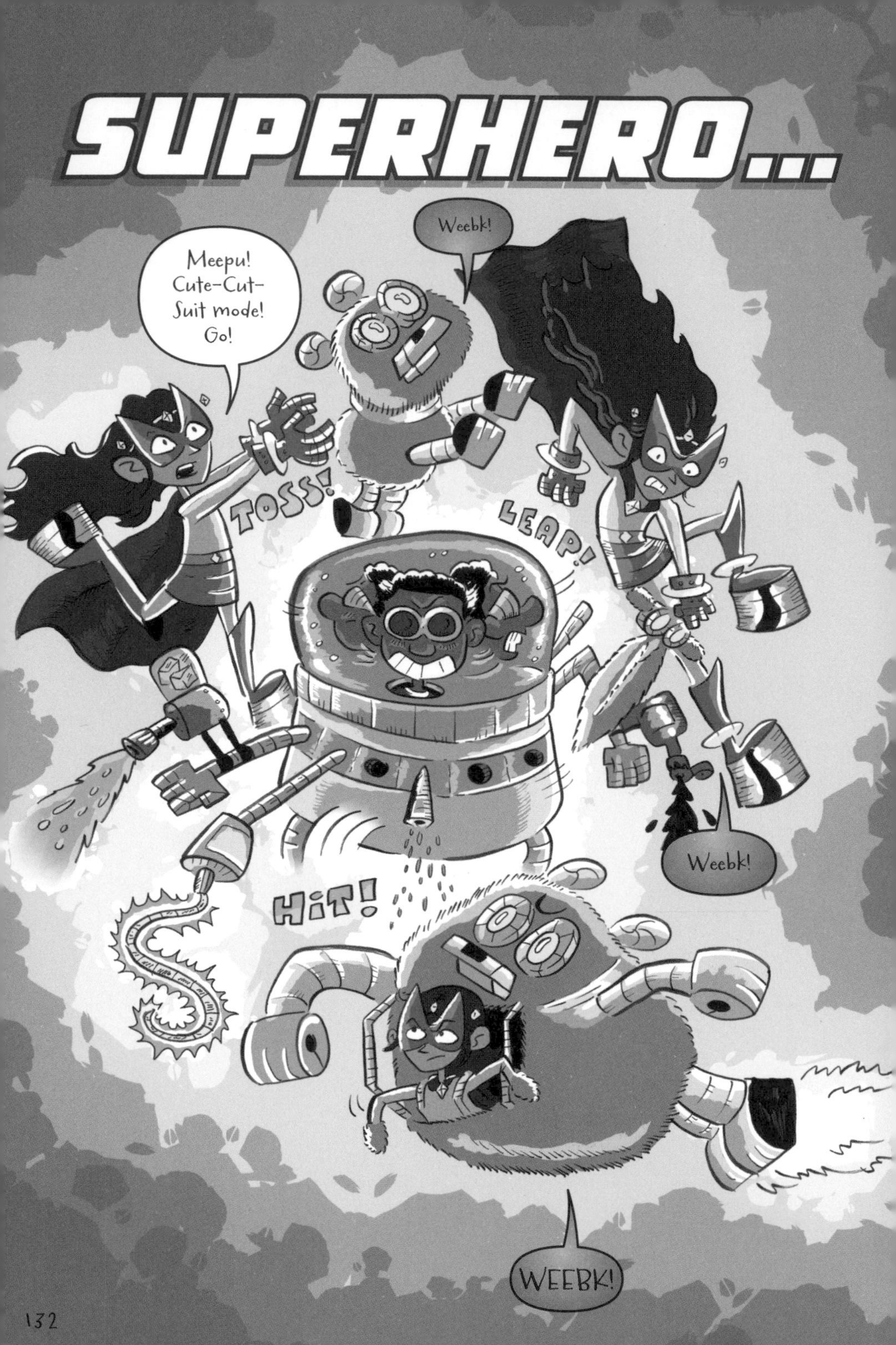
SUPERHERO...
Meepu! Cute-Cut-Suit mode! Go!
Weebk!
TOSS!
LEAP!
HIT!
Weebk!
WEEBK!

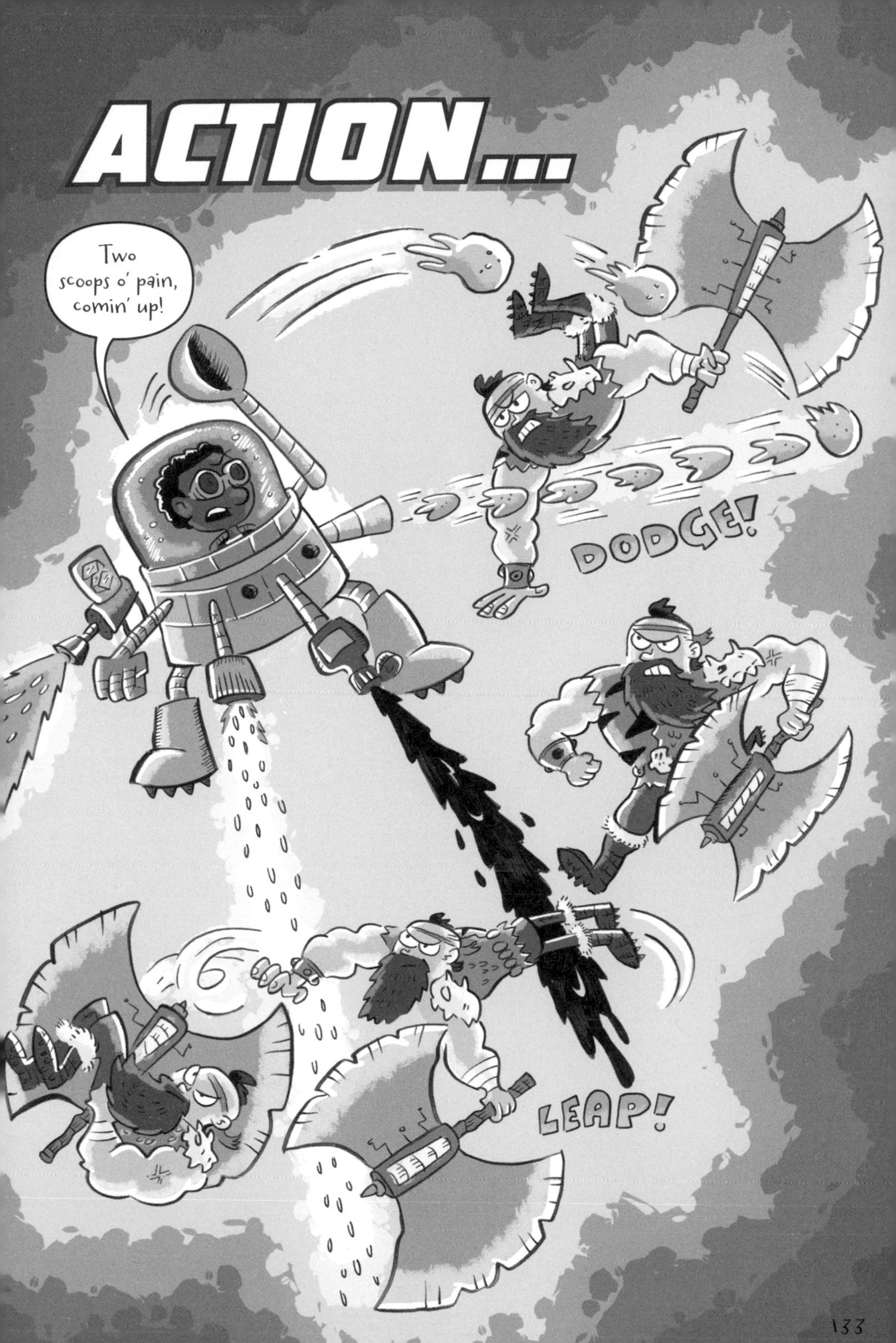
ACTION...
Two scoops o' pain, comin' up!
DODGE!
LEAP!

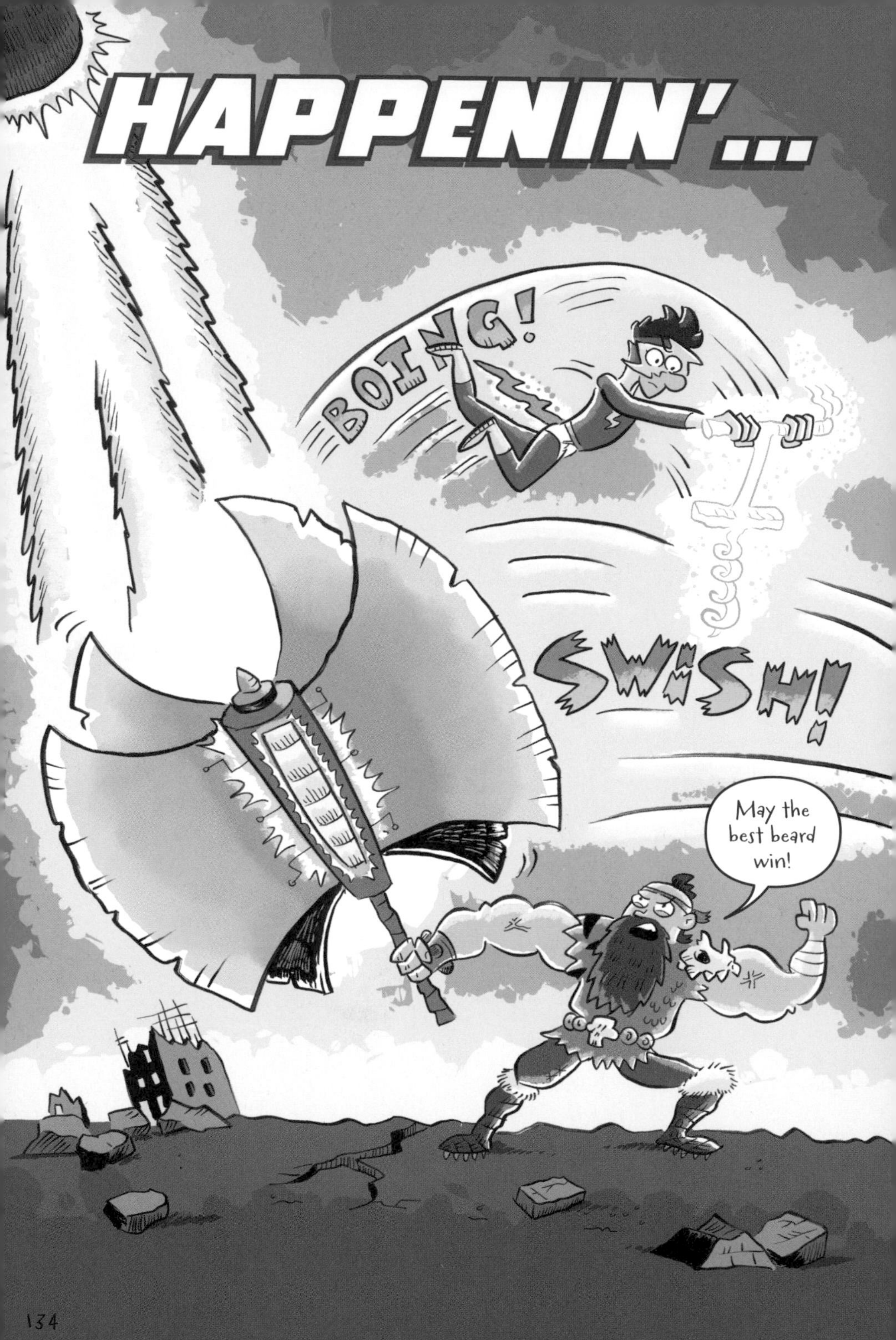
HAPPENIN'...
BOING!
SWISH!
May the best beard win!

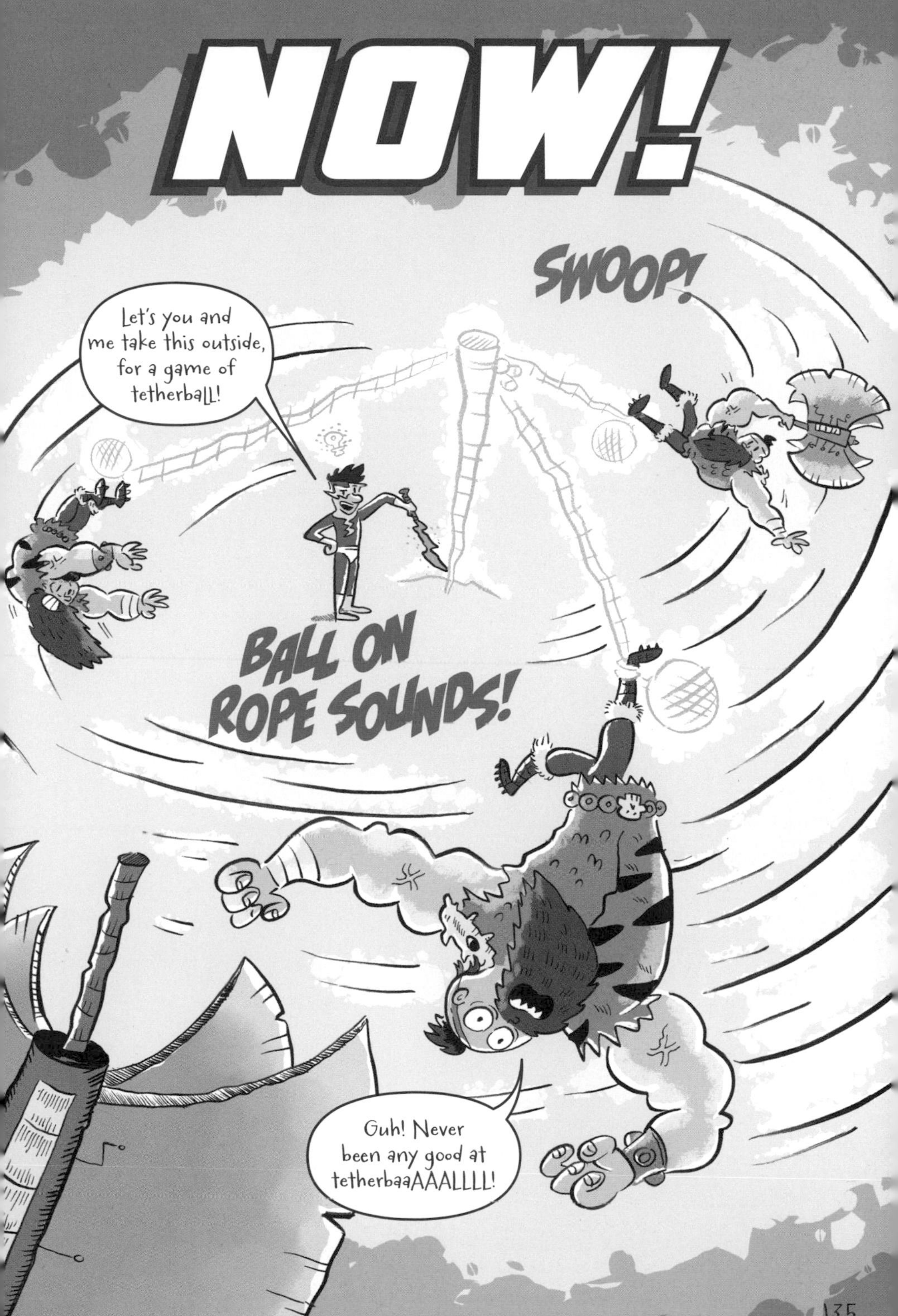
NOW!
SWOOP!
Let's you and me take this outside, for a game of tetherball!
BALL ON ROPE SOUNDS!
Guh! Never been any good at tetherbaaAAALLLL!

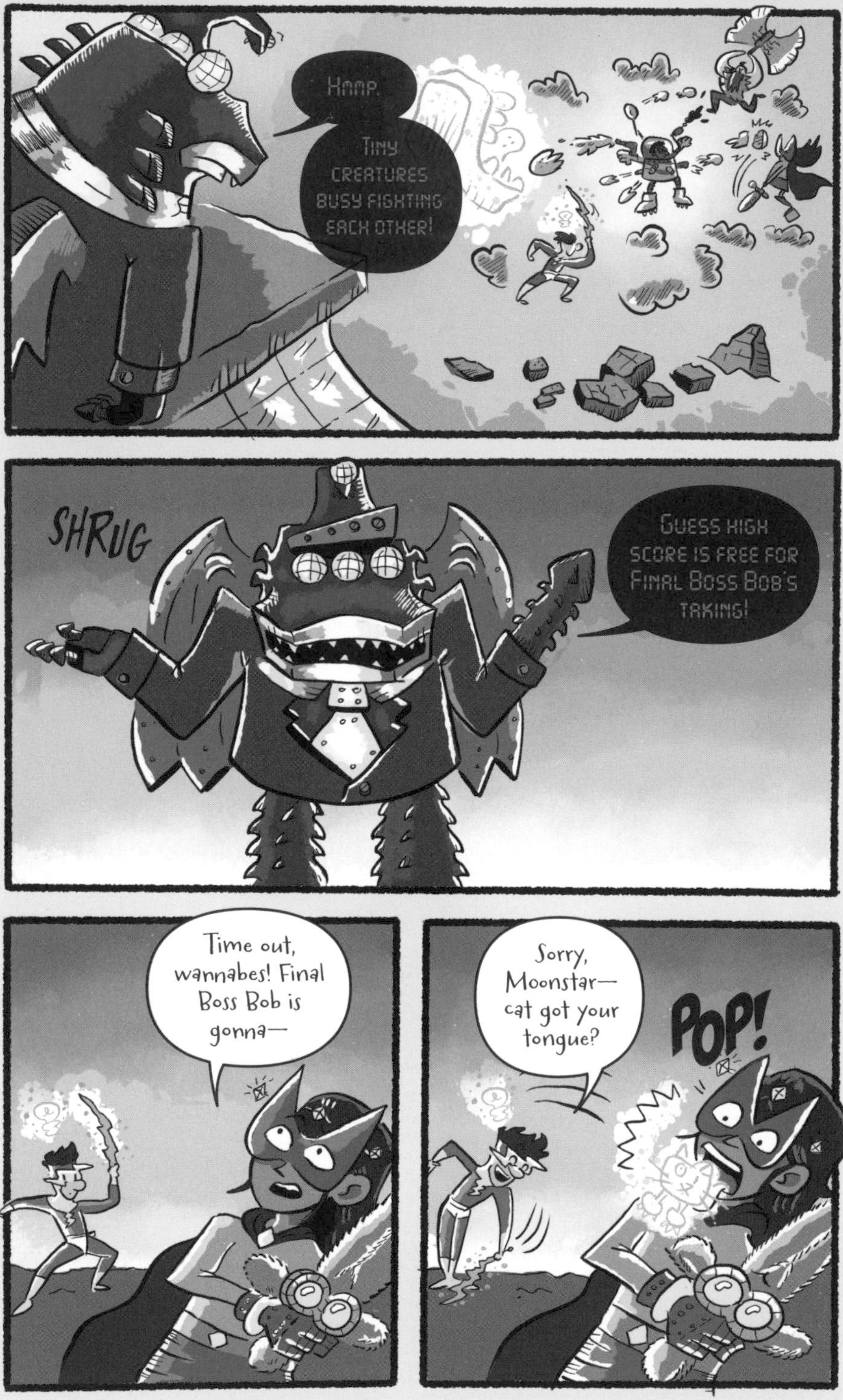
Hmmp.
Tiny creatures busy fighting each other!
SHRUG
Guess high score is free for Final Boss Bob's taking!
Time out, wannabes! Final Boss Bob is gonna—
Sorry, Moonstar— cat got your tongue?
POP!

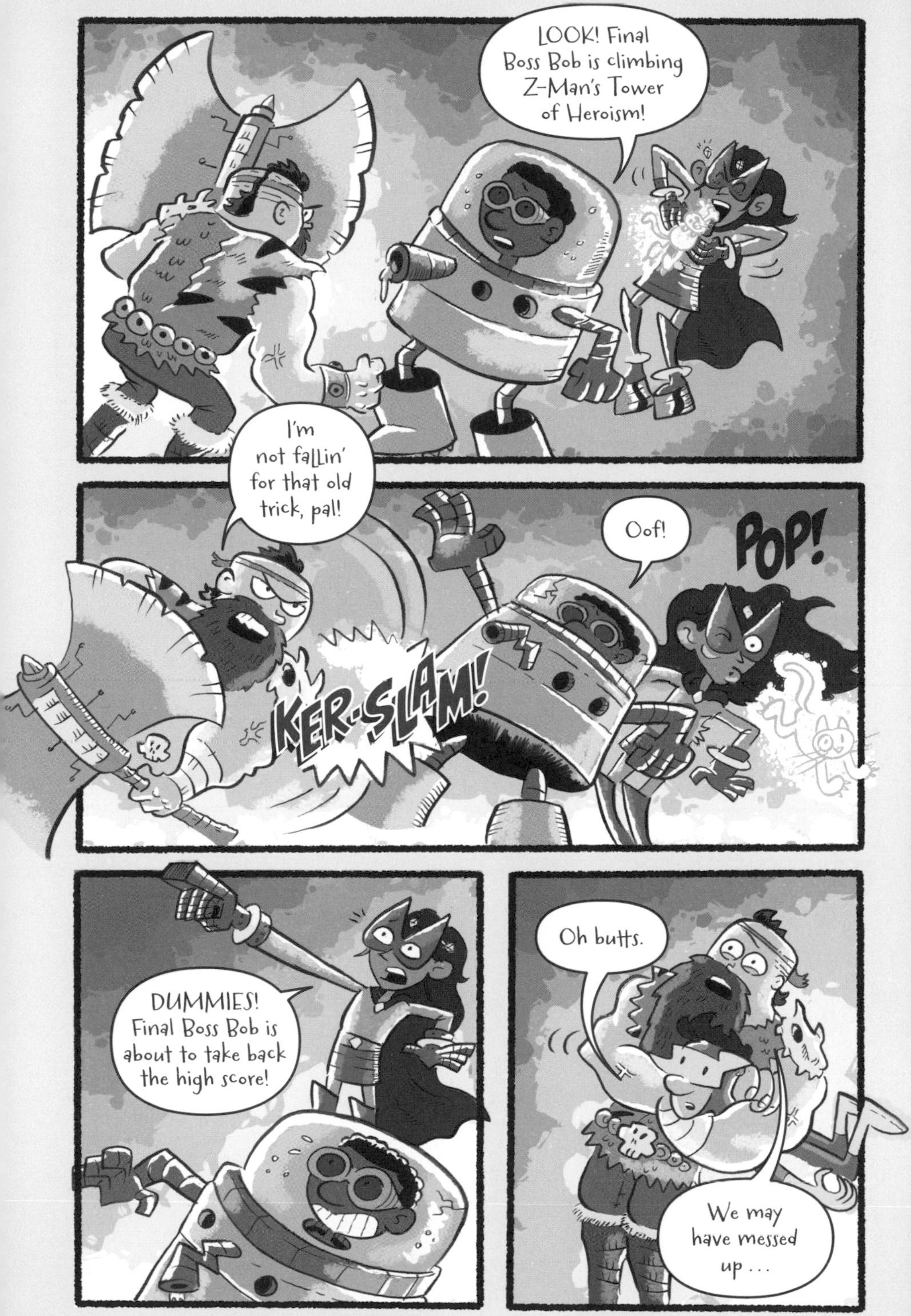
LOOK! Final Boss Bob is climbing Z-Man's Tower of Heroism!
I'm not fallin' for that old trick, pal!
Oof!
POP!
KER-SLAM!
DUMMIES! Final Boss Bob is about to take back the high score!
Oh butts.
We may have messed up . . .

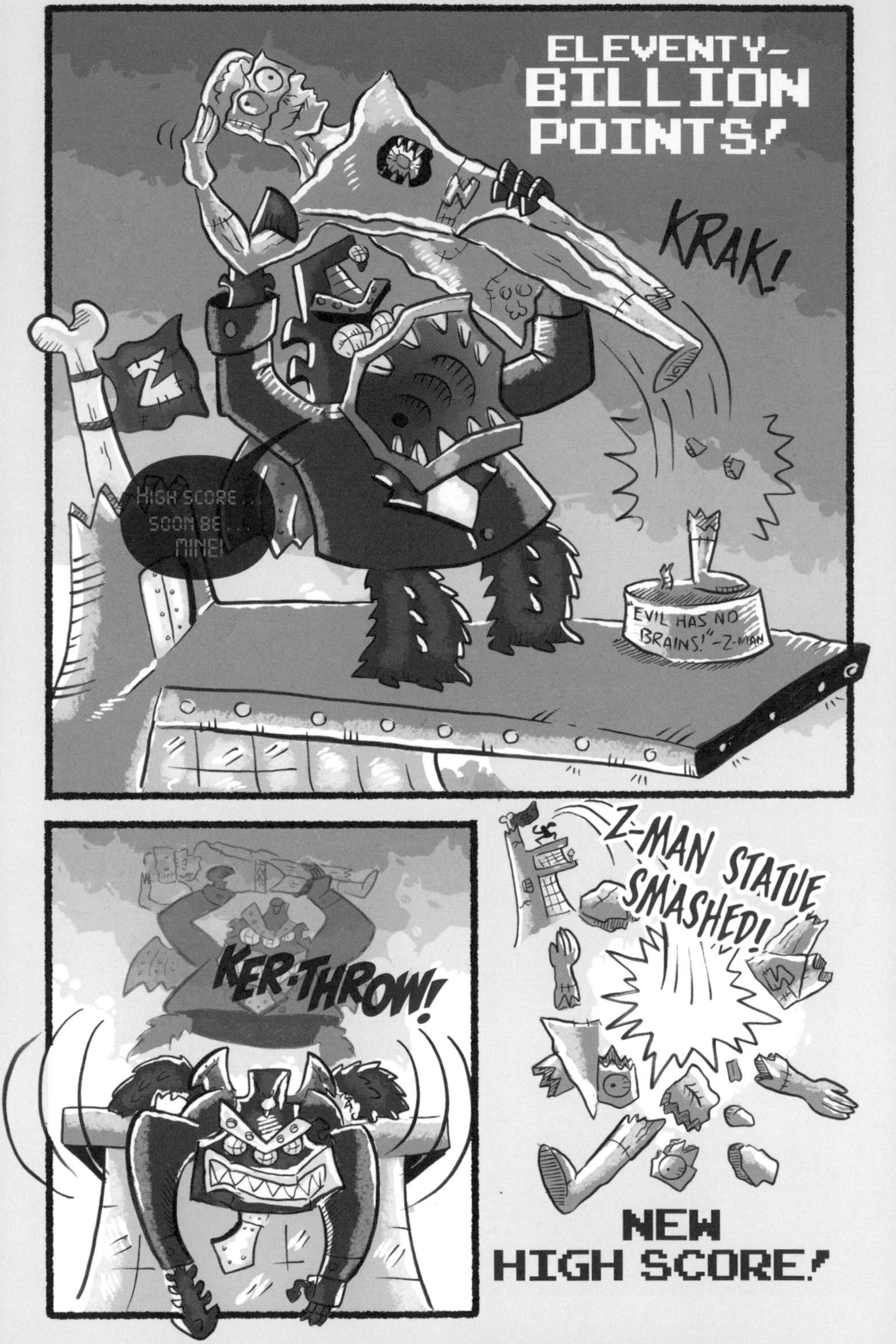
ELEVENTY-
BILLION
POINTS!
KRAK!
HIGH SCORE...
SOON BE...
MINE!
"EVIL HAS NO BRAINS!" -Z-MAN
KER-THROW!
Z-MAN STATUE
SMASHED!
NEW
HIGH SCORE!

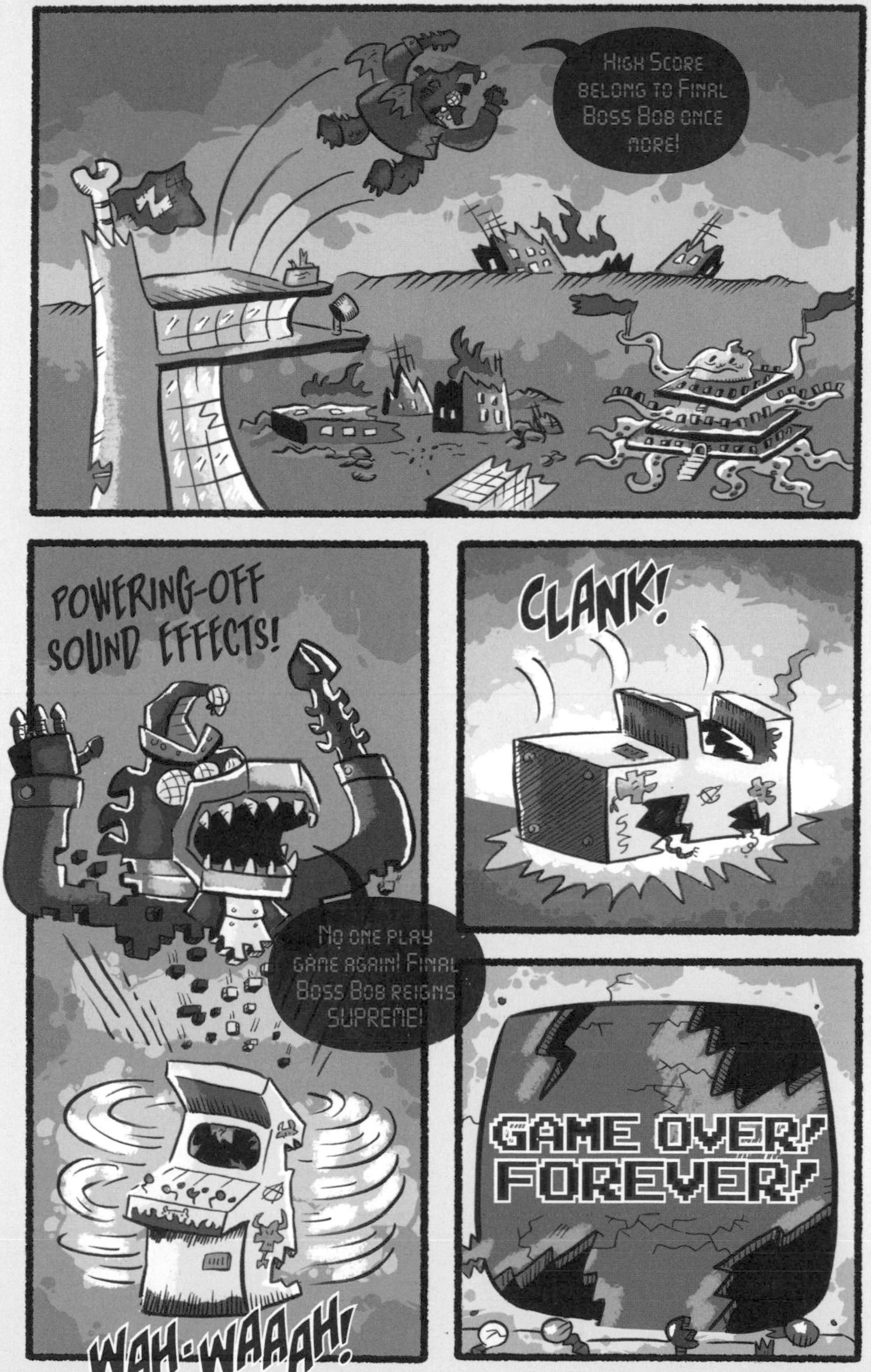
High Score belong to Final Boss Bob once more!
POWERING-OFF SOUND EFFECTS!
CLANK!
No one play game again! Final Boss Bob reigns supreme!
WAH-WAAAH!
GAME OVER! FOREVER!

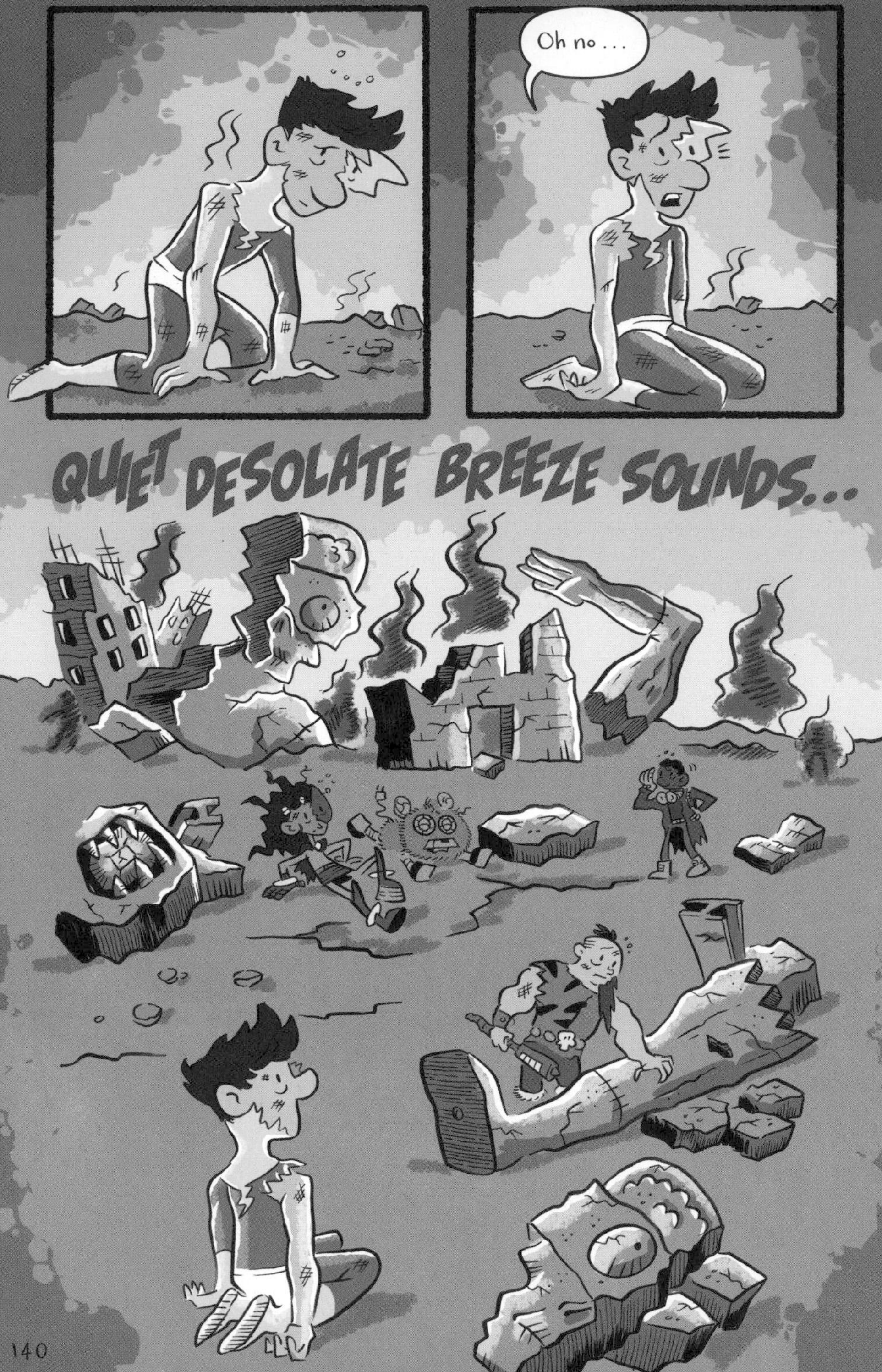
Oh no . . .
QUIET DESOLATE BREEZE SOUNDS...

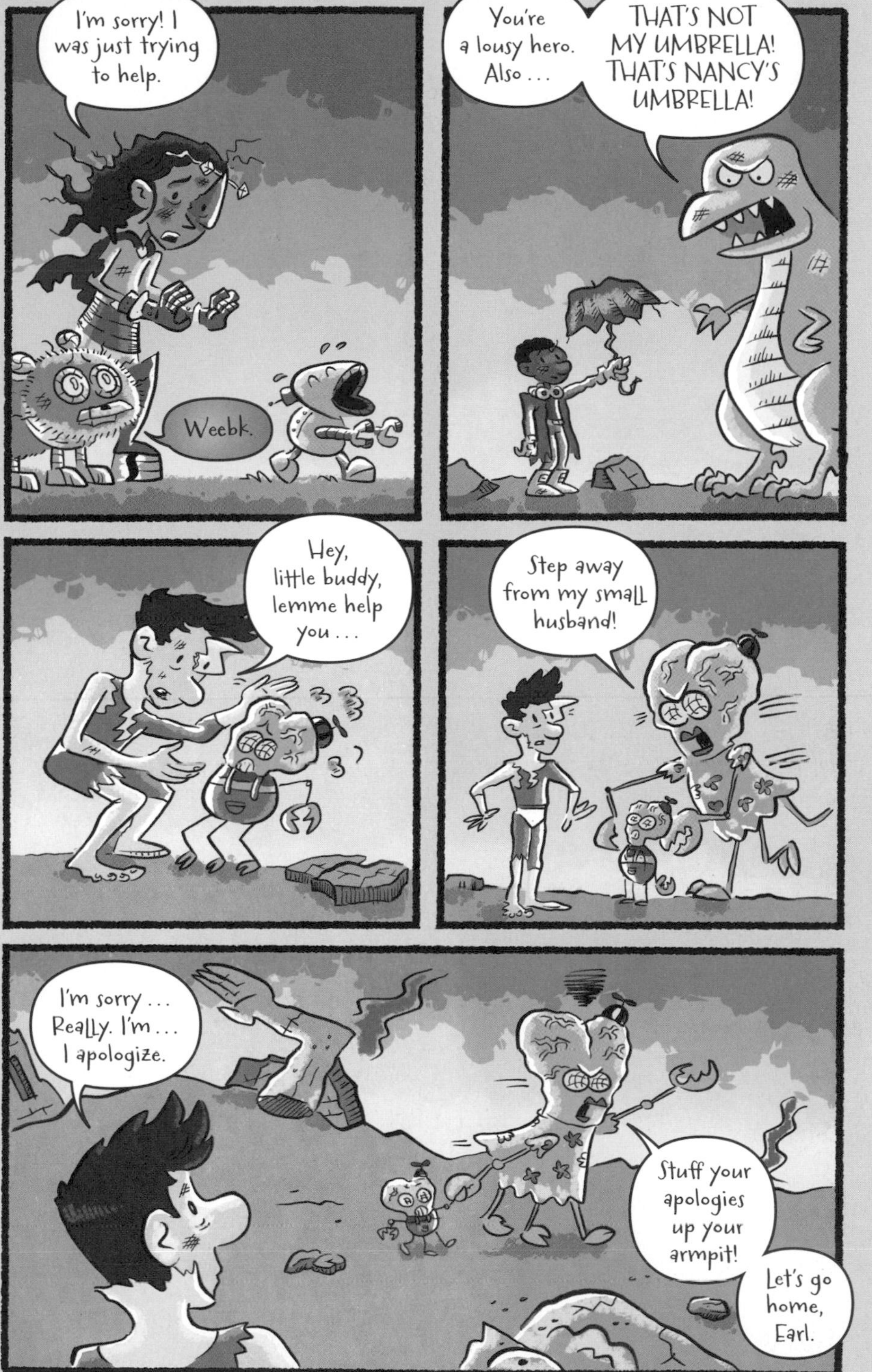
I'm sorry! I was just trying to help.
Weebk.
You're a lousy hero. Also . . .
THAT'S NOT MY UMBRELLA! THAT'S NANCY'S UMBRELLA!
Hey, little buddy, lemme help you . . .
Step away from my small husband!
I'm sorry . . . Really. I'm . . . I apologize.
Stuff your apologies up your armpit!
Let's go home, Earl.

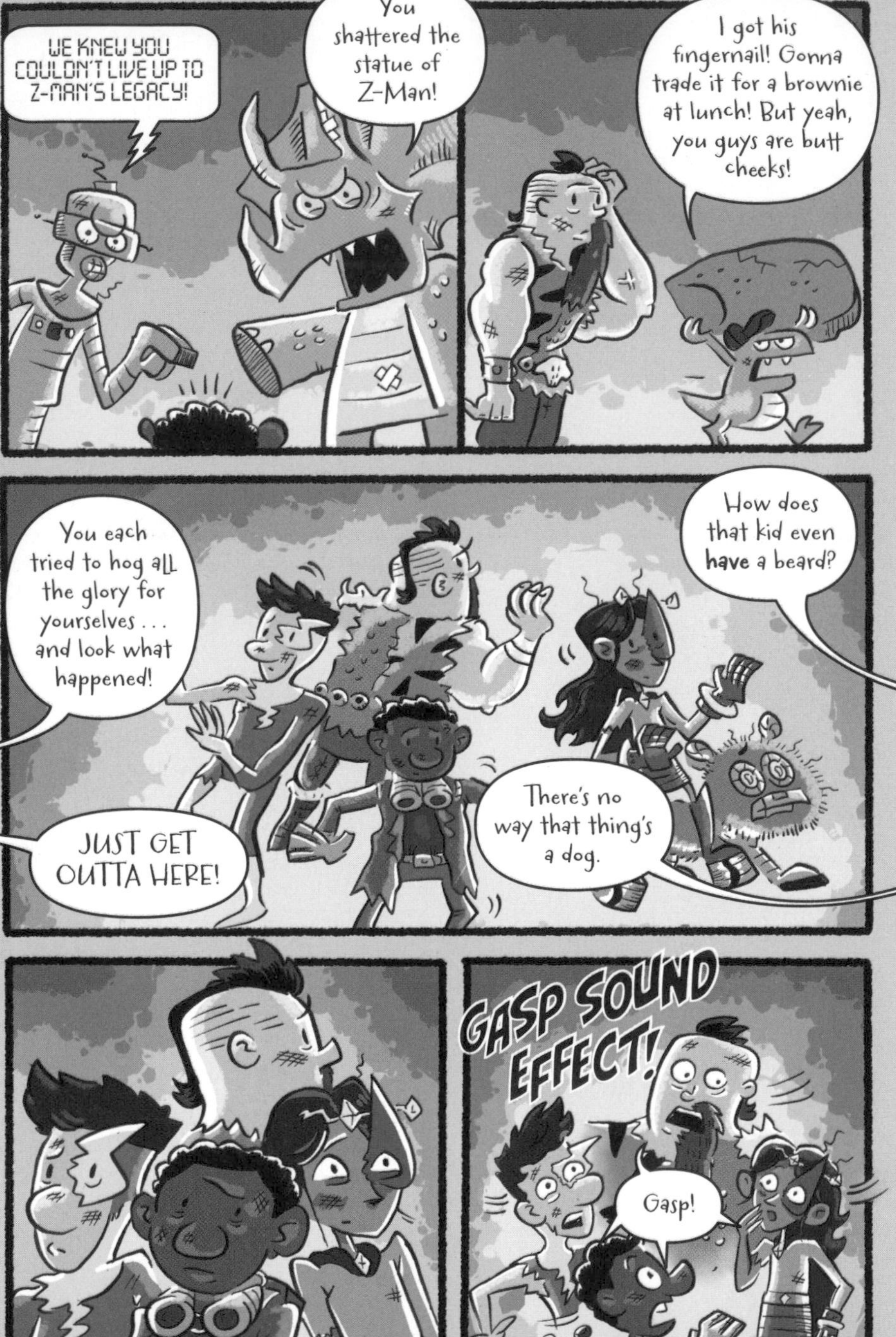
WE KNEW YOU COULDN'T LIVE UP TO Z-MAN'S LEGACY!
You shattered the statue of Z-Man!
I got his fingernail! Gonna trade it for a brownie at lunch! But yeah, you guys are butt cheeks!
You each tried to hog all the glory for yourselves . . . and look what happened!
How does that kid even **have** a beard?
JUST GET OUTTA HERE!
There's no way that thing's a dog.
GASP SOUND EFFECT!
Gasp!

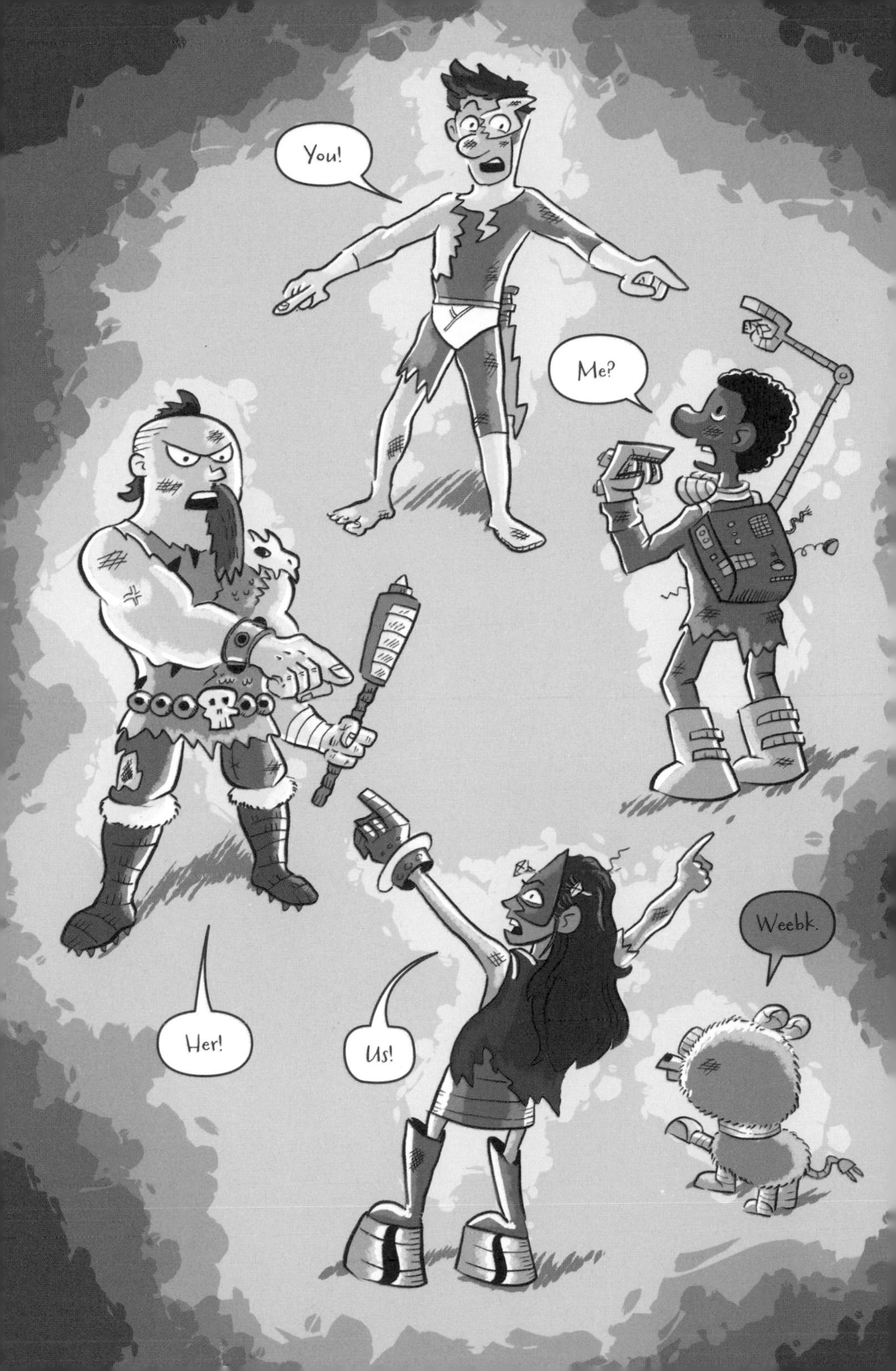
You!
Me?
Her!
Us!
Weebk.

MORE SAVAGE ALONER THAN YOU CAN SHAKE AN AX AT!

CATCH UP ON YOUR SUMMER READING WITH THESE SAVAGE BACKLIST TITLES!

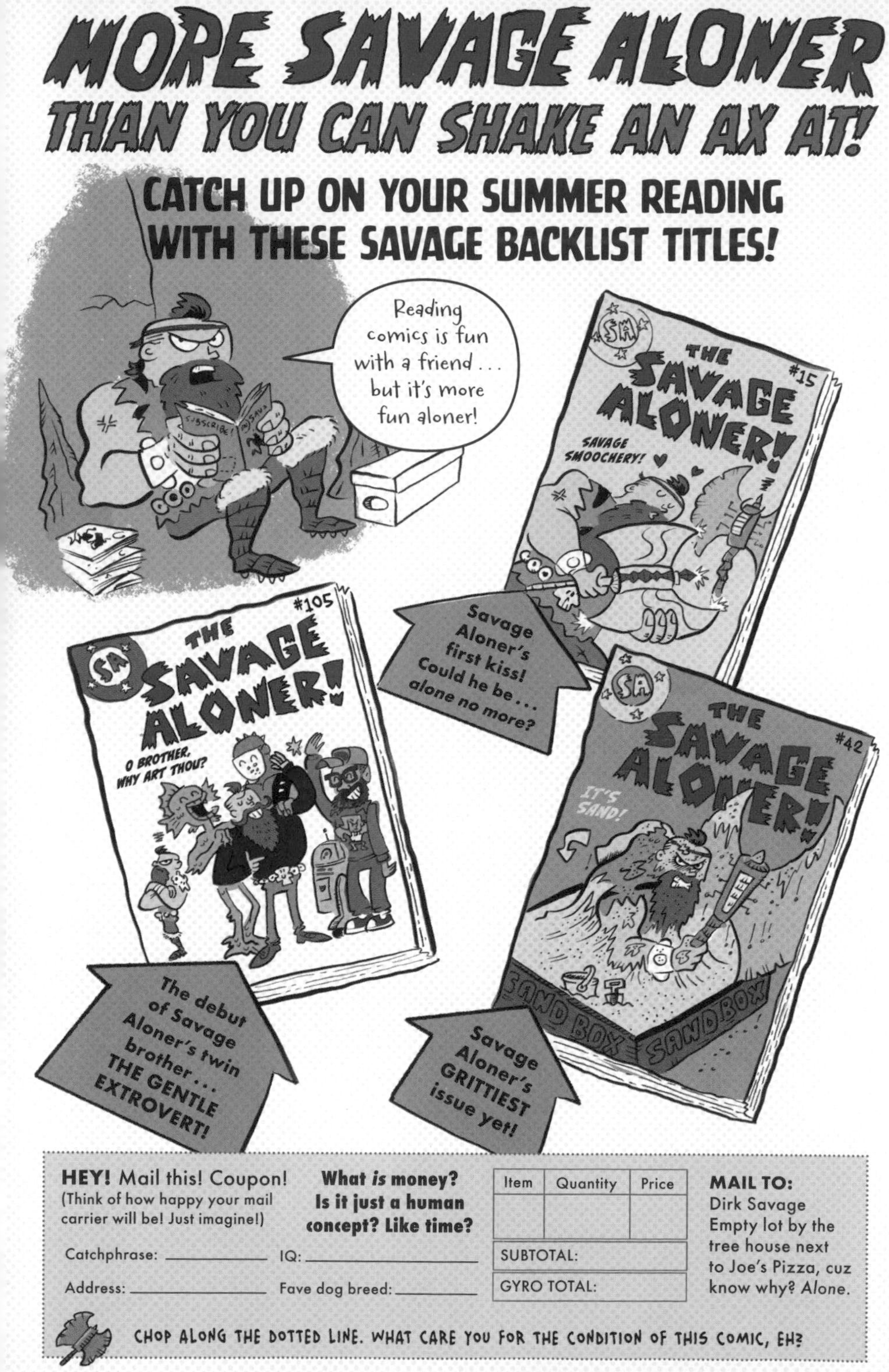

Reading comics is fun with a friend . . . but it's more fun aloner!
SUBSCRIBE!
THE SAVAGE ALONER!
#15
SAVAGE SMOOCHERY!
Savage Aloner's first kiss! Could he be . . . alone no more?
#105
THE SAVAGE ALONER!
O BROTHER, WHY ART THOU?
The debut of Savage Aloner's twin brother . . . THE GENTLE EXTROVERT!
THE SAVAGE ALONER!
#42
IT'S SAND!
SAND BOX
SAND BOX
Savage Aloner's GRITTIEST issue yet!

HEY! Mail this! Coupon!
(Think of how happy your mail carrier will be! Just imagine!)

What *is* money? Is it just a human concept? Like time?

Catchphrase: ______________ IQ: ______________

Address: ______________ Fave dog breed: ______________

Item	Quantity	Price
SUBTOTAL:		
GYRO TOTAL:		

MAIL TO:
Dirk Savage
Empty lot by the tree house next to Joe's Pizza, cuz know why? Alone.

CHOP ALONG THE DOTTED LINE. WHAT CARE YOU FOR THE CONDITION OF THIS COMIC, EH?

CHAPTER EIGHT

SECRETS UNVEILED! HEROES UNMASKED!

HEROES HAVING AWKWARD CONVERSATIONS!

HEROES LYING TO THEIR FRIENDS! SCANDAL!

TALKING DOGS WHO ARE SO OVER IT!

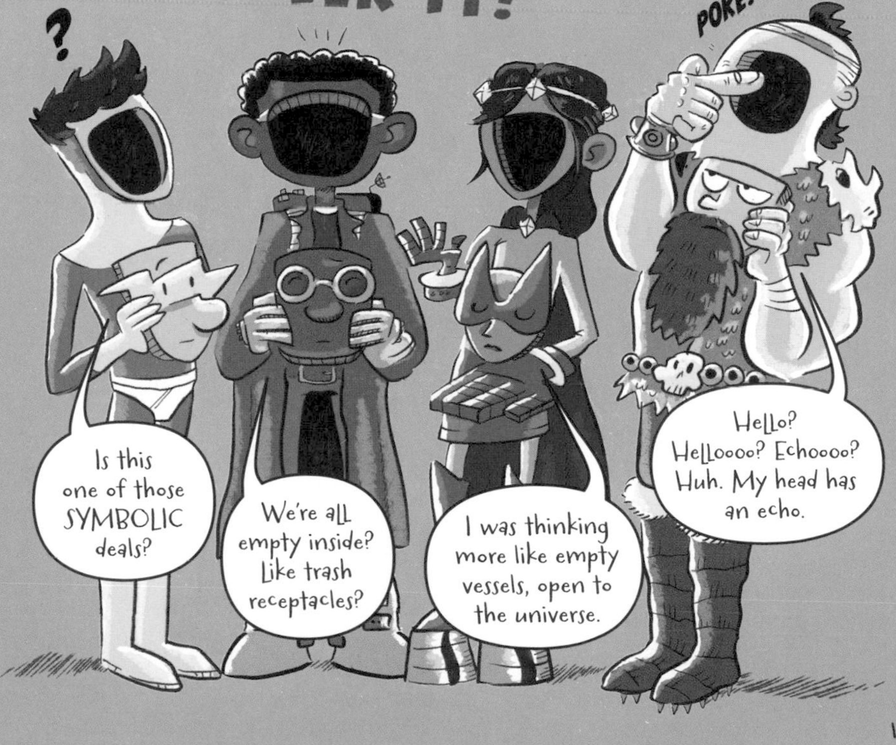
?
POKE!
Is this one of those SYMBOLIC deals?
We're all empty inside? Like trash receptacles?
I was thinking more like empty vessels, open to the universe.
Hello? Hellოooo? Echoooo? Huh. My head has an echo.

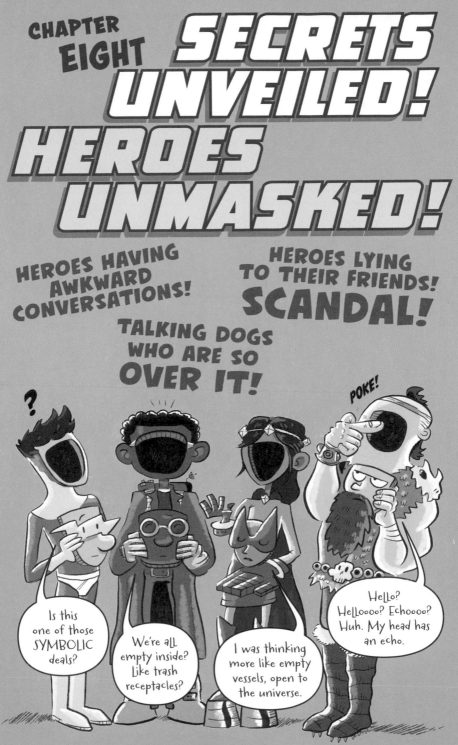

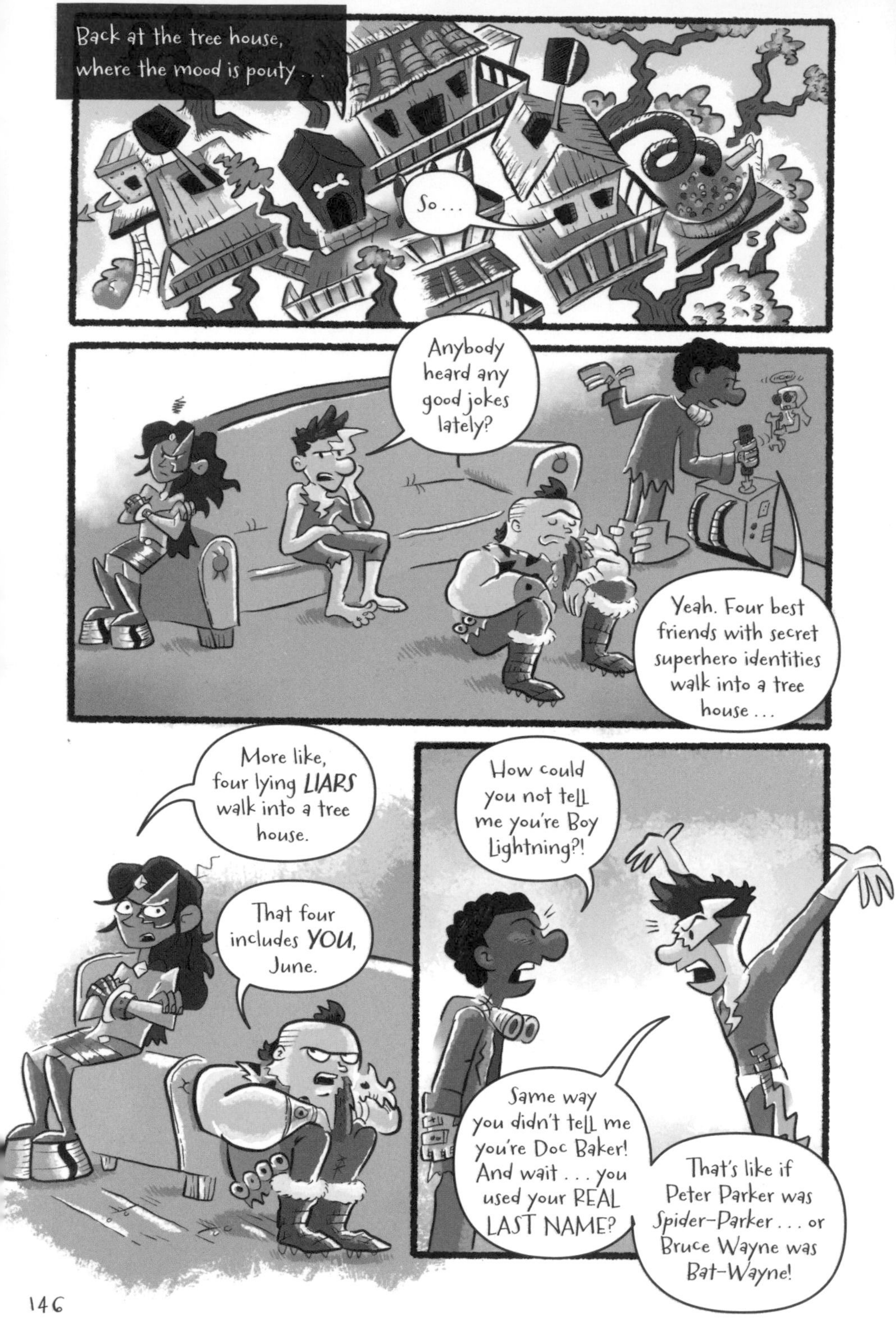
Back at the tree house, where the mood is pouty . . .
So . . .
Anybody heard any good jokes lately?
Yeah. Four best friends with secret superhero identities walk into a tree house . . .
More like, four lying **LIARS** walk into a tree house.
That four includes **YOU**, June.
How could you not tell me you're Boy Lightning?!
Same way you didn't tell me you're Doc Baker! And wait . . . you used your REAL LAST NAME?
That's like if Peter Parker was Spider-Parker . . . or Bruce Wayne was Bat-Wayne!

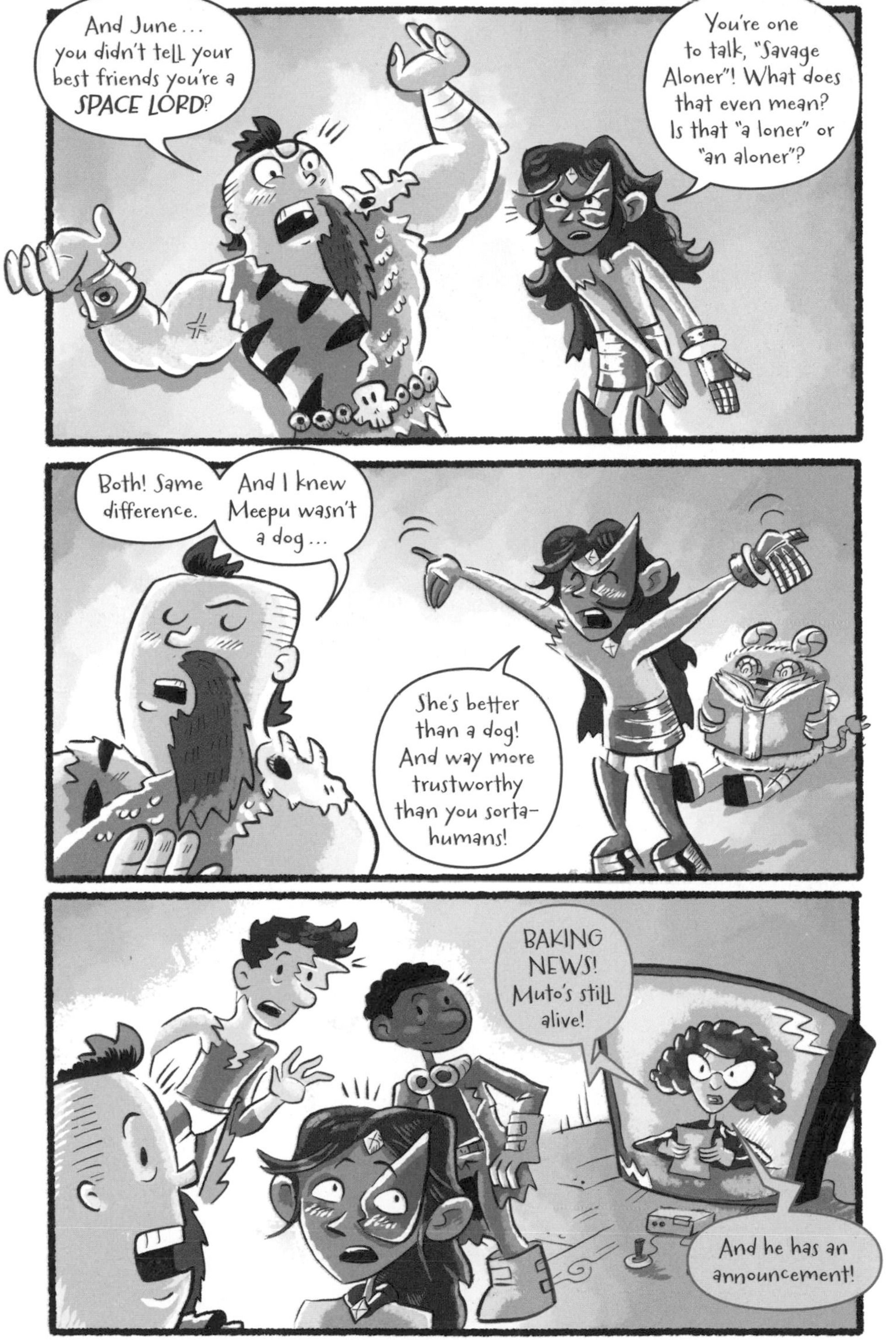
And June... you didn't tell your best friends you're a SPACE LORD?
You're one to talk, "Savage Aloner"! What does that even mean? Is that "a loner" or "an aloner"?
Both! Same difference.
And I knew Meepu wasn't a dog...
She's better than a dog! And way more trustworthy than you sorta-humans!
BAKING NEWS! Muto's still alive!
And he has an announcement!

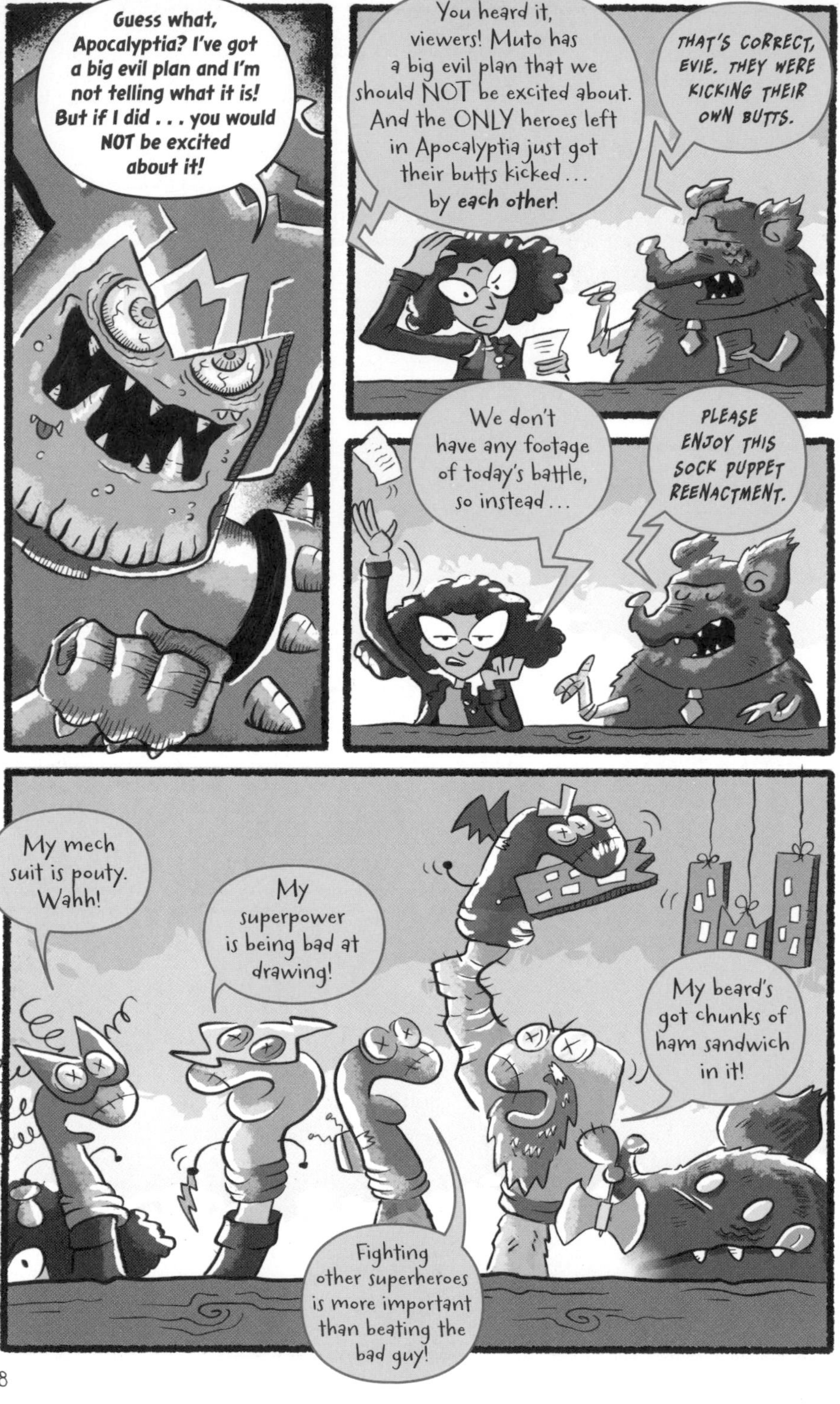

Guess what, Apocalyptia? I've got a big evil plan and I'm not telling what it is! But if I did . . . you would NOT be excited about it!
You heard it, viewers! Muto has a big evil plan that we should NOT be excited about. And the ONLY heroes left in Apocalyptia just got their butts kicked . . . by each other!
THAT'S CORRECT, EVIE. THEY WERE KICKING THEIR OWN BUTTS.
We don't have any footage of today's battle, so instead . . .
PLEASE ENJOY THIS SOCK PUPPET REENACTMENT.
My mech suit is pouty. Wahh!
My superpower is being bad at drawing!
Fighting other superheroes is more important than beating the bad guy!
My beard's got chunks of ham sandwich in it!

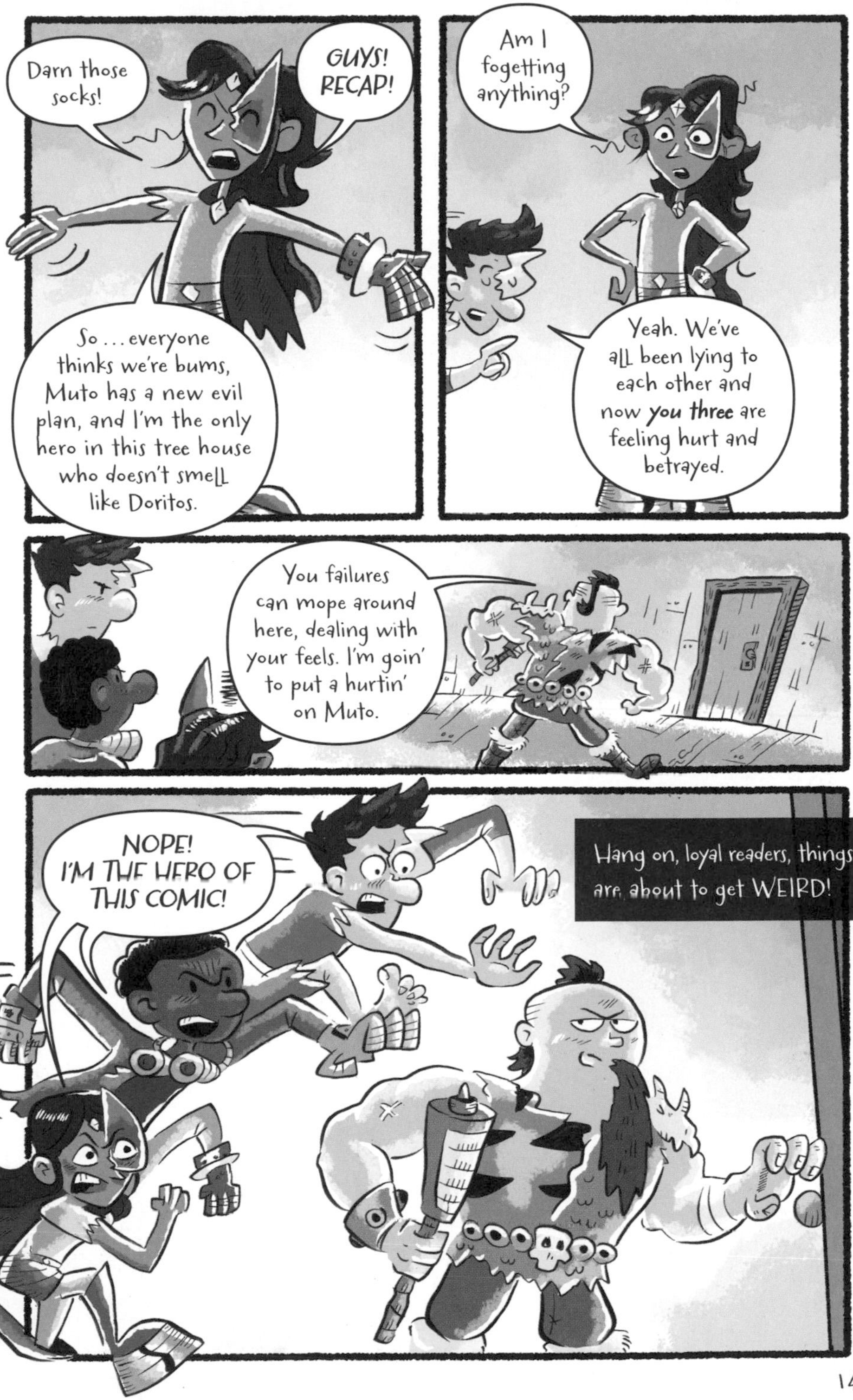
Darn those socks!
GUYS! RECAP!
So . . . everyone thinks we're bums, Muto has a new evil plan, and I'm the only hero in this tree house who doesn't smell like Doritos.
Am I fogetting anything?
Yeah. We've all been lying to each other and now **you three** are feeling hurt and betrayed.
You failures can mope around here, dealing with your feels. I'm goin' to put a hurtin' on Muto.
NOPE! I'M THE HERO OF THIS COMIC!
Hang on, loyal readers, things are about to get WEIRD!

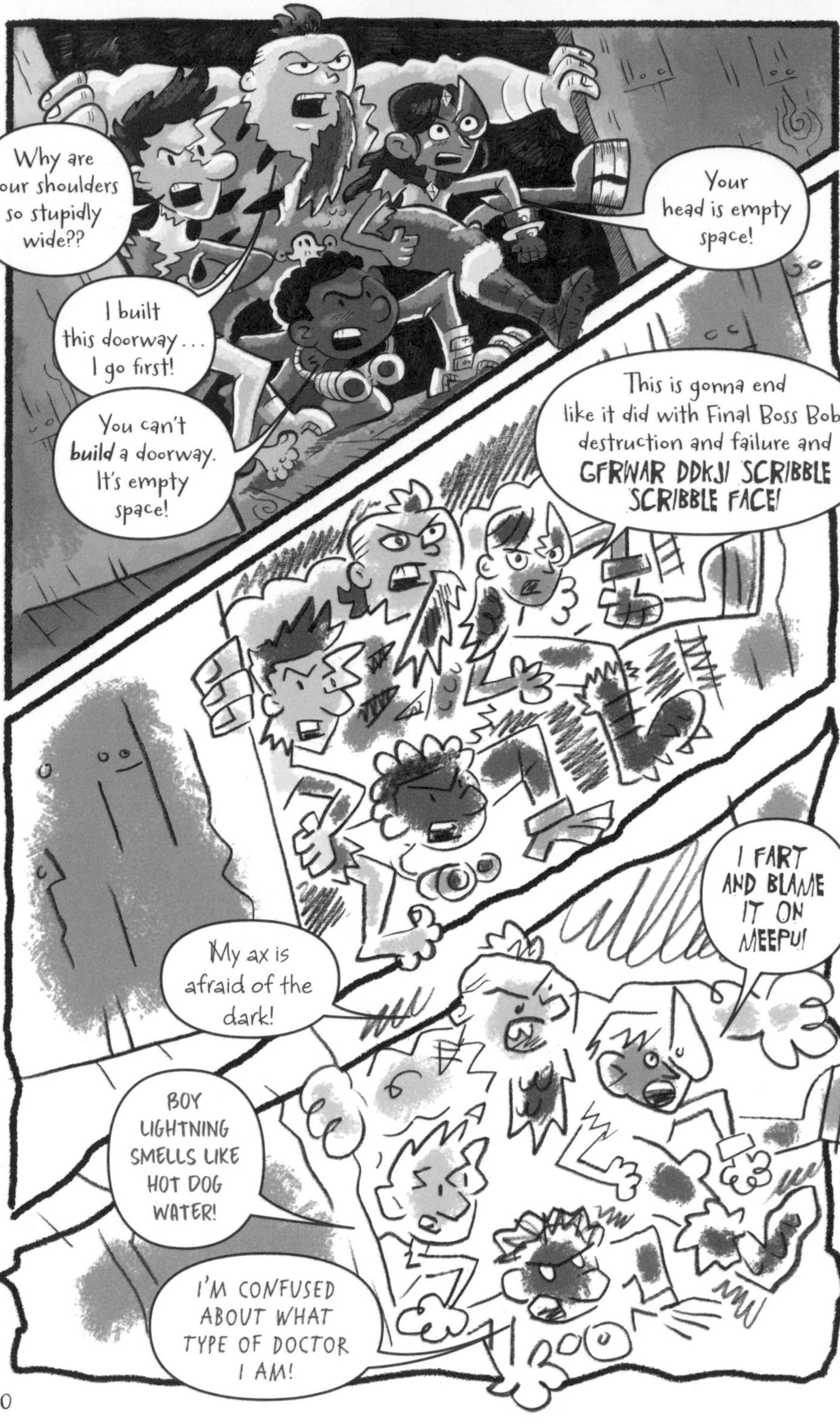
Why are your shoulders so stupidly wide??
Your head is empty space!
I built this doorway . . . I go first!
You can't **build** a doorway. It's empty space!
This is gonna end like it did with Final Boss Bob: destruction and failure and GFRWAR DDKJ! SCRIBBLE SCRIBBLE FACE!
I FART AND BLAME IT ON MEEPU!
My ax is afraid of the dark!
BOY LIGHTNING SMELLS LIKE HOT DOG WATER!
I'M CONFUSED ABOUT WHAT TYPE OF DOCTOR I AM!

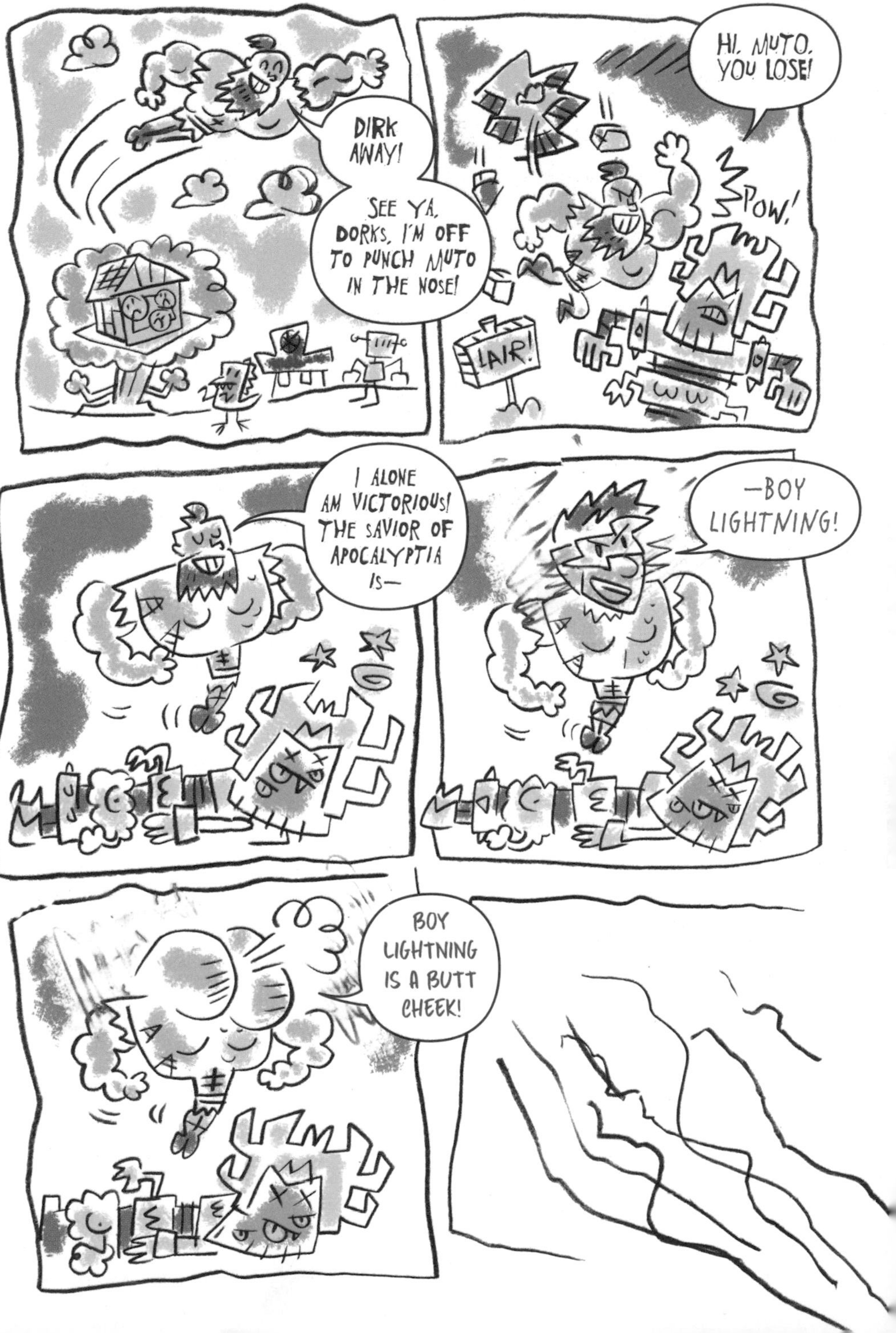
DIRK AWAY!
SEE YA, DORKS, I'M OFF TO PUNCH MUTO IN THE NOSE!
HI, MUTO. YOU LOSE!
POW!
LAIR!
I ALONE AM VICTORIOUS! THE SAVIOR OF APOCALYPTIA IS—
—BOY LIGHTNING!
BOY LIGHTNING IS A BUTT CHEEK!

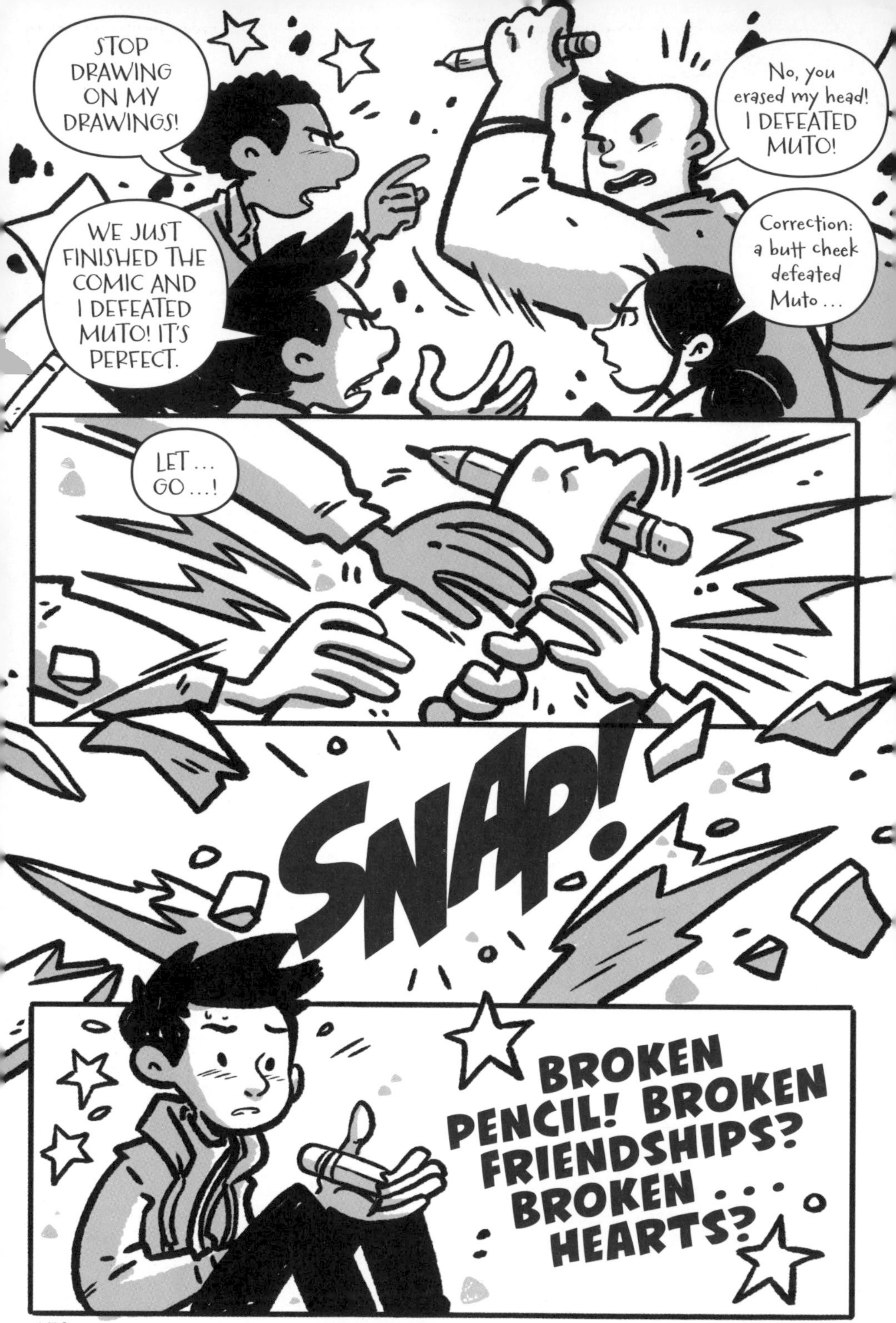
STOP DRAWING ON MY DRAWINGS!
No, you erased my head! I DEFEATED MUTO!
WE JUST FINISHED THE COMIC AND I DEFEATED MUTO! IT'S PERFECT.
Correction: a butt cheek defeated Muto . . .
LET . . . GO . . .!
SNAP!
BROKEN PENCIL! BROKEN FRIENDSHIPS? BROKEN . . . HEARTS?

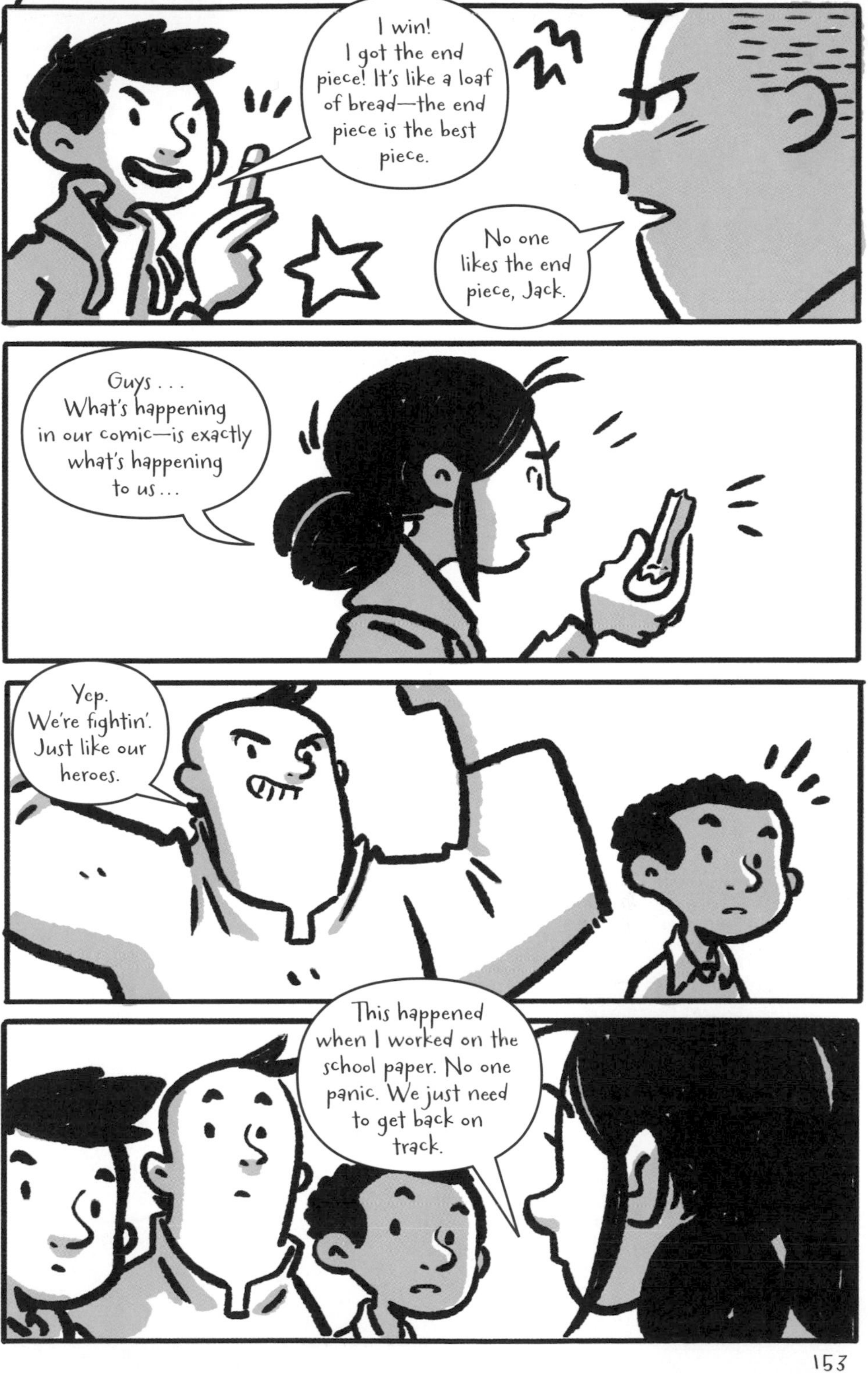
I win! I got the end piece! It's like a loaf of bread—the end piece is the best piece.
No one likes the end piece, Jack.
Guys . . . What's happening in our comic—is exactly what's happening to us . . .
Yep. We're fightin'. Just like our heroes.
This happened when I worked on the school paper. No one panic. We just need to get back on track.

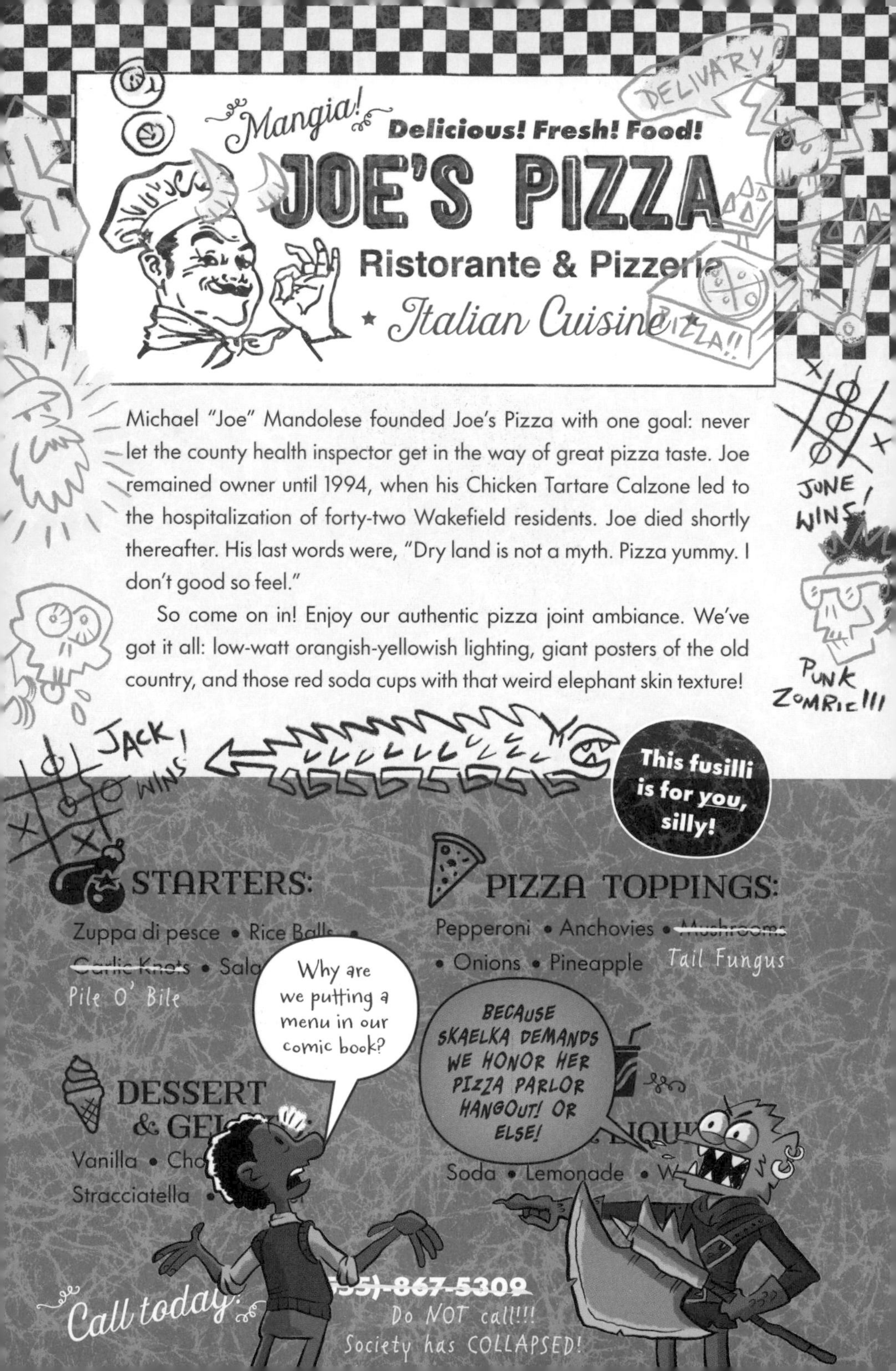

Mangia! Delicious! Fresh! Food!

JOE'S PIZZA

Ristorante & Pizzeria

★ Italian Cuisine ★

Michael "Joe" Mandolese founded Joe's Pizza with one goal: never let the county health inspector get in the way of great pizza taste. Joe remained owner until 1994, when his Chicken Tartare Calzone led to the hospitalization of forty-two Wakefield residents. Joe died shortly thereafter. His last words were, "Dry land is not a myth. Pizza yummy. I don't good so feel."

So come on in! Enjoy our authentic pizza joint ambiance. We've got it all: low-watt orangish-yellowish lighting, giant posters of the old country, and those red soda cups with that weird elephant skin texture!

STARTERS:

Zuppa di pesce • Rice Balls • ~~Garlic Knots~~ Pile O' Bile • Sala

PIZZA TOPPINGS:

Pepperoni • Anchovies • ~~Mushrooms~~ Tail Fungus • Onions • Pineapple

DESSERT & GEL

Vanilla • Cho
Stracciatella •

LIQU

Soda • Lemonade • W

Call today: ~~(555) 867-5309~~

DELIVARY!
PIZZA!!
JUNE WINS!
PUNK ZOMBIE!!!
JACK WINS!
This fusilli is for you, silly!
Why are we putting a menu in our comic book?
BECAUSE SKAELKA DEMANDS WE HONOR HER PIZZA PARLOR HANGOUT! OR ELSE!
Do NOT call!!! Society has COLLAPSED!

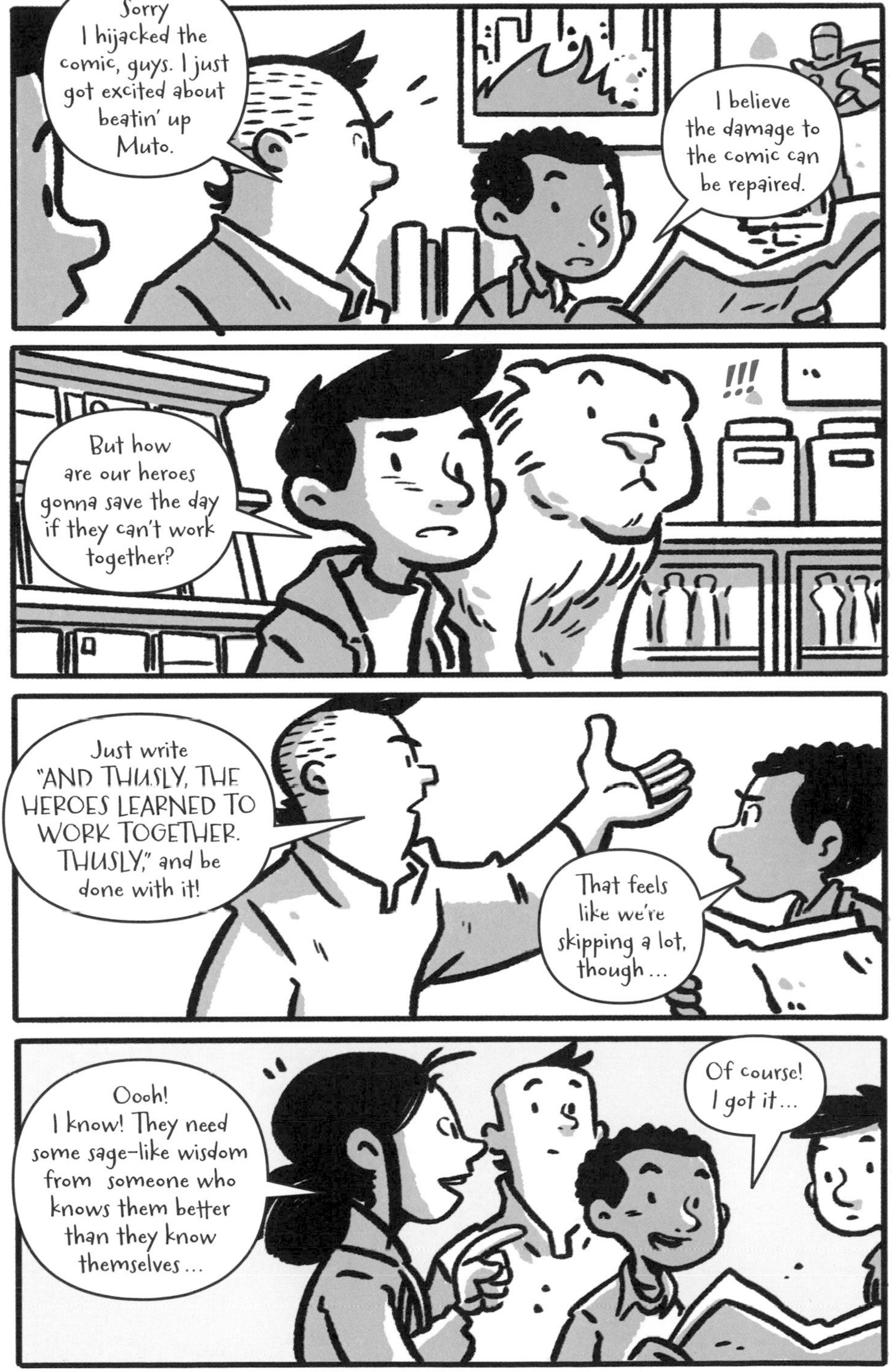
Sorry I hijacked the comic, guys. I just got excited about beatin' up Muto.
I believe the damage to the comic can be repaired.
!!!
But how are our heroes gonna save the day if they can't work together?
Just write "AND THUSLY, THE HEROES LEARNED TO WORK TOGETHER. THUSLY," and be done with it!
That feels like we're skipping a lot, though...
Oooh! I know! They need some sage-like wisdom from someone who knows them better than they know themselves...
Of course! I got it...

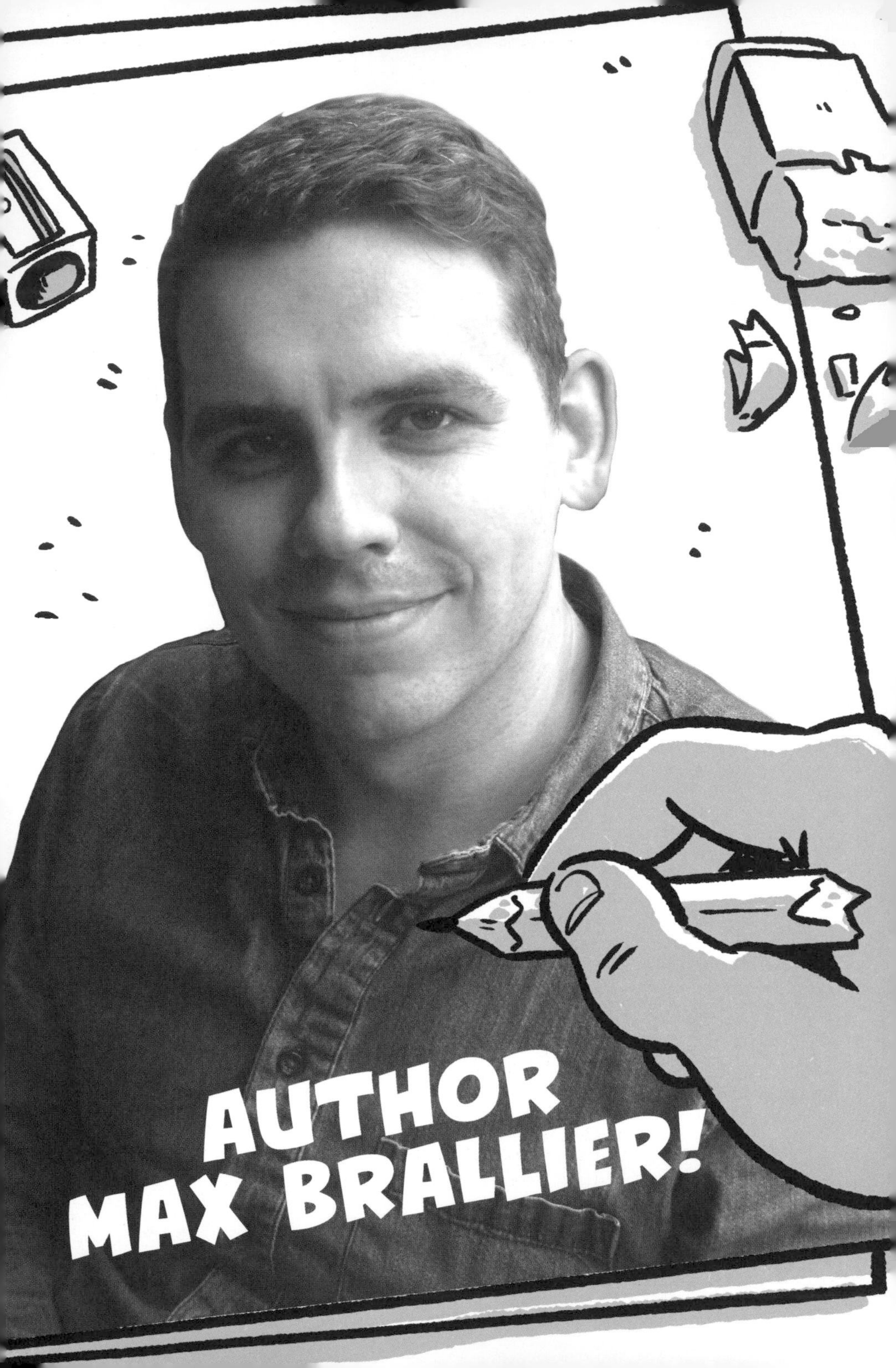
AUTHOR
MAX BRALLIER!

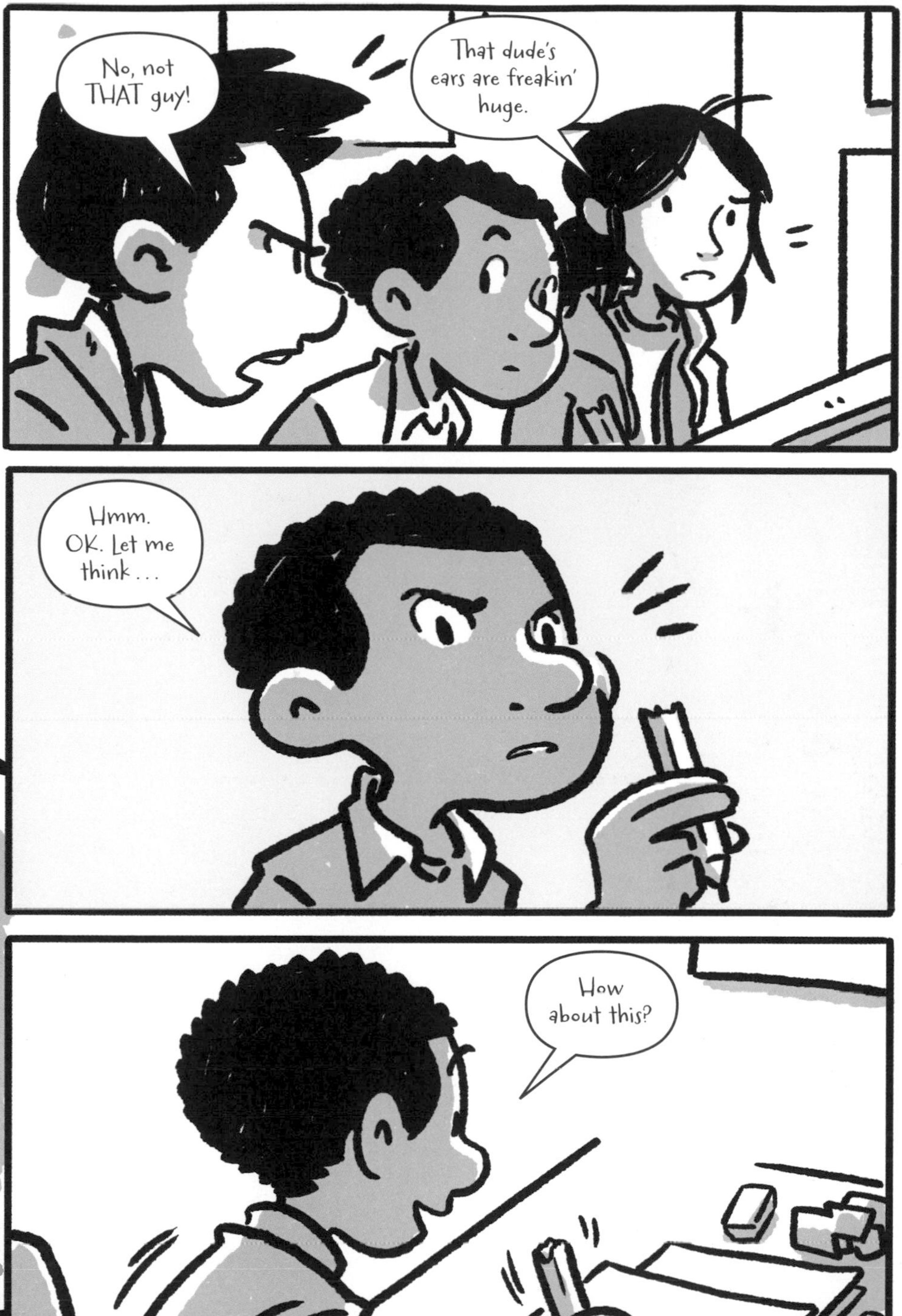
No, not THAT guy!
That dude's ears are freakin' huge.
Hmm. OK. Let me think . . .
How about this?

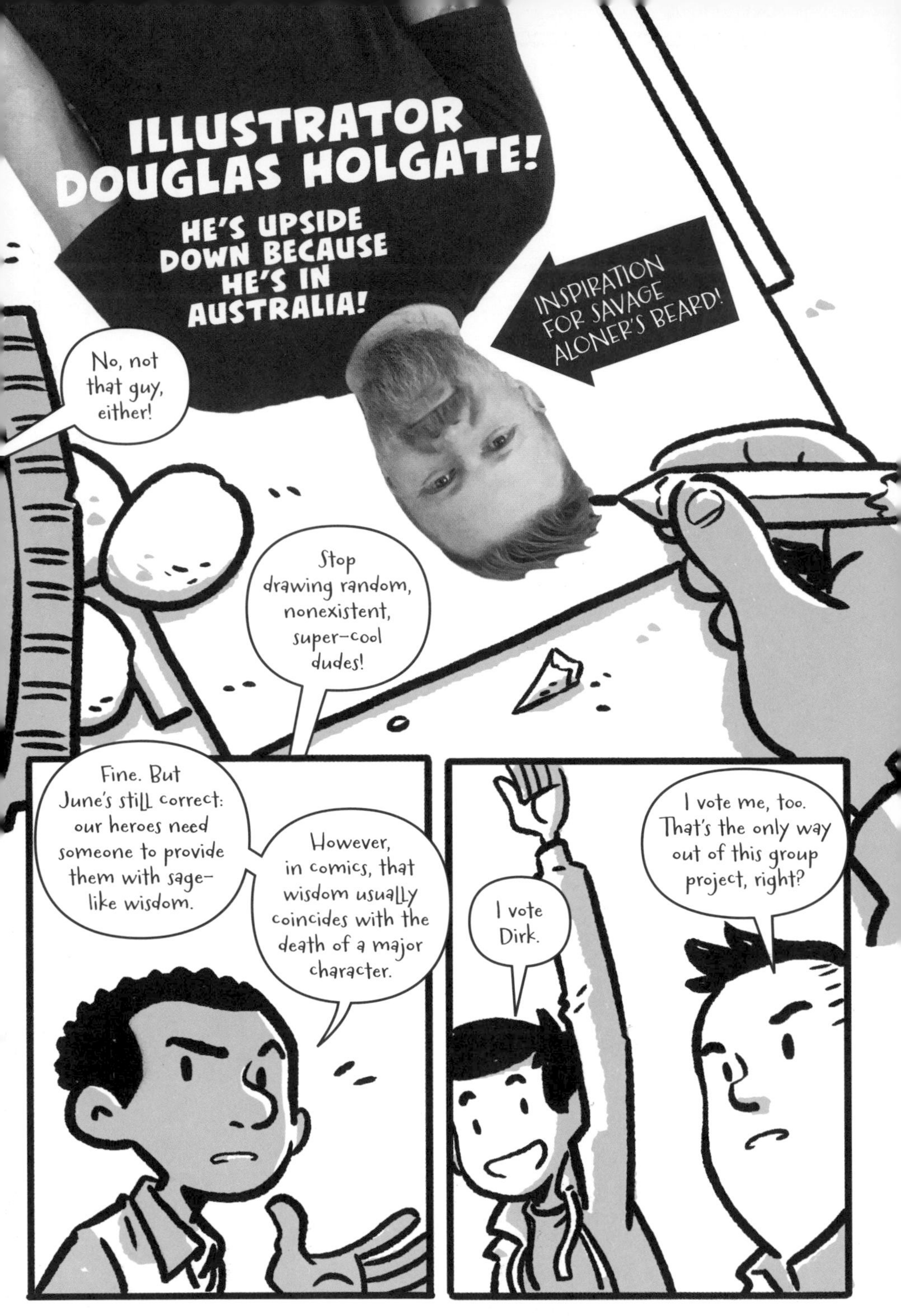
ILLUSTRATOR DOUGLAS HOLGATE!
HE'S UPSIDE DOWN BECAUSE HE'S IN AUSTRALIA!
INSPIRATION FOR SAVAGE ALONER'S BEARD!
No, not that guy, either!
Stop drawing random, nonexistent, super-cool dudes!
Fine. But June's still correct: our heroes need someone to provide them with sage-like wisdom.
However, in comics, that wisdom usually coincides with the death of a major character.
I vote Dirk.
I vote me, too. That's the only way out of this group project, right?

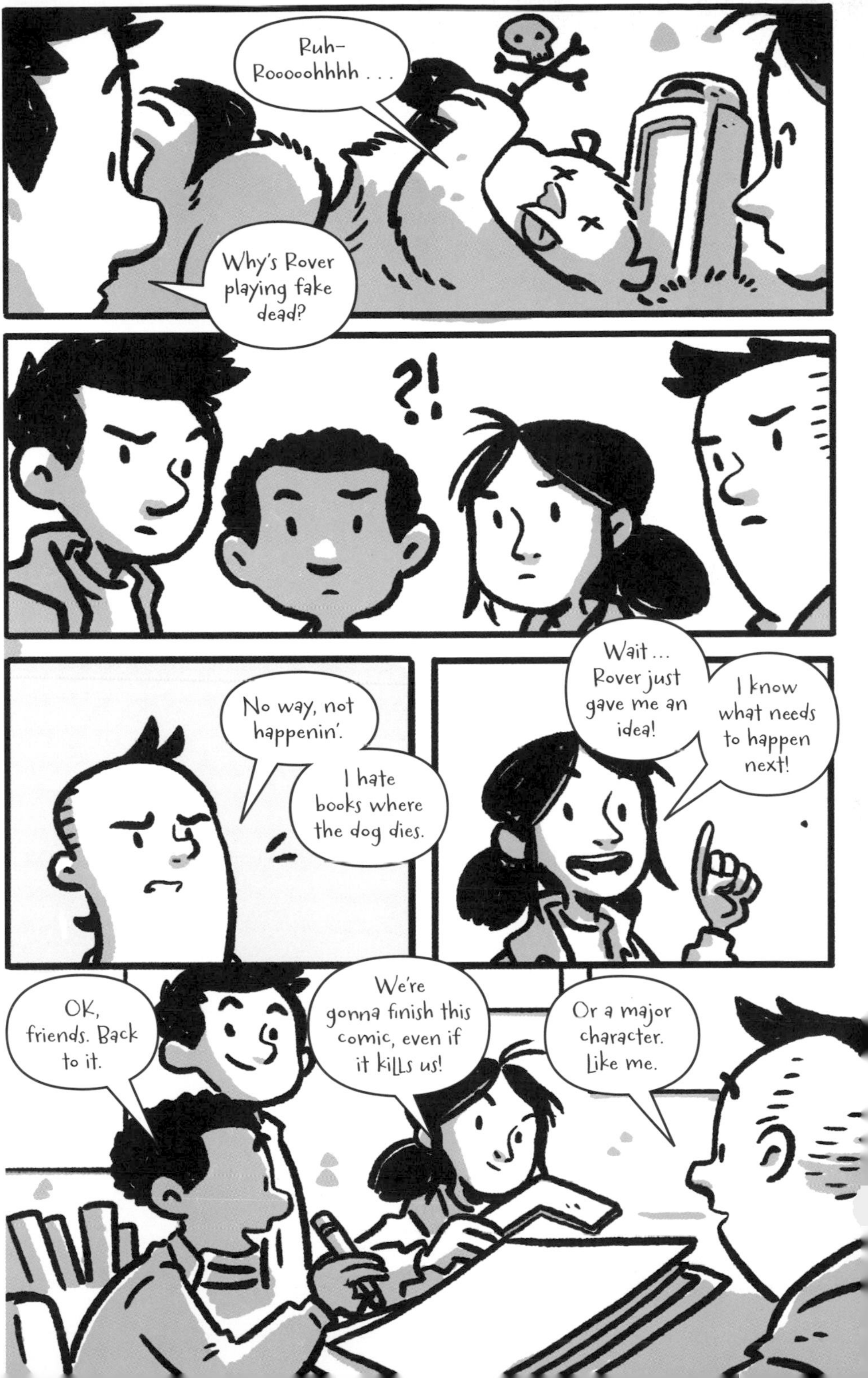

Ruh-Roooohhhh . . .
Why's Rover playing fake dead?
?!
No way, not happenin'.
I hate books where the dog dies.
Wait . . . Rover just gave me an idea!
I know what needs to happen next!
OK, friends. Back to it.
We're gonna finish this comic, even if it kills us!
Or a major character. Like me.

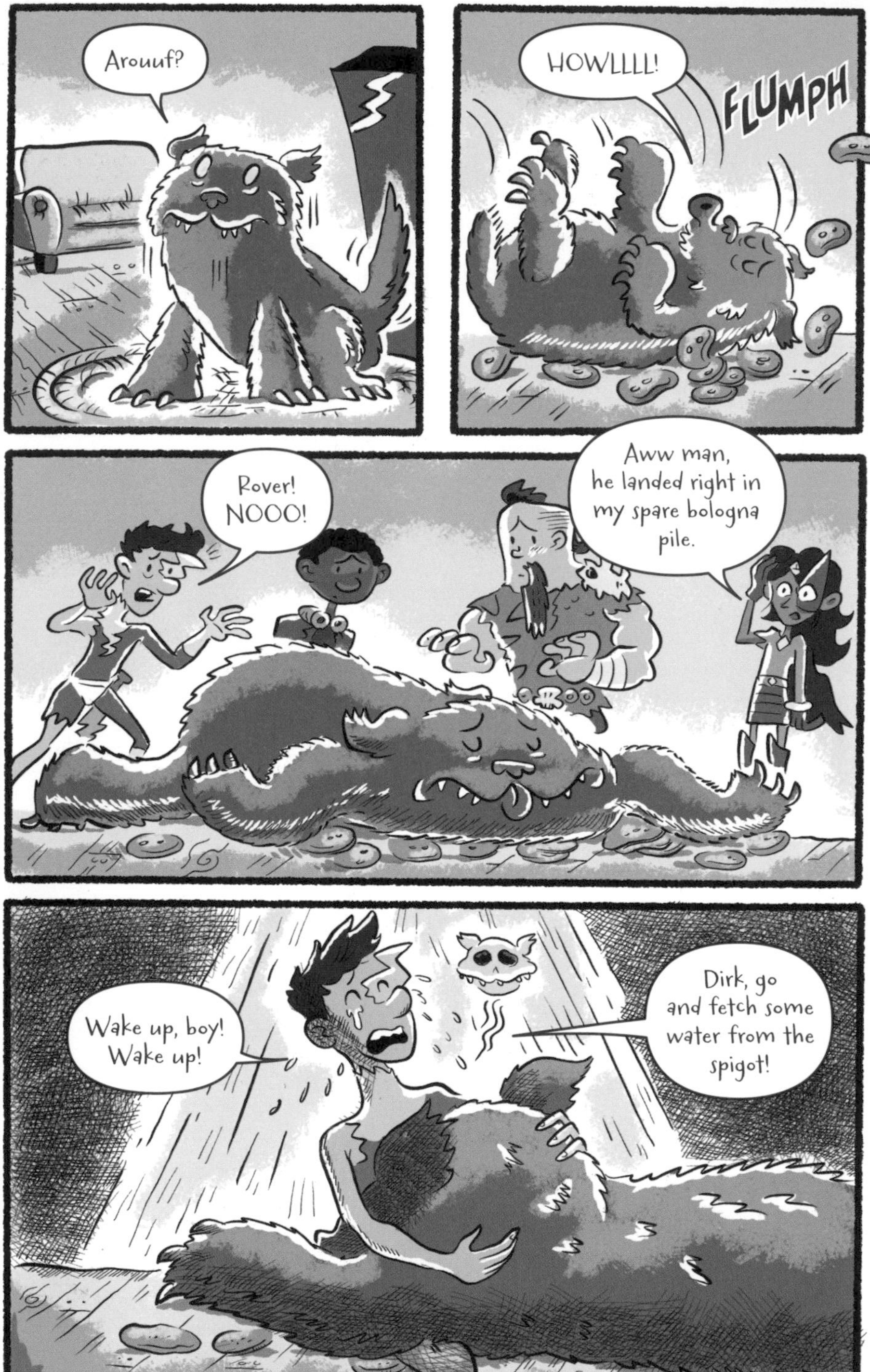
Arouuf?
HOWLLLL!
FLUMPH
Rover! NOOO!
Aww man, he landed right in my spare bologna pile.
Wake up, boy! Wake up!
Dirk, go and fetch some water from the spigot!

ILLUSTRATOR NOTE (QUINT): THIS IS CALLED "CROSS-HATCHING." IT'S REALLY DRAMATIC, BUT TAKES A SUPER LONG TIME TO DO!

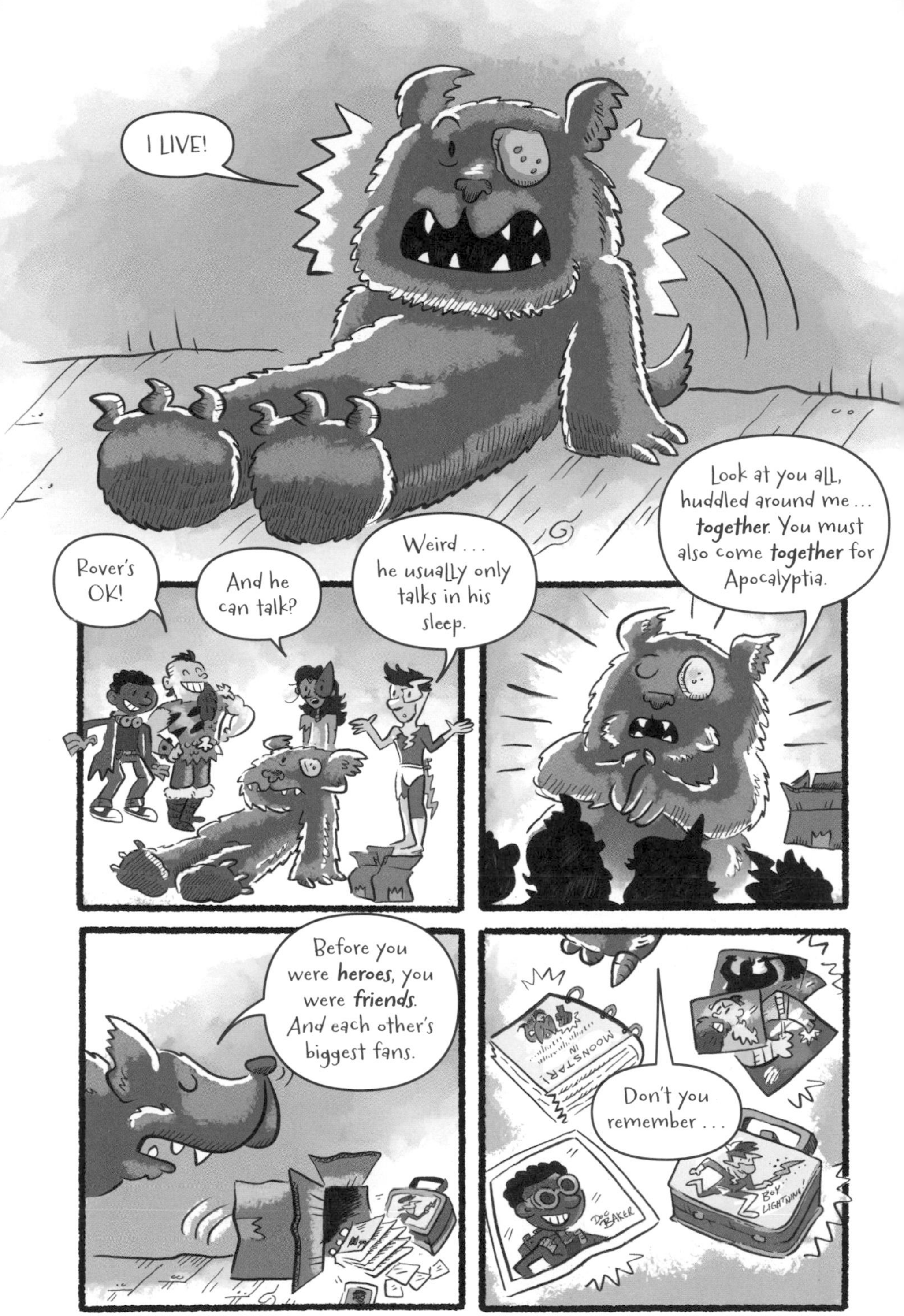
I LIVE!
Rover's OK!
And he can talk?
Weird . . . he usually only talks in his sleep.
Look at you all, huddled around me . . . **together**. You must also come **together** for Apocalyptia.
Before you were **heroes**, you were **friends**. And each other's biggest fans.
MOONSTAR! IN
Don't you remember . . .
DOC BAKER
BOY LIGHTNING

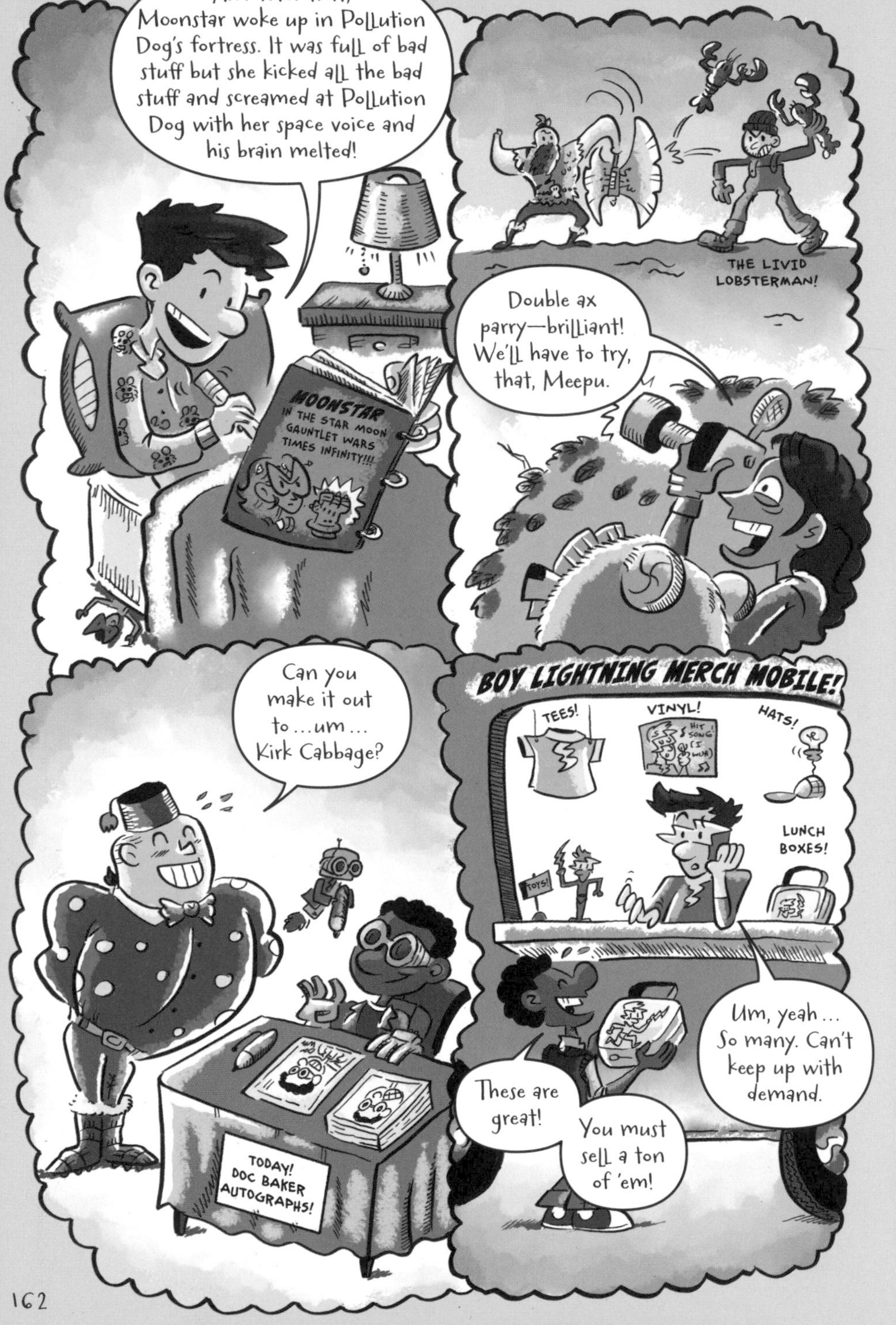

And after that, Moonstar woke up in Pollution Dog's fortress. It was full of bad stuff but she kicked all the bad stuff and screamed at Pollution Dog with her space voice and his brain melted!
MOONSTAR IN THE STAR MOON GAUNTLET WARS TIMES INFINITY!!!
THE LIVID LOBSTERMAN!
Double ax parry—brilliant! We'll have to try, that, Meepu.
Can you make it out to ... um ... Kirk Cabbage?
TODAY! DOC BAKER AUTOGRAPHS!
BOY LIGHTNING MERCH MOBILE!
TEES!
VINYL!
HATS!
TOYS!
LUNCH BOXES!
Um, yeah ... So many. Can't keep up with demand.
These are great!
You must sell a ton of 'em!

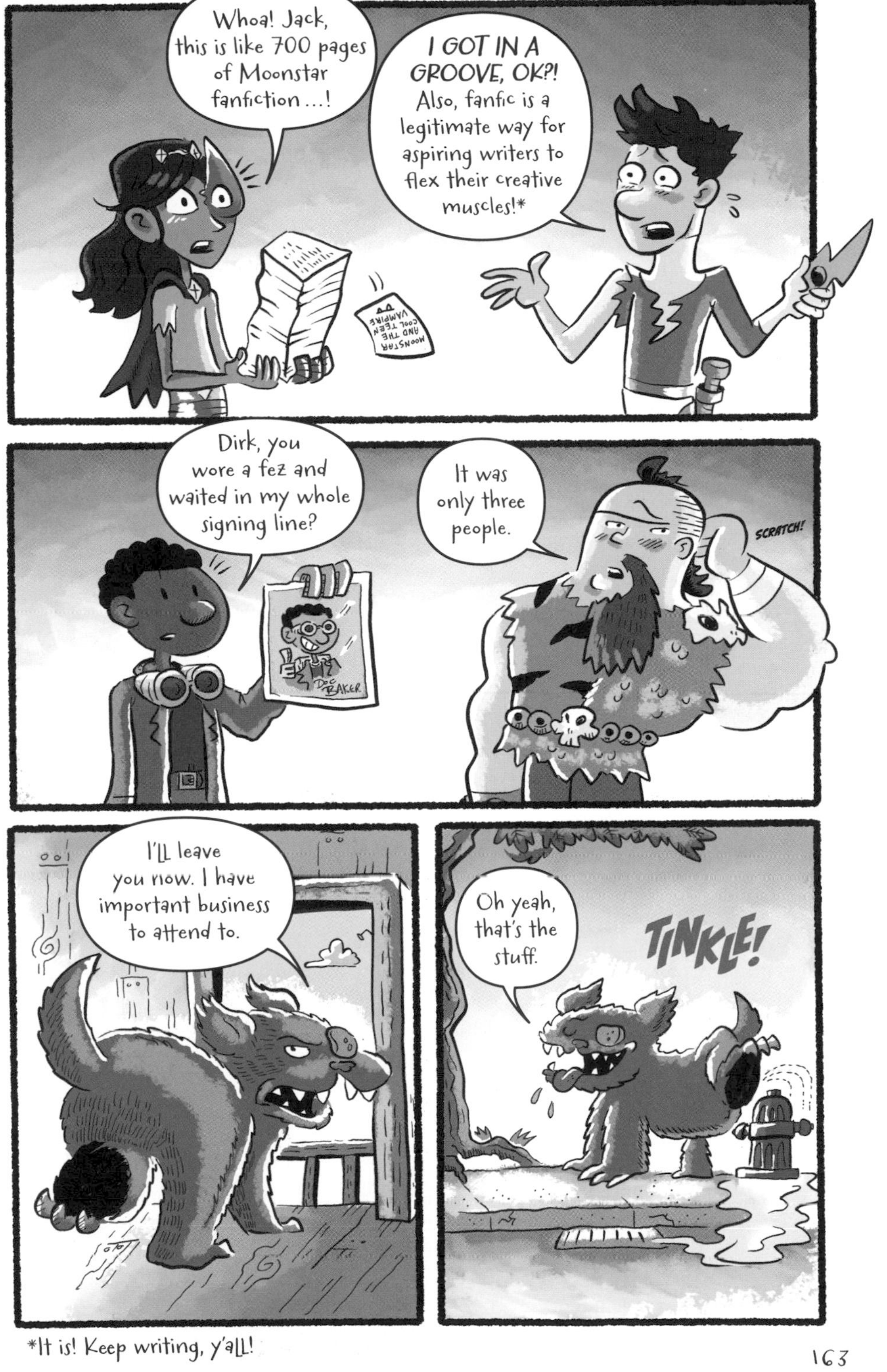
Whoa! Jack, this is like 700 pages of Moonstar fanfiction ...!
I GOT IN A GROOVE, OK?! Also, fanfic is a legitimate way for aspiring writers to flex their creative muscles!*
MOONSTAR AND THE COOL TEEN VAMPIRE
Dirk, you wore a fez and waited in my whole signing line?
DOC BAKER
It was only three people.
SCRATCH!
I'LL leave you now. I have important business to attend to.
Oh yeah, that's the stuff.
TINKLE!

*It is! Keep writing, y'aLL!

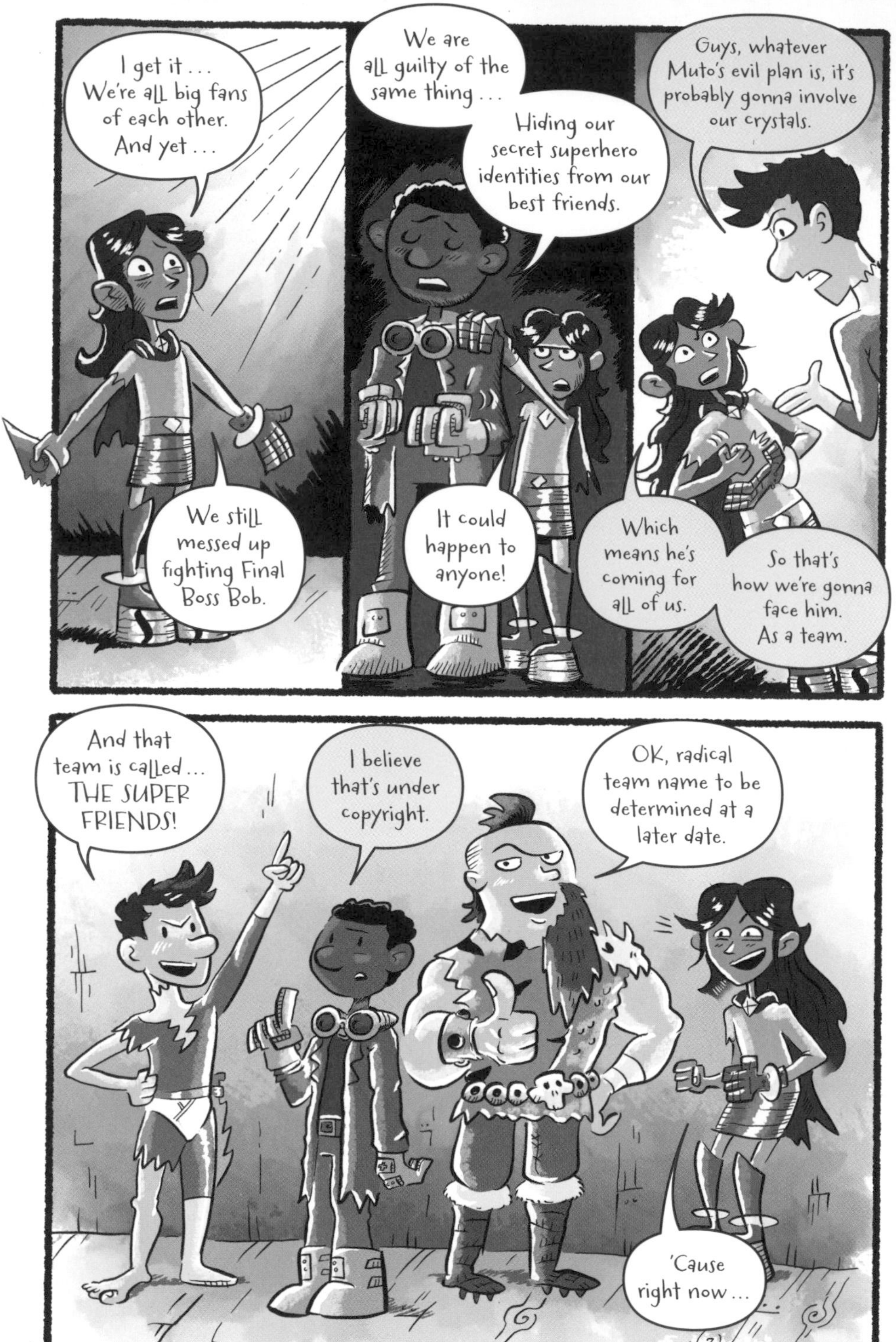
I get it . . . We're all big fans of each other. And yet . . .
We still messed up fighting Final Boss Bob.
We are all guilty of the same thing . . .
Hiding our secret superhero identities from our best friends.
It could happen to anyone!
Guys, whatever Muto's evil plan is, it's probably gonna involve our crystals.
Which means he's coming for all of us.
So that's how we're gonna face him. As a team.
And that team is called . . . THE SUPER FRIENDS!
I believe that's under copyright.
OK, radical team name to be determined at a later date.
'Cause right now . . .

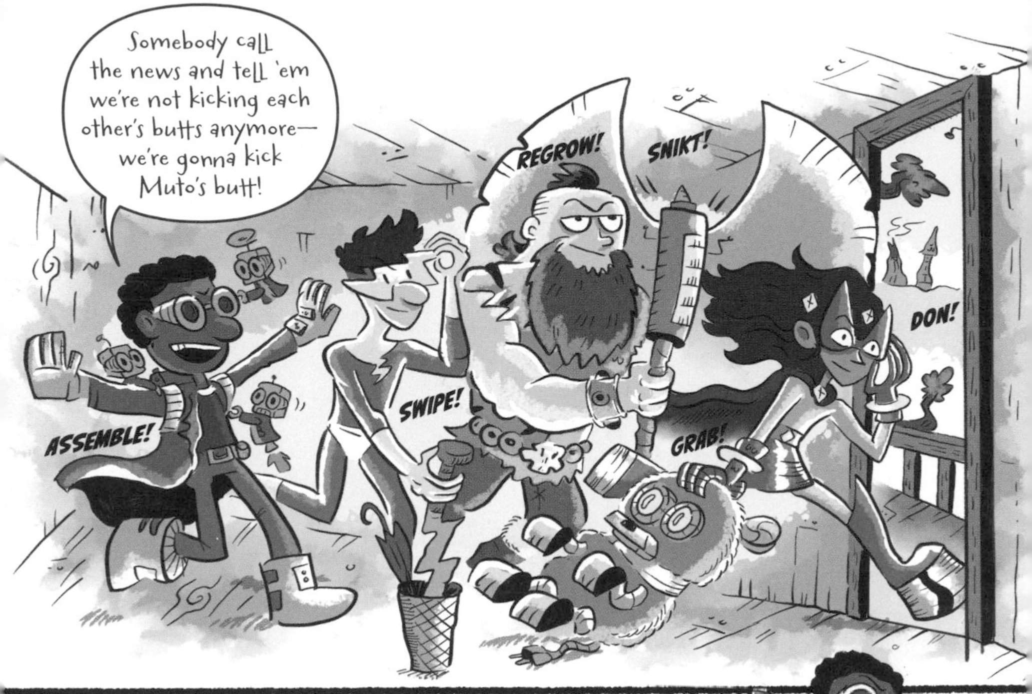
Somebody call the news and tell 'em we're not kicking each other's butts anymore—we're gonna kick Muto's butt!
REGROW!
SNIKT!
DON!
SWIPE!
ASSEMBLE!
GRAB!

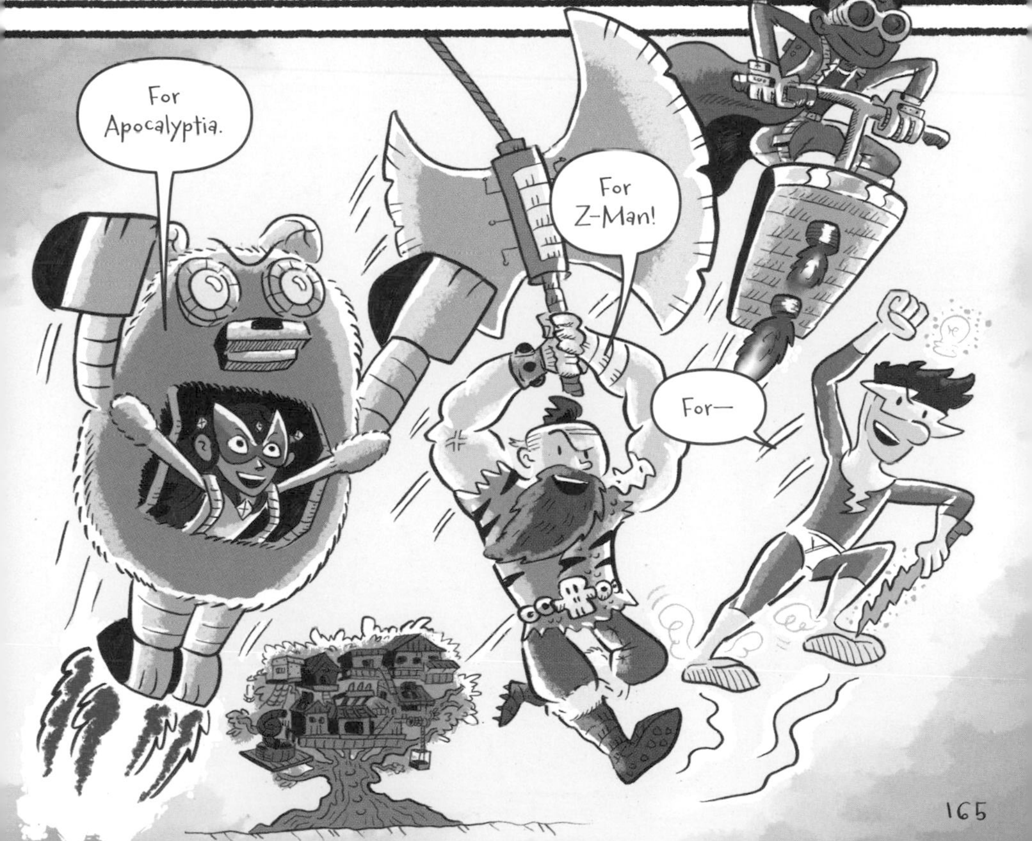
For Apocalyptia.
For Z-Man!
For—

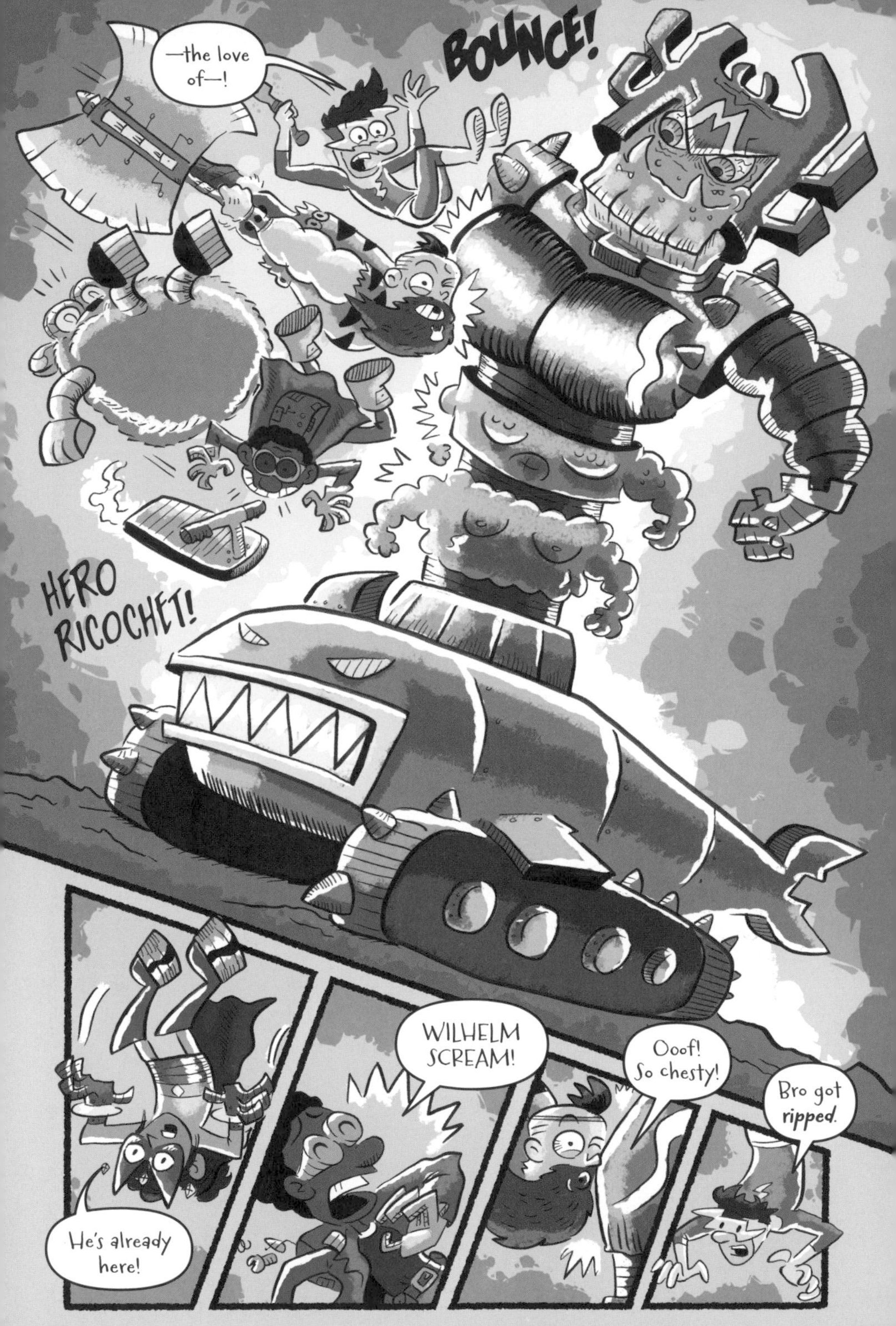
—the love of—!
BOUNCE!
HERO RICOCHET!
He's already here!
WILHELM SCREAM!
Ooof! So chesty!
Bro got *ripped*.

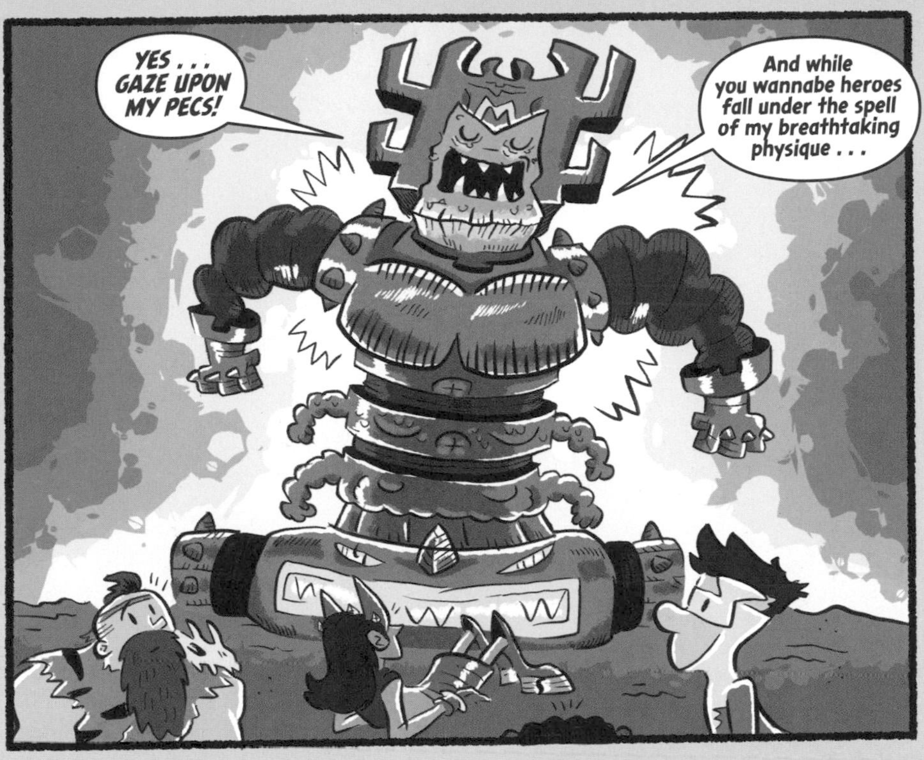
YES . . . GAZE UPON MY PECS!
And while you wannabe heroes fall under the spell of my breathtaking physique . . .

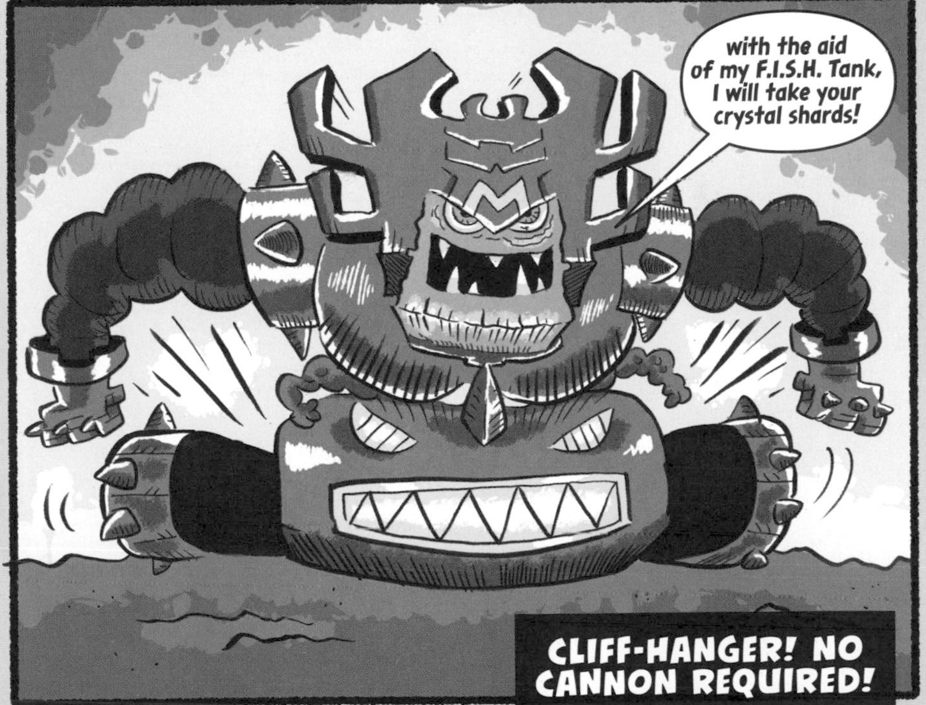
with the aid of my F.I.S.H. Tank, I will take your crystal shards!
CLIFF-HANGER! NO CANNON REQUIRED!

CHAPTER NINE

A SUPERHERO TEAM? YES, AT LONG LAST, A SUPERHERO TEAM!

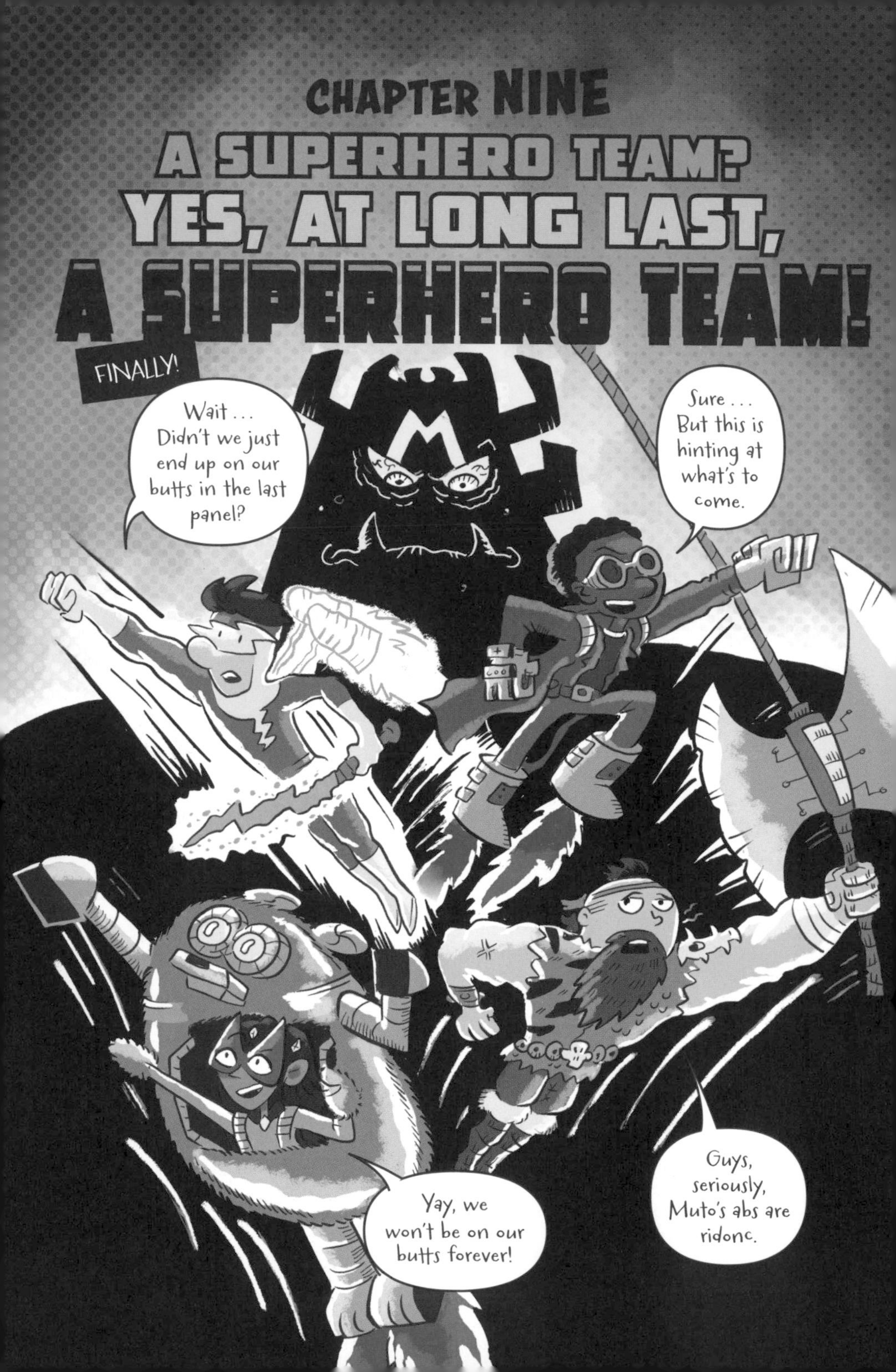
FINALLY!
Wait . . . Didn't we just end up on our butts in the last panel?
Sure . . . But this is hinting at what's to come.
Yay, we won't be on our butts forever!
Guys, seriously, Muto's abs are ridonc.

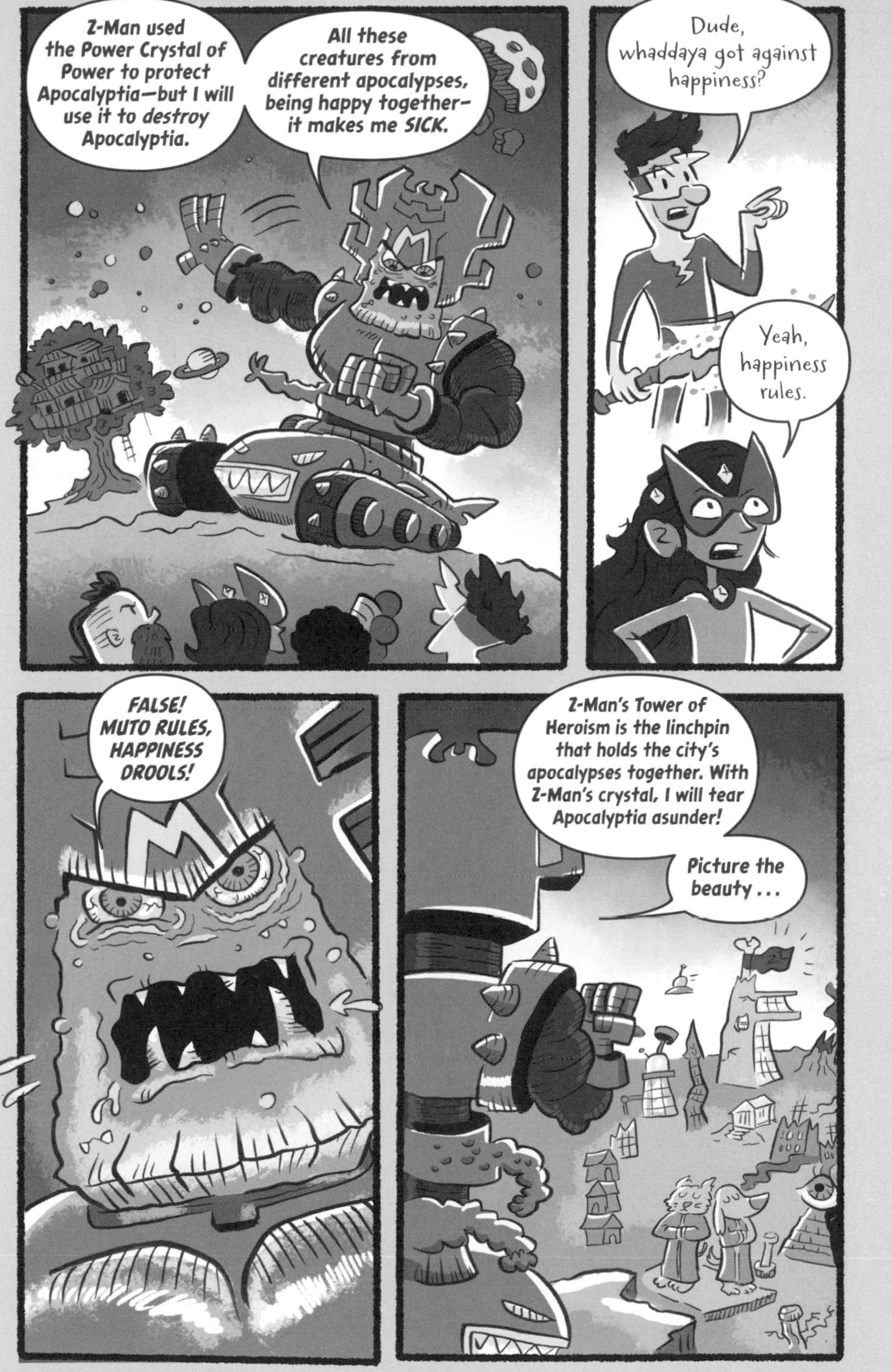

Z-Man used the Power Crystal of Power to protect Apocalyptia—but I will use it to *destroy* Apocalyptia.
All these creatures from different apocalypses, being happy together—it makes me *SICK*.
Dude, whaddaya got against happiness?
Yeah, happiness rules.
FALSE! MUTO RULES, HAPPINESS DROOLS!
Z-Man's Tower of Heroism is the linchpin that holds the city's apocalypses together. With Z-Man's crystal, I will tear Apocalyptia asunder!
Picture the beauty . . .

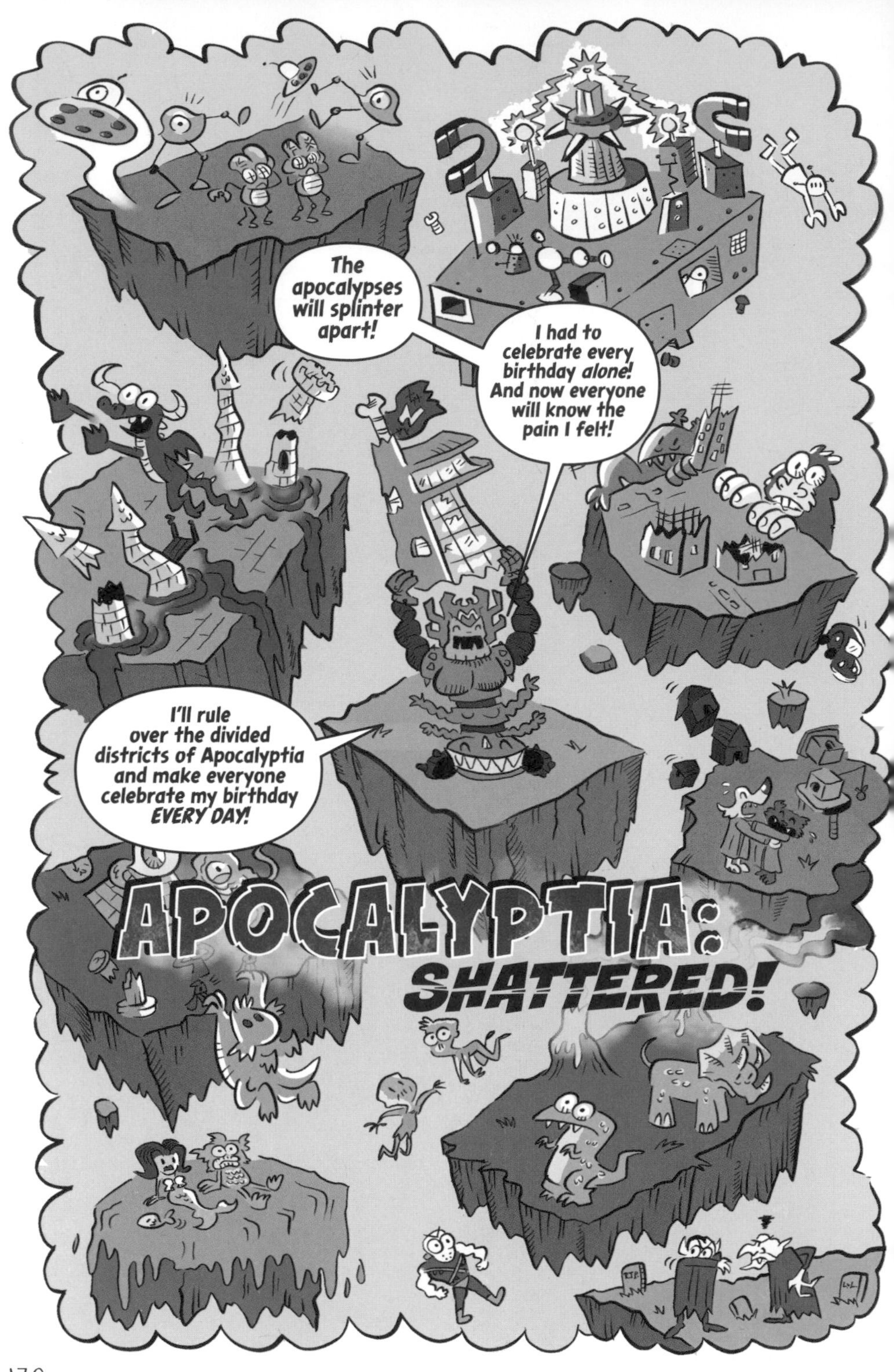
The apocalypses will splinter apart!
I had to celebrate every birthday *alone*! And now everyone will know the pain I felt!
I'll rule over the divided districts of Apocalyptia and make everyone celebrate my birthday *EVERY DAY!*
APOCALYPTIA: SHATTERED!

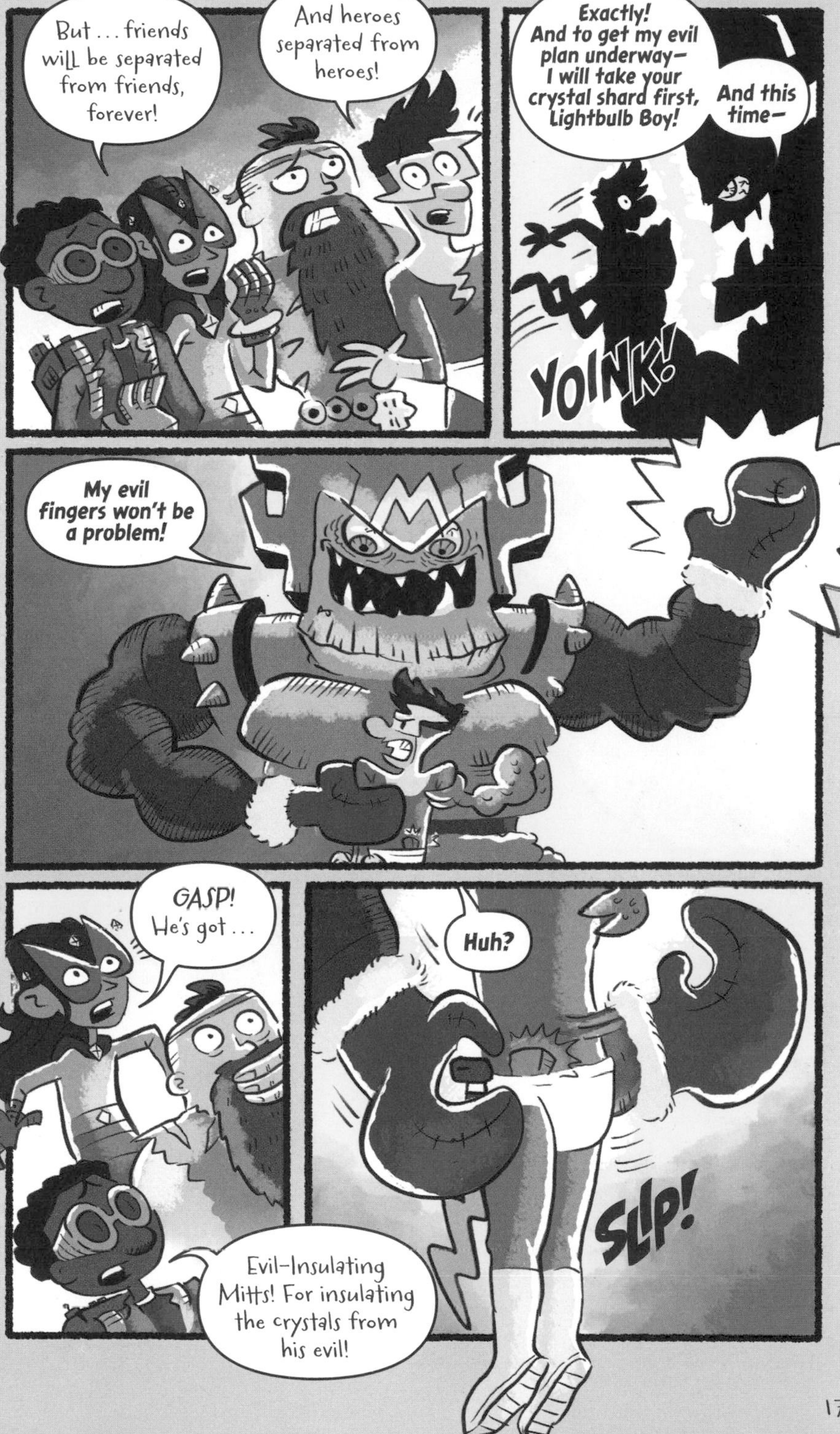
But . . . friends will be separated from friends, forever!
And heroes separated from heroes!
Exactly! And to get my evil plan underway— I will take your crystal shard first, Lightbulb Boy!
And this time—
YOINK!
My evil fingers won't be a problem!
GASP! He's got . . .
Evil-Insulating Mitts! For insulating the crystals from his evil!
Huh?
SLIP!

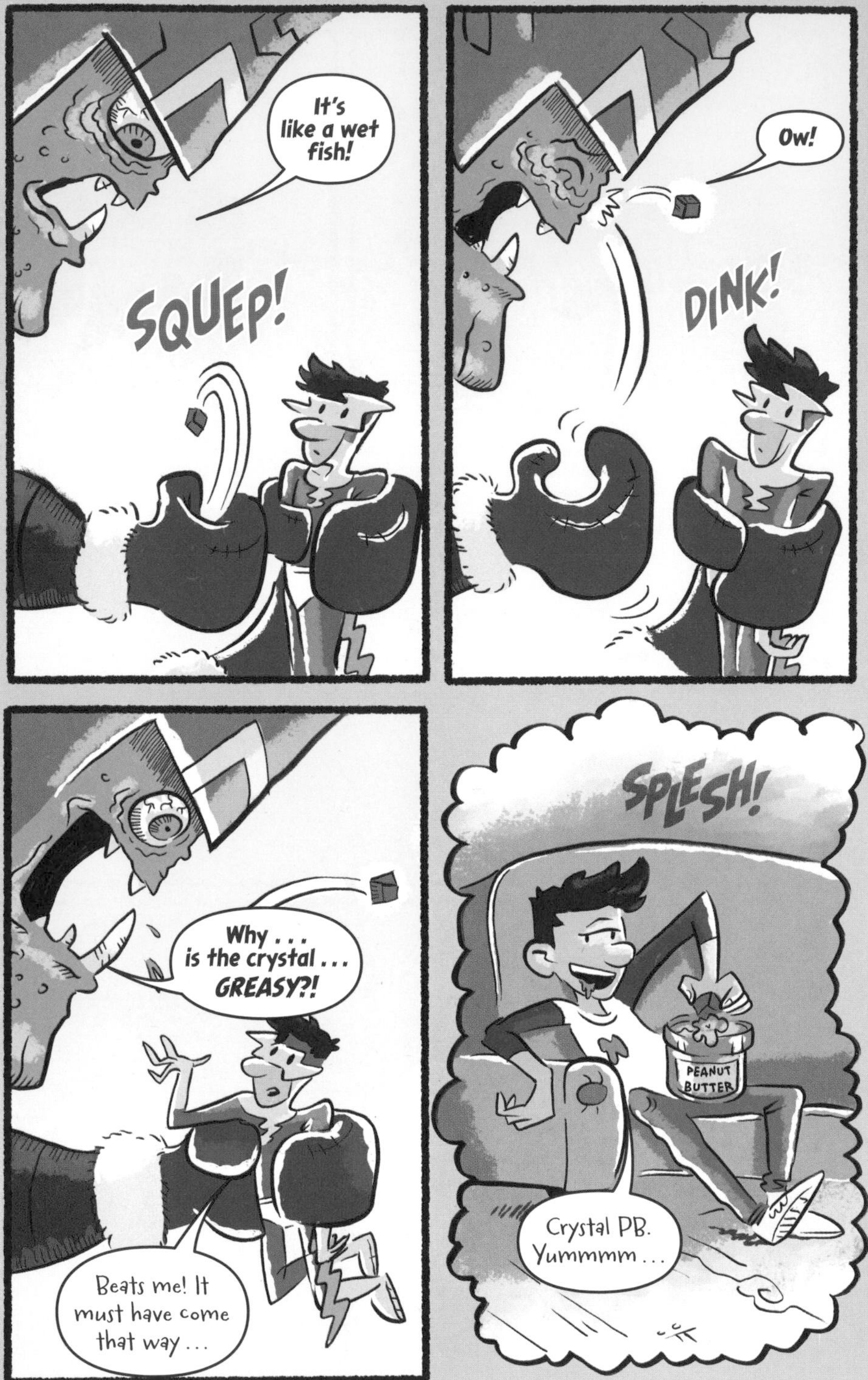
It's like a wet fish!
SQUEP!
Ow!
DINK!
Why . . . is the crystal . . . GREASY?!
Beats me! It must have come that way . . .
SPLESH!
PEANUT BUTTER
Crystal PB. Yummmm . . .

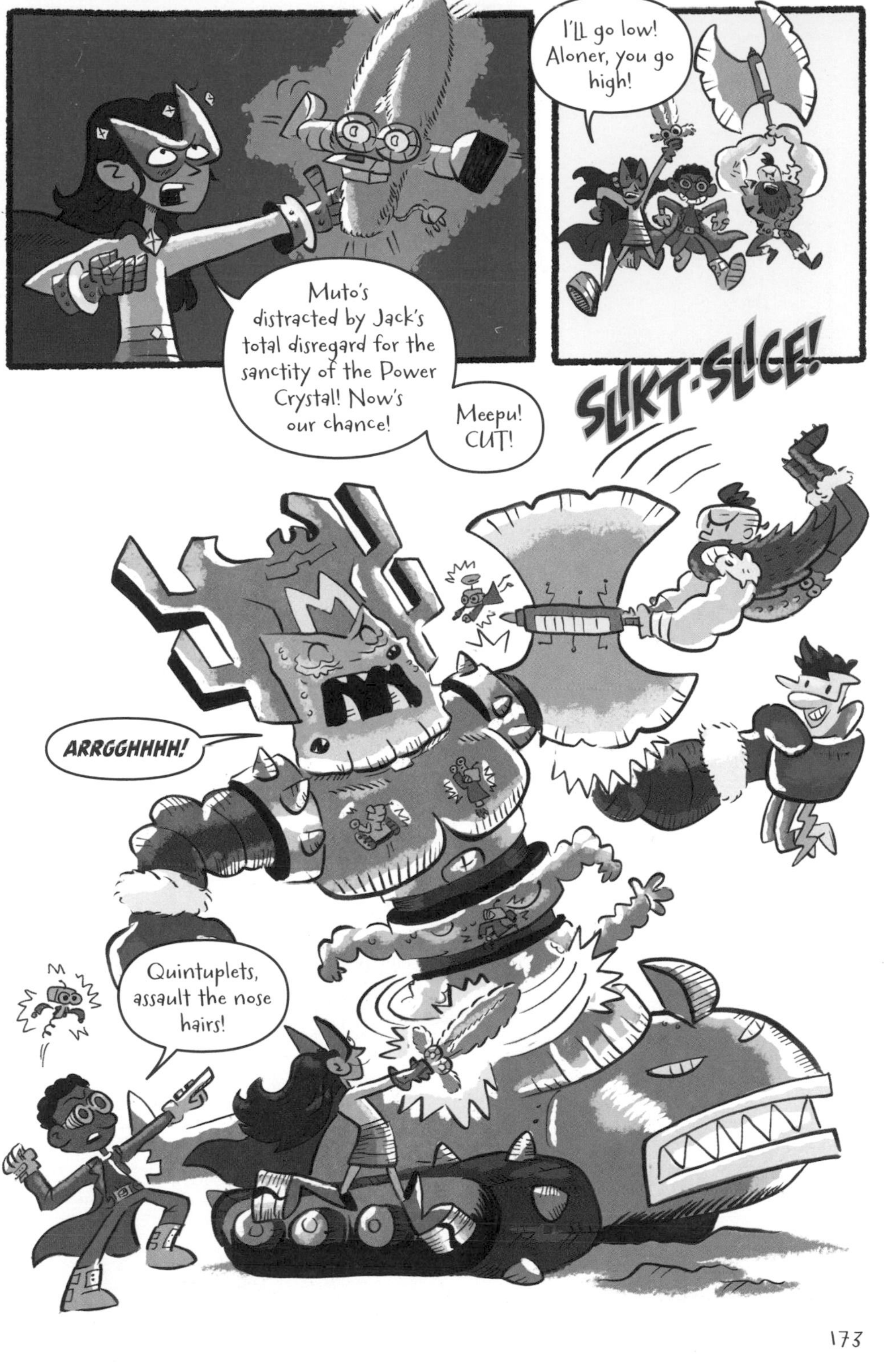
Muto's distracted by Jack's total disregard for the sanctity of the Power Crystal! Now's our chance!
I'LL go low! Aloner, you go high!
Meepu! CUT!
SLIKT-SLICE!
ARRGGHHHH!
Quintuplets, assault the nose hairs!

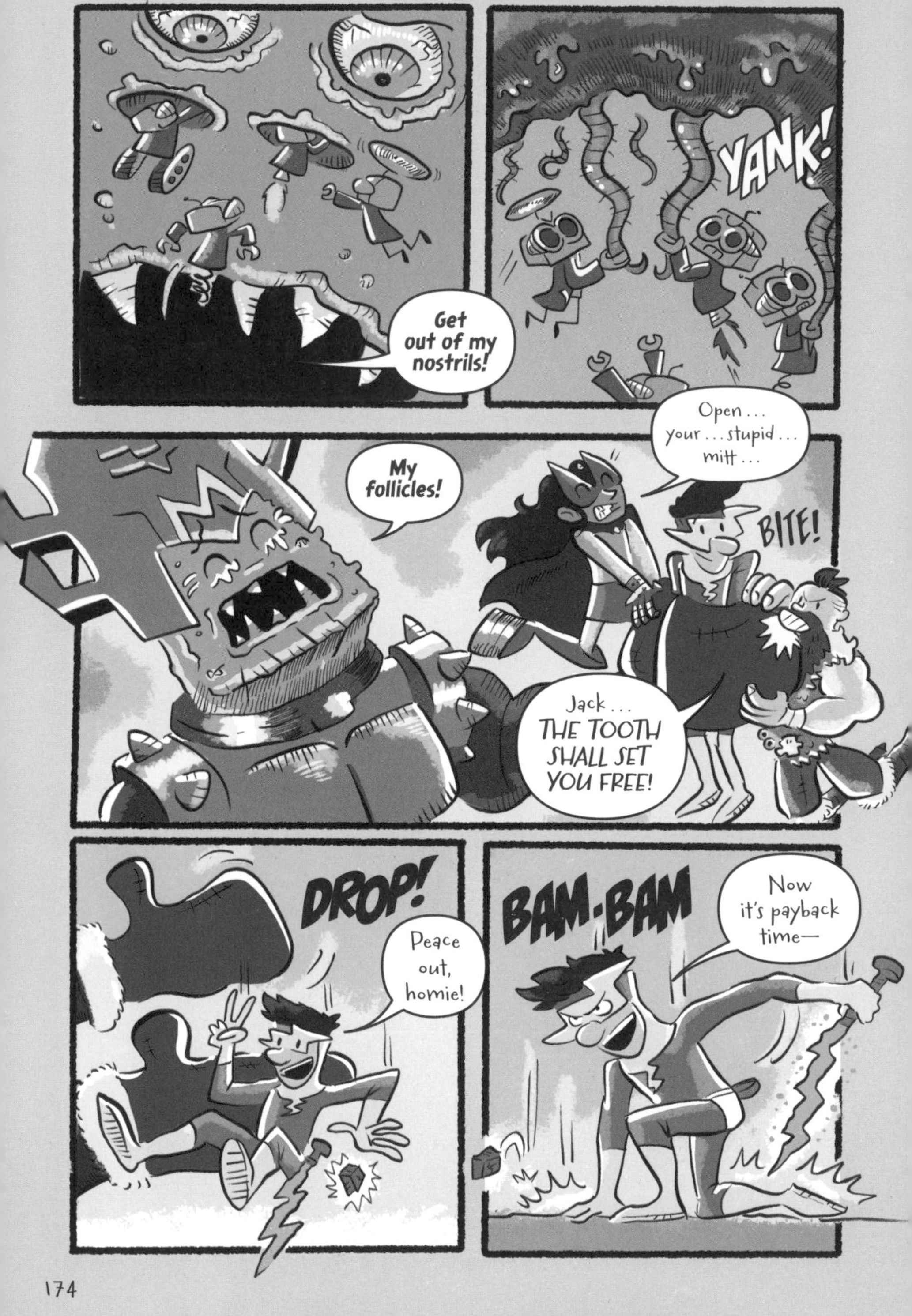
Get out of my nostrils!
YANK!
My follicles!
Open... your...stupid... mitt...
BITE!
Jack... THE TOOTH SHALL SET YOU FREE!
DROP!
Peace out, homie!
BAM-BAM
Now it's payback time—

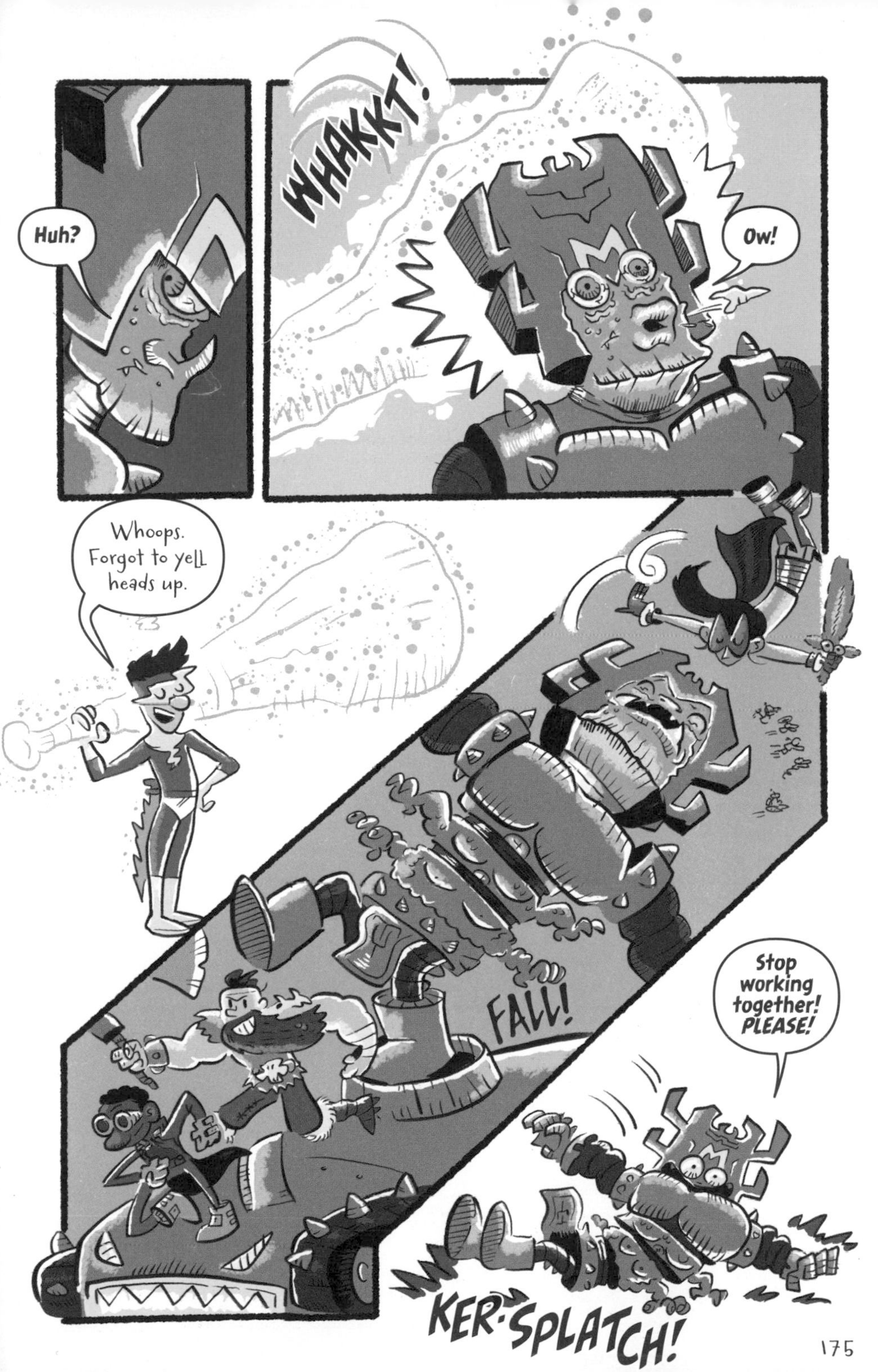
Huh?
WHAKKT!
Ow!
Whoops. Forgot to yell heads up.
FALL!
Stop working together! PLEASE!
KER-SPLATCH!

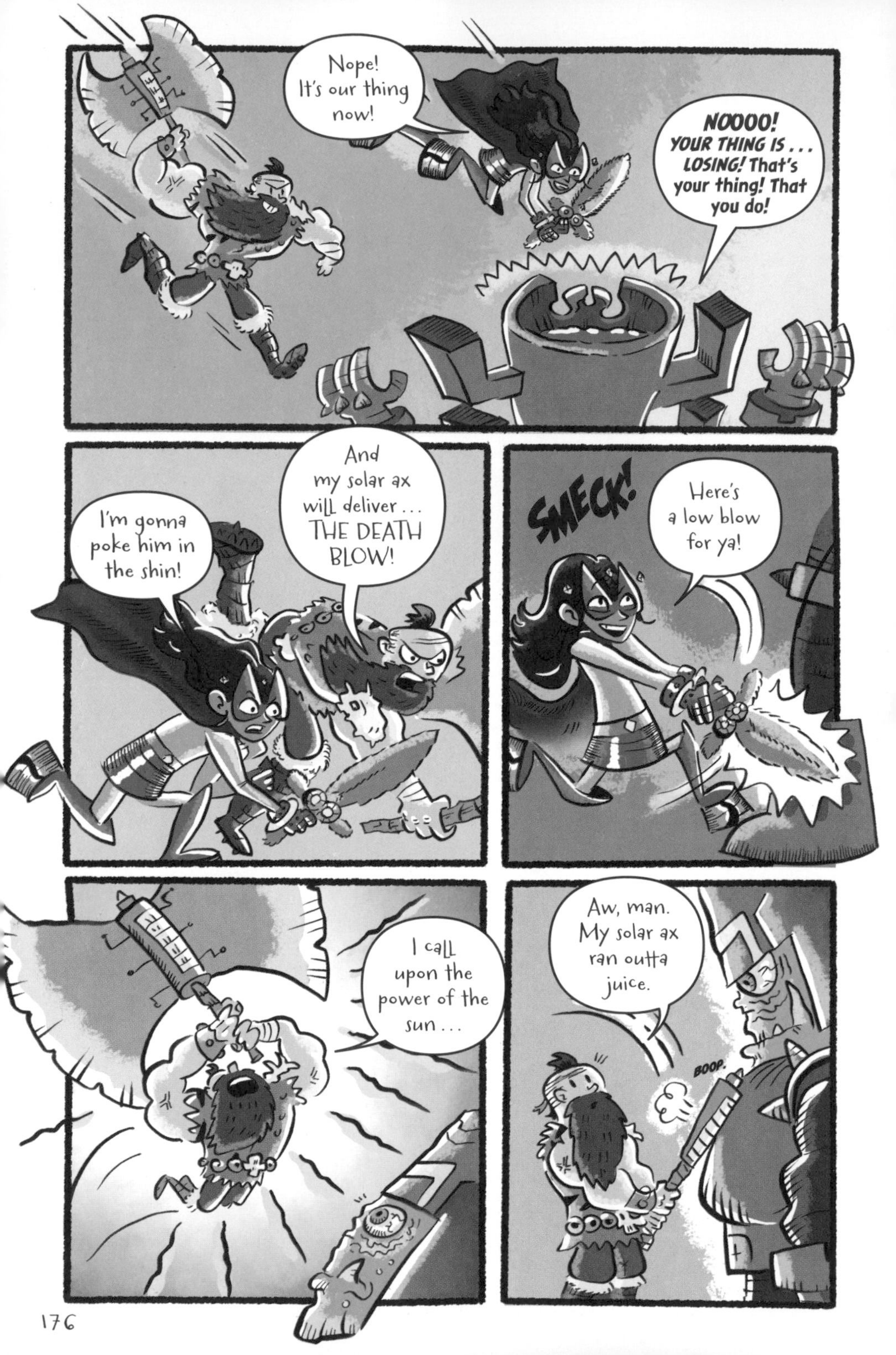
Nope! It's our thing now!
NOOOO! YOUR THING IS . . . LOSING! That's your thing! That you do!
I'm gonna poke him in the shin!
And my solar ax will deliver . . . THE DEATH BLOW!
SMECK!
Here's a low blow for ya!
I call upon the power of the sun . . .
Aw, man. My solar ax ran outta juice.
BOOP.

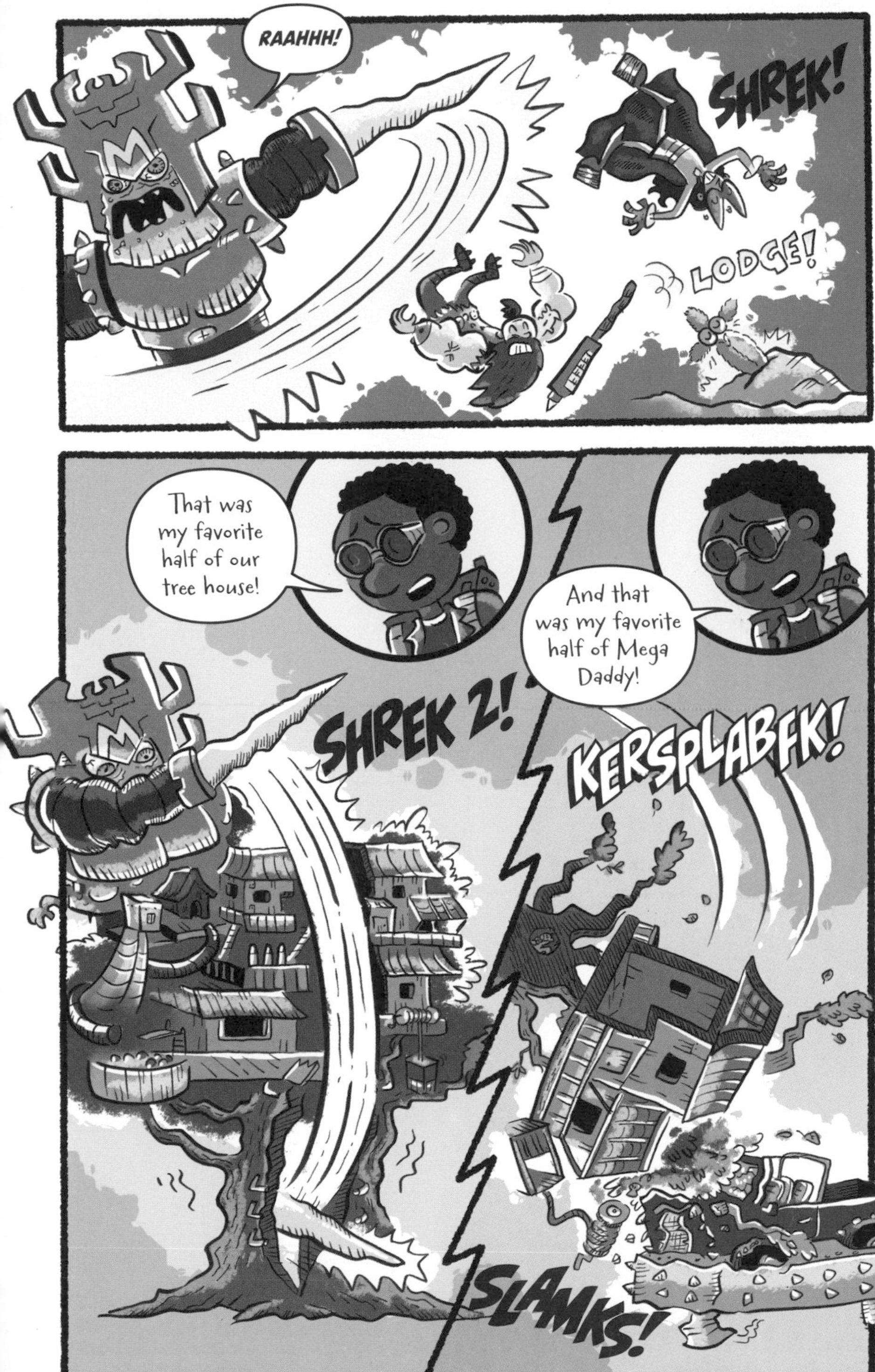
RAAHHH!
SHREK!
LODGE!
That was my favorite half of our tree house!
And that was my favorite half of Mega Daddy!
SHREK 2!
KERSPLABFK!
SLAMKS!

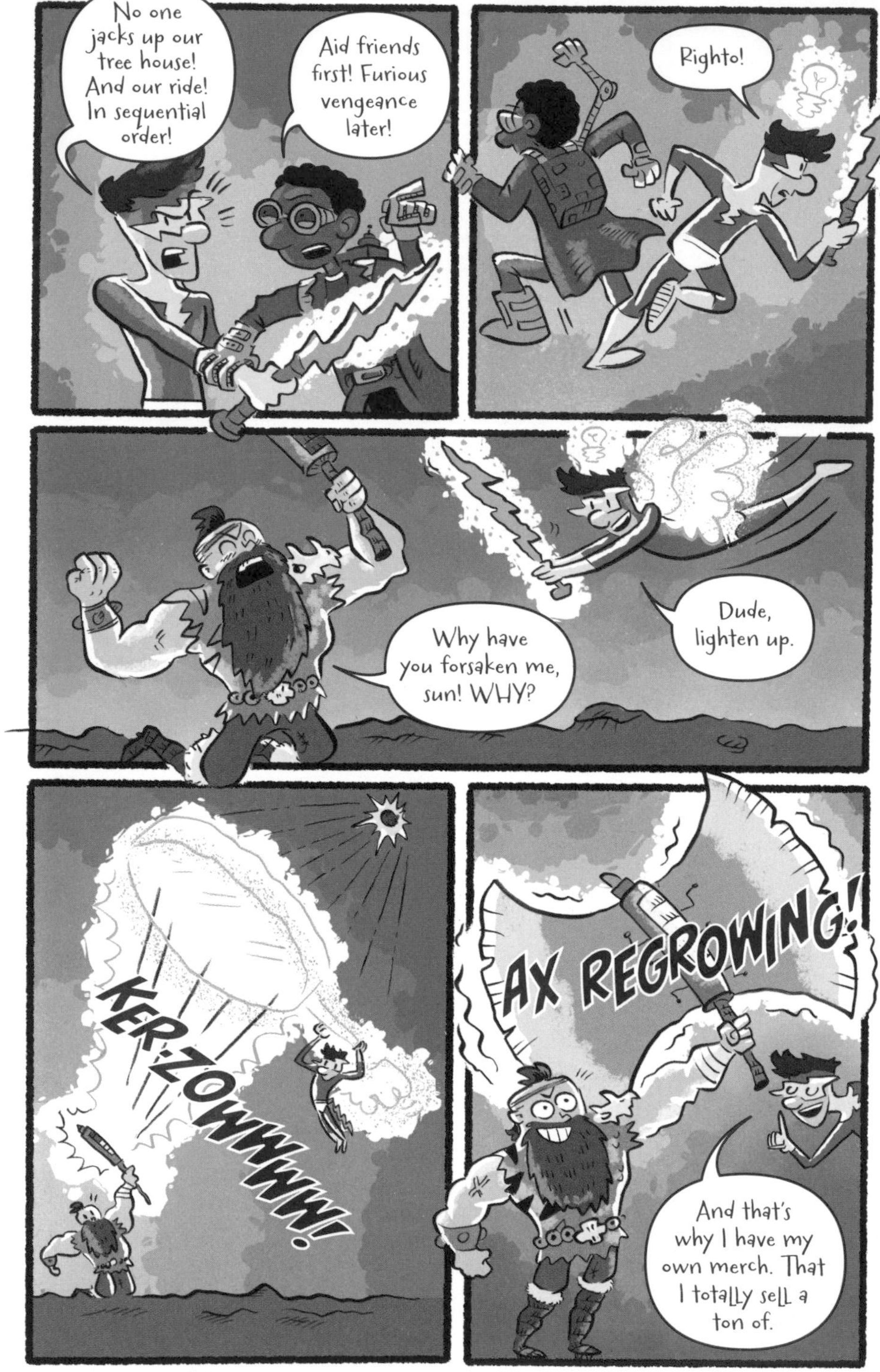
No one jacks up our tree house! And our ride! In sequential order!
Aid friends first! Furious vengeance later!
Righto!
Why have you forsaken me, sun! WHY?
Dude, lighten up.
KER-ZOWWWWW!
AX REGROWING!
And that's why I have my own merch. That I totally sell a ton of.

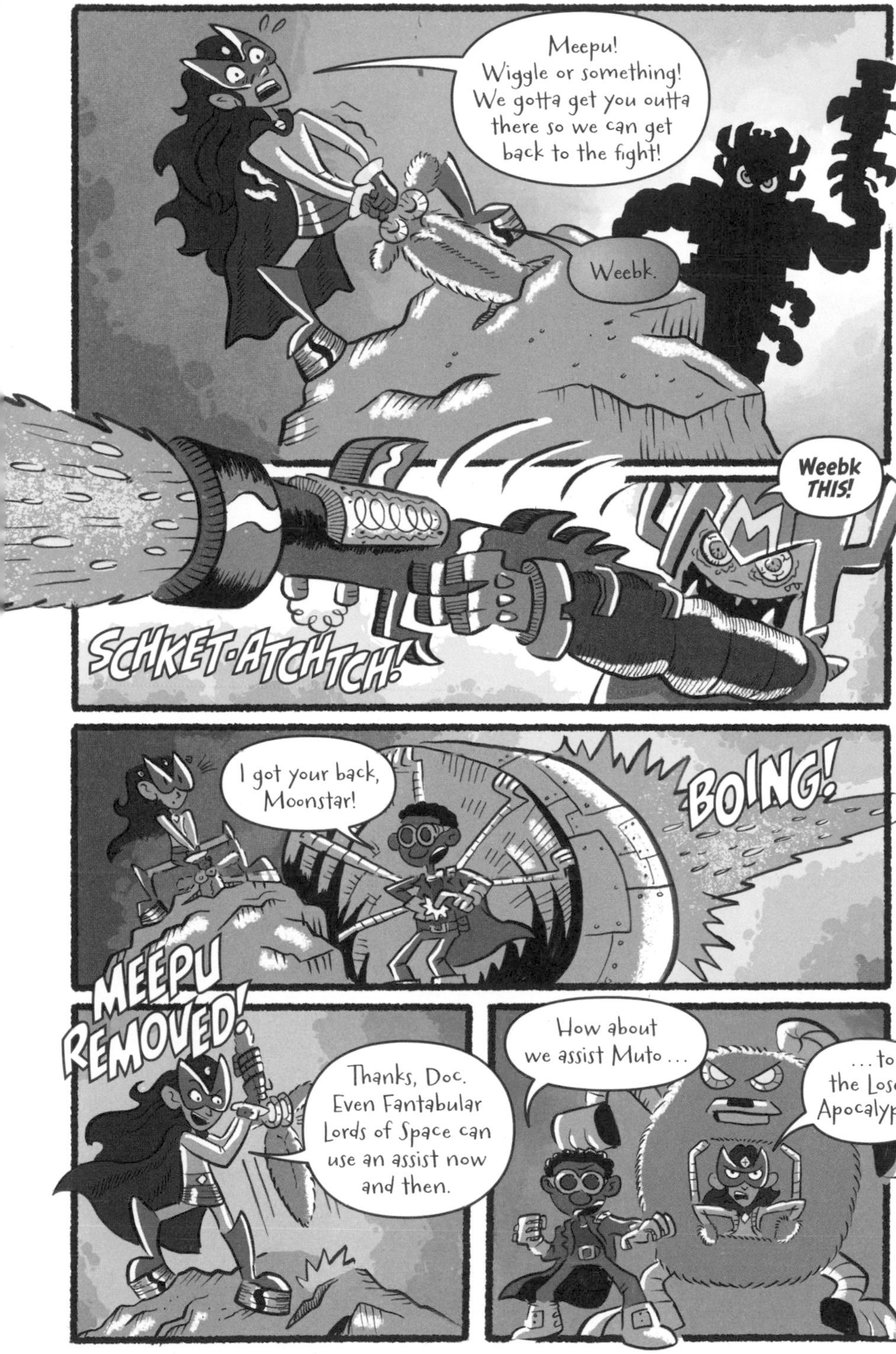
Meepu!
Wiggle or something!
We gotta get you outta
there so we can get
back to the fight!
Weebk.
Weebk THIS!
SCHKET-ATCHTCH!
I got your back,
Moonstar!
BOING!
MEEPU REMOVED!
Thanks, Doc.
Even Fantabular
Lords of Space can
use an assist now
and then.
How about
we assist Muto . . .
. . . to
the Loser
Apocalypse!

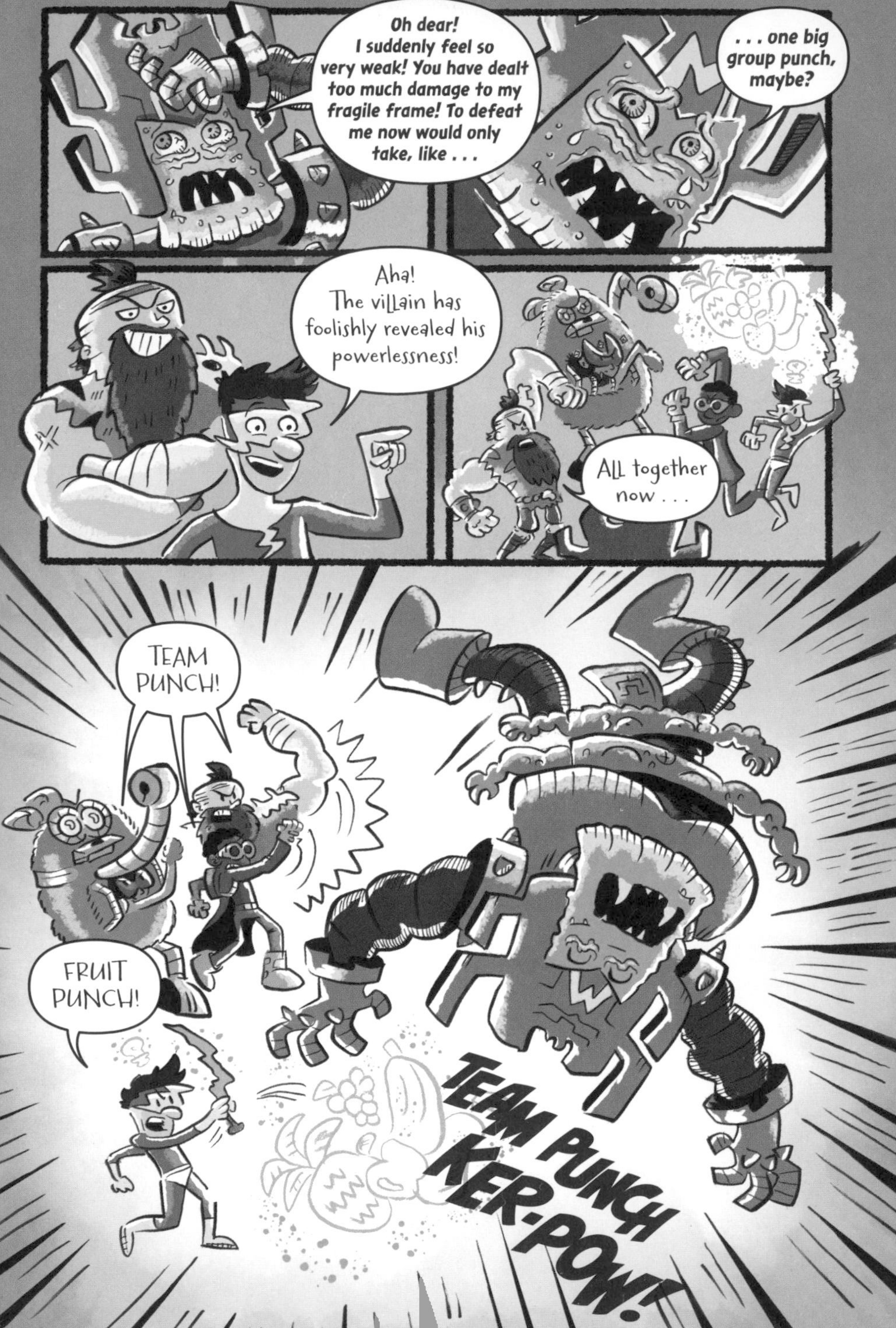
Oh dear! I suddenly feel so very weak! You have dealt too much damage to my fragile frame! To defeat me now would only take, like . . .
. . . one big group punch, maybe?
Aha! The villain has foolishly revealed his powerlessness!
ALL together now . . .
TEAM PUNCH!
FRUIT PUNCH!
TEAM PUNCH KER-POW!

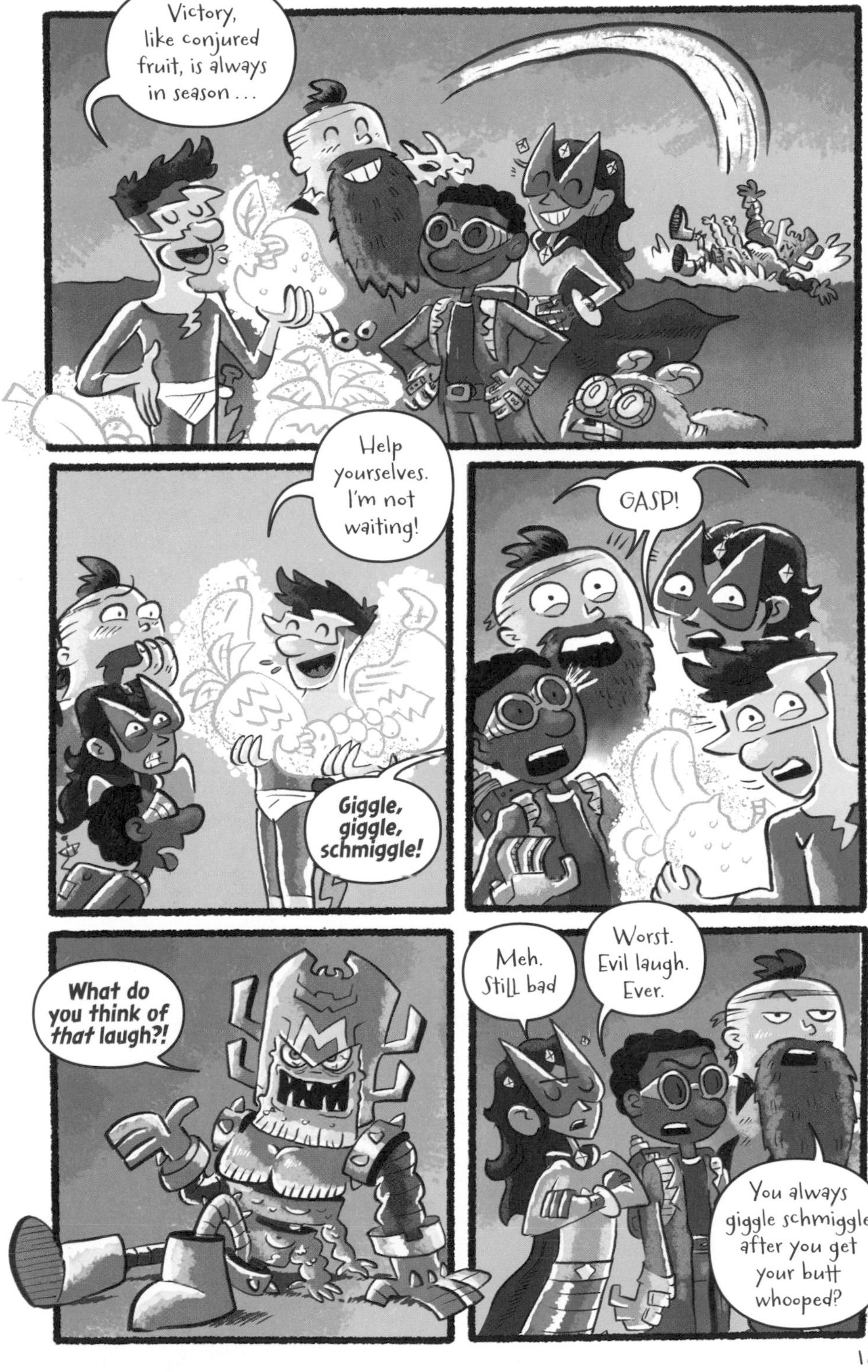
Victory, like conjured fruit, is always in season . . .
Help yourselves. I'm not waiting!
Giggle, giggle, schmiggle!
GASP!
What do you think of that laugh?!
Meh. StiLL bad
Worst. Evil laugh. Ever.
You always giggle schmiggle after you get your butt whooped?

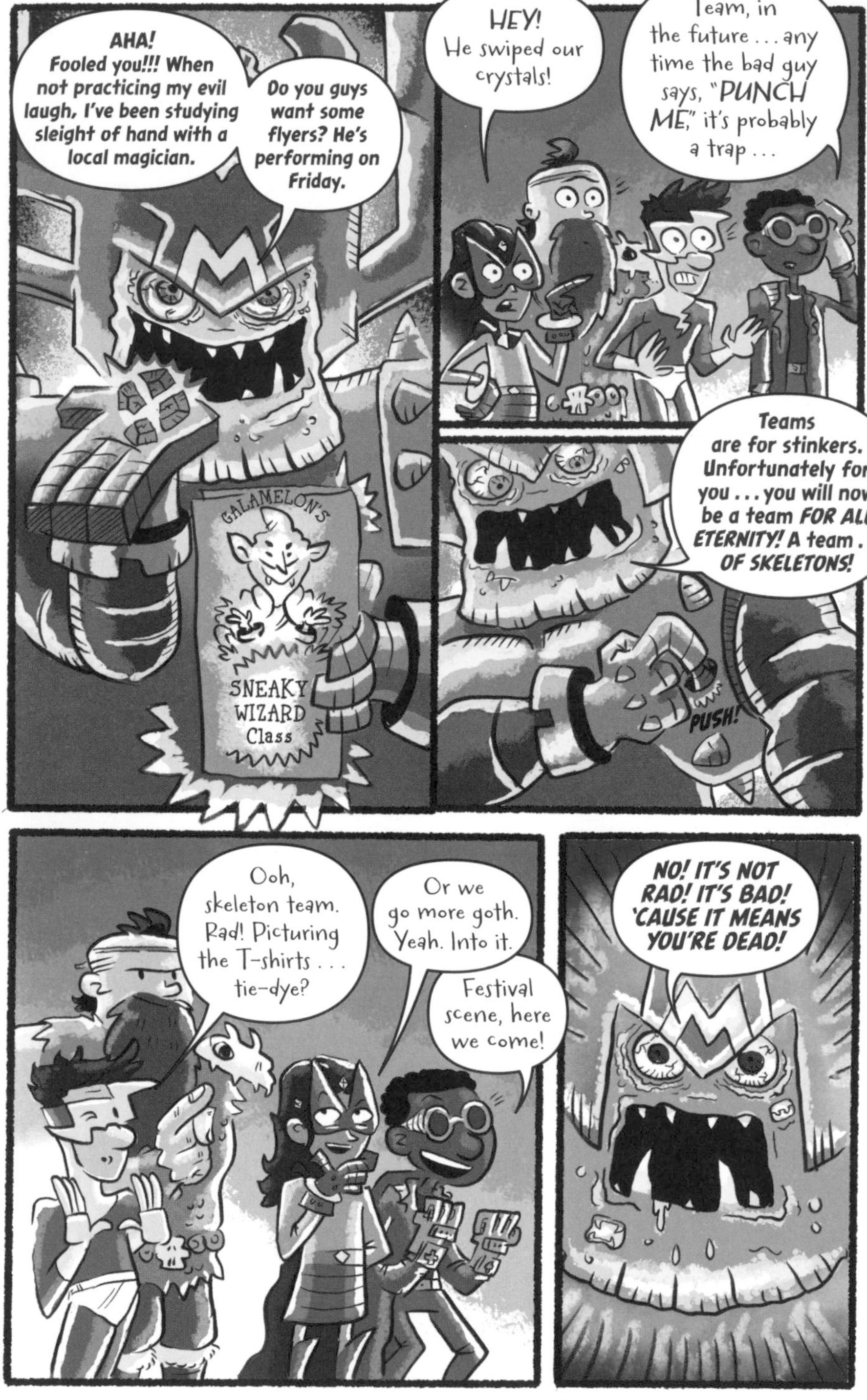
AHA! Fooled you!!! When not practicing my evil laugh, I've been studying sleight of hand with a local magician.
Do you guys want some flyers? He's performing on Friday.
GALAMELON'S
SNEAKY WIZARD Class
HEY! He swiped our crystals!
Team, in the future . . . any time the bad guy says, "PUNCH ME," it's probably a trap . . .
Teams are for stinkers. Unfortunately for you . . . you will now be a team FOR ALL ETERNITY! A team . . . OF SKELETONS!
PUSH!
Ooh, skeleton team. Rad! Picturing the T-shirts . . . tie-dye?
Or we go more goth. Yeah. Into it.
Festival scene, here we come!
NO! IT'S NOT RAD! IT'S BAD! 'CAUSE IT MEANS YOU'RE DEAD!

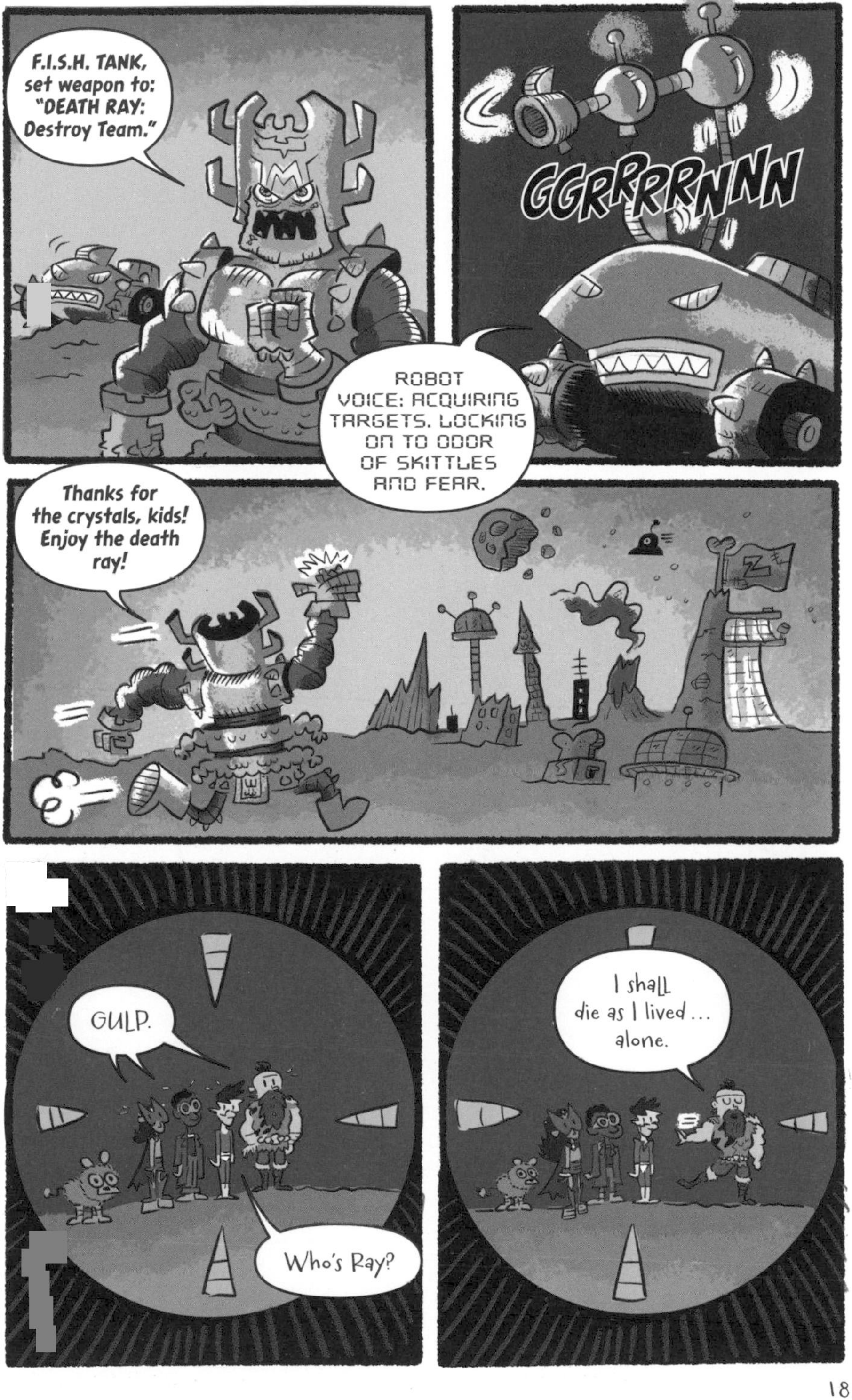
F.I.S.H. TANK, set weapon to: "DEATH RAY: Destroy Team."
GGRRRRNNN
ROBOT VOICE: ACQUIRING TARGETS. LOCKING ON TO ODOR OF SKITTLES AND FEAR.
Thanks for the crystals, kids! Enjoy the death ray!
GULP.
Who's Ray?
I shall die as I lived... alone.

CHAPTER TEN
TEAM SKELETON?

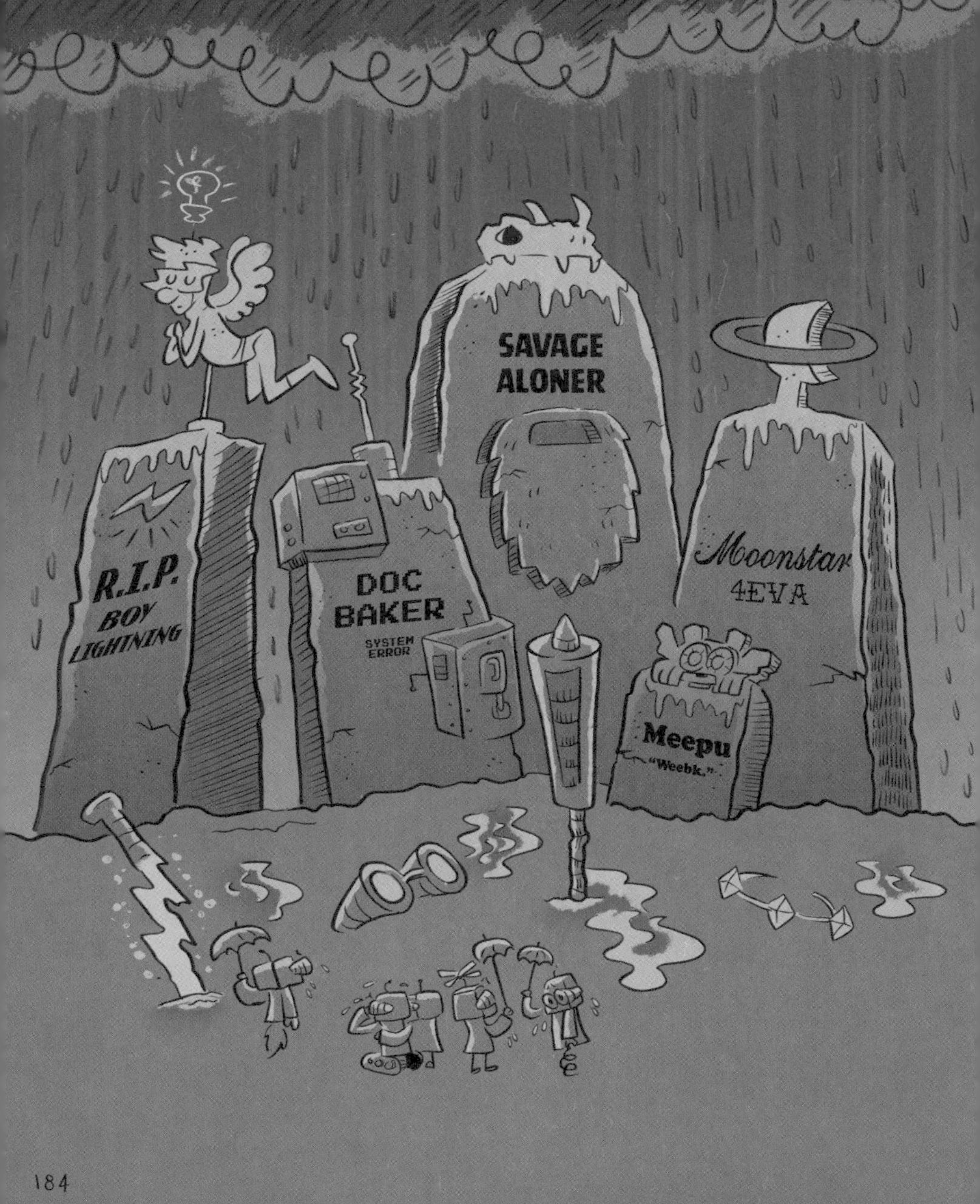
R.I.P.
BOY
LIGHTNING
DOC
BAKER
SYSTEM
ERROR
SAVAGE
ALONER
Moonstar
4EVA
Meepu
"Weebk."

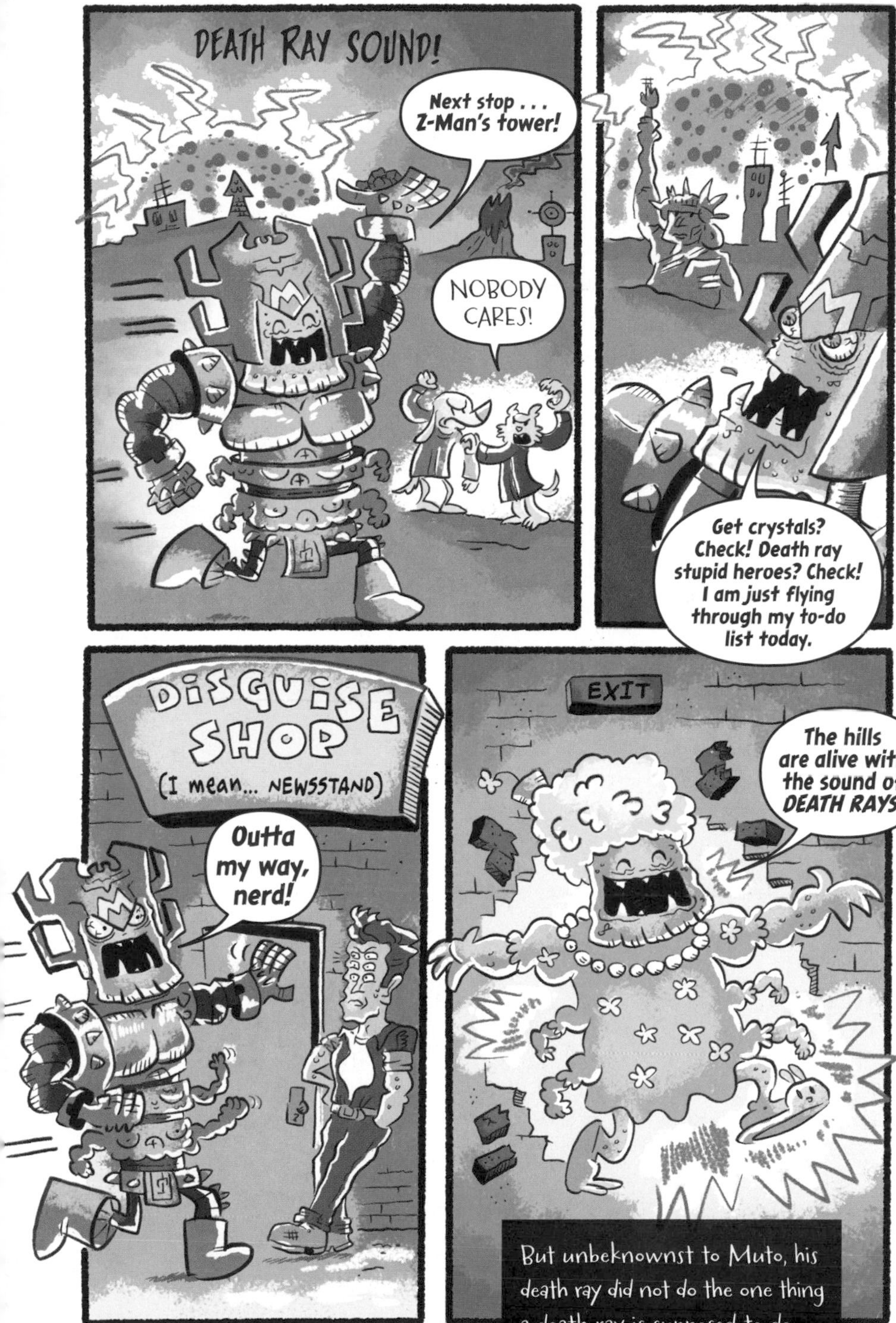
DEATH RAY SOUND!
Next stop . . . Z-Man's tower!
NOBODY CARES!
Get crystals? Check! Death ray stupid heroes? Check! I am just flying through my to-do list today.
DISGUISE SHOP
(I mean... NEWSSTAND)
Outta my way, nerd!
EXIT
The hills are alive with the sound of *DEATH RAYS!*
But unbeknownst to Muto, his death ray did not do the one thing a death ray is supposed to do . . .

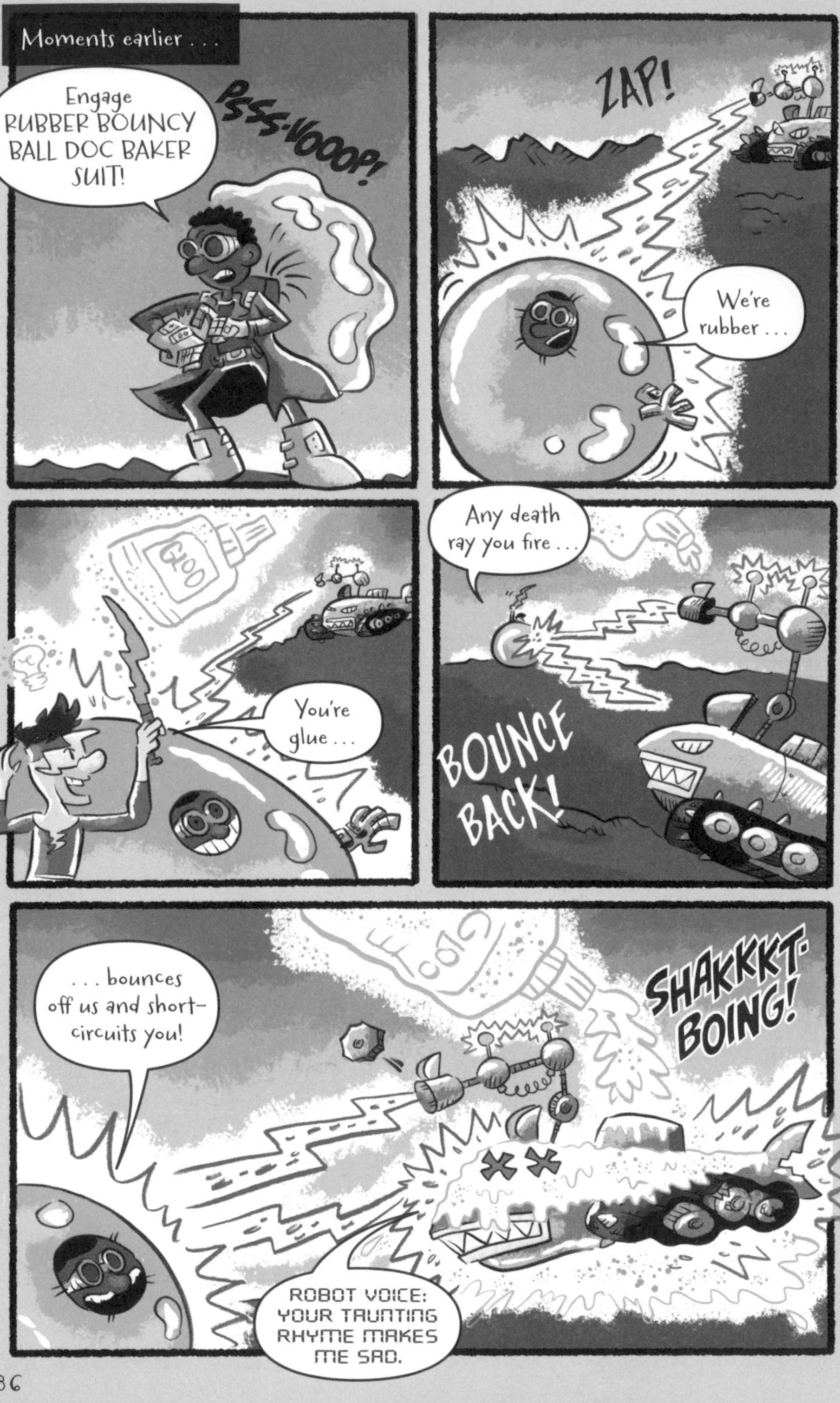
Moments earlier . . .
Engage RUBBER BOUNCY BALL DOC BAKER SUIT!
PSSS-VOOOP!
ZAP!
We're rubber . . .
You're glue . . .
Any death ray you fire . . .
BOUNCE BACK!
. . . bounces off us and short-circuits you!
SHAKKT-BOING!
ROBOT VOICE: YOUR TAUNTING RHYME MAKES ME SAD.

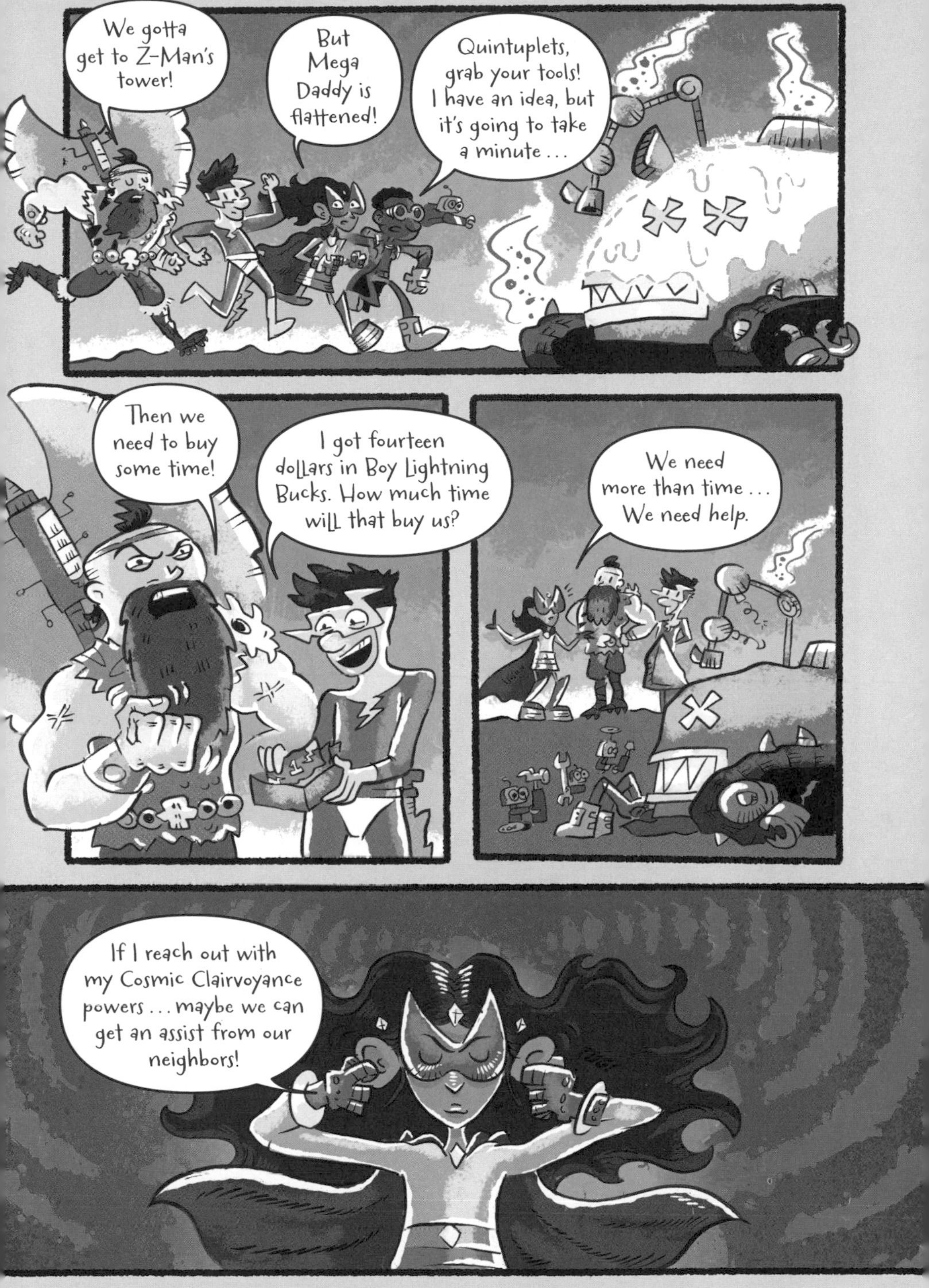
We gotta get to Z-Man's tower!
But Mega Daddy is flattened!
Quintuplets, grab your tools! I have an idea, but it's going to take a minute . . .
Then we need to buy some time!
I got fourteen dollars in Boy Lightning Bucks. How much time will that buy us?
We need more than time . . . We need help.
If I reach out with my Cosmic Clairvoyance powers . . . maybe we can get an assist from our neighbors!

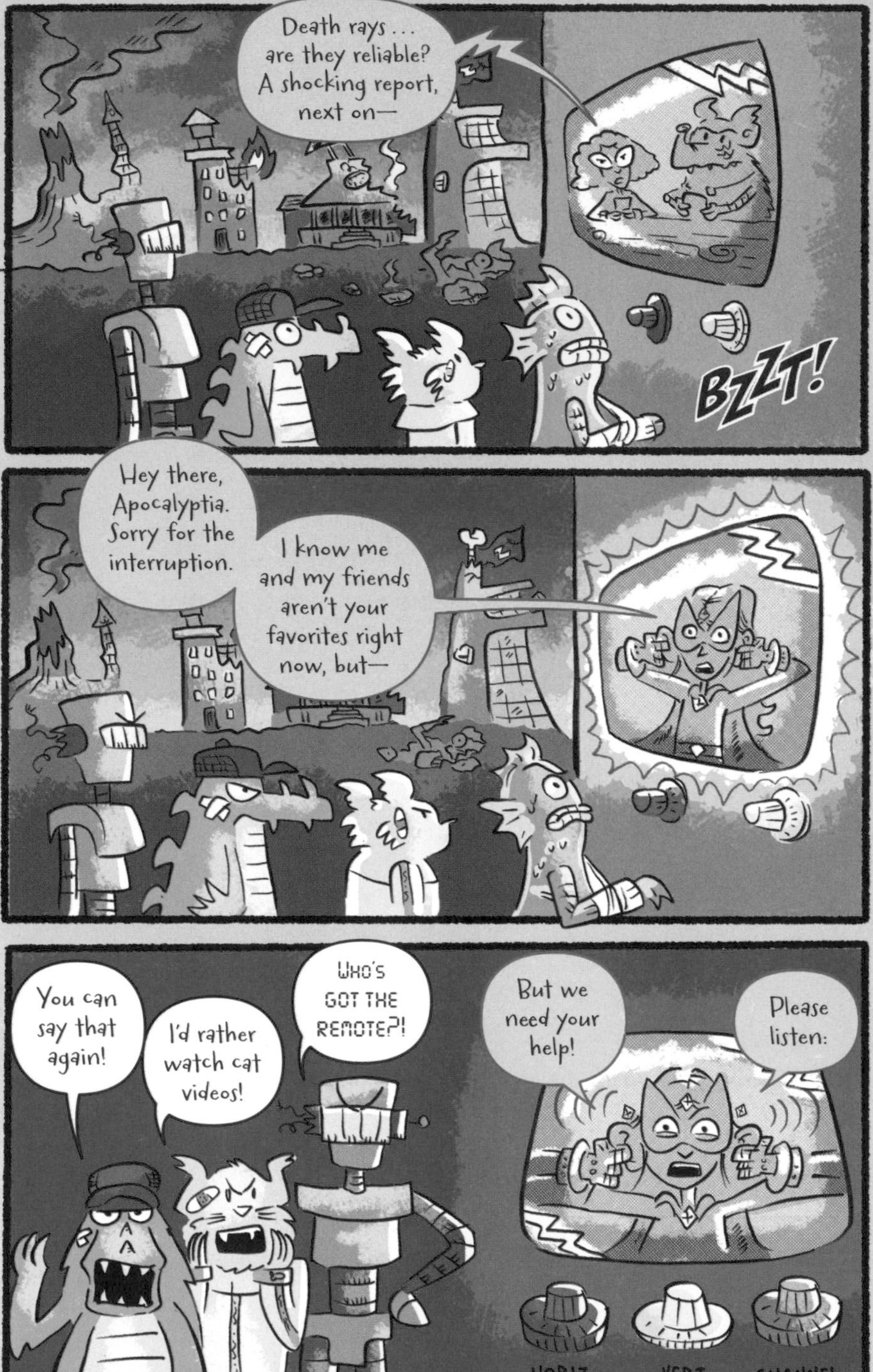
Death rays . . . are they reliable? A shocking report, next on—
BZZT!
Hey there, Apocalyptia. Sorry for the interruption.
I know me and my friends aren't your favorites right now, but—
You can say that again!
I'd rather watch cat videos!
WHO'S GOT THE REMOTE?!
But we need your help!
Please listen:
HORIZ.
VERT.
CHANNEL

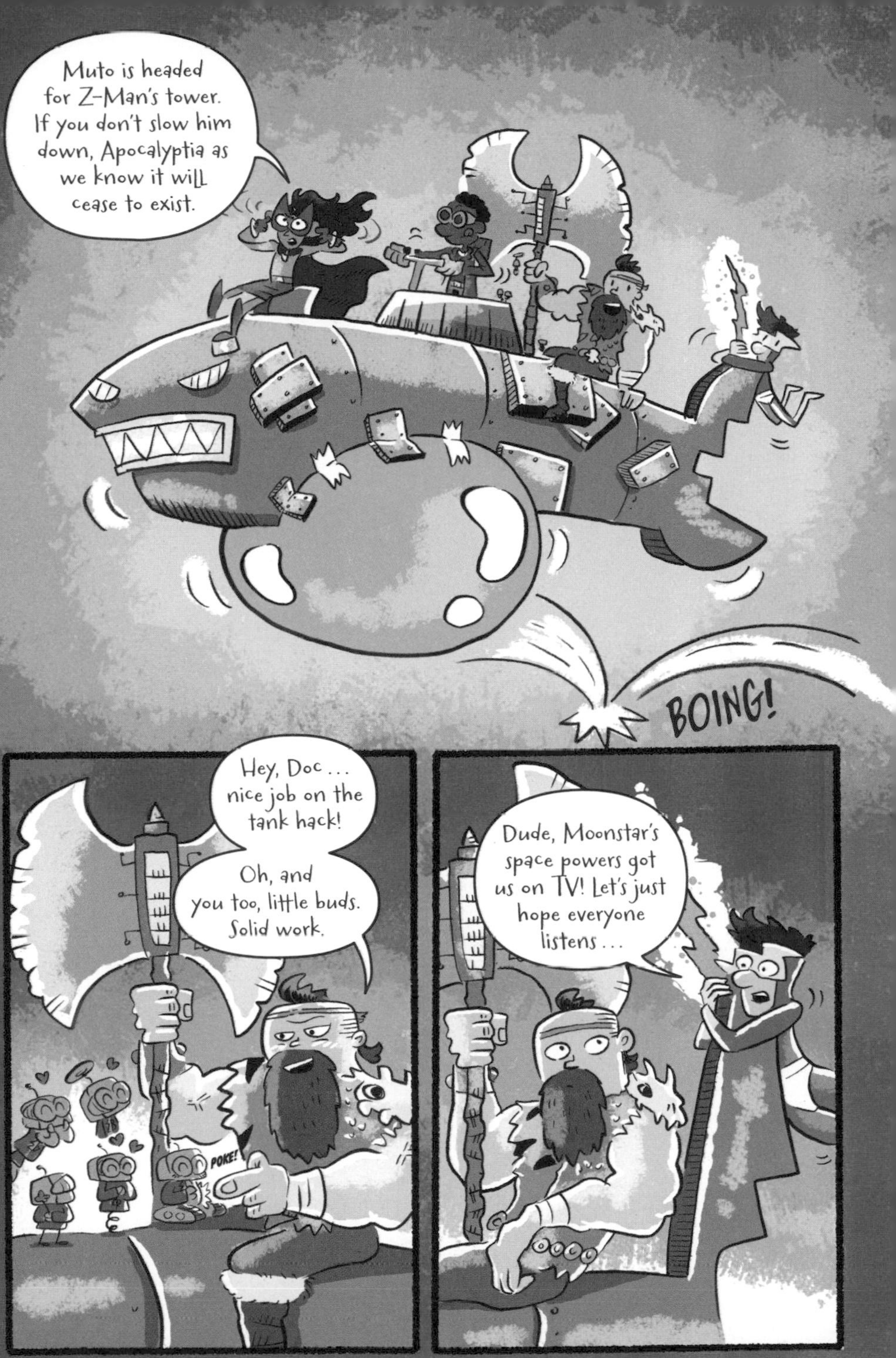
Muto is headed for Z-Man's tower. If you don't slow him down, Apocalyptia as we know it will cease to exist.
BOING!
Hey, Doc . . . nice job on the tank hack!
Oh, and you too, little buds. Solid work.
POKE!
Dude, Moonstar's space powers got us on TV! Let's just hope everyone listens . . .

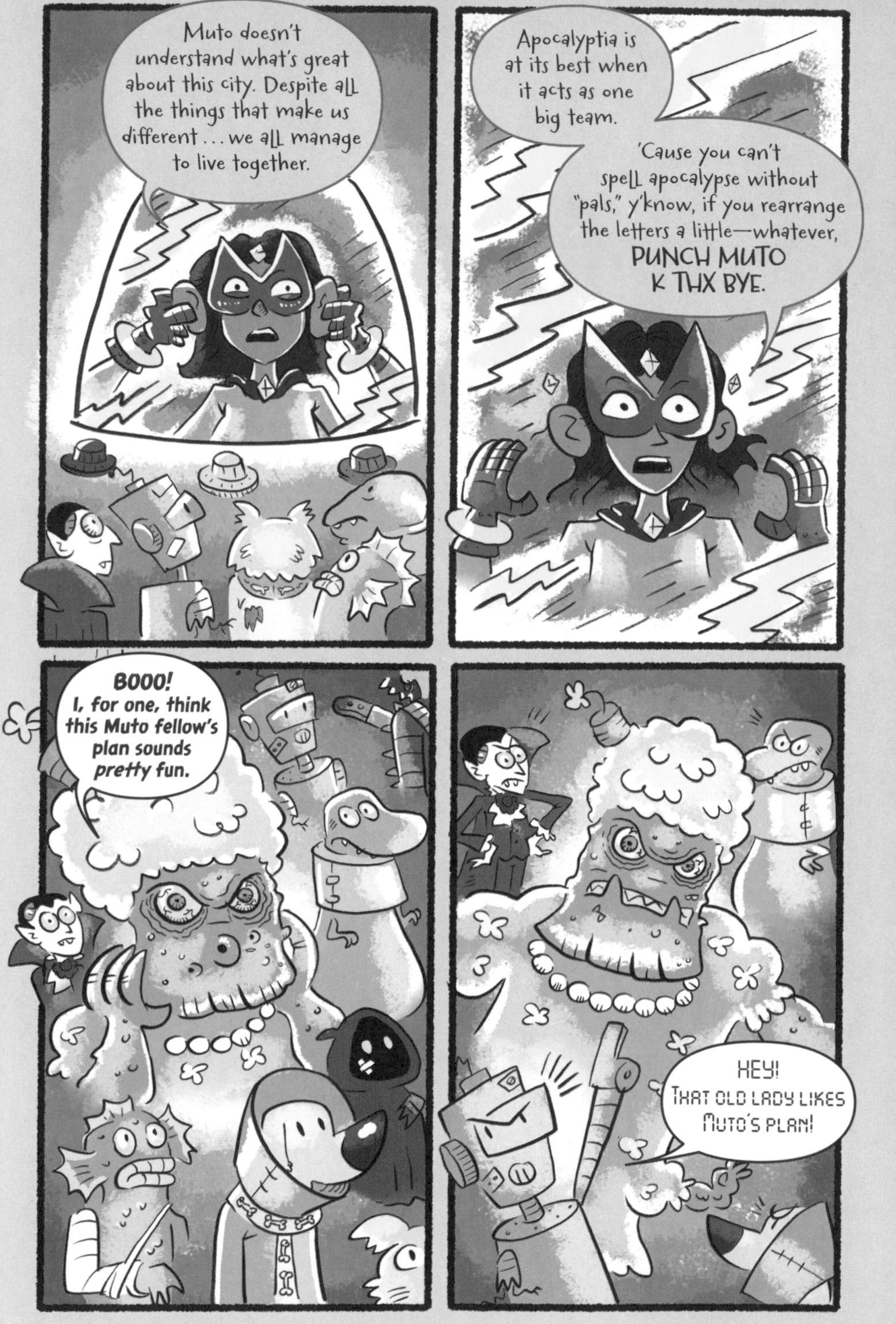
Muto doesn't understand what's great about this city. Despite all the things that make us different . . . we all manage to live together.
Apocalyptia is at its best when it acts as one big team.
'Cause you can't spell apocalypse without "pals," y'know, if you rearrange the letters a little—whatever, PUNCH MUTO K THX BYE.
BOOO! I, for one, think this Muto fellow's plan sounds *pretty* fun.
HEY! THAT OLD LADY LIKES MUTO'S PLAN!

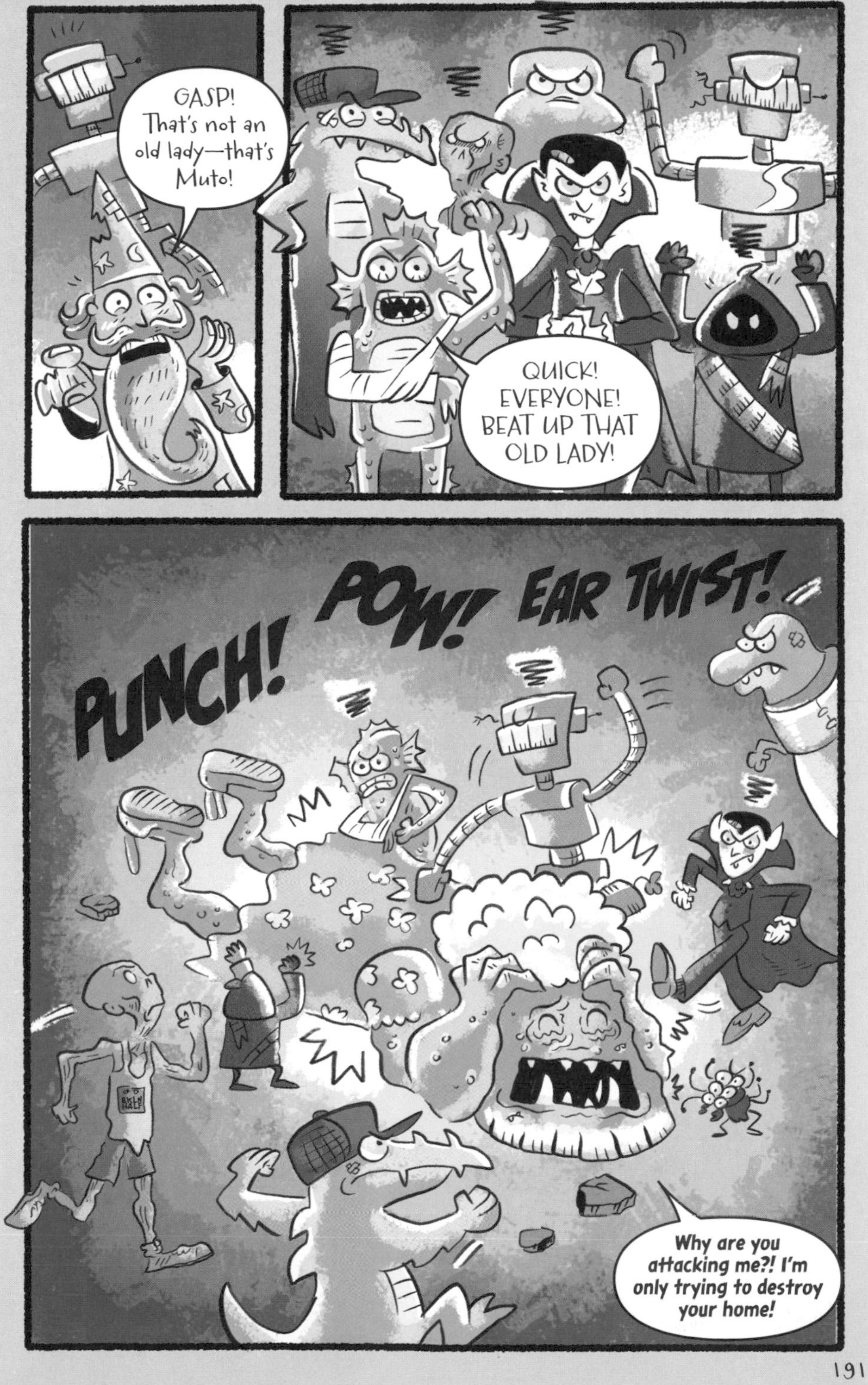
GASP! That's not an old lady—that's Muto!
QUICK! EVERYONE! BEAT UP THAT OLD LADY!
PUNCH!
POW!
EAR TWIST!
Why are you attacking me?! I'm only trying to destroy your home!

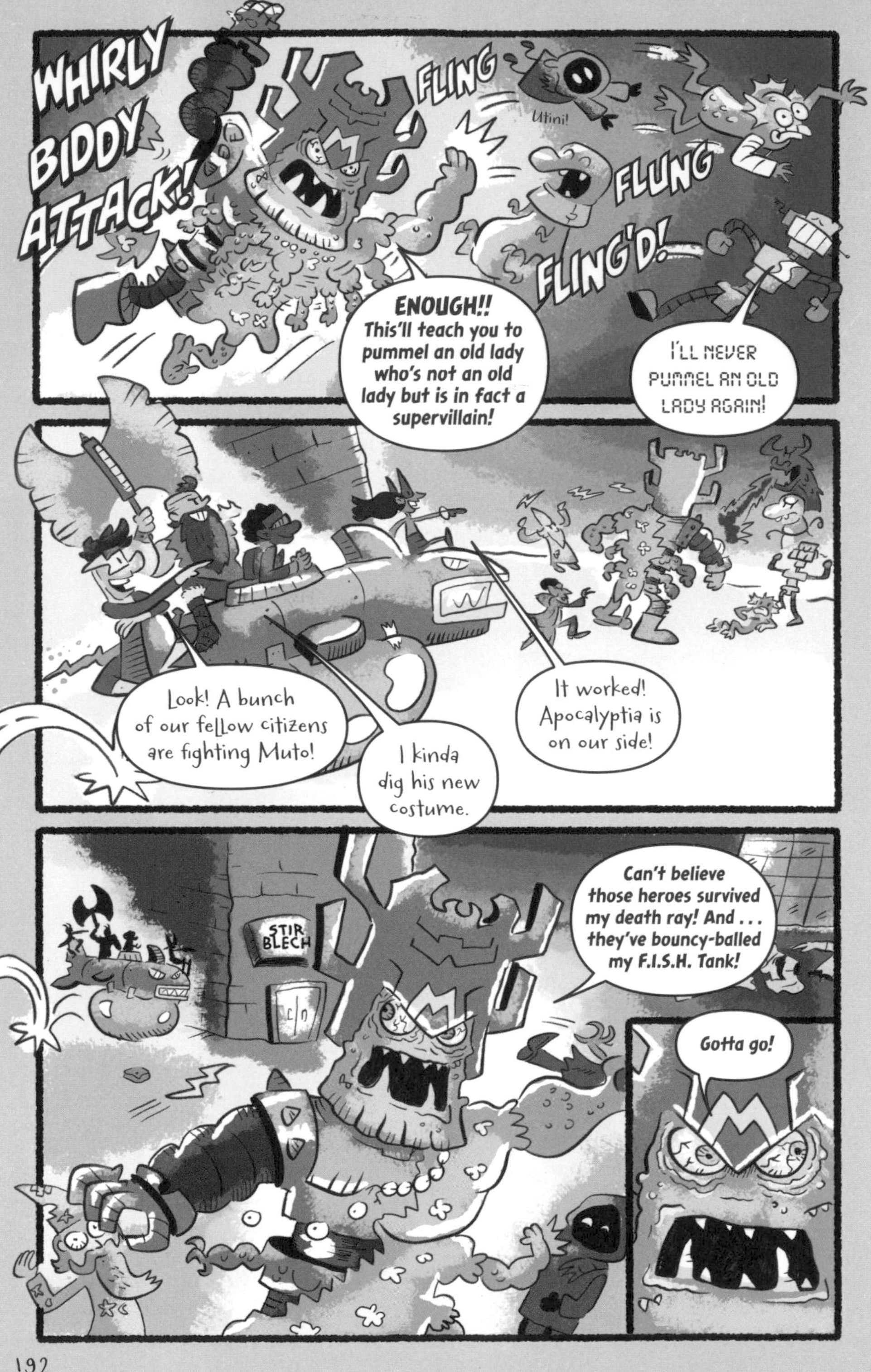
WHIRLY BIDDY ATTACK!
FLING
Utini!
FLUNG
FLING'D!
ENOUGH!! This'll teach you to pummel an old lady who's not an old lady but is in fact a supervillain!
I'LL NEVER PUMMEL AN OLD LADY AGAIN!
Look! A bunch of our fellow citizens are fighting Muto!
I kinda dig his new costume.
It worked! Apocalyptia is on our side!
STIR BLECH
Can't believe those heroes survived my death ray! And . . . they've bouncy-balled my F.I.S.H. Tank!
Gotta go!

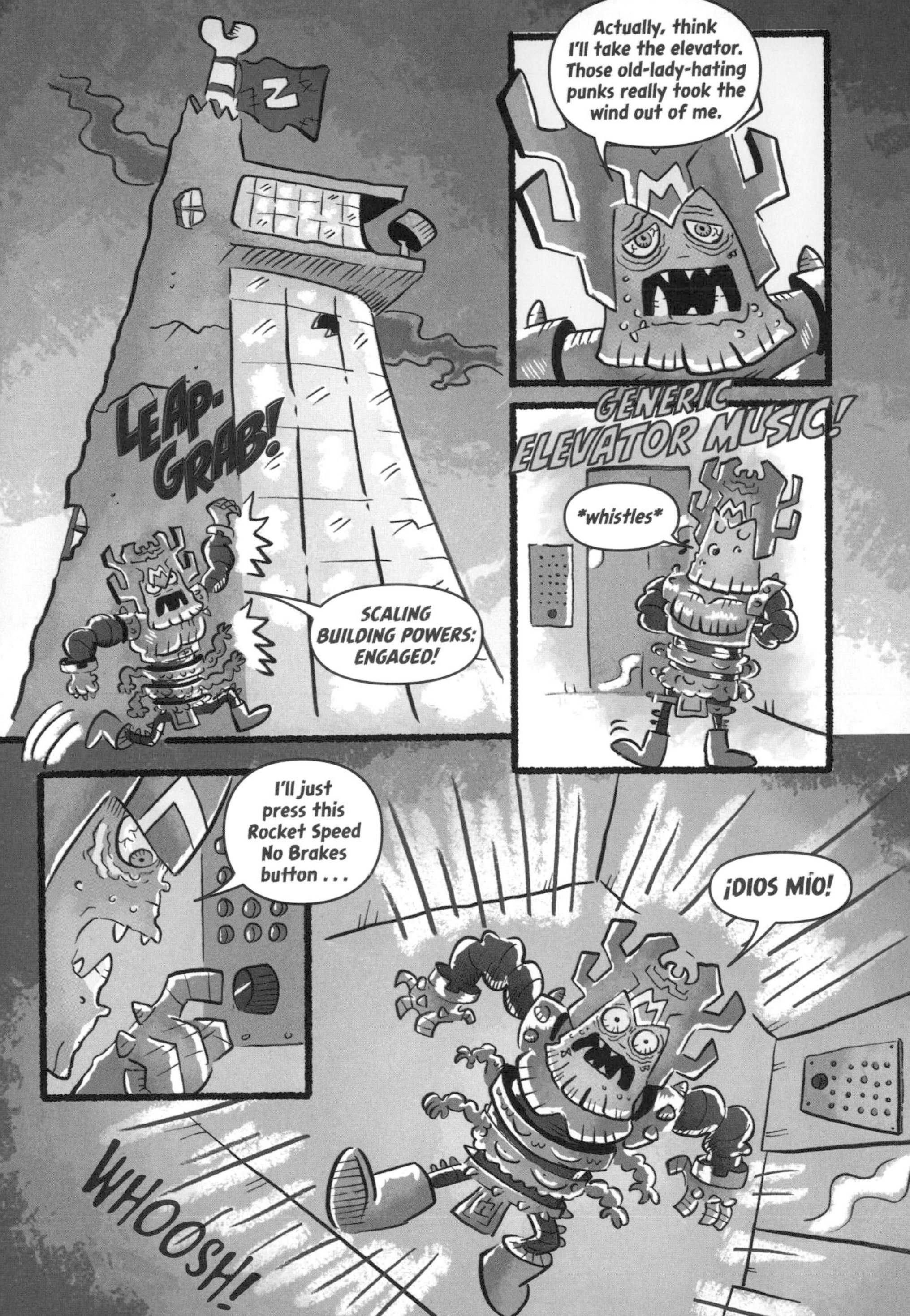
Actually, think I'll take the elevator. Those old-lady-hating punks really took the wind out of me.
LEAP-GRAB!
SCALING BUILDING POWERS: ENGAGED!
GENERIC ELEVATOR MUSIC!
whistles
I'll just press this Rocket Speed No Brakes button . . .
¡DIOS MIO!
WHOOSH!

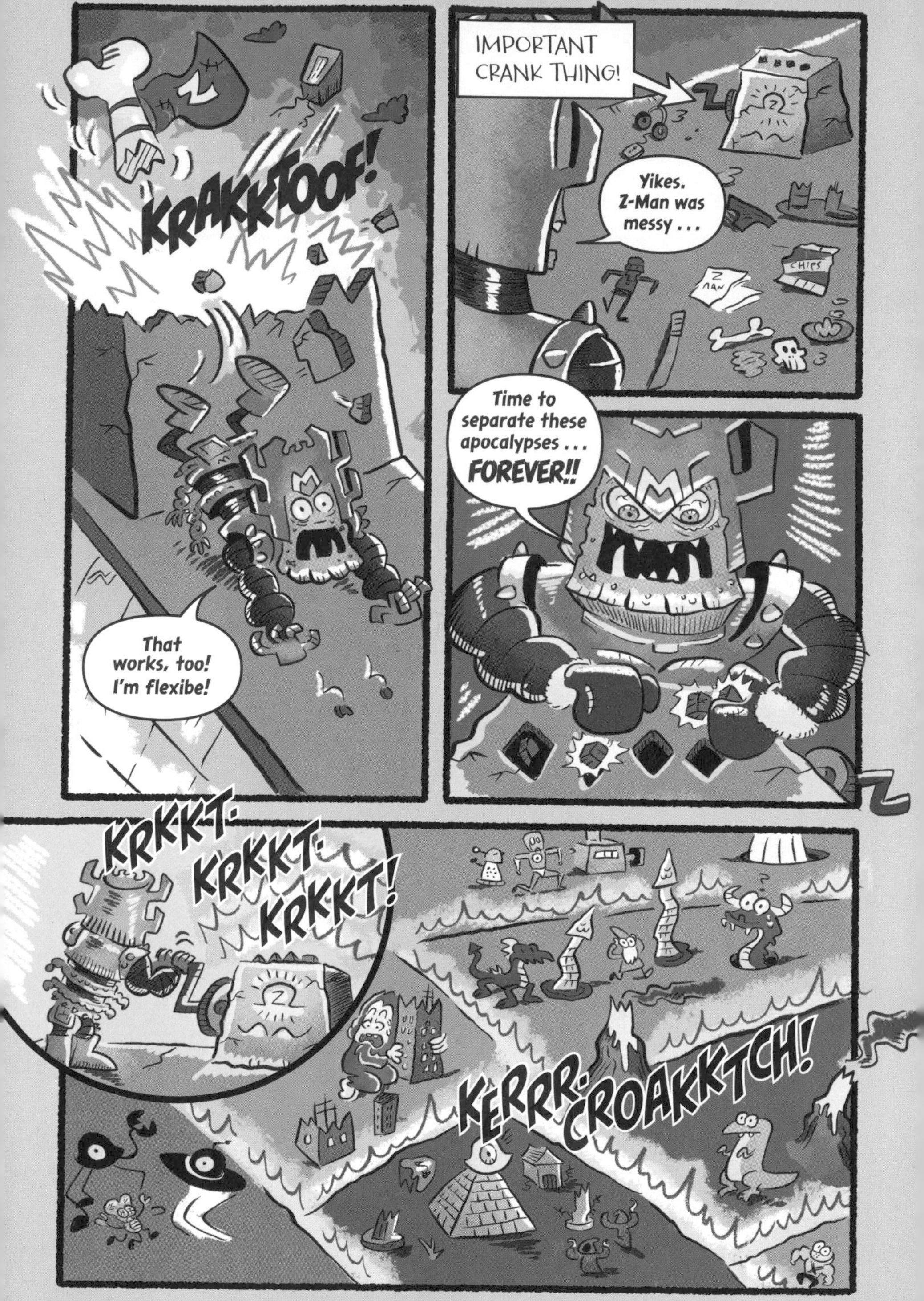
KRAKKTOOF!
That works, too! I'm flexibe!
IMPORTANT CRANK THING!
Yikes. Z-Man was messy . . .
CHIPS
Time to separate these apocalypses . . . FOREVER!!
KRKKT-KRKKT-KRKKT!
KERRR-CROAKKTCH!

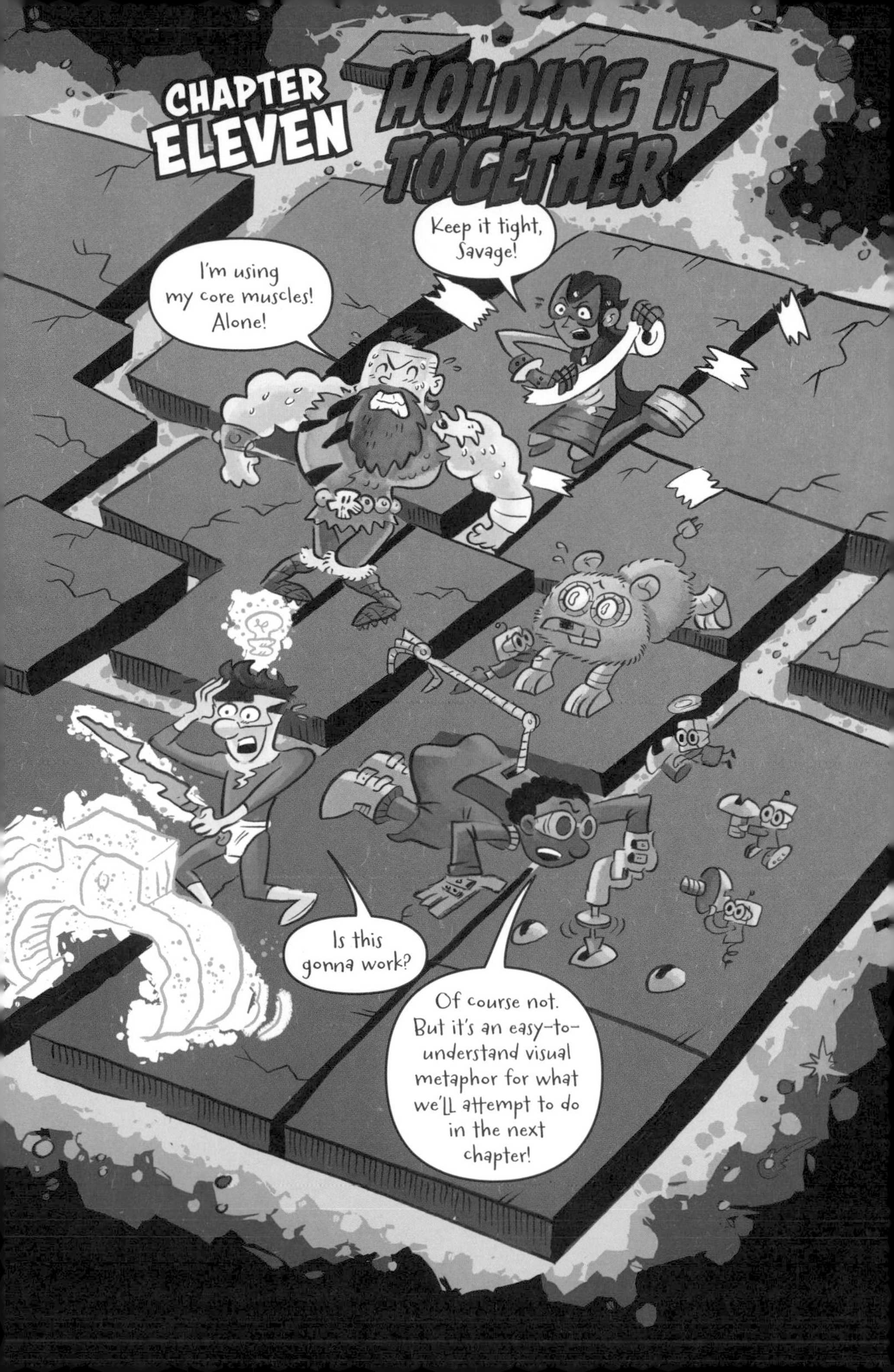
CHAPTER ELEVEN
HOLDING IT TOGETHER
I'm using my core muscles! Alone!
Keep it tight, Savage!
Is this gonna work?
Of course not. But it's an easy-to-understand visual metaphor for what we'll attempt to do in the next chapter!

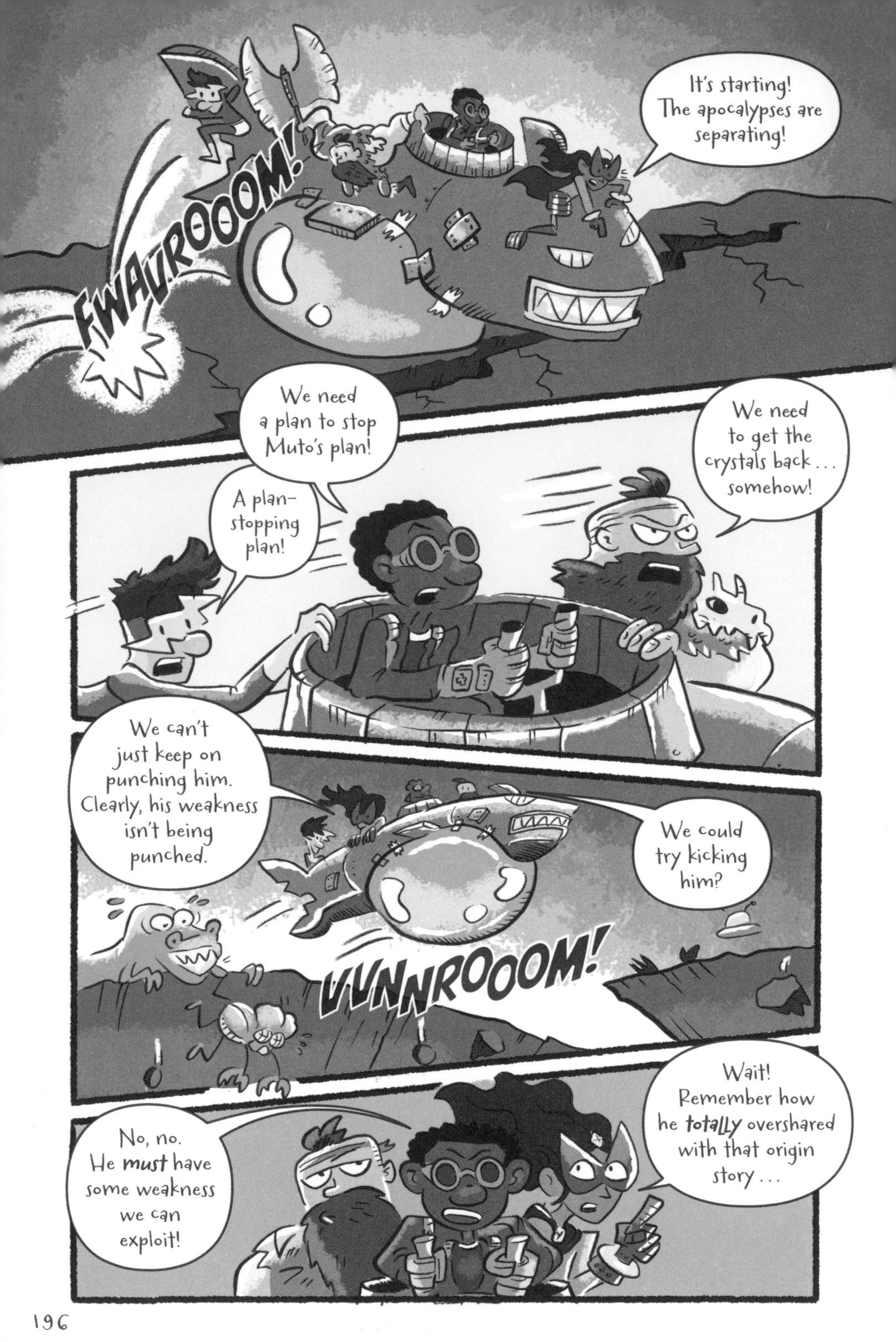
FWAVROOOM!
It's starting! The apocalypses are separating!
We need a plan to stop Muto's plan!
A plan-stopping plan!
We need to get the crystals back . . . somehow!
We can't just keep on punching him. Clearly, his weakness isn't being punched.
We could try kicking him?
VVNNROOOM!
No, no. He **must** have some weakness we can exploit!
Wait! Remember how he ***totally*** overshared with that origin story . . .

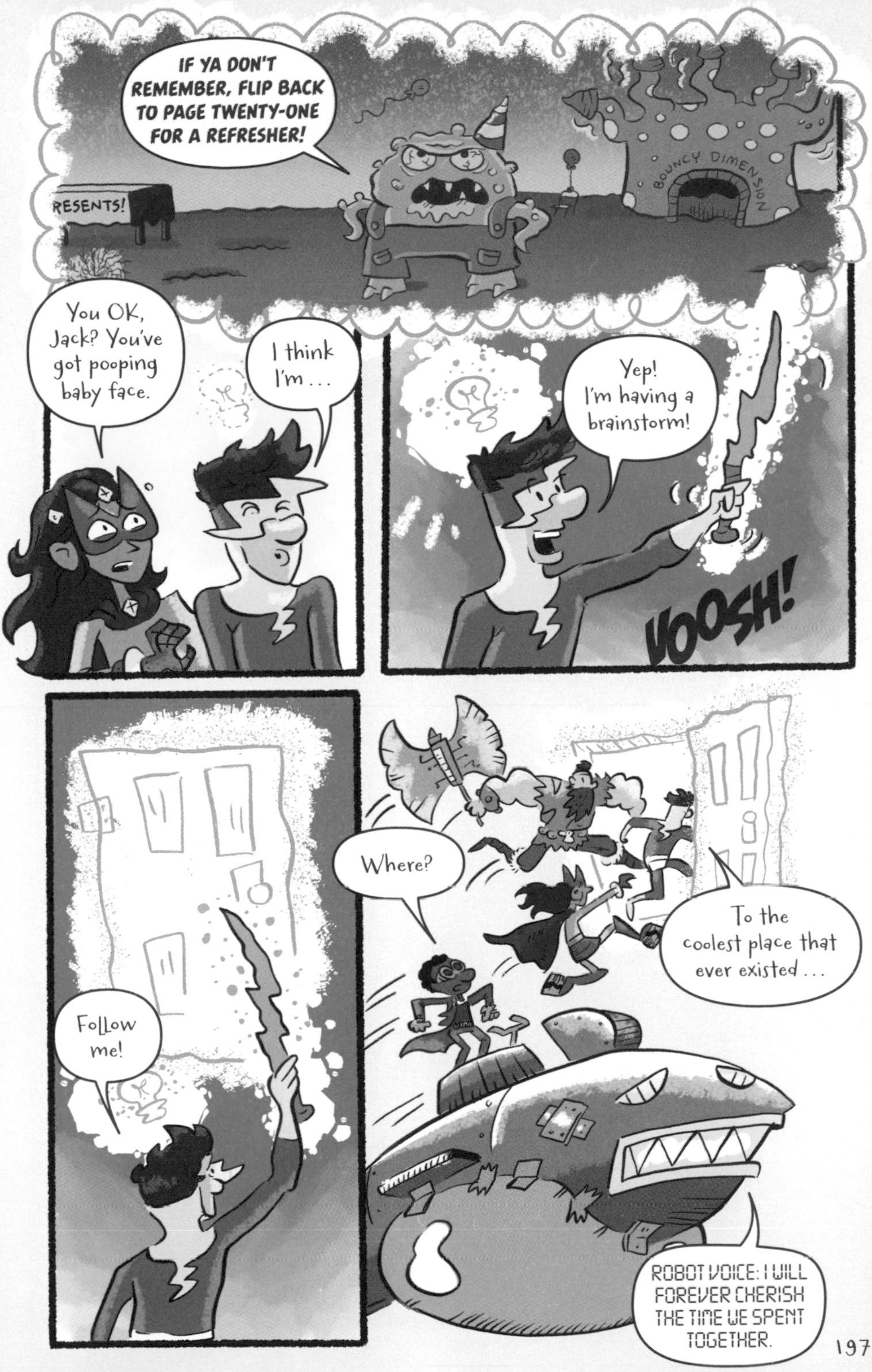
IF YA DON'T REMEMBER, FLIP BACK TO PAGE TWENTY-ONE FOR A REFRESHER!
RESENTS!
BOUNCY DIMENSION
You OK, Jack? You've got pooping baby face.
I think I'm . . .
Yep! I'm having a brainstorm!
VOOSH!
Follow me!
Where?
To the coolest place that ever existed . . .
ROBOT VOICE: I WILL FOREVER CHERISH THE TIME WE SPENT TOGETHER.

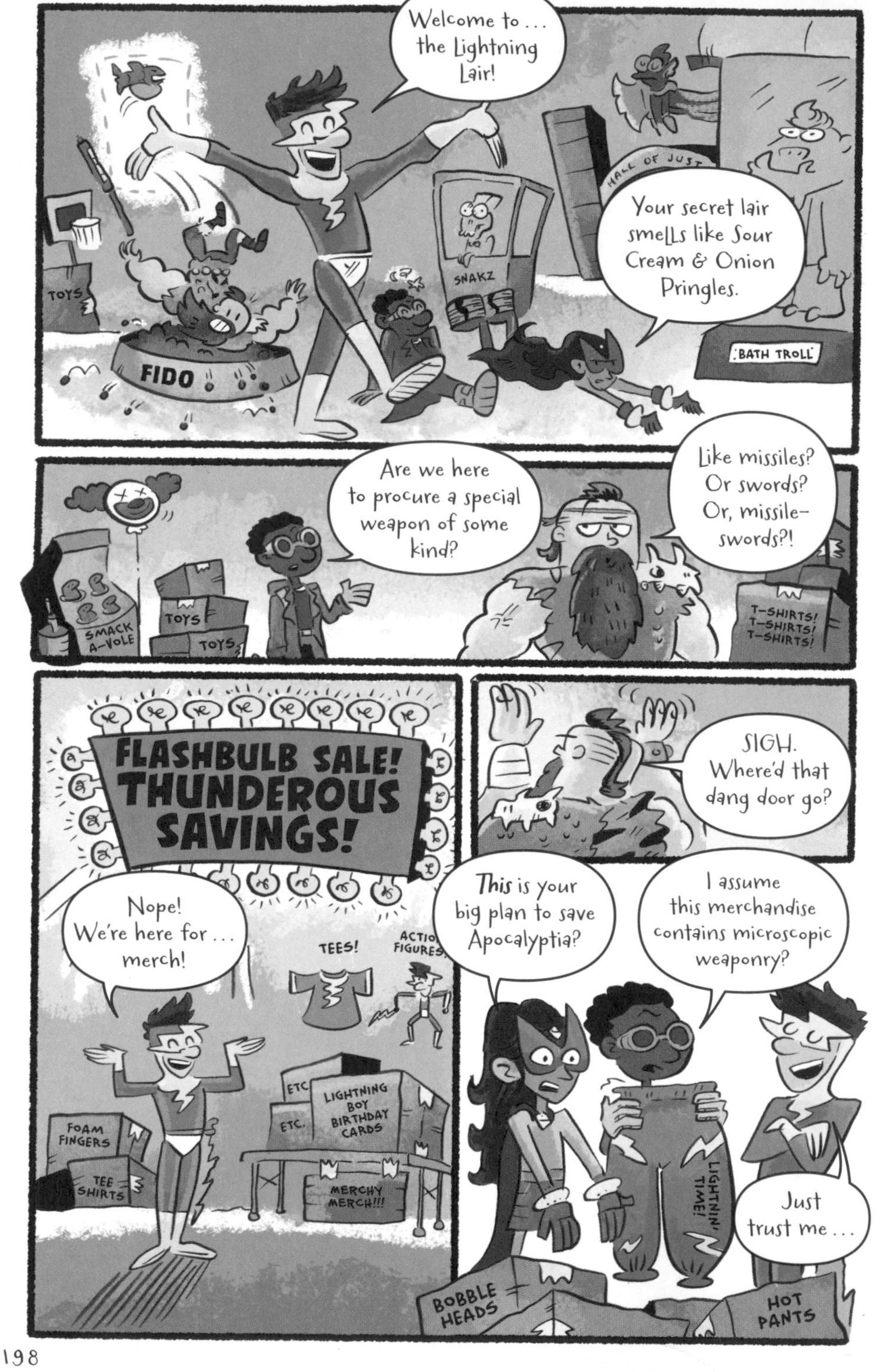
Welcome to . . . the Lightning Lair!
HALL OF JUST
TOYS
FIDO
SNAKZ
Your secret lair smells like Sour Cream & Onion Pringles.
BATH TROLL
Are we here to procure a special weapon of some kind?
Like missiles? Or swords? Or, missile-swords?!
SMACK A-VOLE
TOYS
TOYS
T-SHIRTS! T-SHIRTS! T-SHIRTS!
FLASHBULB SALE! THUNDEROUS SAVINGS!
SIGH. Where'd that dang door go?
Nope! We're here for . . . merch!
TEES!
ACTION FIGURES!
FOAM FINGERS
TEE SHIRTS
ETC.
ETC.
LIGHTNING BOY BIRTHDAY CARDS
MERCHY MERCH!!!
This is your big plan to save Apocalyptia?
I assume this merchandise contains microscopic weaponry?
LIGHTNIN' TIME!
Just trust me . . .
BOBBLE HEADS
HOT PANTS

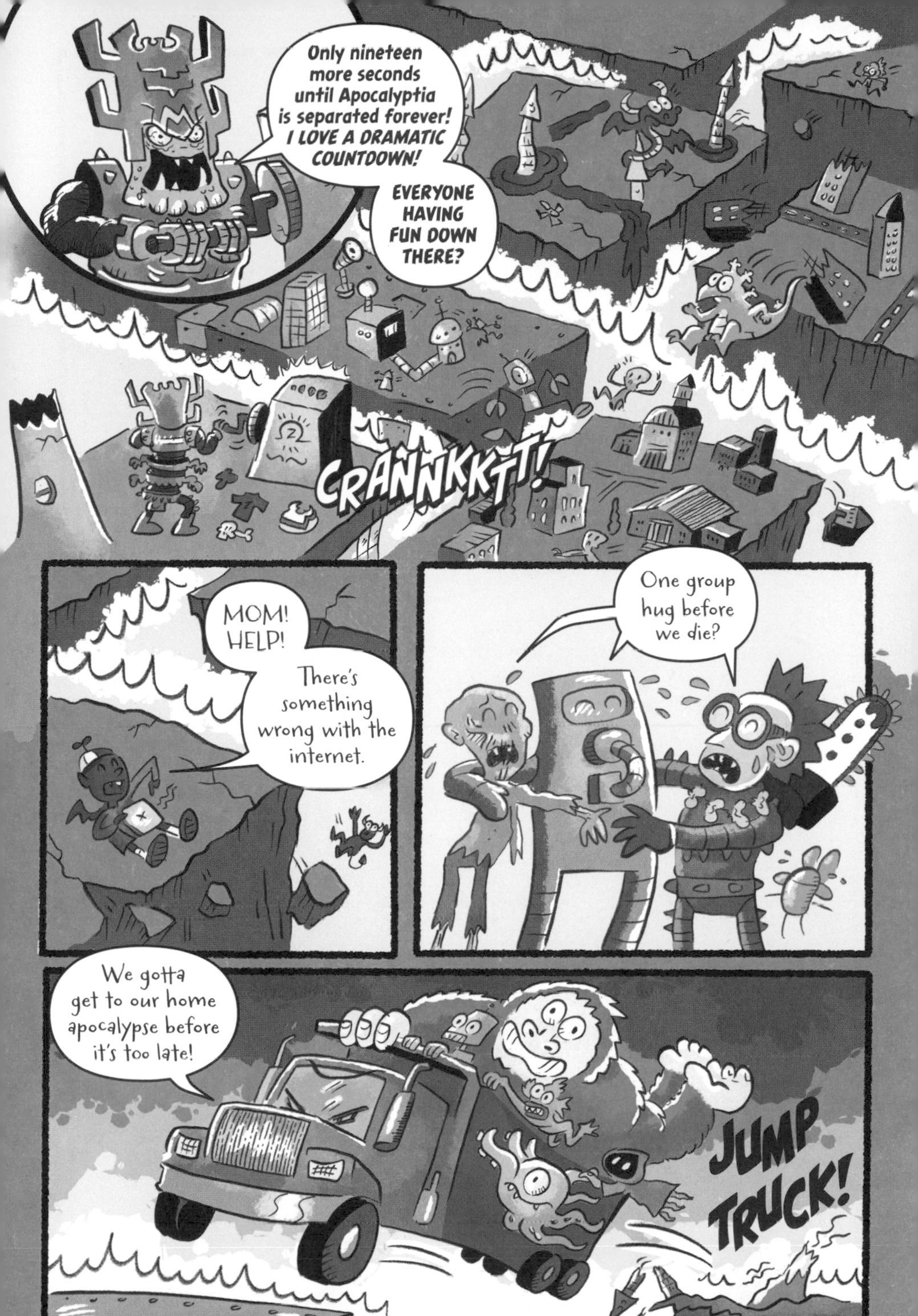
Only nineteen more seconds until Apocalyptia is separated forever! I LOVE A DRAMATIC COUNTDOWN!
EVERYONE HAVING FUN DOWN THERE?
CRANNKKTT!
MOM! HELP!
There's something wrong with the internet.
One group hug before we die?
We gotta get to our home apocalypse before it's too late!
JUMP TRUCK!

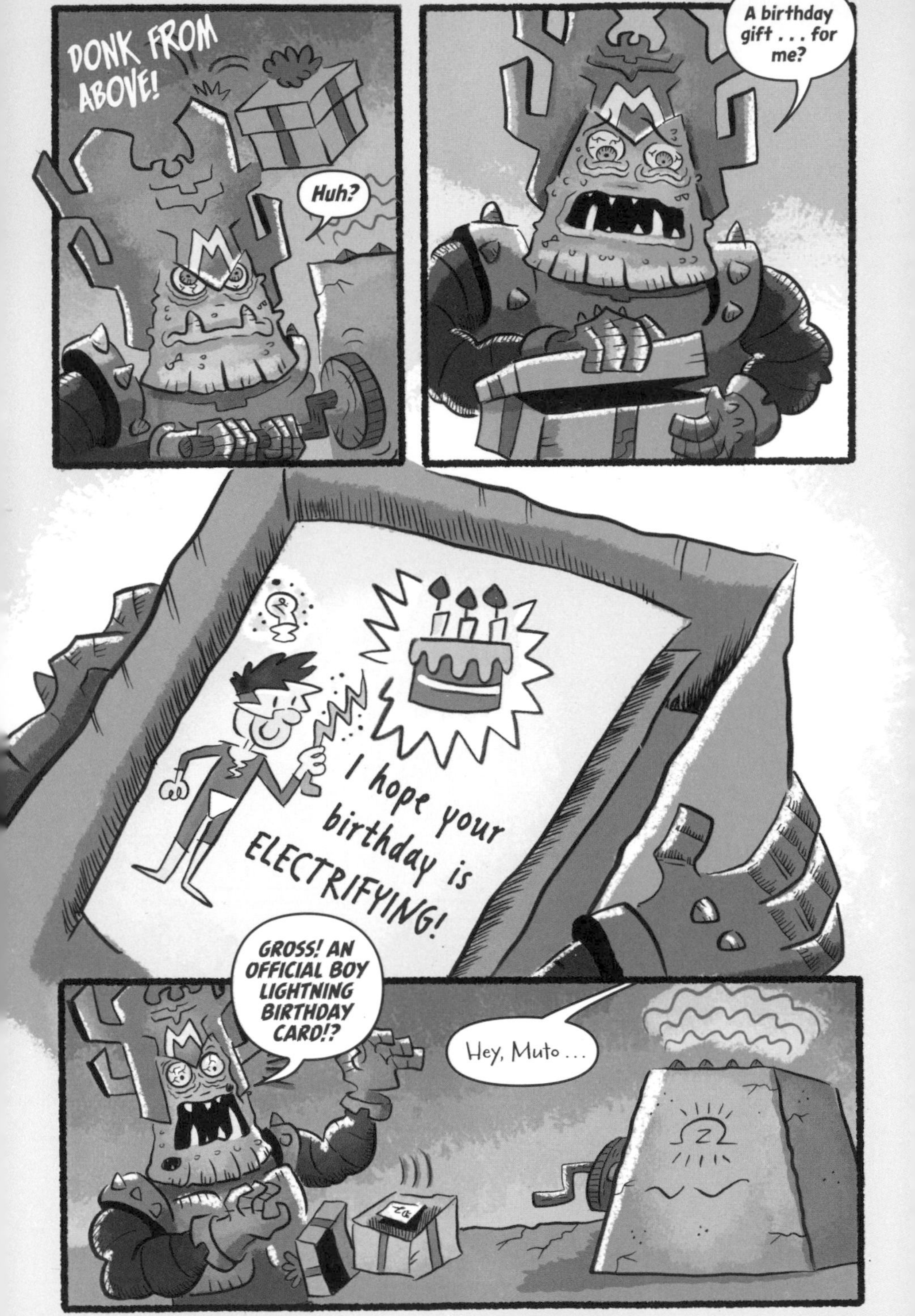
DONK FROM ABOVE!
Huh?
A birthday gift . . . for me?
I hope your birthday is ELECTRIFYING!
GROSS! AN OFFICIAL BOY LIGHTNING BIRTHDAY CARD!?
Hey, Muto . . .

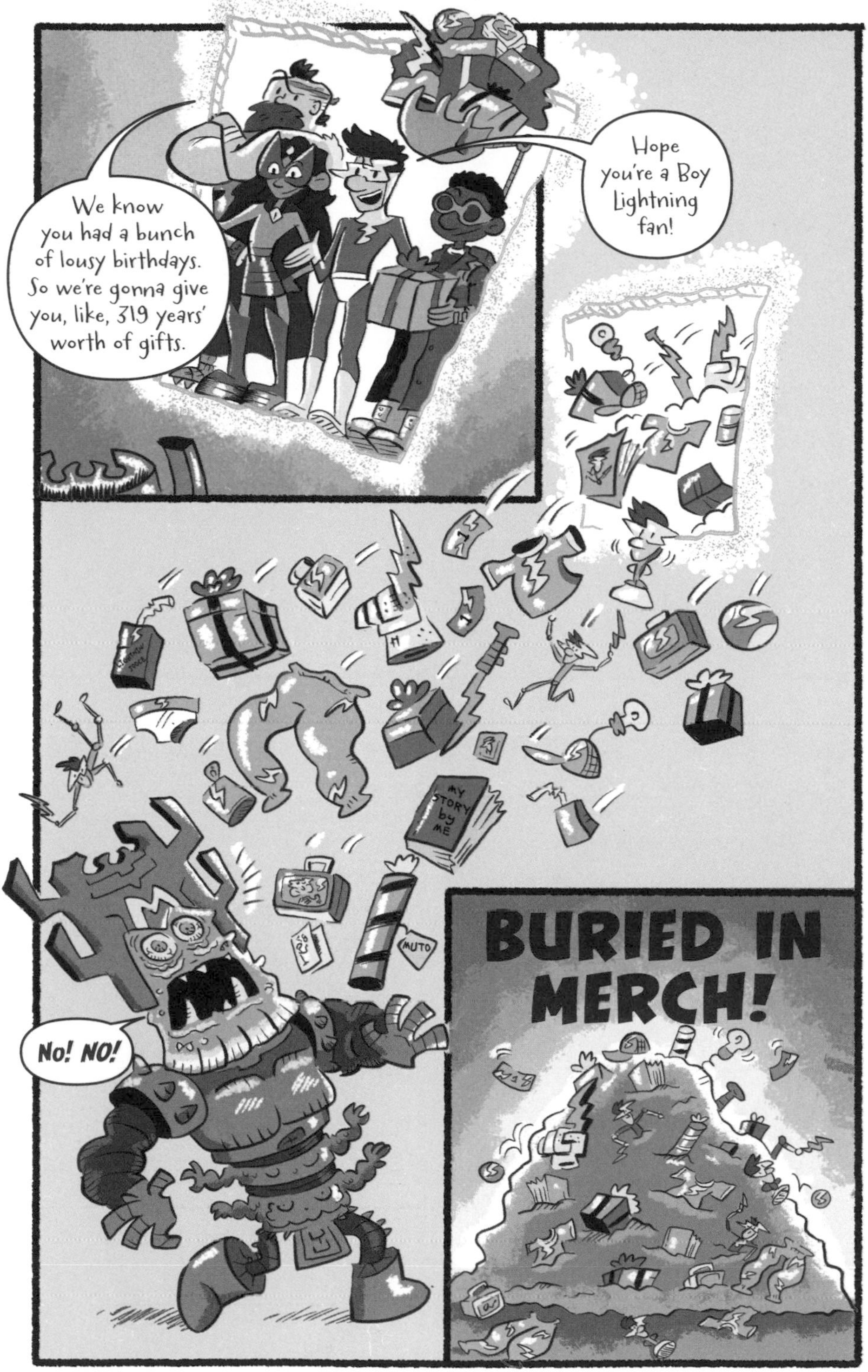
We know you had a bunch of lousy birthdays. So we're gonna give you, like, 319 years' worth of gifts.
Hope you're a Boy Lightning fan!
MY STORY by ME
MUTO
No! NO!
BURIED IN MERCH!

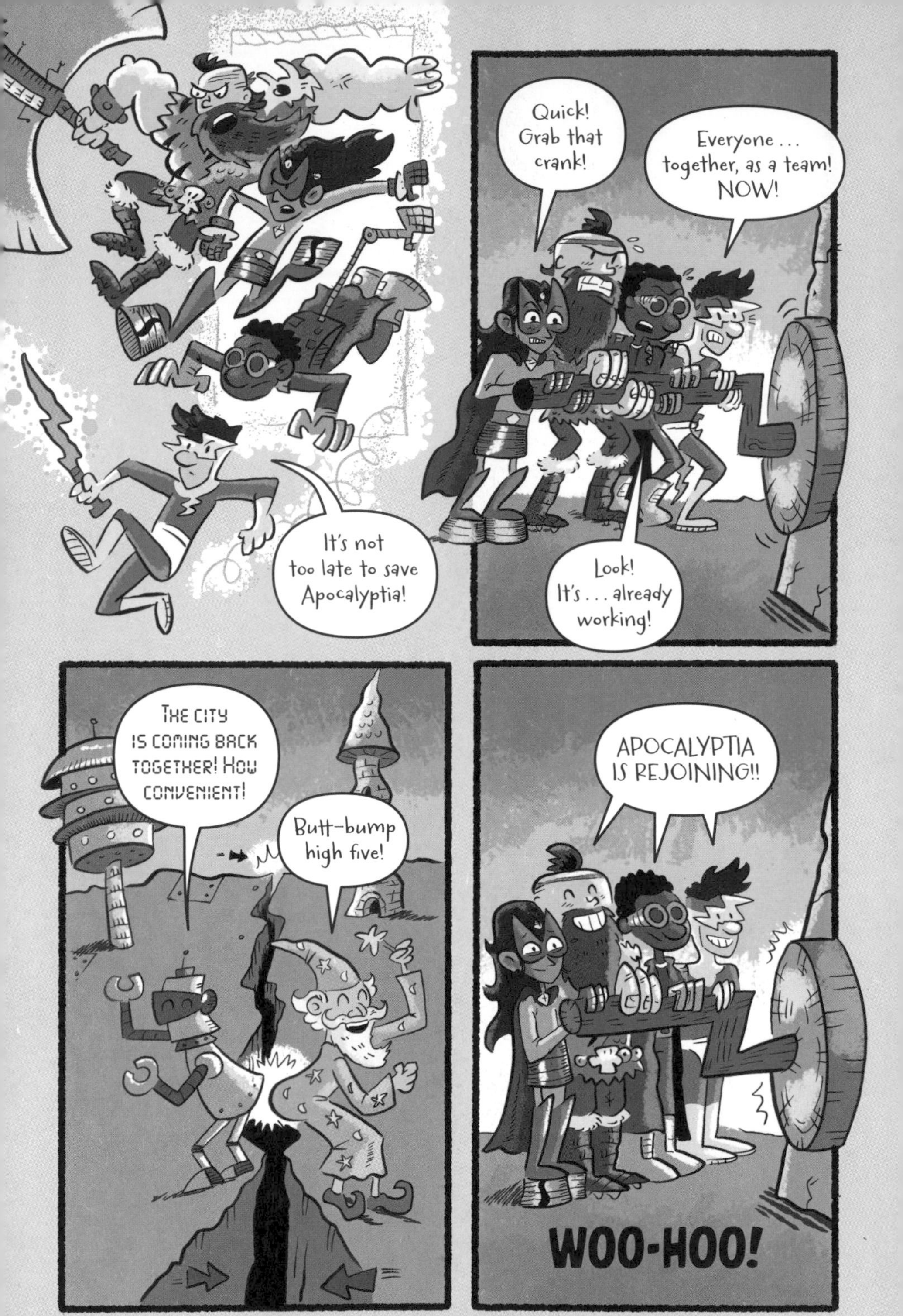
It's not too late to save Apocalyptia!
Quick! Grab that crank!
Everyone . . . together, as a team! NOW!
Look! It's . . . already working!
THE CITY IS COMING BACK TOGETHER! HOW CONVENIENT!
Butt-bump high five!
APOCALYPTIA IS REJOINING!!
WOO-HOO!

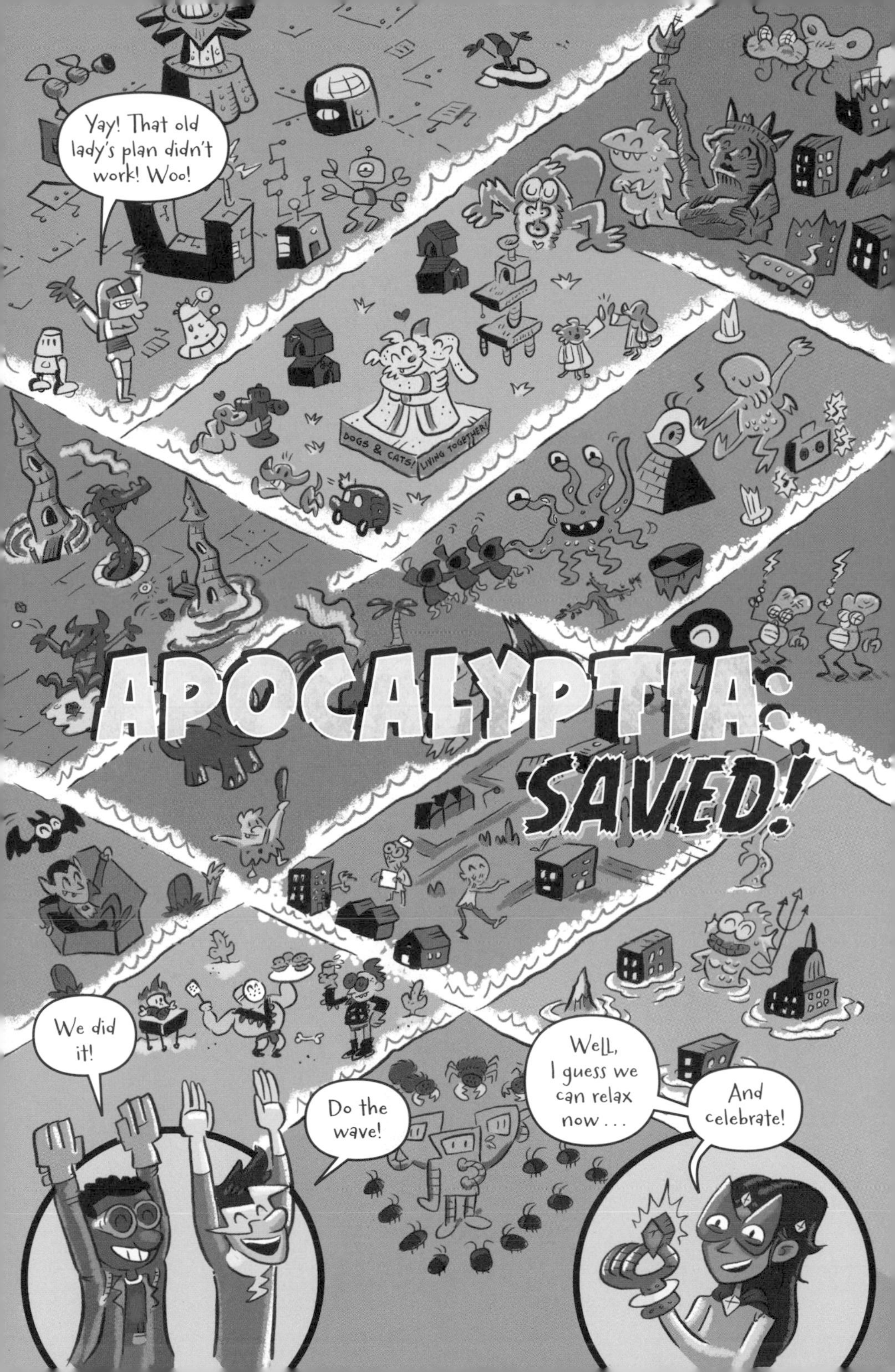
Yay! That old lady's plan didn't work! Woo!
DOGS & CATS!
LIVING TOGETHER!
APOCALYPTIA: SAVED!
We did it!
Do the wave!
Well, I guess we can relax now . . .
And celebrate!

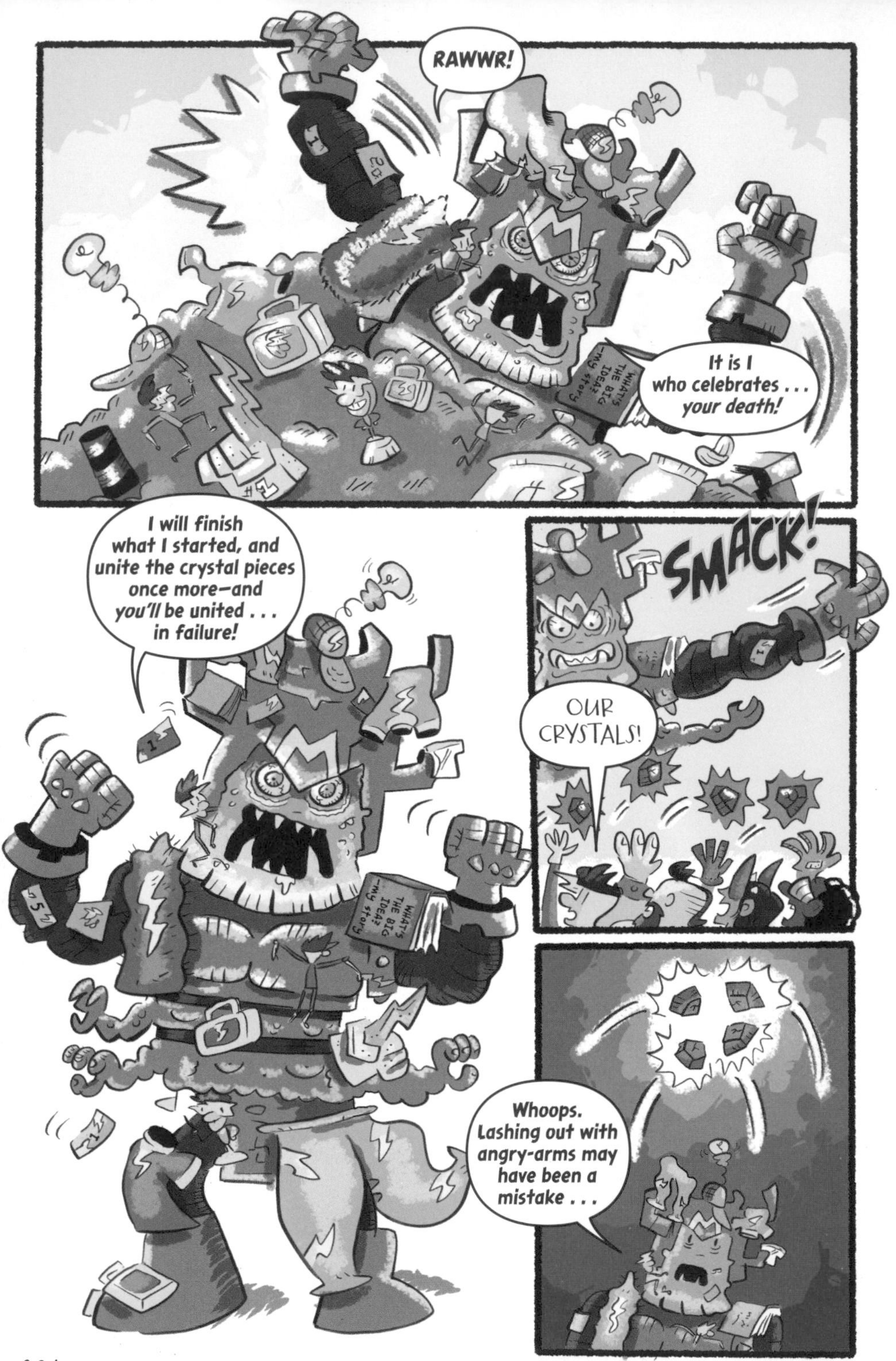
RAWWR!
It is I who celebrates . . . *your death!*
I will finish what I started, and unite the crystal pieces once more—and *you'll* be united . . . in failure!
SMACK!
OUR CRYSTALS!
Whoops. Lashing out with angry-arms may have been a mistake . . .

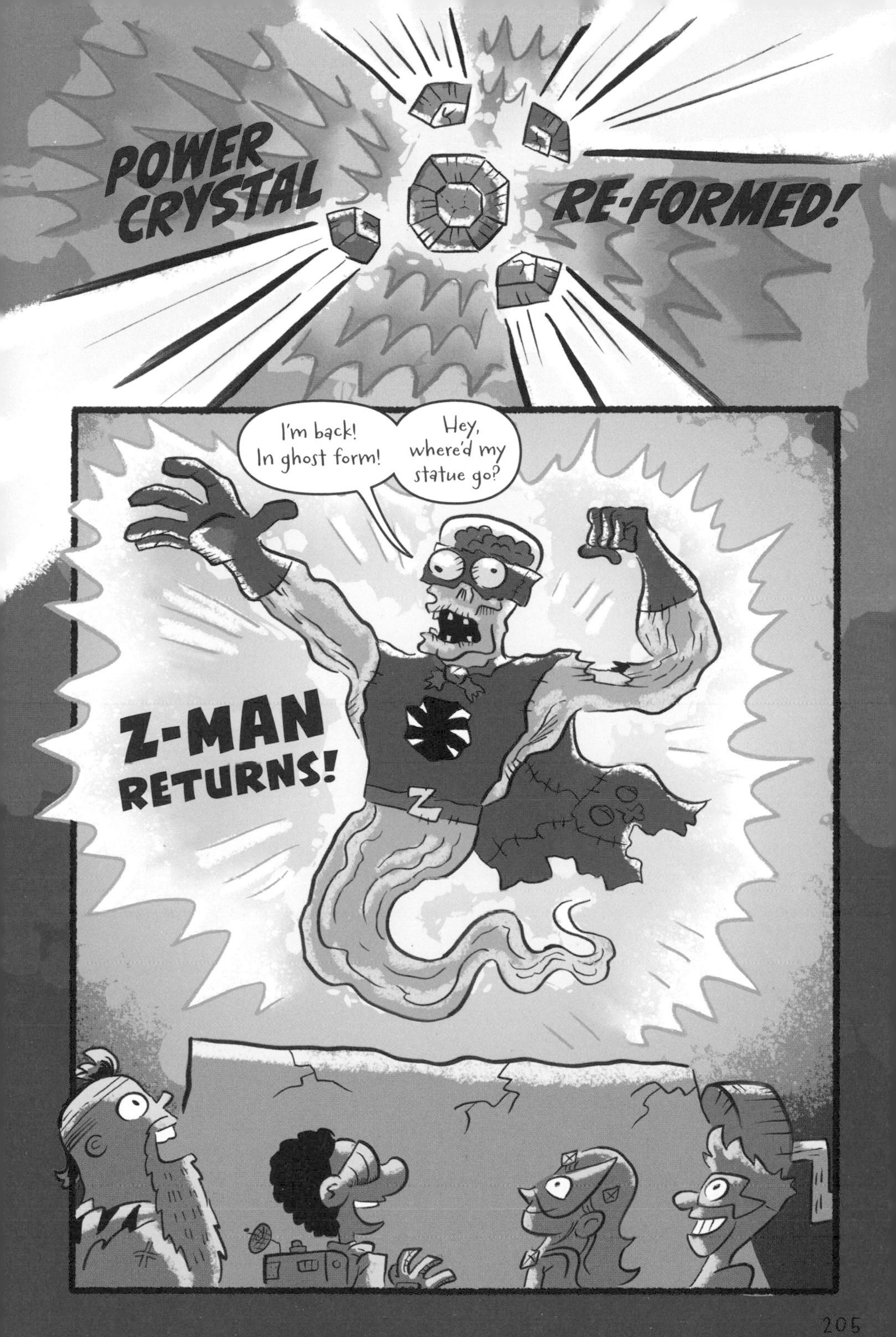
POWER CRYSTAL RE-FORMED!
I'm back! In ghost form!
Hey, where'd my statue go?
Z-MAN RETURNS!

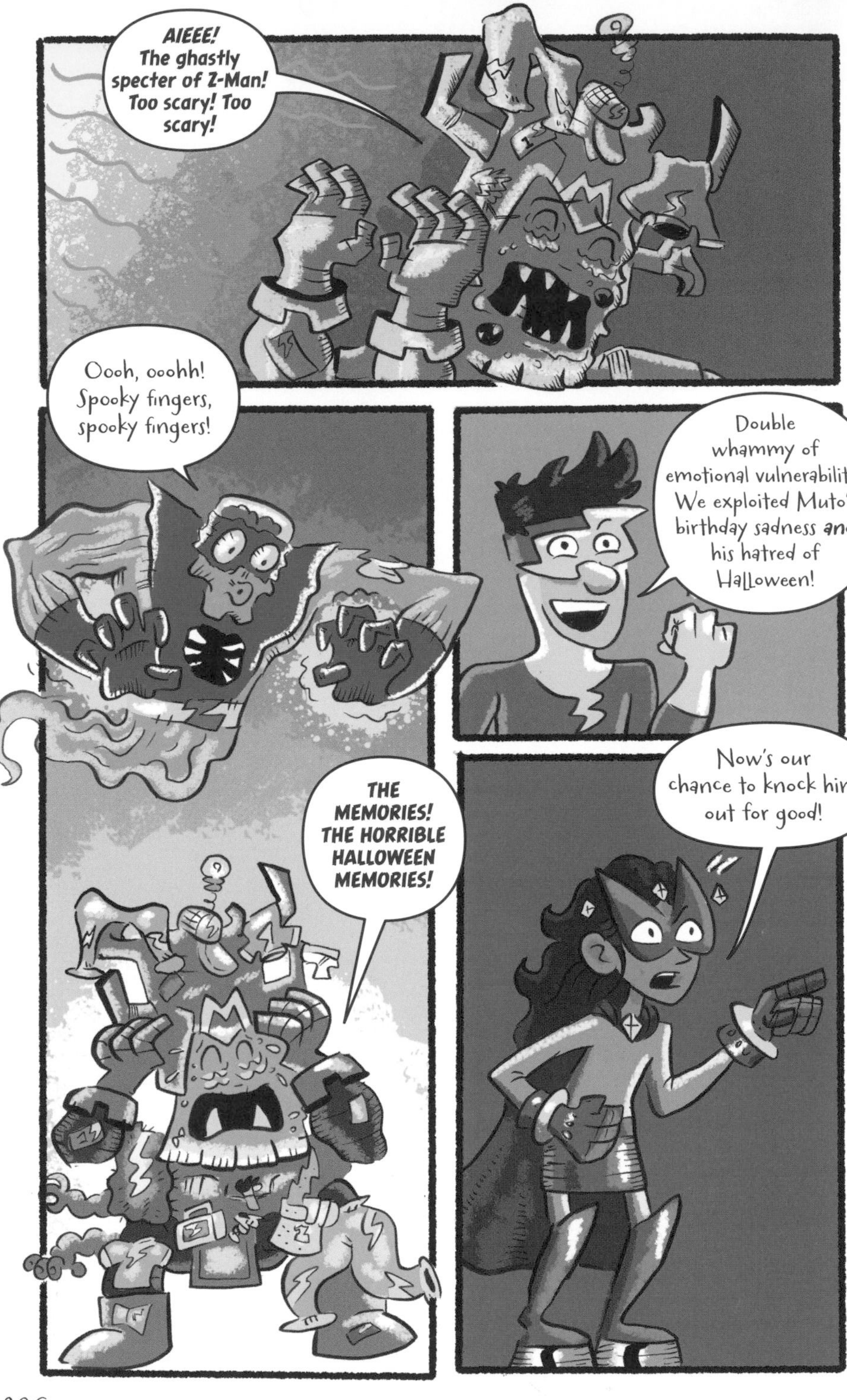
AIEEE! The ghastly specter of Z-Man! Too scary! Too scary!
Oooh, ooohh! Spooky fingers, spooky fingers!
Double whammy of emotional vulnerability! We exploited Muto's birthday sadness **and** his hatred of Halloween!
THE MEMORIES! THE HORRIBLE HALLOWEEN MEMORIES!
Now's our chance to knock him out for good!

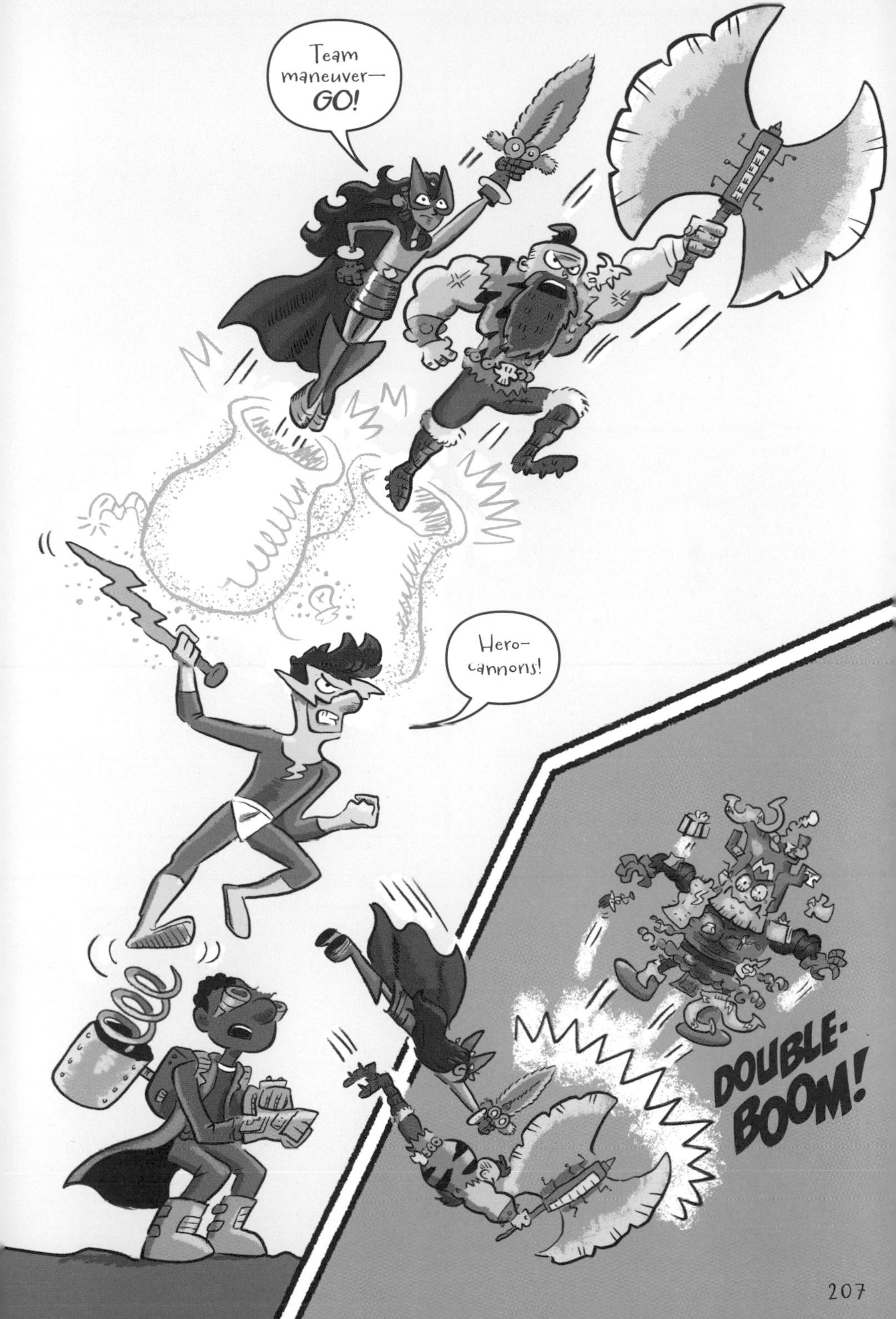
Team maneuver—GO!
Hero-cannons!
DOUBLE-BOOM!

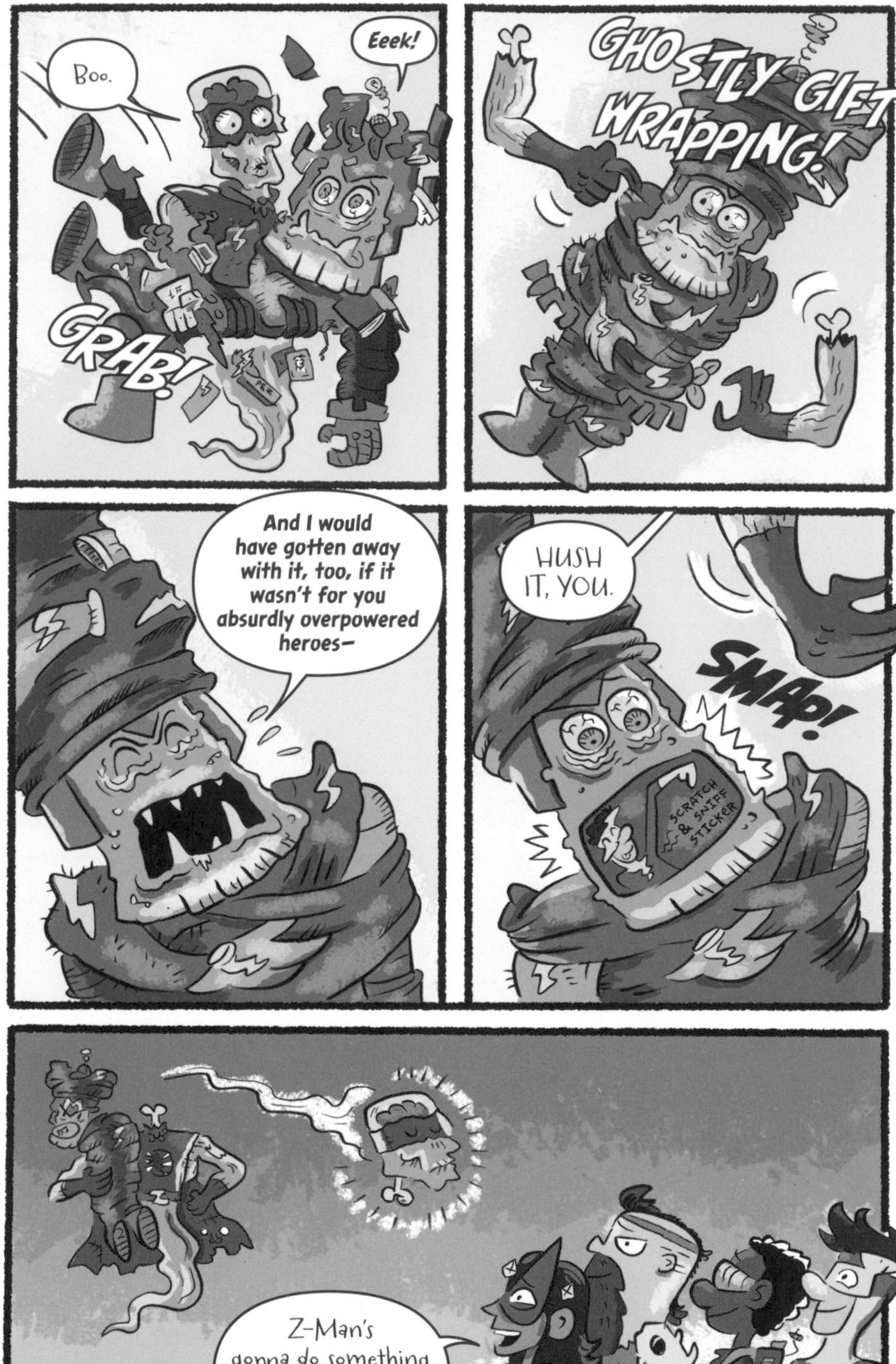
Boo.
Eeek!
GRAB!
GHOSTLY GIFT WRAPPING!
And I would have gotten away with it, too, if it wasn't for you absurdly overpowered heroes—
HUSH IT, YOU.
SMAP!
SCRATCH & SNIFF STICKER
Z-Man's gonna do something really cool right now . . . just wait.

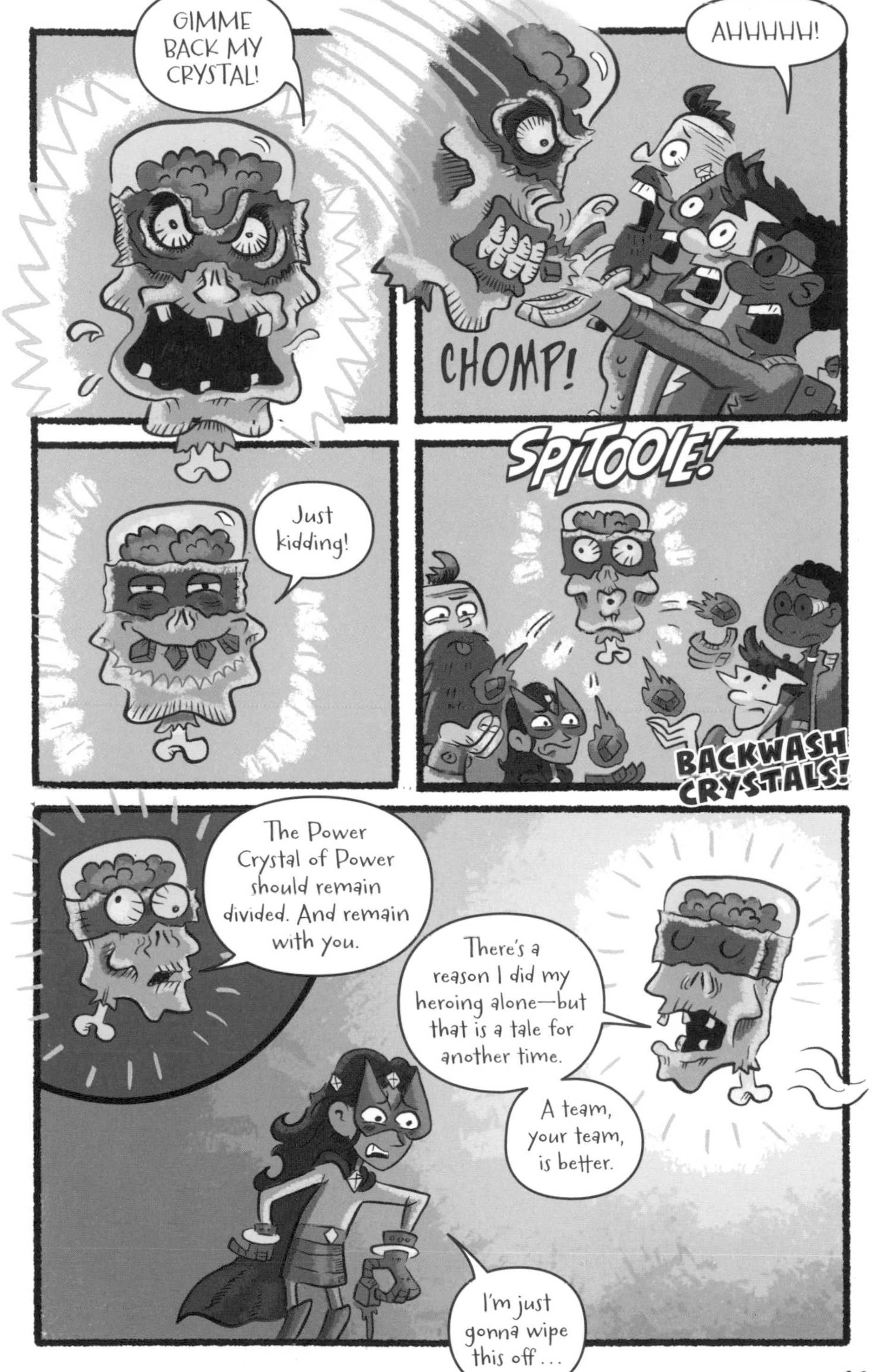
GIMME BACK MY CRYSTAL!
AHHHHH!
CHOMP!
Just kidding!
SPITOOIE!
BACKWASH CRYSTALS!
The Power Crystal of Power should remain divided. And remain with you.
There's a reason I did my heroing alone—but that is a tale for another time.
A team, your team, is better.
I'm just gonna wipe this off . . .

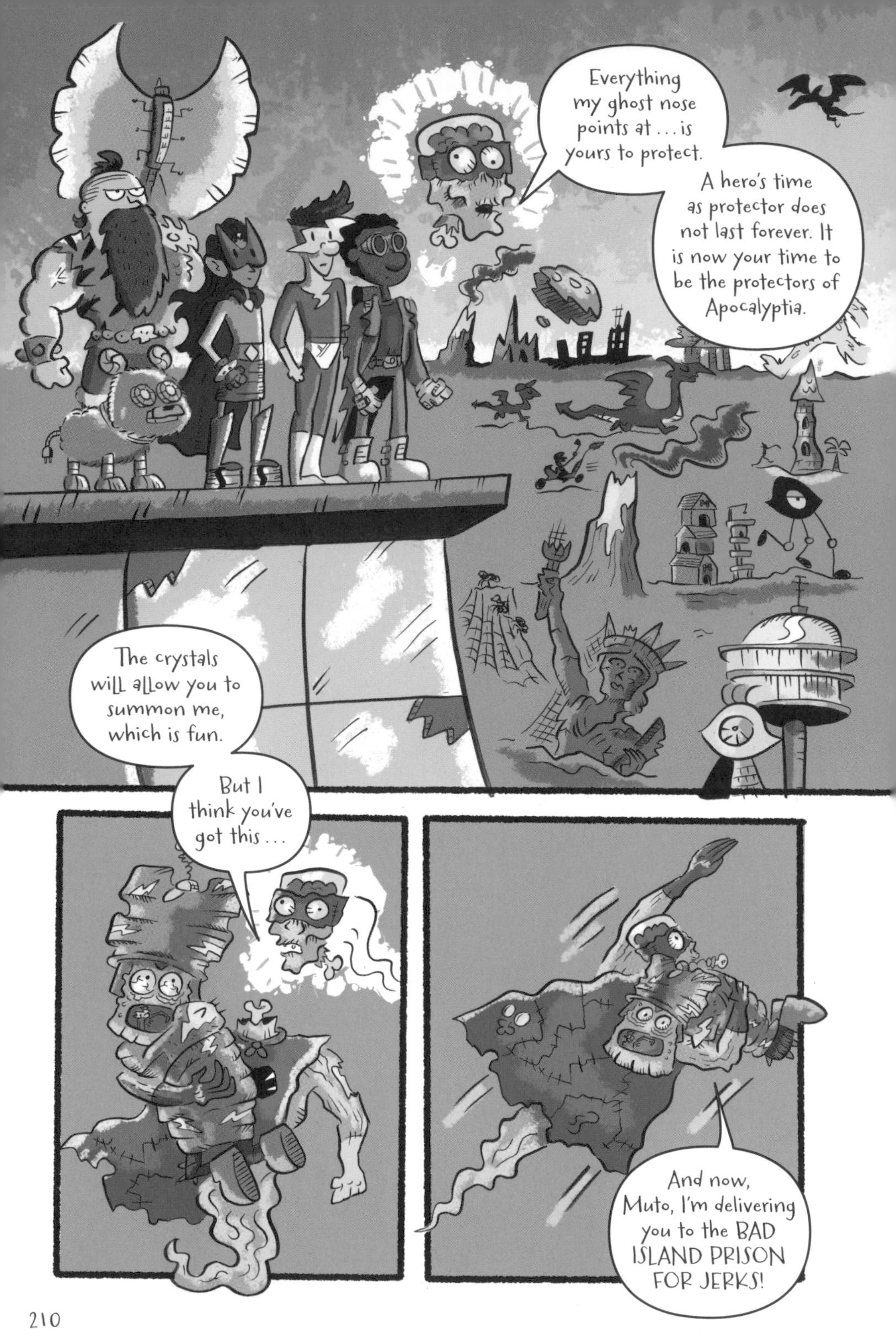

Everything my ghost nose points at . . . is yours to protect.
A hero's time as protector does not last forever. It is now your time to be the protectors of Apocalyptia.
The crystals will allow you to summon me, which is fun.
But I think you've got this . . .
And now, Muto, I'm delivering you to the BAD ISLAND PRISON FOR JERKS!

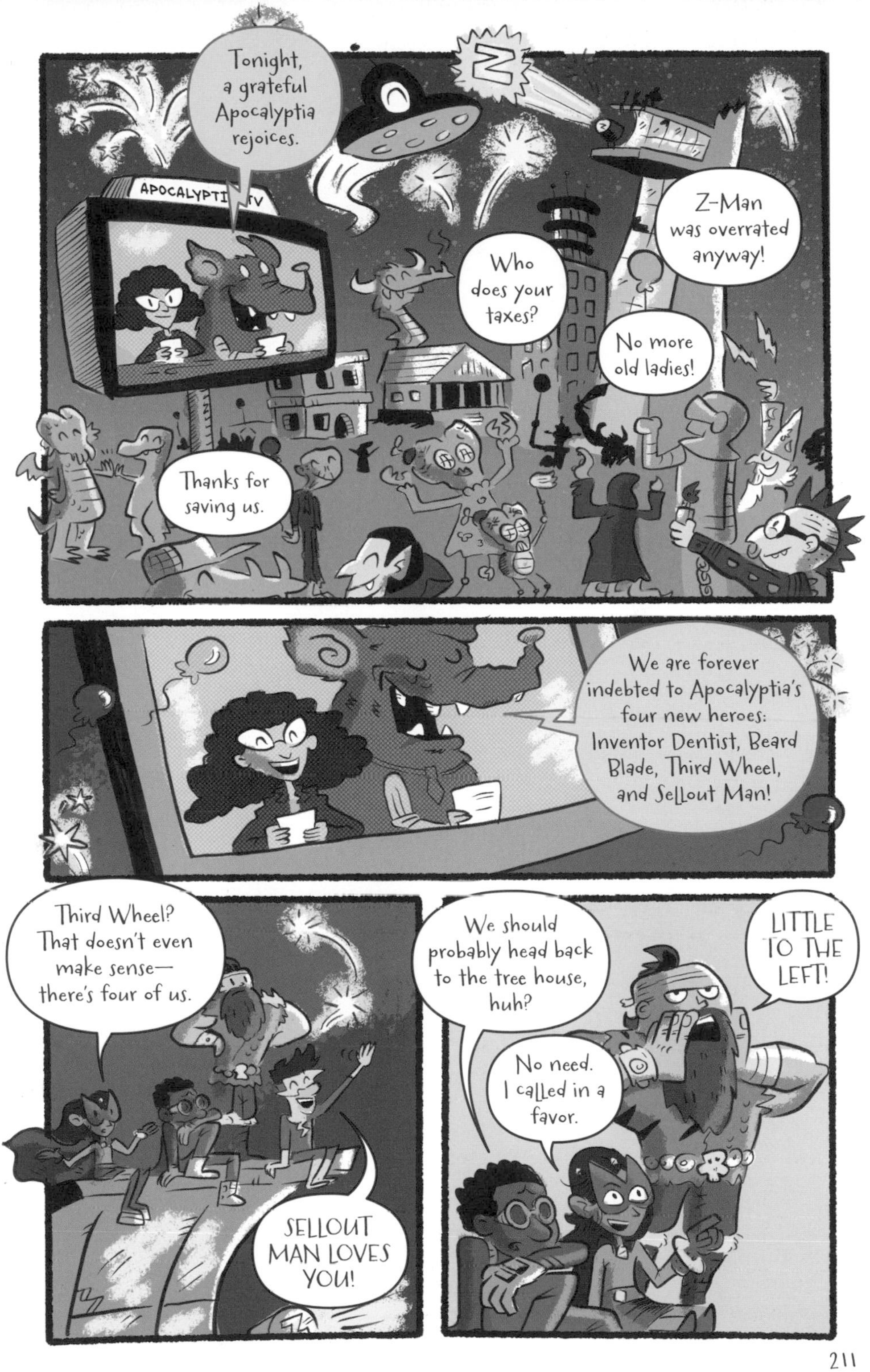
Tonight, a grateful Apocalyptia rejoices.
APOCALYPTI TV
Z
Who does your taxes?
Z-Man was overrated anyway!
No more old ladies!
Thanks for saving us.
We are forever indebted to Apocalyptia's four new heroes: Inventor Dentist, Beard Blade, Third Wheel, and Sellout Man!
Third Wheel? That doesn't even make sense—there's four of us.
SELLOUT MAN LOVES YOU!
We should probably head back to the tree house, huh?
LITTLE TO THE LEFT!
No need. I called in a favor.

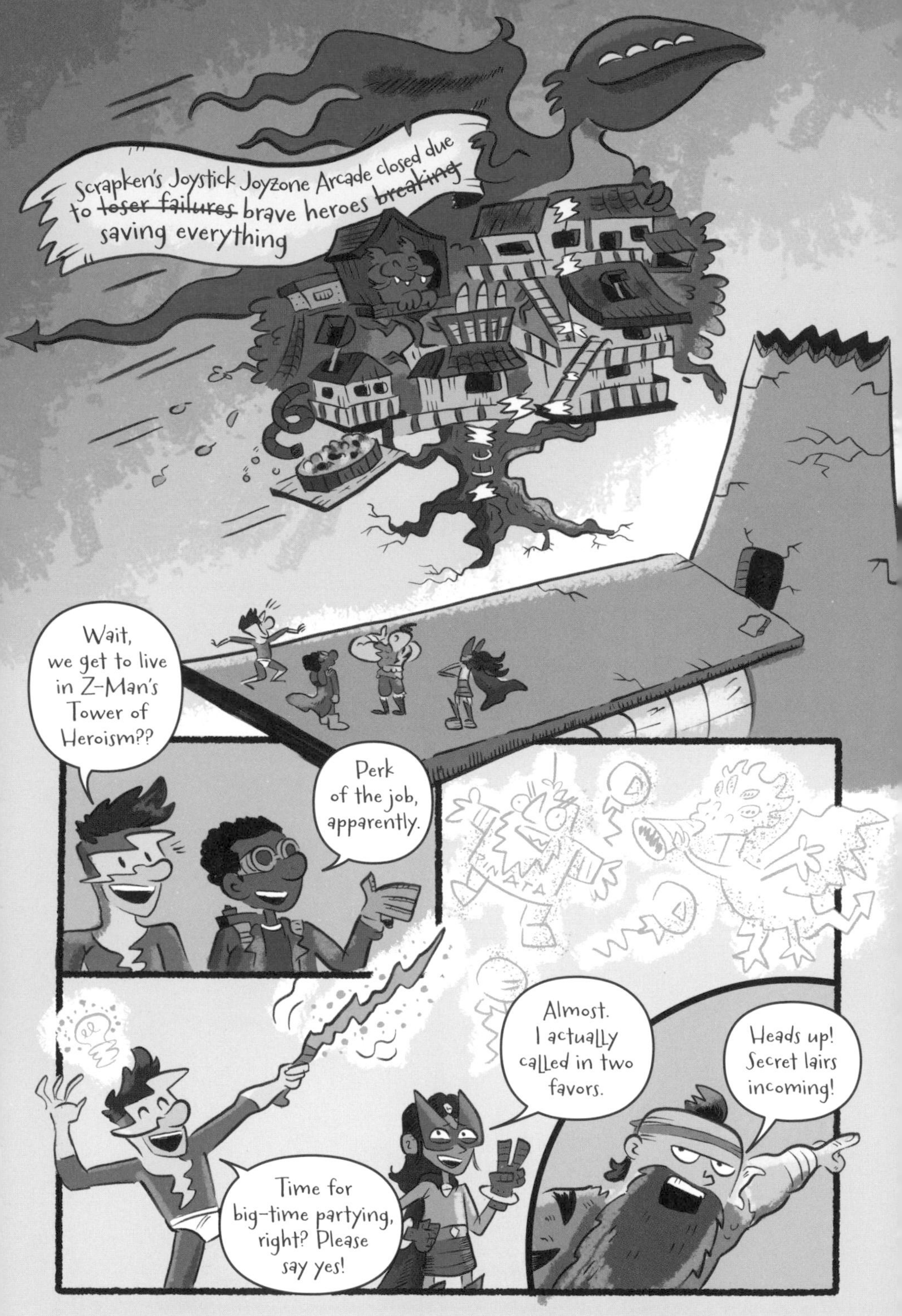
Scrapken's Joystick Joyzone Arcade closed due to ~~loser failures~~ brave heroes ~~breaking~~ saving everything
Wait, we get to live in Z-Man's Tower of Heroism??
Perk of the job, apparently.
PINATA
Almost. I actually called in two favors.
Heads up! Secret lairs incoming!
Time for big-time partying, right? Please say yes!

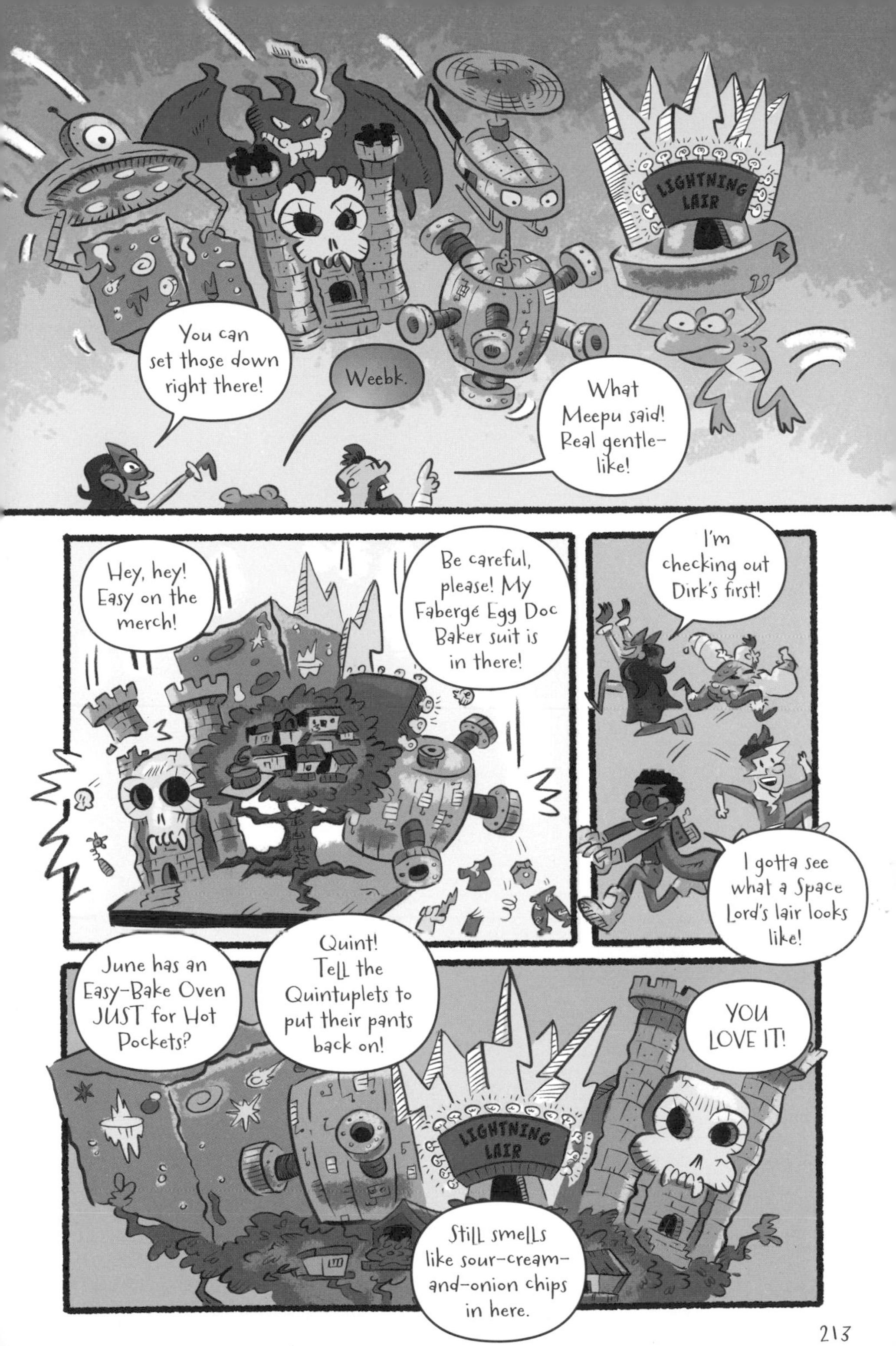
You can set those down right there!
Weebk.
What Meepu said! Real gentle-like!
LIGHTNING LAIR
Hey, hey! Easy on the merch!
Be careful, please! My Fabergé Egg Doc Baker suit is in there!
I'm checking out Dirk's first!
I gotta see what a Space Lord's lair looks like!
June has an Easy-Bake Oven JUST for Hot Pockets?
Quint! Tell the Quintuplets to put their pants back on!
YOU LOVE IT!
LIGHTNING LAIR
Still smells like sour-cream-and-onion chips in here.

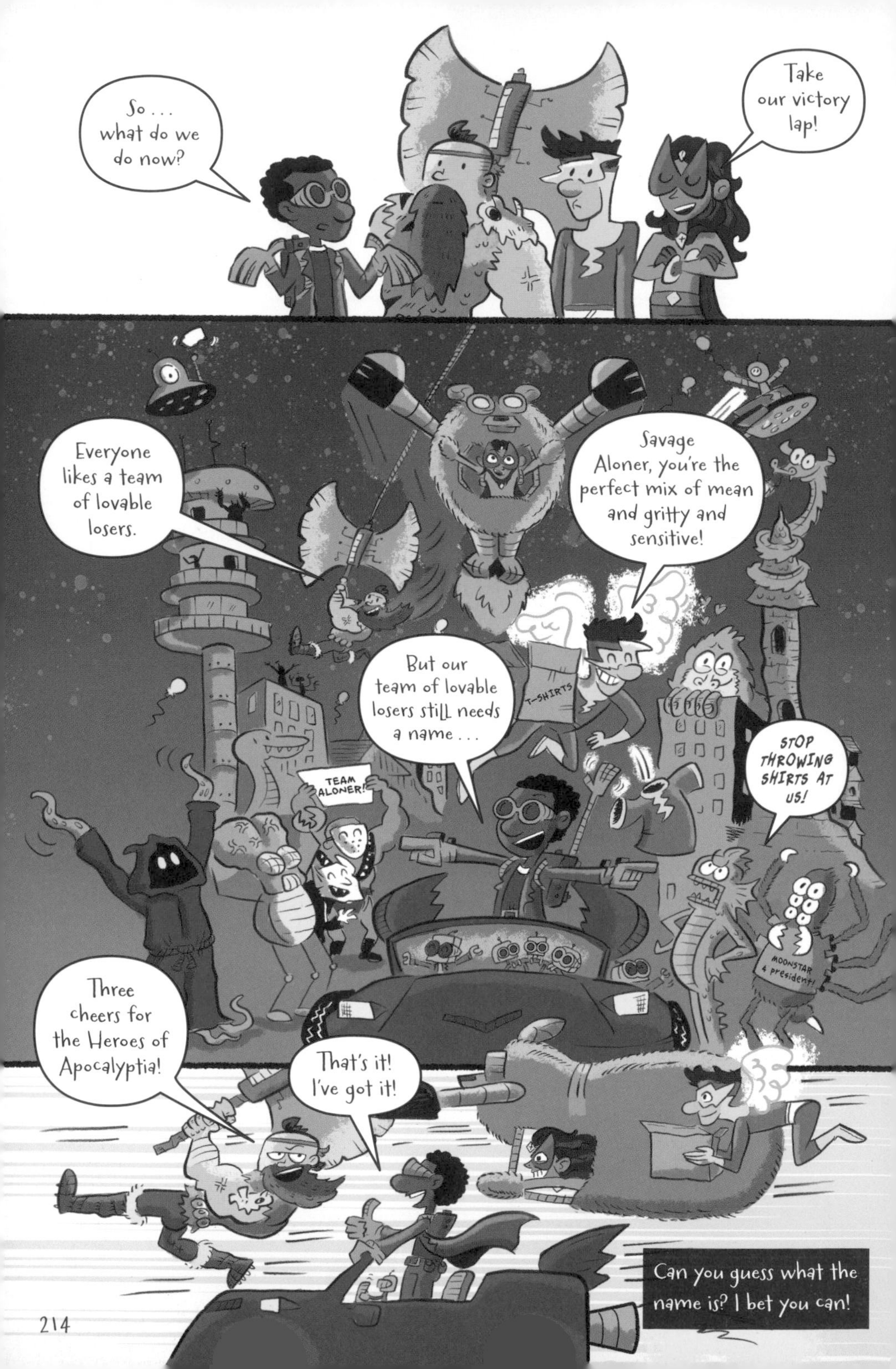
So . . . what do we do now?
Take our victory lap!
Everyone likes a team of lovable losers.
Savage Aloner, you're the perfect mix of mean and gritty and sensitive!
But our team of lovable losers still needs a name . . .
T-SHIRTS
TEAM ALONER!
STOP THROWING SHIRTS AT US!
MOONSTAR 4 president!
Three cheers for the Heroes of Apocalyptia!
That's it! I've got it!
Can you guess what the name is? I bet you can!

CHAPTER TWELVE
HEROES OF APOCALYPTIA!

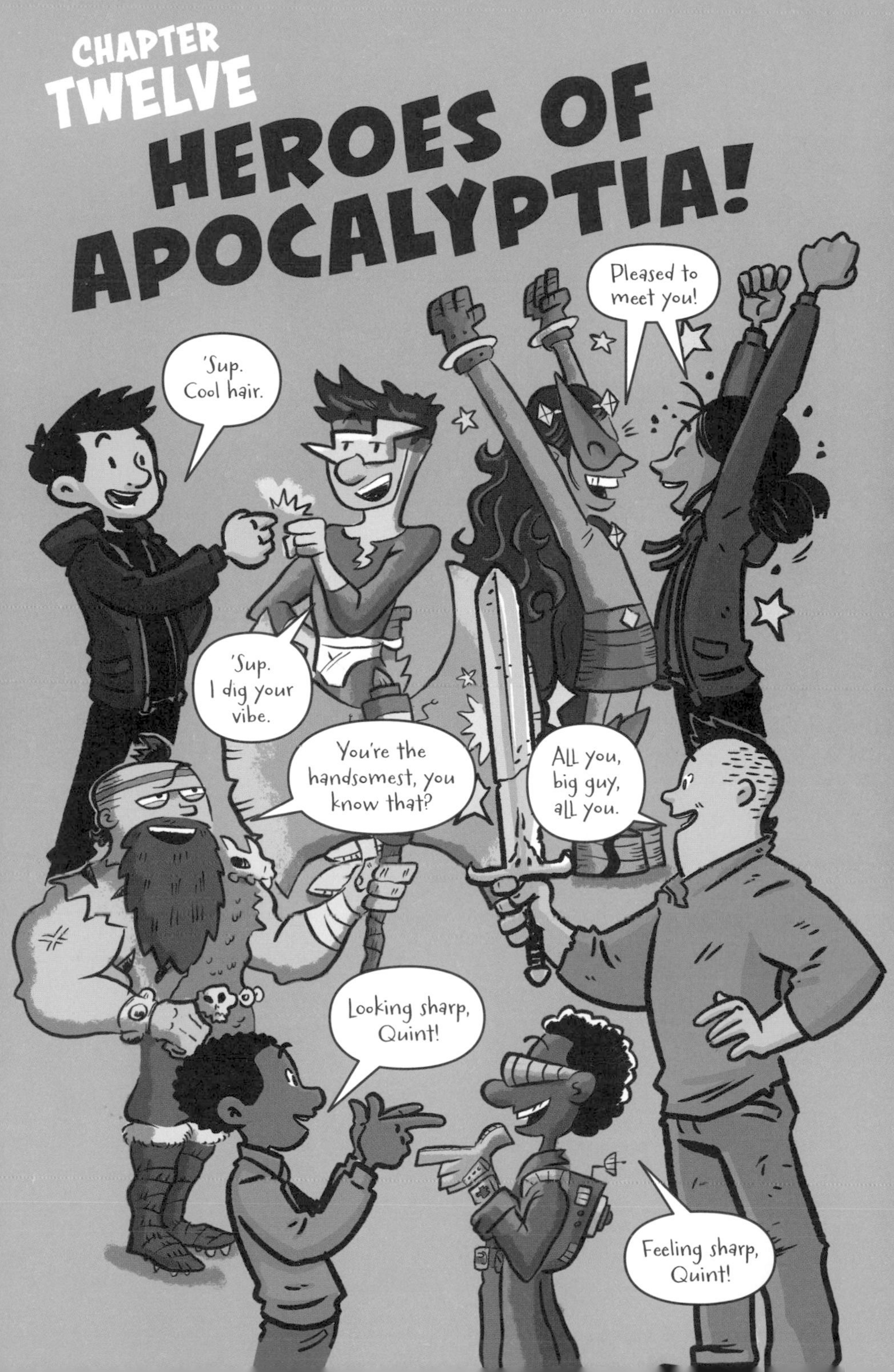
'Sup. Cool hair.
'Sup. I dig your vibe.
Pleased to meet you!
You're the handsomest, you know that?
ALL you, big guy, aLL you.
Looking sharp, Quint!
Feeling sharp, Quint!

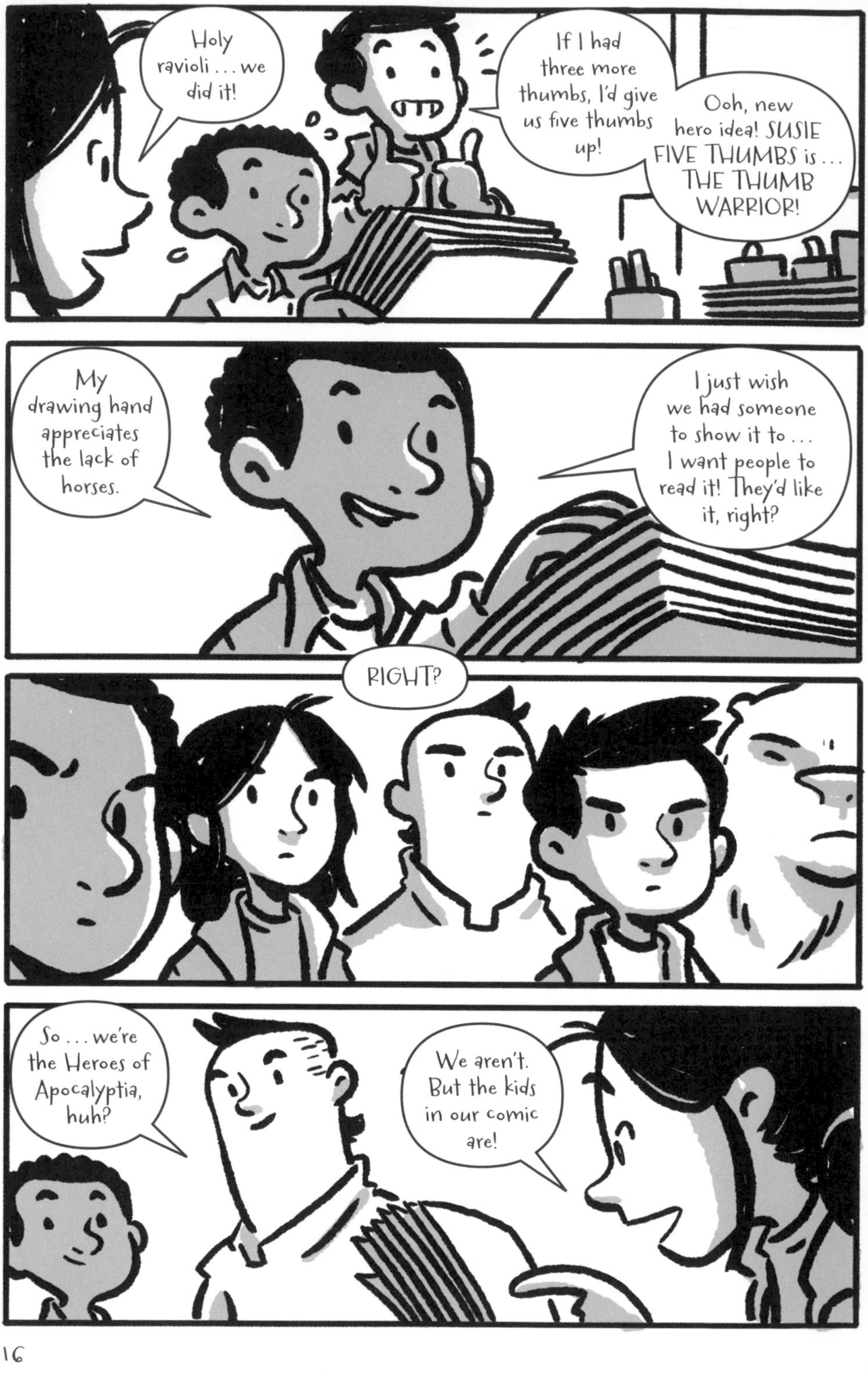
Holy ravioli . . . we did it!
If I had three more thumbs, I'd give us five thumbs up!
Ooh, new hero idea! SUSIE FIVE THUMBS is . . . THE THUMB WARRIOR!
My drawing hand appreciates the lack of horses.
I just wish we had someone to show it to . . . I want people to read it! They'd like it, right?
RIGHT?
So . . . we're the Heroes of Apocalyptia, huh?
We aren't. But the kids in our comic are!

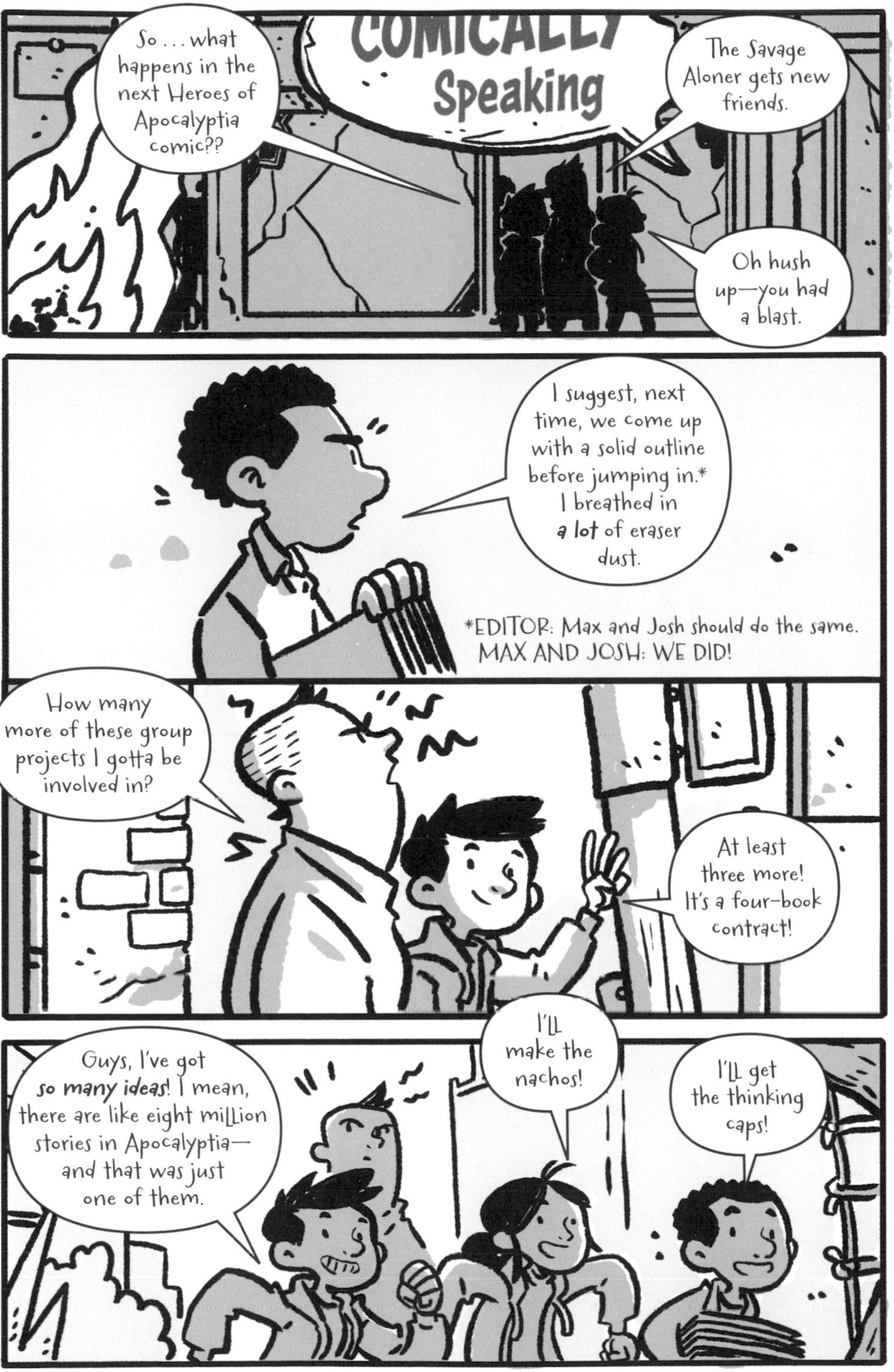
So . . . what happens in the next Heroes of Apocalyptia comic??
COMICALLY Speaking
The Savage Aloner gets new friends.
Oh hush up—you had a blast.
I suggest, next time, we come up with a solid outline before jumping in.* I breathed in **a lot** of eraser dust.
*EDITOR: Max and Josh should do the same.
MAX AND JOSH: WE DID!
How many more of these group projects I gotta be involved in?
At least three more! It's a four-book contract!
Guys, I've got **so many ideas**! I mean, there are like eight million stories in Apocalyptia—and that was just one of them.
I'LL make the nachos!
I'LL get the thinking caps!

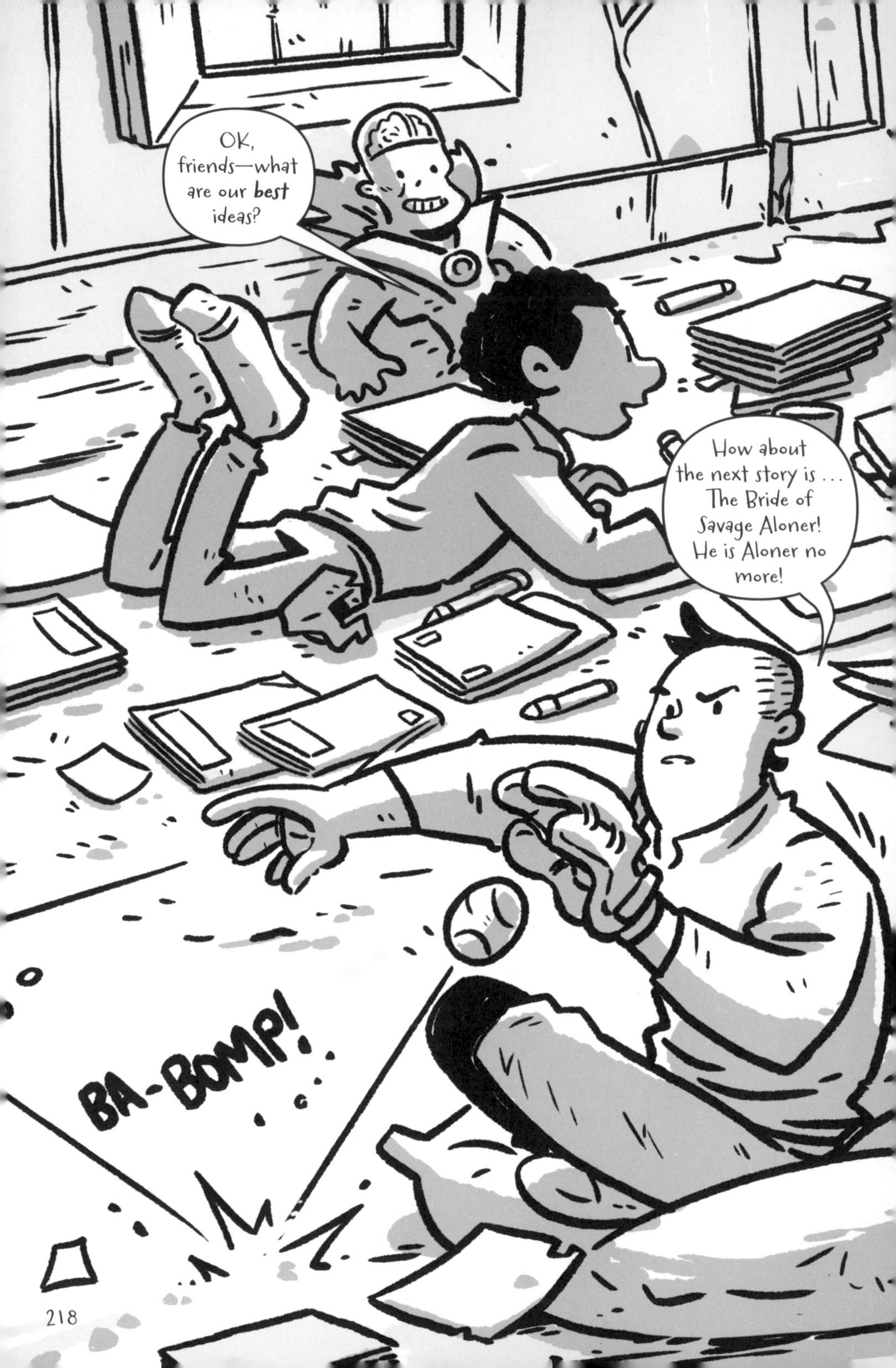
OK, friends—what are our **best** ideas?
How about the next story is . . . The Bride of Savage Aloner! He is Aloner no more!
BA-BOMP!

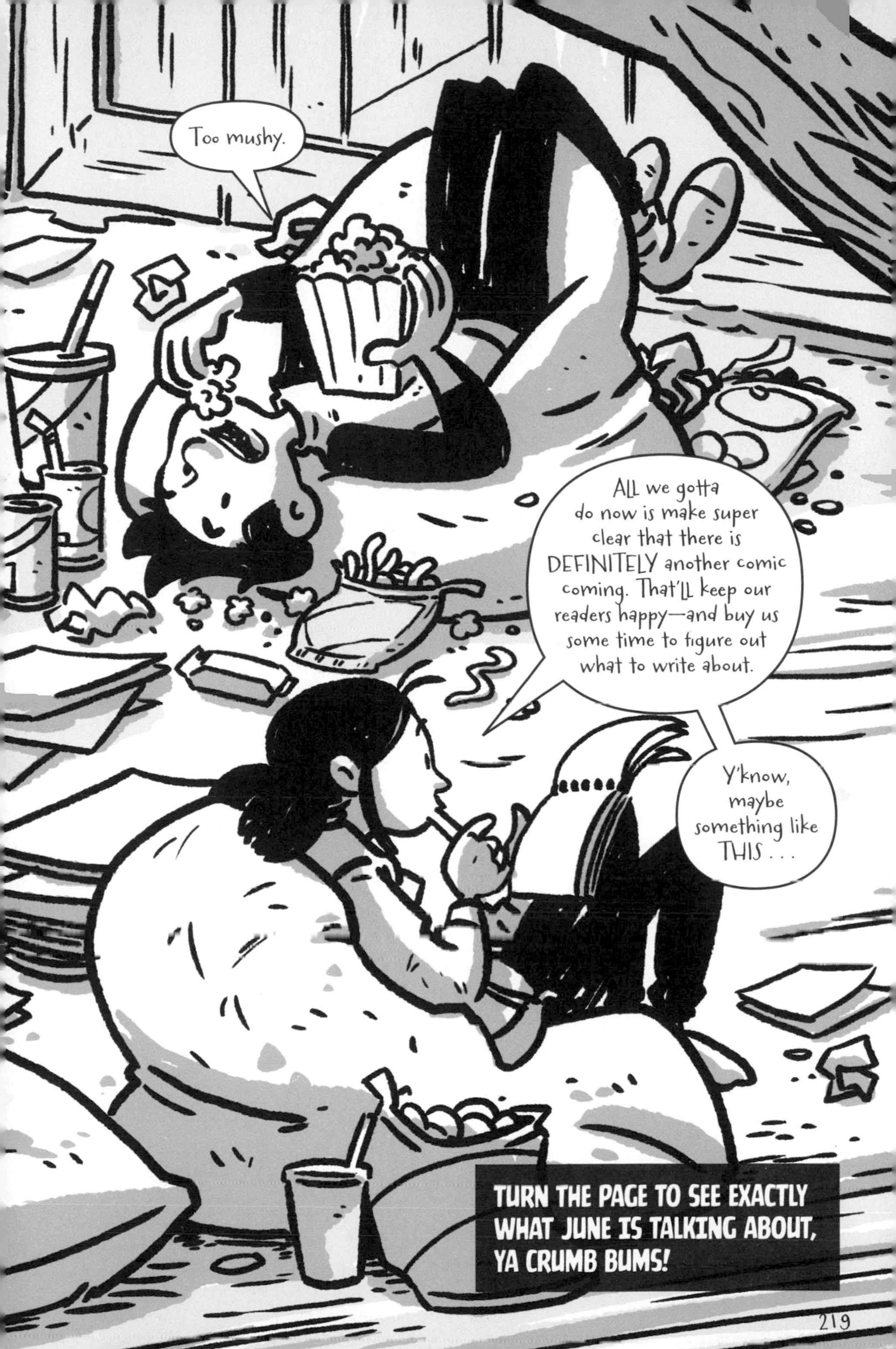

Too mushy.
ALL we gotta do now is make super clear that there is DEFINITELY another comic coming. That'LL keep our readers happy—and buy us some time to figure out what to write about.
Y'know, maybe something like THIS . . .
TURN THE PAGE TO SEE EXACTLY WHAT JUNE IS TALKING ABOUT, YA CRUMB BUMS!

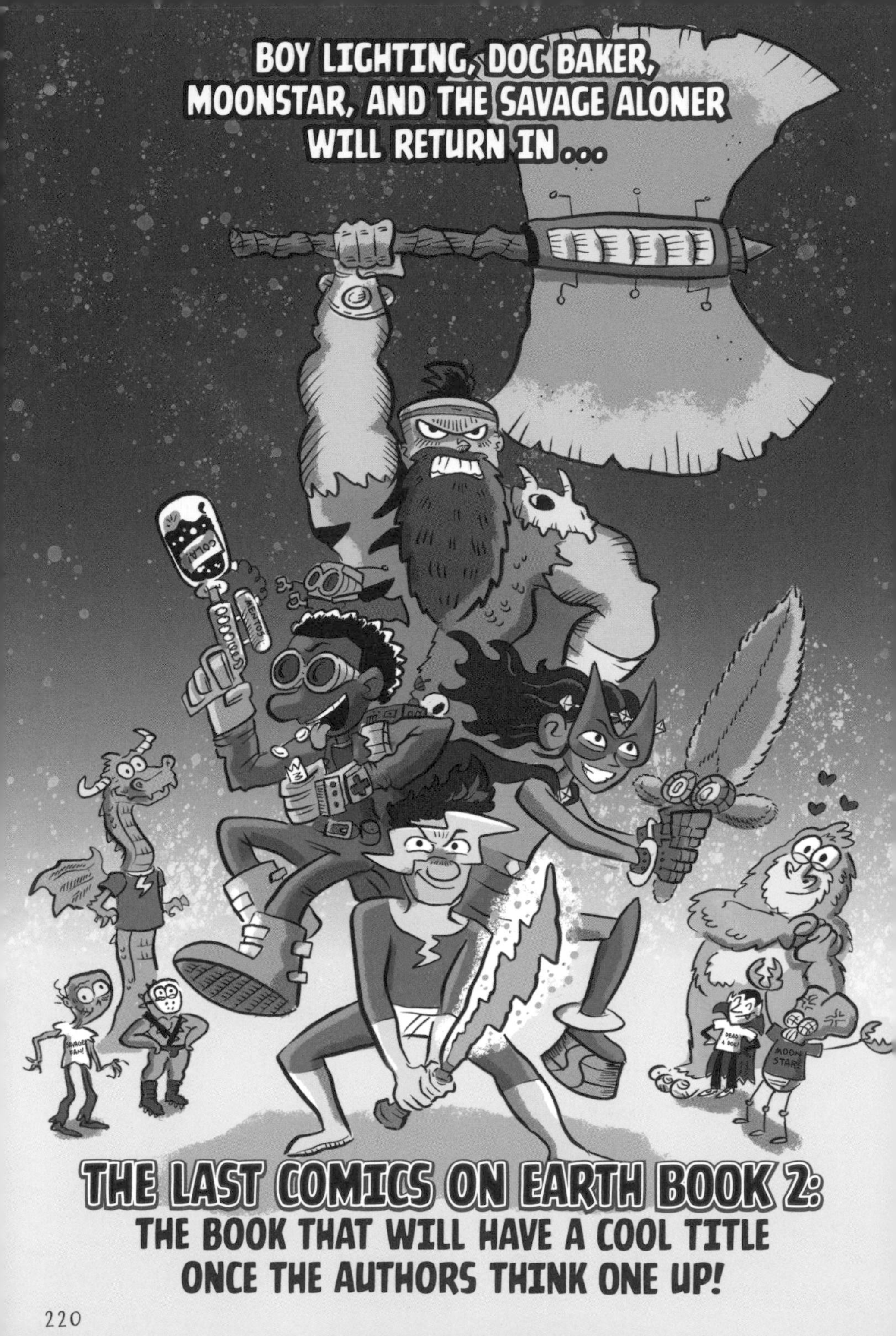
BOY LIGHTING, DOC BAKER, MOONSTAR, AND THE SAVAGE ALONER WILL RETURN IN...
COLA!
MENTOS
SAVAGE FAN!
DEAD 4 DOC!
MOON STAR!
THE LAST COMICS ON EARTH BOOK 2:
THE BOOK THAT WILL HAVE A COOL TITLE ONCE THE AUTHORS THINK ONE UP!

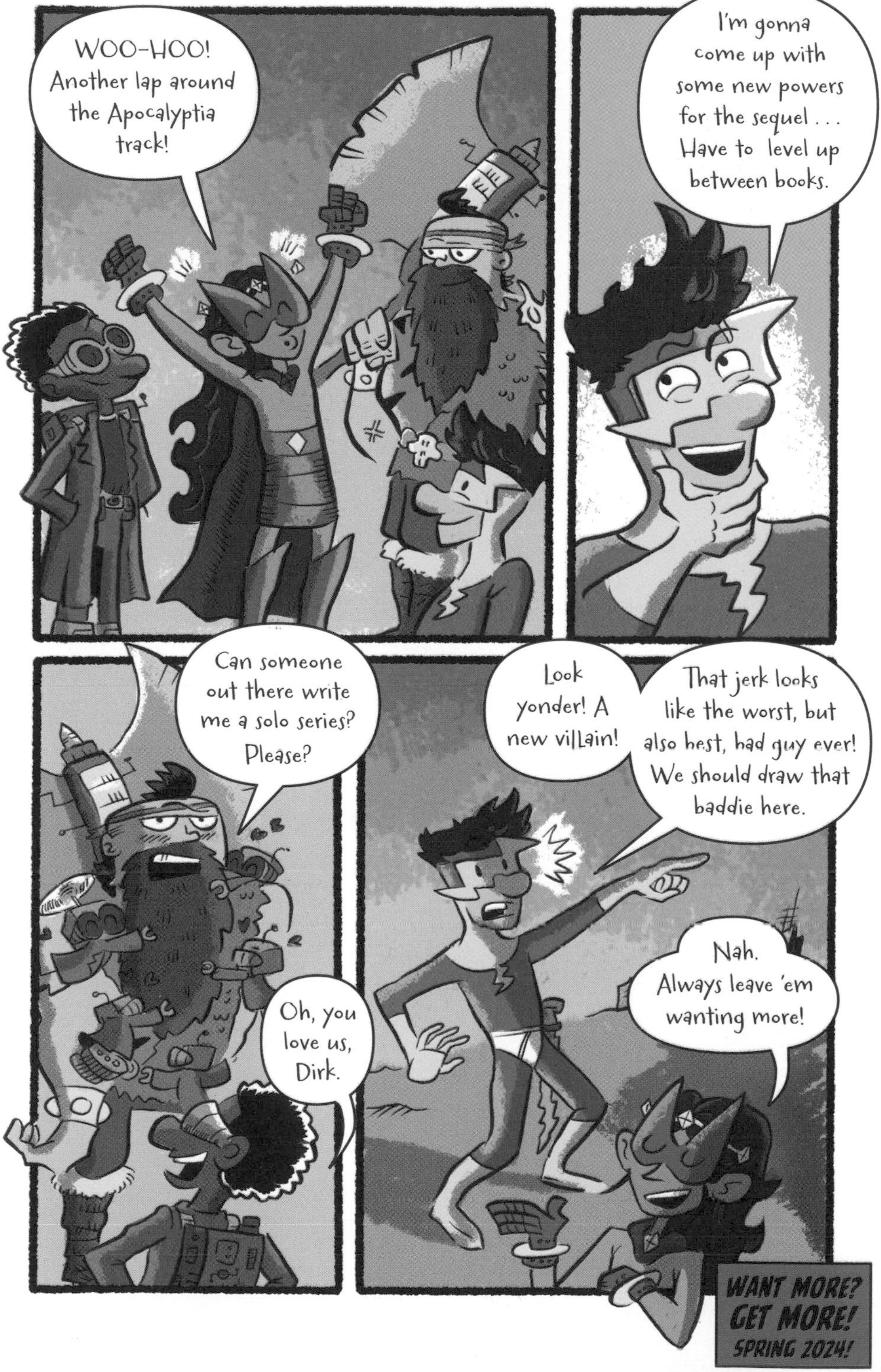
WOO-HOO! Another lap around the Apocalyptia track!
I'm gonna come up with some new powers for the sequel . . . Have to level up between books.
Can someone out there write me a solo series? Please?
Oh, you love us, Dirk.
Look yonder! A new villain!
That jerk looks like the worst, but also best, bad guy ever! We should draw that baddie here.
Nah. Always leave 'em wanting more!
WANT MORE? GET MORE! SPRING 2024!

© Ruby Brallier

MAX BRALLIER

is a #1 *New York Times*, *USA Today*, and *Wall Street Journal* bestselling author. His books and series include The Last Kids on Earth, Eerie Elementary, Mister Shivers, Galactic Hot Dogs, and Can YOU Survive the Zombie Apocalypse? He is a writer and executive producer for Netflix's Emmy Award–winning adaptation of The Last Kids on Earth. Visit him at MaxBrallier.com.

JOSHUA PRUETT

is an Emmy Award–winning TV writer and the only human being on Earth to have written for both *Mystery Science Theater 3000* and *Doctor Who*. Joshua has worked in animation for over fifteen years, inflicting laughter (and monsters) on others writing on Disney's *Phineas & Ferb*, the feature film *Candace Against the Universe*, and the Emmy-winning adaptation of The Last Kids on Earth for Netflix. He is also co-author of *Shipwreckers: The Curse of the Cursed Temple of Curses, or We Nearly Died. A Lot.* with Scott Peterson. Last Comics is his first graphic novel! He's on Twitter: @ZombieTardis.

© Guzman

JAY COOPER

has illustrated over twenty books for kids young and old, including the popular Bots series and the national bestselling *Your Guide to Not Getting Murdered in a Quaint English Village*. Jay is also an award-winning graphic designer of theatrical advertising, and has crafted art and advertising for more than one hundred Broadway shows. He lives in New Jersey with his family and a dog named Bradley Cooper. Visit him at JayCooperBooks.com and follow him on Twitter at your peril: @JayCooperArt.

DOUGLAS HOLGATE

is the illustrator of the #1 *New York Times* bestselling series The Last Kids on Earth from Viking (now also an Emmy-winning Netflix animated series) and the cocreator and illustrator of the graphic novel *Clem Hetherington and the Ironwood Race* for Scholastic Graphix.

He has worked for the last twenty years making books and comics for publishers around the world from his garage in Victoria, Australia. He lives with his family and an adorable young pupper in the Australian bush on five acres surrounded by eighty-million-year-old volcanic boulders.

You can find his work at DouglasBotHolgate.com and on Twitter @DouglasHolgate.

Acknowledgments

Tremendous thanks are owed to about three hundred people for helping make something new and different. The biggest thanks goes to Jay Cooper for making this whole thing look so rad and filling it with jokes and gags and personality—making it so much more than it was on the page. Ditto for Jim Hoover, who continues to do jaw-dropping work despite tight deadlines, my many annoying last-minute changes, and about a dozen other challenges. Doug Holgate, of course, ALWAYS—my faithful companion on this end-of-the-world journey. Joe Eichelberger, for making the world of Apocalyptia stunning and vivid and eye-popping. Dana Leydig, Ken Wright, and Dan Lazar, THANK YOU—and thanks everyone in PYR marketing and publicity and sales. Hugs and high-fives to the team at Atomic Cartoons for continuing to share Last Kids with kids around the world. Haley Mancini—you're funny and neat. And one tremendous thanks and fist-bump to Josh Pruett—I never wrote a book with a friend before; it's a nice thing. —M. B.

MUTO-sized thanks to our amazing team: Jay, Doug, Joe, Dana, and Jim! You put the COMICS in *Last Comics*! Z-MAN-powered thanks to my joke-testers, Catie, Zach, and Amanda! Huge Apocalyptia-sized gratitude to Scott, Matt, Aaron, Catie, Jennifer, Jill, Julian, Haley, Jen, and the rest of the Atomic Cartoons/Netflix *Last Kids on Earth* animated series team! Love you guys. All remaining thanks to Deborah Warren, Dan, and Torie at Writers House, and my eager readers and cheerleaders: Shari, Jim, Molly, Owen, Lincoln, Micah, Nicole, Marie, Laura, Christopher, Autumn, Logan, Hollin, and Peyton! BIGGEST THANKS to Max, for inviting me to the party. —J. P.

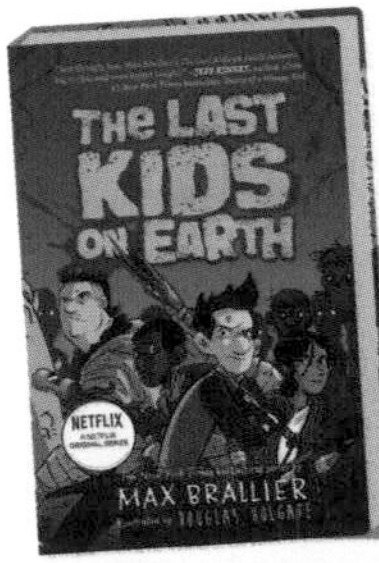
THE LAST KIDS ON EARTH
NETFLIX
MAX BRALLIER

CHECK IT OUT! A TEASER FROM THE FIRST LAST KIDS ON EARTH BOOK! READ IT!

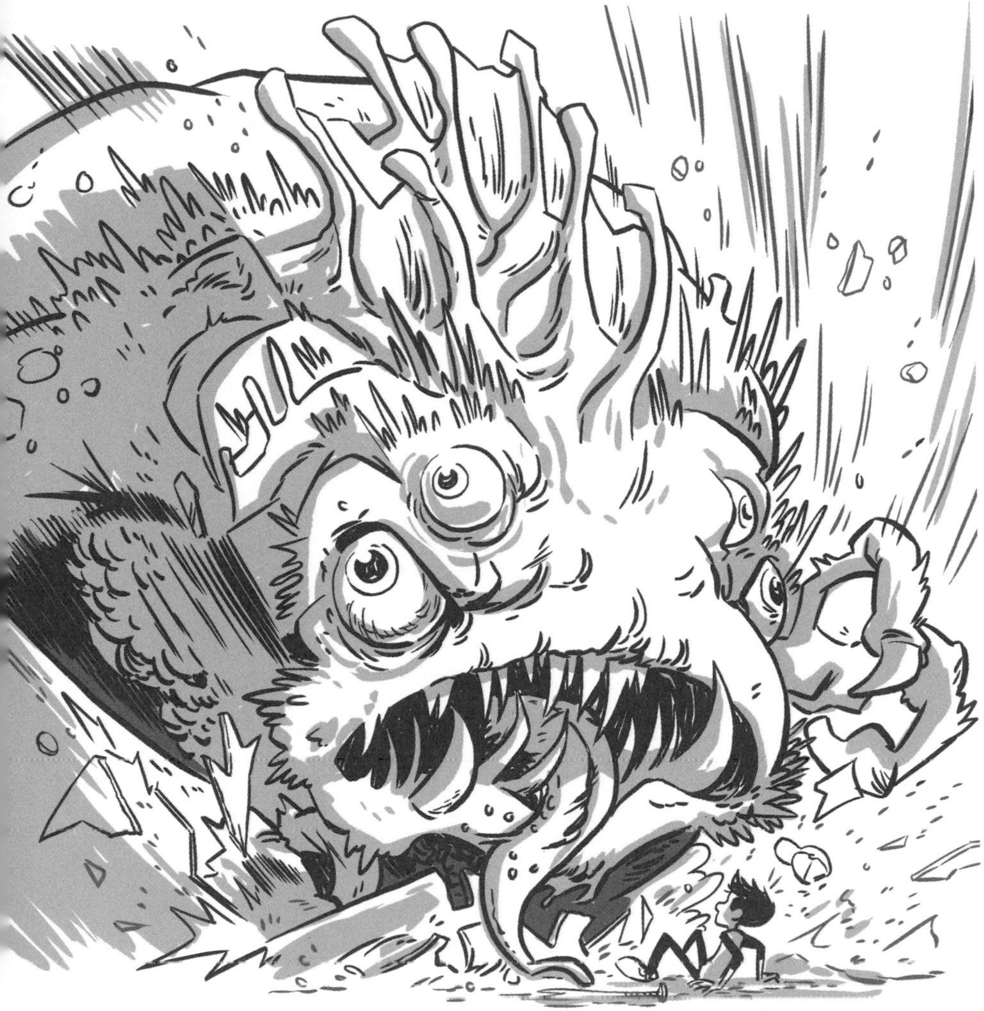

chapter one

That's me.

Not the giant monster.

Beneath the giant monster. The kid on his back, with the splintered bat. The handsome kid, about to get eaten.

Forty-two days ago, I was regular Jack Sullivan: thirteen years old, living an uneventful life in the uninteresting town of Wakefield. I was totally **not** a hero, totally **not** a tough guy, totally **not** fighting giant monsters.

But look at me now. Battling a gargantuan beast on the roof of the local CVS.

Life is crazy like that.

Right now, the *whole world* is crazy like that. Check the shattered windows. Check the wild vines crawling up the side of the building.

All of these things are not normal.

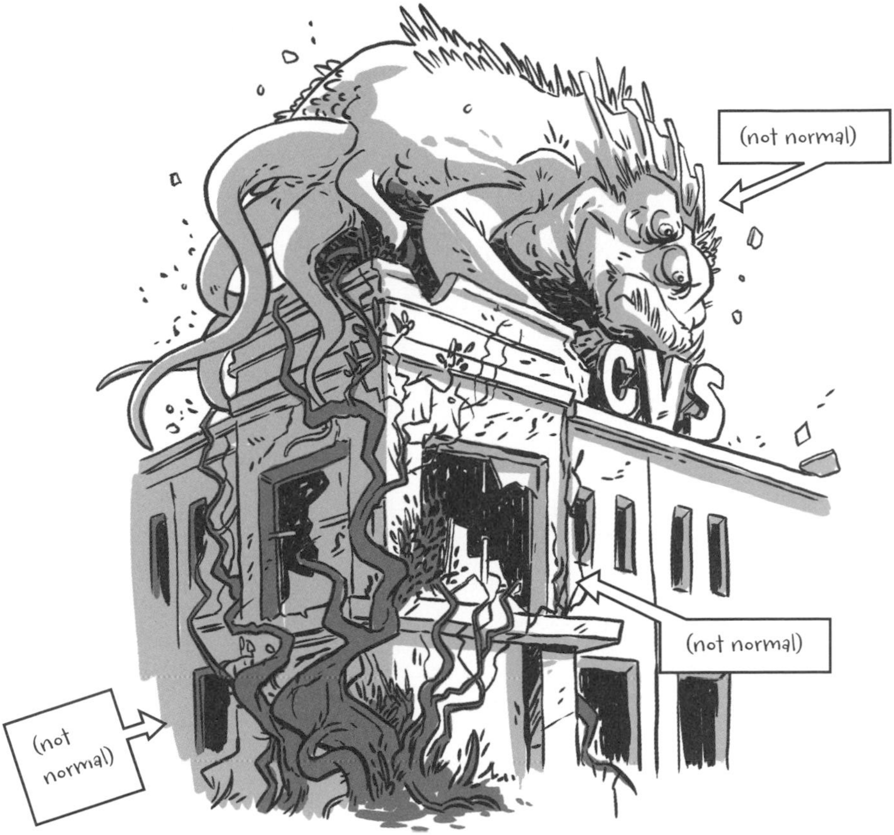
(not normal)
CVS
(not normal)
(not normal)

And me? I haven't been normal, well, ever. I've always been *different*. See, I'm an orphan—I bounced all over the country, different homes, different families, before landing in this little town of Wakefield in December.

But all that moving, it makes you tough: it makes you cool, it makes you confident, it makes you good with the girls—it makes you JACK SULLIVAN.

Oh *crud!*

INCOMING MONSTER FIST!!!

KRUNCH!

CLOSE CALL!

Yikes.

Almost got a monster fist to the skull there.

I'm at CVS because I need an eyeglass repair kit—those little tool sets that dads buy for when their glasses break. I know, that's a lame thing to need. But I have a walkie and that walkie is busted and to fix that walkie, I need a really really *really* tiny screwdriver and the only place to get a really really *really* tiny screwdriver is in an **eyeglass repair kit**.

This was supposed to be a quick, easy trip to CVS. But one thing I've learned about life after the Monster Apocalypse: **nothing's quick** and **nothing's easy**.

This monster here is the foulest, most ferocious, and just plain horrible thing I've encountered yet. He's straight-up—

KA-SLAM!

Yikes! The monster's massive fist pounds the roof until it cracks like thin ice. I trip, tumble back, and land hard on my bony butt.

It's time to stop being this monster's punching bag. See, I've kind of been the world's punching bag for a while and y'know—it just ain't a whole lotta fun.

So I'm fighting back.

I get to my feet.

I dust myself off.

I grip the bat in my hand. Not too tight, not too loose—just like they coach you in Little League.

Only I'm not trying to hit some kid's lousy curveball. . . . I'm trying to slay a monster.

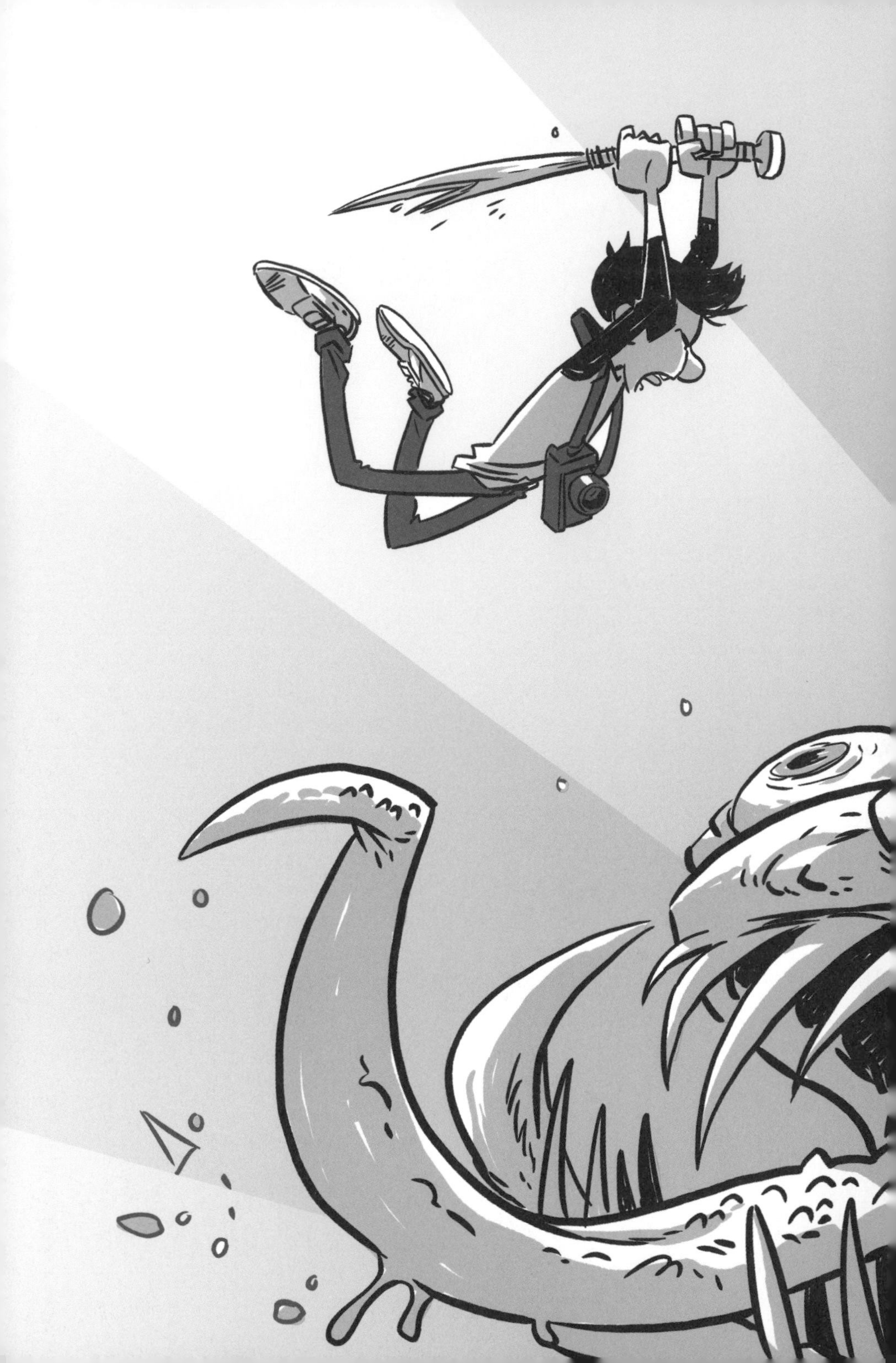

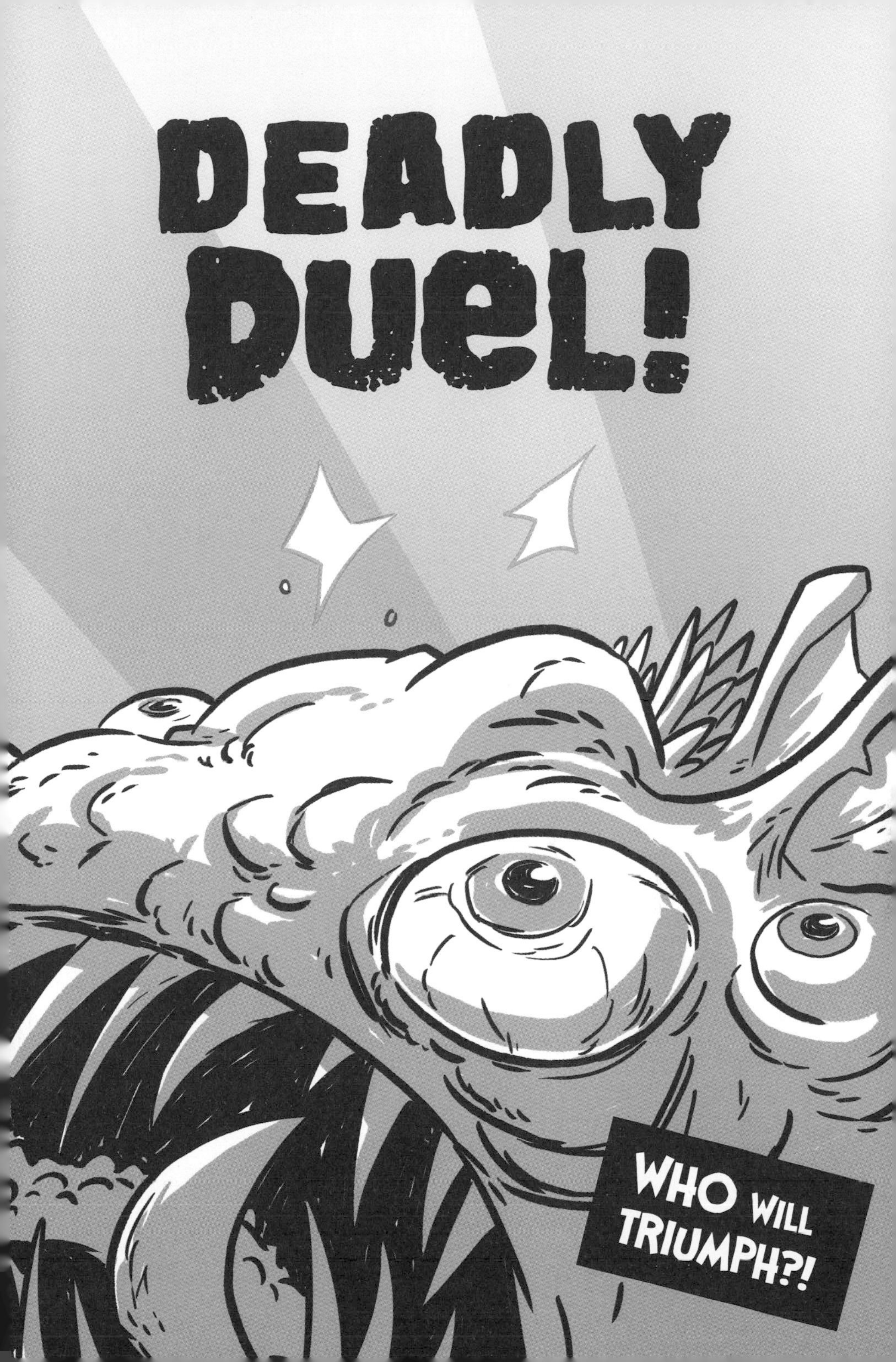
DEADLY DUEL!
WHO WILL TRIUMPH?!

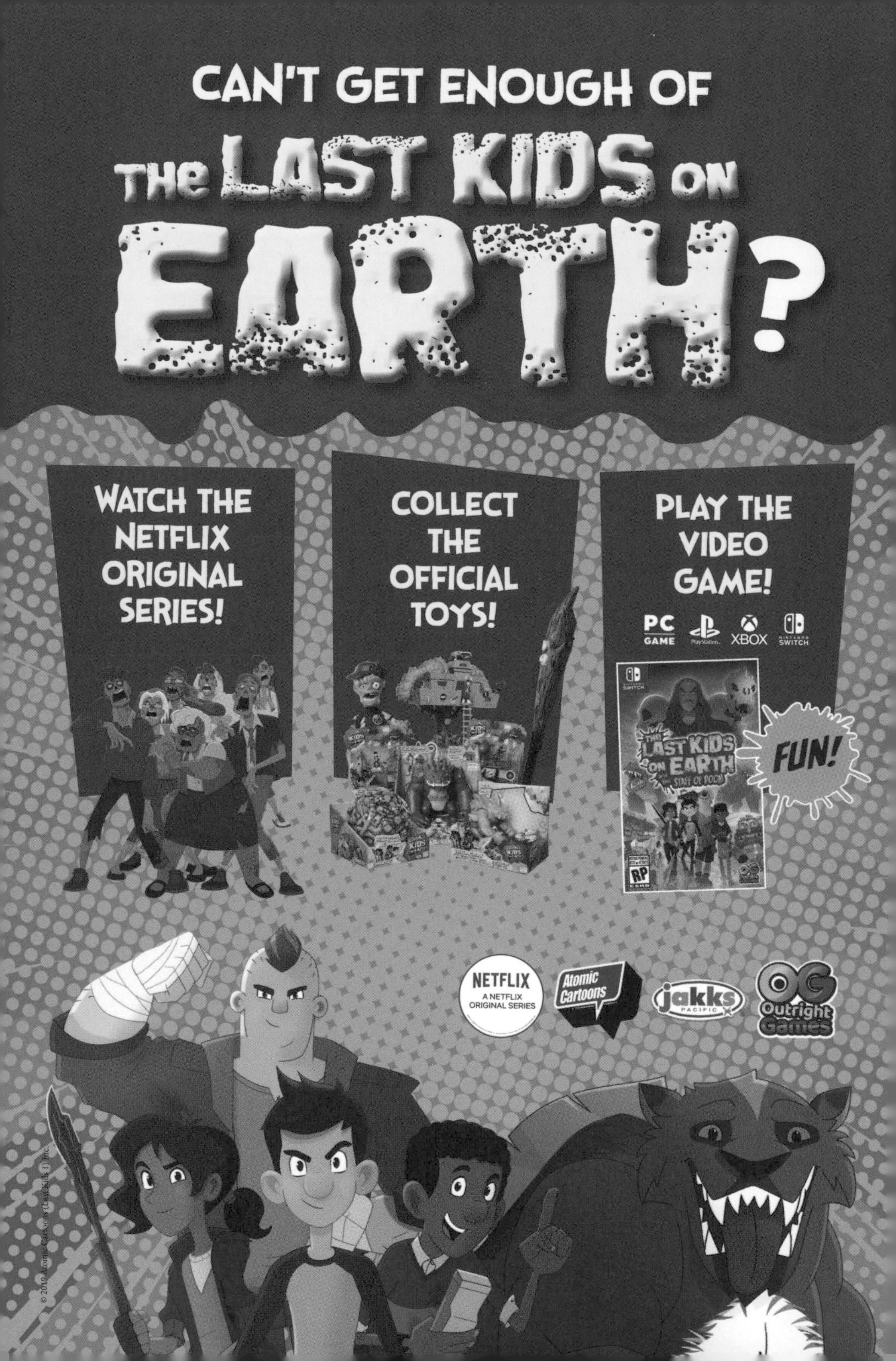

CAN'T GET ENOUGH OF
THE LAST KIDS ON EARTH?
WATCH THE NETFLIX ORIGINAL SERIES!
COLLECT THE OFFICIAL TOYS!
PLAY THE VIDEO GAME!
PC GAME
PlayStation
XBOX
NINTENDO SWITCH
THE LAST KIDS ON EARTH AND THE STAFF OF DOOM
FUN!
NETFLIX
A NETFLIX ORIGINAL SERIES
Atomic Cartoons
jakks PACIFIC
OG Outright Games
© 2019 Atomic Cartoons (Last Kids 1) Inc.

THE MONSTER-BATTLING FUN DOESN'T STOP HERE!

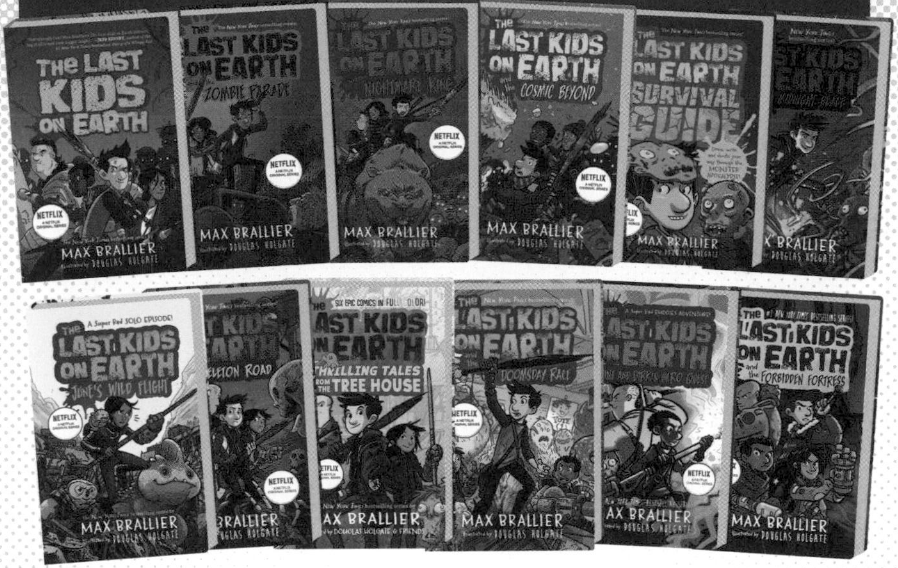

The Last Kids on Earth
MAX BRALLIER
The Last Kids on Earth and the Zombie Parade
MAX BRALLIER
The Last Kids on Earth and the Nightmare King
MAX BRALLIER
The Last Kids on Earth and the Cosmic Beyond
MAX BRALLIER
The Last Kids on Earth Survival Guide
MAX BRALLIER
The Last Kids on Earth: June's Wild Flight
MAX BRALLIER
The Last Kids on Earth: Thrilling Tales from the Tree House
SIX EPIC COMICS IN FULL COLOR!
The Last Kids on Earth and the Doomsday Race
MAX BRALLIER
The Last Kids on Earth and the Forbidden Fortress
MAX BRALLIER

TheLastKidsOnEarth.com

Check out more books in the bestselling

THE LAST KIDS ON EARTH SERIES! HUZZAH!

Jack Sullivan, June Del Toro, Quint Baker, Dirk Savage, Rover, and a whole bunch of monsters will return in book nine . . .

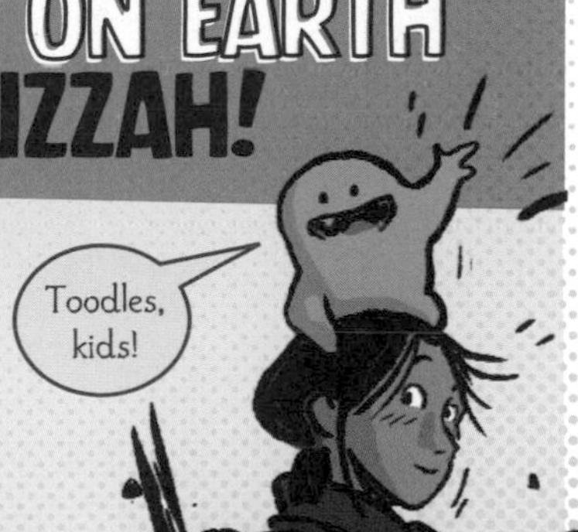

Toodles, kids!

AVAILABLE FALL 2023!

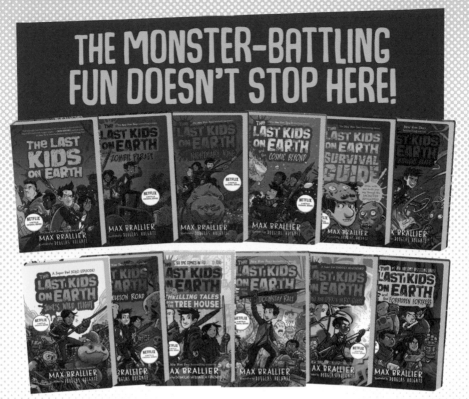

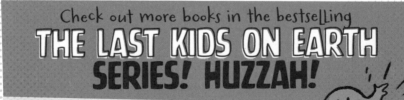

JOIN TODAY!

MAX BRALLIER'S

THE LAST KIDS

FAN CLUB

ON EARTH

Have your parent or guardian sign up now to receive a Fan Club Welcome Kit, exclusive Last Kids news, sneak previews, and behind-the-scenes info!

VISIT TheLastKidsonEarthClub.com
TO LEARN MORE

SCAN QR CODE

TO VISIT TODAY